HEAVENLY DECEPTION

For my father, George Maurice Brooks

HEAVENLY DECEPTION

Maggie Brooks

CHATTO & WINDUS

LONDON

By the same author
LOOSE CONNECTIONS

Acknowledgement and thanks to Janet Brooks
for invaluable help and advice at all
stages of the manuscript.

Published in 1985 by
Chatto & Windus
40 William IV Street
London WC2N 4DF

British Library Cataloguing in Publication Data
Brooks, Maggie
Heavenly deception.
I. Title
823'.914 [F]   PR6052.R5823/
ISBN 0–7011–2864–X

Photoset and printed in Great Britain by
Redwood Burn Limited
Trowbridge, Wiltshire

Chapter 1

Finally the coach scrunched up a long driveway and into the grounds of a large, Victorian house. The doors sighed open and the passengers poured out onto the gravel forecourt, shaking the cramp out of their legs, looking around them with the air of slightly dazed sheep. Carmen took in her surroundings carefully. The house was solid and dignified like a rectory. It was screened and shielded by tall trees and the shrubbery was tended and luxuriant. Rhododendron flowers ballooned pink from their lush, green foliage against banks of larkspur and regulated hollyhocks. There was a feeling of wealth, of care and respectability.

Carmen had spent much of the long journey trying to decide which of her fellow travellers were guests and which were members. Now the members made themselves conspicuous by the purposeful way they were heaving the baggage out of the hold and ferrying the luggage towards the oaken doors, chivvying their charges to follow. The sound of joyful singing drifted out on the fragrant summer air. Carmen tagged on to the line of the other guests as they trotted obediently behind the members into the vestibule. They watched as their luggage was piled into a mountain. She stood slightly apart from the others, aimless and ill at ease, listening to the full-throated gospel song, taking in the portentous gloom of the dark oak panelling, the warm light that filtered through the stained-glass bird vignettes around the door, casting bright shadows on the stone-flagged floor.

'This way,' someone said, and the guests shambled awkwardly after their leader towards the rapturous singing that was swelling from the hall down the corridor.

Carmen hovered in the doorway, unable to get right inside the hall because it was so crowded. The room was laid out with neat rows of scrubbed deal trestle tables. Maybe sixty people, a mixed bunch, a cross-section of races and ages, were singing 'Down By The Riverside' with every ounce of their strength and lung power, swaying ecstatically to the sound they were producing. The room was dominated by a handwritten song board and all eyes were pinned upon it. The sun's departing rays lent a bronze light to their ardent faces and Carmen looked around in wonderment, feeling the power that was pent up in their ardour. To either side of the song sheet, a clean-cut boy in a checked shirt played guitar and another man was beating out the rhythm on a set of tablas. They were smiling. Practically everyone in the room was smiling. In sympathy, a rather nervous simper settled experimentally on her face.

As the song came to an end, everybody clapped and began to cheer and whistle until the noise threatened to raise the roof. It was then that she became aware of Gary at her shoulder. He was smiling too. He guided her gently through the crowd just as 'If I Had A Hammer' was starting up. They began to sing it at full throttle, complete with actions – the hammer, the warning telltale finger, the crossed heart for love and extended arms to encompass the universe. Gary was singing heartily in a good clear baritone and he nodded at her encouragingly and motioned her to sing along. She piped up reluctantly in a muffled mumble, and then he firmly put her hands together and encouraged her to copy the actions. She began to wag her finger with a singular lack of conviction.

As she sang, her eyes roved across the unfamiliar, lit-up faces, half-hoping to pinpoint Lucy in their midst. She couldn't really tie in this sort of thing with Lucy. It made no sense. But then, had any of it made sense? An idle thought occurred to her and she bit her lip to suppress it. It would be extremely ironic if she's picked the wrong cult. What if Lucy was wrapped up in a sari, tagging after a string of bald men with bongoes in Lower Regent Street? Since Lucy had not headed her pathetic little letter, or named any particular group, there had been very little to go on. It was a process of slim research, elimination and half-hunches that had led Carmen here. Whether it made sense or not, she was almost sure that she was in the right place.

When they'd sung themselves to a standstill, the tabla player stood up and, grinning broadly, waited for the applause to die away. He was a handsome man of around thirty wearing a neat, grey suit. He had startling blue eyes and an air of quiet authority. He introduced himself as Matthew, the leader of the Centre, and he began a warm speech of welcome to the newcomers. Carmen's eyes continued to roam restlessly over the faces as she tried to discern the ratio of guests to members. The members, she decided, were somehow *cleaner*. The girls hung on his every word, their eager faces shining like scrubbed apples, and the boys had close-cut hair and poker backs.

Over the door was an oriental insignia formed of wriggly sun rays that seemed at odds with the austere, vicarage ambience.

'I guess some of you are looking around you,' Matthew boomed in a faintly transatlantic version of an Oxbridge accent, 'thinking ... *weird*!'

Everybody laughed. The members laughed inordinately, fondly, as though on a cue, and the guests laughed because they were already wondering what they were doing here, this lazy Sunday afternoon, and how they had allowed themselves to be persuaded to climb aboard the coach.

'What a weird bunch of people, huh? How come they get such a kick from just singing together?' He paced up and down with a benevolent smile on his face. 'But, you know, there's something you'll find out pretty soon here. We all get an enormous kick out of being here together, living as a family: a family made up of all ages, races and colours, a family made up of all different religions. It sounds like some sort of miracle, doesn't it?' He let his smile fade and his face became sombre. 'A multi-racial family. Working together, caring for one another. A family based on *love*. That surely does sound like a miracle.' He shook his head sadly.

'Well, it's a miracle we want to share with you. All we ask is that you put your preconceptions away and travel along with us for seven days. Accept our hospitality, enjoy our entertainment and look at the way we live. That's all we ask.' He grinned boyishly at the clumps of visitors around the room. 'Is that a lot to ask?' There were murmurs of 'no' from all four corners.

'Sometimes people think we have some religious axe to grind. They say, "This family of yours, sure it's great but it's got nothing to do with me – I'm an atheist or I'm a Catholic or I'm a Muslim..." Well, I just want to tell you now, we don't *care what* you are. To us, you're brothers and sisters coming here to see a unique and amazing experiment, living proof that the world can live as one. And perhaps you'll find something very true here, something very profound and moving. You may experience some deep, internal revelation as each of us here in the family has done.'

7

Carmen found herself looking speculatively at the girls, with their hair scraped back from their faces and hidden under peasant ker-chiefs; at Gary staring reverently ahead of him, his face taut with concentration. What had they found here?

'So, we're setting out on a voyage of discovery. It could be a pretty exciting time, huh?' They laughed again, and there seemed some-thing unnatural, something too automatic about their response. They laughed like a studio audience.

'We're all travelling light here. All we ask you to bring is a tooth-brush and an open mind...'

The room erupted into wild applause and Matthew had to shout above the noise, 'If anyone's forgotten their toothbrush, don't worry, the House Mother's got some spares...' and that produced even more hilarity and a renewed volley of tumultuous clapping.

Carmen felt a little left behind. The wild delight was quite out of proportion to the content of the speech and she wasn't used to unal-loyed enthusiasm applied so indiscriminately. She was aware of a rather contemptuous curl to her upper lip and she suddenly felt a twinge of guilt about it. Had he really said anything to sneer about? Was there anything wrong with the notion of racial harmony, of brotherly love? It was churlish to pre-judge them, in the circum-stances. They'd laid on transport and a meal. She'd paid her twelve pound cheque, it was true, but then twelve pounds wouldn't go far to cover a whole week's food and accommodation, and everyone seemed very gentle and kind. She supposed, until she should see a reason to doubt their sincerity, it was only fair to keep an open mind.

There were plates of unappetising pink Spam laid out on the table and she eyed it hungrily, but just as she thought they might be allowed to attack it, a woman's voice began to say a prayer in a marked French accent.

'Feeling such love for you, Heavenly Fazzer, and for each other. Heavenly Fazzer, we are so many nations, Fazzer, yet we can live in harmony and peace as one, Fazzer...'

It was a funny urgent little prayer that went on and on. Her voice was breathy and monotonous, like someone blowing faintly down a pipe. The Deity was invoked at least three times per sentence, as though the Addressed One might otherwise lose concentration and wander off to get His slippers like some senile old gent. Carmen squinted furiously as if she was praying too but, since she didn't believe in God, she felt rather a fraud. After a while, she lifted her head and took the opportunity to squint fuzzily at Gary while he was vulnerable and in repose and available for objective study. His brow was fiercely puckered and he looked like someone with a migraine, but even that couldn't mar the symmetry of his perfect features. With his dark hair and well-defined bone structure he was very good-looking, in a corny sort of way, and she thought again that he might have modelled for a shop window dummy if he hadn't chosen to be whatever he was in the One World Family.

'If it's not a religion, then why does everyone have to pray?' she asked him innocently as she shovelled up the bland, pink chunks of pork.

'No-one has to pray,' he shrugged. 'It's up to the individual. There's a lot of different religions here. Some people like to pray before a meal. It's good to respect other people's views, don't you think?' He looked at her with his polite, enquiring air, waiting for her to agree.

'Yes,' said Carmen. 'But if it's not a church and it's not a political organisation, what is it? A sort of God-fearing youth club without the ping-pong?' Once it was out, it sounded rather flippant and awful, but she'd been trying to get a clear answer out of him for the length of the coach journey. Every time he had come near to answering her questions, the coach had erupted into fresh song.

'I suppose that pretty well sums it up,' he said, without appearing to give the matter much thought. 'But it's not a heavy thing. People don't try to force their views on you. It's very easy going. A bit like a holiday camp, really.'

'And you're the Red Coat?' she asked, doubtfully.

'Yes, I'm your personal entertainments manager,' he answered easily, 'so you just *better enjoy yourself*.' He smiled his lazy smile that was both warm and disarming. Carmen looked at him just a fraction too long. Whenever he smiled at her, she got a shock. Maybe it was because he spent so much time avoiding her eyes, but when he did choose to look at her his gaze was so direct and searching that she was glad when he looked away again. What's more, his eyes were startlingly blue and strange. She found that sometimes it was impossible to concentrate on what he was saying because she was so busy

9

trying to analyse what exactly was so strange and compulsive about them. It was at those moments that she began to wonder if she wasn't just a little in love with him; to wonder whether the small agitation in her chest was not entirely to do with fear of the unknown. As far as Carmen knew, there was no other explanation as to why it should be so disorientating to look into another person's eyes. Now, as he continued to regard her, she suddenly became acutely conscious of how she must look to him. She had scragged her thin, fair hair back into a skimpy pigtail and she could sense that sprouts of it were sticking out absurdly from behind her ears, and that her ears were too prominent and burning red like a schoolboy's. At best, she found herself pale, slight and insignificant-looking, but now she was pink with the heat and her upper lip glistened with sweat. Yet Gary continued to appraise her with frank admiration. She looked away from him, confused. She had met him only three or four times, in cafés mostly, and once at the communal London house. Each time he had afforded her the same degree of intimate concentration, as if she was the only person in the room, the only person in the world. For that reason she felt inclined to trust him, and for the same reason, she didn't trust him one little bit.

At the end of the meal he wandered off in search of a form for her to sign. She noticed almost subliminally that people treated him with a certain deference as he wove his way about the room, and she would have needed to be wiser than she was not to find his constant attention flattering.

'There you are,' he said, when he got back to her. 'Perhaps you could fill it in straight away. They need them for the office work.'

He stood over her with a paternalistic air as she filled out her details. Mostly, they were the normal sort of questions and she filled in CARMEN STONE, age TWENTY, religion NOT REALLY, occupation ART STUDENT in her best italic hand. At the bottom of the page, the questions became more informal and chatty. To DO YOU EVER DESPAIR OF THE STATE OF THE WORLD? she cheerfully filled in SOMETIMES, but her pen faltered over the last one. ARE YOU SEARCHING FOR SOMETHING? Her eyes rested for a moment on the blob of fresh black ink poised on the gold nib. She looked up questioningly at Gary. 'What should I be searching for?'

'I can't answer them for you,' he smiled. 'We find a lot of people who come here are searching for something – maybe they don't even know what it is.'

Carmen knew what she was searching for all right. She firmly wrote YES and, almost immediately, before she could read the small print at the bottom and discover what she'd signed, Gary was folding up the form.

She could hardly demand it back, insist on scrutinising the thing minutely as though it was a crooked insurance policy, so she said nothing and merely watched him as he put it in his pocket, hoping fervently that she hadn't just signed away her badminton racket, her single premium bond and her banal but fairly happy little life.

'Perhaps you'd like to see your room now?' he asked gently, 'Pamela's taking people up.' When she nodded, he got up hastily and moved around her to pull her chair out with the kind of olde worlde courtesy that seemed to be second nature to him.

Pamela was a small, sharp-faced girl who looked harassed and self-important with responsibility. She wore the peasant kerchief that many of the girls affected but from her white eyelashes and freckles it was plain her hair was red. She wore an unflattering matronly dress that hung limp and shapeless on her small, spare frame. She was no more than eighteen and her bare legs were stick-like and splodged with brown freckles, ending in large childish sandals. She looked like a small child wearing a grown-up's dress but her air was one of distracted authority, as though she was concentrating very hard, and there was something middle-aged about her manner as she flourished her clipboard and called out the names. She reminded Carmen of something between a determined, highly responsible social worker and a neurotic sheep dog. That impression was confirmed as she worried the females into the hallway and up the sweeping staircase, keeping up a fearsomely jolly commentary on the history of the house and the delights of the forthcoming week's programme.

The light was fading now. The house was labyrinthine and the corridors both narrow and dark.

'The house used to be a convent and these were the nuns' cells,' she announced. As they passed, they all peered in at the string of bleak, inhospitable cubicles with nothing in them but bleak, horsehair beds.

Carmen was glad that they were striding past them. They looked so melancholy. 'But what with the decline of the Catholic church...' Carmen might have imagined it but it seemed that Pamela gave a rather contented sniff, 'the order declined and Our Founder bought the house.'

At the second landing, Pamela stopped and appeared to listen, as if hearing an imperceptible whistle. Then, as though in response to it, she split the group arbitrarily, syphoning off the main gaggle of female guests along a side corridor and leaving only Carmen and a tall gormless-looking girl in a cowboy shirt and jeans to stare wanly around at the panelling. The moment the footsteps receded, the girl, who had thus far looked exceedingly unpromising with her expressionless features and her gold-rimmed glasses, suddenly sprang into life.

'Are you a member?' she hissed urgently. Animated, her features took on a startling sweetness and an almost comic-book mobility. Suddenly she wasn't gormless at all.

'No, I'm a guest,' Carmen muttered back.

'Thank God,' said the girl. 'D'you smoke?'

Carmen nodded.

'She's confiscated my cigarettes,' the girl said with a heavy, ironic nod at the departed Pamela. 'I came down from Northampton with her. It's been seven hours! I mean, she's as sweet as anything but, frankly, I don't think she understands nicotine withdrawal.'

Carmen looked at her with fresh interest. The girl had short, shiny brown hair and green eyes that gleamed with intelligence behind the thick National Health lenses. Her nose was tip-tilted and her mouth had a deprecating twist to it that made her whole face lively.

'Look,' said the girl, 'we'll just let her settle us in and then we'll slip round the back for a fag, eh? Otherwise we'll have to sing again and, to be honest, my lungs won't stand it.'

Carmen assented swiftly. As Pamela swung out of the corridor towards them, Carmen was intrigued to note that the girl seemed to slump and resume her former posture of dull, virtuous blankness.

'Have you two met?' asked Pamela. 'Apparently Carmen's very talented at art, Jane,' she said as she marched them up the next flight of stairs. 'You two should have a lot in common.' She added to Carmen, in explanation, 'Jane's very good at origami.'

12

Jane rolled her eyes expressively at Carmen.

'There's a film tonight about the Family's enterprises and then a Family evening,' Pamela announced as they chased her up the corridor. They watched her buttocks jiggle self-importantly as she struggled gamely on, laden like a pack-horse with their baggage, the bulk of which she refused to let them carry. As Carmen was to learn, the members were heroically self-sacrificing, but the self-sacrifice usually demanded extraordinary forbearance on the part of its beneficiary.

When she reached the end of the corridor, Pamela waited for them to draw level with her. Then she threw open the door triumphantly and ushered them in with the modest pride of an estate agent displaying the best property on the firm's books.

'It's the nicest room we have,' she said, proudly. 'And it's got the prettiest view of the garden.'

Carmen and Jane stared ahead of them with consummate dismay. Their eyes were drawn involuntarily up towards the ceiling where the bank of three-tiered crate-wood bunks reared grimly to brush against the polystyrene ceiling tiles, obscuring much of the light and giving the impression of some sort of inhumane veal-raising apparatus at a battery farm. The bunks were stacked so close together that there was hardly a hand's space between them, and yet there were sleeping bags laid out in the gaps. In fact, sleeping bags covered every inch of floor space, all in different unpleasant-coloured nylon, giving the floor the look of a festive variegated quilt.

'But there's twenty-five people in here already,' Jane protested aghast.

'Don't exaggerate,' scowled Pamela. 'There's plenty of space.'

Jane and Pamela exchanged hostile looks. 'Why, so there is!' said Jane, and Carmen watched her as she picked her way over the bags to the open window and thrust her head out.

'My, it *is* a pretty view,' her muffled voice came back. 'And there's a little ledge. Perhaps I'll put my bag out here.' She leaned out even further and appeared to size up the outside wall. 'Yes!' she cried, gaily. 'It's OK, Pamela. There's space for my clock and I can hang my soap-bag from the drainpipe!'

Carmen laughed, without meaning to. Pamela frowned, biting her lip, both vexed and hurt.

'I don't think that's a bit funny, Jane. Honestly, there's plenty of room. You know it's a push for space.' She busied herself with climbing precariously to the top bunk, tossing down a bag and motioning to Carmen to throw her own up in its place.

'Won't someone mind?' asked Carmen lamely, watching as Pamela, having levered herself down, spread the displaced person's bag under the U-bend of the sink.

'Not at all,' said Pamela briskly. 'That's something you'll find in the Family. People enjoy giving things. Sacrifice is a very nice way to say "you're welcome", don't you think?' Then, with a very pointed look at Jane, 'People never grumble about trivial things here, in the Family. That's the great thing. It makes it so much nicer for everyone else when people don't grumble about every petty little thing.'

Jane was making an elaborate pantomime of laying out her bag in the single wardrobe and, since Carmen seemed to find this droll, Pamela made an effort to smile indulgently and hide her exasperation.

'Do you want to have a wash and brush-up?' she asked finally, her patience pushed to the limit by Jane disappearing inside the wardrobe and trying to close the door on herself. 'The bathroom's down the hall.'

They scampered off like co-conspirators with their toilet bags and toothbrushes, both determinedly entering into the Enid Blyton spirit.

'But what about all those rows and rows of rooms?' gasped Carmen as they ran. 'Who sleeps in those?'

'No-one,' said Jane. 'Togetherness, you know. Isolation is of Satan, and all that.'

Carmen had no time to puzzle this out. As she leaned on the bathroom door, it burst open on a bewildering array of naked and semi-naked flesh.

'Sorry,' she mumbled, but, even as she withdrew, the door was flung open with hearty invitation and they found themselves facing a girl with a face like a potato who urged them into the crowded little room. There were two naked girls crouched in the bath, back to back, their limbs wet and rubbery whilst another sister hosed them down to save water. There were two at the sink and another perched on the lavatory with her dress hauled up, straining to evacuate her bowels without benefit of screen or curtain. It was this last girl who addressed them directly.

'Just arrived?' she hailed them.

Carmen nodded nervously and fixed her eyes on the plughole of the sink.

'Hi! I'm Virginia.' She gave a cheery smile and leaned forward enthusiastically from the toilet seat, although she didn't get up.

Carmen said her name, grinning rather foolishly the while. She wondered if it was appropriate to shake hands, but decided that hygiene precluded it if propriety didn't.

Virginia hauled a long lug of toilet paper noisily from the holder.

'I think this Seven Day's going to be the best one ever,' she said. 'I helped choose the film programme, and even if I *do* say it myself, they're the most terrific bunch of films!'

Carmen nodded nervously and began to wash her hands, taking advantage of the fact that one of the girls was brushing her teeth so enthusiastically that she hardly ever spat into the basin.

'Wednesday's "The Greatest Story Ever Told" and Thursday's "The Sound Of Music"!'

To Carmen's surprise, they all began to shriek and twitter like so many pink mice in a pantomime. Virginia got up and pulled the chain. 'Hey, let's sing,' she said suddenly, and just as Carmen was about to put her toothbrush into her mouth, they broke into song as though a cue had been given, all rolling their eyes soulfully and swaying from the hips:

> 'I'm on the *top* of the world,
> Lookin' *down* on creation,
> And the only explanation I can find
> Is the love I have found
> Ever *since* you've been around...'

Unnerved, Carmen caught Jane's eye; as one, they zipped up their soap-bags and piled out into the corridor, where they collapsed into a giggling heap, helpless with laughter. After a while, they became aware of Pamela standing over them, frowning as they snorted and squeaked and held their stomachs.

'All freshened up?' she asked. Which only made them laugh more.

'Really,' Pamela said with weary forbearance. 'You won't be able to get into the atmosphere at all if you're going to be silly.' Carmen tried to stop laughing because she suddenly felt rather sorry for Pamela with her worn, pinched little face, her red hands and her worried air of duty.

Pamela escorted them down like a self-righteous Girl Guide leader. The hall was beginning to fill for the evening film show and she found them two seats beside the ancient projector.

'Now stay put,' she said to Jane, 'because I'm watching you.'

Carmen wondered about this; although it was said in a jocular tone, there was an unctuous air of authority in her voice which meant she intended to be obeyed.

The film whirred into motion to tumultuous applause, and there were sounds of overexcited anticipation more suited to a childrens' matinee. Carmen half expected to see the members racing up and down the aisles and dropping ice creams down one another's necks, but there were no refreshments and concentration on the image was touchingly intense considering the quality of the scratched and fuzzy print. The projector whirred in her ears like the beating of a pterodactyl's wings, almost obscuring the commentary, and whenever the film snapped, the audience broke into loud theatrical groans which turned to cheers when the film slurred back into motion again.

The film purported to be an information film about the Family. It was very bland and boring and gave Carmen none of the information that she wanted. The quality was so poor that the primary colours glared from ths screen, gaudy as boiled sweets. The images were of perfect roses in summer gardens and squirrel-like rodents which she supposed were chipmunks, nibbling acorns. Interspersed with these were shots of smiling young Family members with clipboards, accosting passers-by; smiling Family members in boiler suits with smart matching dust carts cleaning up Times Square; more smiling Family members selling fish and ginseng from the Family's business enterprises. The commentary that competed with the lush, maudlin strings of the background music continually returned to the theme that these idealistic young people were changing the world, as though having a clipboard was an innately virtuous state of being, and the clipboard itself a potentially explosive instrument for change.

'Well, what did you think of that?' asked Pamela as the lights went up. Carmen saw that she was beaming with pleasure and that her eyes were very shiny and alive. 'Wasn't it tremendous?'

Carmen was at a loss to answer her at the same pitch. She found Pamela's elation bewildering. The film had ranged from OK to quite dull.

'I thought it was *really* inspiring,' said Jane. 'It was *great*.'

Carmen looked at her, surprised. There was no touch of irony in her voice and she was holding Pamela's arm with a warm, intimate pressure. All around them, people were exclaiming in the same terms, that it had moved them, that it had been inspirational and overwhelming. Just then, Carmen felt a playful pinch in the flesh of her ribs and she looked up in time to catch Jane's wink. Two seconds later, she and Jane were sauntering as casually as they could manage through the crowd of people and out of the door.

They sat on the steps of the large house and watched their cigarettes glowing against the darkness. There were other little glimmers beyond the hedgerow which told of other guests who'd had the same idea. The singing began inside the house and drifted out on the evening air.

'Oh, it's just easier to agree,' Jane was saying. 'You'll see. And why upset her? She's a really nice person. She doesn't get many pleasures. This whole thing's a one-way ticket as far as I can work out.'

'But why is it?' puzzled Carmen.

Jane shrugged. 'I don't know. I suppose they believe it.'

'Believe what?' Carmen pursued.

'Oh well,' said Jane vaguely, 'whatever it is they believe. That's why I'm here, isn't it? To satisfy my curiosity. I mean, I've heard little bits...' It was clear she didn't mean to share whatever it was she had heard. 'But it doesn't hang together. You can't make sense of it – not without coming and doing the course. Anyway, you're supposed to get it in dollops, like a slow revelation. Otherwise it doesn't work.'

'*What* doesn't work?' asked Carmen, her curiosity fired.

'The Principle, as they call it,' said Jane. 'It's so deep, you can't understand it all at once. They have to feed you milk and water before you go onto solid food – that sort of thing.' She waved her hand dismissively as though this was all self-explanatory. 'It's a very profound revelation.' She blew some smoke rings with her snub nose tilted towards the moon. They watched them rise against the inky blackness. 'Or so they say,' she added, '*interminably*.' And then, as though ashamed of her fleeting disloyalty, and as though it was Carmen who'd been guilty of the uncharitable thought, 'But they're *such* nice people. They've been very good to me. I didn't have anywhere to stay and they offered me a bed. I was doing Biology at Northampton and I freaked out a bit around exam time. Lost my place in the hall of residence and they took me in at their Centre. They were great. Then Pamela kept going on and on at me to come on the Seven Day. So I thought...' She looked at Carmen and her eyes were candid and clear. 'I could at least give 'em the benefit of the doubt and find out what it is they think is so important – you know?' Carmen nodded.

'I suppose there are Centres all over the place?' Carmen enquired artlessly. It occurred to her that there might be a list of Centres somewhere. Maybe even a list showing which members were in what Centres. If so, maybe Lucy's name would be on it. Supposing, just supposing, there *was* a list, could she get into the office and lay her hands on it? She was eyeing Jane speculatively and wondering if the girl might be a future ally.

Jane nodded indifferently. 'All over the country, all over the world. It doesn't seem a *bad* life,' she reflected, as if she were considering it as a viable career alternative to life in a bank or the woman's Metropolitan Police. 'They're incredibly warm and kind and there's a lot of foreign travel ... except, well, it takes a lot of commitment. I couldn't really commit myself without knowing what I was committing myself *to* ...'

She said it rather apologetically, as though it was Carmen who was pressing her, as though she needed reassuring that her cautious attitude was not unreasonable.

Carmen hesitated before she spoke. 'You don't think there's something ... well, odd about them?' she asked delicately. 'The members, I mean. You know, the way their eyes fog over when they're talking?'

Jane looked at her, mildly surprised. 'Odd?' she echoed distantly. 'Odd!' and she laughed a very healthy peal. 'Look, Carmen, they're completely barmy. You'd better get that through your head or you'll be out selling "One World" in San Francisco come Tuesday week.'

Just as Carmen was digesting this sudden turn-about, Jane began to tug insistently at her sleeve. 'Watch out,' she hissed. 'Here's yours.'

Startled, Carmen looked up at the porch where Gary stood in the light-spill, frowning. Pamela appeared just behind him. As Gary's eyes settled on Carmen, a broad smile snapped onto his face and he mooched casually down the steps towards the truants.

'Hey, there you are,' he called amiably. 'We've been looking for you. You'll miss out on all the fun if you're not careful. There's some cocoa coming.'

Carmen smiled trustingly up at him as he loomed closer. 'We'll be right with you, Gary,' she promised, 'as soon as we finish our cigarettes.'

'Well, don't be long,' wavered Pamela, her face anxious. 'Everyone's getting to know each other and having a good time in here.' With that, Gary and Pamela turned back towards the house.

Carmen was still smiling when she looked back at Jane. It had been a warm smile, the kind that took a little longer to fade. Jane noted how it lit up Carmen's face and she sniffed suspiciously.

'Is he your Spiritual Father?' she asked, nodding at Gary's retreating back. Since Carmen only looked blank, she pressed on, 'Is he the one taking care of you? The one who found you? Does he stick to you like a love-lorn shadow?'

Carmen hesitated. Was that it? Was Gary actually *required* to treat her like a very special piece of porcelain?

'*I* sort of found *him*,' she said flatly, and she drew hard on her cigarette. Jane continued to look at her with expectant interest. 'There was a whole load of them on the Edgware Road teaching things from blackboards. In the rain. I started talking to him. I was curious,' she lied. The truth was that she hadn't just happened upon them: she had sought them out. The officer at the Missing Persons Bureau had warned her to leave well alone, but she couldn't. Every word of the letter was etched on Carmen's brain – the bland phrases, so stilted, so uncharacteristic of Lucy, and the initials I.T.P.N. above the miserable squiggle of Lucy's signature. It hadn't been possible for her to leave well alone. 'And then I asked so many questions he took me to his Centre.'

Jane's eyes widened in surprised appreciation.

'Apparently that's unusual,' Carmen said in an off-hand way.

'Unheard of,' Jane agreed. 'It's usually *them* going on and on at *you*.'

'Yes.' Carmen got to her feet, uneasy with the conversation. 'Well, I must be an unusual sort of person or something. Apparently it means I've got good ancestors.' She laughed flippantly at the idea.

'Good taste, more like,' said Jane, scrambling after her. 'All I've got is that miserable Pamela hanging round my neck like an albatross, snapping all my Rothmans in half.' Together they made their way into the house where the communal singing was winding down to an emotional ending.

As the applause broke out, the cocoa urns were portentously wheeled in, like ceremonial samovars, and everyone began to mill about at random in great good humour, chatting and making friends. Gary was immediately at her side, confiding two chocolate bourbon biscuits into her hand as though they were somehow very precious. Pamela whirled Jane off to a corner and seemed to be administering some private scolding.

Carmen stood alone, watching Gary as he weaved fluidly through the crowd towards the refreshment table. The situation reminded her of something between a church social in a village hall and an eighteenth-century pump room, and she realised then why she felt so light-hearted. After all, no-one was going to steal her soul, and there was no denying that if Gary wanted to dance attendance on her, was maybe even required to dance attendance on her, then there was no law against her getting some innocent pleasure from it. As it was, she couldn't help but notice that, as he was caught in conversation with Matthew in the scrum, he kept darting nervous glances at her as though to fix exactly where she was, rather like, well, rather like a desperate man at a race course with all his money on one dog. She felt again the uneasy sensation that there was something secretive going on behind his eyes, that he was contemplating tactics in some hidden compartment of his brain.

When Gary had threaded his way back with the polystyrene cups of lukewarm cocoa, he placed himself quite close to her and spoke in an undertone that was confidential and intimate, as though they stood alone in the crowded room.

'You should talk to as many people as you can,' he told her. 'That's what the Family's all about, making a lot of friends. It's good to get to know lots of people. Not just one. Jane's nice, but she's not the only person here.'

'I like her,' said Carmen, surprised at herself. She had not expected to like anybody. She had meant to keep herself to herself, like a spy, somehow thinking that would be safer. But now it occurred to her that it would be comforting to have an ally. 'I thought she was quite amusing.'

'Oh well, amusing...' Gary repeated with a hint of a sneer, as though to be amusing was no particular accomplishment. 'You strike me as being someone that's quite spiritually open – '

'Is that good?' asked Carmen, disconcerted.

He nodded gravely, his eyes searching her face. 'It's good, but if you spend all your time with Jane who has – well, rather erratic spirits...'

She waited with a quizzical expression on her face and he thought better of his speech. He smiled with a self-deprecating candour. 'Oh, well, I suppose what I mean is, I'd like to spend more time with you myself. There's so many things we have to talk about. So much I want to ask you about your life. A week isn't very long to get to know each other ... deeply...'

Carmen coloured, wondering how deep he wanted to go. Wondering what on earth else there was to tell him. How much did he think she'd packed into her twenty years? She'd told him about her family and her background; she'd even told him about Lucy vanishing, although he hadn't seemed to want to know. About Robin and art school and her long line of ill-starred cats. He, on the other hand, had managed to tell her virtually nothing about himself. He continued to stare at her with a brooding intensity, as though he believed there was some dark mystery there that only he could penetrate.

'Well, ask me then...' she said, self-consciously, aware that she was batting her eyelids outrageously. He studied her face for a long moment, and she sensed that what he saw there dissatisfied him.

'No,' he said reluctantly. 'Now's not the time. We'll talk tomorrow.'

People were beginning to disperse now, making their way out of the hall towards their beds.

'I just want you to know,' he said, 'that we didn't meet by accident. There's a connection between us that's very strong and important. We were meant to meet...'

And with that cryptic statement, he said his courteous goodnights and made abruptly for the door, leaving her bewildered in the middle of the floor to stare thoughtfully into the chocolate sludge at the bottom of her disposable cup.

The guitar player was moving around the room, serenading the groups of remaining guests with a firm 'Go-To-Bed' song. It wasn't long before Pamela arrived and herded Carmen out with the other sisters, up the staircase for the long walk to the dormitories.

Chapter 2

At midnight, Carmen picked her way delicately over the contorted bodies, heaved herself up the hazardous step-ladder to her airless bunk and settled into the small, hot air pocket that waited to receive her under the polystyrene tiles of the ceiling. Jane, whose nose was pressed into the skirting board, suggested faintly that they open a window but Pamela, who seemed to be directing operations, pointed out that this had to be a majority decision.

The majority, when appealed to, seemed singularly apathetic, as though such a decision was both beyond its scope and too deeply trivial to deserve consideration. Most of the women, anyway, were either dead to the world or crouched in intense prayer with the rounded seats of their pyjama bottoms uppermost. The general lack of interest confirmed that they were content to spend the night without oxygen, breathing in what their sisters had just breathed out.

At one o'clock, the light was extinguished. The window remained closed and Carmen, mindful that she mustn't sit upright suddenly for fear of knocking herself unconscious on the ceiling, snuggled her face into the meagre pillow and tried to think reassuring thoughts of Robin. It was no good. Her brain was too busy and Robin, through no fault of his own, she told herself, seemed pallid and unemphatic.

Just as she began to doze into a fitful sleep, a thin nasal whistle began to pierce her consciousness, followed by the intrusion of a rich catarrhal rattle that began to counterpoint from a bunk below her. Then, from another corner, as though responding to a mating call, a long drawn-out, self-important pig noise introduced itself with reverberating insistence, laying down the bass rhythm for all the high-pitched whines and snorts and whimpers that almost immediately began to follow. Everyone seemed to have a contribution to make, and no offering was too bellicose or too strangled. Carmen, who often said she could sleep through anything, lay rigid and round-eyed with terror, suddenly aware that her boast was idle. The sounds were inhuman and sinister, like nothing she had ever heard before; it was not the kind of noise that she could sleep through.

At morning light, a guitar began to play loudly and insistently outside the door. A ragged, cheerful, male voice was attacking 'Morning Has Broken, Like The First Morning' at aggressive speed and volume, without fidelity to the tune. The chicks in the roof were squawking for their daybreak worms and Carmen sat up warily, red-eyed and alarmed, wondering where she was. It took her a moment to get her bearings.

Viewed from her precarious eyrie, the unnaturally small sleeping bags below were squirming into life, disgorging their contents like animated toothpaste tubes. It was somehow a relief to see the women in the light of day, after the night's unearthly noises: not farmyard beasts at all but just young women, moving silently and reverently in their quilted housecoats, neatly folding up their bags and reducing their possessions to minimal piles as though for imminent inspection by a sadistic sergeant major. They were pulling on track suits and their heads emerged through the terry-towelling holes like drowsy turtles, half-blind with sleep but responding, mechanically, as one, to an unspoken order.

Carmen relaxed. Her eyelids had just drooped closed and sealed when there was a vigorous movement of the whole structure of the bunks, and she sensed something brushing insistently under her nostrils. She sneezed herself violently awake, nearly dislodging Pamela, whom she now perceived to be looming precariously over her, clinging to the rough wood support with one hand and whimsically brandishing a tiger-lily in the other.

'Wake up, sister. It's a beautiful day!' Pamela announced, faltering slightly in the face of Carmen's belligerent glare.

Carmen made a heroic effort to control her irritation.

'OK, Pamela,' she said, as gently as she could. Pamela levered herself down and moved across the room to torment Jane.

'Come *on*,' she teased, playfully trying to unzip Jane's bag. 'You're such a lazybones, you'll miss all the fun.'

Jane snatched her cocoon stubbornly around her. '*You* go and have fun,' she snarled with her eyes firmly shut. 'I'm queueing for the bathroom and I can do that just as well horizontal.'

A frown crossed Pamela's freckled face. She had no answer since she well knew the bathroom was bulging and the queue went some way down the corridor.

'Well, don't be long anyway,' she said lamely, 'or you'll miss breakfast.'

At the word *breakfast*, Carmen suddenly became alert like a cat who'd heard a can clink. She slithered down to ground level and began pulling on her clothes.

'My God, did you ever hear a racket like it?' Jane called to her. 'I mean, the steam engine was one thing but when the donkey joined in ... where are you going?'

'Breakfast,' said Carmen, and she disappeared out of the door with all the single-minded concentration of someone who has slept one hour out of a possible six and thinks they smell a whiff of bacon.

But there was no bacon. The dining room was deserted and silent. There was no comforting clatter and no sign of cutlery, only the dull margarine smell of scrubbed deal tables and the distant sound of gleeful shouting.

She wandered forlornly out to the garden in search of the source of the raised voice and, sure enough, there they all were assembled on the lawn around the Centre's leader, performing frenetic physical jerks to Matthew's barked commands. It was a childish 'Simon says ...' game, the kind that accelerated to maniacal speed. Carmen took one look and tried to dodge back inside the porch, but Matthew spotted her and boomed out like a Shakespearean actor, 'Ah, another sister! In you come. Don't be shy. Join the circle! Simon saaaaayyyyysss, be a ... wait for it ... *a pair of scissors*,' and they all shot up in the air, scissoring their legs and clapping their hands above their heads with ferocious exuberance. Before Carmen could protest, Gary and Pamela were at her elbows, egging her on, refusing to take no for an answer, and she found herself half-heartedly touching her toes and squatting and leap-frogging with the rest of them.

Finally, the circle broke and formed into a brightly coloured snake. With Matthew harrying from the head, it hared off at break-neck speed through the undergrowth with a protesting Carmen tagged on the tail, sandwiched between Gary and Pamela, sashaying a reluctant conga and pretending to brush her teeth with a singular lack of conviction. She allowed herself to be thus bullied along until a thorn drove into her bare foot and she retired injured and limped off to the shrubbery.

'Come on, Carmen, you must keep up!' It was Marianne, the French housemother. She was standing, arms akimbo, her ample flesh straining against the ungenerous cut of her track suit, her spectacles shining opaque in the early morning sun under a mop of short black hair cut like a German helmet. 'Where are you going?'

'Something in my foot,' Carmen growled.

'Oh, some-sing in my foot,' Marianne mocked in a funny, babyish lisp. 'Poor little bébé. 'Ow will we save the world if we make a big fuss about every little sing?'

Carmen stared at her dumbly, no ready answer at her lips. The woman was perched on a log, her head cocked beadily like a robin, a quizzical, teasing smile on her face. There were several possible rejoinders, none of them cordial, but Carmen merely looked at her with dislike and observed coldly, 'It's not a little thing. It's a great big two-inch thorn.'

Marianne laughed gaily, 'Why, 'Enrietta 'as a torn 'am string and she 'as not complained,' and just as Carmen was stung into muttering, 'More fool 'Enrietta,' Marianne turned abruptly, hopped off the log, her flesh aquiver, and disappeared in pursuit of Matthew's fading instructions.

Carmen limped into the echoing dining room and waited glumly for something to happen. Once the ferocious calisthenics were done, they all filed cheerfully in, their appetites enhanced and hopeful, but no food appeared. Instead, the song-sheet was trundled remorselessly forward and the guitarist struck up the chords of the first number.

Matthew hollered above the joyful chords, 'You know, we have a saying in the Family: "Give *one oh-oh*."' He made the figures with his hand. 'A hundred per cent. What are you going to give it?'

'ONE OH-OH!' they cried jubilantly.

'Mind and body united!' Matthew boomed and he jumped in the air as though to head an imaginary football. Immediately, the whole room swung into vibrant motion as they gave voice to 'Rise And Shine And Give God The Glory, Glory', breaking into a precise and choreographed hand routine, their arms stretched ecstatically to the ceiling, then violently washing windows, clockwise and

26

anti-clockwise, stabbing the air with Black Panther fists then back to finger-wagging mode, all executed with bewildering speed, dexterity and infectious, exhilarating enthusiasm which left Carmen completely unmoved.

'You're not very co-ordinated,' said Pamela with helpful concern, as Carmen struggled to get the sequence right.

'I'm not very co-ordinated because I feel like a lemon,' said Carmen dourly, stung into response as she stabbed when she should have wagged and wagged when she should have washed the windows.

'Well, unless you get it right, you *look* like a lemon,' said Pamela practically. 'Honestly, it's very simple. Last week, we had a man with only one arm and he got the hang of it straight away! But then,' she added as an afterthought, looking at Carmen with a critical eye, '*he* was very spiritual.'

Still puzzling over this information, Carmen redoubled her efforts. It was beginning to dawn on her, as she struggled to perfect her high-speed hand jive whilst singing her heart out, that giving one oh-oh was not an optional extra. Relentless zeal was a compulsory and essential feature of the whole experience. No-one was allowed to hover on the sidelines. It was like a tenth-rate musical where no rationale was needed for the whole cast suddenly to burst into a sugar-coated number like 'Annie's Song' or 'Country Roads' or, as she found at the flip of the song-sheet, 'Consider Yourself One Of Us'. Having taken the hospitality of their nightmare dormitory, she was now obliged to sweep along with the chorus, centre stage, acting her socks off as though they were all in it together. She became aware of Gary at her shoulder, a benign reassuring presence rather like a protective older brother.

But then again, she thought, as she sensed him edging closer, was he being her big brother or blocking her exit?

They sang two more numbers as though their lives depended on them, clapped their own efforts uproariously and groaned in mock disappointment when Matthew vetoed a fourth. Silence fell as he spoke the long Heavenly-Father-studded prayer.

When at last the sixty chairs scraped against the floorboards and they settled themselves at the table, the members crouched immediately into intense personal devotions. Carmen watched as Gary brought his fists up to his eyes and compressed his forehead into a concertina pleat. He trembled with the intensity of his prayer as though he were trying to crack some impossible walnut with the conflicting tensions of his body. This posture was echoed by supplicants all the way down the table and, since it seemed indecent to eat while everyone else was suffering, she stared with steadfast reverence at the free offer of a garden umbrella on the back of the Sugar Puffs box.

'You don't have a prayer habit?' Gary asked her conversationally as he freed himself from his internal struggle and surfaced blinking to the light.

'I used to pray on Christmas Eve when I wanted a dolly,' said Carmen, and then to make sure that the state of her religious convictions had penetrated, 'Atheists don't have anyone to pray to,' she reminded him tactfully. He shook his head as though it was rather a sad little notion.

Now that she was free to eat, she realised wanly that she was no longer hungry. Gary seemed to take the state of her appetite personally and spent the rest of the breakfast pandering to her imagined whims, tipping his own Puffs onto her uneaten mound, jumping up quite unnecessarily to fetch her a serviette, to track down the elusive sugar bowl, all with an embarrassing show of devotion. She half thought he was going to wrap the paper napkin round her neck and forcibly spoon-feed her.

In an effort to distract him from his avowed intention of locating for her one of the congealed fried eggs that were being passed from plate to plate, she asked him about the day's programme. She had discovered that there would be lectures every day. 'What's this morning's lecture about?' she asked.

'Oh, about the World's Problems and how we can put them right,' he said evenly as he poured milk onto her cereal.

'Well, that should take us to lunchtime,' she remarked lightly.

He smiled. 'Yes, it's a pretty incredible thought, isn't it? You wouldn't think we could change the world from this little house, would you? But actually, that's what we're doing. We're making human history here,' he told her matter-of-factly, 'and the lectures provide the key to all the problems of civilisation, so ...' he lifted his straggly eyebrows at her, 'I'll be very surprised if you find it boring!'

28

She continued to stare at him doubtfully. She thought it was maybe a lame joke, but he didn't laugh.

After such a momentous build-up, the lecture could hardly fail to disappoint, and disappoint it did. They filed into the lecture room and, after another protracted bout of singing 'Zip-A-Dee-Doo-Dah' and 'Bridge Over Troubled Water', they sat down on the hard schoolroom chairs to a lecture that was very long, boring, unstructured and unilluminating.

Matthew outlined the problems of modern-day living in a calm, even tone, writing the key words on the blackboard as he talked. There was not enough love in the world. Love was the most powerful, the most creative, the most formidable force in the universe. From Love flowed Happiness, Fulfilled Desires, Perfect Families, Health, Harmony, Joy and Total Freedom; he drew a couple of pink and blue stylised flowers and some treble clefs to add to the general greetings-card effect of the happy scenario. The family unit, he told them, was the perfect expression of Perfect Love, and Love itself should be eternal and unconditional. There was one man for every woman and, with the restoration of True Love, the depressing pyramid which now occupied the dark side of the blackboard, with its apex of Selfish Desires widening out to Divorce, Break-Up Of The Family, Suicidal Thoughts, Crime, Chaos and World War, could be completely eradicated. All the manifestations of sin and suffering could be wiped out just as he wiped them all out now with his blackboard eraser, leaving a flurry of chalk dust dancing in the sunlight around the immaculate pressed seams of his slim-fitting suit. He smiled around the round like a conjurer who had just dematerialised a rabbit.

Carmen found this lecture generally unsatisfactory. How they planned to impose the pink Happy side of the board onto an unwilling and uninterested humanity, she had no clear idea. How they imagined that chalk marks could change the world remained a complete mystery. As they collected their diluted barley water from the main hall in the mid-morning recess, her bewilderment deepened: all around her, people were enthusing over Matthew's message with a uniform uncritical euphoria.

No-one appeared to harbour the least reservation that the results Matthew had just achieved with his blackboard rubber could not be reproduced again and again all over the country.

'Pretty exciting stuff, eh?' she heard Virginia breathing to a pair of stunned-looking skinheads. 'The startling thing is, we *actually* have the means to bring it about. For real!'

Perhaps they planned to send fleets of blackboards out to shopping precincts all over the country, Carmen puzzled. Maybe that was what Gary had been doing with his board and easel in the Edgware Road. And yet, it made no sense at all. Surely they could see that however many blackboard lectures they unleashed on an indifferent world, nothing would change. Gary's crowd that day, as far as she could remember, had been a couple of football fans and some blank-eyed winos. Football fans were notoriously unaffected by World Affairs and had a limited attention span, in her opinion. Winos — well, they'd usually taken a bumpy sleigh-ride down the awful pyramid, past Divorce and into Chaos, and it would hardly be much comfort to them to see it spelt out neatly in coloured chalks. Yet this would be a typical street audience. Shoppers weren't likely to stop for religious freaks. She wandered outside and sat cross-legged and neutral on the grass under the shade of the apple tree and breathed in the fragrance of the summer's day. She closed her eyes and let the sun beat down on her face. The bees were tumbling and droning in the flower border and she concentrated on the sharp red afterimage of the horizon lingering on her retina. She became aware of movement in the grass, and then a soft thump as someone sat down beside her, close.

'Well, how did you find it?' Gary asked.

She squinted at him. He was unlacing his track shoe and trying to redistribute his sock.

'That idea of Perfect Love,' he said, without waiting for her reply, 'that's a pretty amazing concept, isn't it? Have you ever had Perfect Love?' He gazed at her with disconcerting directness.

'No, I haven't, Gary,' she said, mildly.

'You must have had a lot of boyfriends,' he said. 'Did you ever experience anything remotely like it?'

'Well,' said Carmen, flattered by his assumption that so many moths had singed their wings at her feeble flame. She wasn't quite sure what perfect love was. She supposed it would be Robin running across the Yorkshire moors, calling 'Carmen' in a strangled voice, but then Robin would be wearing wellington boots, a tightly buttoned waterproof and carrying an umbrella.

30

'What about your present boyfriend?' he prompted.

She made a huge effort of imagination and invested Robin with the qualities of abandoned spontaneity that she had once believed were his. She planted him more securely on the wind-swept heath – but even so she was aware of his bicycle propped up against the tree. He called 'Carmen' a few more times with peevish insistency and then pencilled a note, pronged it onto the branch of a blasted oak and cycled off, probably to his Spanish evening class.

'Well,' said Carmen, doubtfully, 'before you get to know some-one, it's usually pretty perfect. When you're just stuck on them from a distance...'

To Carmen's way of thinking, unrequited infatuation with an unsuspecting subject was as perfect as love ever got. She eyed Gary speculatively. With his dark good looks, his Byronic intensity and his air of other-worldly mystery he was clearly unattainable, and he therefore presented himself as a promising candidate.

'If it was on offer, wouldn't you want it? Eternal love, total mutual respect? Two people coming together with a bond stronger than life itself? Isn't that how love should be? Don't you want it?' He con-tinued to search her face with a sincerity that she found embarrassing and alarming. He was like a rather glamorous alien in a science fic-tion movie, and, no doubt, his alien masters had planned his mor-phology by watching endless reruns of *Fireball X-L-5*. They had somehow got the eyes wrong and programmed him with a faulty notion of small talk. Her uneasy sense that he was about to requite a passion which she hadn't yet decided to conceive was both intriguing and off-putting.

She looked away, confused. 'Yes, I expect so,' she said politely. 'But I'm not quite sure what it involves.'

To her relief, the handbell began to ring in the distance, with its mournful undertones of schoolrooms and duty.

'I know it's possible,' he said. 'And I want you to have it.'

He jumped to his feet immediately, his eyes fixed anxiously on the house, but he hadn't finished. He began to talk more urgently, hold-ing her there, as though it was imperative that he should get his mess-age across before the bell ceased to clatter.

'I promise you, Carmen. Once you experience a love like that, any other love would seem empty ... compromised ... I didn't believe it was true myself once, but I've seen that it's possible. I know what it means...'

The bell petered out abruptly and the strains of a love song began to swell from the house. She had a surreal sense that she should now catch hold of his arm and whisper softly in a voice choked with emotion, 'Gary, you've convinced me. I want it too!' Perhaps he would crush her clumsily to his chest and bury his thankful face in her straw-coloured hair, but she had no opportunity to test the theory because he was already haring off across the grass towards the open windows of the lecture room.

The lecture rambled on in the same rhapsodic, inconclusive fashion and it seemed that lunchtime would never come. Jane slipped her a note. It read, 'Pamela says the meat went off so it's pearl barley soup for lunch', and then, as a hastily scribbled afterthought which Carmen could just decipher, 'I have an awful feeling Pamela's going to ask me to marry her...' Carmen screwed the slip of paper in her hand, aware that Gary had followed the transaction with bristling disapproval as though he'd caught her secreting chewing gum on the kneeler in a church. And still Matthew droned on.

After the lunchtime sing-song and the obligatory prayers, they were forced to confront the denuded stew. Carmen detected a few meat traces in the thin grey gruel, but this only put the coagulated lumps of pearl barley under suspicion. She baulked at eating what might be maggots, no matter how reproachful Gary's coaxing references to the long-suffering devotion of the sister who had cooked the food.

'Well, I'm sure it took her a long time,' said Carmen reasonably, 'but she's not going to know if I don't eat it, is she? Not unless you tell her.' She didn't want to hurt their feelings but she was beginning to find their interest in her eating habits unhealthily intrusive. One of the pleasures of adulthood was that one could eat or not eat according to whim or fancy. Not since the sadistic struggles of her school days had she experienced pressure over food, and it baffled her. It was not as though it was some moral precept, some idea about not wasting food, for there was scarcely enough to go round as it was.

'I think it's yummy,' Pamela remarked to Gary, ignoring Carmen altogether. 'I always think when something's made with love, you can somehow *taste* it.'

'Mmmm,' Gary answered on cue like a ham actor. 'Yes, this certainly tastes of love,' and he smacked his lips like a husband in an advert and looked pointedly at Carmen.

She suddenly felt uncomfortably like a bright child sandwiched between two elderly adults who both nursed the grotesque notion that she could be fooled into gulping red medicine if they both pretended it was cherryade.

As she looked uneasily from one to the other, she found herself thinking again that there was a curious blandness about the members, a strange uniformity. She couldn't quite put her finger on it. Of course they *had* personalities. Some were more self-righteous like Pamela and the other girl, Virginia, some more serious and intense like Gary, but the differences were not as marked as they were amongst a normal random sample of human beings, or even amongst a random sample of spaniel puppies in a pet-shop litter. And it was dawning on her slowly that it was not only Gary whose eyes were strange and somehow compelling. *All* the members had the same pained, disconcerting eyes.

When she could do so with politeness, she got to her feet, leaving them to congratulate each other on the noxious food, and went outside.

On the lawn, there was a net strung up between two trees and a group of boys were playing a boisterous game of volleyball. She could tell by their terse expletives, by their raucous whoops and their spontaneity that they were guests. They had identifiable quirks and faults, they had mood swings, they varied from moment to moment, they made jokes. The members didn't do any of those things. She sat on the steps watching the players and brooding, pondering on the idea that a group of people could lose their spontaneity, could forfeit their sense of humour en masse.

After a while, a young man lowered himself onto the step beside her. She tensed, thinking it was Gary, and then relaxed when she saw that it was a guest whom she'd met that morning. His name was Peter and she liked him. Not only had he expressed some interest in her injured foot but he had turned his car boot inside out, trying to find his first-aid kit and looking for a plaster.

Now, to her surprise, his voice echoed her own thoughts.

'What is it about the members?' he mused. 'What happens? I have this sense there's something not quite right here. I have this sense they're not like us at all.'

She looked at him with interest. He was softly spoken with a Northern accent. His face was open and his eyes were clear and keen. He looked to her about twenty-two or three, but he wore a close-cropped beard that tried and failed to give his baby face a rugged air.

'They told me we'd be discussing humanitarian prison reform, schemes for drug rehabilitation, urban decay, the Third World. I said I was interested in discussing animal rights and Women's Issues.' He shook his head, puzzled. 'But really all this peace and love stuff, well what's it to do with anything? I mean it only worked in the sixties because people took a lot of drugs...' He looked up at her sharply as though a sudden thought had occurred to him. 'You don't think they take drugs?' he asked.

Carmen shook her head. She was sure that something affected their eyes, but she couldn't think it was anything in the soup. If so, they would have tried to make the food more palatable, surely.

'I think it's something in the lectures,' she said solemnly, although she couldn't imagine what it was.

'Maybe you're right. I'm paranoid,' he said. Carmen shook her head again. She had already looked around the walls of the lecture room for air vents through which they might possibly release some sort of soporific gas. She had listened hard for any telltale noise which might suggest a tape playing subliminally. Because, after all, would Lucy have lasted a day here? Lucy, bright as a button on her own particular subjects, but totally uninterested in religion or any sort of scheme to change the world? Lucy had the boredom threshold of a gnat and she didn't even particularly like singing. She'd been identified as a growler at school and had refused to growl in public ever since.

Carmen said darkly, 'I think they're going to bore us into submission and then make us sing ourselves to death.' Peter laughed.

The boys at the net were calling them to join in, and they got to their feet and entered into the game. That was the nice thing, Carmen thought, reluctantly. People here *were* friendly, and there were no barriers at all. No racial tensions, no artificial cliques, no prejudice between the brothers and the sisters that she could see. Only Them and Us: the inexplicable, invisible barrier that existed between the members and the guests.

It was a fast, exhilarating game and the lads were good-natured and friendly. They were maybe not the kind of friends she would have made in other circumstances – Franklin and Lloyd were soldiers on leave and Franklin, particularly with his tattoos and his strange mixture of blustering aggression and naivety, was not immediately prepossessing, but they were normal, less-than-perfect beings. It made the difference more marked when the spiritual parents appeared.

'Watch out!' said Franklin hoaresely, and he stubbed his cigarette out on the rose bush. 'Here they come. Look happy.' Sure enough, from different directions, the parents were weaving towards them, smiling, affecting to saunter casually as they converged on the group to break it up.

She watched as Franklin's rubber face settled experimentally into a hang-dog look if angelic innocence. He had the air of someone who'd spent hid life submitting to a superior authority and who found it a matter of indifference whether he sucked up to the school teacher, the sergeant major or the fierce Japanese Spiritual Mother who had now come to claim him. Carmen noticed Gary heading for her from the back of the house and she found that she too assumed a meek, mealy-mouthed simper which didn't feel the least bit natural.

It was as though all the guests were in a tacit conspiracy to have as much fun as possible but, for some reason, without letting the Spiritual Parents know. The members had their own conspiracy to protect, and they pursued their aim with the dignified but slightly world-weary air of newly appointed prefects given onerous charge of a particularly mischievous fourth form. They scolded and advised, guided and marshalled, answered silly questions, sorted out pillowcase problems and lost pencils, their mouths smiling but their eyes remote and strained.

'So we *will* be getting on to the Third World problems today?' she heard Peter enquiring. The Korean girl was nodding firmly. 'All these major World problems we begin to discuss today.'

Once the lecture bell had finished ringing, the corridors were emptied as if by magic, leaving only those members whose charges were in the lavatories to stand outside the stalls urging the occupants with increasing desperation to hurry up, as though the world would end if they didn't finish urinating before the rapturous singing should begin.

Chapter 3

Carmen sat through the second lecture with a small, worried frown of concentration on her face. As Matthew chalked up his bizarre diagrams with a piece of blue chalk that squeaked, he expounded his thesis in an even reverent tone of authority. Carmen struggled to jot down every word, dutifully reproducing the cryptic geometric constructions in the childish notebook they had given her. She was determined to get it all down. There was something sinister here, and she meant to get to the bottom of it. Gary noted with approval her alert, upright posture, her bright eyes hungry for knowledge, her hand moving across the page like the needle of a frenzied oscilloscope. If she'd thought this feat of concentration would clarify anything, she was mistaken. It was only after two hours of faithful and frantic transcribing that Carmen's zeal began to flag and her eyes took on a dull and steady glaze. It was very boring but, she had to admit, it was about as sinister as sitting in a laundrette watching the coloureds revolve.

Matthew was trying to prove, by means of completely warped logic, that Adam and Eve had existed, and while she thought this an odd aim for a group who claimed to have nothing to do with religion, it was undeniably *not* sinister.

'God would never deliberately create something to harm man,' he was saying. 'Therefore, this apple must have been a symbol. We've seen many, many times that symbols are used in the Bible, isn't that so? And whatever this eating of the fruit symbolises, we know that it passes from generation to generation. Why do things pass from generation to generation? It's because of genetics, nothing to do with eating fruit. It's to do with genetics.'

Matthew stared solemnly at his feet while this sank in.

'Whatever that apple symbolised, it must be more powerful than life itself. Well...' he raised his head, 'there's only one power that overrides life itself, and we all know what that is, don't we?'

He allowed the question to hang heavily in the air. No-one

attempted to supply the answer, apart from someone in the front row who squeaked, 'Death?'

Matthew pretended not to hear. 'Love, yes, love.'

'The ultimate test that we all go through spiritually is *love*.'

He put down his chalk. 'A lot of you may be thinking...' He put his hands behind his back and paced the front of the class with an air of portentous introspection, 'What have Adam and Eve to do with *me*?'

Carmen looked around the faces discreetly. The members were staring ahead with calm complacency. The guests were variously affecting polite expressions of quizzical wistfulness, dumb indifference, and Franklin, the army boy in the front row, was shielding a gaping yawn. Matthew looked up with a show of sudden power and his blue eyes pierced the yawner, who abruptly froze in mid-yawn and shut his mouth.

'Yes, it all seems a long time ago, doesn't it? But actually what many scientists are now beginning to discover is that it has a direct relevance to our lives today. You see, whatever this serpent was, we know that Eve experienced some sort of love relationship with it, therefore we *know* that the snake was able to communicate with man spiritually, able to deceive man – this being knew of God's command. It was a sentient being, a spiritual being. It couldn't have been a real serpent because he would have died by now, isn't that so? There aren't any snakes in London Zoo who've lasted six thousand years, isn't that so?'

He allowed himself a smile.

'Some people would have us believe this was a talking snake. Now, I don't know if anyone here has ever seen a talking snake...?'

He allowed himself to raise one eyebrow, satirically. There was much laughter as he mimicked a ventriloquist's snake with his arm and said, ''ullo.'

Matthew shook his head firmly as the laughter died down, 'No, I don't think so. We know that this snake is as active now as it was then. Okay, so we look to the Bible.' He turned to the board and began to write the reference as he talked. 'Revelations twelve nine indicates to us the true origin of this being – Satan was cast down onto the earth and his angels were cast down with him.'

He scrawled some more words on his drawing. 'The Bible

particularly mentions Lucifer as the angel who Satan cast down. So LUCIFER...' he wrote the name large beside the wriggle that represented the snake. 'Lucifer was involved in a relationship of lust with Eve...' He linked the two names together with an arrow. 'And that relationship, as Divine Principle reveals, had *direct* and *drastic* consequences for the world we live in today...' He began to tell the story of the fatal love triangle in an intimate confidential manner, as though he were describing a rather difficult marital problem between three friends whom everyone knew and of whom everyone faintly disapproved.

At seven o'clock, everyone poured out of the lecture and mingled aimlessly in the dining room. They all seemed to be abuzz with the lecture, but Carmen suspected now that this was a misleading impression. The members were buzzing ecstatically and the guests were stupefied and puzzled, pretending enthusiasm in order not to be thought impolite or stupid or irredeemably unspiritual. Carmen sat out of the general melée on one of the hard-backed chairs, keeping her eyes fixed hopefully on the trestle table beneath the podium. A crowd was gathered there around Matthew and Marianne and she hoped this meant the tea trolley was imminent. After a moment, Gary made his way over. He squatted intimately beside her, so close that she could feel the heat coming off his skin.

'How are you finding it?' he asked, his arm arched on her chair.

'Oh,' she said noncommittally. 'It's quite interesting.'

'It's very deep, isn't it?' he pressed on, the faintest note of reproof in his voice. 'It's actually quite an astounding revelation when you understand it fully. Some people get quite moved by it.'

'Yes,' said Carmen. 'Well, I can't see why it should *move* anyone really. It's an interpretation.' And then, since he looked so pained, 'An interesting interpretation. *If* you're interested in religion,' she added rather accusingly.

Gary shook his head emphatically.

'No, no. It's not religion. This is entirely logical. Religion's where you believe something. These are scientific facts. It's not a matter of belief. You see, Principle's a logical analysis of biblical facts and it's absolutely water-tight. That's what's so mind-blowing about it. You'll see in the lecture tomorrow, it'll all get clearer.'

Carmen nodded doubtfully. The crowd was milling around the

table but she still couldn't catch the glint of an urn. Gary redistributed his weight slightly, effectively blocking her view and bringing her attention back to his earnest face.

'I'm surprised it didn't affect you at all,' he said. 'Personally I could hear that lecture over and over again and never get tired of it. There's always some new point to pick up on. It just gets deeper and deeper every time. Now, are there any points you want clearing up?' he asked. Carmen looked at him wonderingly as he spoke. There was an urgency, an alertness about him, as though it was tremendously important. There was no doubt that his proximity, and the anxious way he scrutinised her face, was flattering. She wanted to please him. She didn't want to pour scorn on his religious beliefs, if that's what they were but, in the end, what was there to discuss? Like any religious theory, one believed it or one didn't.

'There were a few things that bothered me, if you're trying to say it's logical.' She screwed up her nose. 'But really, it's hardly worth...'

'Let's go over them,' he said firmly. He got up and pulled himself a chair to sit on, while she pretended to run her finger down the page.

'Well.' She stared dully at the page of frantic scrawl and indecipherable cryptograms. 'Look, just on a logical basis, Gary, if the talking snake's ruled out because we've never seen one...' – he nodded tersely – 'then you have to use the same logic for the angels. You can't switch.'

'Uh huh. But, as Matthew pointed out, God only needed the angels while he was creating the world. I mean, for instance, the Bible says God said, "Let there be light." Well, he must have been talking to someone, so the logical deduction is that he was talking to his archangels.' He said this in such a matter-of-fact tone that Carmen could only lower her eyes and nod dutifully, rather embarrassed for him.

'But that's not what I'm saying, Gary. I mean, if you've never seen a talking snake, and that means there's never *been* a talking snake, then logically you have to say we've never seen a man with wings, so there's never *been* a man with wings.' He sat silent, so she assumed she'd won her point. The sound of her own voice was beginning to irritate her. She added more gently, 'I'm not saying there were never

40

any angels. I'm just saying you can't use that kind of argument to prove it.'

'Yes,' said Gary. 'Well, actually they didn't have wings, but I know what you're getting at. The thing is, the angels were only necessary up until Jesus came. You won't find them mentioned much after that. Once the direct communication was established God didn't need them any more.'

Carmen nodded, wild-eyed, at this surreal discussion. 'Yes, I got that, Gary, but maybe he needed a talking snake on the same basis and then he didn't need it any more.'

'But the whole idea of a talking snakes's totally ridiculous,' Gary protested.

'Not if you happen to believe it,' Carmen pointed out. Then, wearying of the whole pointless conversation, she added, 'Which I don't.'

'In that case you haven't understood it,' he said. 'That's OK. It's pretty complicated if you haven't got a scientific brain.' Her eyes levelled on him coldly. 'Now, let's go back to the Tree Of Life...' And to Carmen's astonishment, Gary began to paraphrase the lecture she had just heard, at great length, as though she hadn't heard it at all. As he talked, his eyes took on a strange, opaque, distant look, as though some mental drawbridge had come down, as though he was on automatic pilot.

She waited until he drew breath and then cut in with an air of finality.

'But look, Gary. It's all academic, really. You know I'm interested in hearing the philosophy but, well, since I don't believe in God, it doesn't really matter, does it? I mean there's a hundred interpretations of the Adam and Eve story. This one's as valid as any other. And it *was* a long time ago.'

She smiled sunnily at him to show that it wasn't personal, and then turned a determined gaze towards the table. Everyone seemed to be praying over a big cardboard box. They began to pick out pieces of paper from it, to unfold them and call out names.

Gary shrugged, tipped his chair back and regarded her with dissatisfaction. 'Sure, it doesn't really matter. How d'you know if something interests you unless you're sure you understand it? The main thing is to have a good time and enjoy yourself. This is one place where you can really take some time to explore your personality and make some useful changes.'

Carmen had often explored her personality through quizzes in *Cosmopolitan*. Generally, she found it quite satisfactory as it was.

She was feeling very hungry but she could see that people were beginning to sort themselves into teams like children in a playground. Soon she found herself tagged onto the end of a line and filing with her group towards a Team Meeting, where they were assured of an informal group discussion on topics of general interest. She had a grim sense of foreboding. She was beginning to suspect that there was only one topic of general interest in the Family, and that was the one that she and Gary had just discussed.

There were seven guests, six members and Marianne, their team leader, seated in a circle as though for a college seminar or a psychiatric therapy group. Marianne was smiling around the faces like Nurse Hatchett about to order a lobotomy. They introduced themselves and applauded one another's halting contributions as one by one they explained how they'd been tricked or cajoled onto the course. Some of them seemed to have been frankly press-ganged. Achmet spoke little English and seemed totally bewildered. 'Barbecue,' he repeated. 'He said something about barbecue and I find myself getting on the coach.' Peter told them he was a social worker in Lanarkshire. He'd just split up with his girlfriend and was feeling lonely when he first met Ikuno on the street. She'd been warm and friendly and invited him for a meal. It was only when he got to the house that he realised it wasn't to be just the two of them but a simple informal banquet for twenty-five. Carmen clapped him particularly warmly. She liked Peter. He seemed a pleasant, trusting sort of person who didn't deserve to be brainwashed, if that was what was going to happen. She wasn't quite so sure about Reg, or Wendy.

Reg was a lanky, ungainly man in his late forties with luxuriant sandy hair that kinked naturally into a marcel wave. He had a long, pale lugubrious face and spoke very deliberately with a pedantic, nasal twang that suggested he had never been told that he was boring. Carmen listened to him with awe. He was a man of some stature in his local church, as he was at pains to point out. He ran his church youth club and, since one of his young brass players had joined the Family, he'd come on a fact-finding mission with a completely open mind. Now he delivered his interim findings.

'And I've found it very warm, very God-fearing, very hospitable.' He nodded gravely at Marianne, like a king acknowledging a revered consort. His mind was so open, thought Carmen, that he represented a danger to himself. He was one of life's natural conformists who, given a structured situation, would instinctively ally himself with any authority that presented itself, and he was already turning back-flips and somersaults to get his gold star.

Wendy and Ruth were mother and daughter from a nice, middle-class, suburban home. Wendy wore a velvet Alice band in her hair and a pained expression on her face, perhaps as a result of her sudden, cruel desertion by her husband, which she recounted to the group. Her eyes were already remote and she seemed hungry for the group's approval. Her daughter sat beside her, a pale, unhappy, fourteen-year-old lump with a ponytail and two grave, gentian eyes that were her only beauty. The pair seemed like two shell-shocked survivors, gripping the only raft in a hostile ocean.

And now Reg was giving his careful, measured analysis of the lecture, conceding this point guardedly, disputing that reservedly, producing biblical quotations complete with references to back up his point, discoursing learnedly on the different viewpoints that could be taken on the subject of Original Sin. As he spoke Marianne cocked her head this way and that with a flattering absorption, nodding, interpolating, demolishing his argument with a quick swipe, so charming in her funny, childlike pussy-cat way that Reg hardly registered he'd just lost the battle. Carmen was glad someone wanted to talk, because she'd decided she wasn't going to. The late sun was streaming through the open window, patterning the parquet floor with the soft shadows of leaves. Outside she could see a butterfly hovering around the bed of lupins. The figures in the gloomy room seemed rather insubstantial and flat. Through half-closed eyes she could see a haloed afterimage like a fitted neon round each different head.

'Carmen?' the voice startled her. ''Ow did you find this lecture?'

'Er, I thought he was good,' said Carmen, hoping to give points for style and presentation and miss out on content altogether. 'He explained it all very clearly and he's a very persuasive speaker.'

Marianne nodded, with a hint of impatience. 'The speaker is inspired by God,' she said, and continued to wait with polite interest for more.

Carmen wriggled. She was loath to ask a question when she didn't want to know the answer; besides, Marianne would just repeat the whole interminable lecture over again like a warped record with the needle stuck.

'You listen to this whole lecture and you have no questions?' She smiled with tender, teasing incredulity.

'Well, I've already had a long talk with Gary about the talking snake...' Carmen hid a half-apologetic smirk. 'And he explained all that to me,' she said hastily. 'It all seems to make a lot of sense.'

'What 'ave you found particularly inspiring?' Marianne persisted.

Inspiring. Crumbs, that was a difficult one. Carmen racked her brains. To her relief, Peter broke in and the eyes all swivelled away from her.

'There *was* something I wanted to ask, Marianne,' he said. His rather dogged face was crumpled with earnest puzzlement and a tinge of embarrassment.

'Look, I understand Eve had sex with the angel but I don't see how that would taint her bloodstream, really. I mean, if Adam and Eve were real people, well, blood doesn't mingle during intercourse, does it?' He looked anxiously around the faces as though everyone knew a Fact Of Life that he'd missed out on.

Marianne bridled and looked rather affronted, as though there was something distasteful about anyone wanting to go too deeply into the medical ramifications of the affair.

'An angel is a dirty thing,' she affirmed stoutly. 'This would be like to 'ave sex with an animal, a beast, an ape. This pollutes the pure bloodstream with sin like germs.' And her eyes flashed indignantly at Peter as though he was somehow responsible for Lucifer's dirty actions. 'Eve's blood is tainted with the bad blood of the Spirit Man so that when she 'ave sex with Adam, that sin, it multiplies like germs, more and more, breeding down the centuries like bacteria and this is how we have such a bad situation now.'

Peter nodded vigorously to imply that he was actually on her side and not trying to make trouble. Marianne, seeing his compliance, relented slightly.

'This is how we have sin and suffering in the world today. Lucifer actually spoilt God's beautiful plan. This human history should have been like a factory line producing perfect human beings, but what happens? The factory produces rejects and the fault of this prototype just keeps on repeating, multiplying the damage. This makes a lot of sense for the way our world is today, huh?'

Peter was still nodding anxiously, keen to toss the ball back into general play, regretting he had ever tried to field it in the first place.

Once Marianne had elicited questions from each of the guests and despatched them all with her quiet, inexorable logic, they bent their heads in prayer, all apparently satisfied, while Marianne informed Heavenly Father of how ignorant they all were, and begged Him to make them humble. As they looked up, Peter caught Carmen's eye and she saw that the crumpled, puzzled look was still there on his forehead as though none of it made any sense at all.

The guests filed out like a line of stunned ducklings towards the dining room. 'Well, that was a pretty stimulating session,' Pamela chirruped. 'What did you make of it?'

'Reg is a bit of a bore,' Carmen said, idly, aware that he had stayed behind after class to ingratiate himself further with Marianne.

Pamela frowned. 'We try to look at people through God's eyes in the Family, Carmen. We've all got qualities and faults.' Her tone was quite severe. 'Some of the people with the sharpest tongues aren't always the people closest to God's Heart. It's not nice to be always criticising. If you just try and look through God's eyes for once, you might discover some rather revealing things about yourself.'

Pamela's tart little speech made Carmen feel oddly depressed, as though she was an unsatisfactory sort of person. It was true that she was pretty intolerant. She often had uncharitable thoughts, she often made judgements and sometimes the burden of her cynicism turned inwards as a self-punitive reaction. Perhaps it was true that if one couldn't say anything nice then one had best keep silent. Of course it would also make life very dull and, even with the best of intentions, she didn't think she could keep it up for long.

'Even God'd think that man was a bore,' muttered Jane who was standing behind them.

'We don't like to be judgmental in the Family,' said Pamela swiftly. 'And we dwell on people's positive characteristics.'

'He's nice and tall,' Jane simpered, and she pinched Carmen's arm and winked, but Carmen suddenly realised that she was feeling, for some reason, ridiculously tearful: she didn't laugh for fear her face would crumple.

There was the remains of the stew for dinner, followed by a bright jelly and custard which Carmen refused. After a while, she got up, without being asked, and began to collect the finished plates and carry them through to the kitchen. People were usually invited to volunteer for washing up, but she had worked out for herself that a hundred greasy plates were preferable to sitting staring at an uneaten meal under Gary's disapproving eye. The kitchen was an institutional-looking place, as befitted the kitchen of a convent. It boasted two enormous vats and a monstrous evil-looking gas stove. There were two exhausted little sisters on their hands and knees with their heads practically inside it, scrubbing out its bowels. Carmen found the sound of their brushes chafing and her own clatter soothing and cathartic. It was only the second time since she'd arrived that she'd felt any sort of privacy.

Just as she was beginning to relax, Peter wobbled in with a great pile of sticky plates and he stayed behind to dry up for her as she washed. He was still looking faintly perplexed, still dwelling on the mystifying mechanics of spirit copulation.

'I still can't understand how the sin's supposed to get in there,' he said. 'Did you get it?'

She shook her head. 'Osmosis, I expect,' and she scraped the custard goo and the nauseating glitter of the jelly into the pig-bin. 'What does it matter? If you can believe he was an angel and angels can walk through walls, you might as well believe his other bits can go through walls as well.'

Peter considered this explanation and seemed to find it satisfactory.

'Yes,' he said. 'Well, I accept that the snake must have been an angel. After all, it couldn't have been a talking snake.'

'Of *course* it could,' said Carmen testily. 'Once you decide to believe one impossible thing, you might as well believe seven or eight of them. You don't have to restrict yourself.'

Peter put down his drying-up cloth and began to talk intently. 'Look, as I understand it...' He began to count his fingers, still trying to sort it out in his head.

46

'The Tree Of Life was symbolic. The Tree Of The Knowledge Of Goodness And Evil, this stood for . . .'

'Oh, don't *you* start, Peter!' she cried out in a sudden frenzy of exasperation. He stopped, confused, appalled to realise that he was now parroting the same gibberish that he'd been bombarded with all day. Then they both started to laugh, entirely forgetting the two sisters with their heads in the gas oven. Carmen threw the wet cloth at him and Peter began to spray her with the rubber tap hose until her jeans were soaked.

The heads of the two sisters emerged from the metal surround and they exchanged glances of grave disquiet. Laughter was not much appreciated in the Family unless it was a member who'd made the joke and then on an approved subject. How very far the Fall Of Man was from being an approved subject in the Family, neither Peter nor Carmen, as they fooled around splashing one another, whooping and shrieking, could have guessed. When Gary arrived, they'd begun to sober up, but all the same they looked at him rather guiltily as he strode in.

Gary, too, was ill at ease, strangely off guard, his expression inscrutable. He'd come to fetch them for the Family Evening, a short session because it was already ten-fifteen and everything was running late. Carmen thought that she had glimpsed for a moment, before he snapped on his friendly, big brother smile, an odd expression on his face, an expression that she might almost have judged to be jealousy. Perhaps he suspected her of lining up some perfect love for herself in the kitchen with another suitor, or perhaps he resented a spontaneity which was lost to him forever. Whatever it was, she knew just then that Gary, for all he had found the meaning of life, was not a very happy human being.

They hurried after him to join the jollification in the hall. An amateur talent night was in progress and people were being encouraged to come out to the front and do a turn. The lights were dimmed, with spotlights on the floor area, and it somehow created the excited anticipation of a special children's treat. Carmen huddled up small on her seat, with the natural shrinking of the nervous from any suggestion that they might be required to participate.

When the harmonica player stepped down, Reg was coaxed to take his place. She felt a fit of the giggles coming on, just looking at

47

him. He was threshing his arms wildly in protest, teetering like a tree that had learnt to walk. He was being forced protesting to the spotlight, propelled by three tiny Japanese sisters who pushed and pulled him like Lilliputians manoeuvring an obstinate Gulliver. As he cleared his throat, everyone was clapping wildly and whistling and stamping their feet. He was certainly very popular.

'He has a very good singing voice,' Pamela explained.

Which made it all the more excrutiating when he actually began to sing. 'Bless This House' was a difficult song for the most accomplished singer. Reg dutifully climbed to the strangled upper limits of his range like an old car attempting an impossible gradient, hitting a true note now and then, but more often hitting them a mere fraction off, which was somehow worse than missing them altogether.

Carmen's shoulders began to shake. She was very tired and was beginning to feel a little hysterical.

Whenever Reg sensed trouble ahead, a great frown of concentration rippled across his brow. He changed pitch and then, trapped in the wrong register, he was forced to growl through the low bits with his chins doubling and tripling. When he ground to a halt – and, as is always the way on these occasions, he seemed to know a lot of verses – Carmen was reduced to a shaking heap. The room around her rose to him with a great roar, the applause unrestrained and ecstatically appreciative.

Reg stood there abashed in the spotlight, unable to credit his audience's enthusiasm, stooping shyly and foolishly on one leg, his face glowing red with a painful, boyish pleasure as he began to beam helplessly from ear to ear.

It was then, as his speechless pleasure communicated itself, that Carmen began to feel ashamed. The suppressed laughter unreleased at the back of her throat turned into a strange catching ache and she was aware that her eyes were suddenly hot with unspilt tears. Perhaps she was seeing him through God's eyes, or maybe it was that there is nothing so touchingly vulnerable as someone who can't sing and doesn't know it. Reg was having his moment, and as she looked around at the assembled company, all smiling and clapping and roaring their acceptance, she felt swamped with an emotion that was unquantifiable. There *was* something genuinely moving about people who offered this kind of support, who would love you

48

regardless of what you were like, what you did, what you wore or how witty you were in conversation.

Emboldened by the rapturous response, Reg was now licking his lips as though about to give them another tune but, thankfully, the sisters who had dragged him on now dragged him off before he could push his luck.

'You'll have to sing one night, you know,' Gary said to Carmen in a low voice.

'No. No, I'd be mortified,' she said shrinking.

'Yes. But those kind of inhibitions, what use are they?' he asked. 'Really, they're just a form of self-regard.'

'I sing like a dog in pain,' she said firmly.

'I should imagine from looking at you that you'd have a rather beautiful voice,' he said cordially and then he turned his attention back to the unskilled juggler who had now taken the stage.

In the dormitory at midnight Carmen and Jane lay, unwashed, in their bunks one above the other, each staring at the view above them, their eyes unfocussed, totally high and too exhausted to sleep. Pamela breezed in and began to distribute hand-stapled books of white paper to the sisters in the room. As she handed them up to Jane and Carmen she lingered, waiting for a response.

Carmen looked at hers. It was blank. On the cover was a blue tissue paper crescent moon and some stars. The words 'My Book Of Reflections' had been written oh so carefully at the bottom with a purple felt tip pen.

'I helped make it,' said Pamela shyly. 'I cut out all the little blue shapes.'

There was something so wistful about the way Pamela hovered that Carmen felt obliged to admire it exaggeratedly, rather as though a child had timidly proffered an unrecognisable Santa made from a Dairylea cheese box and milk-bottle tops. But Pamela was not five. She was almost nineteen.

'It's lovely,' said Carmen. 'Did you really cut the stars out? That must have been quite tricky.' Silence. 'What's it for?'

Jane, in the bunk beneath, bit her lip.

'Oh, you write down all your private, innermost thoughts, you know, about the course and anything really beautiful that happens to you...'

'I'll write something really nice in it,' Carmen promised warmly.

At that, Pamela looked quietly pleased, and then she toddled off to the bathroom in her winceyette pyjamas with her toothbrush in her hand.

'You'd *better* write something nice in it,' Jane's disembodied voice warned her darkly. 'They collect them in at the middle of the week and read them.' Carmen laughed.

'You think I'm joking,' came Jane's voice again. 'But I'm not.'

Carmen put her pen gingerly to the first virgin page of the Reflection book. After a moment, she felt the crate heave and Jane's head peered up, level with Carmen's knee. Her face was serious and she spoke quickly and very softly.

'I know I laugh at them, Carmen,' she said, 'but, you know, they're very good people. Can you see what I mean now? They're sort of innocent. There's no harm in them. They're like children.' Carmen recognised the symptoms. Jane was feeling contrite for something or other. 'Yes,' said Carmen. Jane lowered herself again, reassured by Carmen's face that she had really understood, and, in a way, she had. The members had a strange knack of arousing resentment and hostility in the guests and then defusing it just as suddenly by revealing their vulnerability. How could you attack people who were so obviously defenceless? It was easy to laugh at them, but then wasn't it at the same time rather churlish and predatory to share their lives, accept their food and yet to sneer at them behind their backs. Her pen hovered over the page but she couldn't bring herself to write. Knowing that her thoughts were going to be read gave her a creepy, uneasy feeling.

If these people were so nice, so harmless, what was she afraid of? And yet she was a little bit afraid. There was always that sneaking doubt: what if *they* were the ones who were laughing, what if they were the ones who were deceiving? She knew that this was late-night, crazy paranoia, but she decided to be cautious all the same. She christened the silly notebook in an elaborate italic hand.

'Well, what an exciting, inspiring day,' she wrote carefully. 'The lectures are very interesting and intriguing. Of course I have lots of questions but everyone says it gets deeper and deeper and all will become clear as I hear more of Principle.'

This looked a little reserved and cautious when she read it over.

She wanted to give the impression that she was eager to learn and so she tried to adopt Pamela's tone of positive enthusiasm. 'I CAN'T WAIT,' she wrote and then she read it over and over, strangely disconcerted.

What a bizarre state of affairs, to be lying to a notebook. What was the point of it? All the book would reflect back to them, if they wanted to read it, would be a false mirror image of themselves. Thinking that made her feel, just for the odd split second, as though she was dissolving; she lay back searching the pitted, pock-marked ceiling tiles until Pamela came back in.

She turned her head and murmured down to her, 'Pamela, who *runs* the Family?'

Pamela smiled enigmatically. 'No-one runs the Family,' she said. 'That's the miracle. The Family runs itself.'

Carmen thought about it. 'But it must have a leader. I mean the Boy Scouts run themselves but they still have Baden-Powell. Some-one must have started it. There must be *someone* at the head.'

'Questions, questions.' Pamela made a funny, scolding face. 'Well, it's true. It was a very extraordinary man who founded the Family. A very kind-hearted, spiritual man who was also a philanthropist on a big scale. He's like the father of the family. He's like our Baden-Powell.' And then she turned the light off.

'But what's his name?' Carmen persisted in the darkness. All the sisters shushed her and she turned discontentedly on her side. Then she thought she heard Pamela hiss, 'His name is Reverend Moon. Now go to *sleep*.'

Chapter 4

On the following day, after a night of disturbed sleep, reality re-asserted itself. She put the maudlin empathy of the night before down to extreme tiredness and to the twin evils of singing far too much and arguing fruitlessly on surreal subjects. She arrived red-eyed and grumpy at the early morning sing-song and, when she sat down to breakfast, she wilfully declined to pray over her food.

In the cold light of day, the members were once again extremely weird and Reg was *still* a crashing bore. The frenzied bout of singing seemed to have put too much oxygen into her bloodstream and she felt both elated and tetchy.

'The milk's off,' she observed.

'Did you have any interesting dreams?' asked Gary, pleasantly. 'Sometimes people begin to have really interesting dreams when they come here.'

'I'm not surprised,' she said. 'That dormitory smells like a hamster cage and it sounds like a farm yard.' She began to flick the oily flecks from her cup of tea. 'Do they all snore in your one, as well? There's one woman with a really hacking cough and it *sounds* infectious.'

Since Gary just looked pained, she directed her eyes to Reg.

'My bunk's jolly comfortable,' he said with a pugnacious thrust of his chin. 'When things are tight, no-one minds mucking in. That's what you young ones don't appreciate. A bit of esprit de corps.'

Carmen gave a mulish flounce. 'But things *aren't* tight,' she objected. 'There's a great big empty room next door.'

When she looked up, she saw that Gary was no longer listening but had put down his spoon and was crouched into a tense, private prayer.

'And I could really do with a good wash,' she said, discontentedly.

'Looks like another nice, sunny day, Pamela,' Reg remarked breezily across the table.

'Yes,' said Pamela, with a warning glare at Carmen. 'Heavenly Father certainly wants us to enjoy the Seven Day.'

Gary at last emerged blinking from his devotion, his brow furrowed as though the concentration had really hurt him, a pulse beating in his temple from the effort. She stared at him, perturbed.

He leaned over, picked up his plate impulsively and scraped his piece of bacon onto her plate. She thanked him ungraciously and smeared it around in the yolk of the rubber egg, then put her knife and fork together resolutely.

'I'm sorry,' she said. 'I can't eat any more. It's all streak and no bacon and the egg's like a bullet.'

Even to her own ears, she sounded peevish and ungracious, so she got to her feet, mumbled an excuse and went outside into the hallway. It was becoming urgent that she should call her mother. She didn't want to arouse her suspicions or let her worry. She'd told her she was going pony-trekking with a group of friends – a plan so uncharacteristic and unlikely that it had the ring of truth. All she had to do now was say she'd got there safely and hope that no-one started singing while she was actually on the phone.

The coin-box was in the entrance hall. It wore an ineffectual sound-proof hood. She knew it was ineffectual because there was someone inside it, head encased as though under a hair dryer, whispering urgently with a hysterical note in their voice, having a long distance argument, every word echoing and ringing off the walls because of the curious acoustic properties of the hall. The telephone in this house seemed like a kind of coin-operated confessional because everyone who used it was always in a state of distress. The same idea obviously occurred to the members, because they made a habit of hovering round the booth, eavesdropping on the conversations, eyeing the strained face of the occupant, or what could be seen of it through the scratched polythene booth.

Inside was Wendy, the unhappy housewife, and she was arguing about the custody of the daughter. She was clutching her patent handbag like a vice, discarding flurries of bus tickets as she rummaged desperately for more change. To one side of her, a member was pretending to peruse the Home Church pin-board. Carmen wandered up and down the corridor, trying not to listen to Wendy's anguished conversation. It wasn't long before Pamela came out to find her, looking severe. The previous night, with her frizzy ginger hair framing her face she had looked about fifteen but now, in her unbecoming head scarf and hausfrau frock, she looked somehow withered and tired like an ancient midget.

'Look, there's something I want to say to you, Carmen,' she began, and there was an air of hesitation which suggested it wasn't going to be pleasant but it had to be said. 'You know, Gary's trying really hard and, well, it's not exactly *fair* on him unless you try as well ... Gary feels sort of responsible for you but, you know, he can't help you to develop unless you try to help yourself.'

'What is it I'm trying to develop?' asked Carmen, mystified.

'Well, a prayer life for a start,' said Pamela with faint exasperation, as though it was self-evident. 'Honestly, Carmen, how can you *hope* to find out if there's a God unless you try to contact Him?'

Carmen had a vague, uneasy feeling that the ground rules were shifting. Just a short time ago her role had been that of the disinterested observer but now they were pushing her into becoming an active participant. Pamela went on in a quiet, reasonable, admonishing tone. 'Gary's working so hard to help you, and you don't seem to appreciate it all. He goes hungry for you and, well, it's really a bit selfish to let him suffer that way ...'

Carmen couldn't think of anything to say, except that she wasn't asking anyone to pray for her, she wasn't asking anyone to suffer or to give her their food.

'Our hospitality may be simple, but we give it with love and we give it with sacrifice. It's a struggle for us to make ends meet here. Food's a precious commodity. It's nice to have people appreciate what we try to do for them.'

Pamela's eyes were distant and strained, as though she had personally to scrape together the money for all their breakfasts. Her face was pale and drawn like a muzzle. Carmen felt guilty and defensive although she couldn't rationally see why.

'Well, I certainly don't mean to seem ungrateful,' said Carmen. 'It's just – '

'No.' Pamela softened and gave Carmen's arm a squeeze. 'But now you will start to pray, won't you? You will try to join in more and stop being so *negative*? It's such a downer for everyone else, and I know you're not like that inside. Inside, I think you're a very warm, loving person.'

Pamela smiled warmly at her. 'You know, it might be nice if you made a resolution to speak only positive thoughts. You'll be surprised how much nicer the world looks that way.' To Carmen's surprise, she gripped her hand and took a biro from her pocket. Then she began to write in block letters that tickled on Carmen's palm, 'THINK POSITIVE' and she laughed delightedly. Carmen stared at the blue ink, disturbed and affronted, surprised by her sense of invasion.

The bell began to ring and just as the bell-ringer paced down the corridor towards them, Wendy emerged tearful and distraught from the phone hood, into the arms of her Spiritual Mother.

'I just want to call my mother,' said Carmen, turning away, but Pamela restrained her.

'Not now, Carmen, there's no time. The lecture's about to start. You wouldn't want to miss any of it. It's really beautiful. It's one of my favourites.'

Reluctantly Carmen allowed herself to be led along to the lecture room, although she well knew there was plenty of time.

'Your mother sounds pretty over-protective if you've got to tell her every little thing you do', Pamela observed. 'It all sounds a bit stifling.' Before Carmen could contradict her, she found herself back in the lecture room, where the song sheet was set up waiting for the guests to assemble.

Pamela bustled about, finding her a fresh notebook and biro. 'Oh, there was just one other thing I meant to mention,' she said cautiously. 'About the dormitory. There's a very serious and important reason why we sleep together, apart from the fact it's just more fun. You see, the spirits get very active and attack a lot when you first hear Principle. They don't really want you to hear it...' She spoke low and confidentially as though they might be listening now. Carmen shook her head, wide-eyed, as if humouring a mad person. Encouraged, Pamela went on, 'There's safety in numbers. That's why we stick together. Another good tip might be to sleep on your stomach,' she added darkly.

'I'll remember that,' said Carmen, awkwardly.

Carmen gave up on the lecture within the first five minutes. If she found it hard to enter wholeheartedly into the lurid sex life of Adam and Eve and the angel as if they were real people in a soap opera, she found the lives of Cain and Abel, Abraham and Isaac, Ephraim and

Manasseh even less compelling. They covered Noah's Ark and Moses and the Red Sea. The board was rapidly filled with crazy triangles and pyramids, as Matthew passionately put across the message that each of these case histories was yet another of God's desperate symbolic attempts to restore the polluted bloodline and initiate a pure strain. Carmen was beginning to think that their God was a little crazy and, at best, hopelessly ineffectual. If He insisted on communicating with men through such obscure and devious signals, then no wonder man had constantly misunderstood the clues. She rapidly wearied of trying to follow his logic and concentrated on just writing it all down in order to keep herself awake. After two or three hours, it was hard to tell how long exactly, she drifted off to sleep.

She was awoken by a hard, bony finger prodding her in the back, and she sat up and looked around her dazed and indignant. It was Pamela, of course, frowning faintly. Carmen stared dully down at her book. They were onto GOD'S HEART – SIX THOUSAND YEARS OF SUFFERING whereas her notes had petered out on THE PROVIDENCE OF RESTORATION CENTRING ON ADAM'S FAMILY AND NOAH'S FAMILY. She had an awful feeling that he'd skipped five thousand years while she'd been asleep, and that she'd be closely cross-questioned on it all afternoon. She looked across unhappily at Jane, who was glassy-eyed and swaying slightly in her seat. She noticed that Jane's right hand was covered in neat biro mottos like so many weird tattoos. The biggest one, just above her knuckles, read 'NO CONCEPTS!'

Matthew was winding up the lecture. 'So, this is an extraordinary discovery, don't you think? For so many years people thought the events of the Old Testament were just random stories, but once you have the *key* to those events, you can see the very logical way that God has tried to contact us. So Divine Principle lets us see the whole overall pattern of human history. Extraordinary, isn't it, once you begin to see the pattern of the time periods? Has anyone ever been able to explain history to you so logically before?'

Everyone shook their heads, a lot of them without interest.

'OK, who has another question?'

Franklin was being goody-two-shoes up the front, she noticed, waving his hand urgently like a child in school anxious to be teacher's pet.

'Franklin.' Franklin shuffled self-importantly and sat up straight.

'If the whole human race came from Adam and Even, how come Noah's children were all different colours, sir?' he asked and then subsided, pleased with himself.

Matthew smiled gently at him. 'Good question. Good question. You must always question everything because it's the only way to learn. God made Noah's children all different colours because He likes us that way. OK, any more questions?'

Carmen and Jane exchanged a sort of sick look.

With all questions satisfactorily answered, the session drew to a close and Marianne bustled to the front of the class and asked them to volunteer for chores. She drew up a roster on the board and made it clear as she did so that those who wanted to get closer to Heavenly Father soonest were expected to toady for the worst of the chores: those who *didn't* would be identified as slower spiritual developers and therefore, being the most in need of spiritual mortification, would be given the worst chores anyway. It was heads or tails.

Gardening and polishing and dusting were quickly allocated, and the gardeners, dusters and polishers, who'd definitely got off lightly, all scowled ferociously so that no-one would think they were shirkers. The shirkers, on the other hand, all volunteered for the ironing and laundering and labouring so no-one would think them unspiritual.

'And now bathroom,' she said, looking around accusingly at the remaining shirkers. 'Bathroom is unpopular but bathroom loves and serves us. Who will love and serve the bathroom?'

Carmen and Jane responded simultaneously, both with a deceptive air of martyred virtue. The bathrooms were so over-employed that the toilets quickly became blocked and sordid and the job was not a pleasant one. Marianne eyed them with suspicion but she chalked them up on the board anyway. They collected their Domestos and J-cloths and, armed with toilet brushes and bleach, they sprinted upstairs to take a luxurious private turn at the toilet and the bath-hose, each guarding the door for the other. It was less satisfying than they might have anticipated because there was a leak of dark water seeping from the pedestal of the toilet and the air was fetid, but, nevertheless, they could have some privacy at last.

Their ablutions complete, they threw the window wide open,

jammed a chair against the door and smoked their cigarettes, leaning contentedly out of the window. At the suspicion of the sound of Pamela's flip-flopping sandals outside the door, they seized their brushes and flung themselves to their knees, Jane scrubbing the lime stain on the bath, Carmen mopping and swilling the unpleasantness around the lavatory, both of them breathing through their mouths and holding their noses. Her sandals stopped outside the door and they could see her shadow hovering on the frosted glass as though she were listening for sounds of activity. Satisfied, she moved on. Carmen sat upright, at eye level with the splash-back of the sink. She waited for the little while tadpoles to clear from her vision. Jane was muttering, 'You know, I'm going to have to get out of here at some point today. I'm beginning to find it a bit oppressive. I think there's a little country pub down the road ... Maybe this evening...'

Carmen was just wondering if there was the faintest possibility that they could give their Spiritual Parents the slip, when her eyes were drawn to a small, innocuous notice behind the sink. The notice was studded with hand-drawn flowers and announced in a childish, rounded hand: 'SISTERS, PLEASE DO NOT COMB HAIRS OVER SINK. IT CLOGS THE U-BEND AND MAKES WORK FOR POOR BROTHERS WHO HAVE TO UNCLOG IT.' But what had caught her attention, what had set her heart beating a little faster, were the initials that signed it off: 'I.T.P.N.' Those same initials had been on the end of Lucy's half-crazed little letter. She continued to kneel there, staring ahead of her. Well, if she had had any sneaking doubts at all, that surely settled them. Jane noticed her attention and looked at her in mild surprise.

'You only have to love and serve it. I don't think you have to kiss the porcelain.'

'What does I.T.P.N. mean?' she asked, trying to conceal her sudden excitement. She thought of all the days and nights that she and her mother had asked that same question, turning over the sheet of crumpled note-paper, wondering if the initials held some obscure coded clue.

Jane hesitated, then clicked her tongue and sighed. 'It means "In True Parents' Name" but *don't* say I told you. I'm not supposed to know yet. And don't ask me what True Parents are,' she said firmly, 'because I'm not supposed to know that either.'

But Carmen had all the information she needed to be going on with. She had been there two and a half days and already it seemed a lifetime, but here at last was a concrete sign that she was in the right place. Up till now, she'd been working on a mixture of coincidence and intuition, but this was clear confirmation that she was not such a bad detective, that she was following a warm trail and it would surely be only a matter of time before she found Lucy.

Buoyed up by this fresh information, Carmen went into lunch wearing a bland madonna smile. She sang three songs and got the actions right and she squealed emphatically for another along with all the other sisters. When they sat down to plates of jam sandwiches, she crouched first into a long, tense painful prayer and clasped her hands as though she was trying to break the bones of all her fingers, and burst a blood vessel in her forehead at the same time.

Gary watched her with a gentle curious smile. He seemed pleased, almost moved.

'What were you asking Heavenly Father?' he asked softly.

'Oh,' Carmen's eyes became vague and other-worldly, 'I was just praying for my family and friends and ... anyone who knows me.'

'Ah,' he said, looking vexed. She was relieved to see he didn't force any extra food on her. They were strawberry jam sandwiches and she could just manage the two she had. 'In the Family we tend to pray for the Future of the World. When you think of the way people are suffering with famine and wars, you know, sometimes it seems a bit ... egotistical ... to pray just for yourself.'

Carmen nodded warily. She wondered if it was actual policy never to allow a guest to get anything right. No sooner had one been emotionally blackmailed into a certain response than yet another, further modification of the response was required. It meant that one could never actually achieve the reward that was held out and that the carrot of approval just hovered further and further out of reach all the time while the stick was always swishing uncomfortably close behind you making a breeze.

In actual fact, her prayer had been something else all together. She had not addressed it to God particularly but to the Cosmos in general and it consisted of the mantra. 'Tell me what's me and what's them, where I stop and they begin,' over and over like some sort of talisman to ward off danger, although what the danger was, or whether there was any at all, she had no clear idea.

'Are you beginning to make some headway with the lectures?' he asked. 'You know, if you ever get sleepy in a lecture, you can always stand up to keep awake. No-one will mind.'

'Yeah. I only dozed off for a little moment,' she said. 'I don't know why that was because I found it really enthralling. Not a bit boring. Really quite inspiring.'

Gary scrutinised her face, unconvinced. It had been a sad lecture and Carmen looked inappropriately radiant and full of beans. 'Well, let's go over it and make sure you've understood it. What was it you found particularly inspiring?'

Carmen's heart sank. 'Well,' she put her head on one side and looked at him like a precocious child, about to launch into her twelve times table, 'God's Heart and all that.'

He waited for her to go on. Either the speed of her conversion had strained his credulity, or they had reached a new stage now. He no longer just forced her to say things, she was now obliged to persuade him that she *meant* them.

'You know, there He is, trying to put things right, watching everything spiral out of control, and yet his hands are tied. Not that He's *got* hands,' she added hastily, lest Gary should pick her up on it.

'So He just cries and cries,' she went on mournfully, 'waiting for us to contact Him and feeling all these torments. I think that's really sad.'

Their God, as far as Carmen could make out, was like a huge, unhappy barrage balloon, and, when Adam and Eve Fell, it somehow cut His moorings and He floated off out of contact and had some sort of nervous breakdown. It must have been a nervous breakdown, she decided, because any sane God could see that sending coded, symbolic messages through random history was a poor way to make contact with a human race that wasn't particularly looking out for them.

'Yes,' he said again with a quick intake of breath. 'So what was it you found so inspiring?' and he stared at her with a distinct tinge of hostility, as though it were a trick question. She cast around wildly in her mind and put on a false placatory smile.

60

'Well, I think it's really inspiring that you're all here, you know, trying to re-establish that vertical connection with Him. I mean, it's a whole new concept, isn't it? We've always thought God looked after us, but really, what this lecture tells us – ' she was beginning to pick up Family phrasing just by natural mimicry and it certainly helped to smooth a conversation – 'is that now it's up to us to look after Him, isn't it? We have to hold Him in our arms and make Him feel better.'

She looked at Gary so anxiously, as though she would be prepared to bandage God's wounds herself if He would give her the chance, that Gary relaxed and smiled sympathetically at her. Carmen drew a sigh of relief. It felt as though she were talking down a would-be suicide, trying to double-think a psychopathic axe-man.

After lunch, they filed outside to the driveway and formed an amiable, chattering crocodile that straggled out of the gates and wound off down the country road towards a stretch of common ground. It was time for Sport. The teams were picked and names were given. Carmen's side was called 'Heavenly Father's Favourites' and she milled about with her team as they huddled together, apparently deciding tactics. Suddenly she found herself drawn into a circle holding hands, and to her intense embarrassment, because there were normal people on the piece of parkland, playing ball, throwing Frisbees, communing with their dogs, her arm was thrown up with all the other arms thrusting against the sky and they started a strange, violent chant to psyche themselves up into a winning mood.

'CHOO CHOO, CHOO CHOO POW! CHOO CHOO, CHOO CHOO POW! MANSEI, MANSEI. VICTORY TO HEAVENLY FATHER'S FAVOURITES!'

Down and up their arms shot as the strident militaristic mantra exploded from their tight scrum. And, across the way, Father's Fleet of Fighters were doing the same sort of thing.

'*What are you going to give it?*' Matthew yelled.

'ONE OH-OH,' they gave him back. And they certainly did give it one-oh-oh, because it was the most aggressive, violent game of body-ball that Carmen had ever seen. The members threw themselves into the attack like maddened dogs and when Carmen, who made the mistake of thinking they were playing for fun, fielded the ball and loped off excitedly towards her goal, she was brought down in a flying tackle under the bodies of three or four grimacing brothers. Her jaw hit the turf with an audible smack. She lay on her face, momentarily stunned in a splay of flying limbs, but alert enough to continue gripping the ball in the hollow of her groin, unwilling to relinquish it and not quite believing that the violence could have been anything but accidental. This charitable thought was soon dispelled when someone dealt her a sly, ferocious rabbit punch to the kidney at the same time as a glancing foot struck her breast. She felt someone else bodily prising her up to explore the space beneath her while everyone around cheered and jeered in a fever of aggression. Her face smeared with mud, she watched rather dazedly as the ball and the scrum rolled off towards the distant goal. She got up experimentally and limped to the sideline, appalled.

'Come on, Carmen, this is *fun*!' Matthew shouted good-humouredly as he sprinted up and down the pitch, waving his whistle like a sadistic P.E. teacher. She flatly ignored him and sat well out of danger, got out a cigarette and lit it with a shaking hand. Soon Jane got damaged too, and she defected from the game to join her.

'Your Gary's not so loving when you put him in a track suit,' she said, rolling up her jeans and examining a ripe bruise as it swelled. Carmen watched him. It was true. Gary was one of the most ruthless players on the pitch.

The sky was darkening and it was coming on to rain. All the other people on the grass began to pack up their possessions and rein in their dogs but Heavenly Father's Favourites continued to beat the hell out of Father's ferocious Fighters. Carmen decided as the rain streaked on the pitch, that she was a normal person too and she held her windcheater over Jane's head as they tripped back through the pelting rain, laughing and shambling like a two-headed beast towards the welcome glow of the house, its lower lights ablaze against the threatening gloom of the black storm clouds.

By the time of the afternoon lecture, the sky was an awesome sight, as dark as doom, a weird, grey ethereal darkness that dwarfed the sombre, restless line of trees and loomed pregnant with portent above the house like some spectral cathedral. As the storm began to break, they huddled uneasily in their neat school rows, eyeing the rattling windows as the rain beat a torrential clatter on the roof and sheeted down the guttering. The earth gave off a dank smell that permeated the air as they sat cocooned together in the security of the lecture room. Matthew had to raise his voice now and then to combat the booming thunder but the lightning flashes only seemed to add to the theatricality of his measured tones.

He was wrapt in his own vision, spinning out for them in meticulous, lingering detail, aspects of the Crucifixion that were best left uninvestigated. Now the bolts were driving slowly, painfully into Jesus's hands, twisting through sinew, splintering the bone; they heard the doleful, inexorable hammering of the mallet, the creaking of the rough-hewn wood as the soldiers carefully raised the cross with Jesus hanging on it, all the pressure of His body wrenching on His wounds. The laboured, increasingly agonising aspiration as he fought for each breath against the bowing compression of his frail chest cavity, the chest bones ruptured, splintering the flooded lungs, the tearing sound of His arms wrenching from His sockets. The audience sat hushed and spell-bound, curiously fascinated and repelled by the relentless medical minutiae.

In the fading light, with the rain still driving hard upon the sills, Carmen started taking gulps of air to aid the dying man, and a cold shiver went through her. When at last Matthew came to the familiar, magic words, 'My God, my God, why hast thou forsaken...' his voice subsided to a harsh whisper, thickened with emotion. He looked around the room. He cleared his throat and said in an even voice, 'Do you believe that Jesus cried these words?' They nodded. He searched their faces, almost angry. 'Do you seriously believe that Jesus would have said these words if there was any Triumph in the Cross?' He challenged them, his face stark and incredulous. 'Do you believe that God could *possibly* have meant His Son to die this lonely, hideous, ignominious death upon a cross of shame?' Some of the guests looked puzzled. What was he saying? Had Jesus not died on the cross after all? And if so, who was the man that Matthew had just crucified?

'Was Jesus then a coward, that He couldn't glory in a martyrdom that would have saved humanity? Was Jesus less than St Joan, less than St Stephen, less than a thousand martyrs who went to excruciating deaths, uncomplaining and without a word of reproach to Heavenly Father?' He simmered down and stared at the desk, shaking his head.

'No,' he said, 'Jesus Christ was not a coward.

'If the Crucifixion was the only way for Jesus to save mankind, he'd gladly have died on the cross hundreds of times over, don't you think so?'

People were beginning to nod. Reg was beginning to shake his head grimly. 'If He was *predestined* to die on the cross, why did He ask God to take away the cup? Why did He say to Judas Iscariot, "Woe to that man by whom the Son of Man is betrayed"? If it was predestined, then surely Judas was playing out a glorious part?'

Reg was flicking through his Bible with an air of outrage. Once he had located the vital quotes to rebuff Matthew's impassioned argument, he stuck his hand up and began to wave it earnestly in the air. Matthew blinked rapidly as though trying to dispel him from his vision.

'No. No!' he said. 'This wasn't the way God had planned for His Messiah. The crucifixion of Jesus Christ was a grievous mistake.'

Reg was almost out of his chair, so urgent and insistent was his question, so violently was he bobbing about.

'*Please*!' shouted Matthew. 'The speaker is inspired here. Waving hands disturb the word of God.'

Reg faltered under the disapproving glares that showered at him from all angles. He put down his hand, abashed.

Matthew continued, 'There *was* no glory in the Passion. There *was* no victory in the Cross.'

Reg had to swallow his indignation, clasping his Bible to him like a weapon, like a shield.

'No, Jesus was put to death before He could achieve His Father's Mission. And then we have to ask ourselves, what was His Mission?'

He searched the faces. Haltingly, from various parts of the room, the reply was hazarded. Even the most unspiritual guests had learned enough of Principle to work out this piece of logic.

'Yes!' said Matthew, 'That's correct. His mission was to restore the bloodline. Jesus had to marry. His Mission was to restore the pure bloodline and create the dynasty of perfect human beings that Adam and Eve should have created at the beginning of the world. This makes a lot of sense, doesn't it? The Mission of Jesus was to marry.'

There was absolute silence in the room. Only the pitter-pattering from the rain-soaked gutters and the sound of parchment leaves ticking over as Reg fingered through his Bible.

The guests poured out towards the dining room for refreshments, in an absorbed, excited buzz. They milled about the tea urns, unusually talkative and alert. It had to be admitted Jesus was a good deal more interesting as a subject than the Old Testament stuff and at least the lecture had contained the elements of good story-telling – a clean-cut hero, moral dilemma and violent death. What was more, they could understand the argument and, for once, they could see the logic clearly for themselves, which was a great relief to some of them, particularly the intelligent ones because they were beginning to lose confidence in themselves beginning to think themselves terminally stupid. So grateful were they to find a piece of pure and simple logic that they latched onto it with grateful enthusiasm and believed it immediately.

The stupid ones, untroubled by self-doubts and spurred on by the flattery and reinforcement of their spiritual parents, were doubly elated at getting the point straight away, without it being reiterated to them five or six times. As Carmen eavesdropped round the tea urn, it seemed that only the devout Christians were hesitant, and this because they sensed it might affect the Resurrection.

'How did you find it?' asked Gary, as they poured their tea.

Carmen thought about it. If the lectures that induced catatonic torpor rated the word 'inspiring' then the one that remotely engaged her interest deserved some sort of reward. 'Fantastic!' she said. 'I found it really moving.' The truth was she always found the story of the crucifixion moving, but the part she found most moving was the part where Jesus had His human doubts, the part where Jesus didn't want to die, the part they were now trying to take away.

She watched Reg engrossed in conversation with Matthew, Reg clutching his ancient leather-bound Bible, the other nursing his spanking new Divine Principle in its smart red plastic coat. Reg was so tall that he had to stoop to wind himself around Matthew in order to reach the short man's ear.

The conversation obviously restored Reg's punctured self-esteem because she noticed, as she joined her team trooping off to their meeting room, that he seemed to be in a high good humour, anticipating the kind of doctrinal debate in which he shone. Perhaps it had been a breach of etiquette to put his hand up in the lecture but he strode now like a man confident that he would, at any minute, be restored to his position at the top of the class.

The team meeting was lively, now that they actually had a topic of common ground. Reg was in his element. He had an encyclopedic knowledge of both the Old and New Testaments and was ready with a fund of memorised quotes complete with references. None of these, Carmen realised as she listened to the cut and thrust, was any ammunition at all against the bullet-proof brick wall that was Marianne. Reg busied himself with producing quotes and refutations like a salesman fetching samples from a suitcase, while Marianne sat smilingly inflexible, like a woman who had examined his brushes already and found them infinitely inferior to the ones in her cupboard. Every now and then she interposed calmly to correct or contradict, to point out the error in his thinking. Reg only redoubled his efforts, one moment defending the reality of the physical Resurrection, the next providing evidence for the Triumph of the Cross, quoting the temptation in the wilderness to demonstrate the free will and self-determinism of Jesus. As Carmen watched him perform, she felt curiously exasperated with him. He seemed to be under the impression that he was involved in a good-natured, stimulating exchange of views concerning Christian doctrine and that, at the end of the argument, they would shake hands and agree to differ. He didn't seem to recognise that no-one in the Family ever lost an argument, that the possession of an absolute truth did not allow anyone to shake the Family's communal hand and agree to differ. What's more, he seemed to be having the wrong argument. He was like a man trying to plug small holes in a dyke and failing to notice that the dam was breaking.

There was only one argument that Carmen thought worth having. After all, it was one proposition to speculate that, if Jesus hadn't been crucified, He might have married. It was quite another to suggest that He'd been put on earth as some sort of celestial breeding machine.

The fact that Reg was making no headway bewildered him. He still hadn't quite grasped that he could only be top of the class by losing the argument. The guests and members were fidgeting restlessly as he gamely took another futile run at the meaning of the Passion.

'The Bible says . . .' he insisted for the third time, 'not My will but Thy will. The Bible says . . .'

Someone sighed audibly and Reg turned on the culprit with an accusing stare. Marianne interrupted him sweetly.

'Many things in the Bible 'ave been misinterpreted. We are not interested in what the Bible *says* but what the Bible *means*.'

It was part of her skill that she could reprimand without ever raising her voice. She went on: 'The Bible speaks many times of Jesus as the Bridegroom, as the Wedding Feast, isn't this so?' Reg nodded grudgingly. 'This actually is the meaning of the Bible when it talks about the Marriage of the Lamb. This is what the Bible tells us once we understand the Truth. Jesus could not 'ave cried out on the cross from weakness. The truth is that his heart was broken because He had failed in His mission.' She spoke with such mild but firm finality that Reg was left with his mouth open, looking foolish, forced to subside out of common politeness.

'I think it makes a lot of sense,' was Wendy's contribution. 'He was a very charismatic man. Why shouldn't He have married?' and she sniffed as though to say it was the charismatic ones who always got away.

'But, if He needs to restore the bloodline,' Jane objected, 'wouldn't He need to find a perfect woman?' Marianne nodded approvingly, as if Jane had made a very clever point.

'Exactly so,' said Marianne. 'No-one can be cleansed of Original Sin except through the Messiah. But the Messiah brings Restoration of the blood through Perfection of the Spirit. This was His mission. To cleanse a Fallen Woman of her Original Sin, and raise her to the Eve position. Only then could He produce children cleansed of the pollution of Original Sin.' Jane nodded intently as though this clearly solved her problem and then, as soon as Marianne's attention wandered elsewhere, her eyes sought Carmen's and she went cross-eyed. Carmen was trying not to laugh at Jane's expression. It was imperative that she control herself because she had absolutely no idea of what would happen if she actually laughed aloud. Maybe she would be hauled out of the room ignominiously by her earlobe, squeaking protests, and from the severe glances that Gary was casting her way, he might be just the man to do it. She frowned with furious concentration at the floor waiting for the danger to pass.

Peter raised his hand timidly. 'I don't know if this is silly, but, well, d'you think Mary Magdalene...?' He tailed off, delicately.

'Perhaps, yes, this may be the case,' Marianne was saying gravely. 'The Bible does not tell us. The Bible leaves out many things. Also it was written by men who did not understand Principle. They did not understand the Mission of Jesus so they missed things out. Carmen,' she said suddenly.

Carmen froze and looked up guiltily. Marianne's face had softened into a gentle, teasing sympathetic smile.

'Each time I look over to you, you have this *beeg* frown,' and she mimicked Carmen's ungracious glower exaggeratedly with a little hiccough of laughter to show that it was affectionate fun. Everyone else laughed gently too.

'Sometimes, you look so worried. Like a little child who does not understand mathematics. But, eventually you came to understand mathematics, yes?'

Carmen smiled unwillingly and shook her head. 'Actually, no.'

'You have some question about this beautiful revelation, yes?'

Carmen sat forward decidedly. 'Yes. I'd like to go back to the talking snake.' The smile wiped off Marianne's face as though it had never been there. She glared at Carmen as though the girl had been specifically sent from Satan to put an awkward cat amongst the placid pigeons.

'The talking snake was yesterday,' she snapped. 'We cannot keep going back over things we have done already. Someone who has a slow brain must make an effort to keep up. Otherwise they hold the others back. If you have not understood it, you must ask your questions afterwards.'

Carmen flushed at the suggestion that she was slow of brain.

'I did ask questions, but no-one actually answered them. I just got told the same thing over again. It's not that I don't understand it...'

'If you understood it, why do you keep asking questions?' Marianne demanded, her eyes like glittering beads.

Carmen hesitated, at a loss. She had a strange baffled sensation that the word 'understood' had developed two meanings. 'I understood the *logic* of the lecture. I mean I understood it with my brain. I just didn't agree with it.' She nodded to herself as though she had solved her own problem. Understanding and agreeing were not the same thing – well, not in the outside world at least.

Gary put his spoke in now, hurt and rather ashamed of his protégée. 'Look, Carmen, that doesn't make sense,' he said reasonably. 'You say you understand the logic, so you accept that it's logical; so, if you've really understood it, then you couldn't disagree with it, because that would be *il*logical.'

Carmen half-closed her eyes as though running through the convoluted sentence, and then opened them again.

She said carefully, 'I understood its internal logic but I thought there were logical inconsistencies. Things can have their own logic and still not be logical,' she said helpfully to all and sundry, 'especially if you start off from a false premise.' Someone shuffled, as though to say – here we go again, another clever clogs.

'Who else 'as found the Fall of Man lecture illogical?' Marianne demanded, looking around the faces challengingly. They all sat very still.

'And who 'as found it logical?' she enquired, more sweetly. Twelve hands went up, including Jane's which went up without much enthusiasm. Marianne looked back at Carmen triumphantly.

'So here we 'ave a lesson, yes?' she asked sorrowfully. 'You say you have not understood mathematics but you agree mathematics is logical?' Carmen nodded unwillingly. Marianne gave her a pitying smile. 'So, if we find we cannot understand then we have to listen harder to people who are quicker. If you cannot understand it with your brain, maybe you try to understand it with your heart. This is OK. Some people are more intellectual, some people are more heartistic. You know this word "heartistic"? Sometimes Heavenly Father even prefers people who aren't so clever, people who have not the brain power for intellectual study.'

Having awarded a gracious consolation prize, Marianne signalled the meeting to a close by bowing her head for prayer. The prayer was particularly solicitous about people who were set in their ways with closed minds and stubborn hearts and slow people who were not humble. Both Reg and Carmen simmered in silence and said 'Amen'.

As they all rose to leave, Marianne detained them with a small lift of her hand. 'I have something to say ...' She looked rather awkward and girlish as she confided her little piece of news. 'Tonight, we have a special occasion. We 'ave singing and then I give my witness. This is a very special thing in the Family to give witness and so, at dinner, I ask you to say a special prayer for me that Heavenly Father will inspire my words and that I can inspire you with my example.' She smiled trustingly around the circle and they all smiled back, barring Carmen who was flushed and sullen. Even though Carmen knew objectively that she wasn't slow of brain, she deeply resented anyone implying it. It had certainly never been implied before. Well, only in mathematics. And chemistry and physics, and she was forced to add privately, well, only in the logical sciences. She gathered together her books and then saw that Jane was frantically pantomiming 'PUB' and 'KITCHEN' and she answered with a firm, decisive nod.

As Carmen escaped out into the hall, she felt Gary catch her arm. 'I'd like a chat,' he said.

'I have to make a phone call,' said Carmen with a mulish look on her face.

There were several guests queueing for the coin-box and several members hovering around the notice-board, pretending to read it.

'I'll wait with you,' he said.

She sighed irritably and gave a flounce. It seemed as though she would never get a chance to ring her mother. It was difficult enough to have to lie on the telephone to someone whom she never normally lied to, but it was plainly impossible to lie with someone else listening in.

'Well, I won't then,' she said. 'I'll go and...' She stopped. She couldn't think of how to end the sentence. That was the funny thing: never-being-alone got to be a habit. Normally a person consulted the little voice inside them and it told them what they needed. It said 'read a book', 'have a quiet night in', 'go out and have a drink', 'have a nice cup of cocoa', 'take a shower' or 'ring a friend'. Here, where the activities were regimented, where the refreshments couldn't be procured at will, where a bath was no pleasure, where the telephone was never private, where there *was* no place to read a book and no books to read but Divine Principle Study Guides and where a bell would ring if you even started and where privacy was obscurely connected with Satan, the little voice got stunted and apathetic and just waited for the next instruction. Carmen could think of no action to take.

'I'll go outside and smoke a cigarette,' she said lamely.

'OK, let's do that,' he said firmly, and to her annoyance he began to walk with her down the corridor. 'Although I wish you didn't smoke quite so many. It's very bad for your health and it gets in your hair and ...'

She gave a little infuriated squeak and made to turn back towards the vestibule.

'What's the matter?' he asked in a voice of genuine surprise.

'Well, what do you want to talk about?' she asked and then, before he could answer, 'I don't want to do the talking snake again. I've got notes, I'll read them in bed.'

'Why, what's the matter?' he asked in a voice of genuine surprise. He looked so bewildered that she decided it was time for some straight talking.

'You always say you want to talk and then when we talk you always just go on and on at me. I find it confusing,' she said peevishly. Gary stared thoughtfully at her profile as she looked distantly down the corridor.

'People *do* sometimes get confused when they come here,' he admitted, 'but it soon gets clearer. After all, it's a lot to pack into a week ...' He suddenly looked at her anxiously as though a new thought had struck him, 'But it's fun, isn't it? I mean, you are enjoying yourself?'

Her eyes came back to linger on his face.

How could he possibly think it was fun? She could hardly explain that her idea of fun was usually something different. Like going to a club and mixing gins and brandies and bad wine and banana liqueur and then dancing till dawn or until she was sick. She waited for him to go on. He hesitated as though what he had to say was too important to be said while he was standing on one leg in a corridor.

'Look, nobody's asking you to believe anything you don't want to believe, but it'd be nice if you could just listen without making it seem that you're, well, so superior and above it all. I know you're pretty clever, but not everyone here's had the benefit of your sort of education. When you start flashing it about as though everyone else is stupid, you know, talking in terms that people can't generally understand ...' Carmen blinked. One moment she was a dumbo, the next she was superior. 'But those people aren't stupid,' said

Carmen. 'I was talking in just the most basic sort of concepts you learn in simple philosophy.'

Gary heaved a small sigh. 'Well, there you go again. You don't really *understand* philosophy, do you?'

'Well, no,' said Carmen. It had been a very potted short course and it got more complicated and abstract as it went along, so she'd opted for an extra session of art history. 'But then, it's a very complicated subject.'

'So it's really just fashionable jargon.' He saw that she was about to protest and corrected himself. 'Well, maybe you understand it, but if other people can't understand what you're talking about, then really you're just talking to yourself, and it sounds sort of pretentious, like showing off...' Carmen was stung but she considered the criticism as she always considered criticism. If someone could take the trouble to make it, it was probably deserved.

'Just try not to talk in concepts. Concepts get in the way. Principle's really very simple, and it takes a very simple heart to understand it.' Carmen was about to ask what Principle was if it wasn't a series of concepts, but she thought better of it. He might begin to tell her. 'It'd be nice if you could listen without making it seem as though you think it's beneath you. After all, some of us here believe in it quite strongly. I mean, everyone's entitled to their religious views and it's nice if people are tolerant and respect each other's differences.'

Carmen nodded, puzzling it over. But didn't they force her to sit and discuss, didn't they *insist* that she participate in the doctrine discussions? And now he was trying to make her feel guilty for having a different point of view. She looked at his pained, concerned face and, it was no good, she *did* feel guilty. She frowned.

'But, look, Gary, in most religions, people are allowed to express doubts. I mean...' she added hastily, 'I know this *isn't* a religion or anything. But, don't you have any doubts?'

He shrugged. 'Oh well, yes,' he said. 'Everyone has doubts. We wouldn't be human if we didn't have doubts.' Carmen nodded, eyeing him doubtfully. That was her view exactly but she hadn't seen any signs of them, and it was something of a relief to notice that he had nicked himself shaving and there was a spot of dark, dried blood on his chin. He went on, 'But on the whole it makes so much sense. I've studied it for three years now and I just think it has so many important truths to offer – it certainly can't do you any harm just to sit through the lectures and try to be open – ' Carmen nodded again slowly. That explained it. If anyone studied it for three years it was *bound* to drive them crazy.

'Three years,' said Carmen. She was thinking about Lucy. 'Do people join for set periods of time? I mean, will you ever leave, d'you think?'

'Maybe,' he said. 'At the moment, it's the most important thing in my life, but, who knows, if something more important came along...'

'People *do* leave?' she pursued.

'Oh, yes,' he said distantly. 'People dip in and out of it, like everything else in life. We're all free to come and go.' That gave her some small satisfaction. At least Lucy had shown the sense not to join a life-and-death cult like the one where they all drank cyanide in Guyana. Perhaps this was more like some sort of Voluntary Service Overseas, only not overseas and without any good works that she could make out, unless you counted forcing unpalatable food on people who didn't want it.

'We give as much of our time as we can,' he assured her, 'because we feel its such a worthwhile cause.' The bell was ringing for the evening meal assembly and the singing began to rise from down the corridor. As they ambled back, Carmen worried it over in her mind. They seemed to expect some sort of respect for their supposed sacrifice and yet, she couldn't see why. If someone wanted to sing and smile and hear lectures all the time, she wished them luck, but she couldn't see why it was particularly praiseworthy.

'I mean as far as I can see – ' she hesitated, 'no-one really *does* anything...' They stood in the doorway for a moment before they joined the singing. 'I mean, do you look after poor people and rescue humanity or what? Is it like the Salvation Army?'

'Sort of,' he said. 'You know, the Salvation Army are very good people but they're wasting their time. Humanitarianism's no good on its own. It's just a drop in the ocean. We're actually attacking the root cause. It's no good rescuing a few old drunks when the whole world needs saving,' he added with a touch of scorn, and they stepped into the hall and joined the throng that were singing for their supper.

73

Throughout the meal, Jane winked and grimaced urgently from the neighbouring table. The plan was to sneak off the premises and find the local pub. Carmen was beginning to wonder how she could possibly shake Gary off without hurting his feelings. He was as loyal as a pair-bonded duckling and he talked Principle all through supper until she was ready to scream. At the same time he seemed so boyishly enthusiastic that it seemed heartless, as well as quite futile, to try to change the subject.

At length, she volunteered to wash up, thinking that she would be better placed to slope off from the kitchen than from the dining table and that, later on, she might be overlooked in the general confusion of post-prandial milling and bell-ringing. Gary looked a little hurt but he made no attempt to follow her. She noticed that the brothers did very little in the way of domestic chores.

Clattering the mounds of dishes in the cold water of the sink, Carmen could think of no good reason why they shouldn't announce their planned excursion openly and just saunter out. After all, they were adults, they were here of their own volition. But she had a feeling that it didn't work that way. Something about the place engendered secrecy and an awful, undignified, schoolgirlish sense of wickedness that appealed to Carmen's worst instincts.

In the same spirit, Jane, when she sneaked by to collect her, didn't walk openly into the kitchen but hovered in the doorway with Franklin standing somewhere in the gloom behind her, saying 'Pssst' like a conspirator and ogling the backs of the sisters, who were, anyway, preoccupied with their work and with singing the third verse of 'Edelweiss'.

Carmen dumped her cloth surreptitiously and, still singing 'Blossom of snow, may you bloom and grow', slipped out to join Jane and Franklin in the passage. They walked smartly on through the flower-drying room and out of the tradesmen's exit, where Peter was waiting for them, looking guilty.

They ran out into the darkness of the grounds, giggling like delinquent children, only to pull up short at the sight of a band of members standing in a pool of light on the front step. Since they stood no chance of reaching the gate without being challenged, the four of them scampered into the shrubbery and sat hunched together in the bushes, watching the windows while the hall filled up for the Family

Evening. The people inside moved serenely about the room, straight-backed and smiling, selecting their places in the rows of chairs, beginning to sing to the words on the song-sheet even as they chose their spot. The warm light inside gave the scene a homely, Christmassy feel, and to Carmen the faces seemed to shine with an innocent pleasure that was both vulnerable and touching. It felt strangely sinful to peep in at them.

Carmen suddenly felt rather envious. A wave of tiredness came over her and she wondered if it wouldn't be preferable to be safe and cossetted inside that glow rather than nestled in the wet leaves with a chilly breeze blowing and Franklin's burly, tattooed arm digging into her groin, accidentally on purpose. Suddenly the pub didn't seem so inviting.

'I don't know why we're being so secretive,' she whispered. 'They probably don't even care. They certainly won't notice...' But her sentence ended abruptly as she saw Gary standing on the steps urgently calling her name into the thicket near the drive.

Gary went in. Even from that distance, she could see that he was perplexed and annoyed. Inside the house, the song was subsiding and those members who had been out on the steps could be seen straggling into the hall to take their seats. As everyone began to scrape their chairs and sit, Marianne came into view, being led up the aisle, dimpling and bowing, eyes downcast, to the podium. She was wearing the most extraordinarily twee mock-Tyrolean frock.

'Now,' said Jane, and before Carmen could properly register the bizarre, tight bodice lacing of Marianne's national dress, they were all racing full pelt down the drive towards the gate and then out into the pitch blackness of the lane. They ran abreast of each other, their arms and legs flailing, until they stumbled into the deserted snug of the brightly lit pub, out of breath but elated and jubilant.

The landlord looked them over with a cold eye as though he knew where they came from and considered them infectious. He wouldn't let them use the phone, which was the only reason that Peter had come out at all.

It was a particularly drab and colourless little bar with no Olde Worlde charm and few modern comforts to make up for it.

They ordered double whiskeys, plugged a few coins in the juke-box, stocked up on cigarettes, spent an inordinately long time deciding on the flavours of their crisps and then kept changing their mind about the smokey bacon, just to be arbitrary, like children in a sweet shop who wanted to make sure the treat was exactly right. Then, having exhausted the permutations of sinfulness on offer in a country pub, they sat down rather gloomily at the Space Invaders table and tried, with determined jollity, to talk of something, anything, other than Divine Principle. This proved to be well-nigh impossible, since for quite some time now they had been allowed to talk of little else.

'I can't get to grips with it,' Peter puzzled. 'I mean, either I'm incredibly thick or it's just far too profound for me to take in...' He looked from Jane to Carmen, hoping for reassurance. 'And when I ask my Spiritual Mother, she just begins to repeat it all over again just like, well –' he hesitated, 'a tape recorder. And she's awfully nice and all that. She's really kind and helpful but she's always *there*...'

'Well, at least she can't follow you into the toilet and make you sing while you're going to the lavatory,' said Jane, consolingly.

'No,' said Peter, 'but there's a very helpful brother who does that. And you *can't* tell them to push off because they're so *nice* all the time.'

They all nodded in recognition of the common problem. 'Sometimes it makes me want to scream. Like today I was just trying to write a letter to someone and there she was *haunting* me, looking over my shoulder, helping me pick the right words...' He looked at them questioningly as though he wondered if he was being unreasonable. 'I mean ... I wouldn't mind ... it wasn't a particularly private letter, but the words she was picking weren't the ones I wanted and, well, I know she's Korean and her English isn't very good – and it was very sweet of her to help me and all that – but honestly, when I'd finished, the letter looked very odd. Not as if I'd written it at all. So, I just decided not to send it.'

Franklin yawned. 'They don't like you sending letters. It stops your spiritual progress. Same with telephone calls. Same with nicking jam sandwiches from the food cupboard and the same goes for groping sisters during the film shows.'

They all looked at him with awe. The sisters were so pure and other-worldly that the very idea was faintly shocking.

76

'How do you know?' asked Carmen frostily.

Franklin's face took on a pained look. 'Well, she's always following me about everywhere, wanting to have talks all the time, so I thought she must *like* me or something. I thought I'd better do something about it before she went off the boil.'

Carmen and Jane exchanged an amused glance. It was unthinkable that Franklin's bespectacled Japanese minder could simmer, let alone boil.

'Next thing is, everyone's coming down on me like a ton of bricks going on and on about talking snakes and Fallen Nature, confiscating my tobacco tin and making me take cold showers. I mean, I only put my arm around her,' he said indignantly.

'Well, it *is* a church,' said Peter reasonably. 'It's not a massage parlour.'

'She massages everyone else!' squeaked Franklin. It was true: the Oriental girls were happy to massage the other sisters' shoulders in between lectures. Since most of them spoke no English other than Principle they seemed to use it as a form of communication.

'I didn't know it was a church. I thought it was a sort of youth hostel. I only came because it was so cheap,' he complained. 'And then, when the dormitory got too full, I found out why it was so cheap because they've put me in this pokey little brush cupboard under the stairs. It's not a broom cupboard – you couldn't get a broom in unless you took the stick off – and there's two other brothers in there with me. Every time I complain, she says Reverend Moon was in a concentration camp in North Korea and it was much worse for him and at least the cupboard hasn't got *rats*.' He told it with the full weight of his droll incredulity. 'I said to her, I wouldn't mind if it *had* got a rat in, I could have hit it over the head with me Divine Principle Study Guide and tomorrow we could all have a bit of protein. And another thing,' he said, 'I think Principle's a load of rubbish.'

Peter frowned. 'Well, it's what they believe,' he said. 'I don't think you should say it's rubbish. Everyone's entitled to their beliefs. There is such a thing as religious tolerance. Just because *you* don't believe it, doesn't necessarily mean it's rubbish.' He looked at Jane and Carmen for corroboration, but they stayed neutral. 'I mean they're awfully good people. You have to respect their commitment. I'm not saying it's rubbish, I'm saying that sometimes it gives me a pain in my head when I try to think it out.'

Franklin stretched arrogantly. 'Well, I don't believe a word of it. I told my Spiritual Mother I'd give her until the end of the week and I *still* won't believe it. I mean, I don't believe in Jesus, let alone his mission.'

There was something offensively lumpen and bullish about Franklin's posture and his jutting chin.

'Well, I don't think you can dispute Jesus,' said Carmen mildly. 'I think Jesus was historical fact.'

'Jesus was the best man that ever lived,' Peter affirmed, as though he'd take his jacket off to anyone who said any different.

Outnumbered, Franklin backed down. 'Well, I don't believe this stuff about Him marrying and having perfect children,' he said sulkily. 'And anyway, what happened to the last perfect person? Eve was perfect and she got led astray. What if Jesus had all these perfect kids and they all got bored with being perfect and start polluting their blood all over again the first chance they get?' He put his chin up in the air belligerently. 'I know I would if I was perfect...' They looked at his charmless face. The possibility was so remote as to be unimaginable.

Privately, Carmen found his logic unimpeachable but she was reluctant to ally herself with Franklin.

'Of course they wouldn't,' Peter insisted. 'They wouldn't have Original Sin so they wouldn't *want* to pollute their bloodstream with Fallen Desires. We only have Fallen Desires because we Fell. That's the whole point of the lecture.' He leaned back in exasperation.

Carmen couldn't help but notice how one was influenced by the voice of the speaker. Even though Peter was talking nonsense, his modulated, middle-class tones made the thrust of his speech infinitely more palatable than the sense that Franklin was growling in his thick, East End accent. Carmen heaved a restless sigh and rolled her eyes at Jane. If they were going to talk about the Fall Of bloody Man, they might as well be indoors, within stumbling distance of their bunks, having a cup of cocoa and discussing it with the experts.

'Well,' grumbled Franklin, reluctant to drop his aggrieved stance, 'No-one told me they were a pack of Moonies, that's all *I'm* saying.'

The words jarred harshly. The others looked at him uneasily, taken aback. There was something so contemptuous and ridiculous about the word. It had associations in the outside world that didn't seem to fit with that group of serious, committed people within the big house. Like the members, Carmen had begun to refer respectfully to the organisation as 'Unification Church' or 'the Family'. 'Moonie' was uncomfortably like 'loony', and 'loony' was inaccurate and unkind to innocent people who had been nothing if not kind and hospitable.

At eleven, the bell rang for time and they got up instantly, guiltily, looking around as though the landlord might hop out from the bar and direct them to a team meeting.

As they strode back quickly, in pairs, Jane muttered, 'Gary's paying you a lot of attention. I watched him at dinner. His eyes were positively limpid. Has he asked you for your birthsign yet?'

Carmen shrugged, secretly flattered. 'Oh, I don't think so. I mean, that's what they're supposed to do, isn't it? He's supposed to shower me with love and affection so I won't want to leave.'

'None of them do it with quite his dedication though,' said Jane. 'In fact, Pamela seems to lose heart halfway through and starts moaning at me.'

Carmen smiled to herself. So she wasn't imagining the way he kept looking at her. It took very little to win Carmen's heart. Just the merest suspicion of attention from a promising male, backed up by an independent female witness, and she could fantasise about a doomed and impossible romance, the contemplation of which would pass the dreary hours and enliven even the dullest lecture. Of course, in this case, it was someone literally too good to be true, but that was no obstacle to fantasy.

'D'you think he's going to ask me to share his eternal prayer mat?' asked Carmen. 'Just me and him alone in the great dormitory of life, and twenty-five brothers snoring in the background?'

'Well, he could leave,' Jane said practically. 'People have been known to.'

Carmen screwed up her eyes and tried to imagine Gary outside the Family, but her imagination failed her. Then she thought of something else.

'Do you think it's true what Franklin said? D'you think they're really making him take cold showers?'

Jane nodded. 'Yes, some of the sisters do it. Haven't you heard them gasping and shouting?' Carmen shook her head, troubled.

'But no-one can *make* him take cold showers, can they?'

Jane looked at her drily. 'They're very persuasive,' was all she said. 'If you're thinking of having a Fallen Desire for Gary, I should be sure to keep it to yourself.'

As they rounded the corner and saw the lights of the house, they began to run, checking their watches. It was eleven-fifteen, which was fine. The Go-To-Bed guitar started playing around midnight. With a bit of luck, they could slip into the hall unnoticed. But, as they approached the gates, it became clear that this would not be possible. There was a posse of Spiritual Parents in an indignant huddle at the gate and, even as the sinners tried to brazen it out, throwing back their shoulders and looking as if they were perfectly entitled to go out for a walk, the Parents called out their names with stern accusation. Carmen saw that Gary's face was impassive and grim. Pamela pounced on Jane like a real anxious mother and gave her a good shake. The men were led off by their little Oriental girls.

'Hallo,' Carmen said brightly to Gary, as though there was nothing wrong.

'Go into the house,' he said tersely. 'I've got something to say to you.'

'Is there some cocoa?' she asked, cockily. She didn't see that he had any right to order her about.

'I should say you've drunk enough, by your breath,' he said, and she followed him as he strode into the corridor, past the main hall where everyone was drinking cocoa. As she peeked in, she saw several people in a bunch staring at her disapprovingly as though she had been the topic of discussion. When they came to the deserted vestibule, Gary turned on his heel and regarded her with a cold, unsympathetic eye, like a school teacher.

'Look, Marianne was terribly upset,' he said. 'We have a Family Evening and we expect people to come, otherwise it upsets everyone else and it makes all the hard-working members who arranged it feel that somehow their hospitality's not good enough. Besides which I thought that you and I had a talk earlier and we came to some sort of understanding.'

'Well, we did,' she said, suddenly feeling defensive under the weight of his words. 'But you said I should have fun. I just didn't think it'd be much fun listening to Marianne, that's all. I seem to spend all day listening to people.'

He continued to stand there, so righteous, so fearlessly irreproachable, making her feel just by gazing at her that she was somehow squalid and trivial and not worth the effort of being told a great truth. It made her want to excuse herself, to win him over.

'But now I wish I *had* come, because I didn't really have a nice time and, anyway, we talked about Principle all the time so it must have been alright.'

His gaze was frigid.

'And when we were talking today, you sort of implied I was like an impartial observer, and so I thought it was probably alright to go out...'

'Well,' he said drily, 'you seem to be an extremely impartial observer on Principle. But you can't actually experience Principle unless you join in and try out the total experience. However, if you were in doubt, you could always have asked me, that's what I'm here for. I'm here for you. And if you don't want to come to me with your problems then I'm wasting my time.' He looked so tired and defeated for a moment that her heart went out to him. She had a sense that it was a dog's life for them, in those moments when they weren't radiantly happy.

She said, 'Pamela said I should try to look at people through God's eyes more and not be so critical and quick to judge. I don't like Franklin much, I have to say, and I thought I ought to try and look at him through God's eyes and this seemed a good opportunity to find out what it was that God saw in him...' She tailed off lamely. It sounded a bit far-fetched, even to her. 'I was thinking positive,' she finished up, pointing to the fading biro marks. Gary looked at the marks on her wrist and then at her face and she saw to her relief that he was about to relent. He sighed and ran his fingers through his hair abstractedly, as though he didn't know what they were going to do with her.

'Look, Carmen,' he said. 'The point is, we're a Family. We do things together. We're not really knowledgeable enough to decide things for ourselves. We have to be like children and believe that other people know better sometimes. Mmm?'

She nodded as though she couldn't agree with him more.

'We don't go off and do things on our own. That's a selfish way of looking at the world. I mean, think of Communism. Don't you think there's a lot about Communism that's very good in some ways? You know, everyone sacrificing the individual towards the whole?' She nodded. In those terms she could understand it. She wondered idly if this was some front for a Socialist organisation funded by the Chinese KGB or something, but then dismissed it. He went on, 'Satan attacks through individualism, and that's why we ask you to join in the communal activities.'

'But I didn't know that,' she wailed. 'I can only do things or not do things that I know about...' The rules were changing all the time.

'Well, now you know,' he said, and his voice was much more kind. 'But the thing is, you see, I was worried about you, because it's dangerous out there.'

'What is?'

'You're vulnerable when you hear Principle. There are very active spirits. And the alcohol makes you more open. Then, when you have give-and-take with other active spirits it becomes like Multiplication Of Evil.'

'Yes,' said Carmen. 'Well, I can see that Franklin had a few active spirits zipping about there.'

'It's not for us to be judgmental,' he said quietly.

'But you're being judgmental about *me*,' she pointed out, indignantly.

'Yes,' he said. 'But that's because I really care about you. Because I feel close to you. Because you matter to me.' She examined his face, daunted by his obvious sincerity. 'I just want you to do the right things,' he said. He looked up at the sound of the guitar player strumming on his rounds of the nooks and crannies of the hall, singing 'I Bid You Goodnight'. The revellers from the Family Evening were pouring out towards the staircase. 'And the right thing now is to go to bed,' he said firmly, and he smiled at her; a warm, sad smile that lit up his face.

'Goodnight,' she said, and for a moment she was on the point of leaning towards him to peck him on the cheek, out of gratitude for his sudden warmth. She checked herself in time. It didn't seem quite right. And anyway, the impulse only came from over-tiredness, from the hot and cold emotions that she had to run through all the time.

She turned quickly and padded off down the corridor, feeling so exhausted that she almost wished the regression to childhood incorporated a take-home service where someone swept her up like a drowsy rag-doll and tucked her into her little bunk. It didn't have to be Gary, but he was the nearest.

However, nothing in the Family was that easy. When she got to the crowded dormitory, she found that her bunk was occupied and her sleeping bag, together with her Book Of Reflections, had been laid out neatly in a small space by the sink. She crawled into her bag and waited for everyone to settle themselves down. Jane was sitting up, mute and unhappy in the space between two bunks, writing in her notebook under the accusing eyes of Pamela and Virginia, who flanked her like a police escort. Carmen was just about to catch her attention when Pamela's warning glare dissuaded her. Perhaps they'd done enough Multiplication of Evil for one night. Just as Carmen was about to nestle down, Virginia called over in a jolly voice, 'Aren't you going to write in your Book Of Reflections, Carmen? You'll fall behind everyone else.'

'I haven't actually got any reflections at the moment,' Carmen said apologetically. 'I have to wait until they sort of come over me. There's not much point just writing down any old thing, is there?'

'Well, not *any* old thing,' said Virginia, screwing up her face, 'but it's nice to write something down, so you can look back later and see the developments you've made. Don't you think so, Pamela?'

Pamela nodded earnestly. 'I've kept all my old Reflection books and it's really funny to see the things I used to put and then compare them with the later ones when things got clearer. It's like two different people writing.' She snuffled engagingly. 'I used to write down *such* funny questions.' Turning back to Carmen, she said, 'I really think you ought to try, Carmen. You'll be glad you did, later.'

Carmen nodded, warily. That was what she was afraid of: the very thought that Virginia and Pamela, those two blank paragons, had once been two normal, puzzled guests, and something had happened to them. She picked up the biro and held it poised over the page. She wrote the headings: MULTIPLICATION OF EVIL, and underneath it INDIVIDUALISM IS OF SATAN. She stared at the words and then wrote, 'I think it is all bilge and rubbish.' It gave her childish pleasure to think that she had written these words right under their approving noses. But when she read it over, she saw that she had written 'binge and rabbits' and that this was a measure of how tired she was. She frowned and scored it through until the nib went right through the page, so that no-one could see what she had tried to write, even if they held it up to the light. Then she wrote carefully, 'I think these are very interesting concepts. It is *spooky* to find out just how very clever Satan is and how he tries to trick us all the time into doing the wrong thing.' She tucked the book firmly underneath her body. Even if her brain didn't seem to want to spell it, she *knew* that it was bilge and rubbish, she told herself, as she watched the silent sisters crouching to their prayers. Just as long as she and her brain were one, then people could make her lie in her speech, they could make her lie in her behaviour and they could make her lie in her Book Of Reflections, but they couldn't make her lie in her own head or her own heart. With that solemn conviction, she fell asleep.

She woke up in the darkness with a cry of alarm. She stared around her wildly. Her heart was pumping adrenalin and there was a strange tingling in her limbs. She tried to remember where she was, but it was OK, she was safely in the dormitory. The night was humid and airless and the troubled sleepers were showing signs of their disturbance, threshing restlessly and letting out strange disembodied moans and whimpers. Just beside her, someone was on their knees, swaying drowsily in the moonlight, encased in a sleeping bag, apparently praying in her sleep. She suddenly felt a pressing urge to go to the toilet, but the route to the door was like an obstacle course. She asked herself whether her journey was really necessary, but the pressure on her bladder was such that it couldn't be denied for fear of kicking a few sisters in the head. She set out with infinite care, as though traversing a minefield, afraid someone would arrest her progress with the words, 'Where are you going? Well, isn't that a bit selfish?' – but she noticed that some of the bags were empty and both Pamela and Virginia were absent from their bunks.

She padded down the passage towards the bathroom, but as she approached it, she heard the most terrifying noise. It was like nothing on earth, like a dragon making fire in its chest – a series of great hoarse aspirations followed by a fearful staccato death rattle. She stood stock-still in the corridor, her eyes starting out of her head, alert for a supernatural danger. Then the rattle changed to a chain of deep, wrenching, sickening expulsions as though a dragon were simultaneously choking, being sick and breathing fire. She was so frightened that she felt her blood had stopped flowing in her veins, and yet there must be a reasonable explanation.

Summoning all her courage, she knocked on the bathroom door and, since there was no answer, she opened it a crack. All she could see was a huge blue bottom that obscured the sink altogether and a woman hacking her lungs out into the bowl. For a moment she was filled with relief that it was a human, and then she felt chilled again because this woman, the black woman with the hacking cough, was clearly very sick indeed. She poked her head timidly in the door and spoke loudly enough to be heard above the choking.

'Are you alright, sister?' she asked. 'Should I get someone?' But the woman only shook her head as the cough continued to wrack her body till it shook like a great blancmange, making the same terrifying inhuman sounds. 'Sister, you sound so sick,' Carmen persisted.

The woman raised herself with an enormous effort and managed to stop coughing long enough to say, 'Go to bed, sister. There's nothing wrong with me. It's just the spirits,' in such an angry, hostile voice that Carmen could do nothing but withdraw.

She stood there for a moment in the corridor, wondering what to do. Having got this far, she was reluctant to give up the quest. She decided to wander into the main body of the house where there was another bathroom, but as she tried the door which led from the passage to the staircase, she found that it was locked from the outside and the key was in the barrel of the lock. And then she felt a different sort of panic. If they were free to come and go, why should anyone want to lock them in? She paced up and down the corridor checking the windows that led out onto the landing, feeling a growing sense of outrage.

As she paced back to the door, she noticed that it had a glass fanlight above it and the pane was ajar. It was high up but Carmen was slight and wiry, and she had no intention of being confined against her will. The lumber room next to the dormitory contained two sets of bunks and a couple of chairs. She brought one out and climbed up on it, hauling herself up until her chest was level with the lintel and then, using all the strength of her arms, swung her leg up and scrabbled through the narrow space like a cat. She jumped the six foot down from the fanlight without too much impact and then sat where she had landed, on her heels, contemplating the deserted staircase.

She listened for a moment to the noises of the house, to the creaks and whines and the buzzing of muted conversation. She sneaked quietly along to the lavatory and relieved herself, wondering all the time what she would say if she was caught. Perhaps she would say, 'I wanted to go to the toilet' or perhaps she would be aggressive and say, 'I don't actually *choose* to be locked in like someone in a mental home.' That sounded a little unlikely; perhaps she could say, 'I was worried about the sister so I came to find someone.' Perhaps she *should* try to find someone. The woman sounded as though she had a good old-fashioned case of terminal consumption, only it wasn't pale and aesthetic like the old films suggested.

She refrained from pulling the chain and padded back along the corridor. As she did so, she became aware that the low murmur of conversation she'd heard was coming from Matthew's office. The door was open far enough for her to catch a glimpse of them, all seated around a board-room table with Matthew at the head.

Pamela was on her feet, her face tired and strained. She had the attitude of someone giving evidence. Marianne was just visible at the other end, nodding judiciously and taking notes. She saw then that Gary was one of the members seated around the table. It gave her a shock to see them all thus gathered around a table at dead of night. Some of the guests had whispered to her that Matthew had supernatural powers, that he had an uncanny prescience of their innermost thoughts, that some of the members could see into other people's souls, but with this vignette before her Carmen realised that the seering insights more likely came from copious note-taking. She wondered how many of the guests' little confidences were aired openly in these night-time conferences.

She suddenly felt afraid and she glanced quickly around for fear a hand should come down hard on her shoulder, but the corridor was empty. She crept on swiftly and silently towards the dormitory. No-one saw her and no-one had disturbed the key. She turned it and went in. The sister had gone from the bathroom; Carmen wondered if the woman would report the chair that blocked the passage or whether she was too far gone in her suffering to notice.

As Carmen crawled back into her bag, she asked herself what on earth she was doing in this sinister place, what machinations went on behind the enigmatic smiles, whether the risks she was taking were in proportion to the quest. What guarantee was there that she would even find Lucy? And wasn't it likely that Lucy would be glazed and smiling too?

She was too disquieted to sleep immediately and she lay there listening to the little frightened sounds of people sleeping, telling herself that the darkest hours were those before daybreak – that it would all seem reasonable again in the light of day. After all, what did it add up to? A woman had been coughing and the members had held a meeting. With all the frenetic activity from dawn to dusk, what other time was there to hold a meeting but at dead of night?

Chapter 5

'Why do they lock the dormitory door?' asked Carmen querulously at breakfast.

Gary looked at her, surprised. He seemed to consider the question as though it was a child's cute saying. She almost thought he was going to say, 'Why, I don't know, Carmen. Why *do* they lock the door?' and she would lisp back, 'So the spirits can't get in!' But he didn't. He just said in a mild tone, 'They don't.'

'Well, it was locked last night. From the outside.'

He shook his head. 'Seems very unlikely to me. If it *was* locked it was probably just an accident. Maybe it was someone's idea of a joke,' and then he added, 'but I doubt it.'

Carmen doubted it too. People didn't make jokes in the Family.

He turned to Pamela, puzzled, '*Was* the door locked?'

'Not when I came in,' she answered, and she paid a lot of attention to her food. Carmen watched her reactions.

'You came in very late,' said Carmen sympathetically. 'Did you have to have a meeting or something?'

Pamela met her eye, apparently unperturbed. 'Yes,' she said. 'We had to go over some accounts. We have to work out rotas, that sort of thing.'

Carmen nodded, partly satisfied. It made sense, of course. They had to distribute chores.

'Did you need to get out for something?' asked Gary, casually.

'There was a sister in the bathroom and she seemed terribly sick but I didn't know who to tell – so in the end I just went back to bed. But she was awfully ill.'

Their expressions were so bland that she almost thought they hadn't heard her. Not a flicker of interest passed across either of their faces.

'I think she's over there,' Carmen volunteered. 'That big woman. Only she was wearing a dressing gown so she looked different.' She pointed helpfully to the lady in question. 'She really ought to see a doctor...'

'Have you had any dreams yet?' asked Pamela, as though illness was not a suitable breakfast-time topic and 'dressing gown' was somehow a very frisky sort of word. Carmen stopped short. She would have imagined that with all their love and solicitude, they'd have been interested to know that one of their number was dying on her feet. It might give them a chance to love someone who actually needed loving. She pretended to address herself to Pamela's question. The only dream she could remember very clearly had been set in a scraggy field near her childhood home; she had been sticking razor blades into the flesh of a small brown totter's pony. She couldn't remember much more than that, only the way the blood trickled through the chestnut shag of his coat and the forlorn, hopeless gleam in the pony's wet eyes, and the guilt.

'I dreamt I was a daddy long-legs and someone was trying to wash me down the plug-hole,' she said firmly.

An expression of dissatisfaction glanced across Gary's face. As a reflex action, he began to tip his sausages onto her plate. He pushed his own plate away with an air of tense martyrdom and she thanked him grumpily. This meant she was confronted by four burnt lacquer sausages, not two. She was beginning to get the hang of this altruism which wasn't altruism at all, but Family policy. The greater his sacrifice, the more he could open her up to faith, and the more he could open her up to faith, the more heavenly blessings he accrued. This was why all the members went hungry, giving up things that they didn't want to give up to people who didn't want to be given them. In return, all the guests felt oppressively guilty about whatever they'd received — in this case, two additional inedible sausages, pock-marked with gristle specks and swimming in grease.

She wondered if she could double her own heavenly blessings by tipping the things onto her neighbour's plate, and whether her neighbour could increase the blessing fourfold by doing the same. If they did it all along the line, someone would end up with an extremely good foundation of faith and thirty-six sausages.

'Why's everyone so obsessed with my dreams?' growled Carmen. Her dreams, at least, were something she should be able to call her own.

'Heavenly Father sometimes contacts us through dreams,' Gary explained evenly. 'You should always be looking out for a revelation. When you have interesting dreams, you should tell me or Pamela and we'll be able to interpret them for you.'

She looked at him with suspicion. 'I don't like people interpreting my dreams,' she said. 'I'm the best person to interpret them. They're just spill-over from my life. I know about my life. You don't.' She felt a sharp sense of alarm and invasion that they should ever begin to tamper with her dreams.

'I think Heavenly Father knows best, actually,' Pamela corrected her quietly.

'Yes. But I don't *believe* in Heavenly Father,' Carmen said in irritation. 'That's something you both choose to forget.'

They both stared at her but she looked away, disdainfully. As she raised her cup to her lips, she realised that her hand was trembling. She put it down to hyperventilation. They had sung four very strenuous and joyous songs and the intake of oxygen seemed to make her high. But she was also aware of feeling angry. She was beginning to note the symptoms of her own exhaustion with a curious detachment, as though her body belonged to someone else. Her mood swings were too extreme. She seemed to switch abruptly from hostility to the kind of elation that brought her to the brink of tears. It wasn't really surprising. The lack of sleep, the constant bombardment, the poor food – the effect was cumulative. But, most of all, she was beginning to consider the idea that the human brain craved privacy; that privacy was a basic human need, and that when even sleep offered no solitude the brain would just shut down for little periods. Maybe that was what happened here. If her only weapon against invasion was hostility, Carmen could be as hostile as the next person.

'Of course you believe in God,' said Pamela. 'Don't be silly. Why, you pray to Him at least five times a day.' That was true. Carmen prayed because it was the only time she was truly alone with her thoughts. 'Why do you do that, Carmen? If you don't believe in Him, it doesn't make any sense.'

'I pray because I'm told to,' she snapped. Gary gave her a warning stare and she amended her harsh statement. 'I pray so I can find out if he's there.'

'Well, there you are,' said Pamela merrily, as though Carmen really was being an awkward silly-billy. 'You're asking for a revelation, and that's why we need to know your dreams!'

Carmen sighed in exasperation and got to her feet. To her surprise she found Pamela's hand clamped tightly on her arm.

'Oh no you don't,' the girl said with firm bonhomie. 'Yesterday you were silly and selfish and did what you wanted and we made allowances because you didn't know it was wrong. But now you *do* know it's wrong, you'd better start being good and doing what you're told!'

Carmen stared with amazement at the restraining hand on her forearm and the playful wagging of Pamela's finger. She tested the grip experimentally and it was strong enough for a Chinese burn. Carmen sat down again, more from surprise than anything else.

It had not occurred to Carmen, indeed to any of the miscreants, that their trip to the pub was a serious act of defiance against God himself and that they were all in dire disgrace and were to be watched like hawks until they recognised and acknowledged their sin.

It became more apparent in the lecture, when Matthew's eyes levelled severely on each of the truants in turn. 'So perhaps John the Baptist had selfish desires,' he was saying. 'Don't we know this ourselves. What does the selfish heart want to do? The selfish heart doesn't want to listen, does it? The selfish heart wants to think for itself. The selfish heart wants to go to the pub or smoke a cigarette, isn't that so?' Carmen flushed slightly, although she was by no means the only culprit. She saw that Peter was fidgeting uneasily. Jane was pretending not to listen and writing it all down; Franklin was in the front row, chin jutting, taking it like a man. 'The selfish heart thinks only of its own pleasure. But who knows best? The individual heart or the heart of the Messiah? Just as man accepts to live by the rules of the world or he will not be happy, so we have to live by the rules of a house in the same way. Don't think of Seven Day as a holiday camp. This is a very wrong way to think of hearing God's truth. We have to think of it more like the army, obeying God's word...' Just as Carmen felt numbers of eyes swivelling towards her pointedly, he changed his tone and said, 'But John the Baptist disobeyed the rules of God ...' and then he was off on his normal rambling discourse, drawing his complicated pyramids and triangles, happy as a sandboy.

As the eyes returned to the board, Carmen's heightened colour subsided. She felt irritated with herself, but she also felt guilty. It was irrational but it was true. She must feel guilt or she wouldn't be putting razor blades into innocent ponies in her sleep, she reasoned. But where was her guilt? In going to the pub? For ridiculing in her mind their great and treasured Truth? Or was it the dubious morality of being here under false pretences? Because if it was the last, her brain had certainly worked a screw loose. Didn't they say everyone was welcome, no matter what their motivation, and wasn't it *they* who used false pretences? First it was a holiday camp and then it was an army barracks, one moment it wasn't a religion and the next minute they were discussing Jesus eight hours a day. As quickly as the rules became established, another set of rules would take their place; everyone was just too polite or dazzled by the sleight of hand to point to the cards as they vanished up the conjuror's sleeve.

'OK,' he said suddenly. 'Who doesn't believe there's a Spirit World?'

Carmen put her hand up mechanically and it was a moment before she registered that hers was the only one. The other guests had already developed their mechanisms for self-preservation and Lesson Number One was to keep a low profile.

'Looks like you're out on your own there, Carmen,' he said affably, 'What does that tell you?'

'Don't know,' she mumbled.

Matthew's smile faded. He continued to regard her thoughtfully, stroking his chin.

'And who is actually open-minded enough to believe that such a thing as a Spirit World might exist?'

All hands went up without hesitation. Matthew allowed the hands to stay there, pretending to count them until he shook his head as if they were too numerous to check. Then he looked at Carmen.

'Perhaps you'd like to come up and tell everyone they're mistaken, Carmen?' he asked cordially. She coloured. He went on, 'In fact, perhaps you'd like to come up here and take over my place and give the lecture?' Everyone laughed. He grinned around the faces amiably. 'I'm sure if Carmen can explain away our experiences and set us right we'd all like to hear it. What do you want to tell us, Carmen?'

Carmen sunk lower in her chair. 'I don't want to tell anyone anything,' she said, 'I just think we're all entitled to our own beliefs.'

Matthew's face sobered up. He shook his head slowly but firmly.

'No. This is the voice of self speaking. It's the selfish heart that says "I'm entitled" – we're not entitled to deny another person's deep experience. In fact it's a very dangerous thing to do. You deny another person's reality and what happens? You throw them into confusion. You make them unbalanced so they don't know what to believe. When you deny someone's reality, you can even make them go insane. It's a very wrong thing to do.'

He stared coldly at her. 'You tell someone that fire isn't dangerous and what happens? That person puts their hand in the fire and the flesh scorches. No, Carmen, this is not something we're entitled to do. You believe electricity exists, yes?'

Carmen nodded mutely, her face red and resentful.

'Carmen believes she's a very rational, logical person,' he told the class. 'But since she can't see electricity, then it doesn't exist, does it?' There was a ripple of nervous laughter. 'So maybe Carmen would like to come and put a hair grip in the wall socket, huh?' People laughed with more conviction. He threw out the disconcerting challenge with a good-natured smile but the smile was meant for others, not for Carmen. When his eyes came back to rest on her, she quailed at the hostility there. If one by-passed the love of the Family, there was something rather steely and frightening behind it. The people she considered to be her friends didn't laugh: they avoided her eye and offered her no comfort either.

'OK,' he said. 'So. Electricity, there's an example of a power that defies the physical sense. And Spirit World is much the same. So let's look at the way evil spirits try to work with us. When a person has a weak spirit or his ancestors have weak spirits, then he lays himself open to attack, how?'

Carmen had sunk very low in her chair, hoping against hope that he had forgotten her, trying to make herself invisible, but she too joined in with the others and mouthed the answer.

'Yes, through our fallen natures. And these are the results of evil spirit activity . . .' He began to chalk up the words, underlining them as he spoke, 'INSANITY, DISEASE, ACCIDENTS. Now, how can we judge if someone's troubled with evil spirits?' he asked conversationally. He looked around them. 'Well, have you noticed sometimes when there's a guest with evil spirits, how that person comes into a room and everyone feels uneasy? It's like the whole atmosphere's been disrupted? And when the guest leaves the room, everyone feels relieved as though it's not one person that's left but four or five people? Phew!' He wiped his brow comically as though he'd just had to deal with a tricky character. 'Have you had this experience on the workshop so far?'

People laughed and nodded. Carmen nodded too. She was aware that, although Matthew's eyes scanned the faces, they more than once came to rest on her, as though she more than anyone else might take the information to heart.

The lecture was finally over three or four hours later. Carmen rushed outside hoping to shake off Gary, but Pamela was at her elbow almost immediately. 'Where are you rushing off to now?' asked Pamela, in the same teasing voice she had used before.

'Er – I was going to see if I could help in the kitchen,' said Carmen quickly. She was actually hoping to catch a moment alone with Jane.

'No, no,' said Pamela firmly. 'You do too much washing up. We shouldn't always choose the job we like. You pay better indemnity if you choose the job you *don't* like.' Carmen was borne off unhappily to find the hoe and secateurs. They passed Jane and Virginia en route. Jane was carrying an ironing board and a pile of brothers' shirts. She gave Carmen such a comic, woebegone look that Carmen stifled a laugh. Their night in the pub was obviously to be paid for dearly.

The work in the garden was quite heavy although Carmen didn't mind hard work. It was a fine day and the sun beat down. The only fly in the ointment was Pamela, who kept up a constant monologue about the spiritual experiences of the other guests. It was bad enough having to hear someone's dream at first hand, but having to hear it at a third remove with an amateur interpretation, knowing that the poor battered guest had probably made it up anyway to get a bit of peace, robbed the subject of the slightest interest or relevance. Carmen continued to make monosyllabic replies to Pamela's questions.

'You've never *ever* had a spiritual experience at *all*?' Pamela asked, and she sat up on her haunches in mock surprise.

Carmen shook her head and continued burrowing at the roots of a tenacious field plant.

'Not ever? Well, that's very unusual. Creative people are usually

94

the most open to the spirits,' as though this put all Carmen's claims to creativity in doubt.

Carmen was almost stung into repeating one of her spiritual experiences; she had certainly experienced a few but she believed they came from the mind. As it was, she just muttered, 'Creative people always *say* they have spiritual experiences so people will think they're very creative...'

Pamela watched Carmen's back as though it might give her some clue to the best approach. After a while she spoke in a casual tone.

'You know sometimes people have spiritual experiences when somebody dies or something like that. Didn't anyone in your family ever die? Like a grandparent or something?'

'My father died,' Carmen said abruptly, without looking up.

Pamela's face brightened. 'Oh, I'm sorry,' she said wistfully. She was silent for a decent space and then she enquired hesitantly, 'Do you ever feel that he's watching over you? Do you ever sort of sense him, very close?'

'Sometimes,' said Carmen in a voice which gave no encouragement.

'You know...' Pamela hovered delicately as though she was treading difficult ground, 'it may be that he had to die to bring you here. Sometimes that happens. Sometimes the spirits pay indemnity for us to hear the Truth.'

Carmen snorted, deeply affronted. The very idea that her father should have died so that she could listen to their trivial nonsense. If he was watching her at all, he'd be advising her to pack her little travelling bag *tout de suite* and sending the train fare down the celestial wires.

'I know I feel my mother watching me,' said Pamela sadly.

Carmen stopped burrowing in the flower bed and sat back on her heels.

'You know, she was so *negative* about the Family when she was alive but, now that she's in Spirit World, she really understands. Sometimes I feel as if we're even closer now. Closer than we were ever able to be in life,' and she looked at Carmen with a fearful, pleading face, as though she was willing her not to dispel the illusion that sustained her. 'Don't tell me that's my imagination?'

Carmen stared at Pamela's vulnerable little face. Who could be cruel enough to say it was wish-fulfilment?

'Maybe she does understand,' she said. Pamela nodded and suddenly assumed the appearance of equanimity again. She smiled with complete confidence. 'Of *course* she does,' she said. 'She told me so. And so does your father, you can be sure of that. He just wants you to hear Principle, that's all.' She tapped Carmen's hand playfully with the trowel. 'So you'd just better pay attention.'

Carmen stared unhappily at the little tin trowel as it hit her knuckle. She felt that same sense of invasion and disquiet: nothing was sacred to them. Everything, including private thoughts and dreams and grief, everything was just another useful handle. As she looked up, she saw in Pamela's milky blue eyes that same pain, that same remote blankness; all the time she was speaking, she seemed to be concentrating very hard on something else, something very difficult to fathom, very abstract.

As they raked the weeds and the grass cuttings towards the compost heap, Carmen noticed that there were two figures out on the pitch. One of them looked like Peter and he was running vigorously on the spot, hands behind his head, lifting his knees high like someone undergoing commando training. The other man was barking instructions.

'Is that Peter?' she asked.

Pamela nodded, 'Looks like he's doing a Condition.' When Carmen looked blank, Pamela said, mildly, 'You know, once we begin to admit what our faults are, we can work on them by doing some sort of Condition. Maybe we go on a fast or do some physical training – or a prayer Condition, that's a good one. Peter's been doing that today, I think. You know, you pray for a long while and you really concentrate on trying to experience God's suffering. That's a really worthwhile thing to do. Perhaps you'd like to try a prayer Condition?' she asked tactfully.

'I don't think I've got any terrible faults,' said Carmen. 'And I don't believe in God so I can't experience His suffering.'

'Yes,' said Pamela neutrally. 'Well, that might be a good subject for discussion at the Team Meeting.'

Throughout the day it became clear to Carmen that she and the other miscreants were being kept apart. Whenever there was a free moment, either Gary or Pamela would be waiting at her shoulder ready to discuss more brain-baffling points of Principle with gentle insistence and overwhelming patience. Carmen was beginning to feel the pressure building up in her head. Whenever she caught glimpses of Jane or Peter, they too were pinned down by members and engrossed in fervent debate, and both had an unhappy, puzzled look.

At lunch, she was startled to see Jane hurtle past the window at three minute intervals, a comic, haunted look on her face. She seemed to be running circuits round and round the house.

Peter, she noticed, wasn't eating at all, but stayed crouched in prayer throughout the whole meal, watched sympathetically by his Korean mother. And as Pamela wittered endlessly on about the Future Of The World and God's Providence, Carmen wondered how it was that the members could make them do what they didn't want to do.

In the team meeting, all eyes were on Carmen. It was long past tea-time and she was very hungry, although she wasn't sure a jam sandwich would entirely fill the gap. She had been hoping to keep out of the discussion and thus to speed it along to its conclusion, but Pamela had just announced Carmen's continuing atheism to the class and now there was a pregnant silence. One of the sisters gave a nervous titter and Reg had the accusing look of a baffled bull about to snort. Gary was assiduously picking fluff off his impeccable trousers.

'If God did not exist, 'ow did the world 'appen?' Marianne asked pleasantly enough, rearranging her neat print skirt with a precise movement and settling comfortably into her chair for a long discussion. Carmen's heart sank and all thoughts of jam sandwiches faded.

She rummaged around in her brain. It was important to sound authoritative and certain, but the truth was she couldn't quite remember in detail. It was a long time since she'd had occasion to think about it.

'It was some kind of cataclysmic explosion in space,' she said. There was a ripple of merry laughter. Carmen looked around defensively, rather surprised. Since she'd been absurdly tolerant of their views, she expected them to be tolerant of her own. 'It's quite a widely held theory,' she pointed out.

'But an explosion destroys matter, yes?' asked Marianne gently.

Carmen nodded unwillingly. 'Eef this room exploded, this table, this chair, would be splinters, matchsticks?'

Carmen nodded impatiently. 'Yes, but – well you see it's to do with nuclear fission. You split an atom and it turns into heat and light and energy...'

'How could perfect things come from an explosion, hmm? Ptoof...' She threw up her hands and mimicked a mushroom cloud. 'How could flowers, petals, the stamens of a lily, how could they come out of this explosion of yours?'

Carmen struggled. 'Well, this explosion, you see, it created – well, there were molecules ... bacteria ... the seeds of life...' She found it very difficult to explain because it was too remote and enormous to comprehend. Carmen looked around for assistance from the blank, unsympathetic faces but no-one seemed to hold much brief for her theory. They were looking at her as though it were some crack-brained idea that she'd worked out on her own. She tried to think it through afresh. She was pretty sure the Big Bang theory was the most universal explanation, yet when she tried to work it out logically, it didn't sound entirely right. She wished she'd had the forethought to read up on it before she had come.

'... the explosion charged tiny particles of matter and it animated chains of – DNA ... there were sort of cellular structures and algae – and water, I think there was water...'

Marianne continued to eye her dubiously as though trying very hard to understand the ravings of a lunatic. Then she shook her head firmly. 'No. How could any living thing come to make itself? No, this is not logical.'

'But that's how it happened,' Carmen insisted. 'I can't explain it you. I can't imagine infinity. But I know that's sort of how it happened ... some way like that...' she tailed off lamely, embarrassed. The little Japanese girl was pouring water and the trickling sound was deafening in the pause that followed. When Marianne spoke it was in a tone of soft reproof.

'But this is not a very deep belief you have, if you cannot defend it. Where did you get this knowledge from?'

'I learnt it at school,' said Carmen flatly. She was slightly confused because it occurred to her now that cosmogony was just as much an act of faith as religion. She couldn't defend it, she just believed it as the only alternative to believing in God. She could only tell them famous scientists believed it, which was no better than them telling her that famous scientists believed in Principle. Believing in God or in a big explosion: in either case, it took, a leap of faith. Her stomach growled. She looked plaintively at Gary, hoping someone would change the subject. He studiously avoided her eye and his foot was tapping nervously as though she was letting him down in some way.

Marianne continued to transfix her with a glare of disapproval.

'How do you think Heavenly Father feels if you learn in school that his flowers, his trees, his beautiful creation have all just happened from this explosion? When he says to you, "Carmen, you did not listen to your own heart," what will you say?' She affected a childlike, lisping voice. '"Oh, but I learnt this in school, Father..." He will say, "School is for children." You are not a child, are you, Carmen?'

Carmen shook her head, grudgingly. It was the old school-room humiliation – being forced to answer futile rhetorical questions before a hostile class. She felt the telltale colour rising from her neck. Marianne pressed on. 'How will Heavenly Father feel when He hears His child say this?'

They all waited, alert, for Carmen's answer. She knew she was supposed to say that it would cut him to the heart, that he would suffer incalculable torments and cry real tears of suffering. This was one way to expedite her cup of sickly cocoa but on the one hand, she could not comprehend a God so vulnerable, and on the other, it seemed to be rather overestimating her importance in the Universe.

'Upset?' she conceded reluctantly. 'A bit upset.'

There was a blue line of trees reflected in Marianne's glasses and her mouth changed from a thin crack to a little mauve pucker.

'But look,' Carmen said, lurching energetically in her seat, 'I don't care what anyone else believes. That's what the Family's about, isn't it? Tolerance? I mean, since I don't believe in Him, it's hard for me to get involved in His emotions, and if He *did* exist, I'm sure He'd understand that some people, just, well ... find it a tall order.' She cast around vainly for support of this novel notion of an amiable God who made allowances. 'I mean personally, I should think He'd be pretty busy, and ... I don't think he'd really *mind*.' She finished on an apologetic laugh.

Marianne brought her hand down on the chair arm with a loud, decisive crack.

'Ah, you laugh. You make a flippant joke. You think we are here to listen to your silly sense of humour. But you see, no-one laughs.' Indeed they didn't. They were all frozen in attitudes of awed apprehension. 'We hear the laugh of an arrogant person. Heavenly Father does not laugh to see a child he give so much for, put an arrow in his heart... You think you're very clever with your long words and your big concepts which you don't even understand. No-one here thinks you clever. We hear someone who is ignorant and arrogant. We hear a donkey braying...'

Carmen swallowed hard at the insult and coloured to the roots of her hair. She couldn't quite believe the ferocity of the attack after the mellow sweetness that she'd experienced thus far.

'It's like the man who sees only red colours. People say to him, that grass is green; he says no, the grass is red. So the people say you're colour blind, but this man says, "No, all of *you* are blind. That rose is green, that grass is red"...' There was a mild wave of awkward laughter. Marianne ploughed on, 'That man is arrogant, he has the sin of sinful pride. He has blinkers on like a horse... What would you say of that man, Gary?'

Gary was staring vacantly through the window as though he wasn't in the room. He turned unwillingly into the conversation. 'Well, I'd say, after a while, he'd have to make an effort to understand.' Carmen stared at him coldly but he avoided her eye.

'Yes,' said Marianne triumphantly. 'Yes, he would. Otherwise he drives his car and the traffic lights change and *whoof*, hélas!'

She wiped the imaginary unbeliever off the face of the earth. 'He is gone. Ptoof, like that...' The team laughed at her comic expression and her childlike pleasure in the little story; Carmen smiled faintly to ingratiate herself with the group. The blood was rushing to her ears and singing in her bloodstream. 'He says, "Heavenly Father, forgive me, I was wrong. Now I have learnt to be humble. Give me my body back..."' They all laughed openly now at her dumb show of wounded surprise. Carmen affected a crooked simper but it froze on her face as Marianne rounded on her again. There was not a trace of humour on the woman's face, only a naked hostility that was frightening and unmistakable.

'I say this to you so that you know your fault and correct it. If I do not tell the fault, it becomes my fault as well.'

Everyone stared sadly at their shoes, as though not wishing to humiliate Carmen further by witnessing the reprimand. She cursed her lobster colouring that made discomfiture so obvious. She hunched her shoulders carelessly.

'So I'm arrogant,' she said, 'I can think of worse things to be.'

Marianne rapped the chair again, and her gimlet eyes flashed behind the lenses. 'Ah, you like yourself this way. OK, you will talk to yourself. We don't bother with you. It's other people who must suffer. If they have give-and-take with you, they will get infected. Is this how you want people to see you? Oh, that's Carmen: she knows *everything*? Do you know everything?'

There were two red, livid circles on Marianne's cheeks. Carmen shrugged and sank insolently into her chair. 'I never said I did.'

'Do you understand Divine Principle?'

'Yes,' said Carmen moodily, 'I understand it. I just don't believe it.'

Marianne addressed the room imperiously, 'Does anyone else here understand Principle?' They shook their heads like frightened rabbits. Reg said 'No' with a frog in his throat and then coughed. She glared triumphantly at Carmen. 'It's strange,' she said, 'I have been in the Family seven years and I still do not understand Principle. No-one understands Principle but the Lord of The Second Advent. But Carmen does. So she must be the Messiah, don't you agree?' She looked around for assent. No-one moved. 'We must all bow low and take a lot of notice of what Carmen says, huh?' and she bowed solemnly to Carmen. Carmen scowled ferociously and spread her arms wide on the back of the chair.

'How come if you understand Principle you keep talking of explosions and molecules and . . . was it *bacteria*?' She said the word with a disdainful incredulity, but no-one dared to laugh. 'For Divine Principle does not *anywhere* mention this explosion.'

'I read it in other books,' Carmen mumbled.

'What good is it to read other books when you cannot even read your own heart? When you cannot read the hearts of others? You want to know the Truth, or you would not be here. Yes? Yes or no?'

Carmen gave a grim assent. 'I came to find out the truth,' she said as if the words were being wrenched out of her.

'You would not *disdain* a great Truth if you heard it?'

Carmen shook her head.

'Then you must learn that others more humble have something to give you. That you don't know everything. That to Heavenly Father, a humble heart is more important than all the books in the world.'

She gathered her papers together. 'Enough. We waste too much time on this. Now we pray. Pamela?'

They all crouched into devotional attitudes. Marianne watched Carmen as she bowed her head and clasped her hands and began to pray to the God she so casually denied. Carmen welcomed the opportunity to close her eyes and hide her face because her stupid body was letting her down, she was trembling imperceptibly and very close to tears.

When at last the bell rang, Carmen sprang to her feet, desperate to get out of the stultifying room with its smell of polish and its hostile vibrations. Marianne frowned as Carmen bounded out through the door.

She ran across the grass towards the lawn sprinkler and threw herself under the cascade of water, rolling and lolloping under the cold jets like a dog maddened by the heat. Once she was refreshed, she lay wet through and limp, breathing in the summer smell of fresh grass cuttings. A shadow fell across her face and she became aware of someone standing over her.

'What do you think you're doing?'

She opened her eyes. It was Gary, half-smiling, half-stern. Was he being the playmate or the teacher? It was hard to tell with the sun behind him.

'Wallowing in the gift of God's water,' she said.

'You really are a child, aren't you?' he said with a touch of impatience.

'We're all children, aren't we? I thought that was the point. We're supposed to be like children.' She sat up and stared archly at him.

'Together,' he said. 'We're all children together. We don't go off and do things alone.'

'Do you want to come and roll about with me?' she asked.

He continued to stare at her and then he leaned down towards her. She heard him say in a ferocious, angry undertone, 'If you don't start trying, I'm going to have to cut you off.' With that he turned and stalked off towards the house. Carmen sat up, nonplussed, and watched him as he walked away.

At tea-time, the gravity of her offence was brought home to her in no uncertain terms. Everyone studiously avoided her eye. She saw Gary striding towards her, or so she thought, and pulled the chair out for him as invitation, but instead of joining her, he made a very obvious detour to a seat at the far end of the room. A passing sister piled some gristly meat onto Carmen's plate but Carmen sensed this was an act of penitent service, not friendship.

'I wish I'd chosen a vegetarian cult,' she mumbled to Peter as she speared the unappetising knot of meat and investigated its veins. Peter pretended not to hear her.

'Great,' she said. 'Boiled aorta. My favourite.'

As she struggled to separate the gristly tube of innards from the meagre shreds of beef, she distinctly heard Peter say, 'Reverend Moon lived on four grains of rice.'

'He was in a prison camp. I'm not,' she said mildly.

'I don't think someone being tortured in a concentration camp is anything to be funny about,' Peter snapped.

She looked up, completely taken by surprise. She realised suddenly that there was something wrong. His eyes were vague and unfocused and he seemed agitated.

'Why, what's the matter, Peter?' she asked.

'People are very kind here. I don't think it's amusing to make fun of their hospitality, and I'm sick of your flippant comments about other peoples' beliefs,' he said. She saw then that he was serious, his face flushed with rising anger, his movements spasmodic and jerky. It was such a sudden transformation from the kindly, easy-going Peter she had come to like, that she was thrown completely off balance.

'They're trying to help you,' he frothed. 'They're trying to make you feel something very special. These people are good people. They're simple people. Why d'you always have to criticise? Can't you see they're doing their best?' His voice rose to a squeak of indignation. 'They're trying to give you something wonderful, Carmen. They're trying to teach you the meaning of love!' His chair scraped back angrily as he got to his feet. He collected up his knife and fork. 'There are some things in the world that don't just come down to money and grabbing everything you can get. There are some things more important than your comfort, your appetite, your silly comments. These people are giving you something for free with no ties, no strings, and they don't deserve your whingeing cynicism!'

With that he took his plate, scattering processed peas in her jam rolypoly, and stalked off angrily to a corner where the spirits were less active. Carmen swallowed hard, aware that people were staring at her, aware that the chairs to either side of her were conspicuously empty and that the conversation in the room was suddenly hushed.

She pushed away her dinner plate disconsolately and looked around for a friendly face. Reg was sitting some way down the table, so she picked up her dessert bowl and went to join him.

'I don't know what's up with everyone today,' she muttered.

Reg calmly pretended he hadn't heard her.

'Honestly, Reg,' she said in a confidential undertone. 'You don't really think Jesus was meant to have children, do you? Not really?' and she tried to scrape the compulsory congealed custard off the roll. It was lumpen and cold. So fastidiously was she separating it from the sponge that she failed to notice the flush that rose angrily from Reg's neck to lend his earlobes a dulled purple coloration. He gave a loud infuriated snort and she looked up, startled.

'Oh, that's rich, that is,' he said with ponderous irony, 'from someone who doesn't believe in their Maker. I'd say that's pretty rich.' He shook his head incredulously. 'You're too clever by half, miss. Too clever by half.' And he applied himself to his portion of ventricle with a savage show of moral rectitude.

She considered his stubborn, wrathful profile with a troubled expression. On behalf of which God was Reg getting so self-righteous? His God or theirs, or hadn't he spotted the difference? Anyway, if Reg was his old self, shouldn't unbelief be a lesser blasphemy than tampering with Holy Scripture? At least she hadn't given the Redeemer a fiancée and compared him to Adolf Hitler, as *they* had done in one of the lectures.

Since he was determined to ignore her, she mashed the horrible custard into the rolypoly with a sulky, mutinous air, until they bled together in a marbled mess.

She sat there at the long trestle table until the room was quite empty, save for the sisters who were clearing plates. She felt desolate and bereft. She told herself there was no rational reason to feel so low, only that she was exhausted and overwrought. Why should she care what they thought of her? Three days before, she hadn't even met these people, so why should they have the power to affect her so? And yet, hot tears were stinging in her eyes.

After a while, she heard footsteps echoing in the hall and she looked up, defensively, wiping her face, fearing that it was someone else sent to tell her she was selfish and arrogant and worthless. But it was Matthew himself standing over her, and he was smiling sympathetically.

'Hey, Carmen. Is there some problem? Do you want to talk?'

She stared at him mistrustfully, dimly aware that this was a grand honour. Matthew was seen as something of a celebrity in the Family, a person of exalted status who rarely stooped to mingle with lesser spirits. He bore himself like a distinguished younger statesman and he had an air of great inner tranquillity and wisdom. She nodded unhappily, having little choice.

'Well, let's walk outside,' he said.

She fell obediently into step with him as he paced slowly and reflectively down the corridor, his hands behind his back like a prince consort, his eyes fixed on the caps of his gleaming shoes.

'I've been hearing some very interesting things about you, Carmen,' he said suddenly. 'I've heard you're an extremely capable person. Very strong. You're honest and loyal, you have integrity and you're very bright.'

Carmen tried not to adopt an inane simper and began to blink intelligently. He might be laying it on with a trowel but it was certainly better than being called a donkey.

'You hold firm beliefs which you're prepared to defend and you're nobody's fool, am I right?'

'Well.' Carmen coloured. 'I don't know . . .' she said awkwardly.

They stopped at the outer door and Matthew lent against the frame. He scrutinised her face with an intensity that she found embarrassing. His eyes were a dark, wishy-washy blue, and she was close enough to see the striations, the flecks and flaws that studded the iris. His eyes drew her in and made her feel dizzy.

'They're very special qualities, Carmen,' he told her firmly, 'the kind of qualities we value here in the Family. We like people with enquiring minds, we like people who can ask thought-provoking questions.'

Carmen was just going to ask timidly why they never answered them, in that case, when he continued: 'But you know, sometimes people with *your* intelligence have a little more trouble with Divine Principle because they tend to over-intellectualise. You see Divine Principle's very complex but it's also very simple. Sometimes it takes a simple heart to grasp it. People who need to over-intellectualise everything, well, occasionally they find the issues get terribly muddled and confused and they can't see the wood for the trees. Do you think that might be possible?'

Carmen was forced to agree.

'And when I hear that someone with such a lively, active mind as you have can't conceive of there being a God, I wonder whether that's what's happening. Because if so, it's easy to sort out.'

'It's not that I can't conceive of Him,' Carmen objected. 'It's just –' Was it worth fighting this one? She had fought it once already and she was only going to lose.

'It's just that maybe my idea of God is different. Maybe I see it more as a Universal life force or some sort of power for good that makes a pattern out of chaos.' Matthew was nodding approvingly as though this was a good start. Encouraged, Carmen rounded it off with a flourish, 'And maybe if you can feel a sense of that all around you in creation, in human beings, then you might as well call it God because one word is simpler.' She nodded firmly as though she had sorted something out in her own mind. 'Yes, in that sense, I suppose I do believe in God.' What the hell, they were going to make her say it sooner or later anyway. At least this way there was a large element of truth in what she said. 'I believe in God, but maybe our definitions differ.'

'Well, there *is* only one God,' Matthew corrected her, and she supposed he meant their suffering, out-of-control God blundering about the stratosphere like an unhappy barrage balloon with its strings cut. 'But each of us has to discover him for ourselves in our heart. And if you find you're prone to over-intellectualisation, then it might be a good idea to stop asking questions altogether for a while and just concentrate on opening your heart to let Him in. Stop using your brain and see what happens. Does that seem like a good idea?' he asked solicitously.

Carmen's eyes were wary. It didn't sound like a good idea at all, under the circumstances.

'But if everyone tells me Principle is scientific fact,' she began, with a troubled look on her face. She still could not quite get through her head that any attempt at a logical conversation was pointless. She struggled on. 'Well, when scientific fact's involved, how could you ever understand it without your brain?' and she looked at him with doubtful entreaty, hoping quite hopelessly that he would see the paradox.

'Carmen,' he said in a fatherly voice. 'Some of the top scientists in the world have come to look at Principle, and the strange thing is, no-one has ever been able to fault the logic. There've been any number of Nobel prize winners who've tried and failed. So . . .' he looked at her fondly and shook his head, 'with the greatest respect . . . I don't think you need to worry your head about the logic. There are scientific principles at work there and eventually, you'll find everything will just fall into place.'

Since she looked singularly unconvinced, he leant forward. 'Look, let me bounce an idea off you . . .'

She waited expectantly. It was impossible not to be flattered by his air of great confidence in her abilities.

'Say you have a theory and you want to test it out. How would you do that scientifically?'

'Well, you'd test the hypothesis and then study the results. It would depend on what it was,' said Carmen slowly.

Matthew nodded. 'Good. Yes, that's the brain method. But, if you don't want to use that method then, conversely, you can study the effects and then analyse the means of achievement. That's the heart method. In this case you can see the results of the scientific experiment all around you. You see the fruits of Principle: Love, Joy, Freedom, Equality. All very beautiful things. As long as you genuinely want to receive God, you'll find Him. But if you close your heart He can't come in. Do you want to know Him?'

Carmen nodded seriously.

'Knock and the door will be opened,' he told her. 'Seek and you will find.'

She carried it on in her head, with Jim Reeves singing the refrain: 'Ask and you'll be given but leave this world behind...' It was a Fifties song, 'Welcome To My World', and Matthew stood there before her with arms outstretched, welcoming her with a perfect simplicity of gesture to the world they had prepared. The only snag was that one had to take the world sight unseen, the price was as yet unspecified and there were no refunds.

'We have a very beautiful experiment here, Carmen,' he said sombrely, still examining her face. 'I think you could be a part of it. Heavenly Father needs exceptional people, and I have a very strong intuition that you may be one of those.'

Carmen stared past him to the trees on the horizon. The sky was streaked with a deep blush of red as the light receded. However much her heart revolted, she was strangely moved by his kindness, by the value he seemed to set on her. From feeling so slumped and shabby and insignificant, she felt her whole spirit rise up. She put her shoulders back and tried to look like the kind of person he seemed to think she was.

'Promise me you'll try to contact Him,' he said.

The plovers were hovering and swooping in the dusk letting out little mournful cries and the handbell was ringing insistently from within the house. The communal singing started up. She was surprised to feel a lump in her throat and she marvelled at how grateful she felt, and how susceptible the human heart was to unexpected kindness. In certain situations, when warmth was applied like a balm, it could make logic seem a very secondary consideration.

'Yes, I can say that,' she assented, and they smiled at one another like equals who had struck an important gentleman's agreement.

By the time they reached the door of the main hall, the singing was ecstatic and overwhelming. Inside there was a sea of radiant profiles that rippled as the bodies swayed. Matthew paused with her on the threshold.

'Why don't you just say a few words to Marianne when you get a chance?' he said. 'She was upset about her witness, and I think she'd appreciate it if you tried to make amends.'

She nodded bravely. The prospect didn't immediately entice. But there again, if the poor woman had been persuaded to get all togged up in her Heidi outfit to confide her life story, it must have been a bit galling to find the audience on the thin side. Carmen took a deep breath and accompanied Matthew into the hall. A number of heads turned but she kept her chin in the air and walked with a proud spring in her step. Matthew made his way to the front of the hall whilst she stood surveying the rows of seats. There seemed to be no spaces. It was a relief when a friendly hiss penetrated the frantic clapping, and she saw Gary leaning across the aisle and beckoning frantically. She squeezed through the audience towards him.

'I was looking for you everywhere,' he said. 'I kept you a seat.'

She beamed gratefully at him and sat herself down on it. He was miraculously restored to his old self.

'Now, you're going to have to sing tonight,' he insisted. 'It's your turn. You've no option.' She laughed and began to shake her head. There was no way on earth that she could be persuaded to perform in public. 'I mean it, Carmen,' he assured her. 'It's a very little thing and it'll please people no end and show you're not stuck up.'

'Of course I'm not stuck up,' she protested. 'But no-one in their right mind would want to hear me s...' Her voice was drowned by another burst of applause and she craned forward to see Franklin being hauled, blustering and snickering, into the spotlight. It occurred to her then that brute force disguised as teasing fun was quite possible, and she began to ransack her memory rather desperately for a party-piece in an undemanding key. Franklin stood at ease and began to drawl 'Deck Of Cards', his eyes fixed angelically on the light fittings.

When Franklin stepped down, Gary volunteered to sing, smiling at Carmen to show her how little courage it took. She cringed on his behalf as he sat on the stool, fine-tuning the guitar like someone pretending to be an expert, but, as he began to play, she relaxed. She was relieved to find he knew what he was doing. He was much better than the House Guitarist and his voice was confident and practised. It was a love song. His eyes unmistakably sought hers as he performed. Jane gave Carmen a meaningful dig in the back.

Carmen noticed that when he had finished he handed back the guitar with a regretful look, and she noticed also that his accomplished performance was rewarded with a cool sprinkle of clapping which died away almost as soon as it began. She wondered about that.

The next moment, he was back in his seat beside her, clapping encouragement as Peter took his place on the podium and began to play the spoons. As each dubious piece of amateur talent followed the last, Carmen began to hope that she had been forgotten. But, once the brother with the comb and tissue paper had taken his extended bow, Gary leaned towards her and hissed firmly, 'You now. What are you going to sing?'

'I can't *sing*,' she wailed, mortified. Even as she spoke, Pamela and Virginia were at her elbows, pulling her to her feet, laughing and cajoling, refusing to take no for an answer. A great roar of appreciation went up as Carmen walked unwillingly towards the front, finding it more dignified to walk unaided, not wanting to be dragged there protesting. As she turned to the audience, her face was crimson, her ears were livid and her mind a complete blank. She started off falteringly with 'You Are My Sunshine', since it was a Family favourite and hadn't many high notes. Her voice was small and piping. She sang as quickly as she could so that the ordeal would be over sooner. By the third verse, she'd run out of words and was beginning to start rather desperately over again on the first verse, when she decided she'd fulfilled her obligation and stopped.

'That's all I know. I don't think there is any more,' she mumbled gruffly. She was just about to stalk off when the room exploded into tumultuous clapping and whistling, as though she had just sung a demanding aria at Covent Garden. She was quite startled and made to bolt back into the anonymity of the audience but Matthew was ambling towards her like a chat-show host, smiling warmly and clapping her as though she were his guest star. She was forced to stand there, colour flooding her face, until the full overwhelming weight of their approval had registered. She slouched in a foolish, self-conscious manner, trying to hide her pleasure and embarrassment just as Reg had done earlier in the week. She knew they were not clapping her song or her Minnie Mouse voice. They were reinforcing her, telling her that it was warmer inside the group than out of it, that if she conformed she would find acceptance such as she had never known. It was totally bewildering to receive their sanction and yet, even as she wondered how the signal travelled through the group, how they knew when their group approval should be granted or withheld, she found herself responding to it. It flooded over her like some great wave.

When she was finally allowed back to her seat, hands reaching out to pat her on the back, Gary brought his mouth close to her ear and whispered, 'You know you really are quite beautiful.'

She laughed and turned away so that he shouldn't see her blush an even deeper red.

As the evening drew to a close and everyone queued contentedly, chatting around the cocoa urns, Carmen became aware of Marianne at her shoulder. The woman leant towards her with a little burst of confidentiality and squeezed her arm.

'Carmen,' she said. 'This song you sing like a little lark. You make it so beautiful it make me want to cry . . .' and she smiled with a tenderness that lit up her rather prosaic face and gave it a surprising beauty. Close to, Marianne seemed much younger than she had ever seemed in the team meetings and, without her glasses, there was a vulnerability that caught Carmen off balance. Impulsively, Carmen reached out for her hand and spoke warmly to her.

'Listen, Marianne, I'm awfully sorry about the other night. I'm really sorry about your witness. I didn't realise what it meant and, well, everyone told me it was so moving and inspiring and that I felt very sad I wasn't there.'

Marianne smiled with shy doubt, pathetically pleased. 'Did they say this?' Carmen nodded vigorously and then Marianne said, 'I only wished you would be there so I could show you something of me, this Marianne . . .' She touched her sternum gently. 'You see one Marianne and maybe you cannot always relate to her, but inside us, in our 'earts, there is another deeper person, that we want to express. I would like you to know this Marianne inside me because then you would understand me better and perhaps we could be friends. But when you did not come to my witness, I thought, ah Carmen, after all, she doesn't care to know me, she doesn't think I'm a worthwhile person . . .' She looked so crestfallen that Carmen was immediately riven with guilt, and was afraid now that the tears that made Marianne's eyes bright were about to spill.

'Oh, that's so silly,' said Carmen, in a soothing tone. 'I think you're a really wonderful person, why, everyone here loves you so much.' Marianne smiled with childlike pleasure and brushed the tears away, laughing, and they hugged each other in a warm sisterly fashion until Carmen thought she was about to burst into tears herself.

'And now we will be friends?' asked Marianne.

'We *are* friends,' said Carmen recklessly.

Marianne tapped her affectionately on the nose. 'And perhaps we will not argue so much in the Team Meetings? Sometimes there has been hostility between us and this spoils the beautiful atmosphere for others? But now, all will be harmonious, mm?'

'Mm,' said Carmen, her smile fading slightly.

'I think I've found the answer,' Jane whispered from her sleeping bag as Carmen undressed. 'The only thing to do is just to stop arguing with them altogether. Just agree with everything they say and try to pretend you believe it too.'

'Does it work?' asked Carmen, folding her clothes.

'It worked really well this afternoon. I pretended to myself that I thought the Messiah really *was* on earth, and then I just acted out how exciting it would be if you genuinely discovered He was. You should try it. It gets you through the meetings and it's quite effortless. It stops the pressure building up in your head.'

'I'll try it tomorrow,' said Carmen, and as she unzipped her bag and snuggled down for the night she decided it might not be such a bad idea.

She lay in the darkness thinking about Gary and it gave her a certain curious pleasure. She examined it and tried to rationalise it but it wasn't rational at all. He intrigued her. He was so hard to figure out. Like a locked box that rattled, it drove you crazy and you turned it this way and that, trying to puzzle out what was inside. But, if you broke the lock, it was only an old cuff-link and an ancient hair grip and you wished you'd left the box where it was on the mantelpiece.

Another thought popped into her head. She sat up, suddenly anxious. She remembered that she had left her notebook in the lecture room. Normally this wouldn't have worried her, but she had doodled a cartoon of Marianne in it, a cartoon which was rather accurate and which she wouldn't want anyone to find, particularly since she and Marianne were now bosom pals. She got up and pulled on her trousers.

'You don't need your notebook,' Pamela whined drowsily as Carmen climbed over her. 'You can get it in the morning.'

'I shouldn't like it to get lost,' Carmen called behind her and she skipped off before she could be prevented. It would be unfortunate if the thing was found because it showed Marianne in a peaked cap and uniform with shiny leather boots and a swastika on her epaulette. The book had Carmen's name written on the cover in big letters and she had meant to tear the page out. In fact, in retrospect, she felt rather ashamed of it.

She found the book resting innocently on a bench, where no-one was likely to have seen it. Feeling thankful, she ripped the page out and shredded it, then stared at the tiny white scraps in the waste-paper basket. Some impulse made her collect them up again. She put them in her pocket, meaning to flush them down the lavatory. She asked herself what she was afraid of. Did she seriously think some-one would work patiently over the pieces for hours reconstituting the drawing like a jigsaw puzzle? It was ridiculous, but even so she collected each tiny scrap. She wandered back through the empty house and up the stairs, turning the lights off as she went.

At the second landing, her progress was halted by an eerie, whining sound that seemed to be coming from the door marked 'Prayer Room'. She thought, for a moment, that there was an animal inside, unlikely as it seemed. She pressed the door gingerly and stepped into the darkened room. The light from the gloomy passage illuminated an expanse of empty floor; there were framed pictures of Sun Meung Moon and his family spaced around the walls. The whining noise had stopped and now there was just a rhythmic knocking sound, but she could see nothing. She had a shrewd suspicion she was not allowed in this room and that made her jumpy. As she turned back to the door, something moved in the corner and she let out a frightened gasp. As her eyes adjusted to the light, she saw that it was Peter. He was huddled in the corner, behind the door, banging his head and rocking, staring into space with sightless unfocused eyes. Even as she stared at him, his mouth opened and the low keening noise began again. She crouched beside him.

'God, Peter, what's the matter? What is it? What is it?'

He showed no sign of hearing her but just continued to let out that thin, unnatural wail. It was drained of emotion, as though some shock had passed through him and left him hollow. The noise chilled her. She recognised it for what it was, the sound of mourning, of infinite regret for what would never be again. She put her arms around him and tried to make him calm but he threshed against her movements, out of control. He seemed not to know that she was there. She stroked his damp hair in streaks across the furrows of his forehead.

'I felt God's heart,' he said. 'I felt it all at once and it nearly blinded me. I felt all the suffering all at once and it was too much for *anyone* to stand. I saw the boat people. I saw them machine-gunned down. I saw little babies drowning and their mothers jumping after them and wailing, swimming with these stiff, white little babies' bodies in their arms. I heard it all mixed together. The Jews in the concentration camps throwing themselves on the barbed wire; the torture; the experiments; six thousand years of suffering all in one blast, it was too much . . .'

Carmen thought rapidly. Perhaps she should encourage him to talk, or perhaps she should try to turn his mind away from what he'd seen. She wondered if it was like the kind of nightmare children have, where the exorcism lies in retelling every detail. On the other hand, perhaps Peter was mentally ill and then no amount of talking would banish his phantoms. She had no idea what she was dealing with here, and the only figures of authority to whom she might turn for help in this gothic house were the very people who had caused the conceit to form within his brain.

'It was just a nightmare, Peter,' she said. There was no conviction in her voice. 'It's over. Now you're safe. You're here. Everything's calm.' Since he couldn't hear her, he couldn't hear that she was lying. She could only give him the reassurance of her arms tightly around him.

'It was too *much*,' he insisted, anguished. He began to shake his head. She still wasn't sure that he was aware of her presence. 'I saw the bodies flung into heaps like offal, bayonets stuck through children's limbs like kebab skewers. I saw people torn limb from limb, still screaming, their heads pierced on spikes like footballs with their eyes still rolling.'

Carmen wondered how much of this there was to hear and whether she had the stomach for it.

'And all these animals,' he said. The sobs began to choke him and he buried his head in her breast. She tried to soothe him, frightened for him. He seemed to have internalised every newspaper article he had ever read, every news report he'd seen on television.

'They were in cages with electrodes on their heads, dogs with stumps where their legs should be, and howling, howling . . .'

Carmen rubbed his hands, which were fluttering like pigeons.

'You're just over-tired,' she said inadequately. Suddenly, the light was blocked by shadows in the doorway. She heard her name called sharply; dazzled, she got up and moved towards them.

'I think you should go to bed now,' said Gary, and his tone was freezing.

'He seems upset,' said Carmen.

'Go to bed,' he told her. The brothers moved into the room like orderlies in a mental hospital. They didn't seem surprised or overawed. Carmen went outside and, as the door closed, she heard them begin to chant.

She thought it was the name of their founder. 'Sun Meung Moon, Sun Meung Moon, Sun Meung Moon', but the more she listened the more the syllables ran into one another in a frenzied invocation so that the chant might have been anything. Since she could do nothing, and wild alarm bells were ringing in her head, she turned on her heel and ran as fast as she could back to the safety of the dormitory.

She stumbled back into the darkened room, her heart lurching wildly. She picked her way over to Jane's bunk and whispered urgently, 'Jane, I feel spooked. Come out and talk to me.'

Jane sat up smartly and levered herself off the mattress. She wasn't really asleep and, besides, she was the kind of person who responded generously to emergencies. They crept out and into the adjoining lumber room, furtively clutching their cigarette packets. They sat down on the floor with their backs to the skirting board and talked in very low voices in case someone should come to send them back to bed. Carmen related what she had seen in the prayer room. Jane considered it.

'Well, maybe he was upset about his little party piece,' she reasoned. No-one had clapped much. 'He's not actually very good at playing the spoons, is he? I mean, it just sounded like someone rattling cutlery.'

'Don't be ridiculous,' said Carmen. 'He wasn't upset. He was completely out of his head! Did he mention any sort of mental problem to you? I shouldn't think this place is very good for people who're mentally ill, would you? Let's be frank, it's not very good for people who are sane.'

Jane shook her head. 'He never mentioned anything like that. He seemed quite normal to me. A bit upset about the girlfriend, that's all.'

'D'you think that's what it is?' Carmen persisted. 'Is that why people change? They've already got some sort of mental illness and it just makes it worse?'

Jane shook her head and frowned. 'I don't think it's that. They don't seem very keen on people with problems. I know they say they take just anyone but they seemed awfully disappointed with Franklin when they caught him nicking food and he wouldn't admit it. Pamela said he had a reality problem – she said it was much harder for people with troubled spirits to centre themselves properly and sometimes people with multiple spirits just couldn't hear Principle at all.'

They both stared pensively at their outstretched bare feet. Jane's were rather narrow and elegant and Carmen's were long and stringy. If Franklin had a reality problem, what did Pamela and Gary have?

'Did Peter have multiple spirits?' asked Carmen.

'No,' Jane said slowly. 'Pamela said he'd got very accepting spirits and they were quite calm.'

'Well, they're certainly working themselves up into a lather at the moment,' Carmen observed. 'It was all garottings and decapitations and gouging eyes out –'

Jane held up her hand as though the picture was vivid enough.

'Maybe some of Franklin's spirits sort of hopped out onto Peter like fleas,' she suggested helpfully. 'Then perhaps they'll hop out of him and onto someone else. Maybe they'll hop onto Pamela and they'll all drop dead. That's what she reminds me of, a walking sterilisation unit.'

'Just so long as they don't hop onto me,' Carmen muttered darkly.

'Why, you don't believe in spirits, do you?' asked Jane.

'No.'

'Nor do I.' Jane drew hard on her cigarette. 'Well, what is there to get spooked about then?'

Carmen screwed up her eyes. 'Well, look. The members, I mean they're very nice and all that, but they're a bit abnormal. To us, their idea of reality is a bit unreal, and *our* idea of reality is a bit unreal to them.' Jane agreed. 'Now, their aim is to get us to accept their reality as fact. Mm? Now, because the two realities are relatively stable, we can swap into theirs without too much trouble if we want to. But they can't switch back into ours, can they?'

'No,' Jane agreed.

'So say there is a line between their reality and ours...' She was speaking very slowly because it was a strain. 'Something really drastic must happen to fix them there on that side of the line. Something that makes it permanent. Does that make sense?' Jane concurred. 'But they think Franklin's poor material because he can switch so easily between reality and fantasy, so if he swapped into their reality, they couldn't fix him there – he might just flit in and out of it...' Carmen was beginning to confuse herself. Her brain found it increasingly more laborious to handle abstract notions, but she had a feeling it was very important. 'So they seem to think the ones who make good material are the normal ones, the ones with a normal reality, like you and me. And Peter,' she added significantly. She sat back and crossed her arms as though she had made her point.

Jane looked at her slightly mystified. 'So?'

Carmen dropped her rational air of scientific detachment and began to gibber excitedly. 'So, what are we doing sitting here, waiting for something drastic to happen to us and we don't know what it is and maybe it's what just happened to Peter in the prayer room?'

'But Peter was probably over-tired and upset and someone had been battering him and he just freaked out.'

'But I'm tired and upset!' Carmen screeched. 'And people are always battering me. And what if we got stuck in their reality and we couldn't get back?'

Jane thought about it. 'I don't know. You're spooking *me* out now,' she muttered. She was very over-tired and very overwrought herself. It was a combination of factors that, at that particular time of night, always incubated paranoia. She made an effort to be rational. 'But look, no-one could get stuck in a reality. Think about it logically. What is a reality? It's not a country. It's not a place. It's not a lift that gets stuck between floors.'

Carmen began to concentrate very hard on the word 'reality' and the concept that belonged to it until it lost its meaning. She stared anxiously at Jane, eager for reassurance.

'It can't, can it?'

'Of course it can't,' said Jane, soothingly. 'Just think about it. It's silly. It's like Alice falling down a rabbit hole. It's something that only happens in dreams.'

Carmen shook herself out of it. She laughed, embarrassed. 'It *is* silly, isn't it? I don't know what's wrong with me. I must be getting as crazy as they are ... it's just that sometimes everything seems very dark and sinister and weird, and everything they do looks as if they're doing it for some ulterior motive. Then suddenly it all switches and I can see what nice, decent people they are and they seem so innocent and vulnerable – and it just seems so unkind to think they mean anything but the best ...' She looked up at Jane, her eyes brimming, a tearful catch in her voice. One of the tears spilt and Carmen brushed it away and began to laugh at herself. 'And sometimes I feel as if I keep taking a run at a brick wall with my head, and then I can't seem to believe that it's a brick wall, I can't believe it's knocked me out, so I get up and take another run at it ... Do you ever feel like that?'

'Well, I feel as if my brain's bursting, sometimes,' said Jane, sensibly. 'But I think that's just the over-stimulation. I think they're basically good people, but they've just gone a bit overboard because they happen to think they've found out something world-shattering. They think they've found out the Messiah's on earth and they believe it. If He is, then they're doing the only thing they *can* do, they're following Him, and if He's not on earth and it's all a lie and they've been duped, then, what the hell, it seems to be making them very happy. Maybe some of them couldn't fit into society anyway, and this place gives them a sense of purpose – like some great big therapy group.'

Carmen nodded, trying to convince herself. A bunk in the corner cranked and they looked at it nervously, but it was empty. They listened to the soft burr of a car passing on a main road somewhere outside, in the real world of the night. Carmen drew the collar of her dressing gown closer.

'But what if someone you knew, someone who was perfectly normal, someone who really couldn't care less about the Messiah – what if they suddenly just upped and disappeared and walked out of their life as if it was an old cardigan or something? If it was so totally out of character that everyone thought she must have been murdered. If someone like that just suddenly changed, that'd be pretty weird, wouldn't it?'

'Do you know someone like that?' asked Jane, suddenly alert. She sat forward excitedly, reading Carmen's face. 'You do, don't you?' Jane's eyes positively glowed at the idea of a secret. 'Oh, go on, you can trust me. I'm on *this* side of the line,' and she traced it on the floorboard. Carmen studied her doubtfully and then gained confidence. If she couldn't trust Jane, she couldn't trust anyone. She fumbled in her pocket, got out the little picture and showed it to her.

'It's my sister.'

'I *knew* there was something,' said Jane, pleased at her own perspicacity. 'You know why I knew? Because most people who come here are naturally quite trusting, but you've never let your guard down once. Good for you!'

She seemed perversely pleased that Carmen had tricked them.

'She looks like you,' Jane said, approvingly. Carmen craned over her shoulder. It was true. The face that stared back was very like Carmen's. Lucy was two years younger but her facial structure was the same, only she was thinner with mousier hair and a gap in her teeth. There was something puppyish and eager in the way that she stared at the glass in the photo booth, smiling for all she was worth. Carmen carried on talking quietly as Jane fingered the snap.

'She went up to Manchester for an interview. And that was that. She just didn't come home. That was two months ago.' She took back the snap possessively and brooded over her sister's face as though it might, even now, give back some answer.

'Lucy wasn't inadequate. She wasn't looking for anything. She didn't have any problems.' She looked at Jane with troubled eyes. 'I mean, why should someone who was bright and normal and perfectly happy suddenly decide that all the things that mattered to them just didn't matter any more, unless something weird happened?'

Jane tried to think of some simple rational explanation. 'Well, I don't know. When you're seventeen, eighteen, sometimes you get restless, start going through changes...'

Carmen shook her head with an air of certainty.

'No, I would have known. She would have talked things out, she would have told me. If she had any problems, my mother and I would have sensed it. We're a close family. We talk. We're not like people who don't tell each other what we're feeling.'

Jane was looking slightly sceptical. Carmen frowned. It seemed the more one insisted on the closeness of a relationship, the less convincing it sounded. Carmen only knew that what she was saying was the truth. She and Lucy had been as close as two sisters could be, and as far as Lucy's relationship with their mother went, it had been very loving. They'd been the best of friends.

She moved restlessly. 'And anyway, Jane, changes take place over periods of time. We've only been here a few days and people are starting to change all over the place. And when people go through normal changes, it doesn't affect their *eyes*. How come *all* the members have peculiar eyes?'

Jane nodded. It was true. There was no rational explanation for it. They said it was because they were growing closer to perfection, but did that make any sense? They didn't even deny that their eyes were strange. It was only that, as time went on, people ceased to comment upon it.

'Something like that must have happened to her,' Carmen insisted, 'because, if she's here, it means she must have come to believe something that she'd never ever have *considered* believing in a million years! And if it happened to someone as sane and normal as Lucy, well then, why couldn't it happen to us as well? What if a person couldn't *stop* it happening to them?'

'Are you sure she's here?'

Carmen nodded miserably. 'I wasn't a hundred per cent sure at first. We only had this crazy letter to go on, but it was all World Problems and how busy she was, doing all this voluntary work, and she signed it I.T.P.N. The police just said it was probably the Moonies and took her off their files. Everyone we talked to who knew anything about it said we should leave it alone and that there was nothing we could do because the whole thing was impenetrable – we'd have to wait for her to get in touch, and that when someone joins the Moonies, they turn into a different person and they just don't want to leave.' She shrugged. 'Well, I wasn't just going to leave it without knowing if she was alright or if she needed help or something. I tried to find out more about it but there weren't any books in the library. All I found was a news item warning people against it, and saying it was run by a millionaire businessman and that he owned factories – tea factories, pharmaceutical companies and an armaments factory...' She stopped in mid-flow. 'Do you think that could be true?'

Jane frowned. 'It doesn't sound true.'

Carmen went on. 'Well, it seemed strange enough that Lucy'd want to get involved with anything religious, but I couldn't see why she'd want to work free for some millionaire, especially not if he had anything to do with arms. I mean, I'd say *that* was pretty sinister.'

'Maybe it's something the press made up,' said Jane. It was clear the idea disturbed her. 'Pamela says they make up all sorts of lies about the Family.'

'Anyhow, after that I went out on the streets, looking for them. That's when I met Gary. He said he couldn't remember anyone called Lucy, there were too many members to remember all their names. I had this feeling he knew something about her but that he didn't want to tell me. Now, I'm pretty sure he *does* know. After all, they move around a lot. They must get to meet each other. They seem to have a pretty good grapevine. But if he knows where she is, what's there to be evasive about? If everything's above board, what's the big mystery?'

Jane put her head on one side. She seemed determined to put the best complexion on things before she finally succumbed to paranoia. She fixed her eyes on the patch of night sky through the window.

'Well, I suppose it depends on the motivation,' she said doubtfully. 'For instance, you want to get your sister out so you haven't exactly opened up about why you want to hear Principle. *They* want you to hear Principle so they can get you in, so they haven't exactly opened up about having your sister. You can sort of see their point. Say they just trotted your sister out and showed her to you...' She looked at Carmen to check that her logic was sound. Carmen motioned that she was following. 'And then she started wittering on about Eve's Satanic blood and saving the world and all that, you'd have thought she was mad or brainwashed or something, wouldn't you?' Carmen nodded firmly. 'But now, when you find her, she'll seem relatively normal...' Jane faltered. It didn't sound quite right, somehow. 'And at least...'

Carmen finished it off for her. 'At least we'll have something to talk about. Thanks, Jane. That's a great consolation.'

Jane looked at her with a troubled frown. It didn't sound right at all.

'Here, you don't think *I'm* changing, do you? You would tell me?'

Carmen hastened to reassure her, although she wasn't absolutely sure.

'The trouble *is*,' said Jane slowly, 'you'll go to all this effort to find her and, when you do, you may well find she just follows you in and out of the bathroom all day like Pamela and you'll be only too glad to get shot of her.'

'I know.' The thought gave her a sharp, wrenching feeling in the chest. She had come to accept, now, that she wasn't likely to find the same Lucy she had lost. That strange, appalling fact had become more familiar to her but it didn't make it any better. And in the photo, Lucy's face still peered out, trusting and hopeful, as if she was relying on Carmen to get her out.

'Well, it's not *that* terrible,' said Jane lamely. 'It's only the eyes, and the fact they've got no sense of humour. But that may just be co-incidence. I mean, you can't extract someone's sense of humour like it was a tooth!' She seemed to be arguing with herself now. She shook her head. 'No, I bet you'll find her and she'll just be exactly the same, only a bit more religious. I honestly don't think people can change unless they want to change.'

Carmen sighed. 'Reg doesn't want to change. He just hasn't noticed he's doing it. And Peter just wanted a new girlfriend. Instead of which he's got a sackful of Franklin's used spirits.'

Jane laughed involuntarily but it had a hollow sound. As it died away, the noise seemed to be carried on somewhere outside the room like a thin dreary echo. They both froze and listened. There it was again. Carmen relaxed.

'It's OK, it's that woman, Letitia, coughing,' she said. 'She must be in the bathroom again.'

'Let's go to bed,' said Jane. 'We're just freaking ourselves. Every-thing'll look different in the morning. It always does.' She got to her feet and extended her arms to pull Carmen up. 'Tomorrow, it'll all seem as right as rain and we'll wonder what we were worrying about.'

'It will, won't it?' said Carmen without conviction.

'Yes,' said Jane, but as they slipped out guiltily into the corridor she added, 'Still, maybe it's just as well to be cautious.' Carmen looked at her, surprised. So Jane *did* feel it too. However hazy their faintly ludicrous suspicions, the sense of indefinable disquiet was shared, as though they both heard ultrasonic squeaks of premonition flitting round the silent house like bats. Like bats or spirits. And it was just conceivable that, behind their smiling faces, the nice, well-meaning members were out to do them some great, irreparable harm.

In the morning, of course, it all seemed like nonsense. Carmen found that Jane had been quite right. Nothing ever looked so bad in daylight and there was nothing more real than a grey English drizzle. She peered down from the dormitory window as she pulled on her clothes and the flat undistinctive light rendered the lush vegetation and the people milling on the lawn reassuringly familiar and mundane. Intellectualising about concepts of reality late at night was obviously not a very fruitful activity for someone suffering from over-stimulation and lack of sleep, she told herself. Maybe Pamela had a point when she printed 'NO CONCEPTS!' in block capitals on the hands of hapless guests.

Reality was sprinting down the stairs to join in a frantic session of physical jerks, then whirling into the hall with the others and singing three rousing songs to get the spirit up and then crouching to a breakfast prayer at eight o'clock. If you allowed yourself to be swept along with the rhythm and pace of the Family, there really wasn't time to worry about different strata of reality, and she found it something of a relief. Nothing could be more real than the aches and pains she was developing in her muscles from unaccustomed exercise, and the actual physical exhilaration of singing to the full extent of her lungs. Carmen was beginning to feel a sneaking passion for the songs they sang so repeatedly: perhaps she would actually miss them when the week ended; perhaps they would continue in her head as ghost melodies, reminding her of the Family, even when the Family was part of her reality no more. Reality, there it was again. Of course, the songs were not all the same ones that they'd sung at the beginning. The corny pop songs they'd sung when it wasn't a religion had gradually given way to familiar sacred songs, and now they seemed to be moving into a new phase of unfamiliar songs, some of them addressed to a Father whom she could only assume to be the New Messiah.

This seemed a touch premature. It reminded her of a phrase she'd once heard about salesmen's technique – The Early Close – where you sold a punter the brand-new washing machine while they still thought they were having a discussion about the broken pump on the old one. No-one seemed particularly to have noticed that the word 'Heavenly' had been lopped off 'Heavenly Father' and she supposed some of them thought they were still singing to God, some of them thought they were singing to Jesus and some were too over-oxygenated to care either way. The latter swayed and smiled with a mad, intoxicated glint in their eyes. Her private theory was that, all unknowing, they were singing to the smiling, inscrutable face of Sun Meung Moon, who looked as if He would make a good washing-machine salesman if His Mission failed, but then how could they possibly believe he was the Messiah? She decided that they couldn't, and that she was being uncharitable to the members to think them either that imaginative or that *un*imaginative.

At breakfast, she scrupulously observed her promise to Matthew. She didn't like making promises because she always felt honour-bound to keep them, and that was why she now made a dutiful stab at contacting the Universal Principle Of Creation And Humanitarianism even though no-one could see inside her head and check what she was doing. As it turned out, the concept was too vague and random. After a struggle, she compromised and brought it down to a human scale; she gave it a personality that was, in fact, indistinguishable from the God of her childhood. She chose the qualities that she wanted Him to have and He beamed them back at her, magnified as though He were a powerful transmitter somewhere in the darkness. She sat with her face buried in her palms, her body tensed and urgent, in the way that everyone prayed in the Family, but this was just to fool Pamela.

Inside, she was calm. It was like staring into a black space and contemplating all that was good and generous. She was peculiarly objective about the sensation but she found it comforting and self-affirming. It made her realise with a chill that the Family was singularly devoid of the qualities that her God possessed. She had a feeling that, if any of the members could see what she saw, they would shrink away like vampires from garlic, and this strange notion convinced her that, under the circumstances, a warm God was a fine and private ally for her to have against them.

'Are you beginning to feel His presence when you pray?' Pamela enquired with delicate solicitude.

'Yes, I think I am,' said Carmen, and her face had a cheerful radiance that made Pamela hopeful. Carmen wolfed down her corn-flakes. She was feeling very high and full of nervous energy. Her eyes were bright as though she had a fever.

'Can you feel something of His sorrow? Can you imagine how desolate He must feel deep inside?' Pamela prompted anxiously.

'Well, not yet. Give us a chance, I've only just started,' said Carmen in an aggrieved tone.

'No, it's true.' Pamela looked pensive. 'You can't expect a revelation right away, I suppose. Sometimes, I just wish it was that easy. Don't you, Gary? I used to get *so* impatient. I used to feel such a dunce, everyone else was making such great spiritual growth and I was so slow. And then I just used to pray that much *harder*. Did you ever feel that way, Gary?'

Gary smiled and said nothing, since although the question was addressed to him, the information was addressed to Carmen.

Jane sat surveying the three of them, her arms akimbo, a look of dissatisfaction on her face. She had woken up cantankerous and edgy. True, she had managed to soothe Carmen's fears the previous night but, by getting entangled with Carmen's paranoia, she seemed to have awakened her own. What's more, she had just spent some time watching the black woman, Letitia, coughing in the bathroom and she had noticed some flecks of blood in the basin.

As Pamela continued to twitter, both Carmen and Jane became aware of Peter shambling across the room towards their table, attended by a diminutive Japanese sister. The girl settled him into a chair a little way down the table with the aloof concern of a ward orderly. He still seemed dazed and his shoulders were stooped. He had the grey pallor of a man in shock and the loose flesh of his jowls hung like the slack cheeks of a bloodhound. He kept his eyes veiled submissively and when the sister offered him the sugar bowl, he seemed to turn the question over in his mind for some moments, suspiciously pondering its significance. He made no effort to eat and only stared at his limp hands lifeless on the table if he thought they'd been stolen from a waxwork tableau and placed either side of his plate as a warped and grisly joke. He darted a look now and then at the crook of his arm as though to ensure the thing was attached at the elbow. His poor hands were covered with biro-ed mottos.

'Did he get a revelation?' Carmen asked Gary with diplomatic tact, and then, since he didn't answer straight away, 'I mean, that's what we're all praying for, isn't it? And Peter's had one. So everyone must be pretty pleased with him.' She looked at Peter with a kind of awe. 'Well, either a revelation or a nervous breakdown.'

'It's not only God who sends revelations,' Gary said rather abruptly. 'We can't always tell who's sending the revelation. Satan takes a lot of guises.'

'I see,' said Carmen.

'So that wasn't God's Heart he was feeling?' she enquired. 'Some other spirits got in there somehow?'

Gary nodded tersely as though even to talk about it was to court danger. He wiped his mouth with the serviette which was unnecessary since nothing had passed his lips.

'Was it the animals?' she pressed on.

'He'll be OK. He's just got to subdue some spirits. Do some Conditions, you know.' He shrugged moodily. 'Vivisection's not a major Global topic in the Plan. The creation's there to serve us. Eventually of course, once Father's plan becomes actualised, there'll be no need for experiments because there won't be any sickness, so it's not really a priority. It's not really relevant at the moment.'

Carmen nodded doubtfully. She continued to regard Gary's lean, intelligent face, searching vainly for some sign that his reality was her reality. She felt the dull, insistent, nagging sensation in her head.

'How will sickness stop? I mean, it's all very well to say it, but how can it possibly stop in reality?'

'Sickness mostly comes from the spirits,' he said with a trace of impatience. 'Anyway, listen to the lectures and you'll understand. I shouldn't tell you these things till you're ready.'

Carmen looked across uneasily and met Jane's eyes.

Jane sat up suddenly in her chair and entered the conversation with quiet insistence. 'I think Steve needs to see a doctor,' she said. 'And that girl sounds like she's got TB. You can't exorcise TB spirits by chanting Sun Meung Moon and you can't cure paranoid delusions by making someone take cold showers and do a lot of gardening.'

'How far did you get in your biology course, Jane?' asked Gary in a light, ironic voice. 'I didn't know you had such a lot of medical knowledge.'

She flushed at the mention of her failure but she carried on doggedly. 'There's only two things I can think of that could make someone cough like that – TB or lung cancer.' Then she added as an afterthought, 'Or pneumoconiosis. She hasn't been down a mine lately, has she?' She looked at Gary with a great show of innocence as though genuinely seeking information, but underneath it, her anger was palpable. 'I mean, the Reverend Moon seems to own everything else. He hasn't got a coal mine, has he?'

There was a stunned silence. Gary looked so angry that Carmen almost thought he was about to reach across the table and clip Jane round the ear. Carmen looked at her with a rather fearful respect. It took some courage to challenge them in that direct way, making no concessions to their fantasy world, particularly when the repercussions were inevitable. But it was also slightly shocking.

Pamela recovered herself quickly and pretended to be only mildly put out. 'Oh, you're just being silly,' she scolded. 'We've got some very brilliant doctors in the Family. I really think if you're feeling worried about anything, you should have a talk with Matthew. Letitia's perfectly capable of looking after herself and, as for Peter, well, his Spiritual Mother has a really deep relationship with him and she's far more likely to know what's best for him than someone who's only just met him.' Her rather matronly authority quelled Jane effectively.

'It's very easy to get involved in other people's spiritual problems as a diversion from getting on with our own,' Gary observed quietly.

He looked across at Carmen and said in a conversational tone, 'The spirits are very active here at the moment. Perhaps it would be nice to go and do some chores?'

Unwillingly, Carmen got to her feet. She felt she was abandoning Jane to trouble, but Gary was rather firm about it. As she brushed past Peter, she became aware that Matthew had taken the sister's place beside him. Matthew was bent over talking intently to him and Peter's face was flushed with beatific wonderment. He stared at Matthew with doglike, adoring eyes, nodding very slowly, repeatedly, as though he were being given a set of instructions that made everything dazzlingly clear.

Gary strode on towards the door. Carmen plucked tentatively at his sleeve. 'Gary, if vivisection's not relevant and humanitarianism is pointless, what *is* relevant? What's the major objective? I mean on *this* earth...'

'Defeating Communism,' he said absently, and they swung into the passage and out towards the back door. Carmen blinked hard as she walked. Whenever she thought she'd mastered Divine Principle with all its warped but inexorable logic, it veered off in some new direction. What was Communism to do with Adam and Eve? 'But that's tomorrow,' he added. 'God actually means the Kingdom of Heaven to come on the earth, and it's pretty imminent at the moment. That's why we're so busy.'

Carmen nodded as if this answered all her questions.

When they reached the garden, all the urgency went out of his pace and she watched him as he stooped to smell the roses one by one. They were big pom-pom blossoms, drenched with rain and fragrance. The Family seemed to produce flaunting, extravagant flowers and the most luxuriant foliage that she had ever seen outside a show garden.

'Aren't they beautiful? They're *so* beautiful,' he said, and he motioned to her. She put her nose inquisitively into the dew-soaked heart of each bloom and drank in the sweetness, since that seemed to be what he wanted her to do. It was as though they were sharing some intimate sacrament as they knelt together on the wet grass, allowing the disturbing vibrations from the interchange at breakfast to drain away. At length, when she was beginning to feel the tension disperse from her neck muscles, he turned to her. She thought he was going to give her a lecture on the Creation and how they were supposed to love and nurture it, but he merely said in a calm, matter-of-fact voice:

'You realise that we may not see one another once this week is over. I don't know how you feel about that?' He made a show of stripping some of the dead leaves from the tea rose. She watched his face. How *did* she feel about it?

She could hardly tell him that it was a relatively easy thing to do, to leave a fantasy behind. That was one of the beauties of a fantasy: it didn't twine itself around the heart strings like a creeping vine. One swift chop and it was possible to find another fantasy to fix on.

'Well,' she said hesitantly, 'I don't know what you feel about it, either...'

He smiled wryly and looked her in the eyes. 'Don't you? Well, then. You're not as perceptive as I gave you credit for.'

One of the roses was listing on a bent stalk. He snapped it off and gave it to her peremptorily without any great romantic flourish.

'I think it would be very sad if we should lose each other now,' he said in a rather stiff, controlled voice. 'I don't believe in coincidences. I think we were meant to meet and I think we were meant to know each other much better than we do.'

She sat on her heels and looked into the pale, tinted petals of the flower, at a loss for words. He was starting it again. Talking like a character in a book, trying to fool her with a false romantic idyll, trying to tell her what he imagined any silly girl would want to hear. She frowned. She suddenly felt tearful and fractious, resenting the fact that he thought her so gullible.

'You're frowning,' he said. 'You know, when I look at you, when I watched you the other night singing, or just when you're in Team Meetings and you're listening so intently with that worried look on your face, I feel ... I can't explain it ...' If he was acting, he was very good. If he was telling the truth he was too good. 'I feel so close. I feel this very strong connection between us. It doesn't make sense ...' He stirred the soil broodily with his hand. 'As If I've always known you, as if I *will* always know you – it's a very strange feeling.'

She looked at him resentfully. No-one had the right to talk that way unless they meant it, particularly if they were talking to someone who was already fragile from lack of sleep, particularly if they were as good-looking as Gary.

'But maybe,' she said obstinately, 'maybe all Spiritual Parents feel that way about their Spiritual Children?'

He laughed abruptly. 'Is that what you think?' He brushed his hand against his forehead and it left some soil there. 'It'd be convenient if they did, but I don't think it's the case. No, I'm talking about something else. You see, we talk together, we eat together, we seem to get on, but, I don't know, I get this curious resistance from you. I don't feel as if you've made any effort to know me at all. Not really.' He looked at her ruefully. 'So, OK, you see me as a Spiritual Parent, this person who's always telling you what to do and what not to do, and maybe you're glad to get away from me sometimes, I understand that –' She shook her head. There was something very raw and open in his face, and she began to believe that she really had affected him in some way, that maybe, unintentionally, she'd hurt him. It was true that she wasn't always as tactful as she might be around the members, for the simple reason that she thought they had hides like rhinoceroses. It was just a natural assumption that people so hermetically sealed should be impermeable. There was just the smallest, niggling possibility that he wasn't lying, that his emotions were real and that he could only express them in this disconcertingly direct verbal fashion, without the subtle circuitry of normal flirtation.

He carried on rather bitterly. 'I don't think you ever look at me and see that there's a person underneath with feelings and fears and desires, the same as everyone else. You see me as a Family member, as someone strange, different from yourself, but can't you see I'm *not* ... I don't know.' He shook his head wearily; he looked so lost and defeated that she couldn't but take seriously what he was saying. His air of dignified, noble confidence seemed to have slipped away from him, leaving him shorn and human. 'Sometimes the way you look at me – it just makes me feel very empty...'

She stared at him, dismayed. How could she have known that she was hurting him when she didn't even know that he had feelings? She was stricken with guilt and strangely, horribly moved by him. What she really wanted to say was that she couldn't get to the person he was talking about because it was locked away behind his cautious eyes where she couldn't reach it, no matter how hard she tried. And yet, how could a person lock themselves away, and why should they?

'I *do* see you as a person, Gary. I *do* – it's only that, well, you are a member, you are a part of this ... thing.' She indicated vaguely around her as though it was the trees and flowers that contained him within the Family, not his own brain. 'It's so all-consuming. I mean it's wonderful and all that, but it's so...' She tailed off, unable to finish the sentence – it was so all-consuming, and so empty. 'I mean, you've chosen – ' He cut across her.

'There's something you haven't realised,' he said tersely. 'People don't *choose* to join the Family. It's not something I would have chosen. I was doing other things when I stumbled on it. It's not a matter of choice. It's something that happens to you.'

'What – against your will?' she asked mildly.

He nodded.

She found that she was holding her breath.

She suddenly had a wild idea that the old Gary, the one that he had been before the Family, was sending out weak and plaintive signals, telling her that he was reachable, pleading with her to batter down the implacable new Gary that contained him as though he was not trapped inside there of his own free will but bottled up like a genie. Perhaps if she found Lucy, she would find that Lucy, too, had been shrunk and reduced and packaged inside a brand-new Lucy, empty except for a small frightened voice saying 'Look at me', 'Find me'. But Gary didn't have parents, Gary didn't have a brother who had cared enough to come looking. Suddenly she felt that their conversation was not about a depth of feeling or affection that might or might not exist between them but about something far more serious. She didn't know what a soul was, but it seemed to her that Gary had lost one, and that some little part of him was mourning and demanding recognition of its passing.

'And if you want to understand, you have to *help* me,' he insisted. Or did he mean, 'If you want to help me, you have to understand?'

She knew with absolute certainty as she looked at him that Gary was not a perfect person, not an inexplicable, exotic clone, but a normal, flawed human being who had had some grievous violence done to some part of his inner self that should have been sacred and inviolable. When someone was drowning, you didn't stop to tell them it was their fault they'd taken the dinghy out. If that was the kind of love he was asking for, she could give it unconditionally. She realised she would give him anything he needed.

'Look, Gary,' she said carefully, 'if you ever should need a friend...'

He moved impatiently and raised his eyebrows. 'I already have many thousands of friends,' he said, 'in every country of the world. The Family links arms around the globe.'

'I know that,' she said awkwardly. She made another attempt to talk to him in the terms of normal reality. 'But it's a closed system. That's why I can't . . . that's why maybe you feel resistance from me. It's very difficult for us to talk across a barrier . . .'

He answered quickly as though he understood exactly what she was saying, although she had no conviction that they were talking about the same thing at all.

'You could break down the barrier, if you wanted to enough.'

'Could I?' She looked at him wonderingly. 'How could I do that?'

He shrugged. 'I don't know. I feel like there's no time. That there's something urgent we haven't communicated to one another. I feel as if I'm letting something important slip away without a struggle and it's trickling through my fingers like fine sand . . .' As if to illustrate his words, the bell, the relentless bell, began to toll from the house like a conscience that would never be stilled. She watched his face. A shutter came down with the finality, the smooth glide of an electronic gate, as though he had never revealed himself at all. But she was left with the impression that someone had just shown her a gaping wound and then refused to let her staunch it. She felt an awful worried tenderness for him. What Gary had failed to achieve with his slightly surreal romantic talk, he achieved effortlessly by showing her a glimpse of his psychic damage. No wonder everyone had an instinct not to hurt the members, not to challenge their reality. Who knew how finely they were balanced?

As they made towards the house, he said, 'Jane worries me slightly. I don't think she's good for you. She seems to drain your energy. Do you understand what I mean now about erratic spirits? Hers are quite visible at the moment.'

'Well, she probably has some doubts.'

'Doubts don't make people swing wildly about like a pendulum,' he said, crisply. 'I think it might be a good idea if you let Pamela talk to her and give her a bit of space today. It's dangerous to have give-and-take with tricky spirits. You might infect yourself just when your things are beginning to get clearer.'

Carmen nodded sagely.

When the lecture was in progress, Jane managed to smuggle a note to her. It said, 'I've got to keep away from you, we're multiplying evil. You're a catalyst and I'm an incubator. We're positively *seething* with spirits and they've made me promise to give up smoking.'

Carmen sniffed and screwed up the note, then nestled into her chair and tuned in to Matthew's voice. She continued writing but for once she let herself fully relax into it, as Jane had suggested. If imaginative projection could give her a better insight into their crazy world then maybe she would be better placed to find a way to help Gary and Lucy. If it also meant that she'd be able to float through team meetings without making objections or putting up obstacles, it might actually take some of the pressure off her.

As Matthew warmed to his theme, she found that it really was something of a relief to let her resistance go. It eased the dammed-up, clogged sensation that caused the aches and pains in her head. She was cautious, but she couldn't rationally see how it could do her any harm – why should it? It was only something actors did all the time, twice a day. No-one ever heard of an actor who got stuck in his performance.

It was an absurd thought. She tried to think of a better example but her brain refused to process it. The brain, she thought, was only prepared to spend a set amount of time pondering its own mysteries; after that it just sent out indignant protests in the form of twanging reverberations at the temples. Even so, while Matthew was leading them delicately down into the mysterious cavern of the Spirit World, she found herself setting a mental timer with strict instructions to come out promptly when she heard the mental buzzer going off.

He was persuading them that spiritual experiences were common and much misunderstood. She was open-minded enough to give that credence for the length of his talk. In fact she had experienced some strange manifestations herself, if one was minded to view them that way. She thought of them as mind tricks brought about by exhaustion or grief or wishful thinking. For instance, she had heard her father breathing in the house long after the car smash killed him; she had heard his characteristic amiable footfalls on the stairs: she had assumed that they were either left as vibrations in the fabric of the building or that they emanated from her brain. He often came to her in dreams, his face sunburnt and golden in a warm autumnal light, and they would dance a waltz or a polka. It was a feature of these dreams that everyone knew he wasn't meant to be alive, but *he* didn't seem to know. Everyone said 'shush' as though he'd been paroled or allowed to dance the night away like swan prince in a fairytale, but as long as no-one mentioned it then he could enjoy himself. He seemed not to know that his time was limited, or, if he did, he was content and accepting. Sometimes, after one of these carefree nights of dancing, she would wake up feeling curiously happy and be surprised to find the pillow cold with tears.

While she meandered in her private thoughts, her hand zig-zagged across the page. She saw that Peter sat forward excitedly in his chair, drinking in the words and images as they spilled out. Every now and then Matthew inserted bizarre clauses into the framework of the Spirit World that made her frown and gave her pen momentary pause. Reverend Moon had been to the Spirit World. That was how he had been able to transcribe Divine Principle, from the revelation that the prophets, Jesus included, had vouchsafed to him. All the good spirits were frantic to pass on the Truth so that God's purpose could be understood properly this time. Some of them were paying great 'Indemnity' for their failure to recognise the Messiah the first time around, and they were desperate to make amends for this terrible misunderstanding – particularly the Jewish race, who bore the responsibility for killing Him.

There was a complicated system of Indemnities and Conditions operating in the Family's world view. They seemed to Carmen to be rather like the penances and indulgences of the Middle Ages. One could make reparation and pre-pay for grace by positive actions of labour, mammoth prayer stints and fasts or by precautionary self-mortification in the form of cold shower Conditions and by constant acts of silent sacrifice. One could buy grace for oneself, for one's relatives and one's ancestors, so that not a drop of toil was wasted or selfish. But, just as one could spiritually restore one's ancestors to grace, one's ancestors could bequeath problems: someone with a detached retina might go back through their family tree and find that an ancestor had been hung as a peeping Tom. Matthew told this like a joke. The guests laughed nervously, metaphorically fingering their aches and pains. The members laughed confidently to cue but without derision.

'It takes very good ancestors, ancestors working overtime, to bring each one of you to the Family,' he told them. 'Never forget that. When you're wasting time here, or not listening, always remember that someone has suffered very much to bring you to the Truth.'

Carmen wrote it all down and tried to imagine what it might be like really, truly to believe this puerile garbage. It was as though someone were deliberately increasing their tolerance so that they would gulp down a bigger dose of nonsense with each new day.

Matthew was saying, 'And accidents. Now here Principle explains a very common phenomenon to us. Accidents often recur at the same place, don't they? Have you heard this expression 'accident black-spot'? Well, the man who dies without completing his life becomes a wandering spirit. Before he can go to his proper place in the Spirit World, he has to stay at the place where the accident occurred. When we get killed in an accident, we have to make a cleansing Condition to purge our resentment at being killed, and the man who's been killed often does this by putting another person in a situation similar to the one that caused his own death. This is why we have to be constantly on guard, because when a wandering spirit leads us into a dangerous situation, it's easy for us to lose control, lose consciousness and just follow that spirit to disaster.'

As Carmen wrote it down, her writing was getting spikier and more acutely slanted as her drowsy indignation grew. But, ridiculous though she found it, she had the strangest and strongest sense of unease, as though someone was now beginning to tamper with some part of her mind where she wasn't quite in control.

A vision had come into her head as he talked and, hard as she tried, she couldn't dispel it. It was her father camping out on the hard shoulder of the motorway. There was fog. He wore his old mac, a trenchcoat, very battered and stained with blood. He was sitting on an orange box and trying to boil a kettle on a little camping primus. He had an enamel mug in his other hand. There was blood on his ashen forehead and streaks of blood like tacky red paint on his shoes.

He was trying to warm his hands, but he could get no warmth into them for they were a waxen blue colour and bloodless. Every now and then he looked at his watch and then stared out at the folding fog as it drifted in swirls, blanking out his vision like a cotton-wool curtain, with only the smearing jewels of the headlamps as the cars whined past. And then he seemed to choose his moment. He got to his feet and quite deliberately began to move out from the hard shoulder into the three-lane carriageway until he reached a midway point in the blanket white-out. He simply stood there, his face gaunt and blue with cold, and waited for the next oncoming stream of cars.

As the first car hurtled out of the mist towards him, she saw that his face was a bitter mask of resignation and despair. Of course, the car couldn't touch him, but the driver didn't know it, and his eyes widened in horror as he hit the brakes with a great grinding shriek.

A sharp no-nonsense tap on her forehead jolted Carmen into awareness. She was back in the lecture room and Matthew was still speaking. She glared belligerently at Pamela, who had obviously administered the tap. Pamela regarded her with nunlike calm, as though the blow required no explanation. Carmen looked around her to see if anyone else had witnessed the inexplicable outrage, but she saw that many other guests were slumped in sleep-befuddled postures and their members were prodding them or pushing them to their feet. In fact, even some of the members were rocking slightly, and several people were massaging each other's backs to keep themselves alert.

'Jesus's disciples fell asleep. Abraham fell asleep. Even some of us here have this problem, don't we? We mustn't blame ourselves, but we have to fight against it. When we sin a dark spirit comes over us. Satan's spirit brings anxiety, loneliness, insecurity, so maybe it's not our fault but we mustn't do it. If only the disciples had known that the whole of human history could have been changed if they'd stayed awake. Abraham slept and brought down four hundred years of slavery on his people. So, when you come to the lecture, you know you have to stay alert. But, have you noticed?' He laughed. 'It's always at the most crucial part of the lecture that the blob spirit comes. Do you know what a blob spirit is? Does anyone know what a blob spirit is?' There was a mild ripple of laughter at the funny word 'blob', but Matthew was serious.

'Blob spirits sit on your head. You see, the reason we have difficulty hearing Principle is fifty per cent physical and fifty per cent spiritual. You know, I've been lecturing sometimes and the whole room has fallen asleep. If I talk about external things, you know, what film is it tonight? they all wake up but when I talk about deeply internal things...' He laid his head on his steepled hands and mimicked someone snoring.

They were all beginning to pick up now and become alert.

'And d'you know why? Because, in this little house in England, the greatest Truth is being told.' He looked around them. 'Doesn't that send a tingle up your spine? What we're hearing here is the greatest Truth. But we're not worthy to hear the greatest Truth. Our ancestors and our evil spirits judge us, they accuse us. So what happens? A blob spirit comes in the room and lands on someone's head. They knock it off and it moves to someone else, and then on, round the room. I can actually watch the spirit move round, people shaking it off. Blaah!' He wobbled his hand above his head to mimic the jellyfishlike spirit and everyone laughed.

'But this is very serious,' he warned. 'The very moment when those spirits attack, that's the moment when you could learn something, that's the very moment when you could receive the Truth.'

He straightened up. 'OK, we've studied the formal, theoretical aspects of Spirit World, now let's look at the evidence.'

Immediately some brothers stepped up smartly to haul out the projector and the sisters moved silently to draw the blinds. In the darkness, he began to project slides of a series of prophetic paintings that they had found in some old man's house. They were weird, hallucinatory pictures of flowers and birds and spectral faces, not at all accomplished or convincing in themselves. There were visions of Second World War planes, although Matthew said the paintings had been done long before the war. As each slide flashed up, Carmen moved uneasily in her seat. She was used to watching slides, but she had never before seen slides that could glow and pulsate of their own accord. She kept looking at Matthew suspiciously to check whether he was twitching the focus, but he wasn't. They were peculiarly hypnotic and alive, yet the vibrancy was not a property of the slides nor of the unskilled paintings themselves. She kept blinking and rubbing her eyes and staring with all her concentration at the screen, because it made no sense that slides could glow that way.

'This,' said Matthew portentously, 'is a man in Spirit World looking down at his child in the physical world. You see he's actually wearing a suit just as he might have done in life.' The picture was of a pensive-looking man painted in a distinctly Forties style peering through a bubble at a little moppet of a girl. Carmen stared at it distrustfully as it shimmered with significance. Matthew spoke like an archaeologist, as though the images gave the most substantial and irrefutable proof, solid and dateable as the fragments of an Etruscan pot.

Carmen became aware of Pamela leaning confidentially to whisper in her ear, her little face gleaming with pleasure. 'There,' she said. 'What do you think about that? Who do you think that might be?'

'I don't know. Who?' she said morosely.

'Doesn't your father look a bit like that?' teased Pamela.

Carmen resisted the temptation to pull her nose and twist it round. She felt a cold fury rising. But she also felt that Pamela was a poor lost creature and she couldn't do it, however much pleasure it would give her to see the look of pained surprise.

She turned her attention back to the slides. They persisted mischievously in pulsing and glowing like some tantalising magic trick. Matthew's calm voice talked soothingly over the images, conjuring up for the audience the kind of delicious sensation that a person would experience when their five senses were open all at once, when they were able to see, hear, smell, taste and feel the heightened stimuli that vibrated through Spirit World, in one extraordinary assault on the centres of pleasure.

He lingered sensually over his descriptions, rolling the adjectives around his palette, but he tactfully refrained from mentioning what seemed to be happening with the light projections – that the supernatural reverberations were getting more urgent and that the colours were throbbing visibly in the darkness like flickering hazy-coloured neons.

Carmen stumbled out of the lecture in a numb, stupid daze, aware of Pamela still close at her shoulder, solicitous and anxious to be of help. Carmen turned out of the back door and took a gulp of air. Pamela was beside her on the step, speaking gently about the Spirit World, repeating all the things that Matthew had told them. It was a fine, sunny day, but as Carmen stared out across the grounds to the reality of the farmland in the distance, she experienced a darkening, as though she was looking through a micro-fine black gauze, as though she was losing light on the periphery of her vision. She opened her eyes wider, in an attempt to let in more light.

'It's great to know he's somewhere safe, isn't it? It's really good news. I couldn't wait for you to know that. I mean, it must be a relief.'

The meaning of the words dawned and Carmen turned on her with a glare of blank incomprehension. 'As far as I understood it, he was trying to tell me my father was hovering perpetually round an accident blackspot, luring drivers to their deaths, and not safe at all. To be quite frank, I don't find that either comforting or credible.' For a moment, she felt such rage that the blood was buzzing in her ears, and she almost felt capable of hitting Pamela. But there was no point. It would have been like hitting a dumb animal or a post.

'Hey, Carmen,' Pamela protested, hurt. 'Don't be so negative all the time. You never look on the bright side. I'm sure he's in Spirit World by now, especially now you've come to the Family. In fact he *must* be in Spirit World, otherwise why would you be here? You can be pretty sure someone was guiding you here. Maybe later you could ask Matthew to try and find out if he got there alright.'

Carmen expelled a great irritated sigh. 'I don't *believe* in Spirit World!'

'Well, what *do* you believe, then?' asked Pamela with an air of worried exasperation.

'I believe my father's dead and I believe he's happy.'

Pamela's pale brow puckered. 'Well, I can't see how he could be happy if he was dead,' she said slowly and then, since Carmen didn't answer, 'OK, look. You tell me your explanation and I'll tell you if it makes sense...'

Carmen gave a start of exasperation. 'I believe you live your life out and then you just die, like a candle going out. You're there and then you're not there. And then the body gets buried and it goes back into the life cycle.'

'Yes.' Pamela continued to regard her doubtfully. 'But that's not a very beautiful idea, is it?'

'It's not about what's a beautiful idea,' Carmen snapped. 'It's about what's the truth.'

Pamela smiled her maddening secret smile, as though humouring a confused, elderly relative. It irritated Carmen beyond endurance and fired her with a sudden, frightening energy.

'Alright, Pamela. I'll make it more beautiful, OK? The body goes into the earth, ashes to ashes, dust to dust and then it transforms miraculously, through the mystery of life itself, into the most beautiful flowers – you know, roses, lilies of the valley – ' She struggled to make the vision more poetic and then gave up. 'Oh, I don't know, snapdragons or something.'

Pamela nodded, unconvinced. After a moment, she spoke carefully but with a hint of accusation in her voice. 'Mm. Yes, but I suppose I just think – well, if you really loved your father, you'd want the best for him.'

Carmen's heart gave an unexpected lurch. She had a feeling of impotent outrage, a feeling of violation. She felt the veins in her temples filling up. Lately, she was much more aware of the way the blood coursed round her body. Right from the beginning of the course, these things had been more noticeable. Surges of adrenalin at inappropriate times, strange numbness when she thought, as though her body was confused and sending fight-or-flight responses when there was actually no danger. Then, at other times, she had the sensation of walking in syrup, of dragging her limbs through a bog, of pitting her brain in argument against immovable objects, implacably smiling sealed systems.

She could hear Pamela's voice, still tentative but reproachful, 'I suppose I feel, if I really cared about someone, I'd rather they were in Spirit World than ... pushing up cabbages somewhere.'

Carmen continued to stare out at the members, dotted about the lawn, praying like so many statues. She felt Pamela's arm curve protectively around her shoulder. 'And maybe you think it doesn't matter, but actually it *does* matter. I mean ... there's always the possibility that what you said was true – maybe he's wandering about on some motorway somewhere crying out for you, and you're the only one who can help him.'

Carmen stiffened like a coiled spring. For a moment she didn't trust herself to speak. Then she hissed gently through her teeth, 'Leave me alone.' And, since her body was quite rigid and Pamela's soft, comforting arm could feel no give, the girl pulled away reluctantly.

'I don't know if it's healthy to bottle things up that way,' she said. 'Sometimes it does you good to talk about it. But we can talk about it later, if you want.'

Carmen prayed for a long, long time over her lunch. Pamela watched her with a great deal of satisfaction. Carmen was hunched, her face gaunt and crumpled with concentration. She was, in fact, intent on praying the same old prayer that she had always prayed. 'Tell me what's me and what's them. Tell me where I finish and they begin.' Perhaps, if she had been more alert, the increasing urgency of the now familiar prayer might have made her feel alarmed, because whereas before she had emerged from her devotional crouch feeling strengthened, when she blinked her eyes open to the light this time, she had a sinking uncertain feeling. It was the normality of the scene before her, the ordinary everydayness of the happy group eating together that made her own paranoia seem absurd and unreasonable.

What did the words she used in her prayer *mean*? People didn't bleed into each other like ink into blotting paper, that was one of the reasons they had skin. Skin told you where one person began and met the air before it met another skin. Thoughts didn't move by osmosis; they were contained within the brain by the bones of the skull. Beliefs you had always believed couldn't ooze out when you weren't looking; neither could other beliefs ooze in just because you were tired and high with singing and off your guard. It didn't make any sense.

She reached out for the water jug with a trembling hand and as she did so, she noticed Jane's face across the room, peering round the door frame, pasty and anxious. Once her eyes lit on Carmen, the girl began to beckon frantically; then she disappeared. Carmen mumbled an excuse and went out quickly to the step where Jane was waiting in a state of agitation.

'There's something very weird going on here,' Jane whispered urgently. 'Did you find those slides peculiar?'

Carmen nodded unhappily. So she hadn't been imagining it. 'But it doesn't make sense,' she said. 'I don't believe they'd give us a drug...'

'How could slides glow like that? How could they?' Jane insisted.

Carmen shook her head. 'Maybe a very strong projector bulb ...' she was saying when she noticed something else very strange about her surroundings. The flowers of the garden were too vivid, too bright and too perfect, as though they were on the cover of a chocolate box. The colours were the merest shade too acidic, too hyperreal, as though the immaculate blooms were made of silk, but the dyes hadn't quite the subtlety of nature's colouring. There was a corresponding drop in the light values where there were no flowers.

'Do they look weird to you?' she asked.

Jane nodded.

'But what does it mean?' asked Carmen. 'If it's a hallucination, how come we both see it?'

They began to walk along the flower bed, their heads close to the blossoms like a pair of detectives, trying to figure out what strange gremlin had crept into their perceptions.

'Maybe it's hypnotism,' Carmen suggested. 'Although I don't see how they could hypnotise a whole room.' She had a queer, uneasy feeling. Her blood was singing gently and she felt that she was viewing the world through a smokey-grey filter while selected parts of it glowed in garish technicolor.

'The arc lamps are on,' Jane said suddenly. They eyed them speculatively. There were strong quartz-iodine lamps all around the house and they *were* on, but Carmen couldn't imagine how they could possibly compete with the bright afternoon sun. But then, neither could she imagine why they should neglect to switch off the arc lamps when they were so economical, not to say stingy, with their hot water. She had no answers. She just added the questions to the stockpile of unanswered ones that had grown stale and lost their urgency with prolonged storage. She stared dully into the heart of a large apricot rose and watched as a bumblebee tumbled drunkenly in its deep orange folds, nuzzling for the pollen.

'It's so beautiful,' she said. 'Just like a Kodachrome print.' Almost as though it had heard her, the rose seemed to make an added spurt of growth and opened the curl of its petals a shade more, like a speeded-up nature film. The scent was heady and overpowering, like concentrated essence seeping from a smashed perfume bottle. Carmen stared at it in dismay.

Jane laughed abruptly. 'Do you want to know something?' she said. 'I could have sworn that flower just opened up.'

'Yes,' said Carmen dully. 'I know.'

This time they both laughed uneasily.

'Is this a sisters' joke or can anyone join in?' They looked up. It was Peter, looking wild-eyed and crazy, but now at least he was animated.

'Well, how are things looking now, Peter?' Jane asked him, nervously.

142

'Everything looks bright to me,' he proclaimed with the effusive bonhomie of a drunkard just before he falls in love with a lamp-post. 'Everything is very bright. This is a very extraordinary place, you know, lots of spiritual experiences happening all over the place today, people seeing visions and making beautiful discoveries. Everyone's very spiritual today.'

'You don't think you're maybe racing ahead too fast into something you haven't quite looked into?' she asked gently. 'You don't think you ought to go more slowly?'

Peter looked confused. 'Everything's very beautiful. Very extraordinary place,' he repeated. 'Lots of spiritual experiences happening all over the place today. Everything's very very bright...'

'Yes, well, someone's left the lights on – maybe that would explain it,' said Jane.

He looked from Jane to the lights and then back to Jane with a comic 'you're having me on' look on his face. 'Naaaah!' he laughed. 'This is a wonderful inside light, not an outside light: this is the inside going out, not the outside coming in. You don't really think it's because God left the lights on!' He gave a guffaw. 'Dear-oh-dear. Spiritual revelations opening everyone's eyes to see the light, and Jane thinks God left the lights on.' He laughed inordinately, then he stopped suddenly and said, 'Well, it's one way of looking at it. Maybe God did leave the lights on – but, isn't it beautiful, Jane, uh?' He shook his head, weary with over-emotion. 'Isn't it beautiful?'

Just then his minder rounded the corner of the house, accompanied by a tense-looking Gary and an annoyed-looking Pamela.

Jane just managed to whisper to Carmen, 'Look, I think I've had enough. I don't feel safe here. I want to go back to my mum and dad. There's a minibus going up North tomorrow. If they won't take me then I'll have to hitch.' Carmen nodded, glad for Jane but worried for herself. Jane grabbed her arm. 'Can you keep yourself together on your own?'

Carmen smiled. 'Of course I can.' She wasn't quite as certain as she sounded, but she was sure that she wanted Jane to leave. Then the three guests snapped on welcoming smiles as their Spiritual Parents bore down on them and hauled them off.

She tried vainly to talk to Jane again that day, but Jane was always surrounded by three or four sisters, all of whom looked the soul of calm and sweet reason while Jane looked hot and bothered and desperate like a recalcitrant schoolgirl, or a martyr being harried to recant.

Carmen realised, as they filed into the team meeting that afternoon, that Jane had no intention of recanting. Far from it: she was lunging for reality like a drowning man striking out for the shore. Carmen could sense Jane's hostility from the jerky impatience of the girl's movements, the dangerous glitter in her eye. While she could sympathise, she was anxious for the meeting to be over with quickly. What was the point, after all, of combating them? You couldn't change their minds, whereas they were capable of pulling your brain out. They would inspect it, declare it faulty and then carelessly stuff it back all the wrong way round. Carmen tried to shoot some warning glances at her as the struggle began, but Jane continued to inspect her fingernails studiously and bite away at the quicks.

Reg was in the midst of a long emotional reminiscence of his mother's death and the strange spiritual experiences that had accompanied it. Marianne waited patiently for a suitable moment to cut him short.

'It was as though something had left the room, as though a great light had gone out,' he was saying. His eyes were distant and his mind was back in that dark, mothballed bedroom with his mother a small emaciated bundle of crocheted bedclothes. 'I remember a draught blowing but there wasn't a window open and I felt as though her spirit was just brushing past me . . .' he smiled faintly at the memory and his pale blue eyes began to brim, '. . . sort of like a butterfly – just a flutter and a sort of feeling as if something was whirring . . .'

Marianne shifted uneasily in her chair. Reg's three minutes were up and his reverie was now meandering on to the meeting at the Psychic Healing centre when the medium had made contact with his mother.

'Son, she said, Son . . . and do you know?' Reg's eyes met Carmen's and there was a sense of wonder in his face as though the moment was as precious and real to him now as then, a decade ago. 'It was *her* voice . . . *Son, I'm happy now and I feel no pain . . .*'

Marianne availed herself of his awestruck pause to interject. 'Thank you for sharing this experience, Reg. This was a most moving story. Who else has a moving story of the Spirit World?' And Reg was left, hanging in mid-air, with a rather lost expression on his face, his treasured memory robbed of its legitimacy. 'Jane?' she said gently. 'You have something to share?'

'Well, yes, I have actually,' said Jane, sitting upright and staring at Marianne. 'I mean, let's get this straight. Everything in the Spirit World is just the same as here, right?' Marianne signified assent by hooding her eyes imperceptibly. 'I mean, if you've got a house here, you've got a house there. If you've got a car or a job, they're just like here?'

'Everything in Spirit World is the same,' Marianne confirmed coolly. 'Just as things are in the physical world, so they are in Spirit World.'

'And these houses, these spirit houses, have they got furnishings? Have they got little fitted kitchen cabinets, little cookers?'

'Everything is the same,' Marianne repeated with implacable composure. 'But these details are not of interest. Everything is the same but much more beautiful. There are very beautiful, strange flowers, all of different colours – colours we have never seen in the physical world – and they are very fluid. Also there is beautiful music playing, like bells chiming, making tinkling sounds. All very inspiring.' She smiled with childish enthusiasm at the very thought of it. 'There are heightened tastes and lovely perfume smells. Everything is heightened and more beautiful because the senses are open.'

'Yes,' said Jane impatiently,' but let's just go back to the bricks and mortar situation. I mean, let me see if I've got this right. If it's Mock Tudor here, it's Mock Tudor there. If you've got a slum here, you're stuck with it in the forever-after. Everything is the same except the spirits don't go through the doors, they walk through walls.' She laughed harshly. 'I mean what sort of sense does that make? Why don't they get rid of the doors? They can still do woodwork, can't they? Or so you say. Isn't this place . . .' her voice rose to a shrill note of frank incredulity, 'kind of *overcrowded*? Where are all these spirit people sleeping? They can't die off and make some room, they've died once already.'

Everyone sat frozen in their chairs, alarmed and awestruck, but Jane seemed way past caring. Carmen swallowed hard. She had to hand it to Jane; it took some guts. But still – she had a strange uneasy feeling. There was something almost blasphemous about her strident voice rasping out in that room where Marianne held sway, where everyone spoke gently and reverently as though a sacrament was taking place.

'I mean,' there seemed to be no stopping Jane now she was underway, 'What do they do, sleep twenty generations to a bed?'

Marianne turned her chair with a decisive screech.

'Carmen,' she said pleasantly, 'perhaps you have found something inspiring?'

Enraged, Jane leant forward and shouted very loudly in Marianne's ear, 'I'm *asking you something.*'

There was an appalled silence and the shock waves seemed to ripple through it until they came to rest like a fine dust. Marianne turned her head towards Jane in extreme slow motion. When their eyes locked, no-one would have been surprised if the atoms that went to make up Jane had petrified into a granite statue.

Marianne spoke very softly but she delivered her judgement with a terrible, accusing finality. 'We do not have give-and-take with a spirit that wants to dominate. This spirit comes of Satan,' and she looked through Jane's body just as though the statue had crumbled and pulverised itself into a small dry heap of greyish powder, as though Jane was an inconvenient pile of dust which could be dealt with later by means of a dustpan and brush.

'Carmen, you were telling me how you have found this lecture,' she said cordially.

Jane let out a jubilant snort. 'Yeah, you tell 'em, Carmen,' she observed to no-one in particular. No-one dared look at her and since, to all intents and purposes, she was no longer present, she sounded even to herself like a ghostly, disembodied parrot.

Carmen hesitated for a long moment, aware that Jane was staring fiercely at her, that Jane was requiring her to be courageous. Marianne smiled gently, promptingly, from the opposing corner, so that she was caught in the cross-fire of their conflicting wills. Jane's eyes urged her on, but what was the point? She felt so weary. She understood Jane's motives. It was hard to sit by and watch perfectly genuine, innocent people, whose only sin was that they were too trusting, swimming gamely towards a weir that they couldn't see. Jane was making a belated attempt to erect the danger post. Jane seemed to think that if they both went on the attack together, they could unravel the whole careful construct like a piece of loose knitting. But it was not the case.

She wanted to shout across to Jane. 'Leave me out of it. You fight this one. Haven't I fought enough of them? I've come for Lucy and that's my limit. I can't save them all. I'm having enough trouble saving myself.' She had come for Lucy. Lucy, Lucy, Lucy. She had to keep dinning it into her head, because she was constantly being told that the reason why she had come, whatever it might be, was not the reason why she was here. And she was just not strong enough to take them on again.

So, she said none of these things. Her mouth opened and she heard herself say in a little, honeyed voice, 'Why, I think it's a really uplifting idea. If Spirit World exists and it's so beautiful and all that, well, we'd all want to go, wouldn't we? We wouldn't need to be afraid of death because, well, death wouldn't have a meaning any more!' She smiled sweetly around the circle with a wide-eyed appeal that owed much to her having seen a repeat of 'The Inn Of The Seventh Happiness' before she came away.

Everyone relaxed visibly and Marianne nodded, well pleased.

'But not all is happy in Spirit World,' Marianne corrected, lest Carmen should get above herself and imagine that understanding Principle was an easy thing. 'Some people still experience many tortures there. Even Jesus, actually, has experienced two thousand years of suffering in Spirit World. There are many problems. Also many of our ancestors are still suffering torments now because they did not have the opportunity to learn Principle.' She shook her head dolefully.

Carmen wasn't sure what kind of response was required, so she settled on a look of polite sorrow. Reg rolled about in his seat, looking pensive and agitated.

'But that can't be right, can it?' he asked anxiously. 'I mean, a lot of people can't get out and about so they just wouldn't get the chance to hear Principle. Isn't it really hard on people to have to suffer in their Spirit life just 'cos they never got the opportunity to hear it when they were alive?' It was obvious that the thought of his mother was worrying him – his poor mother, who had probably had more than her share of suffering on earth.

Marianne assented sympathetically. She understood his fears. 'This is the way it is, but in actual fact we can help them in this. For instance, you are already helping your ancestors. There are two hundred and ten spirits attached to each individual so, when you come to hear Principle, two hundred and ten spirits have the chance to study Divine Principle. So, actually we educate not only ourselves but we have the chance to help our ancestors, also.' She gave him a happy, encouraging smile.

Reg sat back, relieved. He was only worried about his mother; the other two hundred and nine could go off and study car maintenance for all he cared.

'So, you see, your mother now has the chance to study Principle and she already begins to feel the benefit of coming closer to the Truth. Perhaps –' she paused delicately, 'Per'aps when she told you she was happy, you had already made contact with the Family, hmm? And this was her way of guiding you onwards?'

Reg screwed up his face and made an effort to think back.

'D'you know,' he said, 'I think it was somewhere round about that time that the first lot of members came over and papered my front room...'

There was an explosive snort from the other side of the room. Everyone looked up, appalled. It was Jane bursting out with a spluttering hoot of derision.

'That's the most *ridiculous* thing I've ever heard,' she said. 'How can you all just sit there, drinking in this *tosh*?'

A look of bewildered hurt crossed Reg's face. He didn't find it easy to open his heart and now, just as he had made himself vulnerable, someone was sneering at his memories, making light of his recollections. Carmen felt herself strangely at odds with Jane as she watched Reg's hopeful face crumple.

'"I Know That My Redeemer Lives",' Jane began recklessly. 'That's what she sang, didn't she? That's what you said she sang when she was dying?'

Reg nodded unwillingly, frightened by her overpowering vigour.

'Well, if she believed the Redeemer lived, how could she *possibly* want you to come here and be told the crucifixion was a sham and Jesus was a failure? Huh? Tell me that. How could your mother possibly rejoice that you've had your front room decorated and so now you're giving up the Lord? Well, you sold Him cheap, didn't you? Did they pay for the wallpaper, or what?'

This was too much for Gary. He got to his feet, strode over to Jane and ushered her up, leading her firmly towards the door which a solicitous Pamela was already holding open to smooth their exit. Jane was so astonished that she hardly made a whimper. Her eyes were round with surprise as the circle watched her swift despatch.

Marianne settled her hands into her lap contentedly, as though she had arranged the departure by remote control.

Reg sat slumped in his chair with a devastated look on his face, as though unable to comprehend why anyone should seek to destroy his peace of mind.

'Many times Satan uses us as the mouthpiece for his words,' she said wisely. 'This cannot be held responsible to the person he has used, but we do not tolerate him with us.'

She looked around the troubled faces. 'Perhaps someone has the answer to Satan's question...?' Her eyes roved from Peter's stupefied, glazed face to Wendy's puzzled pucker, across the demure expressions of the Spiritual Mothers and then back to Carmen.

'Carmen, what would you say to Reg here?' asked Marianne, as though deferring to the opinion of an honoured, up-and-coming prefect who might make head-girl if she played her cards right. Carmen squirmed. Reg was watching her with doglike attention, willing her to give him some support.

Carmen kept her eyes on the ground. 'Oh, I don't know,' she mumbled. 'Well, if it's all true and Reg's mum's in Spirit World with Jesus...' she tried not to listen to herself and she got it over with quickly, 'then maybe Jesus *explained* it to her or something like that?' Marianne was nodding approvingly. Reg settled into his seat again, mollified.

'Yes, something like this must have 'appened,' Marianne confirmed. 'How else could she have known to send you that message?'

Carmen looked around the darkening room with a fearful face. She didn't know what would have surprised her least – a bolt of lightning striking her like a finger of fire from the heavens or a cockerel appearing on the window ledge and giving voice to three long protests. She felt utterly deceitful and treacherous. She had never betrayed anyone before, and she had never before been in a situation where it would really have mattered. Here, it mattered.

When the meeting was over, Carmen wandered outside. Reg was sitting on the steps alone, praying. Carmen hesitated, then went over to him, crouched on her haunches beside him.

'Reg,' she said gently. He seemed not to hear her. He was staring at the Bible on his knee. The book mark showed Jesus with his lantern in the Garden of Gethsemane. It was a Holman Hunt. The Garden looked like a really nice suburban front garden and Jesus like a frail but handsome young man.

'Reg,' she said again, hardly daring to raise her voice in case some Spiritual Parents should suddenly appear from the shrubbery, which was not unlikely.

'Reg, don't give Him up,' she said.

He lifted his head a fraction but did not look at her. His long skull rested in his huge hands like a weight, unconnected with his body. She saw a tear trickle from his eye and down his nose. It hung for a moment, glistening, then splashed onto the bookmark, flattening out over Jesus's suffering face with its jewelled crown.

It was a moment before he was composed enough to speak.

'It's hard,' he said. He had been a Methodist all his life and he had done well as a lay preacher: now he was giving up everything to espouse a cause that would bring him only mockery. He cleared his throat. 'It's hard,' he said again, 'but when you see what's right, you have to have the courage to speak for it, to follow it.' He stared at the bookmark. 'That's what He taught me,' he said finally. 'That's what I must do.'

Carmen sat back, hugging her knees and staring out moodily at the fringe of dark trees that bordered the members' land. The sun was setting.

'If I believed in Him, I wouldn't give Him up,' she said stubbornly. But that was the sad thing – if one didn't believe, one was hardly entitled to an opinion. Reg didn't hear her anyway. She was talking to another ghost. She got up quietly and went back into the house.

There was no sign of Jane at the evening meal. Carmen watched the door anxiously but she didn't arrive. Gary came over and sat with her, but he immediately crouched into an urgent prayer and she had to wait until he emerged from it before she could enquire into what had happened. Even then he didn't speak, but just began to lump his stew onto her plate. She put her hand on his to prevent him. He stared at her. His eyes were inscrutable and cold. She moved her hand away as though she had touched a hot iron. He continued spooning the food.

'Where's Jane?' she demanded. 'What did they do to her?'

He smiled in a rather pained way. 'Who's they?' he asked. 'No-one's done anything to her. Matthew just had a long chat with her, that's all. He seemed to sort a lot of things out for her. I saw her about an hour ago and she seemed to be quite straightened out.'

Carmen nodded. This sounded rather ominous. 'Well, where is she, then? In the dormitory?'

He looked vaguely irritated. 'I don't know. I expect so.'

Carmen got to her feet. He grabbed a fold of her sweater to restrain her.

'Really, there's nothing you can do,' he said. 'She's resting.' Now she knew he was lying. In the Family no-one was allowed or encouraged to rest, for whatever reason. Rest and sleep only made a foundation for Satan's spirits to invade. That was why the members didn't do much sleeping. She waited for him to explain.

'She's fine,' he said. 'Unfortunately she collapsed, but...'

Carmen tried to push his hand off and struggle free, but he only held on to the clutch of wool more firmly so that she was forced to hear him out.

'It's OK. It's only very bad stomach pains. But there's nothing you can do. Some sisters are with her and they'll make sure she's alright. Please sit down and let's try to enjoy our meal ... huh?'

She sat down, unhappily.

'I'm sorry Jane's not well,' said Gary. 'But it seems to be the only time I get you to myself.' He settled down to make conversation. 'Marianne tells me you're really making good progress in the Team Meetings, she said you really seem to be joining in with the swing of things. That's great. Spirit World's pretty mind-blowing, isn't it?'

'Gary,' she said in a deadened voice. 'I don't believe it. I don't believe any of it. I'm just pretending I do.'

She waited for his wrath to fall but he only smiled in a cheerful, sunny way and said, 'I know that, but that's OK. I was going to suggest you try that. Still, if you've worked it out naturally, that's fine. If there's anything you have trouble believing straight off, then just pretend you believe it for a while, and after a couple of days, it'll all come clear and you'll wonder where your problem was.'

Her eyes were swimming and she couldn't keep him in clear focus. She buried her head in her hand as though she was praying and massaged her temples, staring into the hand's span of darkness she had made for herself in the brightly lit room.

At eight pm, they filed into the lecture room for Matthew's testimony. Carmen looked around, agitated now, troubled that Jane had been gone for so many hours. Just as the singing began, she hopped up from her chair, announced loudly to the people around her that she was going to the lavatory and slipped out, ignoring the frowns. The house was deserted and she ran up the stairs two at a time, lest Gary should come running out after her. When she reached the dormitory, she heard a strange low humming noise like the sound of bees swarming in a hive. She pushed the door and went in, cautiously.

Jane was sitting on a bunk, hunched. Pamela, Virginia and a Japanese sister were sitting and kneeling around her, holding her arms and her thin wrists.

They were chanting the same soft incantation that she had heard the brothers making the previous evening repeating 'Sun Meung Moon, Sun Meung Moon' very quickly, very urgently. Jane was like a large limp doll, like a marionette with its strings cut.

Frightened, Carmen stepped forward and challenged them. 'What are you doing?' Her voice quavered. She raised it. 'Jane, what are they doing to you?' Since they seemed quite impervious to her presence, she moved forward into the light of the lamp and called out in panic, 'Don't do that to her. Leave her alone. It won't work. She doesn't believe in Sun Meung Moon.'

They began to intensify their chanting, as though to block her out. Jane lifted her head slowly. There was an almost punch-drunk smile on her face but her eyes were still closed. They fluttered open, unfocused.

'There's nothing to worry about, Carmen,' she said softly. 'They know what's best. You don't understand. There's a lot you don't understand . . .' She let her head loll back ecstatically on the stalk of her spine as though she were receiving the most relaxing massage. As the words of the chant ran together and became more insistent, more like the amplified sound of someone chewing, Carmen stood there helpless and appalled. The door swung open behind her.

'Ah, naughty!' Marianne pounced playfully and caught her arm. 'Carmen, always so naughty. You should be in the lecture room!'

The shadows of the room made her smile quite fiendish and fierce. She seemed not to notice the tableau beyond Carmen and her hand seemed to dig right through Carmen's skinny arm to find the bone. She put her finger in a shushing motion to her lips and Carmen found herself hauled from the room and out down the staircase.

Matthew paused as she took her place. His eyes were narrow and extremely hostile. All eyes were aimed reproachfully at her and Gary stood pointedly, vacating his own chair and propelling Carmen into it. Since Matthew seemed to be awaiting an apology, she addressed the room generally in a humble mouselike voice.

'I'm sorry,' she said. 'I felt a little dizzy.'

'Satan often attacks this way to blind our hearts from knowledge,' Matthew observed cordially. 'He doesn't want us to hear God's Truth, isn't that so?'

There were polite murmurs of assent around the room and some gentle indulgent laughs from members. Matthew's eyes crinkled and became more kindly. 'We don't give in to him, Carmen. We have to –' he pummelled the air with his fists as though taking on an enormous unseen adversary, '– tell him where to go, huh, Carmen?' She smiled, relieved. 'Let's see you do it, Carmen,' he encouraged her. Embarrassed, Carmen pummelled the air unconvincingly. This went down well as the brothers bellowed and the sisters tittered.

'You'll never get him that way,' Matthew shouted above the laughter. 'Go on, give him a right hook. Show him who's boss!' Carmen obediently renewed and exaggerated her shadow-boxing, her face hot and red, anxious to turn their attention elsewhere. 'Yes, and there's Carmen in the red corner...' Matthew began an excitable commentary. She feared for a moment she'd be required to enact the whole bout so she executed a few violent punches with the whole weight of her body. 'And, *it's a knock-out,*' shouted Matthew above the gales of laughter. 'Well done, Carmen.' He nodded at her approvingly, well pleased. As the giggles subsided, he steepled his fingers and prepared to sober the group enough to continue.

'Do you feel dizzy now, Carmen?' he asked.

'No,' she said.

She settled down into her seat. It wasn't true. She felt even dizzier. She hunched up and tried to shrink into herself, to become invisible.

Matthew was telling them about his life of wealth and privilege before the Family, but Carmen couldn't follow his words. Her mind kept straying back to the sensation she had just experienced. Because, inexplicably enough, the air had given her back a strange, stubborn resistance, as though an invisible force field had blocked her ineffectual fists, as though – but she didn't want to admit it – an army of spirits was flocked around her, fighting back. She told herself over and over that she didn't believe in the spirits, but all that came back to her were some words that Pamela had said: 'It doesn't matter whether you believe in the spirits or not; they can still attack you ...'

Chapter 6

That evening, she put herself on remote control. When she was required to smile, she smiled; when she was required to clap, she clapped. When they all stood up and went through to the film show, she shuffled off with them, glumly aware of reacting like some cowed mental patient. Just before bedtime, they were called to assemble at the foot of the main staircase, and that was why she found herself standing in the dark at the stroke of midnight as the strains of 'Happy Birthday' struck up on the guitar. Everyone looked around, smiling and expectant.

A young man appeared at the head of the stairs, pinpointed by a strategic spot-light. Carmen clapped along with everyone else although she had no idea of who he was. He looked just like any other Moonie. He sported a very short crew cut and a conservative grey suit that looked like one of Matthew's cast-offs. He looked rather like an American spaceman in civilian clothes. The face was smooth, round and shiny and he wore a blissful, abstract grin. Whoever he was, he seemed very popular, but with all the cheering and whistling that was going on it was impossible for her to catch his name. The crowd at the foot of the stairs parted and a cake was borne in by a flutter of excitable sisters. It took Carmen a few moments to realise that there was only one candle on the cake and that they were singing, 'Happy *re*-birthday to you, happy re-birthday to you, Happy re-birthday, dear Peeeter, happy re-birthday to you...'

She looked at him again, and a chill went down her spine. They had shaved his beard off and shorn his longish hair. He seemed calm and stable. Far too calm, far too dignified and collected for someone who had been trembling on the brink of insanity a short time earlier. There was a quiet noble confidence that she could only assume to be a supreme piece of self-control. Peter made his way down to greet the cake-bearing sisters at the landing. He held his hands up in an accurate parody of Matthew's manner.

'Brothers and sisters,' he said with the fond look of a shepherd overseeing lambs, 'I can't say much. My heart is so full. I just wanna say ... where my soul was in confusion, I have found peace. Where my mind was in torment, I have found release. Where my old life was in little pieces like a torn-up page of writing, you have given me a brand new sheet of paper and I hope Heavenly Father will be able to write on it with His ...' He paused, struggling to finish in the same high-flown terms. 'With His invisible ink ...'

Everyone assumed he meant *indelible* ink and began to clap and cheer uproariously before he could stutter on about the great ink-well of Father's heart. 'He is the glue,' she heard him vainly try to shout above the clamour. 'He is the ink-well and the glue ...'

Then the sisters held the touching little home-made cake up to his face. He huffed with all his breath and, to wild applause, blew out his candle.

Carmen paced silently along the dark corridor, holding a plate with a sliver of Peter's cake on it. It was wrapped in a napkin and bore moulting silver balls. It seemed to her that it represented his past life, discarded like a snake skin. Two days ago, it would have been unthinkable. She was taking it to Jane but even as she paused at the door of the dormitory, she was full of foreboding. She had an irrational premonition that Jane might be swinging lifeless from the ceiling with a noose around her neck. Nothing was predictable any longer. The only thing that was predictable was that everyone would change. Maybe Jane would be inside, dressed in a high-neck small-print dress, her eyes cast down like a demure nun. In either eventuality, Carmen would be equally unsurprised.

As it was, Jane was stretched out on her stomach, amongst the other sisters, writing in her Book of Reflections. Carmen knelt beside her.

'Are you alright?' she whispered.

Jane looked up and gave her a relaxed, sleepy grin. 'I'm fine,' she said. 'Just a bit tired.' Carmen continued to search her face for tell-tale signs. 'I *am*, honestly. Nothing's happened. I'm still the same.'

'Well, what happened? What did they say to you?'

'Nothing happened. Gary made me go and talk to Matthew. I thought he was going to be like the headmaster or something but he was *so* lovely. He can be really wonderful, can't he? And Gary's been very sweet. They weren't horrible one bit, just sort of sorry for me. But that just sort of made it worse…' She looked at Carmen with troubled eyes. 'Matthew really has a way of making you feel ashamed, somehow. Sort of low and dirty. I don't know, I just felt really horrible, and then it *did* seem mean saying all those things to Reg. You know, if he believes it and it makes him feel good, well who am I to… They're so pure and good, they seem so *holy*.'

'And then what happened?' Carmen prompted.

'Well, then I started crying and he just kept on talking in his soft, sad voice as if I really was a hopeless case.' She looked around anxiously to make sure that the sisters weren't listening. 'And I was telling him how wild I felt today. How out of control.' Her eyes were wide, as though it was Carmen she needed to convince. 'I just woke up that way. And he was saying it was the spirits putting up a fight because they didn't want me to believe it and I was arguing and trying to explain why I couldn't accept it.' She looked as if she was about to cry again. 'And then suddenly I got these sharp, shooting pains all over here –' she prodded her lower stomach, 'as if someone had stuck a red hot poker in me and twisted it round. One minute I was just standing there answering him and the next I was all creased up on the floor, screaming with pain. It all seemed to explode inside me just as if there were *were* spirits inside me, as though they couldn't stand hearing what he was saying and they didn't want me to hear it either.' She looked at Carmen wonderingly. 'As if they were trying to draw attention to themselves…'

Carmen nodded wisely. 'So, do you think that's what they were doing?' she asked. 'Throwing a sort of little tantrum?'

Jane gave her a look of withering scorn. 'Oh, don't talk to me like I've lost my buttons,' she said too loudly, and some sisters turned and frowned at her. Carmen relaxed and moved closer.

'No,' Jane whispered forcefully. 'It just *seemed* like that was what was happening. I can't explain it. I mean, there I am rolling on the floor like a demented dog and Matthew praying over me like it's nothing out of the ordinary – and that seemed to quiet them a bit, enough so I could get up. But, later on it started up again, and then the sisters came and chanted and this most strange thing happened…'

Jane struggled to continue against Carmen's obvious hostility.

'Look, Carmen, I know it's hard to believe this. I don't understand it myself, but it was so incredible. As soon as they started chanting, it took the pain away. There were just these rhythmic waves, like labour pains or something, and then it all just ebbed out of me.'

She stared at Carmen, willing her to believe.

'Now how could that *be*?' she asked. 'How could chanting someone's name drive pain out? How *could* it do that, unless that person's name had ... special qualities?'

'Maybe it was just psychosomatic,' said Carmen.

Jane shook her head vigorously. 'It didn't feel psychosomatic. It felt like someone was pulling out my intestines like a string of sausages. And then, wouldn't I have to believe in that chant to make it work? But I *didn't* believe, and it worked! What does *that* mean?'

Carmen stalled. 'I don't know. Well, they could have said anything, like – Peter Piper Picked A Peck Of Pickled Pepper.'

Jane looked sceptical. 'Oh, come on ...'

'Or they could have said "Jesus Christ" over and over again.' She kept her voice very low when she spoke Jesus's name because she had been told that they should avoid using it where possible for fear of causing Him pain in Spirit World.

Jane lifted an eyebrow. 'I said "Jesus Christ" a few times when I was writhing, and it only seemed to make it worse.' She shifted her bag around her as she leant forward. 'Look, I'm not saying I believe any of it. I don't. I'm just saying this is me. Jane. Normal. I'm just telling you what happened.' Her face was so earnest that Carmen had to shake her head.

'I can't explain it,' Carmen said slowly. 'I just know that it's rubbish. It's all rubbish.'

One of the sisters was standing by the light switch. 'Sister, it's selfish to whisper when the others want to sleep,' she said.

'Sorry,' they chorused.

The light went out and the sister picked her way across the settling bodies. Carmen raised herself to her haunches, about to get up, then she leant forward and buried her mouth in Jane's hair and whispered harshly, 'I can't explain anything that happens here. I don't know how it works. I've just got one certainty and that's that it's all rubbish!'

Jane reached out and they squeezed each other's hands for a

moment as though they were sealing a pact. Then Carmen got up and moved blind towards her bunk and went to bed. Once there, she prayed to her invented God for ten minutes as a talisman to ward off the evil that she felt was all around her. Then she said 'Rubbish, rubbish, rubbish' over and over again in her head until the syllables ran together in a meaningless mantra, as the syllables of Reverend Moon's name had run together.

She dreamed that she was in one of Marianne's team meetings. Even as she sat there, feigning interest in the discussion, she went into labour, but she made not a sound, from embarrassment. When she felt the baby emerge, she resisted the temptation to look and pushed it firmly underneath the chair with her feet. Everyone in the room pretended not to notice, and they continued their cordial discussion despite the fact that she was bleeding profusely and the blood made a conspicuous dripping noise as it splashed on the varnished boards. When she got a chance to peek under the chair, she saw to her relief that it was not a baby but a large plastic baby doll with real hair lashes and a red rosebud mouth. It lay there in a bloody mass of afterbirth with the cord twisted around its neck and when she picked it up, the squeaker in its back said 'Maa-Maa', but it sounded more like a sheep. When she had the chance, she gathered up the dolly and slipped down the corridor to the bathroom, her school chemistry overall slippery with brown blood. She felt an awful guilt, an awful compulsion to get rid of it.

There were other sisters in the bathroom, naked at their ablutions, singing in unison, all with garlands in their hair. Her heart was beating very fast as she tried to force the doll head first down the toilet. It was impossible because it was far too big, almost life-size. She began to wrestle with it, trying to snap its legs off. One broke with a horrible crack and she looked around in case they should have noticed, but they were too absorbed. Then she picked up the lavatory brush and began to use it like a hammer until the head disappeared down the U-bend and there was only the problem of concealing the plastic torso with its one remaining leg and a gaping socket where the second leg had been. She tore off reams of toilet paper and stuffed it down as though to bandage it in tissue and make it less noticeable. Then she slammed the lid and flushed the toilet, but it went on flushing until the water welled up and began to spill over onto the floor, carrying with it its burden of blood and bobbing excreta and tissue paper. She began to swab the floor maniacally with the mop but the more she swabbed, the more the water rose. She peered fearfully into the toilet bowl, to see that baby had righted itself and was fighting for life, choking and spluttering, instinctively trying to pull the swathes of toilet paper away from its blind eyes with its tiny ineffectual fists.

As it rose for air, it began to wail. The sisters looked around myopically for the source of the noise, and Carmen, in panic, began to take hefty whacks at its skull with the lavatory brush until it subsided and she could replace the lid. Then she thrust the seat down and sat on it, without mind to the water which was still deluging out, soaking her frock. She began to sing along with the sisters, but, even through the singing she could hear the baby's tiny fist knocking weakly against the lid like something buried alive tapping eerily on the coffin, and she began to sing even more joyfully to drown out the bubbling sound as the tiny mutilated baby groped for air.

Chapter 7

When they woke up, Jane complained of stomach ache again, not sharp pains but a general feeling of malaise. Carmen offered to run down to the village shop and get some Milk of Magnesia for her spirits, although from Jane's whey face, she surmised they needed something stronger. She seemed to have changed her mind about leaving. She said she hadn't the strength, and anyway the course was almost completed. This worried Carmen. She managed to slip past the early morning exercisers and she was almost at the gate before she noticed Gary at her shoulder.

'Do you need something from the shop?' he asked. 'Can I get it?'

'I wanted a paper,' she lied. 'And I wanted to choose it myself.'

He fell into step and they walked out into the shady tree-lined country road. It was a beautiful day and the sun sent dapples through the foliage to dance at their feet as they paced.

'I really don't know why you think you want a newspaper.' He spoke with good-humoured tolerance as if he was prepared to go along with her eccentricities, although this one was more bizarre than usual.

'Why not?' she asked.

'Because, as you start growing upwards, you start drawing away from the Fallen World, and it becomes more and more irrelevant. You won't be able to *read* it,' he said, as though the idea was quite impractical. And then, since she stared at him, he simply said, 'You'll see...'

She thought about it. 'You don't ever watch TV or listen to the radio or anything, do you?' she said, curiously. 'Don't you ever wonder what goes on in the world?' She knew perfectly well they didn't. 'I mean, the world's *happening* out there. You *are* a very small minority,' she told him apologetically, unsure whether this piece of news was welcome in cloud cuckoo land. She felt much freer off their premises, much more entitled to express an opinion. It was almost as though, freed from the claustrophobic atmosphere inside, she might be able to provoke Gary to react normally.

'We're a minority at the moment,' he said. 'But that won't be for long. And anyway we *do* sometimes watch television,' he admitted, 'for a special treat, if there's an uplifting film on. We saw "The Sound Of Music" last month. That was very spiritual.'

Carmen nodded. 'The Sound Of Music' was a favourite Family film and they seemed to watch it quite a lot. She felt terribly sorry for him. The idea of living this life of empty, self-imposed bliss and then jumping up for 'The Sound Of Music', like an eager dog leaping for a Good Boy Choc Drop, was curiously demeaning for a young man at the peak of his powers and intelligence. But then again, she told herself, was it so terrible not to read the newspapers? They were all lies anyway.

'We don't interest ourselves in the news generally,' he said. 'What would be the point? It's only murders and evil and crazy politicians. Sometimes, if I do happen to see a paper, it just seems funny. There they all are, beavering away, multiplying evil in their great big world, feeling so important, and really they're just running round in circles in an enormous bottomless cess-pit, with absolutely no idea that their world is ending and that it's all quite pointless. It makes me want to take out a great big double page advert or something.' He blocked the headline out in the air with his hand. 'WE'RE IN THE LAST DAYS NOW. YOU'RE WASTING YOUR TIME. The kingdom is coming on earth and it's just going to sweep over you like a wave. Get yourself to a Centre while there's still time.'

He laughed, and she smiled as though she shared the joke. He began to hum happily to himself, a Dylan song that the Family had appropriated to themselves.

'Come senators, congressmen, please heed the call...
Don't stand in the doorway, don't block up the hall...'

'But how can it come on earth?' She broke across his tune. 'I don't see anything happening. All you're doing is locking yourself away from the world, Gary, you're not changing it. You're just putting your heads in the sand like a load of ostriches.'

He stared at her in genuine surprise and then he really laughed, a natural hearty laugh of real amusement.

'Carmen, you're impossible,' he said, but he said it with affection.

'Well, you look pretty impossible from where I'm standing,' she retorted, niggled.

He stopped and put his hands very lightly on her shoulders. It was the first time he had ever really touched her, she realised. For that reason, maybe, it felt very strange and awkward and very significant. He looked into her eyes.

'The reason I find it funny is just because you're so clear-sighted in some ways. But when all the evidence is around you, when there are all these extraordinary, wonderful things happening just under your nose, you just can't seem to be able to piece them together and finish the jigsaw. When you put those last pieces in, its going to hit you with a blinding flash – the scale of it's going to take your breath away.'

'Well, tell me, then,' she said crossly, feeling frustrated that there was something that she hadn't grasped. But he just gave her an enigmatic smile and walked on, humming contentedly to himself.

They went into the village store. It was little more than a cottage with a shop window and a lot of antiquated signs for Bone Meal and Winalot. It smelt pungently of cats and reminded Carmen forcibly of how deodorised and sterile was the world of their Church, without idiosyncrasy or variation, just like their individual minds. Gary started humming even more intently and she had an odd sensation that he was humming to ward something off – probably evil, although the old whiskered woman behind the counter looked harmless enough. Carmen pretended to ponder long and hard over the newspapers on offer. There were only the *Sun* and *The Times*, so she took both and mumbled 'Milk of Magnesia' as an afterthought, hoping Gary wouldn't notice. He made no comment, and as they walked back to the house they began to sing in unison. It was second nature to them both.

'You've got such a good voice,' she said, after a while. 'You know, when you played the guitar, you sounded like a professional musician.'

She imagined for a moment that his face fell. 'Yes,' he said. 'I shouldn't do it.'

'You're much better than the house guitarist,' she pressed on. 'Why don't they let you take his place?'

A painful flush spread over Gary's face, but she had the idea it wasn't modesty. 'I gave away my guitar,' he said curtly. 'Sometimes Father asks us to give up what we like doing best, until we can do it with proper humility. The house guitarist is a truly humble person.'

Carmen nodded. The guitarist might be humble but he couldn't play the guitar. When he played his aggressive discords outside her dormitory each morning, she felt like pelting him with track shoes. She didn't venture her opinion because Gary's mood had darkened. He didn't speak to her all the way back, nor did he sing until he was back inside the house, where the quality of his voice could be safely camouflaged by others.

'I had the most bizarre dream,' Jane announced at breakfast. Her face was pasty and Carmen noticed that a crop of small spots had broken out on her chin. She seemed subdued and her eyes were anxious. Gary and Pamela sat up, immediately alert.

'I dreamt I was back in the biology faculty and I'd just done this whole batch of dissections. They were all pinned out – a couple of frogs and a rabbit. Beautiful dissections, and I was mounting them in small glass cases and then there was this other one . . . Everyone kept saying, "What is it, what is it?"'

Carmen studiously stirred her glutinous porridge, wishing Jane would have the sense not to give them material to work on.

'And I said, "It's a soot imp!" It was in a case all pinned out, but it wasn't dead. It was all black and rubbery and squirming with pins stuck through its hands as if I'd . . .' She hesitated, reluctant to say the word, 'As if I'd crucified it. I kept saying, "It's a soot imp, its feet are only bleeding like that 'cos it's got chilblains."'

She laughed nervously and her eyes darted between her listeners. 'And then I said, there's a whole panful over there, and, sure enough, there were masses of them boiling up in the cauldron. I kept trying to hit them with the spatula but they wouldn't die, they just kept squealing. It was horrible . . .'

Pamela frowned and looked thoughtful. 'Was this your old University?' she asked. 'Well, then,' she pronounced, 'I'd say it was a good news dream. You know what I think it means? I think Heavenly Father may be hinting that He needs you in a CARP team. That means the Collegiate Association for the Research of Principle. You go back to your university and go on doing Heavenly Father's work.'

Jane nodded dubiously.

164

'You know, before you were just doing selfish things like cutting up animals for your own store of knowledge, but now you'd be working from inside the University to bring other students to the Family. Father needs lots of University students and professional people, that sort of thing. We do some very high-calibre work on the campuses. There's a lot of Restoration to be done there.'

Carmen pondered this information. 'So, if I joined I could go back to art school?' she asked with a spurt of disingenuous interest.

'Yes,' said Pamela, pleased to reassure her on a point that might have been holding her back. 'You could be a "B" member. So you'd go into art college and make friends and bring people to Heavenly Father that way. It's just as useful to Heavenly Father as being a full-timer.'

Carmen managed to look reassured.

Pamela looked at her speculatively. 'Of course, I don't know that he needs that many artists. We've got a lot of those already, but engineers, technicians, that sort of thing, they're always very useful. For when Father starts his TV network,' she added.

'And journalists.' She smiled smugly. 'We've already bought the *Washington Times*. Maybe we'll get one over here. It'd be nice to get the *Daily Mail*. They're so negative. Satan really works through the *Daily Mail*.'

'Eventually, of course,' she said in a controversial tone, 'we'll buy out all the newspapers, those that don't come to us from choice, and we'll have all media channels so we really will need a lot of people with skills.'

Carmen nodded, a glazed smile on her face. She was never quite sure whether the members suffered from delusions, or whether the Family's claims to enormous and influential holdings were true.

'You really have the *Washington Times*?' she asked uneasily. Wasn't the *Times* a big national paper and didn't it cost an awful lot to buy a national paper? Pamela nodded with equanimity.

'It's very important for us to control the media because, in the end, it's the quickest way to get a message across, isn't it? We're expanding out all over the place now. But with a TV channel we could reach that many more people that much faster.'

Carmen stirred uneasily. 'How many people do you have already?'

'About two million,' said Pamela. 'But that was last week. It's hard to keep track with all these courses running. We should be adding another thirty by the end of the week,' she said with an impish grin. 'And that's just our centre. This is going on all over the country, all over the world.'

'This is a bad week,' Gary explained, 'with everyone on holiday. We expect about four million by the end of the year, if we keep on target.'

'Well, it's keeping pace with unemployment,' Carmen murmured, trying to think it out. 'How many do you need?'

Pamela looked at her in surprise, as though she hadn't realised that Carmen was so slow on the uptake.

'Why, all of them,' she said. 'England's just a small country. It won't take long.' Then she smiled knowingly, as if she was repeating some well-worn catch phrase, 'The whole world just takes a little bit longer. It only needs everyone to get the chance to come to a workshop, and then Principle does the rest.'

'What does Principle do to people?' Carmen persisted.

'Oh, don't be dopey,' said Pamela fondly. 'Principle changes people's hearts. Can't you see it? Honestly, it couldn't be plainer. It's happening all around you . . .' She spread her arms.

Carmen gazed around. The gesture seemed to take in the spaced-out, blissful Peter, as he examined and admired the fresh blue tattoos that had appeared on his hands. Her eyes moved to Reg sitting hunched and morose over his food, a quarrelsome, puzzled frown on his forehead, a pulse throbbing visibly at his temple, and then came to rest on Jane, who sat gazing solemnly back, her green eyes cloudy and ringed with dark shadows in a drawn, bloodless face.

'So the Family just exists to enlarge the Family? That's the work of the Family? To keep making a bigger and bigger Family?'

Suddenly Carmen understood, and then she wondered how she could possibly not have understood before: it was all so glaringly obvious. Just as Gary had predicted, it came to her in a blinding flash – but it was chillingly unwelcome. It seemed simultaneously banal, as though she had really known it all along, and startlingly sinister. The fact was that they *did* seem to have stumbled on an inexplicable but workable method of expunging the idiosyncrasies of the human personality. The evidence was all around her. If their sole aim was to expand outwards and expunge more personalities, and if there were two million of them working on it with every ounce of their ferocious zeal and with total conviction, if they really believed it could happen...

'Is that the whole point?' she asked, beginning to shred her serviette and looking at the little wisps of paper. 'Is that how you're going to change the world?' She didn't have to look. She knew Gary was nodding with a broad grin on his face. She went on, 'So, it's all beautifully self-perpetuating, isn't it? Someone gets a revelation and then they go out and bring in more people to get the revelation? Like some great big chain letter?'

'Until the whole world gets the revelation,' Gary confirmed.

'You're going to need a pretty big Centre for the whole world,' said Carmen with a sickly sort of smile.

'Well, then we won't need Centres,' Gary reassured her. 'The whole world will just be one big Centre.'

'There'll be no sickness, suffering, no evil or crime, right?' she asked with an effort to look pleased about it. 'God will get his plan back, right? You think this is possible?'

'It's coming as a reality,' Gary said firmly.

Carmen shifted in her seat. 'Well, isn't that a beautiful idea?' she said, hoping to jog Jane out of her dazzled reverie and find out which way her mind was wandering.

'Yes,' said Jane dully. 'Really beautiful.' She twisted her mouth imperceptibly so Carmen shouldn't be taken in by her words.

'But maybe not everyone gets the revelation,' Carmen said reasonably, to no-one in particular. 'Maybe there's some people who are just so eaten up with Satan's spirits that they can't get it.'

She heard Jane mutter out of the corner of her mouth, 'I wouldn't be too sure about that. Look what's just walked in...'

Carmen looked over to the doorway where Franklin hovered self-consciously, resplendent in a suit and tie. He had got it wrong somehow. The tie was too wide and bright and the trousers a hint too flared. He looked dressed for a barrack-room dance, but the normal lechery that characterised his face was gone. An expression of haunting humility sat uncomfortably on his bellicose, lumpen features. Every scrap of cockiness had disappeared.

'Well,' said Carmen suddenly. 'This is all too much for me to take in first thing in the morning. I think I'll have a stroll,' and she signalled Jane urgently to follow her outside.

They hid in the shrubbery.

It was a fine, clear day and the sun was already beating down, promising a day of scorching heat. They lay in the grass and kept their heads low so that they were screened by the nodding puff-ball heads of the rhododendrons.

Carmen made Jane swig the Milk of Magnesia and then set her to the task of smoking a cigarette without any pauses right down to the butt. Jane had solemnly sworn to give up smoking and she had kept her word now for almost twenty-four hours. But her body was craving nicotine and she complained of a light-headed floating sensation which was not a welcome addition when her brain was already feeling both starved and over-loaded.

'It does feel a bit awful,' said Jane. 'After all I *did* promise,' but continued to draw ecstatically on the cigarette like a baby sucking at a bottle.

They stretched out and basked in the warmth. Carmen settled down to read *The Times*.

'What's happening out there?' asked Jane, lazily.

'It's hard to tell,' Carmen frowned. She didn't like to admit it to herself, but the paper made no sense at all. The print was dancing about in front of her eyes and whereas normally, in the perfectly automatic action of reading, the eyes scanned the print and the brain engaged with the meaning of the words, now she found that her eyes were scanning as normal but that there was some invisible barrier between her brain and the ideas that were contained in the sentences.

She blinked, shook her head and tried with renewed concentration to extract some meaning from the neat rows of letters.

'Two Tamils killed a policeman,' she said finally with an effort.

'What are Tamils?' asked Jane.

'I haven't got a clue,' said Carmen, and she buried her head in the paragraph and tried to puzzle it out. She might as well have been reading a foreign newspaper in a foreign language. There was a picture of police firing rounds of bullets into a crowd, probably in Northern Ireland, and a picture of a child with its hand blown off in Beirut looking puzzled. None of it seemed at all real or at all to do with her. As for the Tamils, she could only think of small, passive donkey-like creatures with long ant-eater snouts, but that couldn't be right because, when she persevered with the sequence of words, they had planted a car bomb which would have required a certain dexterity with their hooves. She realised then that her knowing or not knowing couldn't make one iota of difference.

She felt rather relieved. That was the whole self-deluding fiction of reading newspapers. Newspapers gave the reader a false sense that knowledge was the same thing as power, that the knowledge somehow gave the reader purchase on the chaos of the world. But if she knew what a Tamil was, she would be none the wiser. Next she would need to know if a Tamil was a Good Thing or a Bad Thing and if the paper told her that, which it generally didn't, then what exactly would she know? She would just be taking one person's opinion on trust, and why should she give that trust? At the end of the week, when she left the cocoon that the Family provided, she would once again be able to read the meanings in addition to the words but would she really be any better off, any more in control?

The Family had an illusion of total control. She was beginning to get a glimpse of the reason why they found humanitarian acts quite pointless. They could take the short, direct route, sidestepping world affairs completely and going straight for the cause of all the problems. Wars were only symptoms. The root cause was human nature and the cure was its elimination. It made sense; it was beautifully simple and it made the conflicts and civil wars that filled the papers quite irrelevant. Once the Tamils and the people of Beirut and the Northern Irish and the Sandinistas and the Iranians – and all the other people engaged in life-and-death struggles – once they came to the Family to have their human natures eradicated, they would wonder what on earth there had ever been to fight about.

There was a movement in the grass and Jane guiltily stubbed her dog-end out into the earth. They peered up like two surfacing periscopes and were relieved to see that it was only Franklin.

'Hallo, sisters,' he hailed them. 'They sent me out to find you.' That made sense. Franklin knew all the hiding places because he'd spent most of the week crouched in them. He had an awful, holy, apologetic simper on his face.

'Time for singing,' he said firmly, and he stood over them, his arms akimbo.

Carmen found his general air of moral superiority so irritating that she leant over and pinched his leg. 'Oh, sit down and have a fag,' she said. 'Whatever's got into you?'

'Given 'em up,' he bragged, and then, since they didn't seem particularly impressed, he capitulated and sat cross-legged beside them, shuffling the *Sun* under his bottom so that he wouldn't get grass stains on the seat of the suit. 'Given up the cigarettes; this is the second day of fasting...' He counted the Conditions off on his fingers. 'Had two cold showers and did a three-hour prayer stint all before breakfast.' Franklin was not a person to do things by halves. 'I've been sacrificing and serving all over the place. I'm running out of things to give up. I gave Lloyd me last clean pair of socks and I gave Achmet me Swiss pen-knife. I'm trying to help people with spiritual difficulties. That reminds me,' he said, looking from one to the other, 'would either of you like a small khaki knapsack with a broken buckle?'

'No, thank you very much,' said Carmen, tartly.

'Or there's some white cotton handkerchiefs,' he said, pulling them out of his pocket. Jane viewed them with disdain.

'They're clean,' he assured her.

'I should hope so,' Jane said, distantly. 'I don't think giving away dirty ones would count as a genuine sacrifice.'

'Well, you wouldn't think pig's offal counted, would you? But I think it does,' Carmen pointed out.

'Anyway,' Jane scolded him, 'you're not supposed to tell people your Conditions or they don't work. If you're proud of doing them, you just start up another spiral of sin and defeat your purpose.'

'Shit!' said Franklin, vexed. 'I forgot. That means I'll have to think of something else to give you, dunnit? D'you wanna digital watch?' He began to unstrap it. 'It's only cheap but it goes. There was a leap year and then the button fell off so you have to do a bit of calculation if you want to see the date. And it plays "Colonel Bogey" at three am on the dot, so you have to put it under the pillow.'

'I haven't got a pillow,' said Jane.

'Oh yeah.' Franklin looked crestfallen and then he brightened up. 'I could give someone my pillow, couldn't I? If I got rid of the watch I wouldn't need the pillow.' He was just about to offer the pillow to Jane, all generosity, when he hesitated. 'Well, maybe I better not give it to you ... there might be some reason why not, mightn't there?'

He tried to think it through logically. 'It might be risky or something.'

They all thought about it. They weren't sure. The idea of transferring a brother's pillow to a sister's head seemed vaguely shocking. None of them were sure whether spirits could travel in pillows or whether there'd be a problem if the boy spirits arrived in the girls' dormitory, and whether the same boy spirits might not start whooping it up and having a wild and disruptive slumber party, running in and out of the sleeping sisters' bodies letting out whoops and causing havoc in their spiritual pyjamas.

'Give the pillow to the same person you give the watch to,' said Jane sensibly. 'They'll need something to muffle it with.'

This seemed eminently reasonable to the three of them.

'What came over you anyway?' asked Carmen. 'I thought you felt it was all rubbish.'

'I had a dream,' he said. He fixed his eyes on the horizon and retold it portentously. 'I was at West Ham football ground and I was being eaten alive by rats. They'd just got me liver out and they were all gnawing at it when someone came and shooed them off. I couldn't see who it was. It was night but he was all lit up like a walking floodlight. It was too bright to see his face but he had a crown on his head made out of brown paper.' Franklin looked at them, rather pleased with himself. 'And then he put me liver back. Matthew said it was a very profound revelation, actually.' He tried to look unconcerned and modest but he was obviously rather proud about it. 'He said it was miles better than what some of the people what had gone to university was dreaming that night.'

Franklin hopped to his feet, an anxious look on his face. 'Anyway, best get back, gotta talk to three people seriously about God. Are you going to come in? Otherwise they'll think I've just been trying to have give-and-take with you . . .' His face was white and drawn from hunger and his eyes were busy elsewhere.

Carmen and Jane sighed and then got to their feet. Franklin bounded on ahead of them, looking straight-backed and self-important as though he had rounded them up with the new authority that was vested in him. As they entered the room and joined in the singing, several people gave him approving smiles, as though he had passed his first sheep-dog trial.

After the singing everyone broke up into their groups in order to rehearse their team sketch for the end of the week party.

'A chance to let your hair down,' Matthew told them with a smile. 'A chance for everyone to show their creativity.'

Carmen was quite looking forward to it. They'd be allowed to rummage through the theatrical chest and fool about, with the idea of coming up with something amusing and inventive, even though the brief restricted them to the subject of God's creation and Heavenly Father. However, it became clear when the chairs were pushed back and they started rehearsal that this was not to be. Marianne had the sketch worked out in advance and it seemed to be the same sketch that each of her succeeding teams performed. They were to sing a Korean song.

'So, although we cannot understand the words we sing,' she told them blithely, 'this is a very beautiful song all about trees and blossom and spring. And Heavenly Father particularly likes this song because the sound of Korean pleases Him. So some of us are trees and some of us are blossoms and together we are all spring!' Carmen and Jane exchanged glances.

Since none of them spoke Korean and it transpired that Korean songs had a strange arhythmic structure, it took them some time even approximately to master the top half of the song-sheet. There was also the added problem that Reg, whose voice was the strongest and most penetrating, had no ear for music and couldn't carry an English tune, let alone a Korean one. As if they weren't handicapped enough, they were all required to wrap themselves in sheets and perform a dignified choreographed minuet, making a complicated set of arches with their arms, weaving in and out of another and pirouetting on their toes.

Reg was six feet four and the little Japanese girl was four feet six, and Marianne had paired them together. Thus, he was trying to remember the Korean words and the tune and the movements while bent at an angle of ninety degrees and, having no co-ordination anyway, he was circling in and out, braying his garbled notion of the words when he should have been arching, and arching when he should have been braying. One moment he would be rotating in ever decreasing circles with a quizzical expression on his face, and the next, he was standing stooped and bewildered in the middle of the chaos he had caused, his ear to the ground as though trying to listen to some private instructions and wailing like a banshee the while. On the fourth circuit, Carmen caught sight of his face, contorted with earnest concentration, his legs splayed out in different directions like Bambi on ice with his Japanese girl trying to lug him into place as though erecting a top-heavy post. Just then Marianne, pink with exertion, ran past shouting joyfully, 'But on the night we do it with boughs of apple blossom!'

This was just about the final straw. Carmen and Jane's eyes met and they both collapsed with laughter in a helpless huddle on the ground, completely unable to control their shrieks of abandoned mirth. Marianne stood over the two miscreants, glaring with fierce indignation and flared nostrils.

'There is some problem?' she asked coldly. 'You have some useful suggestion?'

There was no answer, only hiccoughs and guilty splutters. At last Carmen's voice emerged from the heap, weak and distorted with hysteria, 'Of *course* there's a problem. We look so *ridiculous*...' and they both began to heave again.

'No, this is not possible,' Marianne rapped out. 'Anything that is done with love for Heavenly Father cannot be ridiculous.' She struck her chair imperiously. 'Now, we begin again.'

Carmen was laughing so hard she couldn't rise. It was like some awful spell that held her paralysed. Gary was looking at the pair of them without sympathy.

'We are all held up for two silly people,' said Marianne.

'Look,' said Carmen, righting herself. 'Why doesn't *he*,' pointing to Reg, 'partner *him*,' pointing to Peter, who was shambling like a mental patient with no notion of which direction was which, but waiting all the time to be spun or pushed into position like a big, anxious dog waiting for its master's whistle.

'You should relate to your Central Figure, Carmen,' Gary warned in a stern undertone. Carmen had no idea what this meant, so she ignored him.

'But it's just *sense*,' she pointed out reasonably, forgetting where she was. 'If the tall ones go to the back and the small ones come to the front, then Reg and Peter can be trees and the girls can be the blossoms.' She looked around at the unsympathetic faces. 'I mean, anyone can see he's just too big for a blossom.'

Reg stood there stooping, off guard, looking at her with a slightly hurt expression and said, 'What, me?' which only creased them into fresh paroxysms of helpless laughter.

Marianne reddened with anger. 'Heavenly Father has no time for selfish, dominating spirits. When we feel these spirits, we must subordinate them or they destroy us.' After this diagnosis, she turned angrily away with an imperious, '*Alors* . . .'

Carmen plucked weakly at Jane's arm and the two of them got up and crept towards the door, still trying to control their awful, irrepressible whoops and sniggers.

Outside, they laughed until they were weak and then slid exhausted to the floor, their backs against the wall.

'Well, they may not have managed to give us the Truth,' said Jane, wiping away her tears, 'but you can't say they haven't given us a laugh.'

Carmen had gone beyond rational laughter into the silly, hysterical phase. 'It was when he was going "Choo ni mi won soo i gi sa. Is it alright if I just stop and pull me sock up?"' and she drowned out the punchline with another high explosive squeal and started choking again. Jane's face was red and her eyes were brimming as she squawked, 'Am I holding me bough in me right hand or me left hand?' and they snorted out a fresh burst of muffled hiccoughs. Just then, Jane stopped and let out an almighty gasp. Carmen's head swung round and the smile froze on her face. Jane was staring into the air in front of her, her whole body braced as though against some severe sharp burst of pain.

In that moment, all the colour had drained out of her face. Beads of sweat stood up from her forehead and traced along her upper lip. She shrieked as the contraction went through her, and then she curled up into a ball and began to writhe in spasm, squealing with frightened yelps of agony like a wounded animal. Carmen didn't know what to do. She put her arms round Jane and tried to raise her, but she was too crouched and rigid.

'Jane,' she called urgently. 'What is it? What should I do?'

She looked around for help, but the corridor was empty: what help could they be anyway? 'Hold on to me,' she said, uselessly – so violent were the spasms that Jane seemed neither to hear or see anything

174

outside the mist of her own pain. Carmen released her hand and moved to stand away from her, to go and fetch someone, but Jane managed to clutch at her and said through clenched teeth, 'Say the words, Carmen.'

'I can't,' Carmen wailed. It seemed such a terrible thing to ask, and yet it seemed a more terrible thing to deny her when she was rolling this way and that, locked in her own excruciating torment. She gripped Carmen's arm more tightly. 'Please,' she gasped. 'Just say them. You don't have to believe them.'

Carmen took her hands and held them firmly and began to mutter 'Sun Meung Moon, Sun Meung Moon, Sun Meung Moon...' over and over again, unhappily and without conviction. As the chant became more rhythmic, she made up her mind that, since she was doing it, she might as well pretend she was doing it with conviction. Maybe it was the conviction in their voices that soothed the afflicted subject, not the words. So she put strength and confidence into her voice, and she channelled all her powers of concentration on willing the pain to leave Jane's body. 'Sunmeungmoonsunmeungmoon-sunmeungmoonsunmeungmoonsunmeungmoon' until it meant nothing but a strange garbled oriental noise. And then, Carmen distinctly felt something ebb from her like a wave, and, to her astonishment she could almost watch it enter Jane, as though she herself was transmitting her strength and stillness. Jane's hands ceased to tremble and became limp and pliable. A look of great relief and peace came over her face, and very slowly she sat up and looked around her, dazed.

They sat there for a moment on their knees, not speaking. There was a certain awkwardness between them, for no reason that Carmen could explain. From within the room, the Korean song rose joyfully for about the fourteenth time.

'I think they're getting it,' said Carmen brusquely. She felt embarrassed and she felt sullied, as though she had taken part unwillingly in some black magic rite. And yet, whether by coincidence or suggestion, the chant had worked again. It was uncanny, and she didn't like to be the instrument for it. 'Are you OK now?'

'I'm fine,' said Jane. She had the serene look that comes to a person's face after an epileptic fit.

When they went back into the room, the pair of them were

noticeably cowed and subdued. They allowed themselves to be scolded, and then manoeuvred about with the neutrality of chess pieces, as though their bodies weren't their own to control.

They parroted the Korean words as though they understood exactly what they meant, rolling their eyes with whimsical coquettishness as Marianne directed them. And, for some reason which neither of them could have explained, they avoided meeting each other's eyes, even though they were partners in the dance.

Carmen kept herself to herself at lunch, but there was another small interchange which disturbed her. She heard Pamela saying reproachfully to Jane, 'I heard you were having a cigarette in the grass this morning.'

Jane, who was eating nothing but only staring submissively at an empty plate, looked up, surprised.

'Yes, I did. I'm sorry, Pamela.'

'Oh, I don't mind,' shrugged Pamela. 'It wasn't me you made the solemn promise to, was it? It was Heavenly Father. It's Him you're betraying, not me.'

Carmen intervened, alarmed. 'Did Franklin tell you? It must have been Franklin.'

Pamela raised her eyebrows in cool disdain. 'Why shouldn't he have told me?' she asked. 'We don't have any secrets in the Family. Secrets are just what Satan likes. We're here to help one another. It was his duty to tell someone if he thought you and Jane were multiplying evil. Anyway, he didn't tell me. Matthew did.'

This somehow made it worse. It was disturbing that Franklin had gone straight to the top and sneaked. If he had just told Pamela, then Carmen could have put it down to a slip of the tongue, but Matthew was hard to get hold of. One had to knock on his office door. She imagined Franklin, all self-righteousness, his shoulders thrown back as he apologetically delivered his report. Earlier, she had thought him overly zealous but still on the side of the guests. He was the kind of person who would always be on the side of rebellion. The new information made her revise her opinion. If even Franklin was changing sides, then who was safe?

The lecture called 'Foundation To Receive The Messiah' pulled together the loose threads of Principle. It was hard for her to imagine now that she had once wondered how it could possibly all tie up. The threads had seemed so disparate, once upon a time, but now it was all crystal clear – still nonsensical, but clear in terms of its own logic.

Even Eve had tainted her blood by having sexual intercourse with Lucifer, and then compounded the sin by passing the evil blood to Adam, she had caused everyone from that time on to be born with Original Sin and with Fallen Nature. If the new Messiah took a wife and cleansed her Fallen Nature, the Holy Couple would produce children free of Original Sin.

Naturally, one man could not restore the blood-line alone; it would take too long, so there was another way for quite ordinary people to expunge their Original Sin and this was by relating to the Messiah. Relating to the Messiah meant centring all thoughts on God at all times, thus creating a vertical relationship with Heavenly Father. So, it was possible for everyone in the room, however sinful, to cut off from their Fallen Nature and to grow to perfection. Once perfect, they too could produce children free of Original Sin, and people who achieved perfection were able to love all others equally in the way that God had intended.

To Carmen it seemed impossible to centre *all* thoughts on God, *all* the time, but Matthew clearly meant it literally. He mentioned that the Family had already produced a number of Perfected children.

The idea worried her and she puzzled over it throughout the team meeting. It occurred to her that she was the only person who did not find it reassuring and inspirational.

'Now this lecture makes us feel very dirty, yes?' asked Marianne. They all nodded.

'When we realise that we all have Fallen Natures, we realise we must identify our faults and try to help each other with them so that we can learn humility and begin to change ourselves. This is how it is; when we begin to discover our Original Sin, we have to cut off our Fallen Natures.'

She looked sadly around the faces. 'We are so dirty inside our hearts. This is a shock to realise, huh? Even the trash cans outside are not so dirty as we are, and this evil blood is the result of what happened between Lucifer and Eve, and then what happened between Eve and Adam. Sometimes we say we have understood the Fall Of

Man lecture, but actually, we have not understood until we feel this dirtiness deep inside us. That all this evil blood from those unions has been passed onto us, even by our own parents . . .'

She waited until she had established that everyone was either nodding or looking suitably glum. 'So this is how we must feel, we must feel the sin of Adam and Eve is our own sin, we must feel this sin that has multiplied through centuries many thousands of times, we must be aware of it concentrated in our blood.'

Then she went round the room, asking the members to point out their own worst faults and how Fallen Nature manifested itself in their behaviour. Pamela started the ball rolling vigorously with a sustained attack on her own selfishness, her own desire to eat a lot of food and to sleep when she should be working for Heavenly Father. The members seemed to make the effort to outdo one another in the weight and seriousness of their offences, as though they would be given badges of merit for the faults they could identify. They stated them clearly and matter-of-factly as though they had stated them many times before. The sins sounded pretty puny ones to Carmen. Sleeping wasn't traditionally considered to be a sin. Even in the Catholic church, it was more often *not* sleeping that caused the problems. But she joined in the enthusiastic applause.

'My Fallen Nature manifests itself in the sin of vainglorious pride,' Gary announced. 'Sometimes it makes me do things from the wrong motivation. It makes me do things for my own glory so people will think I'm specially clever or specially talented or something, and this is very wrong. Satan attacks me very much when I give him this foundation to invade.' He looked around for approval from Marianne. 'And then Heavenly Father tells me that we're all the same in God's eyes and that our talents are not our own, so we can only rightly use them for God's purpose. Also I have Fallen Desires, but I'm making a lot of headway with that,' he assured them. Carmen watched his face as he completed his self-criticism. He spoke with a kind of self-accepting humility that was rather embarrassing to witness. Marianne nodded regretfully. 'Yes, we must work very hard against vainglory,' she said. 'Often we think we are a good artist or a good singer or a good gardener and then we want to show off and want everyone to say how clever we are, but when everyone says "Ah, Gary is a good gardener", then it is Heavenly Father who must suffer

178

because someone takes away from Heavenly Father what is rightfully His.'

Carmen had an uneasy feeling then that they were referring to Gary's performance at the last Family Evening. After all, no-one was likely to praise Gary's gardening skills. From watching him, she guessed he hardly knew the sharp end of the secateurs from the blunt end, but there was no doubt he could sing and that his singing gave him pleasure. It was not the singing itself that was a problem, only the nature of his gratification.

When it came to the guests' turn to confess, they had obviously absorbed the lesson of their betters and felt obliged to match the members' self-critical rigour. Reg notched up a respectable total of own goals.

'I have trouble seeing people through God's eyes sometimes,' he said broodily, and his eyes skimmed tactfully across Carmen and Jane. 'And yet I know, logically, that God sees something good in every one of us. I'm stubborn and bull-headed about things. I'm very inflexible and set in my ways. I know I ought to change but I don't *want* to change – this is the problem. I find it hard to accept new ideas and I'm not as open, I'm not as humble as I'd like to be,' he said sadly. Carmen couldn't look at him. Poor Reg. He did himself an injustice. He was quite humble enough, and it seemed to her that he had been infinitely accommodating, infinitely flexible. Marianne nodded warmly at him.

'When we begin to recognise these things in our own hearts, then Heavenly Father is able to do His work and help us change,' she reassured him. 'And everyone here will work to help you, also.'

She was about to move on to Jane when Reg gave a shuffle and began again.

'Another way I see my Fallen Nature working is that I . . . well, at the beginning, I can admit it now, I found some trouble with the lectures. I found I couldn't keep awake.' He looked around fearfully, 'It's amazing to me now, of course, but Matthew had a word with me and I came to realise, with his help, that if we find the lectures boring, this is something that comes from deep within ourselves. The lectures certainly aren't boring. They're powerful and thought-provoking and full of startling truths, so if we find ourselves dropping off in lectures, this is coming from the person themself.

And when I thought about this, I realised that yes, it was me who was approaching it the wrong way. It was me, stuck in that old rut, full of false pride in my Bible knowledge, glorifying in myself and not in Heavenly Father, lacking in imagination even to stretch these old brain cells around a new idea.'

He looked up with a certain proud humility. 'Yes, I think it's a shock to look at yourself and realise that everything about your life is dull and fitted into dry sterile compartments. I looked at myself, and I saw a man who was a boring sort of person.'

There was an uncomfortable silence as his self-judgement fell flatly on the air. No-one was sure whether to clap or not. It was a truly noble admission. There were many faults that added a sort of tarnished lustre to the guilty party, but it took real courage to make that fatal verdict to one's own self. A hearty round of applause would seem to confirm the truth of his observation, so they waited for Marianne to give the lead.

'No-one is boring to Heavenly Father,' she said gently. 'No-one is boring to the Family,' and she turned to Jane before Reg could come up with any other painful self-analyses.

Jane was staring at Reg in dismay, stricken with guilt. Hadn't she been the one who made him feel this way – what right had she to pass judgement on another human being? She had difficulty collecting herself and when she spoke her voice quavered dangerously.

'Well...' She cleared her throat. 'I just want to say my Fallen Nature manifests itself in a cruel sense of humour, and I've realised over the week that to use cruelty in humour, well, that isn't any sort of humour at all, and sometimes it makes me feel very ashamed and I'm going to stop doing it.'

'When something is bad, we mustn't do it,' Marianne encouraged her. 'Heavenly Father likes us to laugh only in a kind way and to make jokes about flowers and birds and heavenly things.'

Carmen was hoping that Jane would leave it there, but the urge for self-castigation was powerful. 'I also want to say that I have sinful pride. That I sometimes feel better than other people, but I'm not. The kind of pride I feel in being cynical or flippant and trying to be clever, that's not the kind of pride I'm proud of.' Her words were getting tangled up in her emotional effusion. 'I just wanted to say that I think Reg has a most incredible humility and I respect it. I hope that I can one day be that humble. I think he's a most extraordinary person and that Heavenly Father treasures the qualities he has. He's an example to us all and to me especially.'

Everyone began to clap her very warmly. Reg flushed to the roots of his sandy hair, incredibly surprised and pleased, looking around as though he had arrived home unexpectedly to find himself in the middle of a surprise party when he had expected to spend the night alone in solitary gloom. So warm was the applause and so generously shared between the two of them, that the tear which trembled on Jane's lash tumbled over and rolled down her face.

Carmen's brain was racing. The moment the applause died down, she would be required to deliver her speech of contrition. Her mind was quite blank. She felt oddly resentful about the scene she had just witnessed. It had moved her, but it had done so in a way she distrusted. The sentimental wallow of remorse and expiation had raised the emotional temperature in the room to a degree where she felt it unsafe to speak. Apart from the fact that her faults were no-one's business but her own, the faults that they wanted her to repudiate were the faults that kept her sane. Marianne's eyes came to rest upon her, trustingly, as though to ask whether anyone could fail to respond harmoniously to this high spiritual atmosphere.

Reg was looking at her with the expectant air of someone who had received a number of surprise presents and was now hopeful at each ring of the doorbell. She steeled herself to disappoint him. With a gulp, she arranged her features into a hang-dog look and began her recitation as though she was reading from a school report.

'I notice my Fallen Nature in lots of ways. Particularly when I'm not serious about things I should be serious about. And I'm very critical and intolerant . . .'

She looked at Marianne timidly to see how this was going down, but Marianne merely signalled her to continue.

'. . . I'm very arrogant and I think I know better than other people round me and I keep trying to work things out with my brain when I ought to be using my heart more and trusting other people who only want the best for me. And I'm very individualistic, and this makes a foundation for Satan to invade . . .'

She looked up optimistically, thinking that this must be enough. It was a heroic effort but Marianne continued to stare frigidly at her; she had still not passed muster.

'And I also keep forgetting and say "God" as an exclamation when it might be nicer for everyone if I said "Wow".'

She closed her mouth with finality. Marianne examined her minutely. The room fell silent and no-one clapped.

'But these are very grievous faults,' she pronounced in a grave voice. 'How do you suppose to change your fallen heart that causes you to do these wrong, dirty things?'

Carmen screwed up her face, rather disconcerted. Something seemed to have gone awry here. Her confessed faults weren't any more dirty or grievous than anybody else's, and if they were shouldn't that entitle her to a bigger and better round of applause? She pretended to think about the question.

'Well, I'm going to try to...'

'No.' Marianne firmly shook her head. 'We cannot try. Heavenly Father doesn't understand this word "to try". To say we try prepares the way for failure. To say we try admits the right to fail. When we understand we have such grievous sins, we have to understand we have no right to fail. You think you have this right?' she demanded.

Carmen shook her head, nervously.

'What will happen if you fail?' She turned quickly. 'Jane, what will happen if Carmen fails?'

Jane wriggled. 'Well, I should think Satan would claim her.'

Marianne nodded. 'You understand what this would mean?' she asked.

Carmen nodded.

'When we can understand that we are selfish and arrogant and full of pride, then we begin to face our Fallen Nature and we have to change. We have to say, "Heavenly Father, I have seen my faults and now I want to change." We have to say this and we have to genuinely want it in our hearts. We have to be humble and lower ourselves and ask Heavenly Father to crush our pride.' She waited to see the effect of this speech register on Carmen's mulish face. 'So, now what will you say to Heavenly Father?'

Carmen squirmed under her relentless eye. 'Er, I'd say, "Heavenly Father. I know I'm arrogant. Please make me humble and crush my pride because I've seen my faults and I want to change."'

Marianne continued to stare at her with dissatisfaction. Carmen had said it with as much conviction as she might have read the telephone directory.

'But look,' Carmen objected, 'could we just go over the meaning of the word "change"? Perhaps there are some things I ought to change about my personality, but I think when you say "change" you're meaning something a bit more radical. I mean, am I asking Heavenly Father to change the little bits or am I asking Him to chuck the whole lot out?'

Wendy let out an audible sigh. Carmen flushed. She was aware that it was selfish to take more than one's allotted time, that Marianne only had so much time for each person, like a distinguished Harley Street doctor, only the ills they brought to the surgery were spiritual ills and therefore much more important. No matter that Carmen didn't actually want to have her symptoms discussed and examined; all the more reason why she should give way to people who did. There was a general air of impatience. She cast around her for support.

'I mean, I want to change but I want to know what it involves...'

'We have no need of our Fallen Natures. It holds back our development. If we compare our spirit to a plant that seeks the light, sometimes we must cut away much growth to give the shoot its chance.' Carmen understood this to mean that her personality and her Fallen Nature were one and the same.

She found it rather shocking that anyone should ask her to erase her personality like a tape. 'So when we all get rid of our Fallen Natures and change our hearts, then we'll all be the same?'

'This is how God intended us to be,' Marianne confirmed. 'This was His original Plan.'

'Well, I can see it's a very worthwhile aim and all that,' said Carmen, with a hint of desperation, 'but wouldn't it be boring if we were all the same and didn't have any problems?'

Marianne fixed her with an incredulous eye. 'You think the Family is boring because we sing and smile and feel happy thoughts and praise God? Have you found the Family boring?' She lifted one frosty, ironic eyebrow.

'Not at all,' Carmen hastened to reassure her. 'No, I've found it very interesting and stimulating and inspiring.'

'Well, this is how the world will be when the Kingdom of Heaven comes on earth. Without sin or suffering or death. In our lifetime we see the culmination of human history. This is a very beautiful thought, huh?'

'Yes, it's very beautiful,' Carmen said. 'But not everyone could change from just hearing Principle. People have got to *want* to change. Not every single person in the world is going to want to change, are they? How could it possibly happen?'

Marianne smiled and nodded at Gary to indicate that he should give the answer.

'That's the point, Carmen,' he said quietly. 'It couldn't possibly happen but that's the miracle. With Principle it *does* happen. Even though people don't know they want it, once they hear Principle they begin to change. That's how we know we've found a very special Truth. The most powerful Truth in the world.'

'But maybe there'd be people – you know, selfish stubborn people – who couldn't see how beautiful it was. Who'd actively *resist* change.'

Everyone in the room was restive. They were quite out of sympathy with her, anxious to proceed, impatient with her insensitivity. The beautiful atmosphere of harmony and brotherly love was being rudely shattered by her endless irrelevant questions.

'This movement is God-inspired and therefore cannot be resisted,' said Marianne smoothly. 'Satan stole God's beautiful Plan and made Communism. Now we restore God's Heavenly Kingdom on a global scale. As the Restoration moves across the earth, all hearts will change, and then we change the hearts of the Communists.'

'But what about the individual hearts?' Carmen insisted. She was less worried about the Communists than about herself.

Marianne spoke softly and deliberately as though she were delivering an unwelcome diagnosis on Carmen.

'If the stubborn, selfish heart refuses to change, then we take that heart and examine it for cracks. Father has said, there is a crack in every human heart. We find this crack and we use a chisel to lever it open. We take a chisel to the human heart and we pour in heavenly love.'

Carmen's hand went involuntarily to her chest. The threat was unmistakable, yet Marianne was smiling at her with sufficient affection to mist up her glasses.

184

'Ah, Carmen,' she said gently, teasingly. 'You look so worried. Perhaps you think you will not have this revelation? But already you come to the Seven Day and we see you begin to change.'

'I haven't changed,' she said defensively.

Marianne laughed. Carmen looked around. The members and the guests were all smiling knowingly at her in an awful superior way.

'Carmen comes to the Seven Day and she doesn't believe in God. At the end of the week, she believes in God. Carmen doesn't accept the Messiah and she tries to tell everyone there can be no Messiah, but by the end of the week, Carmen also begins to wonder and look for the Messiah. Carmen has no faults and by the end of the week she tells us she has many faults and that she wants to change her heart – No, Carmen has not changed.' She pouted comically so that a ripple of laughter went around the room.

Carmen thought it through quickly. It was true that she now believed in God, but that was because she felt so threatened, because prayer was the only thing that offered her any moments of solitude, because her amorphous God was predictable and stable when everything else around her was in a state of flux. It was true she was looking for the Messiah, but that was because they'd run so many appetite-whetting trailers on Him that a false sense of tension had been created. And as for admitting her faults, she was only doing that because they made her do it. But then, they weren't holding a gun to her head, were they? No-one could make you admit things you didn't want to admit, that you didn't even believe, without the use of force. Perhaps she did believe them. She knew that wasn't the case. She tried to get in touch with a few things that she *did* believe – a few absolute truths from her old, familiar reality, but they refused to come into her head. Everyone was staring at her expectantly waiting for her to answer, but all that came into her head were the words they kept repeating over and over again: 'There is no truth without freedom and there is no freedom without the Messiah'.

A heap of toilet-paper roses was piled up on the table and Carmen wound the pink tissue into yet another blossom. The groups were spaced about the hall preparing the props and sketches for the following night's Family Evening. Each group was secretive and excitable, although Carmen couldn't see much point in raising

185

excitement to a fever pitch if the sketches were up to the standard of their own Korean song. All the same, the room buzzed and hummed and everyone seemed content – apart from Carmen, who sat there mechanically churning out roses like someone at an assembly-line bench, muttering to herself as though a dark demon had come into her.

'Jesus, I think it's terrifying,' she said. Jane was busy Sellotaping Carmen's rose output onto crudely made cardboard boughs. 'I don't know about you, but I'm going to stock up with a black beret and a secret radio transmitter.'

Jane smiled wearily. 'Oh, Carmen, why's everything got to be sinister?' she said. 'Maybe it is a bit megalomaniac, but why shouldn't it be? God's a megalomaniac, isn't He? It's only because the traditional churches are so wishy-washy and compromised that we tend to forget it. Don't you think there's something sort of refreshing about a church that actually intends to *do* something about the world, instead of just talking about it?'

Carmen was thrown off balance by Jane's response. 'Depends what they've got in mind for it,' said Carmen. 'If they want to put people in Centres and rearrange their brains, I'd say that was sinister.'

'Well.' Jane shrugged carelessly. 'Any great movement's sinister, when you think about it. Christianity's the bloodiest movement in the history of civilisation. Socialism and Fascism have got about the same body count, I should think. At least this movement's not violent, however sinister it seems. The only movements that don't look sinister are the ones that don't achieve much. A religion ought to have guts, it ought to have fire and conviction. I mean, if you think the aim's sinister, maybe you think the Salvation Army's sinister. Don't you think they've got the same aim? Don't you think they mean everyone in the world to join the Salvation Army?'

'They don't go round sticking people in Centres, forcing them to put on poke bonnets and making the men play trombones,' said Carmen stoutly. 'And they don't go out collecting money and then giving it all to their Wing Commander.'

'Who's to say?' said Jane, as they sat down at the dining-room table. 'Do any of us really know for sure? If you wanted to see the Salvation Army as a sinister para-military movement, I'm sure you could get the evidence to make it look that way.'

186

Carmen scowled. She could see a sort of logic in it. Maybe it wasn't that sinister after all, but the feeling still persisted. And then, the Pope *did* live in a palace like a king.

'Well, I still think there's something not quite right about it.'

Jane sighed. It was then that Carmen noticed the high flush that lent her face a raptured beauty. 'You can't always look at the rose and see the thorn,' she said. 'Sometimes you have to go with something and see where it leads you. Sometimes you just have to smell the perfume and see the way the petals fold. Do you know what I mean, Carmen?'

Carmen stared back at her in consummate dismay. 'Yes,' she said. 'Yes, I see what you mean. Thanks for that bit of advice, Jane. It was really beautiful.' Jane smiled timidly, pleased that Carmen wasn't going to take issue with her. Indeed at that moment Carmen hadn't the strength. She was filled suddenly with the dull certainty that Jane was slipping away and that there was nothing she could do to hold her back.

'You make them so well,' said Jane encouragingly. 'Yours are much better than mine. Yours look like real tea roses.'

'Ah, yes,' said Carmen energetically, in a fair imitation of Marianne. 'So this is a very inspiring idea we have here, huh? 'Ere we 'ave ze most beautiful tea rose but when we examine it closer, we see we 'ave actually an old bit of lavatory paper...'

Jane didn't smile. Carmen felt an insistent dull thudding in her head. Her irritability was sharpened by the awareness that Franklin was walking about with a proprietorial air and that he kept passing back and forth quite close to her shoulder. It made her edgy and ill at ease and she suspected that he was spying on her. She had ceased to trust him, as she had ceased to trust everyone.

'I wish that big moron would push off,' she murmured darkly. 'He's like the Hitler Youth or something. I wish he'd stop wearing that ridiculous holy look. It doesn't suit him.'

Jane smiled with easy tolerance. 'Oh, I don't know. He seems a lot nicer than he was before. He doesn't tell lies any more. Pamela says he's stopped that.'

'No,' said Carmen. 'Now he insists on going round telling the truth about things which are none of his business. Is that really an improvement?'

'I don't know,' said Jane cosily. 'That sounds like a pretty big improvement to me. I'd rather be around people who told the truth, wouldn't you? Lies are a bit unsettling, aren't they?'

'I don't like him hovering round me spying,' Carmen grumbled, keeping her eye on him.

'I think you're being paranoid,' said Jane. 'He really isn't doing anything.'

But Carmen could think of no reason why he should pace about behind her like that unless he was trying to find out snippets of incriminating conversation to pass on so that people would know better how to handle her or how to help her. However muddled she felt, she didn't want to be 'handled' and she felt a strong resistance to being 'helped'. She was frightened she would show where the crack in her heart was. She knew where it was. It centred round her father and it wasn't satisfactorily healed over.

As Franklin passed behind her for about the twelfth time, she leant back angrily in her chair and said in a deep penetrating growl, 'Why don't you piss off? There's nothing at all interesting for you to earwig, as it happens.'

Franklin merely stared at her, surprised and hurt. She realised then that he was doing nothing more sinister than pacing up and down as he memorised his lines.

'You see?' said Jane serenely. 'Now you've hurt his feelings.'

'Well, he sneaked about the cigarette,' said Carmen defensively. '*And* he went and told Matthew we were relating horizontally.'

'But wasn't he right, in a way?' asked Jane. 'After all, there's no reason to have secrets, is there? And he was only trying to help me to help myself.'

Carmen began to worry how safe her own secret was in Jane's keeping. Jane touched her hand and began to talk earnestly.

'Look, Carmen, I know you're resistant to this thing, but I took a look at myself today and I didn't like what I saw. Can't you understand that? I'm not "going over to the other side" or anything.' She laughed softly at the ridiculous notion. 'It's just that if we really want to be nicer people then we *do* have to make an effort to stop relating horizontally.'

When Carmen spoke it was with fierce and clear emphasis. 'You told me to tell you if it started to happen and now I'm telling you.

When I close my eyes, I hear that same whining, wheedling tone. You sound exactly like bloody Pamela, as though half your brain's gone missing.'

There was a startled silence all around her. She had spoken too loudly and it occurred to her too late that Pamela was actually sitting right at her elbow. There was no possible way that Pamela could have failed to hear her. In fact, she was a picture of utter dismay, her eyes big, unhappy and limpid, her mouth half-open with shock.

Carmen struggled inadequately to retrieve the situation.

'I'm sorry, Pamela, I didn't know you were sitting there,' she said awkwardly, as though that made it any better. 'I didn't really mean anything. I only meant she sounded...'

A big, fully formed tear brimmed and fell from Pamela's opaque eyes and spilt down her cheek.

'I had no idea,' Pamela faltered. 'I had no idea you didn't like me. I thought ... I've only been trying to do my best. I thought we were friends...' She got up from her chair, very distressed. Carmen struggled to her feet to restrain her but Pamela sidled past and made her way through the tables towards the door, where Gary and some sisters comforted her.

'Oh God,' said Carmen, dismally. Here she was taking it out on these poor creatures who were only her tormentors in that they had also once been victims. She had an overwhelming sense that she was losing control.

'I didn't mean to...' she said uselessly to Jane, but Jane refused to acknowledge her and continued Sellotaping flowers in a tight-lipped, angry silence.

Carmen pushed back her chair and strode out to follow Pamela. But when she reached the porch, she could see no sign of her, only Gary walking towards her from the darkness.

'She's praying,' he said. 'Best leave her to it.'

'I didn't mean to upset her. It's only that my head's bursting...'

'Don't blame yourself,' said Gary. 'It's not you, that's what you've got to remember. It's your Fallen Nature. But now you're starting to recognise it and cut away from it, you won't find that sort of thing happening any more. No more getting irritated, no more getting angry.'

They looked up at the starred night sky. He handed her one of her cigarettes and lit it for her, which touched her, considering how much he disapproved.

'There's something else that's upsetting you, though,' he said gently. 'And I think I know what it is. It's because the end of the week's coming and you don't know what you're going to do afterwards. It's all a bit of anti-climax, isn't it?'

Carmen only drew on her cigarette with trembling hands. He carried on, quietly. 'It's sad when you're just getting to know people really deeply and you suddenly realise that you're going to lose them.'

She nodded. In a sense that *was* the reason. She had got to know them and now they were all, one by one, slipping quietly away from her over the dividing line where she couldn't follow, where she didn't want to follow, from where they could not return.

'But you see, you don't have to lose touch, you don't have to go off immediately. There's another course, much more relaxed than this one, and I think I could persuade them to let you come along.'

His warmth, his proximity, his intimate solicitude made her feel terribly grateful to him, terribly fond of him. He was always there when she needed solace.

'I'm going on to the Twenty-One Day, and I don't want to leave you behind – I want to know you're coming with me. Can I put your name down?'

She shook her head. It was hard to say no straight out when he looked so doglike and pleading. It was hard to say it but it was not hard to know it very, very surely inside. The time had passed when Lucy was anything like a good enough excuse to subject herself to something she didn't understand but that felt so dangerous.

'This isn't a good time to ask me,' she said. 'I shouldn't be making decisions now, not when I'm so tired and confused and my brain's exploding all over the place. Honestly, Gary, I can't quite explain it to you but I get this very weird baffled sensation in my head.'

He nodded sympathetically and she felt an overwhelming, irrational desire to confide in him, to tell someone how peculiar she felt.

'I mean, I feel like a pin-ball machine. It's like there's a silver ball-bearing inside flipping about loose and it's shooting everywhere and setting off lights and buzzers – that's the only way I can explain it. It's not a good time for anyone to put pressure on me, that's all I'm saying.'

'It's *exactly* the time to make a decision,' he insisted. 'Hold on to that confusion. Don't let it go!' He was nodding firmly as though he recognised the symptoms exactly.

'When you feel confusion in your heart, that's God and Satan doing battle. They're both pulling you this way and that and it creates a feeling of confusion. But if you just go with that, if you persevere and see it through, you know what happens next?'

She shook her head dumbly. He seemed unreasonably intense and excited.

'Suddenly there'll be this most intense moment of clarity and inner revelation, something will just go *snap*!' He clicked his fingers as though her consciousness was no more important than an elastic band.

'It's the most wonderful feeling. Everything suddenly becomes very calm and very clear and what you haven't understood before will just click into place. Hold onto it, Carmen. See it through. Satan wants your heart, but God needs it much much more.'

'It's not my heart, it's my brain.'

'Look,' he said. 'When someone's confused, they have to put their trust in someone who's *not* confused. They have to turn to someone who can see more clearly – isn't that so? You have to *trust* me.'

She looked at his pleading, trustworthy face with infinite distrust.

'Gary,' she said quietly. 'My brain is confused because I'm tired, because I'm never ever alone for a single moment of the day, because everyone keeps battering on and on and *on* and *on* at me, because people keep telling me things that I know aren't true and they keep telling me with such certainty that my brain is going on overdrive and trying to keep up with it all and it *just can't cope*!' She ended in an infuriated squeal. 'I'm not confused! *People are confusing me!*'

'Hey, calm down,' he said. 'Let's just talk this out, shall we?' He guided her gently to sit beside him on the cold stone step. She lit another cigarette.

'Look, Carmen,' he said. 'If you genuinely think that people are trying to confuse you, well,' he shook his head, 'I don't know, but there must be something wrong in your reasoning. Nobody wants anything but the best for you. Do you think I would have spent all this time praying and trying to help you unless I really thought I had something very precious and special to pass on? Maybe I get a bit intense, maybe we all do – but that's just because we're so anxious to share something very beautiful with you. And people think you have something special or they wouldn't want to trust you with it; they wouldn't care so much or feel so desperately anxious for you to have it.'

'Well, everyone's got to have it anyway. So I understood,' said Carmen, sullenly.

'The people who come to the Truth the soonest are the most blessed, and so are their families,' he pointed out. 'You can't just turn your back on a great Truth when you hear it. You can't say, I'll come back later. You have to commit yourself to it while it's on offer. Maybe Heavenly Father doesn't give you a second chance . . .'

The washing machine again. The salesman was making it hard to order and only available to a few privileged customers.

'If it was a great truth,' she said testily, 'people would be able to answer questions about it.'

He looked at her, mildly hurt. 'I've always tried to answer your questions, haven't I? What questions do you want answered? Ask me,' he prompted her gently, 'ask me anything you want and I'll do my best.'

She watched her smoke rise. She had a sense that their conversation was all part of the same closed cycle. Arguing about her confusion and about whether they answered questions or not still allowed him to continue doing more of the same – to continue telling her that black was white. Arguing was integral to the whole methodology of the breaking-down process. The same weary treadmill could go on indefinitely until her poor abused brain would turn traitor and refuse to process anymore. Then things really *would* become calm and clear.

'OK,' she said, once her cigarette had burnt halfway down. 'OK. There's something I need to understand about the Last Days.' He nodded and sat back against the step, his hands locked around his knees, confident that he was primed for anything she might throw at him. She decided to throw the lot.

'The Restoration is coming very soon, right?' she asked purposefully. 'The Kingdom Of Heaven On Earth, that's imminent?'

He nodded.

'Within our lifetime?' she pursued. He nodded again.

'And everyone will be supremely happy. We'll all love each other equally. There won't be any sin or selfishness or crime. Everyone will sing and smile and there won't be any individuals, we'll all be just the same?'

'We'll have faces and personalities,' he objected.

'But the personalities will all be roughly similar...'

'When everyone grows to perfection, there wouldn't be any big differences, no,' he said rather coldly.

'And there wouldn't be any books or plays or culture or anything like that. In fact, the whole of Western culture we could pretty well junk?' she said cheerfully.

'We'll take some of the good things, but not the Satanic parts,' he said. 'There'll be books – God-centred books. God-centred films. Everything God-centred. It'll be like you see here. We have an immensely rich cultural life in the Family. What you see here is the kind of culture that pleases God. So that's the kind of culture we'll have on a global scale.'

'What, old songs and little skits?' she asked. He flushed.

'God likes corny things,' he said. 'The things we do here are the things God likes. But there'll be new God-centred songs too... But honestly, Carmen.' He gave a little start of impatience and re-crossed his legs. 'What difference does it make what the culture is? The point is surely that God's perfect Plan should be fulfilled on earth. Isn't that mind-blowing?'

She nodded. He carried on, 'I mean the old culture would be pretty irrelevant. Culture as we know it in Satan's world, well, it's all based on conflict and struggle. Since there wouldn't *be* any conflict or struggle – even the memory of it would have faded – well then, books and things would be irrelevant, wouldn't they?'

Carmen slowly stubbed her cigarette out on the granite. Her brow was furrowed. She had the feeling that they were discussing something so vital, so fundamental, that she hardly knew where to begin defending it. *He* was telling her that none of it mattered, that books didn't matter. But didn't books represent the storehouse of human knowledge? Weren't they the mirror of an infinitely complex universe, recording what had been and what might be to come? Without books, there would be no reference points, no touchstone for ideas, achievements, mistakes, and no material for independent thought. The world would be the world circumscribed by the Messiah, and any ideas that might circulate about it would be the ideas promulgated by the Messiah. And maybe that man would be a false Messiah, but no-one in the world that Gary described would have the knowledge or the vocabulary to challenge him.

'What are you going to do with the books?' she asked mildly.

He looked rather irritated and taken aback, as though the question was so far off the point he could see no value in following it up.

'Well, I can't see it matters what we do with them. I suppose they'll be disposed of.'

She stared at the rubber toe caps of her trainers against his shiny, pointed shoes.

'Mm. They might as well be, mightn't they?' she agreed. 'If nobody can read them . . .'

He seemed unaware of any irony in her voice. She carried on, 'So there'd be no need of books. There wouldn't be any sort of fantasy or variation. People wouldn't imagine things or dream things or hope for anything.' She was trying to picture it for herself. It was a strange discovery to have a glimpse of heaven and realise that you didn't want it. 'There'd be nothing to strive for.'

'What would there be to strive for?' he asked. 'We'll have everything we want as a reality. There's no need to hope and dream when you have everything you want.'

'But what if it doesn't make us happy?'

'It *will* make us happy,' he said stubbornly. 'If it doesn't make us happy that will only be because we have remnants of Satan's consciousness left. But once we reach perfection and break away totally from Satan, then it will make us perfectly, eternally happy.'

'Wouldn't make me happy,' she said darkly.

'Yes, but that's because you seem to think culture's the be-all and end-all. It seems to me it's a pretty selfish, trivial attitude – to want to stop the Kingdom Of Heaven coming just because you're used to a culture of conflict. "Hold on, God",' he mocked, '"Don't bring perfect happiness on the earth just yet, Carmen wants other people to suffer and struggle so she can read about it ..."'

'I didn't say other people,' said Carmen, 'I'm saying *I'm* prepared to struggle and suffer, because that's what being human *is*. In return, I have the right to dream and hope for things.'

'But your dreams will always turn out hollow,' he objected. 'Your hopes will all get crushed and end in disappointment.'

She was about to object, but he went on, 'Even when we love someone, it turns stale and goes wrong. One person grows indifferent and the other person suffers. Or maybe we have a deep love for a parent or a child and something terrible happens to them or they get sick and die. Yes, you can dream and hope, alright, but don't tell me a world like that can offer true happiness!'

His tone was so scathing that she wondered what the world had done to him to make him despise it so, or whether he'd been away from it too long to remember the small, insignificant human moments that made it a thing of wonder.

'Yes, terrible things sometimes happen,' said Carmen. 'But when you're human, that's the chance you take. Good things happen too. Good things come out of struggle as well as bad things. Loving anything's a risk but you can't not do it just because it's dangerous. Maybe you love someone very deeply and then they die and it makes you think life's very cruel ...' She was going to add lightly, 'that's why I don't believe in a God,' but something stopped her – a certain loyal pact between herself and the darkness she had prayed to lately.

The truth was that, every day, she was coming into closer touch with a source of strength and goodness, and as long as it continued to inspire her actions and protect her, she was becoming less particular about whether she called it God or not.

'That's why some people don't believe in God,' she said. 'They can't believe in a God who's callous, who strikes people down at random – and yet, if I had to choose ...' She was formulating the idea even as she spoke and she was surprised at her own certainty. 'I wouldn't exchange a world where people loved and lost and suffered for one where people never suffered but didn't love at all. So, maybe the balance of love and suffering is *necessary*, maybe God made it the way it has to be.'

Gary was shaking his head quite firmly. 'No, God didn't plan the world to be some terrible, frightening lottery. He intended it to be a world of perfect love, a world where we all love one another equally, where we don't have any understanding of sorrow and we feel no pain.'

Carmen grimaced, trying hard to find the idea beautiful, but it just sounded like living under ecstatic anaesthesia.

'But if you loved everyone equally, it wouldn't be love at all,' she said. 'You have to know what it is *not* to love someone to understand what is when you *do* love someone. If there wasn't any suffering and there wasn't any risk of pain, if you could feel the same emotion towards just anyone – well, that wouldn't be love, that would be something else, some sort of lowest common denominator. Maybe this kingdom of yours is full of something else, like good-natured friendliness or something, but it can't be full of love. You can't love everyone equally. You can't spread love out or it just gets thinner.'

She could sense that he was angry but he veiled his eyes and made an effort to speak in a gentle, warm way.

'Love shouldn't be a tawdry, selfish, individualistic thing,' he told her. 'It shouldn't be something that cuts other people out. When it's as powerful as God meant it to be, it's so strong, you couldn't keep it to yourself, you'd want to share it. You'd want to pass it on. This is the meaning of the Messiah's love. A new kind of love, so over-whelming that we can't appreciate it with a selfish heart –' He meant hers. 'The kind of love you see around you in the Family.'

The kind of love she saw around her, Carmen thought, was only cloying camaraderie. It wasn't the sharp, intense yearning of real love that was jealous of its object. She wondered how he could have forgotten what the real thing was.

He sat forward eagerly to press his advantage. 'This is the dream God wanted us to have,' he breathed. 'The dream to end all dreams – and now, at last, it's coming true. A dream that promises the end to sickness, crime and war. It would be the most incredible perversity to say you didn't want it.'

'I don't want it, all the same,' she muttered.

Gary leant back, staring at her with a mounting, incredulous anger. 'The whole history of theological debate has centred round this one dilemma. If there's a God, why does he allow us to suffer? And now someone solves the whole question, logically and scientifically, and gives you the answer on a plate. An answer that generations of theologians and philosophers have prayed for throughout the history of the world. What's more, He gives you the means to eradicate the ills of mankind and what do you say? You say it was a dumb question and you don't *want* it?' He laughed ironically. 'Come on, Carmen, you're an intelligent girl. That really *is* some arrogance.'

He was rattled. She suddenly had a sense that she was on to something. Maybe everyone who had ever passed through those walls, being carried inexorably onwards towards the light as though on a perpetual conveyor belt, maybe they had argued themselves blue in the face about talking snakes, archangels, God's Heart, the Crucifixion and so on, but no-one had ever dared to suggest that the final vision wasn't beautiful. She felt as though she had just glimpsed a lever.

'When the Restoration comes, what are you going to do with people like me who don't want it?' she asked softly.

'Everyone will want it, everyone will come to be re-educated.'

'But that makes it sound like – I don't know – some sort of Communist thought reform.'

'No,' he said impatiently. 'Communist thought reform is Satan's plan. This is God's Plan.'

'But it's the same bloody plan,' she squealed, suddenly infuriated. 'It's just a different ideology.'

The muscles of his face were taut. She had never seen him so twitchy and ill at ease. And her saying 'bloody' was a personal affront.

'The ideology is the crucial point,' he said. 'We have to *defeat* Communism. Satan stole God's beautiful Plan and now we're justified in taking it back and using it for good.'

She could hardly believe what she was hearing. 'But how are you going to defeat the people who aren't Communists, who just don't *want* God's Plan?'

Gary shook his head as though it was unthinkable.

'That's what would happen, Gary,' she said, insistently. 'Believe me – not everyone would want it. People would resist it like they've resisted every great ideology. Believe me, there'll be small caucuses of people who don't want to come.' She made the caucuses small so as not to tax his credulity. She was well on the way to entering fully into his reality in order to put across her point. She felt for a wild moment that if they could meet somewhere in the vast dark future fantasy that was his reality, she could make him see its flaw, and he would have to reject it. She was using all her powers of visualisation to conjure it up for herself. It was like some great dark housing estate on a hill. It was night but every house was blazing with candles and the people inside were smiling and radiant and their faces were bland and empty. They weren't doing anything, because there wasn't anything to do. Matthew was leading a singing crocodile of members down the hillside. They were heading towards the only darkened house. The house was barred and locked but there was a telltale crucifix in the neglected window, and for a fleeting moment, some pale and frightened faces pulled back the curtain and peered out at the joyful, purposeful members as they grouped around the door, singing with determined menace:

> 'Consider yourself at home
> Consider yourself one of the Family
> We've taken to you so strong
> It's clear we're going to get along...
> Consider yourself our mate...
> We don't want to have no fuss...'

The thought almost made her laugh, although it was not so funny when she thought how bright Gary was, how his intelligence had been warped and harnessed to this impossible dream.

'Believe me, it wouldn't work,' she said sensibly. 'There'd be people who'd resist. You couldn't get them to a Centre, let alone to listen to a lecture. What will the Family do then? Will they use force? And if force doesn't work, will they kill them, or what? If you have Perfect Love, you can't use force, you can't kill people, can you?'

She was so sure that she understood the concept of Perfect Love that she expected him to agree straight away. Gary hesitated. Carmen realised with a shock, then, that Perfect Love did not necessarily exclude force or violence.

'I mean,' she said carefully, her eyes closely watching his face, 'you couldn't get rid of sin and crime and suffering by committing sin and crime and causing suffering, now could you?'

'Well, it would depend,' Gary said in an off-hand way. 'Sometimes God has to use Satan's tools to undo Satan's evil works.'

'Oh,' said Carmen. She thought quickly. 'Is that why Reverend Moon has the armaments factory?'

'Where did you hear that?' asked Gary, but only as though it was of passing interest. He didn't seem shocked or try to deny it.

'I can't remember now. I just heard it,' she said. 'I assumed the press just made it up.'

'Look, killing isn't necessarily wrong, particularly not in wars,' he said. 'And particularly not in the Last Battle, in the holiest war of all. There might be circumstances where a small evil could contribute to the greater good. I'm not saying that's so in the Family,' he added hastily. 'I mean, some of these questions are a bit far advanced for me. You know I'm not very high up in the Family. I'm still only learning myself. The person to ask would be a Centre leader.'

'But you're committed to this. This is going to happen in your lifetime,' she said, appalled. 'Surely you must know what you're committed to? Surely you must have thought it through?'

Gary had a troubled look on his face. She had a feeling that he was really thinking with his old random brain. His eyes were narrowed and he looked almost as though he was in pain. She could almost hear the wheels of the mechanism creaking with disuse.

'When God's on your side,' he said, 'when you're fighting for God and the salvation of the world...' She had the sense that he was running through the lectures in his head in order to make a correct deduction. 'If the whole human race depends on your victory, then sometimes it might even be better for a person that they got killed... I mean, if someone was going to lose their soul to Satan, it might be better for them in the end just to lose their body in this world...' He gave up, his face strained with the effort of thought, and shook his head. 'I'm not sure,' he said in a normal voice. 'You'd have to ask a Centre leader. Ask Matthew, he'd be able to tell you.'

Carmen stared up into the night sky. It was irrational to give their megalomaniac vision any credence but since she had broken through the barrier into envisaging the reality of what they saw ahead, she felt compelled to make him go further.

In her own mind, the jolly band of pilgrims that were bearing down on the shuttered house were now carrying pick-axe handles and beginning to batter down the door. What was more, other cheerful crocodiles of God's soldiers were bearing down on other shuttered houses, in the towns and cities, bearing their inexorable good news, waving free samples of their ginseng tea and brandishing their Korean machine guns. They were dragging people out into the street and loading whole families into Oceanic Seafood fish vans to take them off for re-education.

'What if people put up barricades and burn cars and...' she cast wildly around, 'sabotage the Family's re-education camps? And there you are, standing at your gun post with an Armalite rifle. You might have a bunch of old women and children in your sights. You might have *me* in your sights, for that matter,' she added. 'What are you going to do then, ask your Centre leader? Don't you want to know what you're committed to? Don't you want to know what the furthest extension of your commitment *is*?'

'I don't know,' he said remotely. 'God's Plan is perfectly logical and it has to succeed, so whatever God told us through the Centre leaders, that would be right. Nothing must stand in the way of God's Plan this time, otherwise everything's lost.'

'What if it's me in your sights? Will you kill me?'

He sighed. 'Oh, this is a pointless discussion. You're just pushing it to ridiculous extremes. Why are we talking about killing people? Why can't we dwell on the wonderful happiness everyone's going to experience when the world is free from sin?'

'Because if you're asking me to get involved with this movement, there are certain things I have to know. Things that don't add up. Like, for instance, in the love lecture, Matthew said "Love overcomes ideology" and that's true, isn't it? You couldn't shoot your own mother? If it came down to it, your love for your mother would overcome your ideology.'

His eyes were evasive. 'Love overcomes ideology,' he agreed, cautiously, 'and Perfect Love overcomes *all* ideologies.'

She stopped, confused. Was that logical? Was he saying the same thing or the direct opposite? They seemed to have a trick with words that always made everything mean its opposite. She felt tired and confused again. Suddenly, it didn't seem so shocking, after all. It had only seemed shocking initially because organised Christian religions usually opposed killing. But then, didn't the established churches

sanction atomic weapons which went strictly against the command-
ments, and was the Family's vision any worse than what one read
about Khomeini? It was only a mite more expansionist, that was all.
And then they didn't talk about chopping people's hands off or sum-
mary executions, and what was more, the Family's vision was only a
dream that couldn't be put into practice.

Gary took his opportunity to regain control of the conversation.

'But really, Carmen, I think it's you that's being unrealistic. You
have to take things in by stages or the whole thing will over-
whelm you. You're trying to run before you've learnt to walk.
Principle has to be unfolded gently or of course you'll find it very
confusing.'

Carmen was still turning it over in her mind, still trying to work
out whether it was reasonable to find it disturbing. It seemed to her
that, if the Restoration of the world was possible, which it was not,
then there would be cause to be disturbed, but since it was not possible, it was equally disturbing that these perfectly pleasant and ordinary people around her should be turning themselves, somehow,
into programmed robots for a hopeless cause. But she was not in a
good mental state to decide what was disturbing and what wasn't.
People believed some strange things in the name of religion.

'What if it's a lie?' she asked suddenly.

He seemed to be singing busily under his breath, which she found
an incongruous reaction to such an important question.

'What if it's all a gigantic con?'

Suddenly he stopped singing and looked at her, a direct fierce
proud look, as though her question was both impertinent and beneath contempt.

'If it's a lie, it's a beautiful lie and I give myself to it freely,' he said.
He got to his feet and helped her up. 'But you see, it isn't. And you
know in your heart it isn't. The very fact that you ask means you're
frightened. If it wasn't true, what would there be to be frightened of?
But there *is* something to be frightened of. It's an incredible, frightening beautiful Truth. You didn't ask for it but now you've heard it,
you can't walk away from it – and that's frightening.'

Carmen kept her eyes down. She had no problem at all in turning
down this Truth and she would have even less problem walking
away from it. It wasn't frightening. It was terrifying.

'So,' he said lightly, 'Shall I put you down for the Twenty-One Day?'

She had a wild desire to laugh. She buried her face in her hands to stifle it. It was only late-night hysteria, but the constant switching between enormous global concepts and complete mind-boggling inanity seemed too startlingly absurd. She made an effort to control herself, her hands steepled round her nose and mouth, her eyes serious.

'I'll pray about it,' she assured him, and with that he had to be content. As they walked into the house the laughter captive at the back of her throat subsided and changed into something else entirely sombre. It wasn't funny that he was trapped inside a lie. It wasn't funny that he should live twenty-four hours a day in another reality, without release. It wasn't funny if they'd wrought these violent changes on her own sister.

Once inside the hall, she wove her way towards Jane and hissed in an undertone, 'They *are* prepared to use violence, you know.' But Jane just waved her hand wearily as though she found Carmen's persistence too tiresome.

'Give it a rest,' she said. 'Can't you just appreciate the good things?' She circled her arm affectionately around Carmen's waist and drew her close as the next song began. 'Just listen to the singing. It's so beautiful. How can something so beautiful be wrong?' she asked, and she began to sing.

Carmen began to sing too. It seemed to be the only thing to do, because there was nobody, no-one at all, who shared her view that it was sinister. So maybe it wasn't sinister or maybe it just wasn't worth worrying about. After all, she couldn't change it. It was going ahead anyway, with her or without her: anyway, it was only an idea, and who could be afraid of an idea?

She began to sway with Jane as the voices rose. It was a triumphant, martial song – one of Carmen's favourites.

'Dawn, Golden Dawn
Throughout the shining Fatherland
Brings the tidings of the Rising Sun
That gives us life...'

That night, she was called upon to give in her Book Of Reflections

202

for inspection. She sat on the floor, scrutinising it carefully for slips or errors in her thinking.

The book was filled mostly with lame, vaguely spiritual waffle which she had written to confuse Pamela, who insisted on reading the thing every night. Thus, the latest paragraph read, 'Went to bed very tired after a very powerful day. Lecture very inspiring. What a wonderful world it would be if everyone could sing and smile and look at flowers all day. However, I do have a few questions: 1. If you can't go to Spirit World without a body, how come Adolf Hitler's there? Perhaps he did not die in the bunker after all? What information do we have on this? 2. Dinosaurs. I did not understand what Matthew said. Gary said God was just trying out a few things before He settled on the perfect shape. I think this most unlikely. When I asked Matthew, he said dinosaurs were God's idea of a joke. Who was God having this joke with?'

The questions went down to the bottom of the page in a small, spiky hand which was most unlike her normal writing. There were so many questions and many of them were so bizarre that she had a surreal sense of displacement as she ran her eye down them. It was as though her reality had split off into distinct and separate strands. She spent most of her time now operating in the alternative reality, and even these scribblings which pretended to represent her private feelings were couched in those terms. What *she* considered to be real – the everyday level of life where she was a certain person with a certain past and a certain personality – to the Family, this was not reality at all.

In fact, she herself had no reality for them outside her commitment to the group and its philosophy. Since they dictated the terms on which human interaction took place, she was being forced to spend more and more time in *their* reality and outside her own. She wondered dimly if this could be in any way harmful to her, this schizophrenic flitting between two different systems of thought. It was certainly very tiring, but more than that, she worried whether the alternative reality which was structured, minimalised and controlled from above could come to seem more vivid than the pale and random narrative of normal free-form thinking.

'My, you've been busy,' said Pamela when she took Carmen's book and added it to the pile. Then she bent to zip up Carmen's sleeping bag as though Carmen was a little girl, and wished her sweet dreams.

As Carmen lay in her bag that night, she tossed and turned and thought it over and over. She examined all her fears and found them justified; then she examined them again and found them to be demonstrations of the most extreme paranoia. Why was she so frightened of these people who others continually told her were very very nice, indeed, who *were* very nice? They had confused her, yes, but there was no law against confusing people. They had made her say and do things she didn't want to say and do, but she was a free agent, she could always have refused – only it hadn't seemed possible to refuse at the time. There was no law against manipulating people into doing things they didn't want to: society itself ran that way and people who could do it were admired. Maybe they *had* hypnotised her, but there was no law against that either as far as she knew. They hadn't used it to do any harm, only so that the flowers should seem more beautiful. But it was more likely that she and Jane had just been very overtired and paranoid that day, making themselves more susceptible to hallucination. There was no law against making someone tired and there was no law against serving poor food and there was no law against making people sing. Surely, if there was anything wrong, there would be a law against it. If there *was* no law against it then logically there could be nothing wrong. She flounced over onto her other side and let out a loud sigh. A sister shushed her, although she might have done better to shush the other sisters who were all snoring like pigs. This reality, that reality, it all began to jumble together and sound like nonsense in her head.

And then again the impossible conundrum. Wasn't Lucy the sanest person in the world? Wasn't she one of the two people that Carmen knew most completely? Hadn't Jane and Peter and Reg seemed sane at the outset of the course? But they had each paid their twelve pounds and the miracle had been wrought on them.

Deep down, she was beginning to wonder about herself. She suspected that it was arrogance for her to assume that she was completely sane. After all, she hadn't tested herself against truly sane people for a long long time. Five days in fact. Sanity was relative, and she was beginning to understand that it needed a constant touchstone.

Chapter 8

The following day was the final day: the day when they proved the existence of the Messiah beyond logical human doubt. But as Matthew began his lecture, Carmen felt again that floating, unattached, disorientated sensation, as though she was walking on shifting sand. The idea was to compare the significant dates Before Christ with the significant dates Anno Domini, and thereby calculate the probable date of the arrival of the Lord Of The Second Advent, but as Matthew chalked the time blocks on the board, she had the feeling that historical dates were being shamelessly bent to fit into the pattern, that years were being lopped off here and there, rounded up or rounded down to make the chart look plausible. He was juxtaposing major historical figures and movements with extremely minor ones and giving them all the same weight, so that the time periods appeared to make a rational pattern from Old Testament times right up to World War Two.

She knew it wasn't true, she knew that history did not fall into those neat compartments, but it was so breathtakingly shameless that she could only sit there bewildered with her mouth half open. Yet she knew why no-one protested. The guests were all, by now, so dazzled and befuddled and trusting that Matthew could have told them black was white, it would have made no difference. He could have held up three fingers and told them there were five and they would have nodded. Even those people amongst the guests who looked uneasy, who were shuffling in their seats, couldn't pin down exactly what was wrong, and nor could Carmen. She didn't know the date of Swedenborg's manifesto or the circumstances surrounding the establishment of left-wing Hegelianism, she had never heard of Edward Herbert and her knowledge of Pietism was rather sketchy. She just knew that Matthew's whole time-chart of history, logical as it looked blocked out there in authoritative teacher's chalk, was nonsense.

Matthew was saying, 'In 1818 we have the first of Satan's

Messiahs. In 1848 he published the first Communist manifesto of atheism justifying violent revolution,' he wrote that down, 'which we know took place in 1917, bringing with it the reality of materialistic atheism. This was like the "perfection stage" of Satan's ideology. So, Satan is like the lion in lamb's clothing here...'

At last, he seemed to approach his summing-up. The board was pretty well full by now. 'So we can see from this scientific breakdown of the time periods of history, that there has never *ever* in the whole history of civilisation been more than a two point five per cent error. So this is scientific fact. The Lord Of The Second Advent *has* to come between 1917 and 1930 in order to fit in with that two point five per cent error factor. So this is very interesting, isn't it?'

Interesting? The guests were on the edge of their seats, some stunned and stupefied, taking in the information, some merely alert and watchful, waiting for the expected revelation. The air was electric. The members had the contented, enraptured expressions of children hearing a wonderful and oft-told story that was always fresh with wonder.

'So this is the most significant news that a human being could ever expect to hear.' He gazed sombrely around the room, his eyes strained, as though it was also the greatest responsibility to divulge it. He put down his piece of chalk and carefully dusted his hands before he moved forward to the centre of the room. 'Yes. You're saying to yourselves, "This man is probably alive today." In fact, the Messiah was born in 1920.'

There was absolute silence. No-one coughed, no-one moved. Matthew looked pensively at the ground. The room waited with bated breath for him to continue but he only leant towards the desk for support with the air of a man who was totally drained and overcome.

He looked up and gave a wan, boyish smile. 'This is what the time periods tell us.'

The audience was agog, but Matthew still refrained from naming Him. It was as though he was allowing them to follow a paper-chase trail, teasing them with clues, except that the clues were not so much like hints as enormous, inescapable signposts.

Everyone was buzzing in a fever of excitement as they filed out to the dining room. It was extraordinary to Carmen how this motley bunch of people who, only a week ago, would have had no particular interest in the advent of a New Messiah, or who would have been extremely sceptical if an imminent Korean Messiah had been mooted, were now as excited as a litter of puppies. Maybe it was the fact that the information was so very secret and disclosed to so few people, maybe it was the fact that they'd been forced to undergo so many trials and hardships to receive the information that it was now immeasurably enhanced, and the knowledge seemed incredibly valuable and privileged.

In the main hall groups of members were draping festoons of crepe paper along the walls in preparation for the Family Evening. There was an air of quiet excitement in their terse exchanges, a sense of alert anticipation. They were like children made self-important by the knowledge of a great secret, exquisitely braced by the effort of concealment. Of course she knew what the secret was. It was only a matter of amazement to her that no-one else seemed to have guessed – or maybe they were all playing at being good sports, like wise adults, pretending good-naturedly to be in the dark, allowing the members to unfurl the secret slowly like a drama. Tonight the guests would all ooh and aah at each new revelation like kiddies at a pantomime. She stared up at the portrait of Sun Meung Moon, which two members were manoeuvring into the place of honour. His eyes watched her as she walked this way and that, like the eyes of the Laughing Cavalier but without the roguish twinkle.

At lunch, Marianne stepped forward, trembling with self-importance and excitement. She stilled the babble in the room with a peremptory peal from her small brass bell.

'Tonight,' she said with a beaming smile of contentment, 'tonight, we throw a surprise party for Heavenly Father.' There was an immediate barrage of spontaneous, uproarious appreciation but Marianne put her finger to her lips in sudden agitation. 'Hush, hush, hush,' she insisted in mock distress. 'No, you have not understood...' Silence fell, for otherwise they could hardly catch her little breathy voice. 'It's a *surprise* party. We do not let Heavenly Father know what we plan for Him, or it will not be a big surprise...'

Then everyone looked wise and began to patter-clap silently on their palms, the silent two-finger clap that they sometimes used.

'We put on our very best clothes, the best clothes we have, and look very neat and tidy in His honour. And we must talk very quietly about our preparations so that we make Him cry with pleasure and surprise!'

There was much schoolgirlish giggling and frivolity in the sisters' dormitory as they dressed for the last Family Evening. Sisters in various states of undress were plaiting and pleating each other's hair and lending each other dresses and hair combs. Carmen found the excitement infectious: even if it was childish and silly, there was an air of freedom and fun that gave an enormous sense of relief after the usual atmosphere of repression and constraint.

She was pleased they'd got their Messiah now if it meant that the iron sisters could unbend a little bit.

As she dipped to look at herself in the six-inch square of mirror, her reflection gave her quite a shock. She looked so strange. Her skin was pale and waxen, and her eyes were enormous in comparison with the small, thin face. Her pupils were dilated like cat's eyes, so that the black seemed to take up a great deal more space than ever before, encroaching on the grey of the iris.

She offered her perfume spray around the sisters but they shrank from it as though she were offering them a squirt of paraquat.

The high spot of the evening was the film. It was all about Reverend Moon, only the soundtrack called him Father. He strode around the corridors of the great New York skyscraper, his bland, inscrutable face set in hard lines as he moved with fierce righteousness, scattering salt to right and left, consecrating the floors of his new acquisition, accompanied by a posse of disciples in dark suits who looked like hit men. The soundtrack was Handel's 'Messiah' and it proclaimed him with thrilling conviction as he moved inexorably through the frame, dispersing the evil spirits like Jesus turning over the tables of the money-lenders.

> 'Prince Of Peace
> Lord Of Lords
> Allelujah, Allelujah
> Alle-lu-jah...'

The music rose and swelled, filling the blood of the enthralled watchers, complementing the scenes of the massed stadium rallies where a million people filled the screen like writhing dots underneath his monumental banners. Moon himself stood on the podium, a tiny figure in a business suit, letting out explosive bursts of martial-sounding Korean rhetoric that sent ecstatic shimmers through the great massed army of his followers.

Carmen sat in the darkness, her eyes wide with awe and alarm. Rally followed rally. Washington Monument, Madison Square Gardens, Yankee Stadium, the Rally for Korean Freedom: at every fresh location, a vast blurred ocean of followers acclaimed their diminutive Messiah.

'Six thousand years of history has been waiting for this man to come,' the soundtrack breathed in a reverent American drawl. 'Externally, he's an ordinary man but internally he's quite different. His heart is totally pure and sinless...' The music softened to a lilting sentimental harp piece as the camera moved in on a shot of Father relaxing in a luxuriant garden.

Carmen watched distrustfully as the poor quality film exaggerated the pores of Reverend Moon's face and lent him an unhealthy colour, so that he looked like a green pancake with two tadpole eyes. She could discern nothing benign or trustworthy there at all, no matter how he smiled or joshed around with the cameraman.

The image dissolved to Reverend Moon standing with his bride, a beautiful Korean woman, Hak Ja Han, soft-filtered, bathed in a celestial light, the two of them fiercely proud and regal in their white robes and their paper crowns.

The commentary breathed reverently, 'One man, who comes the suffering way through torment and hardship, to bring on earth God's true mission. One man with the absolute purity to restore the bloodline, to establish the Perfect Family. And, as this great world-wide movement marches forward... As the Kingdom Of Heaven approaches before our eyes...'

The Family of Moon stood before the massed stadium of support-ers. Lord and Lady Moon, the True Parents of the World stared out at the rippling sea of followers, their twelve perfect children lined up before them in their best clothes. '... His mission is almost complete... And, as for us ... It is the great miracle for we True Children of the One World Family, it is the divine blessing that we shall see the culmination of human history in our own life-time, knowing that we have played our part in bringing God's Providence to pass...'

And, as the 'Messiah' began to rise triumphantly over the smiling faces, Carmen was aware of the members around her in the hall rising to their feet with one accord and beginning to clap and howl and cheer and whistle. The noise went on for several minutes after the end of the film had flicked through the projector, plunging them into darkness. When the lights illuminated the room, she realised that those who were not stamping and voicing their appreciation were sobbing quietly.

Even Gary, who sat beside her stunned and still, had his mouth slightly ajar and there were traces of tears on his face.

The graduation ceremony followed. It was an emotive affair. Each guest stepped up in a sprightly fashion to the platform, shook Matthew's hand, received their graduation scroll and made a speech. The atmosphere, at once euphoric and overwhelmingly supportive, spurred each guest on to make a more effusive speech. Carmen merely mumbled an inadequate vote of general thanks and bolted back to her seat with her diploma to muted applause. She was already making the mental leap back to the reality she knew.

Reg broke down on the platform. He was wearing a surprising country-and-western suit with fancy lapels and a tic-tac tie. He got the biggest hand of all, but she was glad and relieved to hear that he was going home because of commitments to his own church.

'I shall say to my brothers in the lay ministry, I have investigated this movement and I have found it good,' he pronounced, his chin jutting out belligerently like Winston Churchill. 'I shall tell the organisers of the Boys Brigade that they have nothing to fear for their children, and the same goes for the Boy Scouts. There's love here, there's true values and there's dignity. I myself have been changed...' and just then his voice cracked and his face crumpled. He was unable to go on, but the room rose to him as he stood there, feebly turning over his parchment scroll, while Matthew supported him.

Carmen turned and slipped away. There was a lump in her throat and her eyes were scalding. She didn't want to hear Jane give her speech. She sat out on the step and unrolled the mock diploma. It was handwritten in a poor but proud copper-plate saying that she had completed the Seven Day Course Of Divine Principle, and there were hand-pressed wild flowers stuck upon the paper. A tear spilt and splattered out across a cornflower.

Someone cleared their throat behind her. She didn't need to turn. She knew it was Gary.

'Are you OK?' he asked in a low voice. She felt him there, some distance away, watching her.

'Yes,' she answered distantly. 'Why?'

'I don't know.' Gary shrugged and ambled closer, his hands in the pockets of his suit. 'All the time, even when you're sitting beside me, I can feel you resisting things. Everything about you says you don't want to know what's going on here. That you think you're not involved – '

'I'm going home,' she said practically. 'That means I *am* uninvolved.'

He sniffed. 'You'll find out just how uninvolved you are when you get back. The strange thing is the Family stays with you long after you leave it.'

She let it pass. She imagined it would be hard to get the songs out of her head, that she would feel withdrawal symptoms from the constant company, that everyday life for some while after might seem bland and poorly paced, but she was prepared for that.

'There's no point in your trying to persuade me,' she began in a warning voice.

'I don't want to persuade you,' he said. 'It's your decision.'

Carmen suddenly felt a little peeved that he was giving up on her soul so easily.

'I know why you're going home,' he said reluctantly. 'I realised it tonight. It's my fault. I shouldn't say this, but . . .'

She waited.

'But, well, you know, it's possible . . . even for members . . . you know, even members . . . even though they've made a lot of spiritual growth – it's still possible for members to relate on a fallen level . . .' He was having such enormous difficulty articulating it that Carmen was riveted. 'There's still the danger, people still have to be watchful – because if they're relating horizontally, then that's a big problem because it's very hard for them to help that person. It may be that, effectively, they even hold them back.'

Carmen watched him with an alert look on her face. 'What does it mean? Explain it to me properly.'

He frowned and tried again. 'Well, Eve and Lucifer shouldn't have been in a horizontal relationship with one another. Lucifer should have guided and instructed spiritually but he had the sin of resentment, and if we examine the idea of the Fruit Of The Tree Of Good And Evil . . .'

Carmen was so irritated to find herself at the receiving end of a lecture, just when she had believed him on the brink of a revelation, that she spoke with more impatience than she intended. 'Oh, don't give me the Fall Of Man lecture, Gary. I'm on my way out, not coming in.'

He recoiled slightly as though she'd insulted him.

'I'm just saying it's my failure, that's all.'

She supposed then that he would have to pay indemnity and set himself some hard Conditions for that failure. She felt responsible once she realised that, and yet, how could she be held responsible for the punishments he was going to inflict upon himself?

'But you haven't failed,' she said gently. 'Can't you just tell them I made up my own mind? I mean, I was always negative. I was negative from the start.'

'That makes no difference,' he said testily, as though she was totally incapable of understanding and he wished he'd never broached it in the first place. 'If you haven't been able to understand, it's because there's something getting in the way. If the Adam figure doesn't raise the Eve figure up, then the Eve figure can drag him down.'

'Oh,' said Carmen. The idea of herself as a femme fatale had a certain tarnished appeal.

Just then, they heard the strains of 'Father' starting up. Gary got to his feet and Carmen followed.

'Don't forget me,' he said. It seemed strange to her that he gave her up so lightly, unless this was some ploy, unless all over the gaunt Victorian house, brothers were haltingly declaring their failures to their gullible female guests, while the sisters fluttered their eyelashes submissively at the recalcitrant males. She didn't think that was the case. For one thing, Gary was sweating, and she had never seen a brother sweat with emotion before, only from a hearty game of sport.

Inside the hall, the guests were swaying like rolling waves in a sea of emotion. Jane affectionately pulled her close and she began to sway with the rhythm of the mass. It was the most beautiful, sweet, sad, addictive song. Pamela came and put her arm round her on the other side and they hung together like that, moving ecstatically to the music and gave full voice to the words.

> 'Father, you went through the nights
> alone
> Opened the way to free the earth
> Father, a Unified World is at hand
> No-one can ever stop you now...
>
> It's a New Dawn
> I see it grow
> Stronger and clearer day by day
> Saving the people
> Bringing the whole wide world
> Into New Hope...'

Carmen gave herself up to the delirium. If they needed this Messiah, why should she begrudge Him to them? They seemed so ecstatic, so alive.

The music seemed to wash over her, cleansing her blood as her heart pumped it to her nerve endings, to the very tips of her fingers. It wasn't a matter of singing in the Family, it was a matter of giving one's heart, soul and body to the massed sound and, in so giving, wiping away all thoughts, all anxiety and manufacturing in its place, as though from nowhere, a great store of optimism, a sense of communal invincibility and overwhelming love for those around who were sharing that unique experience.

When the song finished, Carmen felt quite weak. Her conversation with Gary had lost its significance, nothing seemed important when balanced against that great tidal wave of emotion. Pamela's little hand found Carmen's and squeezed it so that the bones jostled together.

'Have you ever seen love like it?' she whispered. Carmen shook her head. 'When you're miserable and lonely and people let you down, remember this moment. Hold it in your heart. The Family needs you.' Carmen smiled affectionately back at her and there was a lump in her throat at Pamela's pleading, hopeful face, shining with sincerity.

No, sooner had Pamela released her than Marianne enfolded her with soft, pulpy arms and held her close, nuzzling her face affectionately like a puppy. 'Ah, Carmen, you give us many struggles,' she confided, 'but now you see the importance of it all. I have a surprise for you upstairs in the dormitory,' Marianne said.

'Oh, Marianne, you shouldn't have,' Carmen protested. She knew what it would be. A folding padded picture wallet with two gilded frames. It seemed to be the standard gift that all the members gave the guests. At the beginning of the week some of the lucky recipients had misunderstood and inserted pictures of their parents or their family dogs but she had noticed throughout the day that some of the guests were removing their parents and pets now and replacing them with the rightful pictures of Sun Meung Moon and his wife. Now Carmen had, at last, earned one of her own. The picture frame was the only possession that the members carried with them apart from their toothbrushes.

But, as she mounted the stairs towards the dormitory, there was the clatter of footsteps on the stairwell high above her, and then a sharp intake of breath and a voice calling, 'Carmen, Carmen, is it really you?' In that frozen moment she looked up, knowing suddenly that the surprise was not a picture frame, and there was Lucy skidding to an abrupt halt on the landing above, now leaning down from the balustrade, her eyes wide with pleasure, her face gleaming with excitement and the neon behind her haloing her pale, eager face. Carmen felt her heart lift up, for it was suddenly all worthwhile. The next moment Lucy was running pell-mell down the staircase, clasping her in an affectionate bear hug with little cries of delight, and Carmen was laughing too, but she was crying and she found her nose pressed into the creamy soapy smell of Lucy's skin.

'I couldn't believe it!' Lucy shouted. 'I still can't! I just can't believe my eyes! It's really, really you, and you're here!' She held Carmen at arm's length, brushing the tears from her own cheek with familiar, skinny, nail-bitten fingers. 'All the way down here in the van, I kept saying I couldn't believe it until I saw you with my own eyes, and now I see you and I *still* don't believe it . . .' And nor did Carmen.

They stood there, laughing and searching each other's faces as though one or other of them might vanish into thin air before they'd looked their fill.

Carmen felt an overwhelming mixture of conflicting emotions threatening to explode in her chest – with the mawkish sweetness of everything that happened that night, the climax and anti-climax of getting through the week unscathed, and now, just as she had given Lucy up for lost, the surprise and sheer joy of finding she had given up too soon – here was Lucy, standing in front of her. All the things that she had planned to say, the reproaches that were on her lips about the long months when they'd imagined she was in a hospital somewhere or lying injured in a ditch or dead, all just melted magically away. Suddenly there was nothing in her heart towards the Family but gratitude and nothing in her head but the absolute rock-solid certainty that everything was going to be alright. A sure knowledge that the bond between them was stronger than could be broken by any false Messiah; that whatever hold they had on Lucy, she could claw her back.

'What do you think? Isn't it wonderful?' asked Lucy and her face was anxious for a second, as though she was pleading with Carmen to agree. 'Isn't it the most extraordinary place in the world?'

Carmen smiled and nodded. She could afford to be generous to them now. The main thing was to have found Lucy.

'We were *so* worried about you,' Carmen told her gently. 'We went to the police. We were *frantic* with worry. Didn't it occur to you we'd be going out of our minds?'

'But you must have known there was nothing to worry about,' said Lucy. 'What was there to be worried about? I'm home. And now *you're* home...'

Carmen studied her face. It was drained of colour and her hair was drawn back in an unbecoming scarf. She had put on a little weight and there were cold sores round her mouth. But most of all, her eyes were blanched and lighter than Carmen remembered them. They were blank. They were as empty and distant as a clear, blue sky. She felt her heart contract, but Lucy was still bubbling over with excitement.

'I've just been *so* twitchy all week knowing you were here, wondering when I'd see you, how it'd be. What you'd make of everything...'

She embraced her all over again but Carmen stiffened.

'You knew I was here?'

Lucy nodded, surprised. 'They told me you were here but, well, I was busy...' she laughed, half embarrassed, 'Well, the truth is, I wasn't ready. They thought I wasn't ready, you know. And you weren't ready. But now – '

'We're ready?' asked Carmen.

Lucy wheedled her arm affectionately into Carmen's. 'Oh, I think so. I hope so. I mean, if I'd seen you earlier in the week, maybe you would just have been trying to persuade me to go home with you or something but now you've heard Principle, now you know how *important* it is...' She smiled trustingly. 'Well, now it's all going to be such fun and we can go on the Twenty-One Day together.'

Carmen stared at her in appalled incomprehension. 'But I'm not going on the Twenty-One Day!'

A look of bewildered hurt crossed Lucy's face. 'Well, how will you get to see me unless you come? *Of course* you're coming – I don't want to lose you just when I've found you.'

'You haven't found me,' Carmen hissed. 'I've found you, and if you don't want to lose me, then you have to come home. Please, Lucy, just come home. *Please.* Even if it's only for a few days. You can't think clearly here. This whole thing's crazy. How can you think things out with all this madness going on around you?' Her hands were clutching the spare folds in the bodice of Lucy's ugly, ill-fitting little dress and she was shaking her with urgent desperation.

'I don't think that's a very nice thing to say,' Lucy reproved her quietly, and then she disentangled Carmen's hands and assumed a remarkable and uncharacteristic composure. 'Honestly, Carmen, if that's all the development you've made, I don't know if you're ready for the Twenty-One Day after all.'

Carmen could only stare at her with useless, stricken misery because there was nowhere for her fury to go. It just bounced off Lucy. This person *wasn't* Lucy. It was a carbon copy of all the others, mouthing the same phrases with the same implacable, madonna-like calm. Carmen had thought she was prepared for it, but how could she have been prepared to see another person in possession of her sister's body? How could she have been prepared to hear that calm, blank, sweet voice of reason out of a face she knew as well as she knew her own, that was so like hers it might almost have been her own?

'I'm not going on the Twenty-One Day,' she repeated dully. 'I didn't come to hear Principle. I only came for you.'

Chapter 9

After the Sunday morning prayer service, the fleet of silver coaches began to draw out, and Carmen was amongst those who flung their bags into the hold. Jane and Pamela were so delighted she was going with them that they started a round of applause amongst the brothers gathered on the forecourt.

Halfway to Wiltshire, they drove into bad weather, and Carmen sat silent, her thigh pressed of necessity against Gary's thigh, staring moodily from the rain-streaked windows as the towns gave way to country and bleak, angry open skies. Now she had an inexplicable sense of foreboding, as though she were being taken away from all things familiar, being sucked further and further inwards to the centre of something which she didn't understand.

Curiously intense and insistent, the voices filtered through, competing with the high-pitched steady throb as the van sped along the motorway, the conifers that fringed the asphalt blurring into a frieze that ran away from them.

> 'I'm on my way
> And I won't look back
> I'm on my way
> And I won't look back
> I'm on my way and I won't look back
> I'm on my way, Great God, I'm on my way...
> I'm on my way to Freedomland...
> I'm on my way to Freedomland...'

It was half past ten at night when they finally arrived. The journey should have taken five hours, but they had dropped off bundles of their street pamphlet One World to various of their Centre houses, all far off the route. With each stop they had lost their bearings, held animated joyful conferences over the map, and then hared off confidently to get lost in maze-like one-way systems, shooting off with blind and unquenchable enthusiasm to follow signs that led them into eerie deserted empty streets beside high factory walls.

No-one grew down-hearted, apart from Carmen who was so weary and disorientated that she felt like a blindfolded kidnap victim. By the time they reached their destination, they had been travelling for so long that she formed the idea they were somewhere near the tip of Cornwall.

In the darkness, the house seemed very large and quite remote, set back a long way from the country road and with grounds behind it that seemed to stretch for infinity until they merged with the purpling sky. The lights were blazing in the downstairs windows and, as they walked from the coach, kicking up the gravel, a familiar, powerful song met their ears from the hundred throats within. Then, Carmen experienced a queer pang of inevitability, as though they had travelled a hundred miles to find themselves in exactly the same place.

The new house mother greeted them at the door with a cold but cordial smile. She was a crisp American-German woman called Adèle, rather beautiful in a severe way, with startling green eyes and a mass of black, wavy hair, restrained by a neat black ribbon. She wore an outfit like a plain-clothes policewoman, a stern serge skirt, white blouse and heavy shoes, but the clothes only heightened the sensuality of her body. A large tangle of solid keys jangled from her narrow hip as she led them through the gloomy corridor towards the hall.

The weary guests were already beginning to sing along as they trooped behind her, and when they reached the crowded dining room, they romped in joyfully like paddlers jumping in to a pool. Only Carmen hung back, sullen and conspicuous in her lack of joy.

When the meal was served, she and Lucy both crouched fervently in private prayers, each of them praying to their different God: Carmen praying hard that Lucy would decide to leave and Lucy praying thankfully that Carmen had come to stay. Lucy emerged first. When Carmen surfaced, she caught a fleeting look of calculation move across Lucy's face like a shadow, but the next moment she wondered if she had been mistaken, because Lucy's features settled into an expression of doleful reproach.

'You know what I think the problem is?' she said in a cosy voice with a hint of accusation. 'I don't think you're really trying. I don't think you really *want* to believe it.'

Carmen felt a familiar twinge in her temple. She made an effort to control her irritation. Recognising that Lucy's technique was more effective, she tried to adopt the same light, bantering tone of utter reasonableness.

'There isn't a problem,' she said. 'I just don't believe any of it, that's all. And even if I wanted to believe it, that wouldn't actually affect whether a thing was true or not, don't you see?'

Lucy was looking at her with such alert interest that, for a wild moment, Carmen thought she might be getting somewhere. She leant forward impulsively to press her advantage.

'Look, Lucy, no matter how many people believe something, it doesn't necessarily mean it's true.'

'No,' Lucy agreed with a comfortable smile. 'The dictionary definition of truth is "that which is in accordance with the facts". And Father's the only man who's ever been in a position to find out the facts. That's why there's so many people out there . . .' she indicated the fallen world with a nod of her head, 'still believing there's no pattern to the world.'

Carmen let out a small unhappy sigh. There was absolutely no point. It was the same brick wall, no matter how enthusiastically you butted your head against it.

Lucy began to pile meat piously onto Carmen's plate, and Carmen watched the pyramid grow with a sense of despair. 'And once we have the facts, Carmen,' Lucy levelled her eyes seriously, 'we have to face them. We can't pretend we haven't understood. But there's no hurry, and, as you start to grow closer to Father . . .'

Carmen gave an obstinate flounce. 'I don't want to disappoint you, Lucy, but I don't think I can get much closer to Father. I actually don't find him all that sympathetic. I mean, maybe he's very charismatic or something but, so far, I can't see it. When do we get to meet him? Maybe I'll understand it when I see him in the flesh?'

Lucy smiled enigmatically, as though Carmen had said something that was touchingly naive.

'Oh, I've never see Him,' she said. 'He's very busy with the Restoration. He doesn't come to England much. But maybe I'll go to America or Japan or somewhere. I'd *like* to see Him,' she shrugged regretfully, 'but it really doesn't matter. He's actually with me all the time, so seeing Him wouldn't make any difference.' Carmen saw that her face lit up as she talked about him, as though she was describing a lover. 'Don't you think He has the most beautiful, soulful face? It's as though His whole heart's written there. In the crinkle lines around His eyes. In His smile. You can just see continents in His eyes.'

'Mmm.' Carmen sounded as though she was ruminating. In fact, she was chewing her morsel of brisket and waiting for an opportunity to spit it out when no-one was looking.

'And Mother's *so* lovely,' Lucy enthused. She had a dreamy look, like a childish fan talking about some unattainable film star.

While Lucy was distracted, Carmen brought the napkin to her mouth and managed to transfer the offending pellet.

'Well, she's very good for someone with twelve perfect children,' was all that Carmen could volunteer. She managed to nudge the napkin accidentally off the edge of the table. 'She *is* lovely. But then, I expect she can afford to be, can't she? I mean, they're not short of a few bob. As far as I understand it, He's a multi-millionaire.'

Lucy was looking at her reproachfully, her reverie shattered. 'Actually, Mother's always lived in dire poverty and had a really terrible life. I don't think you'd talk like that if you knew what she'd been through. And Father nearly starved to death. In fact, Mother gives away everything that Father gives her because she doesn't think she's worthy. She's an incredibly humble person, otherwise Father wouldn't have been able to raise her to perfection.'

Carmen nodded. She put her knife and fork together decisively and pushed the plate away. Lucy's eyes followed the slice of meat as it slid past her, marooned in its thick sludge of Bisto.

'The food you've wasted there would have kept Him for a month in the labour camp,' she said sadly. 'Maybe two months. And even then He would have probably given it away.'

'Still,' said Carmen with determined cheerfulness. 'He's alright now, isn't he? I'd say he's landed on his feet.' She was in a dangerous, cantankerous mood. Everything was conspiring to make her feel uneasy. It was unnerving for her to be with Lucy for any length of time. It was like attending someone's funeral and chatting cordially with the ghost. All her mannerisms were there – her little nervous laugh, the sharp eyes that darted about and never missed a trick, but there was nothing else. It was as though the interesting parts of Lucy's brain had been vacuumed out. It made Carmen jittery and ill at ease.

'Father doesn't really have anything Himself,' said Lucy remotely. 'Everything He has He holds for us. He has to own material things because those are the things the fallen world respects. Unless He owned things and had money they wouldn't listen to Him at all. But, basically, Father hasn't any interest in material things. He just wishes He could live a simple life, and...' she softened and smiled indulgently at the thought, as though it was the idiosyncrasy of a dear old uncle she was talking about, 'just go fishing. That's what Father likes doing best.'

Carmen smiled a ghoulish artificial smile, as though she too knew the uncle and thought it a great shame that he had to wear himself out owning national newspapers and running arms factories and generally being the Messiah when he'd rather dodder about on a river bank with a rod and a simple tin of maggots. She cleared her throat before Lucy could proffer any more touching little confidences about her True Father.

'Well, your physical mother's not been looking so wonderful lately. She's got bags under her eyes from sitting up waiting for the phone to ring, thinking you were in a plastic bag on a rubbish tip. Her hair's beginning to show some grey and she's not looking like herself at all.'

Carmen thought her sister's face was about to crumple, but then the shutters came down smoothly behind her eyes. She gave a deprecating little laugh. 'Oh, I'm sorry if she got upset. But, you know, it would have been the same if I'd gone away to university.' She rolled her eyes. 'High drama! Oh, my little girl's growing up! How will I know if she's eating properly? What if she gets ill? Who's going to do her laundry? You know what mothers get like.'

Carmen looked blank. Mothers might be like that in a situation comedy, but their mother wasn't like that at all. She was a good-natured, easy-going sort of person with a strong and infectious sense of the ridiculous. She had been perfectly happy for Lucy to go to university and, had Lucy gone as planned, she would have wasted not a thought on the whereabouts of Lucy's laundry. It was as though Lucy had erased the reality of her mother in her mind and replaced her with a simple cardboard cut-out that was easily defused and ignored.

'Yeah, but you didn't go to university, did you?' Carmen persisted. 'You disappeared without a word.'

Lucy clucked and gave a teasing sideways glance. 'Oh, *disappeared*!' she mocked, as though it was the greatest over-dramatization. 'What nonsense. Honestly, I'm an adult. I decided to do something. Do I have to consult the whole world and get permission before I decide to go anywhere or do anything?'

Carmen frowned. It sounded entirely reasonable, and, had Lucy's relationship with them been different, it might have rung true, but the relationship between them had been close and affectionate. What's more, Lucy had been living at home. 'Look, Lucy,' she pressed on, 'if someone says they're going to buy a paper and then they just walk out of their life like it was an old jacket they didn't want any more...'

Lucy sighed with heavy tolerance. 'Hey, let's not talk about it any more, mm? I mean, that was then and this is now and it really all seems a million years ago.' She said it with such good-natured finality that Carmen had to make an effort to go on.

'The length of time that passes doesn't make it any better.'

Lucy smiled distantly, as though the subject was past the point where it could politely be pursued.

'Really, when it comes down to it, it's sort of my business, isn't it?' she asked. 'I mean, no-one can live someone else's life for them.'

Carmen shook her head in bewilderment. 'But just because you decide to walk out of your life, it doesn't mean people stop caring about you. People don't just suddenly *stop* loving someone...' She broke off. Plainly, from Lucy's look of indifference, sometimes they did.

'Well, there are different kinds of love, aren't there?' said Lucy matter-of-factly. 'There's a love that allows other people freedom and there's the love that wants to control the things other people do.' She cast her eyes coolly over Carmen in such a way that it was clear to which category Carmen's love belonged. 'I mean, it's nice to be concerned about people we care about but when it becomes an interfering sort of love, when it means we're trying to stop people we love from making their own choices – '

'Or mistakes,' Carmen interpolated.

'Yes,' she agreed cordially. 'When you love someone you have to let them make their own mistakes, or it's not really love at all.'

Carmen's face was troubled. 'But this wouldn't be just a little mistake, would it? I mean, if this should all be a mistake, it'd be a pretty drastic one – if you were giving up your whole life for it.' Lucy grinned and shook her head as though there really was no room for doubt in her mind.

'No-one wants to control you,' Carmen went on timidly. 'They just want to make sure you're happy.'

'I *am* happy,' Lucy assured her with a tremulous smile. 'I've found a happiness here that no-one else and nothing else has ever been able to give me in my entire life and nothing else, no-one else could ever compete with it. Even if it all turned out to be a mistake – well, no-one could take that away from me, could they?'

Her sincerity was beyond doubt. If that was how she felt, what right had Carmen to say the thing was wrong? And yet, such a short time ago, Lucy would have laughed to scorn the idea that she would want to spend her life singing and praying and raising money for an oriental businessman. And such a short time ago, her eyes had been clear and intelligent and busy, where now they were impenetrable and pained.

It was the physiological change of the eyes which continually prevented Carmen from accepting the simple answers. Maybe group pressures could effect sudden personality change in vulnerable individuals, but group pressures couldn't change the physical functioning of the pupil of the eye. Surely not.

The film treat that night was a very old print of 'Joan Of Arc'. Everyone clapped the title as it came up on the screen. The dialogue was hard to hear above the whirring of the antiquated projector and quite soon Carmen drifted off to sleep. When she jolted guiltily awake, she became aware of more noises in the room, loud moans and sobbing. People were crying openly and someone at the front was wailing inconsolably, a weird thin dry little sound full of desolation. Ingrid Bergman was on the screen, her face bathed in soft supernatural light. She was taking leave of her mother. She was mounted on a farm horse and she wore a simple peasant dress, a kerchief round her head. Her mother was imploring her to stay, clutching at Joan's shirt fearfully, attended by troubled village women.

'Jeanne, Jeanne, don't leave me. Don't leave me. People are saying you're mad. How can you leave me here like this?' Joan's mother

224

turned to the peasant women in desperation. 'She doesn't know what she's doing...'

But Joan was sitting there, radiant and indomitable. The music swelled over her close-up, and her soft, sweet face was suffused with a sacred conviction that could not be touched by human words.

'I have heard His will, Mother,' said Joan. 'I *must* follow the voices.'

Joan impelled her horse forward, and her mother half stumbled in a crazed delirium of suffering and emotion. The music swelled to a crescendo as Joan rode away to her destiny and the choking sobs in the room reached a pitch of hysteria – it was not the sound of people weeping self-indulgently in a cinema but the unmistakable wrenching noise of heartbreak.

After a while, she fell into another doze and it was only when the final music rose that she woke and began to clap automatically. Her hands were the only ones that pattered together as the image of Joan, transfigured in the flames which engulfed her, faded out.

Lucy leaned across fiercely and stopped her clapping.

Carmen was bewildered. 'What's wrong?' she asked. She saw that Lucy's eyes were bright with unspilt tears.

'We don't clap when someone's being burnt at the stake,' Lucy hissed vehemently.

Carmen looked around her, drowsy and perplexed.

'I don't see why not,' she grumbled. 'We seem to clap everything else that moves.'

'You're so insensitive!' Lucy spat at her, and she got to her feet in disgust, the tears still streaming down her face. She blundered and stumbled through the darkness, avoiding the chairs, and disappeared out of the door.

Carmen sighed heavily. She didn't know if there was really any point in following her. It was possible to spend all of one's spare time in the Family running in and out of doors, pursuing and being pursued like someone in a bedroom farce: the truth of the matter was that it was an enormous relief to see the fleeing soles of Lucy's running feet. Carmen was beginning to find it an intolerable burden to have her constantly nudging at her elbow. Yet after a while she felt a stir of pity and went outside to the back steps. She called lamely into the darkness.

There was no reply, but as she wandered down into the blackness she heard the sound of inconsolable, heart-broken weeping.

When she drew level with Lucy, she almost tripped over her. Lucy was kneeling on the wet grass with her nose to the earth, wailing with an anguish that was painful and primal. Carmen knelt beside her and took her wrists.

'Lucy, Lucy,' she urged her. 'It was only a film. They were just actors. It was only moving pictures on a wall.'

Lucy pulled away from her. 'You don't understand,' she wailed.

'What don't I understand?' asked Carmen. 'Tell me and then I will.'

This time Lucy allowed Carmen to put her arm around her shivering shoulders. She gasped it out between wrenching sobs.

'You think it doesn't *hurt* me. You seem to think it was easy for me to . . . give you both . . .' it ended on a fractured hiccough, '*up* . . . It doesn't get easier – it just gets more painful . . . because I know she'll just never ever understand . . .' and she began to cry all over again.

Carmen could hardly console her by saying that their mother *would* understand, because plainly she wouldn't. And neither did Carmen.

'Well, if it hurts you,' she said helplessly, 'if it hurts mother and it hurts me, well . . .' The remedy was so simple if that was the case. 'If it hurts everyone then why do it?'

But Lucy just went on shaking her head and trying to control her breath.

'I mean, you said it was your choice. You made the choice, so I don't quite understand. What is there to cry about?'

It was bewildering. Hadn't Lucy insisted that they should all respect her right to vanish? Hadn't she demanded that they recognise their concern as unacceptable interference? Now when Carmen was half prepared to concede Lucy's strange desire for total, loveless autonomy from her supposedly overbearing family home, she was demanding sympathy for the decision. Carmen thought it downright arbitrary – but then, there was probably some vital piece of Principle which she hadn't understood. After all, it hadn't been one person sobbing in the hall. There had been a whole roomful of them.

'You don't choose the Family. It chooses you!' Lucy insisted, just as Gary had done.

226

Carmen tried to be gentle and patient because Lucy was in a terrible state. She had never seen her so pathetic and vulnerable.

'Well, what is it you want her to understand? Maybe I can get it across to her?'

Lucy shook her head. 'No. She wouldn't see it.' She looked at Carmen desperately. 'The point is,' she said clearly, 'I'm doing more for her here than I can ever do anywhere else, I'm really *helping* her here where I couldn't help her before.'

'But how?'

She thought she heard Lucy mumble 'Daddy' and 'Spirit World' but it didn't seem to make any sense. And then she mumbled 'God's Providence' and something about paying indemnity and the Restoration Of The World.

'Lucy, I know it all makes sense to you, but, you know, how could it possibly help anyone for you to be off somewhere singing songs all day? I mean, apart from the fact that eventually you'll get to save the world...'

Lucy wasn't listening. She had begun to pray and she was muttering under her breath, just as though Carmen wasn't there. Carmen stared at her for a while, but Lucy was completely absorbed in her dialogue with Heavenly Father.

Chapter 10

In daylight the house proved to be a large, rambling mansion, maybe Georgian or older – she couldn't date it, but it was rather beautiful and made of yellow-orange stone. It stood in seven acres and the surrounding farmland stretched as far as the eye could see, until the clumps of trees faded from green to ultraviolet. Pamela said they were not allowed beyond the barbed-wire fence because the farmer persecuted the Church and threatened to shoot any trespassing member that crossed his sights.

The day seemed to follow the established pattern. Physical jerks, then delirious singing and prayers and chores until, at ten-thirty, the lecture began. The lecture course was supposed to be much more profound and revealing than the course they'd heard before, but, after two and a half hours of it, the weary truth descended upon an extremely restless and irritable Carmen. The lecture was exactly the same lecture they'd heard on Day One of the Seven Day. They were going to repeat the same lectures all over again for another seven days, and then presumably they would start the loop again for *another* seven days, and then another seven days, until the twenty-one days were up.

She searched in vain for anything more profound but the only significant difference she could make out was that Robert, the lecturer, was blond and sympathetic, in the mould of a young Robert Redford. But that didn't cover up the fact that he was still talking about Adam and Eve and the sin of the blood, and that he was still expounding the same scientific theory about why Lucifer was Lucifer and why he wasn't a talking snake.

What was making her even more agitated and fidgety was that it didn't sound so ridiculous any more. She recognised now that, with familiarity, the notions lost their power to shock.

The guests were so enchanted by Robert's easy, informal manner, his passionate conviction and his chiselled handsome face, that he could have told them anything. In fact, he was telling them just about anything, she reminded herself. She could only hold on aggressively to the knowledge that she had once found it totally ludicrous and illogical, and she had learnt nothing since to alter that judgement. She had just heard it a lot of times.

As soon as the lecture was over, she went outside onto the grass, looking for Lucy. Groups of people were dotted here and there. Jane stood clasping her Divine Principle Study Guide enthusiastically to her chest, in animated discussion with Peter and Franklin. A sister directed Carmen to the laundry room, which appeared to be one of a group of out-houses on the far perimeter. As Carmen started to walk in the direction of the pointed finger, Jane detached herself from her companions and stepped forward to detain her, a big friendly smile on her face.

'Hey, Carmen, how are you finding it? Is it beginning to get to you yet? Wasn't it just *so deep*?'

There was no trace of irony in her face or voice any longer. Carmen scowled and responded mechanically, 'I found it very moving.' Determined to avoid any discussion, she stalked purpose-fully off towards the distant sheds, her eyes fixed on the steam that was pouring from an extractor fan.

She pushed open the green, rustic door on a grim scene of labour. It was as hot as a sauna, and steam billowed with a sharp, unpleasant smell of starch. There were several sturdy but ancient washing machines, inadequately plumbed and with manual agitators, so that the process of washing the mountainous laundry output of the brothers was an Augean task, requiring constant water changes with leaking hoses and hard physical labour with the agitating handles. Lucy was red and unhappy amongst the soap suds, looking as though she was about to boil herself. One of the machines had flooded and the floor was awash with suds. What was more, some of the large sheets which hung from improvised lines strung across the room were trailing their weight in the mixture of bubbles and grimy slurry on the stone-flagged floor. Lucy made a huge effort to smile as Carmen materialised in the doorway, but she looked as though she was about to cry.

At the sight of her, Carmen's irritation ebbed and she relented enough to pick up the mop and begin to swill the floor. 'How did you get *this* job?' she asked her mildly.

'I asked for it,' said Lucy. 'I wanted to do it.'

'I thought you hated housework.'

'Yes, well. I've changed.' said Lucy, flatly. 'This way, I really do some service for my brothers and sisters instead of thinking about myself all the time. She began to agitate again, as hard as she could, until the meagre flesh of her arm began to wobble and her face was livid. 'How did you find the lecture? Wasn't it inspiring?'

'Well, that's what I wanted to talk about,' said Carmen. 'Can you stop a minute!'

'We can talk while I work,' grunted Lucy, agitating as though her life depended upon it. 'I really want to help you and I really want to get this done before the next lecture so I can help you some more! If there's anything you want to ask, just fire away!'

Carmen found Lucy's forced cheerfulness rather a strain, under the circumstances. The sweat was dripping off them both and she saw that Lucy's hands were red and raw where the powder had set up an eczema reaction on her skin.

'I don't have any questions. I've already heard the answers. How could I have any questions when the lecture's just a repetition of one I've heard already? What's the point of hearing lectures that are all exactly the same?'

Lucy shook her head, puzzled. 'Of course they aren't,' she said. 'They're not the same lectures at all. They're quite different. Maybe you're just not internalising them properly.'

The patronising smile maddened Carmen beyond the point where she could keep her temper.

'I'm sorry, they may not *be* the same but they *sound* exactly the same and that's the only way I can judge. I can only judge by my own ears and I've heard it once already. I really don't see the point of hearing the same lecture over and over again.' What she actually meant was that she did see the point, but she didn't like the implications. 'If that's all that's going to happen I can't see any point in me being here.'

Lucy touched her hand reassuringly. 'Honestly, Carmen, I've heard those lectures many, many times and they just...' Carmen finished the sentence for her.

'Get deeper. Yeah, I know. Well, maybe you need to hear things many, many times. But I get impatient. I only need to hear them once.

I've heard it once and I think I got the point.' She accelerated the end of the sentence so that her irritation reverberated through it. Lucy looked at her with mild amusement.

'That's not what *I* heard. I heard you spent the whole of the Seven Day saying you didn't understand it. It didn't sound to me like you got the point.' There was no rancour in her voice. It seemed to Carmen that Lucy had developed a new social skill. She seemed to be able to deflect hostility by pretending it wasn't there.

'Lucy, things *are* logical or they *aren't* logical. They don't get more logical if you hear them more often.'

Lucy eyed her sympathetically. 'Do you want to run through it again just to make sure?'

Carmen shook her head with surly conviction. The constant, futile arguments were, once again, beginning to weary her. 'You seem to think I'm here for *my* benefit,' she protested. 'I'm *not*. I've got no interest in the lectures. The only reason for coming was to find you, and since I've found you – ' she shrugged. 'And you're perfectly happy ... well, I might as well go home.'

The last thing she felt like was a five-hour trip to London. Besides which, she didn't quite know where she was, but she needed to know whether she had any hold on Lucy, or whether her whole effort was a waste of time.

'Oh, but you *can't* go today.' Lucy looked hurt and rather taken aback. 'You've only just got here! There's a Family Evening tonight and the sisters have baked some biscuits. You've at least got to stay for those. They're going to be yummy!'

Carmen was not tempted by the thought of yummy biscuits. She had never heard Lucy use the word 'yummy' before, and the Lucy she knew had never cared for biscuits. She was feeling acutely depressed and, when she analysed it, she found again that she was experiencing a sense of loss, only more deeply now, like a kind of mourning. She had to accept that Lucy was gone and that there was only this bland, trivial, irritating person in her place. It gave her a dull, sick feeling in her stomach to stand conversing with the damaged travesty of Lucy, across a steaming pile of Family shirts. She made an effort. She took Lucy's red hand and squeezed it urgently.

'I can't say this more clearly, Lucy. This is your life, but I can't stand and watch you throw it away on something – empty. *Think* about what you're doing. Don't throw away everything you ever had for the sake of a lie.'

Lucy flinched and looked down pointedly at Carmen's hand as though it was an intrusion. 'I'm sorry you feel that way. It must be hard for you to realise that we can't relate to one another on our old selfish basis, but, really, as you say, it *is* my life...' and she moved over to the mangle and began to manoeuvre an enormous thick coun-terpane through the rubber roller.

There was such a quiet dignity about her that Carmen could say no more. It indisputably *was* her life. Carmen's natural, libertarian instincts told her that Lucy was entitled to waste her life any way she chose, but something else continued to nag away at her, telling her that Lucy had somehow been deprived of her free will, that she hadn't given up her rights freely and in full cognisance of what the sacrifice entailed.

The veins on her arms were knotted like whipcords as she battled with the bulky quilt. Carmen viewed her impassively. The sight of Lucy as a self-punishing household slave, relentlessly forcing herself on, filled Carmen with despair.

'Here, let me do that. I'm stronger,' she said. As she took over the task, she heard Lucy clear her throat.

'There was just one thing, Carmen.'

'Yes?'

Lucy chose her words carefully. 'I think that if I really loved some-one, and I thought they were really doing something silly – you know, if I saw them swimming or something and I thought they were out of their depth...'

Carmen paused in what she was doing. Lucy's eyes reproached her.

'...I wouldn't just walk out on them. I wouldn't just shrug and say "If they drown, they drown." I think if I loved them, I might stick around and see if they needed the life-belt.'

Carmen continued to stare intently at her. It was the same strange sense she had experienced with Gary – a sense that the old fallen con-sciousness was sending out coded signals.

'Are you drowning?'

Lucy smiled tearfully and tried to make light of it. 'Maybe it just feels like it with all these soap suds everywhere.' But she added, 'And there again, a person wouldn't necessarily know, would they? You get swept up in something that seems so much larger than yourself. Maybe you can lose your objectivity.'

Carmen persisted. 'But you have some doubts?'

'We all have doubts.' She shrugged. 'We wouldn't be human if we didn't have doubts.' It was a ghostly echo of what Gary had said. Carmen had the same certainty that Lucy hadn't just come to believe something, but that something had been done to her. Something destructive. Carmen searched her sister's face in helpless puzzlement. With her hair hanging lank in wet rat's tails and her pleading eyes, Lucy looked impossibly fragile and vulnerable. Was she asking for reassurance or was she asking for rescue?

Carmen wrapped her arms around her. As they clung together, she thought she heard her whisper, 'Sometimes, I feel frightened.'

The next moment, Carmen wondered if she'd imagined the words, because the bell was ringing and Lucy had pulled away, laughing in embarrassment, wiping her eyes, telling Carmen what a lot of fun was in store for her if she only stayed another day.

'What are you going to choose this afternoon?' she asked brightly. 'We have a free period now. We can do sport or singing practice, or we do art and write poems and things. Everyone's very creative in the Family. People are amazed sometimes. They come here and, hey presto, they find they're creative too!' She considered Carmen as though trying to think what would suit her best.

'Perhaps you'd like to do creativity with me. You're so good at drawing. You'll really get a chance to shine!'

So it was that Carmen found herself practising her creativity. To prove that everyone had some creativity inside them, they all sat at the long trestle tables in the gloom of the sombre hall, with fistfuls of coloured pencils, each crouched over their own effort. The windows were very high, so the light only filtered through in long, dust-speckled pencil beams, giving the room the air of a cold but gracious church interior.

Adèle paced the tables like a primary-school teacher with a very docile class. She stooped now and then to give advice over people's shoulders, encouraging and correcting here, advising and congratulating there.

Carmen didn't know what to draw but, since Gary was sitting

opposite her, she took a 2B out of the communal pot and began to sketch him in a desultory fashion. He was reading his Divine Principle Study Guide and his lips were moving, but otherwise he was still and too absorbed to notice. The drawing was poor. For some reason her hand seemed sluggish and she had the crazy notion that there was something slowing up the signals from her brain. Her hand did not respond to her intentions as normal. She did some superficial things to the picture, cross-hatching the tone and then smudging it idly with her finger. This was taboo in real drawing but it was the kind of thing that impressed people who couldn't draw, and she had a strong urge to show off, to prove that she was an individual with specialised talents and excellent at something, and to show them that there was something in her that they couldn't homogenise into their bland melting-pot. She was wrong. It was a rotten drawing. She seemed to have regressed beyond anything she could have dreamt possible, as though her hand was reverting to juvenilia in sympathy with her brain. But still, not to be too hard on herself, it looked like Gary and she thought it might fool someone, especially in comparison to the drawings on either side of her, which looked like the results of a mental ward therapy session or the daubings of an under-five play-group. Big smiley yellow suns and stick men with flowers.

Lucy was composing a poem and she had a strained, 'creative' look on her face, which might have been funny if it hadn't been Lucy's face. When Adèle wafted past in her cloud of carbolic, Carmen leant back fractionally to enable the woman to catch a glimpse of her effort. She was aware of Adèle still and thoughtful at her shoulder, and imagined that the woman's silence was because she was lost in admiration.

It took a little while before Adèle's continued silence alerted her to the fact that this was not the case. Adèle bent and spoke to her in a censorious voice. 'What is this, please?' she asked with a curious apologetic smile.

'It's Gary,' said Carmen, rather put out. It actually was a good resemblance. Gary looked over at the sound of his name and she swivelled the page round so he could see it. He stared at it, but he said nothing. He looked embarrassed and even a little cross and then he looked back at his book as though he had not seen it. She set it straight.

'But what is it to do with Heavenly Father?' Adèle prompted gently.

'Well, nothing,' said Carmen, surprised. 'Except, well, Gary was *made* by Heavenly Father so Heavenly Father's in all his atoms. Doesn't it look like Gary?'

Adèle squinted at it and shook her head sadly. 'This looks like Carmen. This looks like Carmen says "Look at me, everybody, I am *someone*, I am a good drawer". But, actually, no. I cannot see Gary in this picture because Carmen is too big in it. Because there is nothing of Heavenly Father in the picture or in the motivation that made you do it. I see a lot of lines but I see no beautiful ideas like we see here in this picture.' She held up Franklin's pathetic scrawl of a grinning blob person holding an umbrella and apparently kicking his dog up the bottom with his club foot. 'Now here we have a beautiful idea. The rain falls and makes the flowers grow up and the sun smiles like Father. Everyone is joyful, even this smiling dog. But actually Heavenly Father can't come through when we use His talents in a selfish, self-glorifying way and think always how clever we are.'

Carmen flushed. She had been showing off and now she had her come-uppance. Franklin looked particularly gratified and smug, but she could hardly begrudge him his moment. She had had her fair share of life's little compliments and she doubted that Franklin had been given many. The Family evened things up. It was even-handed in its condemnation of anything individualistic or quirky like ability and it raised mediocrity and banality high, as though to make up for the neglect and contempt that those two qualities occasioned in the Fallen World outside. There was a certain justice about that, especially when she looked at the boyish smirk of pleasure on Franklin's podgy face.

'Well, what *should* I be doing then?' asked Carmen, hoping to get points for humility. She felt an instinctive need to win Adèle's good favour.

'Perhaps you could copy someone with more spiritual ideas, like Jane,' she said, and she pulled over one of the illustrations that seemed to have formed the inspiration for Jane's portrait of a pizza. It showed Reverend Moon smiling, wearing a paper crown like someone at a fancy-dress party, clutching his small bride. 'Perhaps you find more inspiration from Father on his own or from True Parents together,' she suggested. Carmen looked at the unpromising oriental features, and stretched out reluctantly for the yellow pencil.

When she tried again, she found she couldn't draw. She had to face the fact that she had only two motives in drawing something – to achieve some self-satisfaction and to have the product praised. There was some truth in what Adèle had said. Her motives were rather tawdry and unattractive, but without those motives, she could see no point in doing it. The aim of drawing in pencils was to create a pleasing configuration of shapes and colours, and if that aim was unworthy too, then she was in limbo. Only if she could discover the correct criterion, and meet it, would her effort be praised. But it would be like stabbing in the dark. How many drawings would one have to do before one lighted at random on the correct criterion? To draw something badly as an exercise in self-humiliation was an experiment at which her pride baulked. Yet she couldn't resent the Family's attitude.

It was true that talent, ability and intelligence were unfairly distributed in the world and their distribution implied no personal merit, so why should those things be considered virtues and elicit praise? The fact that she craved praise, even in a situation where she did not respect the opinions of her peers, gave her a humbling awareness of a weakness she hadn't recognised before, a weakness that was shabby, which she would not want generally known. She felt lowered by the knowledge and, for the first time, she admitted to herself that her faults were not all trivial and forgivable, not if she felt a desire to conceal them from other people's scrutiny. That was the test.

So, she scratched away in a desultory fashion with the yellow pencil, just a patch of yellow cross-hatching more like a doodle than a drawing. When she was bored with doing that, she let her eyes rest dully on the moted light beams as they struck the table, and watched them dance and dapple on the wild flowers sprayed out generously in the vase. As Adèle brushed behind her once more, she picked up the graphite pencil and began to frame her scrawl with black line.

The sisters practising their songs at the piano in the corner had begun 'Ave Maria' in thin, crystal voices, so wistful and plangent that Carmen was close to dissolving into tears. They couldn't quite hit the top note true and this was the only thing that prevented

Carmen from melting away. She didn't know what was wrong with her. She seemed to cry so easily and she had the desire to cry maybe three or four times a day. It was odd, because in the four years since her father's death, she had hardly cried once. It was as though that catastrophe had somehow dammed up her heart. Nine days with the Family had reversed that aberration.

Her eyes came to rest on the picture of Sun Meung Moon. His face was as inscrutable as ever. She thought it was a crafty face. At best, a comic face. He was smiling. His two eyebrows sat on his furrowed brow like curved furry caterpillars, two tiny narrow eyes like tadpoles with laugh lines at the corners, receding hair slicked back with brilliantine, well-padded high cheekbones, perfect teeth. The nose, a long, almost Red Indian nose. The face said nothing to her, only that here was a man smiling, a man who knew that he had plenty to smile about.

She had no idea how long she'd stared at it. She'd come to accept as a matter of course that her sense of space and time was now quite fluid and distorted so it might have been ten minutes or it might have been an hour. Then something rather magical happened. Her concentration had lapsed and she was thinking of nothing, dwelling in a half-conscious region somewhere between sleep and full awareness, when the picture began to blur, and the colours broke down into a smear of printed dots that made no sense in terms of the image they carried but became wheels and whirls of pastel colours like the glass inside a kaleidoscope forming and reforming in patterns, but infinitely more meaningful. Dazed, Carmen was too fascinated to blink or disperse the dancing shapes, and when she finally wiped the tears away, she found the image had reformed in some subtle way.

It was still the same picture but its meaning had changed. The crinkle lines around Father's eyes seemed weighted with a great deal of suffering. His eyes were still inscrutable but now he seemed to stare out with a world-weary, hopeless compassion, and the smiling mouth had a sad touch to it as though he smiled without much hope of the world returning to him the love that he so much wanted to give it.

Carmen pulled her eyes away from it, shaken. Wasn't it what the members had told her, that if you looked at the picture long enough you would see it – you would see his life of suffering in his eyes? Ask and you'll be given, Carmen told herself. That was the essence of it. Seek and you will find. Knock and the door will be opened but you have to leave the world behind. It was disturbing to her to discover that she was not entirely in control of the moments of revelation after all. She looked around her, warily, fearful that anyone could know what she had experienced. It seemed very important that no-one should know about these strange visual dislocations of hers, because, if they knew, they would try to bend the information to their own ends. She concealed them furtively inside her, tucking them away, pretending that they hadn't happened. It was like a secret that she was keeping, even from herself.

She screeched back her chair and got to her feet. The room lurched and then came back into focus, much as it had been before, but marginally darker. Lucy and Jane both looked at her, troubled and perplexed, but Carmen just walked out towards the door, leaving behind her drawing of a yellow balloon.

She had a sense of numbness in her hands. She felt that she was in urgent need of solitude in order to make sense of what had happened: to try to decide whether anything *had* happened. But even as she stared out at the endless stretch of green, sisters and brothers were rounding up their charges and Carmen could see the little pastel figures converging to where Robert stood, blowing his whistle in the middle of the pitch. The next moment, a sister had her arm fondly round Carmen's shoulder and she found herself being alternately coaxed and propelled towards the action. As she drew closer, she saw that a bizarre game was in progress, but it took her a moment to understand it. There was a big circle and each pair of members held their arms steepled so that they formed an arch with their bodies. At their feet, other players crouched, woofing and howling inside the make-believe kennel that their arched bodies formed. When Robert blew his whistle, they all formed a normal circle and began running a circuit as individuals until the whistle blew again, when there was a mad scramble to form new kennels and those who couldn't be kennels became dogs. Anyone who couldn't find a kennel was out. Carmen viewed the antics with a sneer of ill-concealed disdain.

'OK, Carmen, find yourself a kennel,' Robert ordered.

'You're kidding,' she said.

238

He looked at her for an icy moment and then very deliberately put his whistle in his mouth and gave a long *pweeet*. Everyone froze in mid-action and all the dogs pricked up their ears.

'A few words, now,' he drawled with easy bonhomie, crinkling his eyes against the glaring sun. 'Carmen's just raised an interesting point. It's hard for some of us to get rid of our inhibitions, isn't it? But really inhibitions just hold us back. If we want to cut off from our Fallen Natures, we have to become like a child again, isn't that so?' Everybody nodded, impatient to get on, giving Carmen hostile looks because she was preventing them from having fun.

'And when we play games in the Family, we're not just playing games, are we? What are we doing, Carmen?'

'Symbolically restoring the world,' Carmen muttered.

'Yes,' he nodded. 'So even when we're playing games, washing up or peeling potatoes, we can move the Restoration forward with the combined power of our love. So we're not just playing games here, we're helping Heavenly Father reclaim His world. And Satan doesn't want that to happen, does he? So whose side are you on, Carmen? Are you on the side of the Satan or on the side of the Messiah?'

'I'm on the side of the Messiah,' Carmen said.

He smiled approvingly. 'OK, Carmen, then let's try and help Heavenly Father the best way we can.' And he added in amiable undertone, 'Let's see your dog...'

Everyone was waiting tensely for Carmen to do as he said. They were irritated with her, anxious to get on with their dog impressions. Her eyes locked with Robert's. His face was set stern and impassive and he meant business. His authority was not diminished by his ill-fitting track suit, because the authority didn't come from a suit of clothes but from something within him, from the divine purpose which inspired him. As the afternoon sunlight bronzed his face, he was something between a film-star hero and a pure and solemn priest. She hesitated. He stood a foot taller than she did and his eyes willed her to obey him. It was dizzying to try and outstare him when he saw right through her with his strange, compelling eyes. It couldn't be done. Her eyes faltered and broke away but she was thinking fast. She could not, would not, now that it was a battle of wills, go down on all fours to him and pretend to be a dog.

Her heart was beating fast as she thought through what this simple

239

act of defiance would bring down on her head. A lot of concerned people who really cared about her would come and stick to her like glue and try to sort out the problem in her thinking; they would reason with her and persuade her of her fault until she confessed it; they would make her go over the meaning of obedience and why it was required here for the sake of the Universe, and in the end she would agree with them – so why not give in straight away and avoid the wasted emotional effort? His eyes continued to challenge her. Really, she thought, it was only pride that stopped her from backing down. And what use was pride if it just got her into wearying bombardment sessions that she would lose in any case? When she thought about it that way, there was no issue. It troubled her to obey someone, but after all, it wasn't a major moral issue, it was only a silly party game.

So she allowed herself to smile a tight, accepting smile, and she walked over to Gary and Jane's steepled arms, since it was the only position free. She crouched down on all fours and began yelping lamely. Then, as Robert was smiling at her and giving her an affectionate thumbs-up, she thought that, since all pride and face were lost, she might as well do it with abandon and she began to bark ecstatically like the rest of them. And, as she lolloped round in circles, wild-eyed, snapping here and there at people's legs, she felt the deepest, most urgent sense of danger. Something was exploding, pounding like a migraine in her head. There was always the possibility that she had lost control but didn't know it. That she was just as programmed as the rest of them. That, maybe, all along, while she was thinking herself so clever, she'd merely been going through their hoops, responding to the puppet master's strings.

The afternoon lecture began very late. She had the idea that they were starting later and later and that the whole time scale of their life was slipping around in a band.

Perhaps they would find the morning lecture starting at midnight, eventually, and so it would go on until they came full circle. She had given up checking whether this impression was true because she had lost interest in her watch: the little pointers had ceased to have any meaning for her. Now she only judged the time by her hunger or by the colour of the light as it filtered through the long windows and speckled the leaves of the wild flowers in their little yoghurt pots.

'Let's look at my thumb,' Robert was saying, inexplicably. 'It has a very special purpose, hasn't it? Each finger has a special relationship with the other fingers of the hand. Even the little finger's useful. But what if the little finger wanted to marry the thumb? Huh? What would happen then?' He searched their faces.

Several girls shook their heads dumbly.

Carmen stopped doodling the picture of a Spirit Man dancing on one leg dressed in a sheet and tried to focus her lethargic brain cells on Robert's question, wondering where this crucial point led. Robert's voice was becoming more indignant and impassioned.

'What if the little finger wanted to usurp the position of the index finger? The whole hand would be in chaos, don't you think?'

Carmen sneaked a look at Lucy to see if she found the metaphor a mite strained, but Lucy's mouth was slightly open and her eyes were shining with anticipation.

'And *none* of those fingers would find happiness! So everything is in its place. Everything to its own perfection. If there is a God and He loves you then you'll be guided to your perfect mate. God can cross international barriers, can't He? He can find the one person in the world with whom you can share perfect love.' He drew a diagram on the board. 'When the God-centred man mates with the God-centred woman, this is the true situation of God-centred love.' He drew a few arrows between them and wrote 'Perfect Child'.

'This is how it should be between a couple. They should come together and say "Heavenly Father, close your eyes, I want to give you a present", and then the couple come together and take Him in their arms, and the result is a perfect child.'

Carmen had a hazy picture of God like some enormous barrage balloon and the couple trying to link arms in bed around Him, squashing Him out of shape and squeezing yet more tears from His suffering eyes. Robert then roamed off on a long discourse on the Four-Point Foundation which represented the God-centred family. Carmen continued to write notes without really listening and, every now and then, she stopped and stared at Gary's poker back directly in front of her. He had on a dark barathea blazer. The hair was razored close to his neck in a dark teddy-bear fuzz. There was a light sprinkling of dandruff on the severe padded shoulders. His neck was a rich burnt colour and she wondered idly if he had Italian blood. The backs of men's necks were always hypnotic if one was forced to stare at them for long. Even on buses, they seemed so individual, like fingerprints − bull necks, weathered necks, ginger necks, with freckles and big red blotches. If you stared for long enough, the two creases in the nape could make a rather inane or frightening eyeless grin. Gary's neck did not smile. It was of the solid, noble type with two well-defined tendons, and his ears were brown-tipped and loy-ally close-fitting.

She felt an impulse to reach out and brush away the dandruff or to trace her finger down the hollow and make him shiver. He fidgeted and half-turned, almost as though he could feel her eyes boring into his collar, and she bit her lip and gripped her pen determinedly and began to draw a talking snake in case she should find herself touch-ing the close-cropped fuzz experimentally. And it was just then that she became aware of what Robert was saying.

'So when we have selfish attitudes, it's very easy to develop sexual desires. If we have evil desires, we mustn't fulfil them or we accept the standard of Satan. Many, many times, Satan makes a dirty love spring up between us. But that's how He attacks, isn't it? From the inside, playing on our weakness. Where is our weakness? Where was Eve's weakness? Satan stimulated Eve's desire and what happened? She had a relationship that was wrong and dirty, and afterwards they were ashamed of their lower parts because they'd used them for wrong things. And that's why we're in such deep, deep trouble today.'

He moved into more conversational mode as he circled the desk.

'You know, at the end of the Seven Day, a male guest caressed a sister's arm. He had the right motivation, he wanted to thank her, but, you see, he hadn't understood God's Standard. Once we know God's Standard we must always be on guard against false love. So always check your motivation. You brothers...' he raised his voice again, 'when you look at a sister you must think, "That sister is the bride of the Messiah, how can I desire her?" and you sisters...' his eyes met Carmen's fleetingly as they roved across the girls, 'when you look at a brother, you must think, "This man stands to me as the Messiah, how can I desire him?" You don't desire the Messiah, you serve Him...'

Carmen realised then with a queer little shock what it all meant. In fact, she had known for some time, but she was only now beginning to internalise it.

Robert leaned forward, his voice passionate with conviction. 'Our parents transmitted Satan's blood to us, but now we know the truth, we have to stop propagating children of Satanic love. We have to cut off earthly lusts. If we can't be true brothers and sisters to one another, how can we ever be true husbands and wives?'

He searched their faces. Robert was possessed of a humility which shone from his face, a quality which Matthew hadn't exhibited. It undercut his film-star good looks and defused the incongruity of such a handsome man demanding celibacy.

'We have to drive away our Fallen Natures. If you relate to someone on the level of Fallen Nature, are you helping that person? If you touch a sister then it escalates more and more, it accelerates, it gains momentum, until eventually it becomes passion.' He bent his knee and clasped his hands in exaggerated mimickry of a suitor. '*I love you* and then it becomes *I want to marry you* . . .'

A few of the members laughed amiably at his little mime but the guests sat silent, rather shocked. It occurred to Carmen then that many of them had formed secret attachments to their Spiritual Parents, or to the Centre leaders themselves. One or two of the girls were staring with woebegone eyes at Robert himself and certainly Adèle had collected quite a few admirers for herself in a very short time. Robert straightened up. 'But is that True Love or is it just a selfish love that seeks its own gratification?'

He began to pace restlessly. 'How do we know a Fallen desire? We test it. When jealousy comes you know you're wrong. If there's a God and He loves you, then He will guide you to your perfect mate. It's very hard for us to decide for ourselves, we make so many mistakes. We're blinded all the time by our Fallen Nature. Many times people will say, "But I want to choose who to love myself" – "I want to make my own decision", but who is it that speaks with that voice of individualism? It's Fallen Nature that speaks, it's our satanic blood that speaks. Who knows better, the individual selfish heart or the Messiah?'

Robert waited for a response. The company bleated obediently, 'The Messiah.'

'Yes,' said Robert. 'Only the Messiah can find your perfect mate. Perhaps you may never have seen that person before but, after the Blessing, the real miracle becomes apparent, that your mate had been created just for you. Master, knowing God's will for each, has brought them together. When we choose our own partner, what happens? We have a choice of maybe three or four, but God sees so much further. This is how we can form God-centred families. This is how we produce children free from the taint of Satan's blood, free from Original Sin . . . Do you want that?' he asked suddenly.

Most of the guests were looking stunned and unhappy.

'Isn't that what has to happen?' Robert rallied them.

'Yes,' they cried.

Carmen had a sense that everything was suddenly fitting into place, like the pieces of a jigsaw cohering into a most unwelcome pattern. She began to rattle through the pages of her notes and check that she had really understood.

Previously incomprehensible diagrams that she had copied out in a dazed fuddle now offered their own explanations and became crystal clear. She suddenly understood the Four-Point Foundation. She had once understood what cutting off Fallen Nature meant but in the intervening days she had either forgotten or suppressed her knowledge. It came back to her now. Cutting off Fallen Nature meant amputating one's personality in some way. That was the way to perfection, by centring the brain, all thoughts and actions on the Messiah and thus cleansing the blood of all Satanic taints, and eventually achieving perfection. Robert seemed to be telling them now that, once they became totally pure, totally centred, then they would be given in marriage to other pure members, and the result of that arranged union with a stranger would be a perfect, sinless child. A race of perfect, sinless children who would be pure in blood, not just in brain. This was what Lucy and Gary believed to be fact. Indeed, she suddenly remembered, the school already housed fifteen such infants and they were on their summer holidays.

She was internalising it now. It was sinking in, and it appalled her. Lucy was prepared to let this Korean con man give her away in marriage to a total stranger. Lucy was concentrating on cutting off her own past, her own personality, everything that made her an individual. It was as though Lucy was applying a tourniquet to an artery and she would continue to apply the pressure until the blood supply to that unwanted part of her ceased to flow, until her personality should atrophy and drop away. When she had achieved this aim, she would be handed like a blank and hollow possession to another of His blank and hollow possessions and required to produce a child who would be brought up in an atmosphere such as this house, with no stimuli to widen its picture of the world, with only the terror of the spirits to inform its behaviour and the relentless carrot-and-stick discipline that controlled these adults in this room. And what was Lucy's future – growing ever blanker, ever more pure? What was Gary's?

'When we hear this lecture, it shocks us a little, doesn't it?' said Robert. 'We don't want to hear it. We don't have the humility to hear it. We want someone to tell us that it's wrong. We want someone to say, "It's alright, there's some other way." But actually, that shock, it's really a shock of recognition, isn't it? Because when we come face to face with our Fallen Nature, we don't want to recognise it. But, actually, when we recognise the Messiah, we have to serve Him.'

Out on the playing field, something was happening. A guest, one of the black women, was running around in circles, flailing her arms. She was letting out cries that might have been distress signals and some members were circling her and moving in cautiously like dog-catchers without a net. When they had her firm, their lips began to move, and Carmen's interest waned. She supposed they were only exorcising spirits.

The lecture had indeed seemed to send a shock-wave through the group and all around her she could see the signs of its reverberation. Sitting on the steps in little groups, the guests were clustered anxiously round members and the members were showing off their Blessing rings. Carmen had gone up to the dormitory for some peace, but she had come down again because it was noisy in there with the sound of people grieving. Some of them had husbands either in the brothers's dormitory or at home, and they now had to face the truth that their marriages were invalid. They were beginning to internalise Principle and they were facing the fact that, when the Messiah called them to actionise, they would be required to leave their husbands and possibly their children. But then, hadn't Matthew warned them right at the beginning that they were travelling light? The women in the dormitory had been in terrible distress, frantic with the sense of fear and impending loss. It seemed to Carmen that they were like people in a nightmare trance: it was impossible for them to conceive the idea of refusing what had been ordained for them. What they had been told was going to happen was just what was going to happen to them.

Surely it was easy to say 'no' to what you didn't want and nobody could possibly have imagined from their behaviour that they were facing something that they wanted. They didn't want it, and yet it was no longer a possibility for them to say 'no'. The very fact that they railed against their prescribed future testified more surely to the fact that they were about to follow the path as it had been laid out for them, like somnambulists negotiating a dark forest, blind.

Carmen was praying as she stood on the steps. She was praying because she understood it completely. Not in her brain, but in her heart. She felt it herself. A terrible sense of inevitability, as though what they told her *must* happen *would* happen, could not be prevented from happening to her. Her will was no longer relevant or part of the equation. Her head was in turmoil. She felt as though her skull was about to burst open like an overstuffed marrow. How could this be right? How could anyone say that Lucy had chosen? How could one say that the girls who were sobbing in different corners of the dormitory had chosen? They were like doomed moths flittering around a light bulb, like automatons waiting for instruction. When the instructions came, they would buck wildly against them, but in the end there was no question: they knew they would obey.

When the bell clanged its mournful warning, they filed to team meetings. In the dark panelled room where Carmen was, the late afternoon sun poured honey on their faces as though each person in the circle held a buttercup beneath their chin.

They were to have come prepared with guilts like children with homework assignments but Carmen had been too tired for homework and she sat on her hard-backed chair, shuffling, dreading her turn, for she had nothing to declare.

'Well,' she stated mechanically when Adèle's cool eyes turned upon her, 'I'm arrogant and selfish and stuff like that. But really I don't think I have a guilt that matters. I'm not old enough to have done anything that bad.'

Adèle plucked at the fabric of her patterned frock and when she looked up, there was a worried smile around her lips.

'But this is very strange,' said Adèle. 'We all of us are born with guilt. Not to feel this emotion, surely, that is quite disturbing? The people who do the worst crimes are the ones who have no guilt.'

Carmen nodded. 'Yes, well, that might apply to psychopaths or something. I'm not saying I don't feel guilt. I'm just saying I can't particularly think of one right now.'

Adèle continued as though she hadn't spoken. 'Particularly this is strange when someone close has gone to Spirit World. Didn't your father go to Spirit World?' She looked around and received general assent. 'Yes, many times people feel guilt when someone goes to Spirit World. This is actually a normal, human reaction and very common. Your father is in Spirit World, huh?'

Carmen nodded fearfully. She experienced a curious, shrinking withdrawal when her father was mentioned. It was as though they might put their fingers in the wound and wriggle them around and make it bleed. Maybe that was what Marianne had meant when she talked about finding the crack in a person's soul. Carmen always imagined a chisel being hammered into her chest cavity, the hard bone cleaving open like two halves of a coconut and her unhealed sorrow dribbling out in a stream of sweet, white milk.

'He must have been a very good man that you find your way to the Family. How did he go to Spirit World?'

'In a car crash,' said Carmen defensively. 'I've told you before. I don't see what it has to do with anyone else.'

'It has everything to do with everything,' Adèle countered swiftly. 'Perhaps it was that he suffered this way in a car crash to bring you here, and now he hears you say, what is it to do with anything? Maybe he has been in Spirit World guiding you, whispering to you, "Go along to this street corner. Not here, but there," and when you meet a member of the Family, he smiles to himself because all along this is the way he has been guiding you to go. And now, if you turn your back on the Messiah, he begins to suffer again the torments. Many times a spirit goes back to the place where he suffered and experiences the moment again and again. Perhaps he hears the metal and the impact, he feels the steering wheel go through his bone – this is how it is in Spirit World. It's as though you make this collision happen over and over again. You stab your own father in the heart and you turn away from him. Do you want him to suffer this way?'

Carmen stared at her, dry-lipped, unable to understand that someone could torment her in such a sanguine way. It went against all normal sense of decency.

She looked to Lucy for support but Lucy was staring determinedly ahead of her, arms akimbo like someone uninvolved. Jane, too, refused to meet her eye. Adèle continued to talk in her gentle voice.

'Sometimes we learn to harden our hearts this way and then our hearts seal over with something like a thick pad of skin. This way nothing can touch us, this way we become anaesthetised but when we lose our sensitivity, then the Messiah can't get in.' She nodded sadly at Carmen as though this was sad to relate but told for her own benefit. 'But maybe when our heart grows tough like this, like old boot leather, we feel nothing but inside of us something begins to fester. And this way we can really make ourselves ill, because we lock our guilty feelings here inside of us and they eat away into the soft part of our souls. For instance...'

She turned away from Carmen and threw the question to the room, 'Who cried in "Joan Of Arc"?'

The hands shot up, all except for Carmen's. She would have put her hand up, except that Lucy might have shopped her. Adèle turned her eyes sadly back to Carmen as though the fact that her hand was in her lap proved medically, beyond all doubt, the truth of what she'd said.

'Ah yes,' she said. 'But this was a powerfully affecting film. It touched us all in many deep corners of our hearts.' She turned her attention back to Carmen. 'So, Carmen, you have this problem, you have felt no guilt that your father goes to Spirit World for your sake?'

Carmen moved uneasily in her seat. Loyalty to her father decreed that she shouldn't discuss him in this place but her urge to protect him vied with the need to defend herself.

'Well, yes, I felt guilt,' she said. Her throat felt constricted and her voice came out tight and strangled. 'But, as you say. It's a natural reaction. There were things I wished I'd said, things I wished I'd done

– after all, if he hadn't been picking me up that night, he wouldn't have been on the motorway in fog. I mean . . . I was just sixteen then. You can go over things endlessly and blame yourself, but in the end –'

She looked desperately to Lucy's tip-tilted profile.

'I came to terms with it. It was just the way things happened. How could I have known that he was going to crash? It was just a random set of circumstances. No-one was to blame. However badly I felt about it, it wasn't my fault . . .' She ended her little speech lamely, miserably. Apart from the creaking of a chair, there was an uncomfortable, accusing silence. No-one spoke to reassure her. There was only the infinitesimal whooshes of Adèle's hands as they folded and unfolded.

And then Adèle said lightly but with finality, 'Then actually, it *was* your fault. It was a random circumstance perhaps, but if he hadn't been driving to meet you, then he wouldn't have been there, would he? Sometimes we forgive ourselves too much.'

And as Adèle moved briskly on to the next person in the circle, Carmen began to wonder if her own arrogance didn't lie elsewhere. Perhaps it lay in the fact that she believed herself immune. She knew that her head was bursting, that she had a constant, dull insistent pain in her forehead and a fairly permanent furrow just above her eyes. She knew that most of the time she was poised between tears and hysterical laughter, and that the frailties and inanities of the members no longer made her laugh. There had been enough evidence all around her to convince her that sudden personality change was the norm and, yet, for all she had seen its unmistakable signs with bewilderment and alarm, for all she had seen Peter, Jane, and all her friends succumb one by one, she still could not conceive of herself as vulnerable. Such was her confidence in her own strength, her own will, her own spirit, that while she was alert to the danger signals in others, perhaps she had not been sufficiently vigilant for herself.

When the bell rang, Carmen hurried from the room. She had no desire to talk to anyone, least of all Lucy. She felt an urgent need to be alone. But there was Lucy at her shoulder saying, 'Maybe what Adèle said upset you, but actually she has to tell the truth . . .' Carmen shouldered rudely past her and bolted away up the staircase as fast as she could.

Carmen threw open the dormitory door. The sisters crouched on the floor looked up, startled. Robert's voice boomed from the tinny cassette player and they were hunched over it with odd reverence.

'Do you want to be prisoners of love?' the machine demanded. 'That's what we want, isn't it? We all want to be prisoners of love...'

Carmen backed out of the room and pulled the door shut behind her. She ran down the corridor towards the bathroom, for once mercifully empty of half-draped bodies. The bolt had been removed from the door. She cast around wildly for something to use as a wedge. By some chance the brother had left his screwdriver and the bolt was lying discarded under the chair. She began to scrabble for the screws, then changed her mind and rammed the bolt under the door. She screeched a chair against it for good measure and then leant against it. She closed her eyes, listening to the silence until the noises in her head began to fade away.

She felt a band of iron across her forehead. It was as though her head was too small for the activities that were going on inside it, as if that little silver ball was rattling about, being flipped this way and that, setting off lights and bells and circuits like a machine in an amusement arcade.

She took her clothes off quickly and crouched in the bath. She held the hose above her head and let the spray tickle and dance on her scalp like gentle sympathetic fingers tapping out a pitter-patter, then gasped as it trickled icy cold around her neck and down her back. She arched backwards to rest her cramped neck muscles against the cool tiles of the splash-back and surrendered herself to the numbness and the soothing noise of water. She tried to force an image in her head – she was on a blue-white stretch of ice-floe in the Antarctic beneath a monumental wall of ice that loomed against the sky like an ethereal palace. There was no sound, no human habitation, not even a breath of wind – nothing but the blue stillness all around. It was then she heard the tapping at the door become more urgent.

'Carmen? Carmen! Apart from anything else, it's just so *selfish* to lock the bathroom...'

She gave an infuriated shudder and took in a mouthful of water as she jerked herself alert. She summoned up her energy to shout against the sound of spray.

'I just want to be alone, Lucy.' There was fierce conviction in her voice.

Lucy persisted. 'We don't leave one another alone when we've got problems. We *help*.'

Carmen groaned. There was silence, then the little voice started up again, with a wheedling tone, as though cajoling a would-be suicide from a precarious ledge.

'What if somebody else wanted to use the bathroom? I just don't think it's very fair ...'

Carmen turned the water jet to a raging torrent and shouted above it, 'I can't hear you.'

'We do things together. It's not good for you to be alone. Haven't you understood the lectures? Isn't it clear what *damage* it can do?' Lucy was leaning against the door, now, listening. 'I'm not going to leave you on your own when you're feeling mixed up ... *please* open the door!'

She was obviously not going to go away, so Carmen levered herself out of the bath. She rubbed herself down quickly and then began to dress. She could see Lucy as a restless shape distorted by the frosted pane, and the doorknob was moving experimentally as though Lucy was testing how much play there was in the barricaded door. The shadow drew back for a moment, as Lucy braced herself to shoulder it with force, and the next moment, she came hurtling and clattering into the room with far more momentum than was needed, just as Carmen was laconically pulling on her jeans. Carmen ignored her dramatic entrance and merely squeezed a wriggle from someone's abandoned toothpaste and began to clean her teeth with her pasted finger. Lucy recovered her dignity and settled herself gently on the edge of the bath to gaze with wistful eyes at Carmen's back.

'Look, Carmen,' she reasoned. 'Perhaps it was the idea of the Blessing that worried you. Maybe you thought it was a lot to ask, but, honestly, the kind of love we find here in the Family, it more than compensates for the other kind of love we're giving up. When we know the Messiah's on earth, when we understand His purpose, well, really – ' she shrugged, as though it was too petty to be worth discussing, 'it really is such a very little sacrifice, when we think of how much Father's sacrificed for us.' She paused delicately as if a new thought had just occurred to her. 'Hey, is it Robin? You can tell me. Are you having trouble giving Robin up?'

Carmen turned and faced her with dull eyes, the froth still round her mouth like a white moustache. She realised that she had forgotten all about Robin. He had faded so completely into insignificance that she now had trouble even calling up a picture of his face. She had a feeling that things were running on too fast, now. Here was Lucy plea-bargaining with the concept of life-long celibacy when they hadn't yet even persuaded her to accept the talking snake.

'I'm not giving *anything* up,' she mumbled gruffly. 'None of this affects me personally. I'm not involved. What I can't seem to get through to anyone is that I really don't believe it.'

Lucy smiled mischievously. 'Well, you seem pretty disturbed for someone who doesn't believe it. You think when the Messiah's on earth, we can say it's not our business? You think we can meet the Messiah and still say we're not involved?

'Carmen, think about it... You're having to try so hard *not* to believe. Doesn't that tell you something? If it's always such an effort, that must mean that, in some secret part of you, you *do* believe. Don't you understand that? Can't you feel what a strain it is for you to hang on to your disbelief?'

Carmen tried to think about it. It was true that it became increasingly hard to fight them. They were so certain, they were so repetitive and there were so many of them. Maybe she had begun, just by default, to believe something. It all depended on the definition of the word 'believe'. In the old sense of the word, she didn't believe it, but lately she couldn't even remember the facts that she was basing her judgement upon.

She had stepped into the grey twilight middle ground where truth and lies began to wash into a muddy blur.

At first, she had stopped asking questions or making objections out of a sense of self-preservation. It was entirely tactical. But now the thing had washed over her like a wave and she found it difficult to disentangle truth from imaginative projection. It was now only an act of personal faith to disbelieve it. She remembered that it had all seemed nonsensical when she came and there was nothing she had learned since to make it less so. And yet time, strain, tiredness and over-familiarity had dulled the edge of its illogicality.

She knew there had been a genuine problem with the snake, for example, but by citing it so often as the crucial flaw, she had rendered the concept unreal and irrelevant, like pondering on a word too long until its existence in the vocabulary became a matter for doubt.

'Well,' she answered slowly. 'Maybe I do believe it in one way, but "believe" means something different here. "Believe" has sort of changed its meaning while I wasn't looking. Outside it means something different from what it means in here. It's like the Truth. The truth is something you have to believe, but here what you call the Truth is something different. It's all to do with capital letters, and it's not the same truth with a small T that I believe in the old way. There's a big difference – ' She came to a halt. She didn't seem to be making any sense even to herself, and Lucy was staring at her with frank incredulity.

'But how could that be, Carmen?' she asked in a sympathetic, worried little voice. 'How could someone change the meaning of a word when you weren't looking? The truth is the truth, believe means believe. How could those things have two different meanings?'

Carmen sighed unhappily. 'I don't know,' she said, 'but I have this idea in my head that that's how they do it. That's how they make people believe things they don't believe.'

Lucy shook her head. 'I don't think you can *make* someone believe things. And really ...' her hand soothed Carmen's hand, 'there isn't any "they" here, only "we". I'm not trying to make you believe anything, Carmen. Do you think I'd do anything to harm you?'

'No,' said Carmen. She stared unfocused at the pattern of the lino. She had come to work on Lucy but now it dawned on her that the process had undergone a subtle reversal – that, all the time she was trying to work on an impervious Lucy, she was being worked on with infinitely more subtlety herself, by practitioners who were much more skilled. Was that really a possibility, or was it paranoia? She studied Lucy's face as she went on.

'I think I know where the problem is. You tend to think on a very horizontal level, and I understand that because I used to be the same myself. But, you know what would really help you? If you could restrict yourself to really elevated things. You know, watch your vocabulary and try to limit it. You're very cluttered up with ideas and concepts. But really, those things aren't any use. We all have junk in our heads and there's a lot of it we can off-load.'

She took Carmen's stunned attention as sign of a thirst for further knowledge and it fired her to speak with more authority.

'If you could just concentrate on thinking really pure, vertical thoughts, the words would come out more elevated when you speak. I just think it's a good tip to get rid of all that junk in your head and listen to the beautiful poetic things that are said around you.'

She smiled apologetically and waited for some response. Carmen shook her head abruptly and her eyes were wild.

'Lucy, the junk in my head is my *brain*.'

'Oh, of course it's not,' teased Lucy. 'That's the most ridiculous thing I've ever heard. Are you suggesting I haven't got a brain?' She put her hands on her hips and made a comical face. 'Because, if you *are*, I'd like to point out that without one I wouldn't be able to have this ridiculous conversation and I certainly shouldn't be able to interpret your incredibly banal dreams.'

Carmen stared at her, thrown off balance, disconcerted. Something in her voice was suddenly the old Lucy, and the droll, mocking eyes were those of the Lucy she used to know. Maybe after all this was the same Lucy, not some sinister replica. Maybe what Jane had predicted all those long nights ago was true, that this was really the same Lucy, only just a little bit more religious.

'We don't give up our brains,' said Lucy, 'we just use them for the purposes God meant them for. If we all went round giving up our brains, we'd never get God's work done!'

Carmen was thinking quickly. What Lucy said was true. The members were extremely nimble thinkers, responding to complex questions, turning away objections, reacting to naked antipathy with the perfectly judged rejoinder. Lucy saw the trouble in her sister's face and took her advantage. She put her hand softly on Carmen's arm.

'Maybe it's difficult for you to understand this, Carmen, but no-one makes us believe it. This is what I've *chosen*. It's a good life, it's a God-fearing life, and I want you to respect it. I'm only asking you to look around, see how we live and try to understand it. Maybe I've made some terrible mistake, and, if I have, then you're free to point it out, but it really is important to me that I have your approval. Is that so much to ask? Don't you love me enough to *try* to understand it?'

Carmen had a weary feeling that the terms had just undergone a sudden change, but she was tired of thinking about it all. What did it matter anyhow, so long as it made Lucy happy?

'I'm trying. I *am* trying,' Carmen reassured her, and she allowed herself to be manoeuvred gently towards the door.

'Never underestimate the power of love,' said Lucy as they padded down the passage, listening to the eerie shuffle of their soft slippers.

Carmen could only mutter in her own defence, 'How could I underestimate it? It's the only reason I'm here.'

When they reached the dormitory, Carmen went to her bunk to change her clothes, but she found that her bag had been emptied of everything but toiletries and all her clothes were gone. She felt an immediate sense of invasion and panic. Spread out on the bunk was a small-print fawn dress with a high neck and long sleeves.

'Someone's taken my things,' she said.

She had the feeling that the dress was for her, and that they were stealing her identity quietly and hoping she wouldn't notice. Lucy smiled, 'Oh, I put them in the laundry. We're going to do a big wash. You'll get them all back in the morning. You can wear that.' She pointed to the dress. 'Isn't it gorgeous?'

'Oh, thank you,' said Carmen coldly. She didn't like people tampering with her things. It made her feel uneasy. Some of the clothes were dry-clean only and she knew they would come back shrunken. The pink jumper would moult balls of fluff all over the cotton shirts, and the cotton shirts would bleed dye. But it was more the sense of intrusion that bothered her. And she didn't want to wear the demure dimity dress that looked like the embodiment of Divine Principle.

'Whose is this?' she asked, holding it up unhappily against her.

'It's no-one's. It's yours,' Lucy told her. 'We keep our clothes communally in the Family. We just take clean things out of a tub. It's a good idea, don't you think? Saves worrying about what we wear. It's funny how the same thing looks different on different people.'

Carmen stared at her. This was Lucy, who used to spend every spare moment shopping for matching accessories, whose hobby had been spending money, whose wardrobe used to bulge with clever, witty, cheap clothes. Now she understood Lucy's new image, the drab, ill-fitting matronly dresses with draw-strings at the waist, hanging sacklike and seated at the bottom, cheered up by mumsy, synthetic cardigans with a cotton hankie tucked in the sleeve.

For a moment, it seemed to Carmen a terrible indignity, yet another way of robbing someone of their sense of self. The next moment, she shrugged it off. If individualism was of Satan, of course the clothes would have to go – clothes were a certain way of expressing individuality, wasn't that the point of them? Clothes weren't so important. She took her own clothes off and struggled into the dress.

'But what about when you need underclothes or something?' She supposed they didn't throw their knickers in the lucky dip.

'Oh, then we'd ask a Centre leader for some money, and if it's reasonable, they'd give us some. But generally we try to make our clothes last. I used to be *so* wasteful with clothes. As though I could possibly wear twenty different skirts! When you understand the importance of Father's mission, you don't want to waste his money.'

It was only just beginning to dawn on Carmen how it must be always to have to ask someone else for money. Carmen looked down at herself in the dress. It was like a vast maternity smock and the frills at neck and sleeve made her feel like a side of pork decoratively trussed.

'Is there a mirror?' she asked. She realised then that there wasn't a mirror in the whole house, only the little six-inch square by the door.

'I'll be your mirror,' said Lucy, and Carmen allowed herself to be turned like a limp rag-doll. 'There, it *really* suits you,' Lucy assured her. Carmen saw herself reflected in the window. As far as she could make out, she looked like a big pig in a pink sheet, but when she ventured that opinion, Lucy didn't think it beautiful. Some other sisters gathered to take an interest and they chorused in support of Lucy's opinion that it was just the thing for her colouring.

'I'd rather see a mirror, actually,' said Carmen. 'I feel as though I look peculiar.'

'We don't have mirrors in the Family,' Lucy told her gently. 'We don't like them. They make us think too much about ourselves. We try to think more about helping others and not about what kind of impression we're making on people.'

Carmen nodded, feeling instantly at fault, and feeling rather vain and shallow because, after all, what did it matter if it looked like a maternity dress? Who was going to see her? Only a peculiar bunch of people, half of them dressed in maternity smocks themselves. The Family's whole idea was that you saw the person, not their external trappings and, in theory, it wasn't such a terrible idea.

The Family Evening was a night of party games and joyous singing. Carmen quickly adjusted to feeling like a pig at a fancy-dress party, and it took her a while to realise that she was actually the belle of the ball. She had never received so many compliments in all her life. Everyone seemed to be making a special effort to be warm to her.

It was as though the wearing of the dress was a sign to all that she had made concessions, that she was going to stop resisting and try to fit in after all. She felt a bit of a fraud, swanning around looking radiant, as though she were about to give birth at any minute, particularly since she intended to put her resistance straight back on in the morning along with her laundered jeans. Gary danced attendance on her and kept saying how pretty she'd become.

Halfway through the jolly evening, Reg suddenly appeared in the hall, wearing a sheepish expression and carrying a large, brown, battered suitcase. He had come to stay. He'd met a very negative reception from his lay brothers and, already, there'd been talk of taking the Boy Scouts away from him because he'd insisted on talking to them about Satan and it had given some of them nightmares.

He told Carmen when she asked him that he'd found a lot of trouble holding conversations. No-one had seemed to be able to grasp any of the Principle when he had sat down to explain it to them. In fact, he had found himself becoming belligerent and didactic and they had accused him of being brainwashed. It had been a terrible experience. What had shocked him most was the awful, rigid conformity of their views. Their hostility had appalled him, based as it was on prejudice and blind bigotry. What's more, he had kept hearing the songs playing over and over in his head, as though the Family were in the room with him.

'There's nothing out there, Carmen,' he said. 'Nothing at all. That's what I discovered. The world is here.'

The old brown suitcase contained his mother's best willow-pattern china, each piece meticulously packed in newspaper. He was going to donate it to the Family. She realised that it was a very significant gesture to him.

'What good was it sitting on the dresser? Just sitting up there so I could get a selfish pleasure from looking at it. Now it'll be used,' he said. 'Now it'll be enjoyed.' He waved his hand expansively. 'Now it won't just be mine. It'll be everyone's.'

257

Technically he shouldn't have been allowed to join the course two days late, but they considered he'd already made sufficient spiritual growth to overcome the handicap. Carmen thought his growth was quite secure: his grey eyes were as blank as tiddlywinks. He seemed to think that it was markedly auspicious that there were twenty-one pieces to the tea set.

'Your mum would be pleased,' she told him awkwardly, and she turned away because she thought she was going to cry and she couldn't even explain to herself what it was that caused the ache inside her chest.

Reg's re-birthday was marked by a cake. He was so touched by the warmth that surrounded him that he made another of his emotional speeches and again burst into tears of helpless pleasure. If it made him happy, she thought, who could wish it away from him? As she watched his big, red face crumple with expressionless joy, she wondered where else a man like Reg, who needed love, but had probably lived without it for years, would have found such support, such a generous outpouring that could meet his needs and more? Maybe the Family wasn't such a bad thing, after all.

They all sang 'For He's A Jolly Good Fellow' and then Reg announced that he wanted to give his mother's house to Reverend Moon. People clapped uproariously as he cut his tiny, misshapen cake. Peter had given his car. It was a piece of Family history that a couple who had come looking for their young daughter had joined, and given a whole farm complete with land. The daughter had subsequently left and devoted her young life to working for Satan, trying to get her parents out. But still, Reg's little terraced house was not to be sniffed at and many of the guests had only their bank accounts to give. She could tell from their regretful faces that they envied him, that they longed to have something more valuable to offer than just their minds and bodies.

When the film show started, they sat in reverent silence watching the massed rows of brides and grooms that filled the screen. There were seven hundred brides for seven hundred brothers, or so it seemed to Carmen. In fact it was one thousand eight hundred couples who were getting married. The lines of sisters in their wedding veils looked like so many ribbons strung with blossom and the brothers were stripes of black, threaded in between. And there on the podium, with light rays coming from his every movement, was Father, in a white ecclesiastical gown of silk and a high, gold-ornamented paper crown. Mother, too, was blessing the couples as the snake of brides and bridegrooms wound its way up to the stage. It was a strange and awesome sight. So many people, and Father's face taut and strained as though He was summoning up some deep, internal power. Carmen sat forward, hunched with concentration, studying his face at every close-up. She wanted to know if he was the Messiah or just a mad and evil man – he looked like neither one thing or the other, only very tired, someone with enormous responsibilities that weighed him down.

And it was just the look that Jesus might have had, but even Jesus hadn't been required to command mass scenes on this scale.

The commentary drawled worshipfully on. 'Many of them have never met before. But after the Blessing, the real miracle becomes more and more apparent. That God has been planning this meeting all along. Master, knowing God's heart and will for every one of us, has brought together two people, and their mate has been created specifically for them...' and the camera panned along the blank-eyed happy couples in their going-away clothes, the nationalities all carefully mixed and matched. She tried to think it through but the more she churned it over, the more she began to make that mental shrug. So what? In many eastern countries, parents chose the marriage partners for their children. Was it so terrible? And anyway, from what she'd heard the married sisters saying, they hardly ever saw their husbands, what with the forty days' separation from Satan that followed the marriage, and then the diverse missions that Blessed members might be given.

Pamela had spoken of the Blessing as the ultimate reward, which they might not even dare to hope for. It was only available to perfec-ted members who had worked for the Family for at least six years.

'The joy of perfected love surpasses human understanding. It can transcend great distances so powerful and intense a love that it can even transcend total separation. It is these perfect couples who are the hope of the human race, restoring Satan's bloodline to its in-tended purity, cleansing the taint of original, inherited sin...'

As the camera panned across the faces, Carmen sat back and tried to think it through. She supposed it didn't matter whom they married.

A Moonie was a Moonie was a Moonie. They were all the same. Once the imperfections and the individualism were erased, the married couple couldn't find their interests incompatible because they *had* no interests. Only the one overriding, overpowering interest – to make the rest of the world just like themselves. And all at once, it seemed to her that the thing was possible; it was just difficult to comprehend because the scale of the undertaking was so vast. She remembered the two hundred gingerbread men that she had seen laid out in the kitchen on baking trays that afternoon, each one identical with its neighbour, each one glazed with its two blank currant eyes.

'I have a feeling one day that's going to be you and me, up there, wearing white,' Lucy whispered softly, and just as her hand groped to twine itself with Carmen's, Carmen was on her feet and walking mechanically towards the door.

Outside the light was fading and the setting sun hung suspended, bigger than she had ever seen it, like an enormous orange disc. She wandered down past the flower beds, across the playing field and down to where the sun glinted fire off the jagged twists of the barbed-wire fence. On the other side of the wire, in the other reality, the black and white cows were grazing close at the edge of the farmer's brackish pond. Beyond them, the landscape seemed to stretch to infinity, broken up here and there with screens of trees. On the horizon, the plane trees stood like cardboard cut-outs, a dull purple against the deepening red of the sky, and behind them she could see a road where tiny cars streaked by in a reality which was different from the one which contained her. The cows were chomping with placid absorption and, as she drew near, they looked up, still chewing, and considered her.

One of them grew curious and bold. It began to amble heavily towards her and she bent to pull up a clump of dock leaves and held them out. The cow's hooves were caked in mire and it had nothing on its mind but grass. She couldn't look at a cow, she told herself, and believe in the Family's reality. The Family's reality could only be sustained when you were not looking at anything so prosaic – or so poetic – as a cow. It came close enough for her to see the pimples on its great pink tongue but it stayed just out of reach, salivating wistfully as if there was good reason why it couldn't make contact with her, as if the cow too saw the invisible divide.

There were no words for the sensation she was trying to dispel. Maybe no-one had ever needed words for it before, the sensation of their reality – indescribable, unless it was the visual equivalent of the hard-edged, plastic, chemical smell of television sets in a shop. That was the nearest she could get to it. Yet if she inhaled with all her senses open, she could smell manure and loam and fresh-mown grass, so the analogy could make no sense.

Maybe it was like being suspended in amber liquid, seeing everything through a slightly yellow filter, with her brain slowing all its signals and her limbs registering the numbing paralysis that one experienced in dreams. And yet, when she stilled her perceptions and tried to recapture that sense of chemical reality again, her senses perceived only normality and told her everything was fine and that she had perfect control over her movements. So, it was she who was misreading perfectly normal signals and translating them as somehow sinister. It was she who was off balance and out of tune and somehow wrong. If she compared the *here* reality with the *there* reality, they were visually the same – so maybe everything really was OK, but some part of her brain was still misfiring, sending her a spooked sensation when there was nothing to get spooked about, telling her that if she was going to leave, now would be a good time to go. Immediately. Before the gingerbread men were wheeled out with the tea urns.

Even as she watched, the great ball of the sun was slipping down behind the trees, taking the grandiose pyrotechnics with it, dimming the sky to a melancholy, violet dusk.

She felt like someone on a fairground cake-walk with the floor moving rapidly away beneath her feet. When the normal laws were reversed, you put your hand out for something stable and solid. But when Carmen reached her hand out now, there was only the Family waiting to support her, rigid and unbending, immutable as a rock. As real as real, *more* real than the reality that was running away beneath her feet.

'Oh, honestly, what on earth's the matter, now?' called Lucy's anxious voice, and there she was stumbling gamely towards her across the grass. 'I think I ought to tie you down with elastic. I never know where you'll get to next . . .' As the little hand closed like a vice upon her arm, Carmen felt the chill of evening in her blood.

'Carmen, Carmen, always smoking. Heavenly Father doesn't want to live in an ashtray. If you pollute your body, then Heavenly Father can't get *in*.'

'You don't have any doubts, do you?' asked Carmen flatly, drawing on her cigarette.

Lucy stared at her solemnly for a moment and then regretfully shook her head. 'Of course not,' she said simply. 'No-one in the Family has any doubts or why would they be in the Family?'

Carmen's eyes roved abstractedly over to the out-houses. The brothers were building a high bonfire. She could hear the burr of their conversation and the cracking sound as they dragged and stacked the wood. Of course she should have known it all along. There had never been the remotest possibility of getting Lucy back. Lucy was fixed for ever on the other side of that line, as unreachable as a fly in amber. And all the clues and signs that Lucy had fed her, the little glimpses of vulnerability, they had all just been calculated fragments of emotional blackmail.

'But you said you wouldn't be human if you didn't have doubts.' She said it quite remotely.

Lucy laughed lightly. 'Oh, that. Yes, but I thought you understood. We're growing to perfection here. It's our human frailties that have to be erased.'

Carmen nodded. She felt as though she'd swallowed a living blackbird and it was beating its wings in panic in her chest. She had the feeling that her world was shrinking and that every way she turned her head, another avenue would close. Lucy was asserting proudly that she wasn't human and, since Carmen didn't doubt it any longer, she turned and walked determinedly towards the out-house where her identity was hanging on the drying rails, looking innocuous, pretending to be just a line of plain clothes.

'You can't leave now, you *can't*,' Lucy entreated as she flitted in Carmen's shadow like an insistent toddler. Carmen continued, nevertheless, to move methodically around the machines of the laundry room, collecting up wet woollens and jeans and adding them to the pile that was in her arms.

'What's the big, sudden hurry? I just don't see why it's suddenly so urgent . . .'

'I don't feel safe,' Carmen muttered.

Lucy stared at her, aghast. 'You think it's safe *outside?*' she shouted.

The next moment, she was bolting off through the door like a frightened rabbit, out into the darkness. Carmen supposed she was making for the house to consult with someone higher up.

As Carmen scurried back past the bonfire, she dodged behind the bushes for cover, keeping close to the wall of the house. She took the pantry entrance, guessing that the kitchen would be deserted by now. But, just as she slipped into the gloom of the corridor, Adèle loomed before her, framed in the kitchen doorway, her hand on the light switch, her face fixed in an enquiring, sympathetic smile.

'Ah, Carmen. There is some big problem?'

Carmen faltered, looking guilty, her arms full of telltale clothes. She was tempted to swivel on her heel and run back out again but Adèle's shadowed face was welcoming and her arm held the door wide in invitation. Knowing she was caught, Carmen lowered her eyes submissively and walked inside. Adèle swung the door behind them with a firm clang. Carmen turned, alarmed at the sound of the key inserted in the heavy lock. As Adèle secured the door, Carmen's heart began to race and all sorts of wild thoughts ran through her head, that they were going to hold her there by force or maybe starve her – not that she wasn't starving anyway, since the fasting Condition had been laid upon her. Perhaps a small gaggle of Korean brothers would burst from the larder, practising their karate swipes before they tied her up.

'This way no-one will interrupt us,' Adèle explained comfortably. The woman inclined her head and motioned Carmen to take the ingle bench beside the ancient Aga.

'When we have a problem, it's good to talk about it with someone, huh?' Adèle smoothed the seat of her skirt and sat down graciously beside her, assuming the air of a hospital matron condescending to a troubled patient. The keys hanging from her belt jangled with menace against the hard wood of the bench. 'Sometimes talking something out can really help.' She waited tactfully for Carmen to confide her little difficulty. Her expression was at once so solicitous and kindly that Carmen had to remind herself they had opposing interests to protect.

'There's nothing to talk about, really,' said Carmen. 'I just want to go home, that's all. Everyone said I was free to leave whenever I wanted to. And, just now, it suddenly happens that I want to go.'

Adèle considered her with a thoughtful air, then nodded. 'This is understandable. When we face up to what the Messiah asks of us, sometimes we want to run away. Sometimes we get cold feet, huh?' She gave a mischievous little laugh as though she'd often been tempted herself. 'This is very natural.'

'No,' said Carmen flatly, 'it's not that. I just don't believe it.'

'Ah, yes.' Adèle's face became more serious. 'Many times Satan works through our brains putting in ideas like "What if the things they're telling me are clever lies?" and "What if this is not the Messiah?" But, actually, Principle tells us what is true, and so whenever we have this sort of thought, we can know for sure that this is Satan talking, trying to use our brain for his purpose. Satan's very clever and that's how he tries to trick us because he doesn't want us to hear the truth.'

Carmen eyed her uneasily. Adèle's face was very grave and she pressed on with gentle insistency as though it was vital that Carmen should be made to understand.

'But it's very important when he tries to trick us this way that we don't give in to him. We mustn't have give-and-take with Satan — otherwise we let him take control of our brain and we lose that control ourselves. Perhaps this may be the problem you are having now. When Satan causes confusion in our brain, we're not able to think correctly. This is not a good time to take decisions. Perhaps it's better we look to someone wiser, someone closer to God, and let them make our decisions for us.'

'I'm perfectly in control of my brain,' Carmen insisted, shaking her head. 'That's how come I know I don't believe it.'

Adèle studied her with a rather pitying expression.

'What actually matters is not what we believe but what is the truth, don't you agree? And, actually, it is not man who tells us Principle is the truth, but God. When man says a thing is true, we can disbelieve it, but when God says a thing is true...' There was a delicate hesitation. 'Do you think, if God is truly God, we can disbelieve Him?'

She waited for Carmen to respond. Carmen was obliged to shake her head.

'That's not possible, is it?' Adèle coached her. 'God is a God of truth. There cannot be two ideas about the truth. We cannot say something is the truth and also say we disbelieve it. If we try to reconcile irreconcilable ideas, the result is confusion. We mustn't do it. There cannot be two ideas about the truth and if there is Carmen's idea of the truth and the Messiah's idea, whose idea is true?'

'The Messiah's,' said Carmen unhappily.

Adèle sat back, satisfied. 'Uh-huh. When we understand this, we can begin to work on our problems,' she said smoothly. 'The Messiah cannot come in when we have selfish attitudes, so maybe tomorrow you begin to take on some Conditions, huh?' And in a comfortable voice, she began to outline a Condition programme that Carmen might set herself as though all Carmen's problems were solved, all her objections overridden. 'This would be a good way to start, don't you think?' she asked, and she tilted her head on one side, her eyes wide and candid, waiting for Carmen to aquiesce.

'*No!*' Carmen said desperately. She had the feeling she was being hauled unceremoniously on board, with or without her consent. 'It may be the truth for you and it may be the truth for everyone here. For all I know, it's the truth for God Almighty but it *isn't* the truth for me, and I'm going *home*.' Carmen's voice was unnecessarily emphatic and the tremor in her voice gave away the fact that she was not at all in control.

Adèle surveyed her with dissatisfaction for a moment. She leant forward, clasped her hands together and began to speak gently, confidentially.

'Maybe we are stubborn and full of pride. We want to follow our own selfish heart but there are other things I must speak to you about. Things you maybe haven't understood. Now would be quite a dangerous time to leave ... You see, you've stayed here past the point where you could have left safely. When people leave in the growth stage, they're very open. The spirits mass around them and attack. Often such a person will have an accident or be killed. Many times this happens. This is why your physical sister's so upset...' She paused delicately to make sure that Carmen fully understood. 'You know, last week, there was a guest called Katy?'

Carmen nodded. She had heard Katy's friends whispering and crying in the dormitory. She had heard them praying for the girl's immortal soul.

'Well, everyone explained the dangers to her. But she was arrogant, she thought that she knew best. But actually, what happened was she ran out into the road there, and a car came speeding out of nowhere and just mowed her down. It carried her along the road for fifty yards.' Adèle shrugged indifferently. 'Robert tried to locate her in the Spirit World but he couldn't make contact. He only spoke to some other spirits who told him she hadn't managed to get through.'

Carmen watched the woman's mouth distrustfully. She supposed poor Katy was still out there, hovering at the gate with head injuries, waiting to attack another vulnerable person with a fragile spirit. Only she wouldn't be alone. There would be a whole host of other spirits with her and they'd be swarming like an angry hoard of gnats. She shook her head to dispel the unwelcome image.

'So maybe it's best that you listen to others,' Adèle said cordially, 'because, actually, it's not only yourself that you would harm. There is also your physical mother to be thought of. Perhaps she already has some kind of minor illness?' Carmen's eyes were round as she shook her head, mistrustfully.

'Or maybe this would bring some illness on. So this is not only for your own good that I say this but also for your physical family, who might come to harm...'

'It's nothing to do with my mother,' said Carmen tightly. 'She doesn't even know I'm here. How could the spirits hold her responsible?'

Adèle went on calmly. 'Often this happens. Perhaps a relative has some small recurring ailment and when a child turns their back on the Messiah, the spirits attack, and maybe your mother's recurring problem blows up into something very serious, even life-threatening. So this is a big responsibility. Sometimes our selfish actions threaten a relative in a very powerful way.'

'I don't believe that,' Carmen repeated more urgently.

Adèle's mouth set hard with impatience and her eyes became steely. Carmen sensed that the interview was nearing its close. She was running over in her mind the bouts of coughing that had troubled her mother that year, the repeated virus infections. Were they the seeds of something more serious? It was true that she didn't believe it, but, all the same, it frightened her. It was as though Adèle's inexorable pronouncements were very final, as though she was casting a fatal curse on Carmen and everything she loved. Adèle regarded her for a long moment and then shrugged.

'Actually whether you believe it or not makes no difference to the outcome.' Adèle got to her feet as if she could waste no more time on someone worthless. She had done her best. If Carmen wanted to be arrogant, she could face the spirits at the gates alone.

'It's best you wait and think things over in the night. In the morning there will be a coach and it can take you back to London, if you're prepared to take the consequences. There's no point your leaving now. Public transport stops at eight o'clock and you're a long way from the nearest town.'

'Couldn't someone drive a van...?' Carmen began timidly, but she subsided at the naked hostility that was flashing in Adèle's eyes.

'Here people work night and day for the Restoration. We do not spare a van for a selfish person who thinks only of themselves.'

Adèle unlocked the door and held it open. Carmen could feel the icy draught coming from her like the white smoke from a deep-freeze.

'It's best you pray about this before you make a decision you can't undo,' she said. Carmen stood in a daze, nodding, mumbling her thanks, although why she should be thanking someone for laying a curse upon her, she had no idea.

The moment Adèle released her, Carmen bolted off down the corridor towards the stairs, her heart beating very fast. She thought about getting a mini-cab. A mini-cab would just plough on through the spirits and Carmen would surely be invulnerable inside it, at least till the next town. But would Robert let her use the phone to call a cab? Probably not. For some reason, she shrank from walking out through the gates into the darkness to find a call-box. There was also the very real question of money. She hadn't brought her cheque book and she'd given the last of her cash to the shuttlecock fund. Moreover, she had no clear idea of where she was or how to get home. These were mere logistical problems, easily overcome with a clear head and a bit of energy. However, her head was anything *but* clear, while a bit of energy was just what she didn't have. A strange, exhilarating rush of adrenalin had kept her going through the last few days but now, as she climbed the stairs to the dormitory, she was aware that the sheer effort of pitting herself against Adèle's will, of winning her empty victory, had left her drained. An extreme weariness was beginning to wash over her, making her face feel gaunt and hollowed round the eyes.

The thought of trying to cadge money from the hostile sisters, of finding her way to the town, grappling with bus and train timetables in a rural back-water that she had never seen in daylight – all these things seemed insurmountable obstacles. She climbed the second flight of stairs with flagging zeal. There was also the small, niggling premonition that she would be run down by a car. She was very conscious of the way metal would sound hitting flesh and splintering bone. She asked herself whether Gary was sufficiently her friend to help her. She knew Lucy wasn't, but Gary might be prepared to run her to the station. Of all of them, Gary was the weak link; the one she really believed had secret doubts, the one who pined for his guitar, who harboured fallen thoughts and let them hunger from his eyes.

She resolved to pack her bag and seek him out. But, as she arrived breathless at the last landing, she pulled up short, her nose pressed into the buttons of a dark waistcoat. It was Gary, coming down from the prayer room. He was wearing an unfamiliar three-piece suit and, far from looking like her saviour, his features were set in the blackest of frowns. He affected a bantering tone, but there was something uncompromising and menacing in the way he placed his body.

'Hey, Carmen. I'm giving my witness. I think you'd like to hear it.'

'I can't,' she said, simply. 'I've made my mind up and I'm going home.'

He was unsurprised, as though the news had already reached him.

'You can go home any time,' he told her. 'Right now it's far too late for travelling in the dark. Come on, there's no time to waste. The singing's started.' He began to move down the stairs with imperious haste so that she found herself stumbling backwards. Seeing the alarm on her face as she backed away, he seemed to recollect himself. He reached to steady her and spoke more softly.

'It's my witness,' he repeated. 'I don't give it often, Carmen. It's important. I want you to hear it, and if you're leaving this is the only chance you'll get.'

He saw the flicker of hesitation and took his advantage.

268

'It's not a lot to ask, is it? Can't you just stay another night?' His voice was plaintive and his eyes, close to, were strained and bleary. She had the idea that he'd been praying hard and that it might have been for her. Her heart melted a little.

'I'm a bit nervous,' he confessed. 'I could do with some moral support.'

Suddenly he seemed quite normal again and he gave her his most sympathetic, boyish grin. Carmen stared doubtfully at him, wondering which of the Garys that he showed her was the real Gary. And then the fight went out of her. Well, what did it matter? Tonight or tomorrow morning, it was all the same. Perhaps things would seem easier in the morning and the mountains would be molehills in the light of day.

The next moment, he was escorting her courteously down the stairs, his hand softly on her elbow. The house echoed strangely hollow as they trudged through the empty corridors, following the sound of rapturous singing, sweet and distant, from the Family gathered in the garden, and Carmen realised that her heart was light now that she was released from the responsibility of taking independent action.

'The spirit's really high tonight,' Gary remarked lightly as they emerged onto the back steps. It was an understatement.

Carmen stopped still in her tracks, arrested by the spectacle.

The bonfire was blazing high, sending charred remnants shimmering up to heaven in the impetus of the heat-haze. Chairs and benches had been placed around it in a semicircle of regular rows and there were maybe eighty ardent faces lit up in its red-gold glow, straining upwards, giving voice to the hymn.

> 'I have seen him in the watchfires
> of a hundred circling camps
> They have builded him an altar
> in the evening dews and damps
> I can read His righteous sentence
> by the dim and flaring lamps
> His day is marching on...'

The hymn stirred her and tugged at her heart strings, as the Family singing always tugged at her heart strings. An outsider looking in might have thought they were just singing, but that would have been to miss the point completely. Everything they sung was invested with a special, sacred, secret significance. It was Father whose day would come, Father whose truth was marching on.

For a dizzying moment, she had the sense that she was seeing the vignette through the wrong end of a telescope, blurred and distorted. It was if something very important, something very meaningful was being vouchsafed to her in that one concise image, but she couldn't pinpoint just what the meaning was.

They wound their way down through the darkness, towards the beckoning warmth and light. As she walked, she took up the song, until she was close enough for the heat of the fire to bathe her face and her voice blended with the others. People moved to give her room in their circle, but they didn't move in invitation – rather, they shrank from her as from a carrier of contagion. In the Family news travelled like a wave and only Lucy snuggled near to her, smiling with relief.

Gary spoke his testimony haltingly at first. She was curious to hear it because she thought it might reveal some key to him, but it was much like other testimonies she had heard – homogenised and bland. Their pasts, as they recounted them, were deodorised and colourless, shrink-wrapped pasts without texture, peopled with cyphers and re-called without affection or nostalgia. He said the same sort of things she had heard the others say. His parents were well off. They had given him everything but they hadn't been able to give him love.

Since his words told her nothing new, she just allowed herself to be soothed and entranced by the lilts of his voice, hypnotised by the flames as they darted and dipped, now lighting his face from below so that he looked like a ghoul in a horror film, now dancing and leaping so that his face was radiant like St Joan's on her funeral pyre. She had never seen his features so animated or expressive. Who would ever know the truth about any of the Family's pasts? They had confessed everything that was asked them, declared their past lives empty of any value and, on one specific day, shut tight the lid of the capsule as though to say, from now on all that I have confessed today *is* the past. I can get it out for you and parade it to order, but I can't add to it or subtract from it because the past is now sealed. Gary's eyes were shining with enthusiasm now as he dwelt on the episode that never lost its savour in retelling: how he had been tricked and cajoled to the course, how he hadn't wanted to come.

'I thought "Why does this guy keep writing me notes and ringing me up and coming round? Is he lonely or something?"' Everyone laughed with exquisite recognition. Gary smiled too. 'You see I didn't know about Heavenly Deception.' There was another gale of delicious laughter but some of the guests laughed with a puzzled air. 'Do you know this phrase "Heavenly Deception"?' he asked some of the little girls at the front. 'Well, Satan deceived the human race into six thousand years of misery and now God tells us to use Heavenly Deception to bring his children back.' Then the guests understood and smiled delightedly at their Spiritual Parents, beginning to appreciate the well-meaning skill that had fetched them to the Family.

'So I was busy with my own selfish pleasures. I didn't want to know about saving the world. If the Messiah was on earth, it really wasn't anything to do with me...'

Lucy confided her hand into Carmen's and pressed it tightly as if the most exciting part of a film that she'd seen many times was coming up.

'And suddenly He wanted me. The Messiah wanted *me*, and I had to decide if I had the courage and the strength to give up everything I knew to follow Him...' Tears were starting up in his eyes. She could see them glistening by the light of the fire. 'Joining the Family, following the Messiah, that was the only heroic thing I've ever done, and, *yes*, it's a sacrifice...' She saw that other people had tears rolling down their faces as they stared at him transfixed. 'But I had to do it, because otherwise I would have been nothing, I would have been worth less than nothing. You can't see the Messiah and walk away from him. He doesn't *let* you walk away. He binds you in his spell and you don't want to be free. Because there is no freedom without the Messiah.'

It was at that moment that his eyes met Carmen's and she felt that he was speaking directly to her.

'The more precious something *is* and the more we don't want to give it up, then the more precious that gift is to Father and the more we *have* to give it up. Because if we didn't care about giving it up, then it wouldn't be any sort of gift.'

He fell silent for a moment and stared into the fire, almost as though he'd forgotten the words. It wasn't some lecturer's trick. No-one could hear Gary and not believe that his passion came straight from the heart. He made a visible effort to control his emotions and then smiled round the audience, a rather bitter, humble smile as though they ought to understand his weakness.

'And when we've given everything to Father, when we're hollowed out, that's when He fills us with his blessings, that's when we feel the miracle of love the Messiah brings.'

He turned suddenly and nodded to the guitarist. As the musical introduction to his song began, Carmen realised why he had wanted her to hear him. He was effectively telling her that he was a closed book, that whatever other impressions he had given her, he was a Unification Church member and there was nothing in his life but that. He wanted her to understand the sanctity and importance of it. He wanted her to respect it as his fierce triumph, not his tragedy: that was how they all wanted to be seen, because it was their truth. As he began to sing, his voice was weak and thin, trembling slightly with emotion, but as it grew stronger it blotted out the gentle sobbing that floated on the air. His eyes were fixed on the great, dark sky ahead of him, his face shone luminous and transfigured by the flames and every line of the song had a poignancy and a meaning far exceeding anything its writer could have conceived.

> 'To dream the impossible dream
> To fight the unbeatable foe
> To bear with unbearable sorrow
> To run where the brave dare not go
> To right the unrightable wrong
> To love pure and chaste from afar
> To try when your arms are too weary
> To reach the unreachable star...'

They rose to their feet as one body and added their voices to his. As Carmen stood, she felt herself engulfed, borne up by their ferocious absolute conviction that the Messiah was on earth, that they could take on Satan alone. They were the hope for the world, and no personal sacrifice would stand in the way of their mission.

It was impossible not to revere their mad, impossible dream when she considered how much it cost them, how totally dedicated they were to bringing it about. She was so over-tired and confused with her own conflicting emotions, so touched by the pathos and dignity of their futile faith, that she merged with them for a moment. If the Messiah really *did* come to earth, she thought, wouldn't it be like this? This way I can understand it. If this is the whole meaning of the Family, how could it possibly be wrong?

When all the prayers were over, Gary stood slightly apart and people congratulated him, taking turns to shake his hand. It was as though he was some golden, groomed celebrity, and, in his sober three-piece suit and with that easy smile, he looked the part.

Carmen was shy of him now and would not go near him. There was something very separate about him; the purity burned from him like a protective shield. But, even in the confusion, his eyes roved the crowd and found her face. As the group was beginning to disperse, he made his way over to her.

'Do you understand a little more?' he asked, gently. 'Are things becoming clearer? When you have a secret this special, then, the more you love someone, the more you want them to have it too. You want to pass it on.'

'Heavenly Deception?' She repeated the phrase. Separately, the words were not so nice, but put together there was something beautiful and mystical about them. Something mysterious and full of meaning. He nodded. It meant that he had only misled her out of love for her. She understood it now. The more ingeniously he had misled her, the more he must have loved her. She accepted it calmly and without resentment, only thinking how clever he had been to anticipate her every move, to make her feel sorry for him just at the right moment, not to put too much pressure on her, always to seem just that bit more normal than everyone else, making her think he was somehow less of a Moonie than all the others. She wondered if they had an annual prize-giving and if so whether she could recommend him for a small gold egg-cup. They believed it was so important to bring someone to the truth that any means were justified, and she couldn't resent the tactics he'd used because he'd only been acting as he was obliged to act in her own best interests. But she didn't much feel like standing around congratulating him on them, either.

The brothers were lighting wax tapers from the fire and stalking up against the slope of the ground, towards the darkness.

'We're going to the Holy Ground to pray now,' he said.

She shrugged. 'I don't think I will,' she said, 'I'm feeling cold.'

But he swung off his jacket and put it round her shoulders, then propelled her with him to follow the others.

'Really, there's no point,' she protested. 'I'm leaving. . . .'

'It won't hurt you to ask Heavenly Father one more time,' he told her.

She put her head inside his jacket and smelt the warmth of his sweat in the lining. It was the most intimate moment she would ever have with him. When you grew to love someone in the Fallen World, they came closer, but in the Family, she thought, the more you knew them, the more they moved away.

'Is it yours or did you get it in the lucky dip?' she asked. It occurred to her that maybe it wasn't even his warm individual smell she was inhaling, but a pot-pourri of the brothers' bodies who had passed through that particular suit. He ignored her.

When they reached the Holy Ground, he bade her take her shoes off. The grass was wet and freezing on her feet. The Holy Ground turned out to be a patch of land with a grove of trees. It was special because Father had blessed it. The guests and members formed a circle and, to her surprise, instead of praying one at a time as they had always done before, they had to say their individual prayers out loud and all together.

It was difficult for Carmen, at the best of times, to pray in the way the Family did, because praying their way involved praying to a different God.

They were not supposed to bother Him with selfish problems or with any mention of their physical families. She supposed she must ask Him for a revelation. So, against the rapid quick-fire of the other supplicants, she began to demand this of Him quite loudly, because it was necessary to maintain volume if one was going to keep the thread of one's own prayer.

When she sneaked her eyes open, she saw that Gary was watching her. As the voices of the other people in the circle praying became louder and more insistent, she closed her eyes tighter and began to speak more loudly and more urgently. She repeated the same words over and over again, like a chant, 'If this is the Messiah, give me the revelation,' until she had a dizzying sense that she was lost in some vacuum, or trapped inside some old-fashioned wireless in which all the wavelengths on different frequencies were broadcasting at once. It was eerie, that sensation, as if she was a tiny figure in a great void, shouting against the white noise of the different languages that crisscrossed her consciousness. The tighter she closed her eyes, the more brightly burned the blazing tapers in the trees like a red muzz on her eyelids. Fragments of Japanese and French and German competed for her attention until she was literally shouting, 'If this is the Messiah, grant me a revelation,' although the words had become quite meaningless to her and she could hardly hear them. She was aware of the grass which felt like ice on her naked feet.

Then, suddenly, something happened. Her eyes flew open. It wasn't spectacular as she'd imagined it would be.

It was as though three pages of a book turned over in rapid succession. Flick, flick, flick, they went, too fast for her to register the image, although the image was only what she saw before her, the dark tree trunks against the black backdrop of the night. Her perception had lightened and darkened and lightened in the split second that it took to occur, and her brain had captured three distinct and dislocated realities and then settled on the third as a fruit machine might settle on a sequence of lemons. Her eyes were starting out of her head with the concentration that was required to see and understand what had happened in her vision, because, banal as the image was, she knew that there had been something profound hidden between the pages, if she could just recall them and run them through again.

Her world had fragmented and splintered and then realigned itself, the same but also different. There was no self in it. It was as though self and the world were the same thing. There was pain, but also calm resignation. It was as though she was drenched with acceptance and cleansed within. It wasn't at all alarming because she felt she had always known it, and because she had always known it, she knew about the consolation and she understood the sense of enormous promise.

She looked wildly around her to place herself in reality. The wax tapers flared from the trees like flaming swords, lighting the faces of the circle, and the voices jarred and clashed, blending into some strange garbled mantra against the hiss of the wind gushing through the trees.

As her head moved round, she felt herself begin to spin and she saw the circle break up and stretch out into an oblong shape, although neither she nor the other people had moved at all. She looked up to the trees above to get her bearings and saw that they were telescoping up and up, and she felt the bones of her face elongate and then her spectral body stretching so that she was improbably tall without having left the ground. Her head flew back and she let out a loud gasp, half of fear and half of recognition: there seemed to be a brief flash of blinding light and then she staggered back on her heels and crumpled weakly onto the cold wet grass.

She began to cry in long, shuddering sobs and spasms that wrenched through her body, freeing the tension that was jammed up inside her. She was oblivious to everyone around her and they were oblivious to her, except for Gary.

He stood there, some feet away, pretending to concentrate on his muttered prayer, but watching Carmen with a gleam of satisfaction in his face.

As he helped her back to the house through the darkness, he whispered urgently, 'Did you feel it, Carmen? Did you feel that power?'

'I felt something,' she said.

'Don't you think the disciples felt that way when they first set eyes on Jesus?'

'I felt something,' Carmen repeated. Even in her strange dazed state, she fought off believing it. She clung on stubbornly to what literal facts she could find. The disciples had been dazzled in that way by Jesus; *she* had been dazzled by a group of large trees. 'I felt overwhelmed and swept away and I felt *something* . . .'

'Did it all come together at once?' he persisted. 'Did you sense a greater power?'

She began to tremble with cold and over-stimulation. Her whole being felt tenderised and vulnerable. She wanted him to stop talking. She needed solitude to sort it out. But she could feel his breath on her face, feel the heat of his skin as he pressed urgently on.

'Did you feel like a piece of glass in a kaleidoscope, did you feel like you'd suddenly seen where you fitted in the universe? Did you find your place?'

She walked on, huddled up, hugging her body with her arms, trying to veer away from him as he tried to draw closer.

276

'Hey, give in to it, Carmen. Don't fight it all the time. Let it flood over you. Don't resist it. Just let it bear you up, like a sea of love...'

'Leave me *alone*,' she wailed. She turned to him and pushed him away hard with the flats of her hands. The strength in her arms failed, and in pushing him away so ineffectually, the recoil only brought him closer, so that his mouth was almost on her cheek like a lover's.

He whispered, low and urgent, 'When you see the Messiah, you can't walk away from him. Once you know the truth, you can't *un*know it...'

'I don't know what I know,' she muttered. 'I don't know anything.'

'You know everything there is to know. This is what happened to every one of us. We didn't want to know the truth, but the truth came anyway and took us by surprise. No-one *wants* to be called by the Messiah, but He calls us anyway. We didn't believe it but we were given no choice.'

'I have a choice,' she said. She was feeling frightened. 'I have a choice. I can go to sleep and I'll go away tomorrow and it'll be as though none of this ever happened.'

'You can't walk away when you know,' he said firmly. 'You can fool yourself that you don't know, but what good is that? When deep down inside you know something so important, and yet you still walk away from it, then for ever after you're condemned to live a lie.' He took her hands. 'I know you're not afraid of anything. Don't be afraid of this. It's a terrifying responsibility, but it's the most beautiful secret that anyone could ever hold in their keeping. And once you know it, no matter which way you run, all roads lead to Father — there's no escape.'

'I have to find my shoes,' she said, distantly. 'It's very important that I find my shoes.' They were the only flat shoes she had. She would need them in the morning. She couldn't go home barefoot. It was a long way to London. She didn't want their secret. She hadn't asked for it and she wished it could have been taken away. And while Gary busied himself with searching for her track shoes in the grass, she walked on like a somnambulist to the house.

Chapter 11

That night, her father came to the door of the dormitory in the middle of the night. He didn't speak, he just stood there fidgeting in his old lived-in gardening trousers, smiling as if he was quietly pleased about something.

The following afternoon, she sat in the dormitory on a hard-backed chair with a cluster of sisters round her. She fixed her eye on the green geometric pattern of the polished linoleum and watched the pattern of their dresses jostling one another breaking up the symmetry of the floor covering, then watched the hanks of flaxen hair slither and tickle down her bare brown arm and wind into long curls at her feet, listening to the crisp snip, snip of the scissors close to her ears and the whispering of the sisters as they moved around her softly, giggling like excitable ghosts. The linoleum was as fascinating as a piece of malachite, the dark green line fading to a pale green line, the inner diamond darkening to frame a yellow centre. Somewhere in the house a girl's voice was singing 'Amazing Grace' with a heartbreaking sweetness, and the plaintive, insistent tune compounded the mystery and the logic of the self-contained repeating shapes that jiggled up and down in her vision.

Just as everyone had told her, she felt extremely calm and clear. All the struggle, all the confusion, all the thudding pains in her head and the irrational urges to laugh and cry at inappropriate moments, the sense of constant frenzied irritation, all these things that had been part of her prolonged, futile resistance, were gone. After the storm, the still small voice of calm. The revelation brought with it an overpowering sense of release, of letting go, and, in its place, there was an absolute conviction that, strange as it seemed, this actually *was* the truth.

It was a frightening, awesome piece of knowledge and, as they said, once you knew it, you couldn't walk away. They tilted her chin this way and that to even up their ragged effort, and as her eyes

278

searched the ceiling, she wondered why she, of all people, had been chosen to receive it. Why couldn't God have just left her where she was?

Once her hair was neat and tidy, the way Father liked it best, Carmen walked out to the stairwell with her bevy of giggling attendants. Her hand caressed the silk of the bannister as she glided down towards the ring of upturned, joyful faces in the hall. They began to surge towards the base of the stairs and the familiar strains of 'Happy Re-birthday' struck up from the piano. Then everyone began to clap and cheer, calling out 'speech', and she was overwhelmed by a sense of humility and gratitude that they should love her after she had fought so hard against them, after she had ridiculed for so long their sacred truth. Her voice became stronger and more sure as the applause died down. Lucy could only pick up the tail end of the breathless little speech.

'You know, the Bible says, the truth will set you free. Well, I came here to listen to the greatest truth and I can only tell you, I feel a freedom now that I have never known before in my lifetime.' She laughed in an exhilarated, joyful way that was infectious and made everyone else laugh too. They'd heard it so often before. The miracle that Principle could wreak on the most intransigent soul. There was an uproar of clapping and whistling. First Lucy, then Adèle, then Jane, then Pamela stepped forward to kiss her, then a melee of sisters did the same. Through the confusion, Carmen became aware of Gary in the crowd of beaming brothers. He was not smiling but wearing a curious, haunted look.

As she drew level, he reached out and pressed something in her hand, a photograph.

'I want you to have this. There's a space for it in the wallet,' he said. It was a snap of him standing in the grounds. 'Wherever your mission takes you, you can always know I'm with you in spirit, praying for you and watching over you, even though we're far apart.'

She smiled at him, puzzled. Was he going somewhere? Somehow she had imagined they would be able to spend more time together now. She sensed that her education was only just starting. There were a million secrets yet to learn and she had imagined that Gary would be there beside her, along with Lucy, guiding her steps, at her side as she peeled back each mysterious layer and moved towards the heart of the central mystery. Now, it occurred to her that when the end of the Twenty-One Day came, she might be starting the Forty Day without him. She saw that there were tears in his eyes.

'I'm so pleased, so proud…' he began, but then he smiled as though words were quite inadequate to express it all. 'You'll understand when you have a Spiritual Child of your own.'

And before she could ask him whether there wasn't a chance that their missions would bring them together, he stepped back to let Lucy stake her claim. Seeing the radiant pleasure beaming from Lucy's face, Carmen put it out of her mind. Lucy's arms were fiercely around her and their two faces pressed close. Carmen heard her whisper, 'Oh, Carmen! Now, we're *really* sisters. Now we're sisters in the only true sense there is.'

Carmen answered her impulsively, overcome by the emotion of the moment, by the smiling, kindly faces all around them. 'It's so funny. I thought you were lost, but it's me who's found. I thought someone was trying to take you away and all that's really happened is we've come together more completely.'

'You didn't understand,' Lucy cried. 'You thought I was being cold, you thought I didn't love you. It was only because I loved you *so much* that I worked so hard!' Lucy laughed, incredulously. 'You were just *so* difficult! You must have been one of the hardest ones we ever had!'

'I heard you were pretty difficult yourself,' interrupted Robert. She turned and retorted, good-humouredly, 'It took me two days, not two weeks!' She made a comic face and everyone laughed along with her.

She turned back to Carmen and took her hands.

'Remember how I always used to rely on you?' Lucy asked, her voice choked with emotion. 'Now I feel like I've been able to pay some of that back. Isn't it wonderful? Isn't it just the best experience you've ever known?'

Carmen hugged her even tighter. 'It's wonderful,' she whispered, 'and the most wonderful thing is we can share it even more completely than everything we've shared before.'

The next moment, the crowd jostled in and suddenly everyone was laughing and their arms were all intertwined as the sound of a joyful

song began. Tears rolled unashamedly down Carmen's face as she
gave her heart to the words:

> 'I wish for you, my friend
> The happiness that I've found
> On Him you can depend
> It matters not where you're bound
> I shout it from the mountain top
> I want the world to know
> The Lord Of Love has come to me
> I want to pass it on....'

It seemed to her in that ecstatic moment, with all the brothers and
sisters round her, shaking their linked arms, raising the spirit with
their massed voices, that there never *had* been a love like it; that there
could be no more glorious way to spend one's life than in sharing and
passing on this overpowering experience – nothing more humbling
or more exalting than to give one's life to the Lord Of The Second
Advent, nothing more awesome or mysterious or enthralling than to
give one's heart to the Lord Of Love.

'They say we're brainwashed,' Robert thundered indignantly in the
lecture. 'Well, don't our brains need a little scrub? Don't we need to
get the Dettol and the brushes into those deep, dark corners of the
soul, scour it out before we can let the purifying air of the Messiah
in? Because even our brains aren't safe from Satan, are they? And if
the Messiah's mission is to succeed on earth, then we mustn't have
contact with Satan, must we? And yet that's difficult, because –
where is Satan?'

'Everywhere,' the answer came back darkly.

'Yes, he's everywhere, outside there in the Fallen World. And
Satan uses emotional blackmail and deception, Satan has always
used those tools to rule the world. So, many times, someone's physical mother will ring a member in the Centre and say, "You ought to
come home, now. You've heard enough." Maybe this woman will
say, "Come home, I'm in the hospital" or they'll even tell you, "Your
physical father's dying and he wants you near", but how many times
have we found that it was Satan speaking, using that physical parent
to snatch the child back from the truth? This is why we have to be so

careful not to confuse real love, the Messiah's perfect love, with a selfish love that wants only to pollute us and gain control.'

Carmen was trying to concentrate on his words but her mind kept returning to the letter that she had to write. There had already been four or five drafts and Gary had tried to help her with it, but it was so hard. How could she possibly explain the great wave that had overwhelmed her in terms that her mother might understand? Besides which, her mother was still happily under the impression that she was bobbing up and down on a pony somewhere in Talybont-On-Usk. She couldn't hope to convince her mother of what had been revealed to her, the importance of the whole thing for the human race. She was only just coming to terms with it herself. How could someone unprepared, who had not heard Principle, even hope to get a glimmer of understanding?

The letter so far ran: 'Dear Mother, first a piece of really good news! Lucy is safe and happy. More than that, I've never seen her so happy or well in all her life! It may surprise you that I am not in Wales but down in Somerset and that I came here to do a bit of investigating for myself! As we thought, Lucy is with Unification Church but imagine my surprise when I found that they were really a nice, friendly crowd and just the sort of people you would have wanted her to meet! They do a lot of work rescuing drug addicts and working with disadvantaged children...'

Carmen had baulked slightly at this, but Gary insisted that she write it in. What were the new recruits but disadvantaged children suffering under Satan's rule of sin? And, as for the drug addicts, many people in the guilt sessions had admitted to smoking dope at parties.

'And they're very idealistic and hard-working. Now for my other piece of news. This may surprise you, but it wouldn't if you'd met the group of friends I'm with...'

Carmen wasn't at all sure about the uncharacteristic jolly tone or the exclamation marks he wanted her to use, but it seemed to be the house-style in the One World Family. This was the kind of letter that they were advised to write so as not to alarm their physical parents or bring persecution down upon the Family. She sighed. No matter how meticulously she drafted and redrafted the letter, she knew with bitter resignation that her mother would just *never* understand.

'If Satan can even work through our physical families, we have to be cautious, don't we?' Robert was saying.

The members nodded solemnly. Carmen gave a guilty jolt and tried very hard to stop thinking about her mother and the letter, because it was always possible that it was someone else who was putting those thoughts in her head.

'We can take a tip from Satan's book, here. We're justified in using the same tools that Satan used to thwart God's plan. We use love like a fishing rod to bring someone to Father,' he demonstrated hooking someone gently and reeling them in, 'but if that person isn't pure enough to accept the Messiah, that's when we use love like a weapon.' He made a slicing movement through the air. 'That's when we have to cut them off. This is the meaning of Heavenly Deception. Satan deceived the human race into six thousand years of misery, and now God uses Satan's methods to try to bring His children back.

'So, when you're talking to your physical families, don't tell them too much. Don't tell them things that might alarm them. Use your love to try to lead them to the Church. But if your physical parents answer you by speaking against the Family, then remember what Jesus said to Mary when she tried to hold him back. He told her, "Go away now, Mother, I have no time for you. I am doing the work of my Father." This is what our attitude must be. The words of Jesus tell us, "Hate your mother, hate your father," for, if your physical family try to hold you back, then they're no longer on the side of God but on the side of Satan. What we have here is a Heavenly emergency and each of us has to know in our hearts that nothing will stop us from fulfilling our part in the Restoration. For the person who experiences the Revelation, who knows the Messiah, and yet turns his back, that person is cursed and double-cursed. He's cursed by Satan and he's cursed by the Messiah. For such a person, there's no way forward and there's no way back. His soul can only spiral in the abyss like a stone falling into a bottomless well.'

Carmen was giving him her full attention now. The words seemed so mournful, the fate so inexorable and hopeless.

'How much more lost is the man who turns a Heavenly Child from Father, because nothing can protect him from the spirit legions' attack. It's better even for such a man that he should die, better that than to cause a Family member to forsake the Lord Of The Second

Advent. Yes, in God's eyes this is a crime far worse than murder. Better that a man should be murdered than that he lose his everlasting soul. Sometimes selfish parents come to try to drag their physical children back to the Satanic world by force. That's how frightened people are of purity. This is why many of our brothers learn karate because, for their own sakes, these people have to be prevented; they have no idea of what damage they take upon their souls. So, if we love our parents, we don't let them put themselves in danger. If we love our physical parents, we have to protect them from themselves.'

And then Carmen decided how she would finish off the letter. She would say none of the things she wanted so much to explain, about the struggle and the confusion and the blinding light that had hit her in the darkness. She would say nothing about Satan or the Fallen World or Father, but only try to make her mother more inquisitive, and see if she couldn't get her to a Centre. The thought of giving up her mother was quite unthinkable. She couldn't countenance it all. She understood now why Lucy hadn't been in touch after she met the Family. Lucy had been frightened of weakening, frightened of putting them all into a danger that they couldn't understand.

That evening, Carmen sealed her bland little missive and gave it to Adèle. Adèle had already checked it and declared it satisfactory. Then she went and sat cross-legged in the Family Evening and tried to put her mother from her mind. But, even so, a tear rolled down her face, because she knew that this was only the beginning of what the Messiah asked of her.

Gary's group came on and began their skit. She hugged her feet and cheered with all the rest. It was a motley cast, all dressed in bizarre, improvised costumes. Peter and Franklin were gangsters, Reg was an unlikely-looking punk and Jane was a loose woman, smoking a pretend cigarette and lolling about in decadent fashion with a glass of Ribena.

Then Robert came on with a bucket, assisted by Gary who bore a chammy leather wash cloth. They sat the 'clients' down on the waiting chairs and, as the audience waited with mounting anticipation for the punchline, Robert and Gary began to scrub the clients' heads in a choreographed circular movement. Both clients and washers began to echo the same circular motion with their hands, singing to the tune of 'Old MacDonald':

> 'Reverend Moonie had a farm
> Ee ay, ee ay, oh
> And on that farm he had some sinners
> Ee ay, ee ay oh...'

The clients stood up, pretending to be as blank as zombies, while Robert and Gary scrubbed their heads frantically with the scrubbing brushes.

> 'With a brainwash here
> And a brainwash there
> Here a wash, there a wash,
> Everywhere a brainwash...'

The audience erupted with screams of appreciation, and everyone howled with laughter, holding their stomachs, hooting until they were weak. Carmen laughed too. Their faces were so funny. Gary and Robert frowning with desperate sincerity, Jane, Franklin, Peter and Reg all staring out past the audience looking glazed and gormless. The laughter was infectious and irresistible; even though most of the members had seen the sketch many times before, they laughed and laughed until the tears streamed down their cheeks. That was the great thing in the Family – unlike the outside world, where people got jaded and indifferent when they'd seen something a few times, inside the Family the more you saw or heard something repeated, the more intense that thing became.

Carmen felt the buoyancy of their mutual reassurance and their optimism. She felt again the power of the very special kind of love in that room and it made everything else fade away to nothing. She decided not to think about her mother. That was a problem – no, not a problem, a challenge – she was yet to meet. If she faced up to what the Messiah would require from her, it would take all her mental strength and it would spoil the day. After all, it was *her* day. The past was over. Everything that had gone before was unimportant. This was Day One. Her entire life started from today.

Then she began to make the circular washing movement like the rest of them and her eyes sparkled as she took up the jovial refrain.

Chapter 12

Carmen's mother sat in the dingy waiting room, stroking her jugular in a strained, neurotic fashion and then shredding a paper handkerchief into tiny feathers of lint that stuck to her beige pleated skirt. There was an unhealthy smell of germs and baby's vomit. The Christmas tinsel hung torn and half-hearted across the grimy picture rail and the receptionist's cards sat on the unlit Calor stove, although it was several days past Twelfth Night. Unlucky, thought Ellen automatically, but when she thought about it, she'd always been careful to take her own cards down on time, and fate had still seen fit to visit on her every kind of weird, bad luck.

After all, it wasn't common to have two daughters disappear in the space of a year. Since then, what? One strained, surreal visit where the two prodigals sat on the settee like polite strangers, regarding her with secret, unfamiliar eyes; occasional chirpy postcards full of exclamation marks but lacking any information, and one packet of ginseng tea that had arrived in the post unannounced and unaccompanied by any word of explanation. So much time had passed, yet time hadn't dimmed Ellen's sense of unreality or made it easier to accept and understand. And now, at last Carmen had deigned to come again, but this time she had come alone. Her news was that Lucy had left for North America to become a missionary with the International One World Crusade. Carmen seemed to have no idea when or if she was ever coming back. Nor did she seem to care.

A cross-eyed boy was running around the surgery, completely out of control, careering into the old ladies' outstretched, arthritic limbs. He was overseen by a charmless girl with cold sores on her lip. She looked about fourteen but nursed a puling baby and rocked another in a battered Silver Cross pram complete with rusty springs and egg stains. It was exactly the same pram, thought Ellen, that she and Tom had bought when she was expecting Carmen. It had a high-sprung carriage and fringed canopy. She could remember the summer's day when they'd gone out to buy it. How bright and hopeful everything had seemed then as they'd stood looking in that shop window, arm in arm.

Now Ellen started methodically plucking the fragments of tissue from her skirt and pulverising them with her finger tips. She wondered if it was a good sign that Carmen had been closeted with him for so long. She even nursed a forlorn hope that the doctor might hold some magic key to it all, might spring her mind open like a stubborn lock on a suitcase, and that Carmen would appear in the doorway, grinning sheepishly, perfectly normal once again.

In reality, Ellen knew these wild fantasies were just that, and all she could realistically hope for would be an element of doubt and a psychiatric referral; the next problem would be to keep hold of Carmen long enough to make her see it through. But the doctor must surely see for himself the frightening limitations of her new vocabulary, the curious shrinking that went on in her distant eyes, the extraordinary, blank equanimity of the new robotic Carmen.

This last hope faded as, with a sinking feeling in the pit of her stomach, she heard the healthy peal of Carmen's laughter through the thin partition walls, followed by the lower timbre of the doctor's laugh. The two voices sounded so easy and relaxed that they might have been the voices of two old friends reminiscing, and Ellen wondered what they could possibly find to laugh *about*. At length, Carmen reappeared, glowing with good health and smiling. She looked at Ellen – or did Ellen imagine it? – with a slightly ironic arch of the eyebrow. She sat down sedately beside her.

'He'd like a word with you now.'

Ellen fussed to her feet, brushing off the paper pieces, dropping her gloves, then tipping up her handbag so that it emptied a clatter of coins upon the floor.

'You go, I'll pick them up,' said Carmen kindly, and she knelt to collect together the cache of coins. 'Honestly, Mum, there's nothing to be nervous about.'

Ellen stared dumbly at her, tempted to reach out and clip her smartly round the ear. Maybe a blow to the head was the only way to force the needle of the stuck record past the groove. But she resisted the urge and only walked with as much dignity as she could muster into the consulting room, knowing already that it was hopeless.

Carmen sat there making big eyes at the baby, dandling its rattle, but the infant was lack-lustre, smeared with oatmeal and nose drip. Its blue sleep-suit was stained with food. Carmen listened with a sympathetic air to the conversations going on around her, to the mother's peevish complaints about the housing office, the benefits and the social services, but, though she nodded and tutted cordially, her eyes were alert and dancing with the secret knowledge that it was all unnecessary suffering, that she could just lean forward to the girl who was whining now about the dangers of the lift shafts, and whisper to her, 'I know a way to solve every one of these problems and it doesn't lie with the welfare state...' How would the girl react? What if she told every one of those depressed, sick people, young and old, that their sickness wasn't of the flesh but of the spirit? That almost every sickness could be overcome by working hard and by chanting Father's name? How would they respond? Her eyes lit up at the thought.

It seemed intolerably sad that the truth had to be revealed so slowly, that one couldn't just impart it quickly in hurried conversation. 'Hey, trust me. I can change your life. I have the answers to the questions that have plagued mankind through history.' Who would believe her? And yet she hugged to herself the wonderful, the incredible, the impossible knowledge that had been vouchsafed to her, the most earth-shattering secret that the world had ever known. Who would believe that she, simple, ordinary Carmen Stone, was one of the chosen few trusted to propagate it, thereby helping to restore her physical family, her nation and the world itself?

It almost made her want to leap up there and then and begin to teach Principle to this little band of people with their fearful, worried eyes. She felt like shouting out loud to them, 'Look, there's no need to be unhappy — throw away your medication and your walking aids and your doomy, gloomy faces. There's very little time. We're in the Last Days now and it's no time to be complaining about your high rises and leading your self-centred, Satanic lives. We're moving towards the defeat of Communism now, we're moving towards the Third World War. The Kingdom Of Heaven is coming on earth and it's coming *soon*. Change your hearts while there's still time...'

How marvellous it would be when the time came that people could hear Principle immediately, without the preparation of the courses.

If that were the case now, this whole waiting room of Satan's children would surge up after her and she would lead them down the road and off their housing estates like the Pied Piper leaving Hamelin. Even as she sat there, she felt so high. She felt high all the time. To live life at such a pitch was a privilege granted to few people. Her life, now, was a breathless, relentless, ceaseless campaign to sell more copies of 'One World'.

At five am she would jump out of bed and, like the others, prostrate herself before Father's portrait, repeating the pledge to give her life to Father and Korea. From then on it was all uphill, shouting her impossible financial goal, each day more ambitious than the last, pouring, with her Sisters, from the bus onto the street corner, praying all the time to reach her target. The work, far from making one exhausted, made one more alive: all the time her heart would be thud-thud-thudding with the urgency, the importance of their greater goal. It was no longer an effort to cut off Satanic, selfish thoughts because if you worked with the ferocity that Father demanded, there was no time for the Fallen thoughts even to surface. And all the time Father's words would pound in her head as she stood on the inhospitable pavements, 'We must be like a big selling operation. Unless we work like a big machine, how will we bring in the harvest? It costs at least one pound a head to bring a person to re-education so how many million pounds do we need to re-educate everyone in England? How will we finance the Restoration unless we give every ounce of our strength? This is how we have to feel, that the whole Restoration depends on ourselves alone...' So bigger, better, wilder goals, more effort, forget the blisters, they're Heavenly Father's badges, and then the corresponding bitter tears, the sense of worthlessness and failure if the target wasn't reached. It was all she could do not to whip out the copies of 'One World' from her duffel bag and start selling straight away in the surgery.

Her fingers drummed under the seat of her hard-backed chair. Her mother was being an awfully long time. She hoped the doctor would set her mind at rest. Something of Carmen's elation faded at the thought. It seemed to Carmen that her mother was becoming rather neurotic and edgy and looking older. Of course Lucy's abrupt departure hadn't helped. Carmen had tried to get it across to her just what an inspirational opportunity it was for Lucy but her mother had only wanted to look at it from a selfish point of view, shrugging listlessly and handing Carmen the greetings card she'd been writing out for Lucy's birthday, suggesting that Carmen forward it to America when she learnt the exact address. Carmen had studied the glossy picture – a basket of roses dotted with forget-me-nots under a big gilt flourish that spelled 'To My Darling Daughter'. It had been on the tip of her tongue to reassure her mother that Lucy honestly wouldn't *mind* if it was late because she no longer celebrated her physical birthday – the birthday was just a reminder of her shameful blood inheritance and hardly a matter for celebration – but then Carmen had caught the haunted look in her mother's face and thought better of saying anything.

She wished her mother would make more effort to see it from someone else's point of view. Lucy hadn't necessarily gone abroad for ever and, even if it turned out that way, Carmen couldn't see how it particularly affected her mother who never saw her anyway, at home or abroad. For herself, she hardly thought about Lucy now. She tried not to. Whenever she thought about her, she was aware that a stubborn twinge of feeling persisted despite the fact that a lot of time had passed since they'd cut each other off. At first, they'd just stopped acknowledging the fact that they were physical sisters. But later came the hard part, when they'd set out to erase their sense of emotional connection which was an unwelcome by-product of their shared, Satanic blood. Eventually, they would discipline themselves to love one another no more and no less than any other Family member, but in the meantime they represented to each other a constant source of danger and were best apart. Carmen had thought recently that she was beginning to make progress, particularly since Lucy was on the other side of the Atlantic, but now she wasn't quite so sure. Her mother *would* keep harping on and on about Lucy and the past all the time, and it wasn't helpful. After all, what was so riveting about the past that they had to keep going over and over it?

Inside the consulting room, Ellen was sitting hunched, listening miserably to the doctor's homily. He reasoned with her in a soft, censorial tone.

'Of course sometimes it's very hard to let our children go. Especially when we come to middle life.' He made it sound like some dreary, inevitable illness, although Ellen was an elegant and youthful forty-five. 'The child-bearing years are over. The nest is empty and sometimes that causes a certain amount of regret, a feeling of emptiness. It takes some adjusting to, admittedly, but it's no good hanging onto them – clinging sometimes forces them further away. You know, the wisest mother is the one who can say, "You're free to make of your own life what you will. You're free to learn from your own mistakes".'

As he expounded his tedious problem-page analysis, he warmed to his theme, taking her silence for submissive acceptance. She felt an overwhelming desire to reach across the desk, to seize him by his pressed lapels and shake him till his perfect bridge-work rattled. Her natural reverence for the medical profession warred with her seething resentment at the patronising assumptions of this handsome young man with his manicured hands and his ski-pole poking mischievously out from behind the sombre medical cupboard. It was the multi-purpose, mid-life crisis speech, women for the instruction of. And the most insulting thing about it, beyond the fact that he simply wouldn't accept her assessment of her own daughter, was that there was a great mass of women who had grown to middle age and who could still expect to be submitted to a lecture on life by some privileged young blade from social class A who had no first-hand knowledge of the thing as it was lived. She was aware of a dull sense of humiliation. His charming insouciance filled her with rage, but it was important for her to control herself because he was her only option and she needed him on her side.

'You don't understand,' she repeated. 'This isn't any normal sort of problem. I'm not frightened of losing them. I'm frightened when I see how much they've changed. The Carmen you just saw isn't the one who went away.' She tried to keep any note of desperation from her voice. 'It seems to me she's undergone some kind of personality change. She's locked away inside herself, somewhere where she can't be reached. I can't explain it, but everything – her language, her thought processes, her reasoning ability – '

The doctor stirred. His sympathy was waning. 'Yes,' he objected, 'that's all very well, but basically what you're saying is that your daughter believes something you don't believe and therefore she's mentally ill. If we followed that logic through the wards would be full of Jews and Catholics...' he left the implications floating, 'and that's a scenario we've heard somewhere before.' Ellen sat back, defeated.

'What exactly is it you're asking me to do?' he asked in a voice that seemed more kindly. She made one last effort.

'Please, couldn't you just let a psychiatrist examine her? Let someone see her who understands these things. There *are* people who understand it, apparently.'

The doctor's eyebrows knitted. The slur on the breadth of his medical knowledge only increased his irritation, besides which Ellen was impassioned and he was not trained to differentiate between passion and clinical hysteria. For all he knew, this was just one of a long line of hysterical women out there in the crowded waiting room. Carmen had been a breath of fresh air in comparison with the normal run of things. He spoke emphatically.

'Why should I recommend a perfectly healthy young woman, sound in wind and limb, perfectly rational and, if I may say so, with an engaging sense of humour, for psychiatric appraisal? What possible use would it serve? Now,' he said firmly, 'I'm going to give you a letter ...'

'Well, am I crazy?' Carmen asked serenely, but Ellen only swept up her bag and gloves and swung out of the glass door towards the street, leaving Carmen to skip after her.

In the high street, Ellen kept pretending to look in shop windows to check the state of her red, blotched face. Carmen hovered behind her, shifting uneasily. She no longer had any interest in material goods and the banks of clocks in the jeweller's only reminded her that she was wasting precious time, that the minutes were ticking away, that every hour made a day, and every day was crucially important. So, even though she wanted to comfort her mother, even though she wanted to say something that would cheer her up, she could hear the perpetual, insistent voice nagging in her head. 'Hurry, hurry. The only way you can help your mother is to get her to a Centre. That's the only long-term way to make her happy. The Restoration of the world will make her infinitely more happy than a new clock could ever make her. Your desire to make your mother happy, that's a selfish, individualistic desire. That's a desire that'll take too long to fulfil, that's a desire that's puny in relation to the greater overall world goal, whereas the defeat of Communism, this is something that's well within our grasp. The Third World War is in our sights now. Satan and God will have their final conflict on the holy battleground of Korea. When you've offered yourself to die for the sake of the world, when you've vowed to be a living sacrifice, then nothing in Satan's world must make you swerve from your course...' All this was going round and round in Carmen's head like a complete lecture as Ellen vainly streaked and smeared the wet make-up round her eyes, reflected back in the shop window.

'Did he prescribe me something?' Carmen queried.

'No,' said Ellen. 'He said you were short of vitamin C, over-tired and mentally confused.' Her gloved hand in her pocket crumpled up the letter that referred the mother, not the daughter, to the psychiatric clinic. She poked a vindictive finger through the Diazepam prescription.

'That's odd,' Carmen reflected thoughtfully. 'I don't *feel* confused. I've never felt so calm and clear in all my life.'

'Yes, that's what he thinks is odd,' snapped Ellen, avoiding her eye. Carmen smiled beatifically to herself. She wondered if Jesus' disciples had been sent to physicians and she thought they probably had.

They wandered down the street, neither of them observing anything around them, for their different reasons. For Carmen the whole street was bristling with the Satanic vibrations that she always sensed when she was out in the Fallen World. Ellen felt so depressed and at her wits' end that she was past caring about anything other than the problem. The sky was bleak. Only a few, bare stripling trees reached to the sky in their protective wire cages. The human figures in the urban landscape stared fixedly at their boots, faces pinched and blue with cold.

'Did he have any advice?' asked Carmen solicitously, as though the problem under discussion was something she could help with.

'Yes,' said Ellen tersely. 'He suggested I join a parents' support group.'

'Oh, what a great idea!' Carmen beamed, and then she appeared to think about it. 'But, hey, look, I know, why join just any old parents' support group when we run an absolutely fantastic one of our own?' She pretended to turn it over in her mind and then find the idea good.

'Yeah!', she said, as if it had only just struck her what a perfect proposition it was. 'It wouldn't be difficult for you to get to the Centre – or maybe they'd send a minibus! And there's singing and games, and lots of different people with different outlooks on life, lots of other parents trying to learn more about what their kids are into. You might find it really gave a boost to your social life!'

Ellen eyed this ghastly impostor masquerading as her daughter with a stony stare.

'Thank you very much, Carmen,' she said bitterly. 'I think I'll find one for myself, if it's all the same to you. If I wanted to join an alcoholic's support group, I wouldn't join one associated with the Licensed Victuallers.'

'You *do* seem to be drinking quite a lot,' Carmen observed mildly.

They walked on towards the pedestrian precinct where the old age pensioners sat out, feeding the birds. After a while, Carmen said slowly, 'Actually, it's *not* all the same to me which one you join.'

Ellen cast her a sidelong glance.

'Well, look, Mum, there's just one thing I ought to say. If you joined a support group that was hostile to our movement, I'd sort of have to draw the line.'

Ellen ground to a halt. 'And *what* does *that* mean, *pray*?' she demanded, making her words very distinct. 'Oh holy one.'

Carmen made an effort to control her sense of unease. Her mother's tone was so hostile, so uncharacteristic that she had a disorientating sense that Satan was speaking directly through the mouthpiece of her mother. It sounded like the sort of thing Satan would say. She regarded her mother severely and willed the evil spirits to be subdued.

'It means, well...' She put her hands on her hips as though, frankly, it was obvious. 'I mean I'm hardly likely to be able to see you if you join a hostile group.'

'*All* the groups are hostile,' Ellen pointed out. 'If the parents agreed with it, they wouldn't need to form a group. As it is I should think they all band together and sit around, chain-smoking, discussing how strange their children's eyes are.' Carmen didn't seem to be taking anything in, so Ellen gripped her arm and repeated it more loudly. '*All the groups are hostile, Carmen.* Perhaps that might suggest something to you?'

'Yes,' said Carmen distantly, 'it suggests that there's a lot of persecution against our movement. But I wouldn't expect my own mother to join in persecuting me, not if she loved me.' Carmen frowned. 'Not if it meant we couldn't see each other any more.' She stared intently at her mother so that her meaning could not be mistaken. 'I really love you and I wouldn't want not to see you.'

Ellen felt something contract in her stomach region. She felt suddenly so weak that all her anger drained away. And still Carmen's distant eyes challenged her as though she'd just issued an all-important ultimatum. Ellen ran it through in a bewildered fashion in her head. After all, what could she usefully threaten in return? She could say to Carmen, 'What point is there in my seeing you if you're a different person from the one I love?' She could say 'suit yourself, it's your life. Throw it away if you want to, see if I care . . .' and walk away with her nose in the air but, if she did so, Carmen would take her at her word. And the truth was Ellen *did* care, whereas Carmen's ascendancy came from her manifest indifference. There seemed to be no section in Carmen's new brain marked 'compromise'; everything was an absolute. If Ellen called her bluff, the tie would be severed, and that tie was the only link with reality that Carmen had left.

For her part, Carmen, although she continued to stare at her mother with icy composure, was not calm. Her heart was beating against her rib cage as though it wanted to get out and she was praying very hard. What if she had to cut her mother off? Why could her mother not see the obvious? — that unless she made some concession of positivity towards the Family then the severance was inevitable. The very thought of it gave Carmen an acute stabbing pain in her chest. It made her want to gasp. It had been hard enough to sever her ties with Lucy, but at least Lucy had shared an understanding of the wisdom that required it. Her mother understood so little. And what if this was the test they'd talked about — the kind of test that Father had to set? Would she be able to bear it? But then, hadn't Father borne much more suffering, much more self-denial in His harrowing years in the North Korean prison camp and since?

Ellen's gaze faltered. She had no threats or promises that could shake her daughter's terrifying equilibrium. She decided in that moment that there was nothing left for her to do for Carmen but to be a touchstone of the reality that was the past, a reminder to Carmen of her own history. As she stood there, lost for words, she thought just for a fleeting second that she saw something vulnerable, something pathetic in Carmen's face, something that reminded her of the old Carmen.

On impulse, she reached out to her and held her tightly, feeling a surge of hopeless tenderness as the silken head brushed under her cheek. They stood there, closely intertwined like one lonely, deformed figure against the dreary expanse of pink and white paving stones. All around them, the ravaged pigeons preened and foraged in the council plant tubs, squabbling over the crisp packets and the clean-picked chicken bones.

'I love you both. I love you more than anything else. Do you understand that?'

Carmen nodded, but she could not relax into the embrace. Her mother continued talking softly and carefully into her hair. 'Whatever happens, whatever you might do, whatever hurtful things we might say to one another, that always stays the same. Wherever you are, you can always know that I'm there for you if you need me. You can know I love you and nothing will ever change that.' She buried her nose in Carmen's parting. 'Tell me you've heard me.'

'I've heard you,' said Carmen, but she gave a heavy sigh. The truth was that she would never again need anything from her mother because her mother no longer had anything viable to give. Her mother, with the most generous of hearts, could only offer debased, Satanic love, a fallen love that wanted to control and dominate, a love that was frightened to let go of its possession. Once a person understood the *true* meaning of love, as Carmen did, then the kind of love her mother was describing sounded like the mean covetousness of property ownership.

Carmen could sense something of her mother's desolation so she didn't try to put these thoughts into words. She knew her mother wouldn't be able to understand them straight away. It gave Carmen some heart to know there was still a fingerhold; there was still some leverage if Carmen could just find the right way to handle her. She'd have to guide her gently. Everything depended on Carmen because Carmen was the only one with any gift to give. It was up to her to use all her wiles, to channel all her love into making sure her mother would receive it. Just as they'd told her it would be, so it was. Her mother clung to her with a kind of desperation, almost like a child, thought Carmen remotely, and she, herself, was the parent figure, having to think for both of them, guiding her mother towards the Messiah, towards a destiny that, at first, her mother would resist.

The blowing newspapers whipped dismally against their legs and the few old people on the bench stared blankly at them wondering if they were trying to keep warm or if one of them was going on a journey. Ellen hugged her daughter more urgently, hoping for a sign that her words had penetrated and been understood, but Carmen's body was unresponsive as if she was merely humouring her mother's need for physical intimacy and waiting for the mood to pass.

Since it was hopeless, Ellen gave a world-weary sigh and let her go.

As they dragged their feet past Marks and Spencer's, Ellen turned and said, 'Do you need clothes? Is there anything you want?'

Carmen thought quickly. In the past she would immediately have said 'no' but the last few months of relentless frugality, the chiselling for Heavenly funds, gave her a new greed.

'You don't have much money, do you?' she asked.

'I've got about eighty pounds or so spare. You can spend it if it means I can know you're warm and dry,' said Ellen. It was in fact the last of her savings and she'd been thinking of using it to take a weekend away, but she said nothing of that. There weren't many ways left for her to express her love. She had exhausted them all.

'Thank you, that would be great,' said Carmen, and no sooner had she spoken than she was swirling through the doors like a hurricane, trailing Ellen behind her.

'What I really need is five skirts and an assortment of underclothes. Maybe some jumpers if it'll run to that,' said Carmen. She darted from rail to rail, ignoring the young section and heading straight for the middle-aged frumpy things.

'Wouldn't you like something with a bit more style?' Ellen murmured uselessly as Carmen brushed past her, clutching her booty, eyes gleaming with purpose as she hurtled off towards the stirruped slacks.

'Really, it doesn't matter,' Carmen breezed, as Ellen chased her down the aisle. 'God likes us to look nice and tidy, that's all.' She began to throw polythene packets of old lady's winceyette briefs into her basket, moving with a speed that defied Ellen to keep pace.

Ellen gave up and just rested wearily against the pillar in the centre of the store, watching without much interest as her Belgian Mid-Winter Break converted itself into bottle-green tweed skirts, a powder-blue, Crimplene dirndl, a twee Princess Diana blouse with cake-frill neck, four pairs of ankle socks and some senior citizen's carpet slippers. She just summoned up the energy to rendezvous with her at the cash desk when Carmen whooped, 'Oh dear, I could do with some towels and flannels.'

'I should have thought the organisation ought to provide those,' Ellen objected. 'After all, you get dirty on their time.'

Carmen shook her head with a cheery smile. 'It'd be nice if they could, wouldn't it? But we have so many calls on our money. I mean, when you think about it, it's a registered charity not a three-star hotel...' and then she whisked off adroitly through the shoppers, leaving Ellen to oversee the totting-up nervously. Only halfway through the pile they reached fifty-five pounds ninety, and Ellen looked distractedly around to point the fact out to Carmen. It was just as the packing assistant was removing the labels that Ellen noticed all the sizes on the clothes were different. At first she thought it was a mistake. Carmen was tripping towards her with a little stack of hand towels.

'Carmen, what are you thinking about? All these things are different sizes...'

'That's how we *are* in the Family,' said Carmen brightly. 'God's children come in all different shapes and sizes. Don't ask me why. I suppose that's how he likes us.'

It was then, as it dawned on Ellen that she was buying for a whole pack of anonymous Moonies, that something inside her just went snap. She felt the blood rushing to her ears and she shouted much louder than she meant to, 'I'm not kitting out the whole crazy outfit! Get Reverend Moon to pay for them. He's the bloody multi-millionaire, not *me*.'

The assistants stood stock-still, their eyes widening with interest, electrified at a hint of passion in a place where a new influx of flannel blazers was the only drama.

Even as she shouted it, she knew she had transgressed the unspoken boundary. She knew she'd made a mistake that she'd regret.

'I'm sorry you feel that way,' said Carmen evenly.

In that moment, Ellen saw the blinds go down on Carmen's eyes with a curiously visible finality. In a daze, she wrote the cheque. Her daughter hovered some way away, suddenly indifferent.

She stood on the pavement in the gathering gloom of falling dusk and watched Carmen scurrying across the road into the tube station laden with carrier bags. She watched the little figure of her daughter buy a ticket. Carmen even turned to give a cheery wave. Ellen raised her hand, although she didn't really feel like waving. As Carmen disappeared beyond the barrier, Ellen continued to stand there in the cold, looking at the empty ticket hall, and when she gave up the idea that Carmen might suddenly, for whatever reason, reappear there, she knew she would never see her again.

SOLUTE◆POKER.COM

STRAIGHT FLUSH

ALSO BY BEN MEZRICH

Nonfiction

Sex on the Moon

The Accidental Billionaires

Rigged

Busting Vegas

Ugly Americans

Bringing Down the House

Fiction

The Carrier

Skeptic

Fertile Ground

Skin

Reaper

Threshold

STRAIGHT FLUSH

The True Story of Six College Friends Who Dealt Their Way to a Billion-Dollar Online Poker Empire— and How It All Came Crashing Down . . .

BEN MEZRICH

wm
WILLIAM MORROW
An Imprint of HarperCollins*Publishers*

HarperCollins books may be purchased for educational, business, or sales promotional use. For information please write: Special Markets Department, Harper-Collins Publishers, 10 East 53rd Street, New York, NY 10022.

FIRST EDITION

Designed by Jamie Lynn Kerner

Library of Congress Cataloging-in-Publication Data has been applied for.

ISBN 978-0-06-224009-5 (hardcover)
ISBN 978-0-06-227771-8 (international edition)

13 14 15 16 17   OV/RRD   10 9 8 7 6 5 4 3 2 1

For my dad, who inspired me to follow my dreams, and for Arya and Asher, who make me smile every single day

AUTHOR'S NOTE

Straight Flush is a dramatic narrative account based on multiple interviews, numerous sources, and thousands of pages of court documents. In some places, details of settings and descriptions have been changed to protect identities, and certain names, characterizations, and descriptions have been altered to protect privacy. In some instances I employ the technique of re-created dialogue, based on the recollections of interviewees, especially in scenes taking place more than a decade ago.

STRAIGHT FLUSH

CHAPTER 1

Ten minutes before 5 A.M., a gray-on-gray sky was pregnant with the remnants of a passing storm, a thick canopy of clouds marred by occasional daggers of tropical blue and orange—and suddenly seven years disintegrated in a flash of reflected sunlight across the spinning glass of a revolving door.

Brent Beckley stepped through the threshold of the Central American country's main airport and into the poorly air-conditioned terminal. A little over six feet tall, with boyish features, a square jaw, and blondish-brown hair cut short over a wide, boxy forehead, Brent was moving fast, his five-hundred-dollar Italian-leather shoes clicking against the shiny linoleum floor. He was wearing a conservative dark blue suit with matching tie; there was a briefcase in his right hand and a heavy winter coat thrown over his left shoulder. Anyone looking his way might have assumed he was just another young, eager expat businessman on his way to an important meeting up north; business-clad

Americans strolling through Santamaría International were a common sight, symbolic of the expat community that had grown exponentially in the near decade since Brent had first arrived in the tropical country.

But the truth was, Brent Beckley was not on his way to a business meeting. In fact, he was quite possibly on his way to a jail cell. And the journey from where he'd started to where he was going was anything but common. He looked calm, cool, collected—shoulders back, head up—but on the inside he was terrified. He could feel the sweat running down the skin above his spine, and it required all his willpower to keep his knees from buckling, his body moving forward.

Ten feet from the blue-rope labyrinth that led through to Immigration and Security, Brent spotted a man strolling determinedly toward him and slowed his gait. At first glance, the man didn't look like a spy: thin, angular, with narrow cheeks, a sharp triangular nose, long legs lost in the folds of khaki pants, spindly arms jutting out past the cuffs of a white button-down shirt. The man was smiling, having recognized Brent immediately, though the two had never met. Brent tried to smile back, but the fear was playing havoc with the neurons that controlled the muscles of his face.

Brent was barely thirty years old, a small-town kid from backwoods Montana, a former frat boy who'd spent most of his adult life working for what he considered to be an Internet company; he'd certainly never expected to find himself rendezvousing in a tropical airport with a smiling spy.

Then again, the man wasn't *necessarily* a spy. From what Brent remembered from the letter he'd received the week before, detail-

ing how the meeting would go down, the man's official title was some sort of "liaison" with the U.S. State Department, based out of the embassy in San José. And up close, even despite the sharp contours of his face, he looked much more like a kindly accountant than a menacing secret operative.

But if Brent had learned anything over the past seven years, it was that there were very few things in life that were *actually* black or white; most things tended to be a mix of both.

"Good morning, Mr. Beckley," the man said as he intercepted Brent a few feet from the entrance to the maze of blue rope. "My name is David Foster. It's nice to meet you."

Brent shook the man's hand, trying to think of a response. When none was forthcoming, Foster extended his other hand, offering two documents. The first was instantly familiar: Brent's U.S. passport—the same passport he had turned over to the State Department three days earlier. Glancing at the document, Brent felt his mouth go dry. He could see, even without looking closely, that someone had punched three holes through the center of the cover. Each dark circle tore at the pit of Brent's stomach. There was something so permanent and real about the sight of that passport; its mutilation seemed like such a malevolent and unnecessary act.

A week earlier, when Brent had first made the decision to turn himself in, the U.S. Embassy had requested a copy of his passport. Brent had been happy to accommodate, offering them the original document so they could copy it themselves; they had promptly confiscated it. Now he could see the result.

It seemed to be just another step in a deceptive game. Brent had already agreed to surrender, and he was in the process of

moving his family to the United States—yet even that wasn't good enough.

Foster appeared to read Brent's thoughts and quickly shifted the invalidated passport to the side, revealing the second document in his hand: a thin, similar-looking passport, this one with its cover still intact. Brent took both documents from the man, inspecting the second, smaller booklet—and saw that it was dated for a single day's use. Brent was still free to travel like any other American citizen—*for the next twenty-four hours.*

There was a moment of awkward silence, and then Brent finally shrugged, shoving the two passports into his suit pocket.

"What now?" he asked.

Foster's expression turned soft, and he jerked his head toward the blue ropes behind him.

"We've got an hour to kill before your flight. You want to get a cup of coffee?"

It wasn't quite what Brent had expected—but again, none of this could have been anticipated. He nodded and followed the thin man toward Immigration.

It was the fastest Brent had ever moved through the Costa Rican airport; usually, security took forever, especially for young Americans like him. In Brent's experience, some of the native immigration officers seemed to take a special pleasure in hassling young American men traveling to and from the States. Brent assumed it had to do with the massive inequities between the two cultures; to the average Costa Rican, Americans were rich, entitled, and usually obnoxious. From what Brent had seen of the mobs of northerners who kept the local tourist economy alive—usually large groups of men who spent mornings splayed out across the pristine beaches like bleating, bloated, bleached,

and beached marine animals, and evenings carousing through the legal brothels that put red-light districts around the world to shame—well, maybe the immigration officers weren't that far off. At the moment, Brent could only marvel as he was towed through Immigration and Security at a near-Olympic pace; Foster seemed to know everyone who worked at the airport, and even more helpful, the man's Spanish was impeccable. He spoke like a native—though from what Brent could piece together, it appeared that Costa Rica was just one stop on a colorful, government-sponsored road trip that had extended from a military academy in Virginia, through a five-year stint in Iraq, to a half dozen embassies across South and Central America. Even if Foster wasn't a spy, he'd certainly lived like one. Yet by the time Brent lowered himself onto a stool in a quiet corner of a dingy coffee shop—just beyond the last security checkpoint before the waiting area for Continental Airlines, the carrier that would take him out of his adopted home, possibly forever—he felt as comfortable with the man as one could possibly be, under the circumstances. Foster wasn't a bad guy, and he wasn't the enemy. He just worked for them.

Foster ordered for both of them, making small talk as the uniformed waitress brought them Styrofoam cups filled with tar-black coffee. The first sip put strength into Brent's knees and warmed his throat enough to make the words come a little easier.

"This is just so crazy," he said, the most words he'd strung together since he'd stepped into the airport. "I'm not even sure what I'm doing here."

Foster smiled, sipping his coffee. "Getting on a plane to New Jersey."

Brent must have given him a look, because Foster laughed.

"Kid, it really does help to keep things simple in your head. Take it one step at a time. Right now, you're drinking a shit cup of coffee in a shit coffee shop. An hour from now, you'll be boarding a 737 to Newark. Real simple, like that."

Brent nodded. The guy was probably right. Keep his thoughts simple, keep focused on the moment, the little picture—because when he let his mind go after the big picture, well, things got really dark and confusing.

"It just doesn't seem fair."

Foster shrugged. "To tell you the truth, I don't understand why they want you either. But that's not my job."

It was good to hear, but Brent couldn't help finishing the man's thought: Foster's job wasn't to understand why Brent was being prosecuted; it was to facilitate the situation. Or more bluntly, make sure Brent got on that airplane. Brent couldn't help wondering what Foster would do if he suddenly changed his mind—just turned and headed for the airport exit. Would Foster try to stop him?

Brent immediately chided himself. He was letting his fear get to him. He'd already made the decision. The wheels were in motion.

But still.

"I'll probably get some points for surrendering. I mean, I could just stay here in Costa Rica, right?"

He'd spoken to enough lawyers to know that technically, for the moment anyway, he was correct. One of the key points for extradition was that the crime you were accused of committing had to be illegal in both jurisdictions. As far as he—or his lawyers—could tell, what he'd done, what he was accused of doing, was

legal in Costa Rica. Hell, it was legal pretty much everywhere in the world—except for the United States. And even there—well, he and his legal team still weren't entirely clear.

"Maybe," Foster agreed, shrugging his shoulders. "I mean, we probably couldn't have extradited you. But that doesn't mean we couldn't get you."

Brent looked at him. There was a glint in Foster's eyes as the thin "liaison" leaned close, over the table.

"When we really want somebody, we work with our friends, in whatever country we happen to be. A few phone calls, a little back-and-forth, tit for tat. We get them to cancel your immigration status, and next thing you know, you're being deported. Guess where?"

Foster was still smiling, but his thin features didn't seem quite as amiable as before. Brent stifled a shiver.

"Put a bag over my head, hit me with a truncheon, shove me into the trunk of a car?"

Foster laughed. "Come on, kid. You've been in Central America too long. This is the U.S. government you're talking about. We're civilized."

Brent pretended to ease back against his stool, but his muscles were tense, his nerves once again feeding rubber into his knees. When the U.S. government wanted to lock someone up, they didn't need black bags, truncheons, and trunks of cars. They simply passed a law to make whatever their target was doing illegal. Then they punched holes in his passport.

Brent exhaled, taking a deep drink from his coffee.

"So I guess I'm doing the right thing. It's just . . . well, this wasn't how this was supposed to have gone down."

Foster shrugged again. He'd heard the line before, probably many times. The thing was, in Brent's case, it was more than a cliché. Seven years earlier, when he'd strolled through this very airport for the first time—a kid barely out of college, on his way to join four of his best friends chasing a dream that at the time seemed so real and possible—it had felt like the beginning of a grand, exotic adventure. And in many ways, those seven years had been just that—grand, exotic, exciting, and at times unbelievably profitable. Brent and his friends had built something amazing.

And then, just like that, in a flash as quick and blinding as sunlight on a glass pane, it had all come crashing down.

"Yeah," Brent said, and sighed, crumpling his now empty Styrofoam cup in the palm of his hand, "maybe we were stupid, but none of us pictured it ending like this."

Two hours later, Brent toyed with the recline lever of his first-class aisle seat, trying and failing to find a setting that might relieve the dull ache that had settled into his bones once the narrow-bodied Continental 737 had reached its cruising altitude. He knew his efforts were futile; his discomfort had nothing to do with the seat, or the fact that even in first class, his legs were pretzeled together. His body hurt because now that he was alone in the confines of the airplane, his mind couldn't help whirling forward, to what was coming. And even at his most optimistic, Brent knew that it was going to be one hell of a hard landing.

He desperately wanted a drink, but alcohol would be a bad idea. His head needed to be clear. Even his seat was a source of mild anxiety—he had purchased a ticket in coach, but someone

had shifted him to first class, front row, aisle. He wasn't sure if federal agents were going to get on the plane and take him off in handcuffs or if they'd let him walk through the Jetway under his own power. Either way, the gnawing thought of what was awaiting him would make this the longest flight of his life.

As the plane began to jerk and jag through a spot of mild turbulence, Brent shut his eyes, forcing his head back against the faux-leather headrest. Eyes closed, he was not surprised to immediately picture his wife and two young sons; at that moment they were probably beginning the process of setting up residency in Salt Lake City, where he planned to eventually join them. That little family was, without question, the most treasured part of his life. They were the reason he was on that 737. The reason he'd surrendered—even though in the minds of some of his friends, surrendering was akin to giving up without a fight.

The bottom line was, Brent's wife was Colombian, his kids Costa Rican; if he was going to have any chance of giving them a life in the United States, of having his kids become full citizens like their father—he was going to have to make a deal.

And in a way, that had made his decision easier. There had been other options—and not just staying in Costa Rica. His older brother—stepbrother, technically, whom Brent idolized and respected more than anyone else on earth—had gone a very different route. Scott didn't like to use the word *fugitive* because, in truth, he wasn't running, nor was he exactly hiding—the U.S. government just couldn't get him as long as he stayed within the borders of the tiny Caribbean island he now called home. But for Brent, returning to the States had always been the endgame; the government's offer to assist in his family's relocation had tipped

the scales, and despite the anxiety Brent felt about his own future, at least for his family, he was pretty sure he was doing the right thing.

For the moment, he did his best to cling to that minor solace. He had to believe that whatever they did to him, he had made the best decision for his family. He kept his eyes closed, that thought firmly in place, until the plane finally began its descent into Newark.

It wasn't until he heard the quiet rumble of the Jetway moving into place that he finally opened his eyes. He watched the flight attendant going to work on the door; a few clicks and a grunt later, the attendant stepped back, revealing the orange-lit tunnel stretching forward into the depths of Newark International Airport.

Brent gave it a full thirty seconds before he decided it was okay for him to be just another passenger, at least for a little while longer. He retrieved his briefcase and overcoat, then headed for the Jetway.

It wasn't until he'd reached the end of the long, angled tunnel that he saw the immigration officers. He quickly counted six of them, all in uniform—and every one armed. Nobody had a gun drawn, but even so, the sight of those leather holsters, pitched high on each officer's hip—it was enough to take Brent's breath away. He did his best not to stumble as he made it the last few steps to the end of the Jetway.

The closest officer held up a hand, palm out.

"Are you Brent Beckley?"

Brent nodded. The man turned his hand over.

"Passport, please."

Brent fumbled with his coat for a second, then retrieved the single-day passport and gave it to the officer. The officer checked it, showed it to one of his colleagues, and then all six moved forward, taking positions around Brent. The lead officer gestured with his head—and suddenly they were moving forward through the terminal in what appeared to be a diamond formation, with Brent right in the middle.

Christ. It was the most absurd feeling. The officers were walking fast, and Brent was nearly skipping to keep up. People stared as they went past—pointing, whispering, a few even snapping cell phone pictures.

The mobile diamond advanced unimpeded through Customs and out into the main baggage claim area. On the other side of baggage claim, the officers finally broke formation, and Brent was handed off to two middle-aged men in white shirts and dark ties. One of the men showed Brent an FBI badge, the other a badge marked HOMELAND SECURITY. The officers were exceedingly polite, but by this point Brent's heart was pounding so hard, he could barely understand what they were saying. They walked him out of the baggage area toward the terminal exit.

Frigid air splashed against Brent's cheeks as they stepped outside onto the sidewalk, shaking some of the fog out from behind his eyes. He immediately saw a vaguely familiar face, a woman in a dark suit hurrying toward him from the curb, a forced smile on her lips. Brent recognized her as one of the low-level associates from the law firm he'd hired to handle his criminal proceedings. While Brent stood between the officers, she retrieved his briefcase and overcoat. Then the FBI agent pointed at his watch.

"Better take that too. And his belt, and cuff links."

Brent swallowed, then slowly went to work on the watch. He suddenly noticed that his fingers were shaking, and it took a good minute to get from the watch to the cuff links. His belt was a little easier, though his pants felt strange without it; luckily, he'd put on an extra pound or two in the anxiety-filled weeks leading up to his surrender.

After he handed over the items, the FBI agent reached into his back pocket. Out came the handcuffs, like a fist to Brent's gut. When the cold metal touched his wrists, then closed—tight, too damn tight—Brent fought the urge to break down. It all seemed so goddamn unfair.

But instead of complaining, Brent didn't say a word. He let the officers lead him to a waiting black sedan. The Homeland Security officer got behind the wheel; the FBI agent slid into the back next to Brent. A moment later they were off, tires rolling against pavement, winding their way out of the airport and onto the Jersey Turnpike.

Brent tried to find a comfortable position, but the tight handcuffs made it nearly impossible. Instead, he tried to concentrate on the sound of his own breathing. His chest felt constricted, his mouth dry as cotton. He felt himself losing all sense of time as the gray turnpike flickered by outside the tinted window to his left. Was it still morning? Afternoon? How long had they been driving? Were they in New York, or still in New Jersey?

Eventually the silence began to get to him, and he quietly cleared his throat.

"So, are you guys just here to process me today? Or have you been working on my case for a while?"

The agents shared a look in the rearview mirror. Then the FBI agent grinned.

"We've been onto you for a long, long time, Mr. Beckley."

Brent forced a smile of his own.

"Well then, I guess it's nice to finally meet you."

As he turned back toward the window, the sight of something in the distance made him blink. Tall, rising out of a faraway mist, reaching toward the sky: the Statue of Liberty. Brent was seeing it for the first time. *Handcuffed, sitting next to an FBI agent.* He felt the haze of unreality coming back. Once again, he lost all sense of time.

The next hour went by in flashes. An FBI processing center, somewhere in midtown Manhattan—they'd driven in through a gated basement entrance, then gone up in an armored elevator to a cubicle-filled office full of printers, copy machines, and many more agents in white shirts and dark ties. Fingerprinted, photographed, then back into the elevator, returned to the sedan—and on to another faceless building, another gated basement entrance. At that point, the two officers handed him over to a pair of U.S. marshals, who took him into a similar elevator. The marshals were decidedly less polite than the two previous agents; they were large, burly men, with crew cuts and matching cruel grins. When one of them noticed Brent's expensive shoes, he pointed a thick finger at the silver clasps.

"I'm gonna need to rip these off," he said. And a second later the marshal was on his knees, yanking at the clasps with his meaty paws. After a few minutes of grunting and groaning— while Brent did his best to keep from toppling over—he eventually gave up.

Then they were in another processing center—more fingerprints, more photographs. Brent was handed off to different officers and eventually led via a tunnel to another building. Finally,

nearly eight hours after he'd taken off from Costa Rica, he arrived in a jail cell.

Barely larger than ten by ten, it had a low ceiling, white walls, a pair of steel benches suspended beneath a tiny barred window. There was a scruffy-looking man sleeping on one of the benches; as the barred door slammed shut behind Brent, the man momentarily looked up before going right back to sleep. Brent moved a few feet into the cell, then just stood there, staring at the walls, the window, the bars. Everywhere he looked, he saw rivets, some of them rusted, some of them shiny. Rivets, thousands of rivets, running up the corners of the walls, around the window, along the door. So many goddamn rivets.

Brent felt his shoulders begin to sag.

He truly hoped that he was doing the right thing. Because it was suddenly very obvious: he wasn't getting out of that cell until somebody came and let him out. It was maybe two in the afternoon; he had a whole day ahead of him. He was barely thirty years old; he had a whole life ahead of him.

It wasn't supposed to end like this.

It wasn't supposed to have ended at all.

In the beginning, it had been something so special, so wild and cool—and simple. A group of best friends and two brothers, who had set out to do something different.

None of them could have ever imagined how quickly something so simple could become something huge—or how equally quickly it could all come crashing down. They had risen so far—Christ, at one point, they had been days away from being billionaires.

Now Brent was counting rivets in a prison cell, his brother had sequestered himself on an island the size of a Minnesota

shopping mall, and the others had scattered all over the world, facing futures as uncertain as his own.

No, Brent thought to himself as he once again shut his eyes, picturing his wife and his two little boys.

This isn't how it was supposed to go down at all . . .

CHAPTER 2

Here they come, boys. Give me your tired, your hungry, and your wretched. Especially your wretched. Some of my best friends are freaking wretched."

Garin Gustafson grinned as he rose from the front stoop of the SAE fraternity house and tossed a half-empty beer can over his left shoulder. The can arced upward like a Scud missile, hung in the air for a full beat, then spiraled down in a flash of spinning aluminum. Pete Barovich and Shane Blackford, seated two steps up the dilapidated front porch of the aging frat house, cursed as they ducked in tandem. The can hit the edge of the step behind them, then pinwheeled back into the air, spraying beer as it went.

"The only thing wretched is your aim," Pete said, coughing. "It's no wonder you've stayed with the same girl since high school. You can't hit the side of a barn with a tin can. What chance you got making a college girl smile in the dark?"

Garin held up a middle finger without turning around.

"If I'd been aiming for the barn, you'd be picking shingles from the roof out of your hair. I was aiming for the two chicken-shits on the front stoop. I'm hearing a lot of squawking, so I couldn't have been too far off."

Garin raised his arms above his head, stretching his spine, as his two friends wrung beer out of their Sigma Alpha Epsilon sweatshirts. *Goofballs.* And they had the temerity to question his aim. He had taken the house to how many intramural hoops wins in his two years with the fraternity? He could have put the beer can right through the second-floor window above the porch, set it down smack in the center of the desk in Shane's nearly OCD-level, immaculately clean room.

Not that Garin wanted to put another hole in the sagging, multistory monstrosity they called home. As much as it looked like a pretty white barn, all gussied up for the first night of the University of Montana's infamous Greek Week, structurally, the frat house was as rotten as a cow with intestinal worms. From the outside, it was something right out of *Pleasantville,* fitting in perfectly with the dozen other frat and sorority houses that lined the bucolic stretch of suburban Missoula, kitty-corner to the main campus. But if you stuck your head past the door frame, craned your neck just a little bit—well, it was a different story. Loose wires hanging from sparking sockets, stairs that disintegrated beneath your feet, ceilings that drizzled down plaster, toilets that backed up sewage every seventh night like it was some sort of Sabbath ritual—one more beer can through a window might just bring the whole goddamn thing down, and how the hell would that look? Garin's first Greek Week as house rush chair, and him responsible for the demolition of the SAE

house? While Pete, SAE president, and Shane, maybe the most liked member of their class, looked on?

That wouldn't do at all. Garin would never intentionally do anything to harm his beloved SAE. He could still remember the first time he stepped into that house after he'd survived its notorious Hell Week and stood shoulder-to-shoulder with the guys who would become his brothers overnight. Hell, back then he'd been straight out of farm country, plucked from a small town in the middle of nowhere called Conrad, way up near the Canadian border. A place where life revolved around high school sports, farming, and cows. He'd been a wide-eyed kid, shocked by nearly everything he saw. To him, Missoula had been a damn big city.

He'd changed a lot since then; he was more confident, better with the girls. He'd kept his six-pack and his farmer's tan, but he liked to think he wasn't nearly as naive. He certainly wasn't the same bumpkin who'd sold a cow to buy his first car—a rear-wheel-drive Mustang that was completely pointless in the Montana winters. But he was still, at heart, 100 percent country.

He wasn't social chair because he could play basketball. He was the one they sent out onto the street during Rush Week because inside, a part of him would always be that wide-eyed, small-town kid.

"Well, you'd better get cracking," Shane chimed in. "Find us some new pledges. Someone's got to pay for the upkeep of our coop. Us chickenshits get restless, and when we get restless, things get broken."

Garin jibed left, even before he heard the can whistle toward his back. It spiraled harmlessly past his shoulder, then skipped

across the loosely paved street that ran between the frat and sorority houses. He laughed, then followed in the can's wake, finally taking up position a few feet past the edge of the curb,
facing the campus.

It really was a beautiful sight. The whole block was congested
with college kids, most moving in large groups, some in twos
and threes. Everyone seemed to be coming down the center of
the tree-lined street, which had been closed off to car traffic for
the occasion. On either side, beyond the mailboxes, manicured
hedges, and the odd pickup truck sporting bales of hay shaped
into a patchwork of Greek letters, the houses were alive with everything that made this place the center of social life at the state's
biggest university. Parties were already sliding toward full swing
at nearly every other house on the block, even though it was
barely 6 P.M. and still reasonably light outside. But SAE liked to
wait a bit before tapping the multiple kegs lined up behind the
bar in the basement. Pete liked to say, you have to let the night
breathe a bit, like a fine wine, before you started popping corks.
From Garin's vantage point on the street, it looked like corks
were flying all over Greek Row. But he wasn't worried. SAE had
a reputation that drew a respectable crop of pledges every season.
By 10 P.M., he knew, the house behind him would be throbbing
with good music, foaming with decent beer, and, most important
of all, teeming with pretty girls. And girls, of course, were the
currency that held the whole system together.

At that very moment, he knew, two stories above his head,
a trio of sorority sisters were taking their seats on the deck that
jutted out above the SAE front porch. All night long, the girls
would smile and wave at the groups of guys wandering by—a

little tease of the night to come. Girlfriends of three of the fraternity brothers, the girls gave the place a bit of a Mardi Gras feel. Of course, the balcony babes had been Pete's idea. Garin had to give him that: he was one hell of a marketing genius.

And already the girls were working their magic, as the first few groups of guys passed by. The girls laughed and waved, and the freshmen ate it up. Garin had to smile—he understood those freshmen; he knew them well. They were all pure Montana, from Billings, Missoula, and the thousands of smaller towns scattered across the wide farm and ranching state. Mostly lower-middle-class kids from squat in the middle of a depleted country economy—not on food stamps, but not rich either. Maybe their parents made forty thousand a year. They played sports, they drank beer, they liked cars, and they loved girls.

Garin let the first group move by without stopping any of them, then did the same with a second. He wasn't being picky; they were all good prospects. The truth was, this particular year it would mostly be a numbers game. The house was falling apart, so they needed lots of new blood. Basically, a minimum number just to pay the bills. But Garin didn't want to start his first recruiting night with just anyone. He was a born athlete, had been playing sports at a near-elite level since before he could read, and he knew what it meant to build a winning team. His job as social chair was to put together a pledge class that would last, as brothers, for a lifetime. And every athlete in the world knew that a good team began with a strong anchor. Garin intended to start his night by finding that anchor.

So he did his best to ignore Pete and Shane, who were shouting epithets in his direction—a mix of idiotic insults taking aim

at everything from his elongated physique to his small-town origins. No matter how hard they pushed him, he was going to do this right.

And then, right in front of him, not four feet away, moving down the center of the street at the tail end of a group of guys—this kid was definitely something different. Big eyes, intensely green, flicking back and forth as he took in everything around him, like it was all just a show put on for his benefit. Chiseled features under longish locks of auburn hair. Good-looking but not effeminate, obviously an athlete of some sort, though not as tall as Garin or anywhere near as ripped. At the same time, there was certainly something off about the kid, especially in the way he was dressed.

He was wearing a black leather jacket that was at least a size too small for him, the sleeves barely reaching halfway down his forearms, over a white polo shirt with the collar popped up, partially obscuring what looked to be a thin silver necklace. Below the jacket, faded dark jeans, torn and scuffed around the knees, but not in the stylistic way that you might pay double for at a department store—torn because at some point those jeans had seen him through some sort of trouble. And then, below the jeans, brown boat shoes with no socks.

Who the hell dressed like that? And yet, though the kid looked absurd, he didn't seem insecure at all. In fact, he appeared positively cocky, grinning, puffing his chest out, cracking jokes to anyone who would listen. The kid made a damn good first impression.

Garin waited until his target was just a few feet away before making his move. He stepped forward, effectively blocking the

street, and offered a hand along with his most gregarious smile. At six three he towered over many freshmen, but he was lean enough not to be threatening. Not that this kid looked like he could be easily intimidated. He nearly crushed Garin's hand with his own.

"Garin Gustafson," Garin said. "Rush chair, SAE. How's your night shaping up?"

"Got some idea how it's gonna start, no idea how it's gonna end. So I say it's shaping up pretty damn good. Scott Tom. Nice to meet you."

Garin laughed. "I'm sure you've heard about us, so I'm not going to bore you with some clipboard crap about diversity, history, or school spirit. SAE is a great bunch of guys who like to have a whole lot of fun."

Scott pointed toward the girls on the balcony.

"Is there more where they came from?"

"Right to the point," Garin said. "Save the small talk for the ladies—I like that. Come back in about four hours. The party should be in full swing by then. I don't think you'll be disappointed."

There was a flash of mischief in the freshman's eyes. "I just might take you up on that. And I hope you're right—you wouldn't like me when I'm disappointed."

Garin couldn't tell if the kid was joking. It was such a strange thing to say. Before Garin could respond, the kid was already moving away, catching up to the group he'd come with. Garin made a quick decision and took a step after him.

"Hey, if you're thinking of heading downtown to pregame, maybe this will help you out."

Garin fished in his shirt pocket and pulled out a plastic card. It was a Montana driver's license that he'd found floating at the edge of the river when he was out tubing with a beer cooler earlier that week. Most likely a fake ID that someone had discarded after a drunken night—maybe the original owner hadn't had the confidence to pull off the role of a twenty-four-year-old organ donor from Billings. Garin was pretty sure Scott would not have that problem.

He tossed the license in Scott's direction. Scott picked it out of the air with a flick of his wrist, looked at the picture and the date of birth, then gave Garin a thumbs-up.

"Cool. Thanks, man. And I thought I was going to have to get by on my natural charm."

With that, the kid turned and headed back on down the road, leaving Garin wondering if the moment had been the start of something interesting—or if he'd never see that strange, confident green-eyed kid again.

CHAPTER 3

Fifty-seven minutes. I shit you not. Paid off half the house debt and got myself banned from the Missoula County Fairgrounds for three years. But it was a hell of a party."

Pete Barovich crossed his arms against his chest as he leaned back against an aging mahogany upright piano, shoulder-to-shoulder with a brunette in a midriff-baring halter top and low-rise skinny jeans. The girl had to be a volleyball player, she was so damn tall. She had a few inches on Pete, even without her three-inch chunky white heels, and Pete was seriously concerned that the two of them were testing the structural integrity of the antique instrument behind them. After all, the piano had already lost most of its keys, and two of its legs were so chipped and worn they looked like they'd been gnawed upon by a giant rodent.

Certainly, the thing hadn't worked as a musical instrument since Pete had entered the house—which meant it fit right in with the rest of the vast living room's décor. The place was ac-

tively falling apart, and now that the inaugural rush party was in full swing, even the floor beneath Pete's feet seemed to be bucking and swaying in rhythm with a few hundred drunk college kids rapidly being whipped into an alcohol-lubricated frenzy.

"A thousand goldfish in fifty-seven minutes?" The brunette gasped. "That's disgusting."

She covered her mouth, feigning nausea. But Pete could see from the look in her eyes that she was actually impressed. He was pretty certain she'd heard the story before; it had fast become legend across the University of Montana campus and was one of the reasons Pete had been elected president of the fraternity while only a junior. Throwing a party like tonight's was one thing, but throwing a party that would be talked about for years to come was an accomplishment that made it onto your résumé.

The Goat Barn Party—as it had become known—had taken place a year earlier, shortly after Pete had been elected SAE's social chair. The house had been in desperate need of money; a cocaine scandal the year before had nearly gotten the frat kicked off campus and had put the place six figures into debt. Pete had decided the only way to save the house was to party their way out of debt. He had rented out a nearby state fairground, known for its working goat barn, and arranged the delivery of forty kegs of beer, a live band, and plenty of publicity. The goal was to get a ton of kids to attend—and charge them all—but in a place like Montana, that was easier said than done.

So Pete had come up with a unique plan. He'd gone to the local pet store and purchased five thousand goldfish. Anyone attending the party had a choice. Either pay full price—five dollars a head—or swallow a goldfish and get in for one dollar. Girls who swallowed a goldfish got in for free.

"Talk about setting the mood—swallow a goldfish at the front door, and by the time anyone set foot in the goat barn to hear the band and drink some beer, their inhibitions were gone. By the time it was over, I think nearly every cop in the city had made an appearance. The only reason I didn't spend the night in jail was at least half the police force went to my high school."

The girl laughed, wriggling a little closer. Pete felt the warmth of her bare shoulder against his arm and immediately bumped her up in his mental rankings. Garin wasn't the only one assembling prospects that night.

Sliding a hand around her waist, Pete glanced out across the crowded living room. He tried not to grimace as he scanned the pathetic attempts at furniture: a handful of ratty couches strewn about the scuffed hardwood floor, the sofas upholstered in a clash of haphazard colors, pillows stained so deeply it was impossible to imagine what the original shades might have been. Shelving units that looked like they'd been plucked out of the trash were cluttered with old books, beer cans, and various trinkets that seemed collegiate—cloudy glass steins, broken sports trophies, old college yearbooks. The walls, where they were visible between the shelves, were cracked and peeling; the worst cracks were vaguely covered by oil paintings purchased at various garage sales and flea markets, depicting everything from sailboats to farm animals. No dogs playing poker, though a bit of framed velvet would have classed up the place enormously. Everything looked old while somehow avoiding any pretense of gravitas.

And yet Pete and his brothers loved that house. From the looks of the raucous crowd filling every inch of the living room, the feeling was infectious, at least enough to have attracted a good assemblage of the freshman class.

Pete momentarily forgot about the brunette leaning next to him as he surveyed the new talent Garin had invited into their carnival. A few faces he recognized from one or another of the various sports teams, whose recruitment had often included a tour of the houses on Greek Row. Others he recognized from the street outside. As a group, they seemed to be having a good time, reveling in the abundance of free alcohol, ear-shattering music, and the few dozen sorority girls whose main function was to draw the attention away from the state of the house itself.

Yes, if Pete said so himself, he sure was a marketing genius. He caught sight of Shane standing between a pair of girls in matching jeans shorts, both wearing shirts that may as well have been bikini tops—and raised an eyebrow. The prospects seemed good indeed.

And then Pete's gaze settled on another recognizable face, a few feet behind Shane, in a corner of the room between an over-turned loveseat and an oversize plaster bust of Gary Cooper that one of the brothers had won in a card game.

Scott Tom.

Even if Garin hadn't taken a special interest in the kid ear-lier that evening, Pete would have given him a second look, and probably even a third. He was still wearing that ridiculous leather jacket, the cuffs inches above his wrists, as well as those damn boat shoes. And his eyes were still the same pools of green, taking in everything at once, constantly searching, scanning—like he was mentally disassembling all the furniture and putting it back together in a way that made more sense. This kid was different.

"Hold that thought for a moment," Pete said to the brunette next to him, who now had a hand running up his right thigh. "I've got some house business to attend to."

The girl followed his eyes, and then a look crossed her face. "Not him. Anybody but him."

Pete looked at her. "You know him?"

"We all know him. And not just my sorority. Go ahead, ask around."

"Really? It's only his first semester. How much damage could he have done this quickly?"

"Two rooming groups, three girls each, that I know of in my house alone. Slept with one roommate, then the next, then the next—all in the same weekend. And I heard that he's already been banned by both Sigma Tau and Pi Theta E."

Pete whistled low. *A new town slut.* The brunette's warning was having the opposite effect on him than she'd intended. Pete was even more intrigued by the kid. He himself had built up quite a reputation, beginning back in high school—when he'd been known as Porno Pete, first, because of an uncanny resemblance to a famous porn star with the same first name, and second, because he'd racked up pretty good numbers in his school district, even before he'd won a couple of wrestling trophies.

Pete patted the girl's hand, then delicately lifted it off of his thigh.

"Sounds like I'll need to be careful with this one. Don't worry, I'll make sure he's on a strict leash tonight."

The girl rolled her eyes as Pete pushed off the piano and strolled across the room toward the far corner. Along the way, he was shaking hands, slapping backs, pausing a few times to share a beer. Eventually he wound his way past Shane, admiring the two bikini girls, then made his approach. Scott was still standing alone when he got there, but if the kid felt insecure in any way, he certainly didn't show it.

His handshake was firm, his smile strong.

"This certainly looks like the place," he said, in way of a greeting. Then he gestured toward the brunette who was still against the piano, leaning back to reveal even more of her criminally flat stomach. "I think her name is Julie, right? Phi Beta? They serve a great brunch on Sundays. Maybe I'll run into you there, one of these weekends."

Pete laughed. This kid was not going to disappoint. And from the way he was looking around the room, noticing every girl, it seemed clear where his priorities lay. Fair enough; most guys joined a fraternity for the girls. Brotherhood usually came as a surprise.

"Pete Barovich," Pete said, introducing himself. "I'm from Billings. Basketball, football, wrestling, and tennis. Maybe we played against each other at some point?"

Scott shook his head. "You're big city. I'm one hundred percent trailer park. The only way you might have met me in high school is if your mom worked for child services."

Pete blinked. It took him a minute to realize the kid was serious. If he thought Billings, Montana, was a big city, he probably really had been brought up in a trailer. Which could be good or bad. Garin had stepped right off the farm, and he was now one of Pete's best friends. Though a kid from a trailer park might not help that much with the house's bottom line. It was the annual dues that kept the place afloat, after all.

"Dad's an insurance salesman," Pete responded. "Mom is a nurse. But I like to say, doesn't matter where you start—"

"Only matters where you end up. Better yet—who you end up with."

Scott grinned, jerking his head toward the brunette who was still crawling up the piano. Then he gave Pete a punch in the shoulder.

"Don't worry, I keep my scars on the inside. Except the ones you can't really hide, like the cigarette burns and the razor wounds."

Pete opened his mouth, but Scott waved him off.

"Kidding. My dad got me out of that hellhole before I turned into a sociopath. He's an investment banker in Seattle. If you let me into your house, I'm sure you'll meet him. He's almost as good at getting kicked out of sorority houses as I am."

Pete laughed. Talking to Scott was like riding upside down on a Ferris wheel—you had to keep your hands on the fucking safety bar. He gave Scott's shoulder a squeeze, feeling the thick leather of that distressed jacket.

"I got a good sense about you. If the rest of the guys like you as much as I do, and you somehow survive Hell Week, I think you could end up giving me a run for my money with the girls. And I sure as hell like a challenge."

"Then cut out the chitchat and get me a motherfucking beer. The night is just getting started."

Pete caught sight of Shane again, over Scott's shoulder. Shane gave him a thumbs-up; there wasn't going to be much debate about this one.

Maybe Scott Tom had grown up hard, but Pete had a feeling the kid was going to fit in well with the SAE brothers. Hell, with a smile like that, and his almost obscene level of confidence, maybe one day he'd be running the whole goddamn house.

CHAPTER 4

So this is how it ends, Scott Tom thought as he struggled to disentangle himself from the heavy blanket that someone had tucked much too tightly around the corners of the queen-size mattress in the center of his room. For a brief second he pondered who might have been responsible for the blanket, because he sure as hell hadn't tucked it in himself—but then there was that sound again, an ear-shattering roar that seemed to split the very air, and the whole house was suddenly trembling around him.

If it really was an earthquake, he didn't want to die like this, half-naked and trapped under a blanket. Even worse, down by his feet he could feel what seemed to be a sequined tube top. And up by his elbow, a pair of jeans, with a pair of thong underwear still inside.

Kicking as hard as he could, he finally got himself free of the blanket. The roar went off a third time, nearly knocking him onto the floor. He pushed himself to his feet, using the shiny

chrome stripper pole he'd installed next to his bed for leverage. He'd always known the pole would come in handy, despite what Pete and the rest of the brothers thought of his home-decorating tastes. A stripper pole just made sense—especially since he'd painted the walls a searing bright red and installed those mirrored panels along the ceiling. But then again, what the hell did he care what his frat brothers thought of his room's décor? In the semester and a half since he'd moved into the house, he'd discovered that he was by far the most imaginative of the group.

Using the pole as an axis, he flung himself toward the door. Just as his hand reached the knob, he heard another cacophonous burst.

But now that he was closer to the source, it no longer sounded like an earthquake. Flinging the door open, he found his suspicions confirmed—though his initial confusion and thoughts of impending doom were understandable.

Scott had seen plenty of crazy things since he'd moved into the SAE house, but the sight before him was pure bedlam. Half a dozen brothers were out of their rooms, lining both sides of the third-floor hallway, most in similar states of undress. And there, like an untamed beast pawing through the hall carpet and into the very floorboards, some idiot on a four-hundred-pound Harley was in the process of taking out half the banister as he spun the massive steel-and-chrome motorcycle in a wheelie. With a warrior's cry, the guy suddenly headed back down the stairs, carpet and wood splinters spraying in his wake.

Christ. At least the idiot was wearing a helmet. Scott shook his head, rubbing the last vestiges of sleep out of his eyes. He was about to go back into his room to try to solve the mystery of the

tucked-in covers and the disembodied thong when he saw Pete coming toward him from the end of the ruined hall.

For a brief second, Scott considered stepping back into his room anyway, locking the door behind him. Over the past few weeks, Pete had visited him more than a few times to discuss various complaints that had come his way, usually regarding one or another sorority house that Scott may or may not have upset. Hell, it wasn't his fault if certain girls had unrealistic expectations; if Scott was anything, he was always brutally honest. After all, the walls of his room were painted bright red, and there was a stripper pole suspended from his mirrored ceiling. Even more clear, right behind where his hands were resting on the outside of his door there were Roman numerals imprinted in the wood: XXIII. Although Scott didn't remember anything from the night before, he was pretty sure, based on the thong in his bed, that he was going to have to get out his carving knife and add another number to the door.

Pete reached him just as the Harley skidded its way to the ground floor, aiming toward the main entrance and, beyond that, the front lawn.

"That's something you don't see every day," Pete said, as he peered over what was left of the banister to survey the damage. "Now maybe we can get that damn carpeting replaced. It's soaked up so much spilled beer, it's like walking in a marsh."

"I always chalked that up as part of the house's innate charm."

Pete grinned. "First day I toured this place, they were taking me down a hallway on the second floor when a door hinge came loose and the door swung open—and there was one of the brothers, banging his girlfriend up against his dresser. Whole group

of us freshmen standing there in the hallway, and this guy just kept right on going. Yeah, it's hard to imagine anyone making a fuss about the crappy carpet. As long as the girls keep coming through the entrance, nobody gives a damn."

Pete pointed past Scott to the numbers on his door.

"But I don't think I have to convince you."

Scott looked at him with innocent eyes.

"I wouldn't know anything about that. However, you wouldn't happen to have seen number twenty-four wandering around the house somewhere—maybe a little bit naked, save for the odd sequin or two? Unless you're here to break my balls about some sorority house—in which case there wasn't any girl here last night, and she didn't leave her thong in my bed."

Pete shook his head. "Actually, this time I'm here because of your brother."

Scott glanced up, confused. Brent—his stepbrother, actually; Scott's mother had married Brent's father, and Brent had grown up with his stepfamily, saving him from much of the hell that Scott had the misfortune of calling his childhood—was renting a small room on the second floor of the house, on Scott's urging, partly because the house needed the revenue but mainly because Scott hoped Brent would end up at SAE when he matriculated the next year. Scott had always done his best to look after his younger stepbrother; Brent had grown up so dirt poor that the neighbors in his fundamentalist Mormon hometown, just outside of Salt Lake City, would leave baskets of food and clothing on his front porch. Now, Scott's father, Phil, was helping him pay the rent so he could get out of that environment.

Scott himself had only recently reconnected with Phil, who'd

enabled him to go to college in the first place, offering him tuition money and convincing him to write a letter to the university describing the harshness of his background, to explain why he might not have had the grades or the opportunities of the other kids. But he'd had no one to look after him when he was a kid, and he didn't want Brent to ever feel as helplessly alone as he once had.

The idea that Brent could be causing any trouble at the frat house—having only just arrived a few days before—seemed laughable. Brent was just about the sweetest, quietest, most humble kid Scott had ever met.

"Don't tell me it was Brent on the Harley?" Scott joked.

"Of course not," Pete said. "But—well, maybe I should just show you."

He gave Scott a minute to grab a shirt and a pair of sweatpants, then led him down the hall to the stairway. They had to walk carefully over the torn-up carpeting and the splintered wood; the tire tracks from the Harley were clearly visible, the rubber burned into an almost cartoonish circle at the top of the stairs.

When they'd made it to the second floor, Pete led Scott to the fourth door down the hall, the room Brent had been assigned in exchange for two hundred dollars a month. As Pete pulled the door open, Scott could see that the room was probably worth only half that; it was little more than a ten-by-ten closet with enough space for a small desk, a twin bed, and a coffee table; a bare light fixture hung from the ceiling.

Brent was at the coffee table, sitting cross-legged on the floor. His appearance was a stark contrast to both his Mormon background and the common SAE fraternity look. Dirty-blond hair rained down over his shoulders, freshly released from a

ponytail—strands so grungy-looking they seemed halfway to dreadlocks. He was wearing a torn jean jacket over a hemp shirt, and pants that were so baggy they could have doubled for a skirt. His face was covered in three days' worth of beard growth, and he looked like he hadn't taken a shower in a month.

But Pete wasn't pointing at Brent's appearance. He was pointing at an object on the coffee table in front of him. Scott's eyes went wide. A mushroom—a *gigantic* fucking mushroom, about the size of a loaf of bread—was growing out of the middle of a plastic tray.

Brent looked up and saw them in the doorway.

"Hey, guys. Did you hear something this morning? Like, a motorcycle or something?"

Scott looked at Pete, then back at the mushroom.

"Um, Brent? You doing a little farming?"

Not that any of them had anything against a little weed on a Saturday night, or maybe some shared Ritalin from one of the ADD kids in the house. But a mushroom the size of a small dog?

Brent saw where they were looking and seemed to notice the giant fungus for the first time. Then he laughed, grinning wide. Without a word, he reached out and pulled off a chunk of the mushroom. He held it up in the air, then took a bite.

"It's not what it looks like," he said between chews. "It's for eating. Like, for a salad or something. I mean, it's pretty big, but it's not going to get anyone high."

Scott watched his brother wolfing down the mushroom. Brent was a vegan, after all. Still, he wasn't surprised by the concerned look on Pete's face. Most of the house was like Pete, Garin, and Shane. Good-looking, athletic guys who would probably eventu-

ally do well in corporate America. There were some druggies, to be sure, but there was a constant battle between those elements and the sort of country boys who gave the house its heart.

Scott knew that he himself was something a little different. Nobody in the house lived like a Rockefeller—except maybe Shane, whose family had a little money from a tractor dealership—but Scott was pretty sure that nobody else in the house had picked up his mother from rehab nine times by the age of fourteen either. And he was certain that nobody else had ever watched his mother stumble across a trailer, bleeding from deep razor cuts to her wrists. No one else in the house had ever been made to kiss his mother's fresh miscarriage before yet another suicide attempt, this one involving a meat cleaver. Maybe Brent would have to do a little adjusting to fit in, but if Scott could better himself enough to be one of the more popular guys in the house after what he'd been through, anyone could improve himself.

Scott cocked his head toward Brent. "Just try and keep the fungus from eating any of us."

He shut the door and stood next to Pete in the hallway.

"Really?" Pete said. "You think he's going to make it through Hell Week?"

Hell Week was the infamous last seven days before you became a full-fledged member of the fraternity house. Your future brothers spent that time hazing you nonstop to see if you really had the guts and drive to be in SAE. Though it varied from frat house to frat house, there might be things like military-style 4 A.M. wake-ups, with all the brothers gathered around wearing masks, beating drums, holding baseball bats; then you

might be dragged out into the snow, stripped down, hosed off, maybe expecting those baseball bats to rain down upon your head. You might be asked to drink cases of beer, then made to do the most disgusting things: clean shit off the floors, march into town wearing nothing but a summer dress, memorize every detail of the house's history and recite it while being pelted with various objects. Your assigned Big Brother acted as a guide and refuge through the process. Scott's Big Brother had been Shane, but even Shane had indirectly gotten in on the action, urging other active members of the house to give Scott a hard time—especially when he noticed how enthusiastically Scott had taken to being hazed.

Then, finally, if you survived Hell Week, you made it into the house. And everything changed from hell to heaven. You were part of the group.

After all that hazing—maybe because of some of that hazing—Scott now considered his housemates the closest people in his life. Shane, Garin, and Pete were really his brothers. He desperately wanted that same experience for Brent. Brent deserved to have people in his life who were loyal and supportive of him, no matter what happened.

"I'll give him the hose myself," Scott said. "And he'll come out smiling."

There was no doubt in Scott's mind that Brent would survive Hell Week and make it into the house. Having a future to look forward to was something Scott and Brent had never experienced before. Given where he and his brother had come from, things could only get better.

CHAPTER 5

LIQUOR UP FRONT—POKER IN THE REAR.

"I guess it doesn't get any more straightforward than that," Garin said as he stood next to Scott, Pete, and Shane beneath the pulsing red-and-white neon sign, surveying the façade of the nondescript building in front of them. "Doesn't look like much from the outside."

Scott grinned, reaching up to put a hand on Garin's shoulder. No, it sure as hell didn't; other than the sign and a couple of beer and Coca-Cola logos above the dark glass windows that ran along the first-story storefront of the two-story building, there was very little to indicate that the place was even open for business—let alone that it was one of the oldest bars in Missoula. The structure was concrete, paneled in slabs that were a mix of peach and vanilla, very 1970s construction. The sign—which read STOCKMANS CAFE BAR and sported a sketch of a longhorn glaring out angrily over the dark downtown sidewalk, daring anyone to step

inside—was far from inviting; the motto scrawled in circular script across the darkened plate-glass window—shoulder-high for a regular-size human, waist-high for a giant like Garin—was, on the other hand, pregnant with temptation.

"It's a real game?" Shane asked, sounding a little nervous. "I mean, legal?"

Shane was a pretty straight eagle. Sure, he knew how to enjoy college, was great with the ladies, drank like everyone else—but he rarely got into trouble, kept his room immaculate, and often cleaned up Scott's messes when Pete and Garin weren't around to do the sweeping or explaining. But in this instance he had nothing to worry about. Scott had done his research. He'd discovered Stockman's about a month earlier—nearly a full semester into his junior year and just a few days after they'd welcomed Brent into the fraternity—on a late-night jaunt into Missoula with another frat brother. They'd been looking for cheap beer and even cheaper girls and had stumbled into heaven instead.

"Perfectly legal. It's a single table, nine seats, and they have to keep the pot below three hundred dollars. They've got real dealers and everything."

"What about the players?" Pete said.

Scott was beginning to get impatient, standing out there on the street, people walking by and looking at them like they were fucking tourists.

"A few college kids like us, who sit down with twenty bucks and try to double it by the end of the night. And then a lot of regulars, guys who sit down with a couple hundred and play until morning."

Scott reached for the door before any of the Three Stooges could ask another question. Then he ushered them inside.

The front section of Stockman's was about as inviting as the angry longhorn on the neon sign. The ceiling was low and covered in graffiti, mostly people's names, a few hearts with arrows through them, a handful of mini diatribes against one perceived wrong or another. To the right, a long wooden bar ran down one entire side of the rectangular room, lined with red stools, only about a quarter of which were occupied. To the left, a wood-and-glass wall studded with old photos and framed pictures, everything from horses to cows—if it had hooves, it was on that damn wall.

But Scott wasn't there for the bar or the pictures; he kept moving, quickening his pace lest one of his friends lose his nerve on the way to the rear door, still a good ten yards away. Sure, the place had plenty of cheap beer. Better yet, if you could present a piece of paper that even insinuated that you were twenty-one, you could drink there. But there were plenty of establishments in Missoula where you could drink; this was the only place Scott knew of where you could also play cards.

When he reached the rear door, he ushered his three friends inside.

"Say hello to your new second home."

The back room was only a minor improvement on the front: another low ceiling, more framed cattle on the walls, some actual sawdust on the floor—and an oversize circular poker table situated close to the back wall, surrounded by uncomfortable-looking wooden chairs. The table had a real felt cover, drink holders, and a cabinet built in for the dealer's chips. There was also a slot cut into the table next to where the dealer sat, leading to a box that hung beneath the lip of the felt.

The table was nearly full. All men, most of them in their twenties, a few trending toward middle age. At least half were

wearing baseball hats low down over their eyes. None were particularly well dressed; a couple were college kids, like Scott and his friends. A couple more probably worked construction, or were painters, or maybe electricians. Scott doubted any of them were professionals—though in a place like this, nobody was going to ask for your résumé. If you had a few bucks in your pocket, you could play.

A couple bucks—that's all it had cost Scott to get started, the first time he'd wandered into Stockman's that late night about a month ago. The stakes were real low—you could play a hand for as little as a dollar, with the pots topped at three hundred, to stay within the law. That first night, Scott had been more than a little green. The game was Texas Hold'em—the most popular form of poker, the one that nearly every college kid and almost 50 percent of high school boys played regularly, that almost 70 percent of men in the country had played at least once for money, that was practically an American institution, on par with baseball, basketball, and beer. A seven-card game, in which you used five. The play itself was pretty simple. Each player got dealt two cards, then, over the course of the game, five more would be laid out in the center of the table, faceup; each player used three of the center cards to make a hand, and the best hand won. But though the play itself was simple, the *game* was much more complex.

As the cliché went, the game of poker wasn't really about the cards, it was about the players. You had no control over the cards you were dealt—that was pure luck. But what you did with them—or more specifically, how you wielded them against the other players at the table—that was pure skill. Which made the game itself much more about skill than about luck. Over time, a

good player would consistently beat a table of bad players, regardless of how the cards were dealt.

That first night, Scott had been anything but good. He'd lost twenty bucks—a small fortune to him, at least one missed meal that week, maybe two—but he'd found himself hooked on the action. The idea that you could look across that table at a total stranger, try to get a read on him just from the way he looked at his cards, or how he fingered his chips, or how he bet, aggressive or cautious or just plain dumb. It was an awesome feeling, an incredible high.

The next day Scott had headed directly to the school library, a place he had seldom gone before. He'd picked up a book called *The Winner's Guide to Texas Hold'em Poker,* and had studied it intensively over the next three days.

Then he returned to Stockman's. Phil, his rediscovered dad, had begun giving him a four-hundred-dollar-a-month allowance—for food, books, and spending money—which had left Scott just enough extra to play cards. And over the course of the next week, he had become a Stockman's regular.

Now he was going to introduce his three best friends to the hobby that was rapidly becoming a welcome addiction. He wished Brent had been willing to come along, but his younger brother hadn't been interested. Since entering the university and joining the house, Brent had been on a nearly 24/7 mission to transform himself, and he was hardly recognizable now. His hair was cut short, and he often wore a tie; he'd even gotten the house involved in a handful of charities, including a soup kitchen in Missoula. Even Pete had admitted that he'd been 180 degrees wrong about Brent.

Scott glanced over at his frat brothers, his three best friends. Shane was still near the door, eyeing the table and stacks of multicolored chips in front of each player with obvious suspicion. Pete was a few steps ahead of him and seemed to be concentrating on the dealer, on the way he counted up the chips in the center of the felt—the pot—and how every few hands he swept a couple of chips out of the pot and flicked them down the slot in the felt. This was the *rake*, the house's little cut, which was a few percentage points of the total bets placed—a few bucks here, a few bucks there. But Garin was already reaching for his wallet. Scott grinned, because he recognized the glint in Garin's eyes. Maybe Pete and Shane could resist the lure of the cards, but Garin was a goner, just like him.

THREE WEEKS LATER
2 A.M.

There was no greater feeling in the world.

It was a frigid night outside, wisps of icy wind drifting up through the floorboards and poorly paneled walls of the cryptlike back-room poker parlor. Pulling a scarf tight around his throat, Scott fought to control his breathing and to contain the spikes of adrenaline that ricocheted up his spine. It was a sudden, primal thrill, hardwired into his nervous system. The minute the dealer had first flipped over the cards, just a few seconds earlier, something inside of Scott had fired off—a chemical reaction surging up from the animal portion of his brain. Anyone who'd ever placed a bet would understand the feeling. Beyond logic,

beyond math, beyond statistics and practical thought and strategy was a fire that drove him to play—and win.

It didn't matter that tonight it was mostly his friends—Garin, Pete, Shane, and a couple of his other brothers from SAE—crowded around the felt in the corner of the dimly lit back room. And it didn't matter that Scott was halfway to drunk. He was still lucid enough to recognize the cards—two in his hands, the rest lined up in the center of the table for everyone to see. His cards, on their own, were decidedly unimpressive: a six and a seven, both of clubs. But when you added them to the three cards on the table—that was something else. An eight, a nine, and a ten, also of clubs.

A goddamn straight flush.

That was the opposite of unimpressive. That was something you never, ever saw.

Scott didn't care that the entire pot—a metropolis of colored plastic chips rising like a miniature Technicolor skyline above the center of the round table—came to a little less than sixty dollars. A straight flush was a miracle, whether you were playing for pennies or for millions.

He loosened the scarf a little, letting the cold air bite at his lungs. The other players were watching him, so instead of returning their looks, he watched the dealer—who was in the midst of taking another rake. Just as he had done after every raised hand throughout the night, the man—midtwenties, with a well-trimmed goatee, too many rings on his fingers, and wearing a white-and-red Stockman's sweatshirt with that angry bull stitched across the dead center—swept a few chips out of the pot and slipped them into the slot in the felt. And as usual as of late,

Scott more than noticed the ritualistic move—he found his mind replaying a narrative he'd been writing in his mind for the past week or more.

A few chips to the house, every hand. Pennies against pots made up of dollars—but over the course of an evening like this one, the rake would certainly add up. Scott had struck up a conversation with one of the dealers a few days after he'd first introduced his frat brothers to the bar—and he'd learned that over the course of a year, that one table's rake added up to more than two hundred thousand dollars. The number seemed crazy, impossible. A single table, with a dollar ante, a pot capped at three hundred dollars—two hundred thousand dollars of pure profit a year?

When he'd told Pete about the number—because Pete, a marketing major with a real head for economics, had seemed equally intrigued by the rake—Pete had voiced his own thoughts. If only there was a way they could run a table like that. But of course, without licensing from the state, that would be illegal—a boiler-room operation, illegal gambling, the kind of thing you could go to jail for.

Even so, Scott was more and more possessed by the idea. If one little table in the back room of a bar, limited by the bar's hours and the number of players who stumbled in, could earn six figures a year—what if there was some way to bring the game to more players, maybe many more players, whenever they wanted it—and somehow do it legally? The profit you could make seemed infinite.

At that moment, as the dealer finished with his rake and turned back toward the players, Scott had something more immediate to keep him occupied.

With a flourish, he turned over his cards.

The table went silent. Then Garin whistled low, impressed. Pete stared, stunned. Shane laughed.

Scott grinned, rising halfway out of his seat.

"Pay the man!" he shouted.

With a sudden swipe of the back of his hand, he toppled the metropolis of chips, then scooped them across the felt, toward his own growing pile.

It was a feeling better than sex.

And still, he wondered.

What if you could somehow tap into that on a worldwide scale?

CHAPTER 6

"Look at this, I'm killing this guy."

"I think he's going to cry. Talk about his girlfriend again."

Pete had just made it to the top step of the three-story walk-up, still a good ten feet down the institutional-style hallway from Scott and Brent's new apartment, a few blocks from the frat house, but he could already hear voices, laughter, and the clink of glass bottles. Moving closer, he saw that the apartment door was hanging wide open, allowing the noise to travel unimpeded through the dilapidated building. No doubt the neighbors had grown used to this sort of thing, even though the brothers had moved in only a few weeks earlier. Still, whatever was going on inside the apartment at the moment seemed particularly raucous. He wondered if his friends had gotten into his Ritalin prescription again.

Once he was inside the apartment, he shut the door behind him. There wasn't much to the place—a cubicle of a living room,

with a pair of couches that made the ones at SAE look positively regal, a glass coffee table cluttered with beer bottles, various remote controls, and a pair of potted plants that hadn't been watered, leaves fraying and brown, stems dry enough to be smoked. All three of his friends—Scott, Brent, and another fraternity brother named Cal Teller, who often joined Scott at Stockman's on his now regular visits—were gathered around Scott's desktop computer, which had been set up on the plastic bar that served as the dining room table. Scott was at the keyboard, Brent and Cal at either of his shoulders. All three of them were drinking, and from the number of bottles on the coffee table, Pete could guess that they had been at it for a while.

"What the hell are you guys doing?" Pete asked when none of them even acknowledged that he'd entered the room.

"Tell him he's got a small dick," Cal said, still facing the computer screen.

"Yeah," Brent added. "Tell him you're sitting outside his window with binoculars, and that you can see his dick, and that it is very small."

Pete removed his coat, looked for a hook or a hanger, then dropped it onto the floor.

"Really, guys, if that is some sort of interactive porn site, you're all truly pathetic."

Scott glanced back over his shoulder, saw Pete for the first time, and waved him forward.

"No, man, you gotta check this out. This is so cool."

Pete walked across the room and pushed in next to Cal.

The computer screen in front of them was filled with something that was definitely not porn. Whatever the site was, it was extremely rudimentary; everything on it was a dull sandy color,

and all the writing was fairly blotchy. In the main area of the screen there was an oval object surrounded by little cartoon-character faces seated in suede chairs, with names beneath each one. And in front of each face, on the oval, a pair of cards, facedown. In the middle of the oval, three cards were laid out faceup.

It took Pete a full minute to realize what he was looking at. It was a Texas Hold'em game in middeal.

Scott was furiously typing—something about somebody's dick and how small it was—and the words were appearing on the bottom of the screen, beneath a squiggly green border. When he stopped typing, another line of text appeared—the response, a lot of angry words, obviously from someone who didn't like being told that his penis was small.

"Is this some sort of a chat room?" Pete asked. "And is that a poker game you're all watching?"

Scott's reflection was grinning in the glass of the computer screen.

"It's a poker game, all right. Real people, playing poker for real money."

Pete laughed. "You've got to be kidding me. You're playing poker over the Internet?"

"Well, no," Scott said. "You have to have a credit card to put real money in. We're just chatting with the douche bags who are playing. There's no one editing the chat feature. It's pretty funny how mad people get."

Pete headed toward the refrigerator to look for beer.

"You guys must be pretty drunk."

"Yeah, maybe, but this is freaking awesome. We've got to do this."

Pete found a Budweiser, went to work on the cap.

"You are doing it. You got a total stranger worried about his manhood. Mission accomplished."

A beer bottle sailed over the top of the computer screen and narrowly missed Pete's head, crashing into the wall of the kitchenette. Scott was out of his seat now.

"No, you idiot. This poker website. It's awesome. I mean, the software really sucks and the graphics are horrible. These are supposed to be palm trees, and the faces all look the same. But this website—it's genius. Even though it's crap, there are like fifty people playing. And they're taking a rake from every table, all night long. They're minting money."

Pete came over to stand behind Scott again. He looked at the computer screen, a little more carefully this time. The graphics really were awful. But now he could make out the palm trees, and he saw what looked to be sand, and beachy waves in a corner.

"What is this site? How did you find it?"

"I made friends with one of the dealers at Stockman's, and the guy told me he'd been making like three hundred dollars a week playing online at this site. It's called Paradise Poker."

"I guess that explains the palm trees."

Scott went back to the keyboard, waxing philosophic once more about one of the players' anatomy.

"I mean," he said, his fingers rattling against the keys. "We would do a hell of a lot better. Come up with something much more sophisticated and clean."

Pete pointed at the cards on the oval table. "You really think people are going to play poker on the computer? More than a handful of dorks with nothing better to do? Poker is a social

game. It's about reading the other players, it's about the face-to-face competition. You know that way better than me. You're at Stockman's every week."

"But if I didn't have to leave the house, I could play all the time."

"If you had a credit card," Brent added.

"Well, yeah, obviously. But most college kids have credit cards. And not just college kids play poker. If it were a sport, it would be the most popular in the country. More people play cards than baseball. And worldwide—God only knows how many people play poker around the world."

Pete shook his head; he just wasn't buying it. Most intelligent people he knew would be terrified at the idea of putting their credit card on the Internet. It was 2000; the Internet had a long way to go before most would feel comfortable *shopping* over the computer, let alone playing poker. And then, of course, there was one even more important question.

"Is this even legal?"

"Sure, why not?" Scott said. "Everyone pretty much agrees that poker is a game of skill. And this isn't like owning a casino—nobody is playing cards in your house. I mean, we have to do some research, make sure everything is by the book. I think this website is run out of South America somewhere. But I don't see why anyone would have a problem with a poker website."

Scott went quiet, and Pete could see that he was deep in thought. Maybe he was a little drunk, but he wasn't just kidding around.

Still, Pete was far from convinced. Even if it was completely legal, and you found a way to convince people it was safe to use

their credit cards over the Internet, Pete couldn't help repeating what he thought was an insurmountable flaw.

"I just don't see it. Nobody is going to want to play poker over the Internet. No matter how many palm trees you fit on the damn screen."

In his mind, the issue was settled. But Scott's face was still giving off a glow. Pete couldn't tell if it was the result of something internal that had sparked to life, or just the reflection from the screen.

CHAPTER 7

Ladies and gentlemen, we've begun our initial descent into Seattle-Tacoma International Airport. Please begin powering down any electronics as the flight attendants move through the cabin to prepare for landing."

Scott jerked awake as the cabin lights came on with the last few syllables of the pilot's announcement—nearly upending his tray table with one knee while hastily reaching for the small leather attaché case that had slipped off his lap somewhere over the coast of California. The case felt so damn foreign against his fingers as he lifted it back up; he'd never owned anything that nice before. The material seemed too elegant and sophisticated. On its own, it would've been a great graduation gift, and Scott had been completely shocked when he'd learned that the case was really just an appetizer.

The attaché once again resting securely on his lap, Scott stretched out against the full leather of his business-class seat,

careful not to let his boat shoes flip over too far into the aisle to his right. The flight attendants were scurrying about, collecting the last remaining plastic cups from the passengers around him. For the hundredth time since they'd taken off, he couldn't help registering how hot the attendants were—tall, tan, veritable amazons, probably wearing nothing besides bikinis beneath their pale blue uniforms. Scott grinned at the closest of the crew—a staggering blonde who was leaning over the passenger across the aisle to help with a difficult window shade. As she bent, her long skirt rode halfway up the back of her calves, revealing stockings and the heels of a surprisingly sexy pair of red shoes.

A fitting end to an incredible trip. Scott turned away from the aisle, toward the window seat to his left. He was surprised to see that his dad was still fast asleep, and even then, Phil had a wide smile on his face. Though they had reconnected as father and son four years earlier now, it was still kind of amazing to look over and see those features, so similar to his own. Phil was a head taller than him, graying a bit at the temples, but nobody would've had any trouble picking him out as Scott's dad. And probably because they had reconnected as adults, they behaved more like best friends than like father and son.

Which was a big part of why the trip had been so incredible. Under normal circumstances, who the hell would want to go to Rio with his dad? But Phil—that was another story. The attaché case was a nice appetizer, but with Phil along, the trip had been one of the best graduation presents in history. *No-holds-barred Brazil.* Two weeks of pristine beaches, late-night parties, fancy restaurants, and uncountable bottles of fine wine. They took turns playing wingman whenever a string bikini was in sight.

And even with twenty years on him, Phil was almost as good at chatting up girls as Scott. The flight back to Seattle was the longest that either of them had slept uninterrupted in two weeks.

Scott almost felt bad letting his elbow fly over the armrest between them, gently poking at the soft area below his dad's rib cage. There was probably still another fifteen minutes before the plane touched down, but now that the trip was over and they were on their way back to the real world, Scott couldn't wait any longer.

For months now, he had been getting his thoughts in order. He had spent hundreds of hours in the university library. And he was finally ready to take the next step.

"Please tell me the plane had some sort of mechanical problem and had to return to Rio," Phil said, yawning as he rubbed his eyes. "I can't possibly wait until Brent graduates to make that trip again."

Scott laughed, though he knew his dad was serious. Even though Brent wasn't actually related to Phil, the man was generous to a fault. And he had the money to make good on that generosity; he was one of the top investment bankers in the Seattle area. More important to Scott, Phil had built himself up from nothing. He was a true believer in bootstrap ideology—a staunch fiscal conservative who really and truly believed in the American way. Which was why there was no question in Scott's mind about where he had to turn first. With the two of them trapped together in an airplane, even if only for another fifteen minutes, it seemed like the perfect opportunity to make his case.

He carefully unzipped the attaché case and retrieved a stack of computer papers. Then he turned in his seat to face his dad.

"I want to show you something I've been working on," he said, his feet alive against the airplane floor. He could hear the gears in the wings churning; he knew he didn't have much time. But the truth was, if he couldn't make his case in a few minutes, it wasn't going to be something that was worth doing anyway.

"Please don't tell me you want to try and save the world," Phil said.

"We can leave that to Brent and his soup kitchens," Scott responded. "No, this is something a bit more practical. Take a look at this."

He handed his dad the first page from the stack on his lap. It was a screenshot of the Paradise Poker website. Beneath the shot there was a row of numbers, detailing everything that Scott had learned about the site.

As his dad digested what he was seeing, Scott gave him the rundown. His senior year at Montana—just like at colleges everywhere in the country—everyone was talking about Internet ideas. The entrepreneurial spirit had captivated almost every dorm room, and Scott was no different; but he was pretty sure he'd come up with an innovative way to build a company that no one else had yet done right.

"Poker?" Phil said, looking up from the paper. "Scott, I love playing poker as much as the next guy—but as a business?"

"Not just a business," Scott responded. "Big business. International business. Look at Paradise Poker. They've got about a hundred and fifty tables, maybe fifteen hundred regular players. They take a rake out of every game—nearly every minute of every day. Figure just a five percent rake, an average of sixty dollars per pot—that's three dollars per game. If one table deals around one hundred hands per hour, that's three hundred bucks an hour.

Multiply that by a hundred and fifty tables, that's like forty-five thousand dollars a day."

Phil looked at him, then back at the paper. Scott started handing over the rest of his research—calculations based on different gaming parameters, analyses of the handful of casinos that had poker rooms, which were really a tiny minority, because poker as a game of skill wasn't considered a big money earner in Vegas. Even a short history of the game itself: how it had evolved from an eighteenth-century card game played by French royalty, then traveled to the Mississippi steamboats in the 1800s. And he finished with more research into how many people enjoyed the game today: college kids, high school kids, adults, distributed across all incomes and cultures.

Phil took it all in, waited until Scott got quiet before asking the question.

"And you're confident that this is legal?"

Scott nodded. He had spoken to lawyers at the University of Montana and even had a couple of meetings in Seattle. There was a consensus that if there wasn't a law that said you couldn't do it, it was presumed to be perfectly legal. The law that was usually applied to gambling, whether it be online or over the phone, was the infamous Interstate Wire Act of 1961. But every lawyer Scott had talked to was convinced that the Wire Act did not apply to poker. Scott pointed to a page halfway into the stack; on it was printed the entire federal statute. He encouraged his dad to read at least the first few lines:

> *Whoever being engaged in the business of betting or wa-*
> *gering knowingly uses a wire communication facility for*
> *the transmission in interstate or foreign commerce of bets*

or wagers or information assisting in the placing of bets or wagers on any sporting event or contest, or for the transmission of a wire communication which entitles the recipient to receive money or credit as a result of bets or wagers, or for information assisting in the placing of bets or wagers, shall be fined under this title or imprisoned . . .

"It's pretty clear that the Wire Act was designed to inhibit games of chance, specifically sports betting. When you look deeper into it—how it was passed and why—this seems even more obvious. Robert Kennedy was trying to take on organized crime, so he convinced his brother to make it illegal to bet on sports. That's what the lawyers say, at least."

Phil leaned back in his seat, clearly impressed. He could see the passion in Scott's eyes, and that was winning him over even more than the research. Phil was a businessman, and he knew that passion was more important than any numbers. You could sell an idea on passion.

"This is some impressive work."

The seat belt light had just gone on over their heads, indicating that they were on the last leg of their approach into Seattle.

"Okay, Scott, you make sure this is legal. And then you do it. I'll write you a check for twenty-five thousand dollars to get you started."

Scott did his best to take the number in stride. To him it was an enormous sum of money. But he knew his dad wasn't just being generous. The twenty-five thousand dollars wasn't a gift; it was an investment. This was Scott's one chance—and he

intended to take advantage of it. And to do this right, he wasn't going to be able to go it on his own.

As the plane touched down onto the runway with the screech of tires against pavement, Scott's thoughts were swirling forward. By the time they reached the gate, he knew exactly who he needed to call.

CHAPTER 8

I guess this is what you would call a real upstairs/downstairs kind of operation."

Scott gave Shane a friendly shove through the open elevator doors and followed two steps behind him. Even with the basement's high, vaulted ceilings, the thick carpeting, and the well-constructed cement walls, the sounds of the party upstairs could still be heard, probably drifting down through the elevator shaft. Upstairs, Scott knew, it was all caviar and champagne. A cocktail party in full swing, even though it was barely seven in the evening and his dad had just gotten back from a business trip overseas. But down in the basement, it was a different scene altogether.

The basement was large and rectangular, with no windows, no paintings on the walls, and almost no furniture. Shane had stopped a yard from the elevator, which had since closed behind them; it seemed like Scott's frat brother was fighting the urge to

turn and try to run back upstairs. The basement certainly didn't look like the office of a fledgling Internet company—maybe more like some sort of terrorist hideout. There was a whiteboard in one corner, covered in fairly arcane computations and sketches, and stacks of papers like the teetering walls of a hastily constructed fort, set in a semicircular pattern around a pair of matching computer stations. Both monitors were on, dueling screens of sand and green. Without a doubt, Shane immediately recognized the squiggly palm trees from Paradise's website, even from that distance.

"I really like what you've done with the place," Shane said. He pointed toward a pair of closet doors along the back wall of the room. "Is that where we keep the hostages?"

"Actually," Scott said, crossing to the closest stack of papers, "that's where we sleep. There's a cot in each closet."

"You've got to be kidding me."

Scott grinned. He wasn't kidding in the least. And he knew that despite Shane's rumbles of discontent, his friend was completely on board. The basement was a stark contrast to the incredible mansion upstairs—but it was all theirs. When Scott's father had offered him the use of the space for his fledgling company, he'd jumped at the chance. The beautiful home above it—a sprawling estate on Lake Washington with more bedrooms than Scott could count, manicured grounds, and even a fully operational golf course where his dad held one of the area's premier annual charity events—acted as aspirational motivation. Scott intended to own a house like that one day. This basement operation was how he was going to get there. Besides, it wasn't going to hurt that his dad would be entertaining wealthy colleagues and clients upstairs. Scott had agreed not to pitch himself to

Phil's clients in any overt way—but if someone wondered what the heck was going on in the basement, well, Scott would be more than happy to give him a tour.

Even with living out of the basement, twenty-five thousand dollars wasn't going to last very long. If Scott was going to make his company a reality, he was going to need to raise more money. And before he could go after additional funds, he needed personnel.

Shane had been an easy first choice. Scott trusted him implicitly, knew he was a hard worker—it didn't hurt that he was the most anal-retentive of the fraternity bunch—and his eye for detail would be a great help. Equally important, his family had a tractor dealership; they had the ability to invest in a new business venture. Most important of all, Shane had coincidentally already moved to Seattle for a job that hadn't worked out—which made him eager and willing. When Scott had pitched him the idea over lunch at a kitschy place called Chang's Mongolian Grill, Shane had been enthusiastic from the beginning; when he'd opened his fortune cookie at the end of the meal and read his fortune out loud, he'd been completely hooked: "A confidential tip will clue you in to a great financial deal." Scott couldn't have planned it better if he'd tried.

Scott pulled one of the sheets of paper off of the closest tower and handed it to his friend. Shane saw that it was a list of names—all of which he recognized.

"And here I thought I was just really, really special. It looks like half of our fraternity is on this list."

"Just the best, brightest, and those who come from a little bit of money. Look, it seems pretty obvious to me: Why go knocking on doors when we have this incredibly deep bench—SAE?"

"Have to admit, down here in the basement it does feel a little bit like we're back in the fraternity house."

There was even a pile of beer cans in a corner, along with a row of empty Red Bulls. Why not extend the frat house feel? The SAE house was one of the greatest experiences of both their lives. There was no reason to change a model that had already been proven to work.

"Who are you going after first?" Shane asked. "Pete? Garin?"

"I already spoke to Pete. He still isn't on board with the idea of people playing poker online. And also, well—he did just get married."

At least Pete had agreed to act as an informal consultant as they moved forward, but he wouldn't be moving into the basement. He'd married his college sweetheart, and she probably wouldn't have liked living in a closet anyway.

"And Garin?"

Scott grinned. "He's driving his Mustang up next week."

"And who else? You're not going to get Brent to drop out of school early, are you? He just got elected president of the house for next year."

Scott shook his head. He was damn proud of his brother—it was amazing, the transformation the kid had undergone. Now he was going to be president of the whole goddamn frat. Scott watched as Shane lowered himself in front of one of the computers and started poking around the keyboard. Now that he had a little money, Scott had opened an account on the website—so they could play along and see how flawed and imperfect Paradise Poker seemed to be. He was already coming up with ways the site could be improved. But to get there, they needed money—because it was money that would lead to new software.

None of the SAE brothers were computer programmers. In fact, none of them had ever taken any computer courses at all. Which probably made them the least qualified people to start an Internet company.

But that would soon change. Scott was determined to put together the perfect team. They wouldn't leave the basement until they had a working business plan and an avenue to the software that would make it all sing.

Garin was the next piece in that puzzle, and even though he had only been hired a day ago, he had already proven himself invaluable with a simple suggestion of who they could go after next.

Scott was going to let Garin make the call himself.

That's pretty cool," Garin was saying as he squatted against a beanbag chair in the corner of the basement, a cordless phone held in the crook of his neck. "A whole semester abroad in Paris? Can't imagine what that would be like. I'm not even sure I could find the place on a map."

Garin looked up from the phone and across the room at Scott and Shane, who were seated next to each other at the computer stations. He gave them a thumbs-up. A semester abroad in Paris was the kind of thing that none of them could ever have contemplated; it was obvious that the kid on the other end of the line would make an important addition to their team.

"Welcome back," Garin continued. "I know it's been a while since you left Montana, Hilt, but I've got a little proposition for you. Shane and Scott are here too, and we're working on a poker business. Yeah, online. It's an Internet company, where people can play poker."

Garin launched into the pitch that he, Scott, and Shane had developed—a sort of mini business proposal that they had put together from the research they had compiled. Scott could tell, even from across the room, that Hilt was at least listening. If he liked what he heard, they'd be in great shape.

Oscar Hilt Tatum IV had attended the University of Montana for only a single semester—racing back to Florida, where he had grown up, because he hated the cold—but in that short time he'd made quite an impression. He'd rushed the SAE house, gotten accepted in no time—and then had shown up with a BMW M3 convertible on the back of a truck. That sight still stood out in Scott's mind years later.

Hilt came from money. His parents were prominent in the St. Petersburg medical community, and his family extended deep into the professional field. Hell, he had a Roman numeral after his name. The only Roman numeral Scott had ever been involved with had been carved into his frat-room door.

If any of them aside from Shane had access to people with money, it was Hilt. When Garin finally finished his conversation and hung up the phone, Scott could hardly stay in his seat.

"Did he seem into it?"

Before Garin could even answer, the phone, still in his hand, started ringing. Garin stared at it, then finally put it to his ear.

A few seconds later he hung up, then rose to his full height and clapped his palms together.

"He said he'll be here in three days. And he's going to bring a hundred thousand dollars in investment money with him. He wants in, and he wants a piece of the company. I think we damn well better give it to him."

Scott tore across the room and caught his friend in a grip that was half tackle, half bear hug.

They had just quintupled the value of their company with a single phone call.

The next six weeks flashed by at ten thousand RPMs, bolstered by a constant stream of Red Bull, adrenaline, and a shared determination to one day get the hell out of that basement and onto a bigger stage.

Very quickly there emerged a strict daily routine. Scott, Shane, Garin, and Hilt were all at their computer stations every day by 7 A.M. Punching keys, doing whatever research they could, writing away at the business proposal that was growing line by line, paragraph by paragraph—all through the day, until 9 P.M., when one of them would break first, sliding off a stool or beanbag chair and onto the floor, ready to crawl toward one of the cots in those damn closets. None of them had ever worked so hard. Entire weeks went by without any of them stepping outside. It got so bad that eventually they decided to create a ritual night out: Wednesday, because Wednesday was ladies' night at a favorite bar in downtown Seattle, a place with *Billiards* in the name.

As a team, they had learned to function even more efficiently than Scott would have thought possible. Once Hilt had arrived in the basement, he had immediately been assigned the task of headlining their money-raising efforts. Polite, soft-spoken, and slight of build, especially compared with Garin, he had an amazing affinity for numbers and all things economic. He was also

an intensely logical person who spoke faster the more excited he got. He quickly developed an incredibly convincing pitch of his own, which he plied over the phone as often as possible, starting with family friends down in Florida and extending through the fraternity network to anyone he thought might be willing to invest.

They made their goal simple: $750,000, which they intended to raise within three months. That, they believed, was the minimum amount they would need to launch their company. Garin, Shane, and Scott, who were focused on editing and constantly revising their business plan, had come up with the number by both analyzing Paradise Poker's financials and extrapolating using what data they could find about the market as a whole. In the year since they'd discovered Paradise Poker, more companies had entered the business, and a couple in particular were growing at a fairly rapid rate. PokerStars, run out of the Isle of Man, was well capitalized and seemed like it was going to rise to the top of the heap. Another, Party Poker, was growing by leaps and bounds, and was also well financed—its founders had made a pile of money on 1-900 sex lines and had poured that capital into a first-rate poker site.

The one common denominator that they had found among the sites was that they were all based outside of the United States. Even though every lawyer they met with continued to assure them that there was nothing inherently illegal about running an online poker website, it seemed that all of the companies were being run overseas, even though the large majority of their customers were American.

Scott and his team hadn't yet come to any conclusions, but

they began to see the many benefits of launching their company overseas: cheap labor, governments that were okay with licensing a gaming website, experienced platforms. If they were going to run an international business, there was no reason not to think internationally.

Before any of them would be getting on a plane, however, there was one more pressing issue: they needed to come up with a name for their website. On the Internet, your future was only as strong as your domain name. It was more than just words on a monitor; it was your location, your home, and your brand. Paradise Poker, PokerStars, Party Poker—they were all strong choices, because all of them left you with a feeling, an emotion. Paradise—that was self-explanatory. PokerStars gave you a feeling that just by playing there, you were some sort of poker celebrity. Party Poker—well, wasn't that what it was really all about? An online party with friends and strangers that never had to end.

Scott wanted something just as powerful. Something sophisticated, something that brought to mind a classy operation, a place where you might have a martini and a cigar and play a round of poker.

But despite their efforts, a good name eluded them. In recent days they had grown so desperate, they had taken to leafing through the dictionary, just throwing out words, adding *poker.com* to whatever they found. CallPoker.com, JackPoker.com, PlayPoker.com. Nothing seemed good enough. Before they did anything else, they had to solve this problem.

An Internet company without a name was like a bar that no one would ever be able to find.

I t was a Wednesday night, a little after ten o'clock, and the BMW 5 Series sedan was positively throbbing. Techno music reverberated through the speakers built into the dashboard, making the very windows rattle as Scott navigated the sleek automobile down a dark stretch of highway. Trees were flashing by on either side and there were mountains in the distance, but it was hard to concentrate on anything other than the techno. Garin and Hilt, in the back, and Shane, in the passenger seat, had all been complaining about the music since they'd pulled out of Scott's father's driveway. Scott had left it on just to spite them.

It was Garin who'd made the obscene suggestion that the radio had been left on a techno setting by one of the girls Scott had brought home the week before. Scott was seriously offended by the idea that he would sleep with a girl who liked techno; he was pretty sure that it wasn't one of his conquests to blame, because his dad had been on quite a tear recently. The blonde whom Phil had brought home a few days earlier was wearing the kind of high heels that would have fit in well at a rave.

So he left the music on, to punish Garin for his comment, and was fully enjoying the looks of pure agony on his friends' faces in the rearview mirror. They had been driving for thirty minutes, which meant there was still a good ten minutes to go before they reached the billiards bar and ladies' night. Unless one of them picked up a girl with better taste in music, Scott was going to make sure the techno continued for the ride home.

Five minutes later, he had grown so used to the bitching of his passengers he almost didn't hear that one of them was shouting at him from the backseat. It wasn't until Hilt repeated what

he was saying a third time that Scott realized he wasn't yelling about the music. Scott immediately reached for the volume, and the car went dead silent.

"Absolute Poker!" Hilt shouted again.

The words reverberated off the windows and leather seats of Phil's car. Eventually, Shane spoke.

"It's not bad."

"Sophisticated," Garin added. "Cosmopolitan, kind of a lounge feel. You think there's any way something that simple is still available?"

Scott could feel the engine of the BMW pulsing through the steering wheel beneath his fingers.

"Only one way to find out."

Without another word, he yanked hard on the wheel, sending the car careening into a skid. He made the U-turn by inches, the two right tires spitting up gravel, grass, and pavement. Ladies' night was instantly forgotten.

Twenty-five minutes later the four of them were hunched over one of the computer stations as Scott punched in the words. It took less than five seconds before they got a response.

Scott leaned back and lifted his hands into the air. His friends high-fived behind him, and then he quickly punched in the information to buy the domain name. Twenty-nine dollars to lock it down—and AbsolutePoker.com was officially born.

CHAPTER 9

That's got to be him."

Scott shielded his eyes from the late-afternoon sun, which seemed to hang like a vast and flaming Christmas ornament just inches beyond the mostly open-air glass entrance to the airport. Trying to see where Shane was pointing, he could make out the mass of taxi drivers, swarming like flies whenever anyone who looked even remotely North American exited through the revolving doors. Scott himself had briefly stepped out to the curb before being beaten back by the aggressive cabbies; for now he was satisfied to stay in the safety of the baggage claim area with Shane, Garin, and his dad. The trip to Brazil—his first outside the United States—had certainly opened his eyes to how different a foreign culture could be. But even from his brief moment outside, his first tentative steps into the Central American country of Costa Rica—lost in the jumble of drivers shouting at him in Spanish and broken English, the thick, humid air catching in

his throat and filling up his lungs, the smoggy scent of the nearby urban jungle that was San José, the country's capital—gave him the feeling that this place was a world apart.

"Most definitely," Garin said, in tune with Shane. "There can't possibly be two people who look like that in this hemisphere."

Then Scott saw him too, pushing his way through the crowd of taxi drivers and into the revolving door—and whistled low. Eric Tuttle was truly something to behold. Elongated to an almost comical extreme, with gangly limbs like a humanoid spider and spiky red hair above a paper-white forehead, he snaked forward in a gray business suit with wide, anachronistic lapels and an even wider eighties-style tie.

Eric saw them pointing in his direction as he broke free of the door and entered the airport lobby. He smiled, revealing a set of oversize veneers, and raced toward them at full speed.

"Now, where the hell did you find this guy again?" Scott's dad coughed as he leaned back against his designer suitcase. He was the only one of them who had packed a case—the rest had small duffel bags slung over their shoulders. To Scott, seventy-two hours in a tropical country meant three T-shirts, three pairs of boxers, one pair of jeans, and a box of condoms. But his dad was decidedly more urbane.

"The Internet," Garin said, grinning. "Of course. Lots of websites talk about him—he's supposedly the best gaming consultant in the area. Supposedly works with most of the sports books, and people say he used to be a little involved with Paradise when they first opened up here. He's also pretty cheap."

"You had me at cheap," Scott interrupted. "Now, shut the fuck up. We've got three days to learn everything we can about this place, and he's as good a guide as any."

The recon trip had been Scott's idea; even though they were still far from reaching their financial goal of $750,000 in investment seed money, they were at the point where they needed to make some firm decisions. First on that list, now that they had a company domain name, was settling on a location for their headquarters—a home, as it were, where they could incorporate and begin building their brand.

Costa Rica seemed the natural first choice. Paradise Poker was located there—and in addition, the country seemed to be ground zero for the online sports book business. Which meant there would be a lot of experienced people who knew the tech and the industry. As with many Central and South American countries, Costa Rica could also provide lots of cheap labor—but in Costa Rica, that labor would be well educated. From the research they had done, Scott had learned that it would be fairly easy to get incorporated in the country and to secure a gaming license. The location lent an air of credibility. And from the pictures he had seen in the guidebooks Garin had brought home from the Seattle library—well, it didn't hurt that the place was a tropical paradise. The idea that they could all move there—start their company, breathe life into AbsolutePoker.com in such an exotic locale—it was pretty fucking exciting, and very fucking cool.

The bizarre-looking consultant was breathing hard when he finally reached them.

"Welcome to Costa Rica, gentlemen. We have a full schedule, so let's get moving. The car is just outside. Ignore the taxi drivers, they're just part of the place's native charm."

And with that, the man spun on his heel and strutted back in the direction from which he'd come. Scott glanced over at his team; they all seemed about to crack up, and he scolded them

with his eyes. This was serious business, and they were supposed to be acting professional. Even if, from the looks of their skeletal consultant as he moved away, they were about to embark on something akin to Mr. Toad's Wild Ride.

Eight hours later, the ride was beginning to feel a lot more like a merry-go-round than a roller coaster. The five of them were jammed into Eric's bright orange Fiat, speeding along palm-tree-lined highways, with Eric all the while aiming a hand left, then right, then forward, pointing out buildings that ranged from low, boxy warehouses, to ranch-style houses, even to the odd multistory apartment building. Each one, according to Eric, was the home of a sports book or an online casino. They asked him repeatedly about Paradise Poker, and eventually, as they were riding along one of the steeper roads leading up to the base of the hills above San José, he pointed toward a two-story house with gated windows and white shutters, mostly hidden behind a high security fence. He told them that the guys who ran Paradise Poker were essentially shadows in San José; everyone told stories about them, the gringos who lived up in the hills and rode around in black Escalades, throwing money around like it was toilet paper, always traveling in packs protected by bodyguards, surrounded by girls. Nobody ever really saw them, and who knew if the stories were even true? But supposedly, these were their offices, behind that security fence.

Unfortunately, Paradise wasn't one of their destinations that day. Instead, Eric had arranged for them to meet with a slew of sports book owners who were bringing in the lion's share of busi-

ness in the gaming industry. And even though Scott had repeatedly explained that they weren't interested in sports gambling, Eric had maintained that the sports books were the place to start.

So again and again, Eric parked the Fiat in front of one of the nondescript warehouses or the low ranch houses and ushered the four of them inside. Each time the setup was the same. Cubicled call centers spread out across bland spaces—hell, if you walked into a call center at Hewlett-Packard or Cisco, you'd expect to see the same thing. Once they got into the back offices, they found that most of the operators behind the sports books were Americans, while the front-office staff was usually Costa Rican.

But the most remarkable thing about the sports books—and the thing that they all seemed to have in common—was the seedy element at the top levels. Most of the American operators seemed like criminals—the way they dressed, the way they spoke, the way they offhandedly mentioned associates back in New York and Vegas. By the third and fourth book they'd visited, the seediness was reaching almost cartoonish proportions.

Around 4 P.M., at the last stop before they were to break for dinner—and start a night of festivities that Eric had assured them would rival anything they had experienced at the fraternity house—they pulled up in front of a warehouse at the edge of an urban sprawl of similar rectangular buildings. Eric parked the car and led them through the front door, past a security desk, then a pair of secretaries who didn't even bother looking up from the Spanish newspapers they were reading. Then through an unmarked wooden door and into a corner office. And there, the man behind the desk was right out of a Martin Scorsese movie.

Overweight, in his midfifties, with an angry, pug-like face

and a ring of graying curls barely covering the expansive dome of his skull, he was wearing a polyester suit right out of the seventies, all brown and burnt orange, and he was holding the biggest cigar Scott had ever seen.

The minute they sat down, the guy started in on them—the same broken-record song and dance they'd heard from every sports book owner they met. *Poker is a lost cause. There's no money in poker. Sports gambling is where it's at. You're going to lose every penny of your investment money . . .*

When Scott pointed out that running a sports book as an American citizen was clearly illegal, that sports betting was clearly against the Wire Act, the man just brushed his concerns aside.

"It's a new era. The Internet changes everything. We're not bookies, taking bets off of some pay phone in the back of a bar. This is the Wild West. And I don't see any sheriff knocking at our door."

As he spoke, Costa Rican employees filed in and out of the room, putting papers in front of the man for him to sign. Most of the time he just waved his cigar at them, only pausing now and then to add his scrawl to a paper he deemed important enough to warrant his attention. Scott had no idea who the employees were, but he got the feeling from the way they were dressed that at least a couple of them were lawyers.

His suspicions seemed to be confirmed when Garin pulled a small tape recorder out of his pocket and placed it on the man's desk in front of him. Garin had been using the tape recorder to help them keep track of everything they were supposedly learning, but it was the first time he'd taken the thing out midconversation.

Almost immediately, all hell broke loose. The two Costa

Ricans who happened to be in the room at the time began shouting in Spanish, one of them waving his papers so violently it seemed he might take flight. The sports book owner looked up, saw the recorder, and jabbed at Garin with his cigar.

"You want to holster that, buddy? My guys get a little antsy around wires."

The type of people who referred to a tape recorder as a wire weren't usually paragons of good business practices—and for Scott that pretty much summed up the visit. The sports book business was shady, and it didn't look like it had changed much since Robert Kennedy had gone after it with the Wire Act.

Scott wasn't interested in sports betting. Poker was his interest, his passion—and that was all Absolute Poker was going to do. If there wasn't real money in online poker yet, it was simply because nobody had done it right.

don't think we're in Montana anymore."

Scott would've traded every colón in his pocket—and half the blackjack chips stacked in front of him at the semicircular gaming table—for a photo of the expression on Garin's face. Garin had gone from young American businessman in a shirt and tie to shocked farm boy in the space of less than two seconds. Scott couldn't blame him; it wasn't so much that the girl had reached out and grabbed Garin's crotch—it was the nonchalant way she had done it, as if it were the most normal thing in the world. She had been walking by their table, hanging on the arm of a guy who looked like he was at least sixty, and she had just reached out with a smile and given Garin a little squeeze.

Even more bizarre—the guy on her arm hadn't cared. In fact, he'd laughed, and given Garin a thumbs-up.

"You weren't kidding about this place," Phil said. Scott's dad was seated to Scott's left at the blackjack table, Eric standing right behind him, hands crossed against his narrow stomach. The dealer was in the midst of shuffling, but even he cracked a smile.

"There's something for everyone at the Del Rey," Eric said, quite seriously. "People come from all over the world to take part in what's on offer here. Which, if you haven't guessed, is just about anything."

Scott had to admit, Eric hadn't been exaggerating when he'd promised to show them a time they'd never seen before. When they'd first pulled up in front of the seven-story, 1940s-style pink building at the corner of a narrow, crowded street in San José, Scott hadn't expected much. But once he and his crew had pushed their way through the street urchins, past more of those damn ever-present taxi drivers, and finally through the glass entrance into the Del Rey's lobby, he could see that Costa Rica was going to leave Rio in the dust.

With three bars, a casino, a dance club, and a restaurant across the street, as well as a 108-room hotel above, the Del Rey might have looked like any retro Central American resort in a brochure, but three steps into the place, Scott could already tell that it was much more than that. The front area had a sort of tropical sports-bar feel, with soft couches, carved mahogany furniture, potted plants, and televisions blaring from every wall. But the clientele was mostly women—and damn, every one of them was eyeing Scott and his group with palpable intensity. Hot pants, tight jeans, belly-baring halter tops, hair spray, bright red

lipstick, and so much silicone you could take your eye out if you weren't careful—there was no question in Scott's mind what this place was all about.

Ahead of the lobby area was the cashier's cage, and next to that, a floor-to-ceiling mirror—in front of which stood a few more girls, checking themselves out, making minor adjustments for the night ahead. Beyond that, the small casino, filled with table games, a roulette wheel, and a handful of slots. On the other side, the Blue Marlin Bar, which, Eric reported, had the hottest bartenders in all of Central America. And beyond that, the hotel reception desk, staffed by a handful of Costa Rican natives. Eric explained, as they pushed forward, that it was ten dollars to the hotel for each girl you took upstairs—and around a hundred bucks more to the girl, though that was often negotiable.

"On a good night," Eric said, "there could be two hundred girls in here, all for the choosing. From Colombia, Panama, Dominica, even Eastern Europe."

"Holy crap," Shane responded, taking a deep swig from his beer bottle. He had been drinking since they'd sat down at the blackjack table; they'd chosen the relative calm of the casino portion of the resort, because it seemed that the girls were mostly congregated in the front lobby, the bars, and by the hotel desk. But obviously, with so much talent in the place, nowhere was really off-limits.

"It's like Disneyland for whores."

"In that analogy," Scott said, "I think we're the whores."

Shane reached out and grabbed another passing girl—about five foot five, built like a water slide, with blond highlights, a denim skirt, and glitter shining from every inch of exposed skin.

"Hell, yes, we are!"

Scott had to laugh. It was amusing seeing Shane—usually the most self-contained of the group—losing his shit like that. But it wasn't surprising. This place was the new Wild West, and it seemed like anything was fair game. The girls, the gambling, the booze—as Scott focused more closely on his surroundings, the more he let his eyes adjust to the frenetic motion, the deeper he could see into the crags and corners of the place. Girls handing off little paper bags in exchange for a handful of bills, customers palming plastic-wrapped cubes that were either green and leafy or white and powdery—even the odd plastic pipe, shoved into a back pocket. From the guidebooks Garin had shown him, Scott knew that unlike prostitution, drugs were illegal in Costa Rica. But from what he could see, just sitting there at a blackjack table in the most festive bar he could imagine, the place looked pretty damn lawless.

He glanced over at Shane, half off his seat, the girl he'd grabbed now draped across his lap with one hand gripping his thigh. He looked at Garin, who was chatting up a pair of Colombian girls who could have been sisters, sporting matching red hot pants, leather boots, and strikingly identical silicone bolt-ons. He saw his father, leaning away from the table as he lit up a Cuban cigar.

Christ. Building a business here was going to be a unique experience, to say the least. Scott and his friends unleashed in a place with no restrictions, no rules—it was more than a little terrifying to think about. But it was also kind of perfect.

He wasn't opening a hardware store; he was launching an online poker site. He was there to break ground. He intended to turn an industry on its head, build a business around a game

that everyone was telling him couldn't make money. The energy around him, the Wild West feel—it was exactly what he needed.

Poker, the way it was played in America, had been born in Mississippi in the Wild West era. But Scott intended to take it into the modern age, to turn it sophisticated, to make it as tempting and addictive packaged in electronic bits and bytes as it was on a felt table over a sawdust floor.

Sports betting—that was a different business. It was call centers taking phone calls all day long; it was dirty, mobbed up, and illegal. Poker was sophisticated, young, and hip. To capture that, Scott knew the key was going to be the game itself—the software.

Now that he had his core team, was on his way to finding financing, and knew where he was going to build his empire, the next step was to figure out how.

CHAPTER 10

Mission accomplished," Garin said as he rejoined Scott in the waiting area of Sea-Tac's international terminal. He pulled a plastic bag out of his duffel, which was slung over his left shoulder because his right shoulder was still bruised up from an impromptu pickup basketball game they'd gotten into in a corner of the basement the night before while Hilt had booked their last-minute plane tickets—*coach, damn the cheap little bastard.*

"Blue Label, baby. Class all the way."

Garin lifted the neck of the bottle of Johnnie Walker out of the bag so that Scott could nod his approval. Two hundred bucks, but if the information Garin had pulled off the Internet was correct, it would be money well spent.

"If we can keep our hands off of it for the fourteen-hour flight, at least we won't walk in empty-handed."

Garin reached into the bag and pulled out a second item—a Seattle Mariners baseball cap, emblazoned with the number 51.

"And this too. An Ichiro Suzuki hat. They're gonna love it. Hometown hero and all."

Scott stared at his friend.

"Dude, Ichiro is Japanese. We're on our way to Korea. They're different fucking countries. And I think they hate each other."

"Shit." Garin tossed the hat back into the bag. "We'll leave it on the plane."

"You can be pretty stupid sometimes."

"It's because I'm so athletic," Garin joked. "I never had to do no learnin'. Seriously, Korea, Japan—aren't they all Asian?"

The airport intercom coughed to life above their heads, letting them know that their flight—Continental, nonstop to Seoul, Korea—was getting ready to board. Scott reached for his own duffel, tucked between his feet against the dull green carpet. It felt light—even for a forty-eight-hour trip, most of which was going to be spent in the air. One professional outfit, including a single dressy shirt—that was pretty much it. Like the recon mission to Costa Rica, this wasn't a pleasure trip; it was pure business. And besides, they were on a shoestring now; as much as he wanted to give Hilt a hard time for the coach tickets, he knew they couldn't blow any of their budget on extraneous expenses. Especially after the check they'd just written.

Fifty thousand dollars. Even now, days later, after Scott had gotten the chance to digest the number, it still seemed insane. A fifty-thousand-dollar check, made out to some dude in Korea they hadn't yet met, who ran a company they knew very little about. But the little they did know had forced them to move forward—because without the Koreans, they had nothing but a domain name.

It was Shane who had first made the connection with the Koreans; he'd been searching the Internet for poker and gaming software and had kept coming up with addresses in Seoul—over and over again. It seemed that most of the good software was being written in Korea. Eventually he'd narrowed down his search to a company run by two brothers—C. J. and Christian Lee. The materials on their website looked pretty good, and on the phone, C.J.'s English was almost flawless, and his presentation good enough to convince them that he was competent, somewhat experienced in gaming software, and, most important, eager to help them launch a unique site. The thing was, he had insisted on being paid up front—fifty thousand to start, with another fifty thousand when he delivered what they were looking for—the beta software—and then yet another fifty thousand when the software was complete.

A small fortune, but Scott knew that the software was going to make or break them. So he'd written the check. It was half of the money Hilt had brought with him to the company, but Hilt had assured his partners that money begot money. Already, their compact business guru had made inroads to a handful of other family members and friends down in Florida, who had reacted positively to their work-in-progress business plan. And even more significant, Shane's mother and uncle had made critical investments, totaling a quarter of a million dollars. They now all felt sure that with a good software package to present to potential investors, they would quickly be able to reach their goal of $750,000.

All of which meant that Scott was going to spend fourteen hours in a tiny airplane seat fighting the urge to down that bottle

of Blue Label. According to Shane and what he'd found on the Internet, it was a tradition in Korea to give a gift at a business meeting, and supposedly Koreans were nuts about scotch. They probably weren't nearly as nuts about Japanese baseball players. Still, even though he could be a fool sometimes, Garin was the best choice to go along for the software meet and greet. Hilt was the business guy, Shane the conservative research man. Scott was the ringleader, the showman, the guy in the top hat. And Garin was the meat and potatoes. Sometimes more potato than meat, but at least he was always enthusiastic.

"Just for the hat," Scott said as he led Garin toward the line of people that was already forming at the entrance to their gate, "I'm taking the window."

"Go right ahead. I'm gonna try and flirt my way into first class. Maybe one of the stewardesses is a big Ichiro fan."

"Just don't get yourself arrested before we reach Seoul," Scott said with a grunt. "We've got about fifty bucks in traveler's checks to last us through two days, so nobody's getting bailed out of airport jail until we get our damn software."

Three A.M., Korea time, and they hit the ground running. Thankfully, there was a uniformed driver with a sign waiting for them after they passed through Customs, because otherwise they'd have been completely lost. Every sign they passed was in Korean—squiggles that might as well have been hieroglyphics, because even with a Lonely Planet guidebook, neither one of them could have translated their way to a subway.

The airport was a good hour from the city; the modern high-

ways that looped through tunnels, down ramps, and along over-
passes might as well have been northern New Jersey, for all they
could see out the sleek sedan's tinted windows. And then *blam*,
there it was: a modern pincushion of frighteningly bright lights,
towering skyscrapers, glowing bridges, crowded boulevards—and
so much goddamn neon the whole place looked like a spaceship
that had crash-landed, flipped over twice, and caught on fire. It
was beautiful, strange, foreign—and totally futuristic. Scott was
jet-lagged, his head still throbbing from the canned, dry airplane
air, his legs cramped from the coach seat—but looking at the
lights of Seoul, he felt his insides come alive.

A kid who'd grown up in a trailer at the mercy of a mentally
disturbed, majorly addicted single mother, literally dodging frying
pans, irons, razor blades, and the odd shotgun blast—and here he
was, speeding through the streets of Seoul, in the back of a Mercedes sedan, on his way to a business meeting. All those hours
spent jammed in that basement downing Red Bull and crunching
numbers were suddenly worth it; this was really happening.

He looked at Garin, whose face was striped with reflected
neon.

"This is *Blade Runner* shit," he murmured, and then he
pressed his face against the side window, letting the rumble of
the Mercedes's engine play deep into his bones.

Floor-to-ceiling windows; high-tech, chrome-and-leather er-
gonomic office chairs; thick, blindingly white wall-to-wall
carpeting; giant glowing TV screens hanging from the ceiling;
and a burnished redwood boardroom table running the entire

length of the room, supporting a half dozen state-of-the-art computer monitors and keyboards.

"This is quite an operation," Scott said as he followed two steps behind C. J. Lee's mechanized wheelchair, flanked on his left by Garin, whose jaw was down to his chest, gawking at every damn detail like he'd just stepped off a tractor, and on his right by Christian, C.J.'s younger brother. "And everyone in here is going to work on our account?"

There had to be twenty people in the place—at least eight in the boardroom, already waiting for them, gathered around the monitors, some clattering away at the keyboards, and another dozen or so scattered throughout the rest of the fourteenth floor of the glass-and-chrome skyscraper in downtown Seoul—where the Mercedes had taken them after they'd showered, changed, and gotten a couple hours of downtime at the Hyatt, where C.J. had insisted they stay.

"Software is a lot more labor-intensive than people realize," C.J. responded. His English was near perfect, which made sense, because, as he'd explained over coffee in his corner office, down the hall from the boardroom, he'd gone to high school in L.A. and had even spent a few years at Berkeley developing an obsession with software development. "And gaming software has its own unique complications. But we're very good at what we do."

Christian nodded vigorously, a cigarette dangling precipitously from the corner of his thin lips. Nearly everyone they'd seen was smoking—and not just socially, not just a cigarette here and there. These guys were chain-smokers, constantly pulling packs out of back pockets, tossing butts toward the numerous ashtrays situated on every windowsill, desktop, and computer

tray. The air was thick with smoke, but somehow it didn't bother Scott—maybe because of those windows, and the spectacular view of downtown Seoul, which made the place feel airy and clean, even though he was basically breathing in pure exhaust.

"Complications, complications, complications," C.J. continued, navigating his wheelchair to the head of the long boardroom table. He waited for Scott and Garin to sidle up next to him, then nodded at Christian, who grunted and said something in Korean to the other employees. The door shut behind them, and all of the employees rose from the keyboards and monitors, standing at a sort of attention, hands clasped behind their backs.

Scott felt like he was back in college, surrounded by new fraternity pledges. He watched as C.J. touched buttons on the armrest of his wheelchair, moving himself close enough that he could just barely reach out with a finger and touch one of the nearby keyboards.

Scott and Garin had been pretty shocked at first by the wheelchair. C.J. had almost immediately given them the whole story—how he'd gotten into a bad auto accident while in high school, hit his head on the windshield and severed his vertebrae, leaving him a quadriplegic. Even so, he seemed to cope extremely well; he could speak, move his head a bit, and use his hands. As a software designer, he'd explained, he didn't need much else. Scott was extremely impressed by his resilience, and especially his optimism. He was all smiles behind his constant cigarettes, and with his mop of jet-black hair, his animated features, and his wide smile, you almost forgot about the chair.

His brother was much quieter—lean, tall, with narrow features and a sharp, almost beak-like nose. Not particularly friendly;

the only conversation Christian had initiated since they'd arrived at the offices was about the next fifty-thousand-dollar payment— and what it was going to take to get it sent as soon as possible. Scott had assured him that as soon as they put together a good beta version of the poker software, they'd get that check.

"And especially," C.J. continued as he used the keyboard to pull up what they'd been working on since getting the first payment, "since you're so set on poker. A sports book—now, that's something you could get in no time. That's where the money is."

There it was again, the same damn refrain. Scott vigorously shook his head.

"Poker."

"Poker," Garin added, almost simultaneously, as he leaned over the other side of the redwood table, looking toward the screen. "And like we said on the phone, real sophisticated-looking, James Bond kind of shit. Like, you order a martini, you smoke a cigar, and you play a little poker."

C.J. did his best to nod. He flicked a finger toward the screen, which had now lit up with a primitive-looking website. "This is just a mock-up. We still have many questions, and I do apologize, we're not yet as familiar with the game as we need to be."

Although the site was truly basic, Scott immediately recognized some of the design cues that he and his team had suggested to C.J. over the phone. The oval poker table in the center of the screen was a deep royal blue. The chairs looked like red velvet, and there was a little cityscape in the background—very cosmopolitan. It had a long way to go, but it was a thrill to see even the most basic elements up there on the screen.

As soon as the digital cards began being dealt, however, things went rapidly downhill. Everything seemed sluggish, as if the cards were floating through a thick soup. And the game play was just flat-out wrong. All the cards were being dealt faceup— so that they could see what was going on—but even from the start, Scott could tell that the Koreans had no knowledge of the game itself.

"I think we're going to have to go over the rudiments of Hold-'em again—" Scott started, but Garin was a lot less subtle.

"Why are there five aces?"

"That too," Scott said. "Look, I'm not telling you anything that you don't already know, but poker is even more complicated than I think you realize. You need more than just software that can make transactions. With poker, it's all about game play, and there are a lot of important timing issues: when you put your bet in, how long it takes for the chips to get there, how long it takes to deal the cards, everyone getting info at the same time. And everyone's using a different type of connection—dial-up, DSL. And what do you do when someone loses their connection? What do you do when someone goes offline?"

Scott was rolling now, and the room had gone real quiet, everyone just watching him and smoking. He knew he wasn't telling them anything magical, but if he was going to pay these guys $150,000, they were going to have to indulge him.

"You play poker with a bunch of your friends, you expect shit to happen. Someone misdeals, someone spills a drink, someone gets upset and turns over the goddamn table. Over the Internet, everything has to work a certain way. There has to be a flow. And most important of all, nothing can interrupt the play. The game

has to be available to anyone who wants it, whenever they want it. If this seems too complicated for you, if these problems seem too difficult—well, we can take our business elsewhere."

Scott hadn't meant to end his diatribe on such a hard note, but, well, there it was. This wasn't a game to him—this was his life.

If C.J. was put off by Scott's tone, he certainly didn't show it. In fact, his face seemed to light up behind his ever-present cigarette.

"Complicated doesn't have to mean impossible," he said. "In software, music, in life, it's the complications that make a thing worth doing."

That, and one hundred fifty grand, Scott thought. Even so, looking at that computer screen, seeing that blue table and those pixelated velvet chairs, it was hard to stay cynical.

After all, given enough time and guidance, a guy who could run a software company out of a wheelchair could certainly learn to play Texas Hold'em.

The girl was only five foot two, but at least half her height seemed to be legs. They were bare all the way to the thigh, her skin so smooth and tan and toned that it almost seemed shiny, and the rest of her draped in a white-on-white silk gown that shimmered around her long, lithe lines, revealing way more than it obscured—everything about her was damn near spectacular. And she was right up next to Scott on the leather banquette, close enough that he could smell her floral perfume, could see his own reflection in the glassy black strands of her shoulder-

length hair. It took every ounce of his willpower not to reach out and touch her, but C.J., his wheelchair rolled up next to the low glass table in front of the banquette, working his way through his second pack of cigarettes, had been extremely clear. Unlike the Del Rey, this was a look, don't touch, kind of establishment.

Officially, C.J. had explained when the black Mercedes had deposited them at the front entrance, the place was a karaoke bar. A rectangular, warehouse-style building, it was outfitted almost entirely in leather and glass, with multiple levels connected by an open, ascending spiral staircase, attached to the underside of which was the most obtrusive speaker system Scott had ever seen—giant, conical woofers and subwoofers dangling like futuristic barnacles. Still, Scott didn't have to be a genius to realize that karaoke wasn't the place's main draw.

To be sure, there was a stage near the back of the giant hall, bordered on two sides by enormous projector screens. There were microphones set up, and a constant stream of inebriated Korean men stumbling up the four steps to that stage—taking turns at the mike, warbling incomprehensible words as images flashed across the screens—but the karaoke was really just a background screech.

Once they were seated at the banquette, first came the bottles of whiskey—brands Scott had never heard of, with price tags he couldn't believe. And then came the girls—brought to the table in groups of three and four by a hostess in a clingy blue dress. C.J. had explained, almost apologetically, that the girls were there to be looked at, to giggle at your jokes, and to pour the whiskey. If Scott and Garin were looking for more, C.J. assured them that he could take them to places with less restrictive menus.

Scott was happy right where they were. They weren't in Seoul to get laid; they were there to build a partnership. He was content to let the beautiful Korean girl sitting next to him pour his drinks. Besides, it was obvious that she didn't speak a word of English. Still, the way she was smiling at him, intermittently letting her hand brush against his thigh . . .

Scott turned away from the girl, forcing himself to concentrate on the two Korean software programmers on the other side of the banquette. C.J., in his wheelchair, up against the glass table, knocking back cigarettes and scotch. And Christian, next to Garin on the two-seater directly opposite Scott. Christian was in midsentence, again going on about the second fifty-thousand-dollar payment. Garin was assuring him that the money would be there when the site was ready. If it had been Christian alone, and a team of Koreans who couldn't speak English and didn't play poker, Scott wouldn't be going back to Seattle with any sense of confidence.

But looking at C.J., who seemed to be perfectly at home in the karaoke club, with the screeching singing in the background and the goddesses strolling past the banquettes, Scott felt much more at ease. His gaze drifted to C.J.'s hands, the way his fingers almost imperceptibly bounced up and down against the wheelchair's armrests in rhythm with the music.

Then he felt another brush of motion against his leg and turned to see the beautiful Korean girl holding yet another bottle of scotch. Her eyes were low, not meeting his, but again there was a smile pulling at the corners of her lips.

No common language, a culture so different she may as well have been an alien—Scott smiled right back at her.

Even if the software still had a long way to go, it was clear that he and C.J. at least agreed on one thing.

He let his hand glide along the banquette, let his fingers rest against the girl's bare thigh.

Complicated doesn't have to mean impossible . . .

CHAPTER 11

Well, this is encouraging," Scott said as he climbed down from the rickety bus, staggered through a thick cloud of exhaust mixed with yellowish dust from the poorly paved road, and stepped up onto the sweltering curb. "Nothing says international banking mecca like a guy pissing in the street."

"At least he's aiming for the grate," Hilt responded, exiting the bus behind him. Hilt had his suit jacket off, his tie flung back over his shoulder, but still his white oxford shirt was nearly soaked through with sweat. Being from Florida, he hadn't uttered so much as a single complaint during the two-hour, un-air-conditioned bus ride from the tiny island airport, but Scott had to believe his stoic friend had suffered just as much as he had. "I think that kid sitting next to you on the bus was pissing right onto the floor."

"And could you blame him?"

The bus ride had been an ordeal, and not simply because of

the heat. Once they'd left the grounds of the small island airport, the road had been almost entirely unpaved, winding in and out of what appeared to be undeveloped jungle. Even as they'd entered Roseau, the island of Dominica's capital city, the ride hadn't gotten much smoother; the road remained unpaved, even as untouched jungle gave way to urban poverty, punctuated every now and then with a glimpse of the Caribbean. They knew from brochures that there were a handful of resorts on the other side of the city, situated on white-sand beaches, but the bus had given that part of the island a wide berth.

Scott and Hilt were the only two Americans taking public transportation, but everyone had been polite and friendly. Even the man now standing not ten feet away, urinating toward the sewage grate in the center of an intersection just beyond the bus stop, was smiling. In fact, the guy caught Scott's stare and paused long enough to offer him free advice.

"You can do it too!" he shouted in a heavy island accent.

Scott laughed as Hilt joined him on the curb, straightening his tie while peering past the pissing man to the small row of buildings behind him. By the time the city bus had pulled away, its balding tires kicking up a new cloud of dust and dirt, Hilt had found what he was looking for—pointing his free hand at what appeared to be a tiny, single-story building set behind a pair of palm trees. The place couldn't have been more than one or two rooms, with brick and cinder-block walls and only a tiny, barred window. There was no sign out front, no parking lot, not even really a driveway—just another strip of dirt leading up from what was supposed to pass as a road.

"That's it?" Scott said.

"You were expecting the Taj Mahal?"

Hilt pulled his suit jacket over his shoulders. Scott shook his head. A guy pissing in the street out front, a building smaller than your average Burger King—he'd set his expectations low, but this was kind of ridiculous. He nervously patted at his lapel, feeling the thick checkbook that was secure in the inside jacket pocket. To him, that checkbook may as well have been made out of solid gold. He could feel Hilt looking at him, and he knew that his friend understood exactly what he was thinking.

It wasn't just a checkbook; it represented six months of their lives, and more hard work than either of them had done in four years of college. They had sweated and bled—sometimes quite literally—for every penny in the temporary account associated with that book. Phone calls, letter-writing campaigns, flights to and from Florida, New York, Washington, D.C.— hours and hours chasing down possible leads, potential investors. Slowly building toward their goal. Once they'd hired the Korean software designers, it had been easier to start securing real commitments. But not a single dollar of the $750,000 had come easy.

Just a week earlier, minutes before a presentation to a group of wealthy real estate developers in northern Florida, Scott and Garin had actually come to physical blows, after Garin had inadvertently left a piece of their presentation in the hotel room. Hilt had been forced to jump in and physically restrain Scott before they completely trashed the rented conference room. They had still managed to finish the presentation, Garin's jacket ripped right down the middle, Scott's hair askew—but the flare-up of tempers had only proven to them how much they had all per-

sonally invested in this. It was a shared passion, and sometimes inspired people did stupid, stupid things.

Hilt finished with his jacket, then led Scott toward the small building. As Scott followed, he only hoped that this wasn't one of those stupid, stupid things. The island of Dominica was a speck in the Caribbean that none of them could have found without Google, and yet here they were, in the island's only real city, checkbook in pocket, potentially ready to place all the money they had raised into the hands of complete strangers.

When the Costa Rican lawyers who were handling their incorporation had suggested that they use the Caribbean bank, Scott had understood the logic behind the idea. Absolute Poker was going to be an international company, with worldwide clientele. And despite what every lawyer had told them, the fact was, American banking laws and practices seemed to shift week by week. But now that they were actually there, strolling up a dirt path toward an unassuming wooden door, it was a lot harder to stay logical and relaxed.

The lawyers had given them three island banks to choose from: the Loyal Bank of St. Vincent, Bank Crozier of St. Lucia, and Bank Caribe of the Commonwealth of Dominica. They'd immediately crossed off the Loyal, believing that if the company had to put *loyal* in its name, it probably wasn't. Which left Dominica and St. Lucia. They'd decided to check out Dominica first, for the simple reason that the flight from Seattle had been cheaper. They were going to head to St. Lucia the next day. In between, they'd be staying in a hotel just around the corner, a disgusting little place Hilt had found on the Internet that offered tiny un-air-conditioned rooms teeming with cockroaches—because every penny they had would be going into that check.

Hilt paused at the door, giving Scott a chance to fix his tie one last time. Then he led the way inside.

I have to admit, this all looks pretty good."

Hilt was leaning forward in the seat next to Scott, at the edge of the mahogany desk, poking through the huge stack of papers in front of them. Balance sheets, financial statements, asset allocations—all of it printed out at their request by the bank manager, who had now stepped outside to give them time to look through things in private. Even more important than the papers, to Scott, was the manager himself; Scott hadn't been able to stifle his surprise when he first stepped foot into the island bank and caught sight of the well-dressed, midfifties American, with his neatly combed silver hair, traditional-looking wire-rimmed glasses, and impeccable gray suit. The man had been accompanied by his son, a younger version of himself, with similar glasses and a similar suit. They both seemed extremely sharp and knowledgeable about the banking structures for the gaming industry, and once they had all situated themselves in the manager's office, the two men had been very open about all aspects of their work. Bank Caribe handled many gaming sites, from sports books to online casinos, and they had even worked with Paradise Poker. They also handled money from many Wall Street firms, including dozens of American-run hedge funds. Everything the men told them seemed proper, professional, and satisfying.

Now, forty minutes later, it was time to make a decision.

"What do you think?" Hilt said, leaning back from the papers and looking at Scott. "Half here? And half in St. Lucia, if it seems equally professional?"

As usual, there was almost no inflection in Hilt's voice. To him, this was business, and now that he'd seen the papers, he was able to put his emotions aside. Scott wondered if he himself would ever be able to be that levelheaded. For the moment, though, as he reached for the checkbook, he could feel his fingers trembling in time with his rapidly increasing heartbeat.

"Call the manager back in. It's time we open our first real bank account."

Finally, Hilt cracked a smile.

"You think he'll offer us champagne, to take back to our lavish hotel suite?"

"For three hundred and fifty thousand dollars," Scott said, breathing hard, "I'm going to hold out for a goddamn toaster."

CHAPTER 12

O h, man, this is never going to work."

"Shut up. Act casual."

"Dude, abort. I'm telling you, this is gonna end bad."

Garin gave Shane a shove and a glare, then quickly pushed his oversize luggage cart a few feet ahead, following the long line of tourists toward the double doors at the edge of the baggage and customs area. Shane hissed more terrified warnings after him but slowed his pace, letting Garin drift a few places ahead in the moving line.

Scott wanted to laugh at his two friends' antics, but he was a bit nervous himself. Looking at Garin's luggage cart—weighed down by so many cardboard boxes that the little steel wheels of the cart were twisting and turning against the tiled floor, emitting odd squeals that seemed to echo off the walls—he found it hard to believe that he was going to make it through. Scott himself had three cardboard boxes on the cart he was sharing with

Hilt and Shane. But his boxes contained only assorted clothes, shoes, and a handful of bathroom products that he thought he might have trouble finding in Costa Rica. The cardboard boxes were a hell of a lot cheaper than a suitcase, and he'd be able to throw them out after he unpacked at the house—in case, like in his dad's basement, they eventually decided to turn the closets into bedrooms. Though if the house was anything like Shane had described it after he'd gone down, a few weeks earlier, with an IT guy to set up the phone lines and computer wires, well, Scott doubted they were going to have any issues with space.

But five yards ahead and closing fast on the double doors that led out into the airport proper, Garin's cardboard boxes weren't just full of clothes, even though the scrawl of Magic Marker across the cardboard seemed to indicate just that. In reality, the goofball had packed away his entire desktop computer—monitor, hard drive, modem, keyboard, even a pair of speakers—and then piled clothes on top. Nobody had asked him any questions when he'd checked the heavy boxes in at the airport in Seattle, but now that they had landed at Santamaría, well, God only knew what would happen if the customs agents—who were milling about behind a long metal table just ahead of the twin doors in a group of about nine, in full uniform, with sidearms strapped to their hips—decided to pull Garin out of the line. Was a desktop computer something you were supposed to declare?

Looking at the other people in line—almost all of them tourists, a mix of families, young couples on honeymoons, groups of guys on their way to party, golf, or fish—it was obvious that almost every American heading to Costa Rica was on vacation. Nobody else, as far as Scott could see, had packed up what constituted their entire lives—for what amounted to a one-way trip.

Scott had no idea how long they were going to stay, now that they were actually there. The house that Shane had found was rented for a year, at four thousand dollars a month. According to Shane, the living room was big enough for a half dozen cubicles, which he and the IT guy had set up after multiple trips to the Costa Rican equivalent of Home Depot. And supposedly, there was even a pool out back.

"Shit, I think the one with the mustache is going to nab him," Hilt hissed, interrupting Scott's thoughts, from a step behind.

Scott followed Hilt's gaze and saw the customs agent eyeing Garin as he approached the steel table. For a brief moment it looked like the agent was going to say something—but then he shifted his attention to a middle-aged man in a heavy down jacket, just ahead of Garin, signaling the man over to the table. Garin plodded nervously on. Even from that distance, Scott could see the sweat beading on the back of his friend's tautly muscled neck. Somehow he was still moving forward.

Just as he reached the double doors, he turned his head the slightest bit to give Shane a big smile—and a silent "Screw you." The screech of the cart's wheels still echoed off the walls.

Finding a taxi that could fit all four of them and Garin's computer was a true test of their patience; there had to be two dozen of those damn drivers grabbing at them as soon as they'd stepped out of the airport onto the sidewalk, some so aggressive and even threatening that Scott was worried one of his friends might start throwing punches. But eventually they were able to find one who spoke enough English to figure out that four athletically built guys and a half dozen cardboard boxes weren't going

to fit in one of their compact little clown cars. For a handful of colóns—the Costa Rican currency, which was colorful, the wrong size, and looked like it had come out of a board game—he brought them to a friend with a van, who was nice enough to help them load the boxes into his trunk. Even so, by the time the boxes were all loaded and they'd jammed themselves into the backseat—literally on top of one another—they were all covered in sweat. The heat and humidity were intense, even though the driver had the van's air-conditioning turned all the way up and there was a pretty stiff breeze coming out of the hills beyond the city. But the heat was something Scott knew he would get used to; like the Spanish music that was now blaring out of the van's crappy speakers, so loud it made the windows shake, it was just another detail of their new environment.

Then they were off, the man driving like a maniac through the thick airport traffic on his way to the city proper.

"Give the man the address," Scott said to Shane, trying to find space in the back of the van between Garin's cartoonishly long arms and Hilt's spark-plug shoulders.

"There isn't an address," Shane responded.

"What the hell do you mean?"

"I mean in San José, nobody has an address."

Shane leaned forward so that the driver could hear.

"We're going to Escazú. Start with the Tony Roma's restaurant, go a hundred meters west, a hundred meters south. The white house on the corner."

Scott stared at him. "Really?"

"That's how it works here. You'll see."

The driver wasn't arguing, so obviously he didn't have a prob-

lem with the directions. Scott leaned back against the seat, trying to find a comfortable position. Outside, the city flashed by. It was midafternoon, just like the last time he'd arrived in San José, but the roads seemed even more congested, traffic going in every direction. As before, he was amazed at how alive the place felt, how it seemed to throb with energy. So many cars, people, noise—even above the insanely loud music pumping through the van's speakers, the sounds of the urban sprawl felt like a hand, reaching right through those trembling windows, grabbing at Scott's skin. This was it. He was really here; this was actually happening. It was goddamn exhilarating.

Nearly an hour later they were still engulfed by the thrill of it all when Shane shot a finger toward the window by his head.

"This is it. Casa Absolute Poker."

The house was situated on a low hill, in a pretty, leafy residential neighborhood in one of the more upscale suburbs of the city. From the outside it wasn't anywhere near as lavish as Scott's dad's house, but it was big, and there certainly was a pool. And the neighborhood was pretty nice—though there didn't seem to be any nearby transportation, supermarkets, or even a general store, and they didn't have a car. But as they exited the cab, the driver handed them a card, telling them they could call his company anytime. Scott tipped the man well—he had a feeling they were going to be taking a lot of cabs for the time being, whether they liked it or not.

Shane led them inside with a proud sweep of his hand. And once Scott was through the high Spanish door and into the living room, he had to admit that Shane had done pretty well for them.

The living room had high ceilings, a good number of win-

dows, and plenty of natural light. The floors were carpeted, the walls bare, but the interior was exactly as Scott had hoped. Shane and the IT guy had put up a half dozen prefab cubicle walls, converting the room into a serviceable office space. There were wires running everywhere; bright orange and green rubber snakes, some as thin as Scott's fingers, others as thick as garden hoses, running between the cubicles, along the walls, even through the doorway into what looked to be a galley-style kitchen. It was an electrician's nightmare—but, as Shane had explained already, a truly necessary endeavor.

When Scott and his team had first been told about the house, they initially thought they could buy computer servers and build a small server room in the house's basement, or out back by the pool. But Shane and the IT guy had quickly discovered this wasn't an option. Within twenty-four hours of being in Costa Rica, Shane had found out that the Internet crashed at least once a day; likewise, power was something that could go off and on at random. So instead, Shane had located a professional third-party server hosting—a place with the fairly ridiculous name Hosta-Rica. HostaRica was, it turned out, the country's largest hosting site, and Shane had been told it handled most of the gaming concerns in the area.

So instead of servers, Shane and the IT pro had spent their time setting up workstations for desktop computers, which would be Scott and his team's bread and butter. Each cubicle had been outfitted with enough wiring to handle a computer, a modem, and a separate phone line, and even though the Internet and the power would be going on and off at random, at least the servers running their software would presumably stay on.

Aside from the wiring, Shane had installed in each cubicle a basic desk and little shelving units. Five of the cubicles also had desk chairs, but the sixth contained just a desk and shelves. Scott had to smile as Garin headed straight for the chairless cubicle, lugging his boxed-up computer behind him. When Shane had been setting up the house, they demanded he call them in Seattle so they could approve any expenditures over a hundred dollars; the chairs, it turned out, were a hundred and fifty bucks a pop. The discussion had turned into a heated argument, with Garin finally exclaiming that they didn't need any goddamn chairs, he'd sit on a rock for all he cared.

So Shane had bought chairs for everyone—except Garin. But to his credit, Garin didn't voice a single complaint. He just went to work unboxing his computer and began the long process of wiring the damn thing back together.

Meanwhile, Scott continued his tour of the house.

The upstairs was as clean, sparse, and acceptable as the downstairs—more high ceilings, a pair of reasonably modern bathrooms, and five empty bedrooms. Shane had picked the biggest bedroom, which also turned out to be the only one with an air-conditioning unit built into the window. He'd also installed separate phone lines in all five bedrooms, which was a huge plus. In a pinch, they'd be able to use their bedrooms as offices as well, which meant they could double their staff without having to think about moving. Scott had no idea how fast the company could grow, but this was as good a first headquarters as he could have hoped for.

When he was finished with the tour, Scott gathered his team back in the living room. Hilt passed out beers from a cooler Shane

had left in the kitchen, next to the refrigerator. Scott guessed the cooler had something to do with the shaky power grid, but he tried to put thoughts like that out of his head. There would be plenty of time to worry about such things in the weeks, months, and maybe years ahead.

Right now, it was time to get things started.

"Gents," he said, raising his beer, a long-necked bottle covered in Spanish writing. "This just might be the start of something beautiful. So let's set up some ground rules."

"Maybe no alcohol around the computers?" Garin said, eyeing Shane's beer bottle, which was resting on the edge of the cubicle wall closest to his newly unboxed monitor. "These wires look pretty shady to me. I feel like my testicles are shrinking just from being this close to them."

"Your testicles are less important than the wires," Shane shot back. "And *you* try and set up a computer network in a third-world country. Just be glad we have running water and the toilets work."

Scott shut them both up with a wave of his beer.

"Testicles aside, Garin makes a good point. Once the computers are set up, booze stays upstairs, outside, or in the kitchen. The living room is for work. And that's what we're here for—to work. Everyone needs to be at his station at seven A.M. Eventually, we'll have to work in shifts. Six P.M. here is nine A.M. in Korea, so we'll have a team designated to deal with the software people once we launch the beta test."

The guys all nodded. Scott pointed to a small wooden side table Shane had set up outside the cubicles, near the door. There was a phone jack next to the table, and a place to plug in a modem.

"For now, that's going to be our Customer Service Department. We'll take turns manning it. From what we gather, there are going to be a lot of complaints coming when we launch the beta, with the power going in and out and the Internet going down. So there will be a lot of angry e-mails and phone calls. Always be polite. Always be professional."

"And on that note," Hilt said, standing at the entrance to the cubicle he had chosen, closest to the stairs leading up to the bedrooms, "no girls are allowed in the house."

Garin immediately groaned, and Scott raised his eyebrows. Then he thought about it and realized Hilt was probably thinking smart, as usual. If they were going to be running a business there, they had to keep their professional and personal worlds as separate as possible. This wasn't the SAE house, after all.

"Hilt's right. No girls in the house."

"What about the pool?" Garin asked. "Can we keep girls in the pool?"

"The pool is part of the house."

"Even if they can hold their breath for a really, really, really long time?" Shane asked.

"Those are usually the best girls," Garin added. "The ones who know how to hold their breath—"

"Shut up," Scott said. "No fucking girls in the house."

Garin shrugged. Shane sighed. Scott smiled and held up his beer.

"So that's settled. Now let's toast—because goddamn it, we made it this far. And I can't freaking believe that we're actually here."

They all shouted and drank. Then Garin placed his empty

bottle gingerly on the floor beneath his computer desk and clapped his hands together.

"If we can't have girls in the house, get that cabby back over here."

"Why?" Scott asked.

"Because someone needs to take us out on the town. It's time to celebrate."

Scott grinned. Garin was absolutely right—that was something they could all agree on.

It was time to fucking celebrate.

CHAPTER 13

Should we do a countdown or something?" Shane said from inside his cubicle. Like the rest of them, he was hunched over his computer, eyes glued to his screen.

"Don't be stupid," Hilt responded from the cubicle to Shane's left. "This is just a beta test. It's mostly friends, family, and SAE alumni."

"Still, it's like, momentous. We're going live."

Scott stretched his neck. He was in the cubicle next to Hilt's, looking at his own computer. His fingers were poised over his keyboard, and he noticed the slightest anxious tremor in his pinkies.

"I wouldn't call it live," he said quietly. "It's more like artificial life. We're going to stay in total control of the beta, make sure it goes as smoothly as possible. This is a test run, but we want people to come back when we're ready to launch the real thing."

Artificial life—that seemed like the right term for it. It would

be AbsolutePoker.com, with real money from real accounts, maybe fifty or sixty of them spread out, mostly around the United States—well, mostly in and around Missoula, Montana, with a few in St. Petersburg, Florida—but they were going to monitor every second of play. The Koreans had created a handful of employee accounts, numbered accounts so they could keep track of the game play. They would also be able to observe player information, how the shuffle was working, how smoothly the tables were being filled. And after the fact, they'd be able to review the cards and the play in a timed log. For security, the Koreans had built a delay into the review process, so you weren't actually seeing any cards until after each round was over; but later on, Scott and his team would be able to monitor the game play to observe where it needed to be improved and how things could be made smoother.

The Koreans had done a pretty good job so far. It had been six months since Scott and Garin met with them in Seoul and four weeks since he and the crew had moved into the house in Costa Rica. In that time, together with the Koreans, they'd worked nearly round the clock getting ready for this day. And for all of them, it had been a truly brutal routine. Rolling out of bed, heading right to their workstations. Plugging away until nightfall, when one or two of them would begin the second shift, working with C.J. and Christian to hammer out the software details.

The Koreans had nailed the visuals almost from the beginning, but the game play had taken a lot longer. The main problem, as Scott had pointed out when he first met with C.J. and Christian, was that the game had to be smooth—the players must be able to sit down and play wherever they were, whenever they wanted to, even though they could be signing in from cities

all over the world, with different modem speeds, hard drives, and Internet providers. When you got down to it, the software was endlessly complicated—and Scott was sure there would be plenty of issues, especially in the beta phase. The superuser accounts would be helpful in calling out some of those issues, but there was also going to be a lot of feedback coming in from the players.

Which was why at the moment, Garin was sitting cross-legged on the floor in the area they'd designated as Customer Service. In front of him were a computer and a telephone. The 1-800 number that led to that phone had been inserted into the beta introduction page, so for the moment Garin was their call center, ready for action.

"Okay, I guess it's time," Scott said. He signaled Hilt, who began to type into his computer, communicating with the server hosts at HostaRica, then with the Koreans, who would be monitoring the beta test as well. As Hilt had pointed out, it really was mostly friends and family—though they had also sent out notices through a few of the more public poker forums, advertising themselves in a decidedly grassroots manner. No hype, no giant promises—for now, just an offer of good, sophisticated tournament play in what they liked to think of as a uniquely cosmopolitan environment.

As Scott launched the software on the computer in his cubicle and the screen instantly shifted to the AbsolutePoker.com beta site, he couldn't help but smile, bathed in the deep blue of the table that dominated the center of the screen. In the middle of the table, the Koreans had added the Absolute Poker logo, which was a red diamond. Scott thought it looked great, set against that cosmopolitan blue. The chairs around the table were still velvety,

with little tables between them—after all, you needed someplace to set down your martini glass. The room itself was carpeted in gray, but eventually there would be many room choices. And the cityscape that greeted players when they logged on would change too; the key, Scott felt, was to keep the game modern and interesting, and that meant there would probably be constant changes to the look and feel of the site.

But again, the visuals would be secondary to the game play. Paradise Poker, to him, had always felt clunky and primitive. Absolute Poker was going to be something different.

"And go!" Hilt said.

And then it happened. Slowly, one by one, the seats at the table filled. The players were represented by cartoonish avatars— but that too would eventually change. Scott envisioned that people would be able to pick and choose their own avatars, and maybe one day even upload their own photos. But for the moment Scott didn't care about the avatars. He was watching the cards, because the deal had just begun—and it was fucking beautiful.

"It's working!" he shouted. "They're playing. Look, that guy just made a bet. And that guy is gonna call—"

And then, suddenly, Scott's screen went blank. He heard shouts from the other cubicles—and then, a second later, the lights in the house went out.

"Christ no!" Garin shouted. "The power just went down."

"Is it just the power or the Internet?" Shane asked.

"I think it's the Internet too," Hilt said, his voice tight. "Crap."

"What do we do?" Garin asked. "Is it just us, or is the game gonna be screwed up?"

"The game too," Shane said. "Because the way we have the

beta set up, we need to be connected for it to work. Garin, get on the phone with the server—"

"Wait," Hilt said, as suddenly the lights flashed back on. "We're back online."

And Scott could see that they were. His screen was back up, the blue table in front of him again—but the game play had frozen middeal, a card floating halfway across the table, like part of a magic trick gone bad. Scott leaned back in his chair, his face reddening. Inside, he was furious. This was ridiculous. So fucking unprofessional. If anyone had lost money because they went down, they would have to reimburse it. He was sure any minute now Garin's phone would start ringing with complaints, and the e-mails would be coming in.

Scott leaned forward, resting his elbows on his computer table, his head in his hands. *Christ, what a way to start.*

And then, just as he'd expected, Garin's phone blared to life, a metallic, noxious sound that seemed to reverberate through the whole house. Scott watched as Garin grabbed the receiver, cupping it to his ear.

"AbsolutePoker.com," Garin started. And then he stopped. "Hey, Scott," he called. "It's for you. It's Glenn."

Scott looked at Garin, surprised. He had expected it to be a complaining player; Glenn Dwyer was one of the company's first new hires, an SAE alum who'd been a top student in the frat. Glenn was a CPA and MBA who had specialized in accounting, so they'd set him up as their nominal president, based out of Los Angeles. Really, his job was to handle their accounting and officially manage the $750,000 they'd gotten from their investors. He didn't usually call the house; Scott called him whenever they

needed access to the money or had to make a particularly large purchase.

Scott felt Hilt's eyes on him as he crossed to the phone. He took the receiver from Garin and pressed it against his ear.

"Hey, Glenn, now isn't a great time, we've got some fucked-up issues going on with the beta—"

"Scott, we've got a major problem."

Scott could tell immediately from Glenn's voice that it wasn't going to be a little issue. The guy was one of the most mild-mannered people Scott knew—and at the moment, his voice sounded almost frantic, at least an octave too high.

"What is it?"

"Well, see, it started last Thursday. I was catching up on the banking receipts, and there were a few things I needed clarified, so I called over to Caribe to check with them. And nobody answered the phone. I tried again all day Friday—and again, no answer. I figured, hey, it's the Caribbean, people are pretty laid-back in the Caribbean, I can wait until Monday—"

"Glenn," Scott interrupted, "what the hell are you trying to tell me?"

"Well, I called back today. A guy from Pricewaterhouse-Coopers answered. He told me that Caribe Bank has gone insolvent."

Scott's throat constricted. "What?"

"The bank, man. It went under. Just folded. I mean, it's gone. That money's all gone."

Scott couldn't feel the phone in his hand. He looked up and saw that Shane, Garin, and Hilt were all staring at him. His face had gone white.

"What happened?" Hilt asked.

"Caribe Bank went under."

The air in the room seemed to freeze, like a leather belt snapping tight.

Then Scott lurched forward and vomited all over the floor.

CHAPTER 14

Brent Beckley tossed the last three spoons into the large plastic shopping bag, ignoring the cacophonic clash of metal against metal, then twisted the bag shut and slung it over his right shoulder. The thing was heavy, bulging at the bottom, and there was a very good chance it was going to rip right open, spilling three years' worth of collected silverware all over his bare kitchen floor. But he didn't have much choice. The guy who'd come for the potted plants had taken his last box, so the bag would have to do. Besides, the silverware was pretty damn shitty; most of the forks were bent beyond use, and the knives were so dull they might as well have been spoons. But for three bucks, it really was a case of buyer beware. Besides, Brent had been exceedingly honest in his Craigslist ad; he'd described about everything in his apartment as junk—and yet still, there he was, bagging up the very last of it. Every last thing had sold, from the tattered couches to the soap dispenser from the bathroom. Who the hell bought a used soap dispenser?

Brent shook his head, then headed to the front door. Outside, he carefully placed the heavy plastic bag of silverware on the floor of the hallway, where the welcome mat used to sit, before he'd sold that too. He thought about leaving a note taped to the bag—then decided it wasn't necessary. Nobody was going to steal a plastic bag of bent forks, and the guy who'd paid for it wouldn't have any trouble finding it; there was literally nothing else there.

Brent took his apartment key out of his pocket and stuck it in the lock. He said a mental good-bye, then turned and headed for the stairs.

Twenty minutes later he was sitting in the front seat of his rust red Buick Century, hands on the steering wheel, staring straight ahead through the windshield. He wasn't thinking, exactly, more like counting ahead. Seconds, minutes, hours—a sort of psychological exercise to calm his rapidly unraveling nerves. It was a terrifying thing, saying good-bye to everything you knew, starting fresh. But it was also exciting, the kind of thing you wanted to contemplate and remember.

Unbelievably, it was finally, actually happening. He couldn't begin to count how many times he'd called his big brother over the past six months, begging Scott to hire him, to let him drop out of school and come down to Costa Rica to join the crew. Again and again, Scott had responded the same way: *Absolutely not.* Brent shouldn't have been surprised. Scott had nearly forced him, kicking and screaming, to go to college in the first place. Without Scott, he would have probably ended up selling weed to rebelling Mormon high school kids in Salt Lake City for the rest of his life—well, until he ended up in jail, or in hell.

Instead, he had finally made it to graduation from the University of Montana. He'd cut his hair, traded his hemp shirts for oxfords with matching ties. He'd actually changed so much, cleaned himself up so thoroughly, that he'd been elected president of the frat house for his senior year, following in Pete Barovich's shadow.

And then, less than a week ago, the phone had rung. This time it was Scott calling him—with a job offer.

"Director of customer service," Scott had said. "We can only start you at two thousand dollars a month, but you'll be running your own department. If things go well, there will be a lot of opportunity for forward motion."

Brent had nearly dropped the phone. Director of customer service. That sounded like a pretty big title. Running his own department right out of college? It sounded like an incredible opportunity. Then Scott had dropped a bombshell.

"We need you here tomorrow."

Brent had laughed, thinking it was a joke. He'd just barely graduated; he had an apartment, things, a car. But Scott was dead serious. Brent knew the company had just gone through a huge trauma involving a bank failure, but obviously Scott and his team had decided to power through, and they weren't wasting any time. But packing up his life in twenty-four hours, moving to a foreign country to live, perhaps for a long, long time?

"Scott, I don't even have a passport."

Scott had paused for less than a second.

"Okay, by the end of the week. You get here by Friday, or you're fired."

And with that, he'd disconnected. Brent knew immediately that his brother hadn't been joking. Scott could be intense, to the

point of manic, and though he liked to play hard, he did not fool around when it came to something important. He wouldn't think twice about firing his own brother if he screwed up. Especially with whatever had gone down with the Caribbean bank—and what Scott and his team were trying to do to survive after a blow like that—Scott obviously wasn't playing games.

So Brent went right to Craigslist. He'd sold everything in his apartment—down to the goddamn silverware—and then told his landlord that he was leaving. The guy had tried to argue about a lease, but Brent was paid up through the month, and there was simply nothing else he could do about it. Then he'd gone into downtown Missoula to get an expedited passport.

And now, three days later, and just a few hours before his flight—Missoula to Minneapolis to Houston to Costa Rica—he had just one more thing to take care of before he was in the air.

He tapped his fingers on the steering wheel for a few more seconds, contemplating what lay ahead, step by step, then yanked the keys out of the ignition and stepped out onto the curb.

The sun was high above the tree-lined street, barely any breeze pulling at his white shirt or his loosely tied paisley tie, the day beginning to bake, but Brent didn't feel warm at all. He felt ready.

He walked to the back of his car and got down on both knees. Then he pulled a screwdriver out of his back pocket. It took a few minutes to get the license plate unscrewed, and then he was back on his feet.

He crossed the street and headed toward a two-story building with glass front doors and smoky picture windows. There was a uniformed guard just inside the doors, but Brent walked right

by him, heading straight through the marble-floored lobby. He'd been in the bank a dozen times before—usually to fill out forms, manage student loans, once in a while to deposit checks. It was also where he received wired money from Scott's dad to help him with tuition, insurance, and, of course, car payments.

Brent took a deep breath, tasting the air-conditioned air, then headed straight to the nearest teller; behind the window, the woman looked to be in her midthirties, with short auburn hair and too much lipstick, wearing a stiffly tailored pantsuit. It was lucky that there was no line, because today Brent wasn't sure he'd have the patience to wait.

He reached the window and, without pause, placed his car keys and the license plate on the counter in front of the woman.

"What's this?" the woman asked.

"Your car. It's parked out front."

The woman stared at him. Her red lips opened, then closed. "Sorry?"

"You own it," Brent said. "Twenty-eight hundred dollars to go, and I can't pay it—so it's yours. It's out front."

"Sir—"

"Call it a voluntary repossession. Be careful, the ignition sticks a little bit. I'd love to stay and chat, but I don't have the time. I'm moving to Costa Rica."

Before the woman could respond, he turned and headed back toward the glass exit, smiling as he went.

My God my God my God this is awesome, Brent thought as he spilled out of Santamaría International and into the

overwhelming chaos, noise, and heat. He felt himself pulled in every direction at once, with people jostling him as they looked for their rides, taxi drivers yanking at his sleeves, kids trying to sell him handmade trinkets, people whispering offers to him for everything from booze to drugs to girls—and then he broke free from the crowd for a moment and saw Scott and Hilt over on the other side of the curb, leaning against a guardrail and just watching him. Both had big grins on their faces.

Brent composed himself as best he could and strolled toward them, flattening his tie against the buttons of his shirt. His backpack—all he had brought with him, filled with the few items of clothing that he hadn't sold—was sticking to his back because of the heat and humidity, but he didn't care. Seeing Scott there, waiting for him, took all the worry away. He'd have followed his older brother to the ends of the earth—which, looking around, seemed to be exactly where he was.

"Welcome to Costa Rica," Scott said, leaping off the guardrail to shake his hand. "And I see you came dressed to impress."

"I figured you'd want me to hit the ground running," Brent responded, greeting Hilt as well. Then they led him to a taxi that was waiting a few yards down the curb. It was obvious Scott knew the driver, who greeted him with a smile and a few words of Spanish. Brent couldn't tell whether Scott understood the guy, but either way, a moment later the three of them crowded into the back, and the cab took off like a rocket, zero to warp speed in less than three seconds.

"I mean, I've almost been fired once already, and I haven't even started working."

Hilt laughed, glancing at Scott. "You almost fired your own brother?"

"Hell," Scott said as the taxi narrowly avoided a truck carrying what looked to be bushels of bananas, then took a curve so fast it felt like they were up on two wheels, "we were all almost out of a job a week ago. Half our money, gone in the blink of an eye. Only managed to save the other half by pulling most of it out of the bank in St. Lucia, before it went bust like the one in Dominica."

Brent had heard about that from Phil. He'd told Brent how Scott had narrowly avoided full ruin by getting about three hundred thousand dollars out of the St. Lucia bank—only to hear that the St. Lucia bank then went under as well, just a couple of hours after he'd succeeded with the transfer.

"Even so," Scott continued, "that was nearly the end. We almost packed everything up and went home."

"But you didn't," Brent said, pressing his face against the window to get a better glimpse of the low buildings flashing by.

"Nope," his brother said, his eyes narrow. "We did the fucking opposite. We went all in. Decided to launch the site anyway, and then hit the investors up again, as hard as we could. Put a whole new valuation on the company, brought in as many new shareholders as we could find."

Brent was impressed, though he knew his brother well enough to understand: Scott didn't give up—no matter how bad things might be, well, he'd been through worse.

"We've revalued the company at four million," Hilt explained. "And the investors pitched in another seven hundred fifty thousand, so we've got over a million to spend on advertising and development. So we're kicking things up."

"And the site?" Brent asked. He'd logged on to it every night, waiting for Scott to finally hire him. He loved the way it looked,

and although he wasn't really a poker player like his brother, he enjoyed the game play. He mostly lost, but never much, maybe thirty or forty bucks in total.

"Starting small, but still, the money has started to trickle in. We've been registering about fifty players a day. Most of those are playing for fun, but about one in ten puts down a credit card to play with real money. It's adding up to about a hundred bucks a day in our rake, but it's a start. As long as it keeps the board of directors happy, it's all good."

Brent looked at his brother. "We have a board of directors?"

Scott pointed to himself and Hilt. "And Garin, Shane, Phil, and a bunch of Hilt's people back in Florida. We're doing everything as by-the-book as we can, even though there isn't much regulation from anyone outside the company. Hell, we'd love some regulation, but the industry seems to work this way, so we need to do these things ourselves."

Brent had just graduated college—he didn't know much about business or how a company like this was supposed to be structured. But he could tell Hilt and his brother took these things very seriously. Then again, they weren't much older than he, and they were building their company on what felt like the edge of the world.

Outside the window, the scene was becoming increasingly urban, with storefronts and boxy apartment buildings, traffic jams and blinking streetlights. This didn't look like the upscale residential suburb his brother had described on the phone.

"Are we heading to the house?" he asked. He really was eager to get started working. As Absolute Poker's new director of customer service, he had a whole department to run.

Scott winked at him, then pointed out the front windshield of the cab. "Not exactly."

Brent squinted against the sun and saw a huge pink hotel rising behind a crowded sidewalk. His gaze slid up the seven stories to the marquee at the top of the building.

"The Hotel Del Rey," he read cautiously. "Are you checking me into a hotel?"

Again Scott winked.

"Not exactly," he repeated.

Six hours later Brent opened his eyes just in time to see the sidewalk hurtling toward his face. He managed to get one hand out, catching himself inches before he hit, and rolled onto his shoulder, then over onto his back, his feet straight up in the air. Above his leather loafers, he could see that the sky had somehow gone black. He had no idea how it had switched from day to night in what felt like a few seconds; the last thing he remembered clearly was stepping into that damn pink hotel, his brother and Hilt urging him on from behind. He'd lost sight of them when the first girl grabbed him by the hand, right inside the Del Rey's entrance, and he hadn't seen either of them since. Twelve hours ago he was handing his car keys over to a bank teller in Missoula, Montana. Now he was on a Costa Rican sidewalk, the sky between his feet. All in all, it had been a pretty good day.

Then he heard laughter, and female voices speaking Spanish. He followed the sound and realized why he was lying on the sidewalk. He'd obviously fallen out of the taxi when one of the girls had opened the door. There were two of them, the girls: one

tall with dark skin and incredibly long legs, made even longer by
her six-inch see-through heels; the other only about five feet tall,
with short blond hair and enormous breasts. The girl in the heels
was paying the taxi driver—out of Brent's wallet, he realized—
while the other one leaned over Brent, poking at his chest.

"You fall down," she said in heavily accented English.

"I fall down," Brent responded. He let her pull him to his
feet. He was wobbly, but to his surprise, he found that he could,
in fact, stand. As the taxi pulled away from the curb, he took
the shorter girl in one arm and the tall, dark-skinned girl in the
other. He had no recollection of where or how he had met them,
but he could see that they were beautiful, and that they liked to
share. Maybe this sort of thing had happened to guys like Scott
in college, but Brent had never been in this situation before. And
he liked it.

"Is your house?" the shorter girl asked.

With some difficulty, Brent peered out through the darkness,
making out what appeared to be a two-story home directly in
front of them. It looked just like the house Scott and Hilt had
described when they'd given him the directions he was to use
with the taxi drivers, but still he was amazed that he had gotten
there on his own. Well, he'd had a little help. He had no idea
how much he was going to have to pay the girls, but the fact that
the taller girl was still holding his wallet was a pretty bad sign.

"I have no idea," Brent said honestly. "I hope so."

He pulled the two girls tight to his sides and started up the
hill to the house's front door.

The porch light came on as he got close, and before he could
even knock, or find a doorbell, or just kick the damn thing in, the

door swung inward. Garin was standing in the doorway, all ten feet of him, with a goofy smile on his face.

"Brent, man. You made it. Welcome to the house. Scott was about to send out the Costa Rican air force to find you."

Brent smiled back at him and started forward, but Garin held out a hand, blocking his way. "Sorry, man. You can come in, but the girls can't."

Brent stared at the hand. It looked ten times as large as it was supposed to. "What do you mean?"

"No girls allowed in the house. It's an official rule."

"But . . ." Brent started. He gestured at the tall girl, then the other. "Two of them, Garin. There are two of them."

"Yeah, I can see that. You'll have to call them a cab."

Brent couldn't believe what he was hearing, but Garin only shrugged. "Sorry, man. House rules."

It took another fifteen minutes for the taxi to return to collect the girls. By the time Brent finally made it inside the house, he was halfway to sober. Still a little angry, but clearheaded enough not to make a big deal out of it. If Scott could acquiesce to the no-girls rule, then he certainly could. He was Mormon, after all.

He took in the cubicles that sectioned up the living room, counting the wires and computers. It was an impressive sight. He spotted Shane at one of the cubicles, plugging away, his ear to a phone. Maybe he was on with Korea, or perhaps he was dealing with the server. A couple of the other computers were on and running, the screens filled with numbers. One of them, Brent knew, was keeping live track of people signing on to the site and especially new registrations. Every morning, Scott had told him, they looked at that number, and if it was high enough,

they had a mini celebration. It was a sort of ritual—no matter how drunk they got the night before, the team checked the registration numbers together.

"This place looks great," Brent said. "So where's my department?"

Garin's smile got even wider. With a flourish, he pointed to a short side table right inside the door. There was a computer on it, and a phone right next to the monitor. Someone had placed a low stool in front of the keyboard, set almost all the way down to the floor.

Brent stared at the table, then back at Garin. "You've got to be kidding me."

"Welcome to the Customer Service Department."

Brent closed his eyes. The whole department was *him*. He didn't even have a desk. His chair was a stool.

"That computer has about two hundred e-mails on it, most of them complaints," Garin continued. "There will be a hundred more tomorrow, guaranteed."

Brent opened his eyes, sighing. Scott was probably getting a big laugh out of the situation, but Brent decided then and there he wasn't going to say a word; he was just going to take it in stride.

"So what do I do with those e-mails, exactly?"

"You answer them."

Garin patted him on the back, then headed for the kitchen. Drunk as he still was, Brent lowered himself onto the stool. He was determined to look on the bright side. He still was the director of customer service. Even if it was a department of one. He was the director of himself.

He couldn't help laughing as he powered up the computer and started answering those damn e-mails.

CHAPTER 15

Six months flashed by in a blur of eighteen-hour days: Brent chained to that coffee table; Scott, Garin, Shane, and Hilt camped out in their cubicles. Every morning they rolled out of bed, then gathered around Scott's screen to see how many new players had registered, how many new real-money accounts had been deposited. Then phone calls with potential investors, shareholders, board members. Reading through e-mails from the Koreans. Impromptu meetings about new promotional ideas—free roll tournaments, where players could join for no charge and play for cash prizes, advertising opportunities on various poker blogs, in online poker magazines, via e-mail blasts . . .

Every now and then, when someone realized the refrigerator was empty, straws were drawn to see who would make the five-mile walk to the nearest supermarket, lugging home energy drinks, rice, beans, pasta, and beer in oversize plastic bags.

And when there was something to celebrate—the thou-

sandth account, the first day with three hundred dollars in rakes, a good review in a poker blog—late nights at the Del Rey, and then, when that started to get old, scouting trips to a half dozen other clubs, bars, and casinos that pockmarked downtown San José. Sometimes the party went all night long, ending in some hotel room with a half dozen naked *ticas*—Costa Rican girls, some of whom became girlfriends, others who were just there for the alcohol—and a buffet of other vices.

Even so, the focus was always on their work. No matter how late the party ran, there was an unwritten rule in the house— you were at your post the next morning, or you weren't getting paid. At first, the salaries were paltry—a couple thousand a month, barely enough to cover their lifestyle. As the site grew, and its valuation doubled again, those salaries began to change. Three thousand a month, then five thousand. Back in the States those numbers still wouldn't raise many eyebrows, but in Costa Rica the guys were fast on their way to becoming what all the *ticas* assumed they were—rich expat Americans, living the expat way.

Brent knew that something had changed, that the bootstrap feel of the company was being left behind, when Scott had a BMW 3 Series convertible imported—delivered directly to the house by a driver who actually asked if they were the legend-ary gringos who had founded Paradise Poker, telling him the same story Scott and the group had heard when they first toured the country about the shadowy foreigners who supposedly lived somewhere in the hills above San José and were shuttled around by bodyguards, though in this retelling it was Range Rovers with tinted windows instead of Escalades. When the BMW was fol-

lowed by the purchase of two souped-up motorcycles, a Kawasaki Ninja for Shane and a bright red racing Ducati for Scott, it was just more evidence that things were building faster than any of them had expected.

Still, though the money was changing and the site was growing in popularity—getting more good reviews all over the Web for being clean, fast, and trustworthy, always paying its accounts quickly and honestly, even in an industry that was completely unregulated—Brent's life revolved around those e-mails. He got complaints about everything from Internet outages to slow deals, from nitpicky objections to the visual layout of a game table to reports of perceived abuse from other players. And, of course, numerous accusations of cheating by other players, by imagined robot players—artificially intelligent software that some magazine or another had suggested might be trolling the fledgling Internet sites—and sometimes even by the site itself. It was an early lesson for Brent, one that he assumed every casino operator in Vegas had learned the minute they offered their first game: when people lost money, their first instinct was always to suspect foul play. Game of chance, game of skill—it didn't matter; it was rare when players took losing gracefully. But Brent always did his best to address the complaints, no matter how arbitrary they seemed.

Even so, it was a mind-numbing, soul-crushing job. As more money came in, as Absolute Poker went from a fledgling little company with a handful of players to a viable business with enough investment to support a valuation nearing six million dollars, Brent decided it was time for a change.

Thankfully for him, he wasn't the only one to feel that way.

A nd we are up and running!"

The applause was near deafening, accentuated by the low ceilings and the freshly painted, newly plastered walls. Someone popped a bottle of champagne, the cork flying in a low arc that narrowly sailed over the bank of cubicles and threaded between Scott and Hilt, who were standing at the head of the long, rectangular room. Behind them, a pair of windows looked out over a poorly lit parking lot. From where Brent was sitting, behind a computer screen at one of the cubicles, he could count at least twelve cars in the lot, including Scott's BMW, as well as two motorcycles—Shane's Ninja and a Honda owned by one of the directors of the sports book that took up the top two floors above them.

The building wasn't grand—it was really just a concrete, glass, and plaster box in a strip mall near downtown San José— but it was a hell of an improvement on the home office. Instead of seeming like a fraternity, the company now felt like a corporate business. Other than the dress code, that is; the Costa Rican employees, who made up two-thirds of the room, were mostly in short-sleeved shirts, shorts, and even flip-flops. Scott was dressed similarly; he'd taken to wearing flip-flops almost everywhere, even when they went out to fancy restaurants—which they did almost every Friday, now that things were going so well.

But even with the flip-flops, nobody would have mistaken the place for the SAE house anymore. There were at least thirty people moving about, engaged in some sort of job or another. Thirty people who were getting paychecks, having their health and dental paid for, setting up company trips to the beach, even

taking part in the homeless charity—centered in a soup kitchen in one of the more depressing San José slums—that Brent had talked the other guys into helping him set up. They were a part of the community now, and Brent felt it was important to make sure their lives revolved around something other than printing money.

Which was exactly what it felt like Absolute Poker was doing, now that it was up and running. Every time they refreshed the screen that displayed new registrations, there were twenty or thirty more—and now a good portion of those included credit card payments, mostly through Neteller, one of the biggest online depositors around, and also PayPal, maybe the most respected online commerce facilitator on the Web. They were the real deal now, still lean compared with a handful of competitors that had moved into the market since they'd opened their doors—hell, it seemed like a new poker company was appearing out of thin air every second of the day—but making money hand over fist.

But despite their extreme success, their new digs were indicative of how professionally they were handling the cash flow. Other than the moderate salaries they were now paying themselves, almost all the money was flowing right back into the business, and nearly all of it was being spent on marketing. Because the most important thing they'd learned was that advertising and marketing were the lifeblood of their business. At the moment, Garin and Hilt were handling most of those concerns, but Brent knew that building a marketing department was just one of the main things on their wish list for the coming six months.

As for his own role in the company, things had finally shifted in a positive direction. He'd handed off the customer service job to a pair of Costa Rican employees with better-than-basic English skills and had moved into "fraud protection"—a kind of creative way of saying that his job was to monitor both the game play, looking for anomalies, and, more important, the financial flow coming in through the depositing agents. He was spending a lot of time on the phone with the online credit companies and the various big U.S. banks, making sure all their accounts were in order. Although there were a few banks that eventually decided not to accept transactions pegged toward gambling, most, including many of the biggest banks in the United States, were very happy for the business.

And why not? Business was good and getting better. Brent couldn't help but feel amused when he thought back to Pete Barovich's belief that nobody would be comfortable playing poker over the Internet for real money. The truth was, people were *begging* to play poker over the Internet for real money. And not just college kids, though they made up a huge part of their market. Adults were turning what started as a hobby into a profession; some of the bigger accounts they'd received were earning close to six figures through careful and skilled daily play. Some players were playing eight, ten hours a day—and earning hundreds of dollars a session. AbsolutePoker.com was making good money off that rake, but to Brent, it was also providing a market of sorts—really, directly akin to a stock market, or any other market that provided a place where someone with a lot of skill, and a little luck, could earn a good living.

Everything was coming together, better than Brent could

have imagined. As he knocked back his glass of champagne, letting the bubbles caterwaul down his throat, he locked eyes with his brother, still up at the front of the room next to Hilt. Scott looked tan and happy but certainly not content. But that had always been part of Scott's allure—he was never entirely content, because he was always driving forward. And always driving fast.

CHAPTER 16

The thick, humid night air whipped against the face shield of Scott's motorcycle helmet as he hunched forward over the slanted steering column of his bright red Ducati racing bike, trying desperately to keep the damn thing in the middle of the road. He didn't dare look at the speedometer; he could tell by the way the bike was trembling against his body that he'd passed seventy miles per hour when they'd hit the last straightaway, and there was a good chance they were way beyond that now. His headlight was little better than a flashlight at that speed, and against the inky black of the long, desolate stretch of blacktop that bisected what looked to be sugarcane fields on either side, it was almost as useless as shouting into the wind. Which he was doing anyway, though he knew there was no way in hell that Shane could hear him.

Shane was about a hundred yards ahead, streaking through the blackness on his Kawasaki Ninja, visible only by the tiny, jerking blur of his taillight. Scott was desperate to catch up to

him, but even though the Ducati was a much more powerful bike, he didn't dare try to push it any harder. He was only thankful that they had chosen one of the few paved roads in the area; had they taken a left at the last turn instead of a right, they'd probably both be dead by now.

In retrospect, of course, neither one of them should ever have been in this situation. Going much too fast, driving recklessly—in Costa Rica for such a short time and already *living* recklessly. And with Shane, specifically, Scott and the rest should never have let it get to this point—and Scott definitely blamed himself. All the signs had been there, and anyone who wasn't blind or stupid should have been able to see them for what they were.

Sure, it had started simply enough, way back at the Del Rey that first time. Shane, drunk off his ass, pawing at the hooker strolling behind their blackjack table. The kid they'd all known as a straitlaced, under control—if a little obsessive—social star breaking character in the face of sudden, unregulated temptation. Looking back, of course that was the first sign, but hell, pretty soon they were all drinking just like he was; they were all grabbing cookies from the cookie jar until they couldn't eat any more.

When Shane had shifted from alcohol to weed, again nobody raised any eyebrows. They'd all smoked a bit in college, and now that it was basically a phone call away, there didn't seem to be anything wrong with a joint now and again. After all, they all worked so hard, and as long as everyone made it to their desks on time, who cared what they were smoking when they got off work?

But the cocaine—that was where it had all started to go wrong. It had begun real simple—in the back of a cab, asking the driver if he could get them some more weed. Well, what about

coke? And the driver had simply smiled, pulling a plastic bag out of his glove compartment. Eventually, for Shane the taxis became a personal delivery service, bringing whatever he asked for, whenever he wanted.

In retrospect, all of them should have seen it happening. Shane's gradual deterioration, his leaving the bar a little earlier each night, having these strange side conversations with the taxi driver when he thought nobody was looking. Then, when the rest of them got back home at 3 A.M., Shane would still be wide awake, alone in his room with the air conditioner on full blast, talking a mile a minute to himself. Eventually, as he began showing up later and later at his computer station, he reacted angrily when someone pointed it out.

And after that—well, after that it just got weird. Scott would never forget the day they'd all come into the house to find a long blue cable stretching all the way from the power outlet in the basement, across the living room, up the stairs, then under Shane's door; he'd moved his computer station into his room so that he could stay there day and night. And that's exactly what he did. For weeks on end, nobody saw him. And when he did finally come downstairs, he looked worse than shit. Skinny, his hair falling out, his eyebrows completely gone. Had he plucked out the hairs in a neurotic coke haze, or had they fallen out naturally? Regardless, he was clearly out of control.

The final straw came about a week later, when Scott and the others officially moved out of the house—Scott, Brent, and Garin to the house Scott had rented in the hills, Hilt and his girlfriend into an upscale apartment in a gated complex near downtown. Everyone had just packed up and moved out. And then, a day

later, Shane had finally wandered into the new office and asked if anyone had had a chance to pick up any groceries for the fridge. Everyone had just stared at him, shocked. They'd cleared the entire house out—even the furniture—and Shane hadn't even realized that they'd gone.

At that moment, every one of them knew that something had to be done. Scott knew he shouldn't have waited another minute—at the very least, he should have sat Shane down and said something. But instead he'd decided to give it another day to think the next step through.

And now here he was, screaming into his helmet as the three-hundred-pound aluminum-and-fiberglass beast between his knees fought to stay on the pavement, chasing a little red flash of taillight in what seemed to be infinite darkness. As far as he could tell, Shane hadn't been on drugs when he'd shown up at Scott's house, helmet under his arm, wearing nothing but shorts, a T-shirt, and a pair of flip-flops, revving the engine of his Ninja, asking if Scott wanted to join him for a ride. But even though he was sober at that moment, Shane was in the midst of a growing, dangerous addiction. Still, when Shane had donned his helmet— thank God—and taken off down the driveway, Scott had only grinned and torn right out after him.

And then, right there, as Scott leaned into a soft curve, it happened. One second he was looking at that taillight, red and wobbly, and then suddenly he was seeing Shane's headlight shoot straight up into the air. There was a terrifying squeal of metal against pavement, then a fountain of sparks sprayed out above where the headlight used to be.

Scott hunched farther forward and took the last fifty yards as

fast as he dared. As he pumped the brakes, putting himself into a controlled skid, he caught a glimpse of the scene in front of him in the glow of his own light. The road had curved to the right—and Shane had been unable to take the turn or stop in time, hurtling directly into what appeared to be a highway construction site. A long braided wire hung at about waist level; Shane had managed to lay the bike down—and the Ninja had skidded out and gone under the wire. Shane had gone over.

It took Scott a full beat to see where Shane had landed—a good ten yards from where the bike had gone down. Shane was lying facedown on the dirt, his hands splayed out at his sides, not moving.

Scott cursed, tearing off his helmet as he leaped off the Ducati. He hurdled the braided wire and raced toward his friend. *Christ,* he thought, *he can't possibly have survived that.*

And just as he reached Shane's side, Shane rolled over onto his back and started trying to push himself up off the pavement. His T-shirt was shredded, and there was blood everywhere, spilling from gashes and cuts up and down his chest, arms, and bare legs.

"Dude," Scott gasped. He couldn't think of anything else to say. He looked at Shane's helmet and saw the huge crack across the front shield, running all the way to the back. But other than that, and the road rash up and down his body, Shane didn't look broken, at least not on the outside.

Before Scott could stop him, Shane yanked the helmet off. His eyes were glazed, but he was conscious. He tried to stand, but Scott stopped him with a hand.

"You're a fucking mess," Scott said. "You need to stay still."

Shane mumbled something—an apology, it sounded like, though he wasn't making much sense—and Scott told him to shut up and try to stop bleeding so much. At that, Shane cracked a little smile. Scott didn't know whether he wanted to punch his friend or grab him in a hug.

First he had to get him to an emergency room, to get X-rayed, scanned, and stitched up like a rag doll.

And then he had to get his friend the hell out of Costa Rica.

It was a hard phone call to make. Scott, Garin, Hilt, and Brent gathered around the receiver as one of them dialed, then they took turns with the phone, because at first Shane's mother refused to believe what they were telling her. They finally got her to understand how bad things had gotten. Since the motorcycle accident, Shane had grown even more isolated, the bandages that covered half his body a perfect excuse for him to lock himself in his room for days on end. His mother had immediately connected them to Shane's uncle, who was a rehab counselor and a former addict, clean and sober twenty years now.

Shane's uncle didn't ask any questions—he simply bought a ticket to Costa Rica and got on a plane the next morning. When Scott picked him up from the airport, Shane's uncle showed him a first-class ticket back to the United States with Shane's name on it; he wasn't going to leave without his nephew.

The intervention took place at the small apartment Shane had moved into after he'd finally realized that nobody else was living in the house anymore. They surprised him in the kitchen; when he eventually came out of his room, looking for something

to eat, they were all gathered around his kitchen table. Although Shane's uncle led the conversation, by the end nearly all of them had gotten emotional; Shane had been there since the beginning, and it was crazy to think of the group without him. But he needed to get help, and he needed to get better.

By two in the morning, they were all helping him pack. When his uncle led him to a waiting cab, to take him to the airport for his flight back to the States, he had his head down, watching the ground beneath his feet. Hunched over, skinny, covered in bandages, eyebrows gone—he was a sobering sight for all of them.

But as the cab pulled away and they headed for their own cars, there was little talk of slowing down; if anything, Scott felt it was time to step things up. Shane had shown them—in the world they lived in, if you lost sight of where you were going, you ran the risk of ending up facedown in the road.

CHAPTER 17

Two months later, January 2005, and the party was just getting started.

It was the end of a regular workday. Brent followed the team back to Scott's newly rented house high in the hills above their former home office. Brent and Garin would be staying there as well, and although Brent had toured the place a few times since Scott first moved in, he was still awed by its scale. The building itself was massive, an old Spanish-style mansion with at least six bedrooms, a living room that could have doubled as a ballroom, and multiple decks overlooking downtown San José—a vista of sparkling lights, bolstered by the pulsing flare of the constant traffic that threaded between the buildings, like a radiated circulatory system feeding that ravenous urban sprawl.

The party was mostly confined to the house's massive pool deck. A DJ had set up shop on an elevated stage, the music from his spinning CDs blasting out of massive twin speakers

that had been built right into one of the house's exterior brick walls. At five minutes to midnight, Scott strolled through the party, pulling everyone he could find out of whatever trouble they had gotten into to lead them to the farthest railing that looked out over the city. There was a Colombian girl on Scott's arm—Brent hadn't quite caught her name, but he thought it might be Clara. She was wearing a black bikini bottom and nothing else. There was a tattoo of a tiger on her lower back, and her dyed blond hair was tied back in an elaborate ponytail, held in place by a band that sparkled with what may very well have been diamonds.

By the time Scott made it to the railing, Brent, Garin, and Hilt were right behind him. Shane, just back from rehab, followed a few feet after, a bottle of water in his hand. Although Shane walked carefully, still on the road to a full physical recovery, the color was back in his cheeks; now that he had returned to the team, he was dividing his time between the office and NA and AA programs. A living, breathing, walking reminder of what life in a place like that could become if you let yourself lose control.

When the team had gathered around him, Scott leaned back against the railing, his arm around the topless girl's shoulders. Brent, Garin, Hilt, and Shane made a small semicircle, wondering why he'd brought them to the edge of the deck.

"You know all those stories we keep hearing about the crazy gringos who live up in the hills, living like rock stars, spending money like they're printing it themselves?"

He waited a beat, then grinned his trademark grin.

"From now on, those gringos are us."

And right on cue, the midnight sky above their heads exploded in a brilliant wash of fireworks, streaks of Technicolor sparks raining over the city below, so many explosions in such rapid succession, it seemed like the show could somehow go on forever.

CHAPTER 18

Ten hours in the air. Three more in a rented Mercedes convertible, going seventy miles per hour with the top down, buffeted by a fierce wind heavy with the scent of lush hills, ancient lakes, towering pines—the Pacific Northwest distilled and funneled through the senses.

By the time Scott found himself standing next to Hilt in the leather-paneled elevator, racing up the spine of a glass-and-steel office building in the heart of downtown Portland, he should have been exhausted. But in the months since Shane's rehab and return, Scott had been operating on less and less sleep. Every minute of the day had been dominated by the company; despite the initial skyrocket of growth that had put them on the map as one of the premier online poker sites, things had started to turn—and not for the better.

"We're simply not getting enough for our ad dollars," Hilt was saying, continuing the conversation that had carried them

through much of the trip from San José. "I've done the calculations. With all the Web ads, the promotions through the poker blogs, the magazine pullouts—we're paying about three hundred fifty dollars per player. It's just not sustainable in the long run."

Scott grimaced, his palms feeling the cool leather of the elevator walls. He knew Hilt was right. Over the past few months, he'd grown much closer to his business-minded friend. Hilt had become more and more his consigliere—the guy he turned to first when he had questions about the business. Garin had been there from the beginning and was his oldest friend, but especially since their intervention with Shane, in Scott's opinion—though Garin probably felt quite differently about it—Garin seemed to have taken a step back. Maybe Scott was reading too much into things. After Shane's stint in rehab, there were plenty of discussions about being careful, maybe trying to attain a little more balance rather than continue with their full-throttle, business-first mentality. But Scott had only one setting, and balance had never been one of his strengths. And Hilt was fast becoming his day-to-day partner.

Another part of the shift had to do with girls. Hilt had recently coupled off with an old girlfriend—a spectacular five-foot-seven blonde who had graduated college in three years with honors, a scouted model who was now in school to be a teacher. She had come to Costa Rica so they could be together, and they were moving rapidly toward marriage. In contrast, Scott had fallen into a relationship of his own with a hot-blooded, exceedingly jealous Colombian he'd met at a club in San José. For whatever reason, Scott's girlfriend had taken an immediate dislike to the girl Garin was dating, a pretty Costa Rican, and instead

had been pushing him to spend as much couple time as possible with Hilt and his likely future wife. Maybe Scott's girlfriend was hoping that Hilt's relationship stability would rub off on them; whatever the case, the fact that Scott's and Garin's women didn't get along meant less time spent together.

"And the landscape has changed," Hilt added. "So many more competitors now. Another poker site popping up every day. And they're passing us by."

That was an understatement; not only were there now hundreds, if not thousands, of online poker sites, but a handful of them were dwarfing AbsolutePoker.com. Specifically, Poker-Stars.com and PartyPoker.com were monsters in the industry. To be fair, they had both been well capitalized from the beginning; neither had started in some frat house in Montana. Party Poker's founders had their 1-900 sex line fortune and had rolled that cash into building what was now probably one of the biggest online companies, in terms of straight revenue, in existence. And Poker-Stars was following right behind.

Absolute Poker had certainly grown dramatically from its humble beginnings. Now valued at more than thirty million dollars, it was bringing in about eight thousand dollars a day in revenue. But with the competition, and the price they were paying to sign up new players, they needed to figure out how to leverage what they had, and expand exponentially.

Which was why they were in the elevator in Portland.

"Hopefully Greg can tell us what we're doing wrong," Scott responded as the elevator slowed at the fourteenth floor. "Because God knows, he's done everything right."

Scott had met Greg Pierson, CEO and founder of Ultimate-

Bet.com, one of their competitors—which was now valued in the hundreds of millions, one step away from the PokerStars and Party Pokers of the industry—when Greg had tried to sell him on a software partnership. Greg was a computer guy, a programming whiz who fell into online poker sideways; at the time Scott had first spoken to him, Greg's company, ieLogic, was creating skin sites for the gaming industry—basically, software that allowed instant, pop-up gaming on the Internet without downloads. Scott had remained in contact with the man and had always thought he was one of the smartest guys in the business. So when Greg had invited him to come by their offices in Portland, Scott figured it would be worthwhile to pick the man's brain. Ultimate Bet had streaked right past Absolute Poker, and Scott needed to know why.

The elevator doors opened, spilling them out into a brightly lit modern lobby, staffed by a woman in an impeccable suit seated behind a smoked-glass desk. After a brief wait they were led to a corner office with large picture windows overlooking downtown Portland. Pierson rose from his leather chair to greet them, and it was instantly obvious that things were going very well for the former software geek. He was a compact man in an off-brown suit, and his face was glowing beneath his crown of reddish hair, eyes beaming from behind his wire-rimmed glasses. He looked like he'd just won the lottery.

He ushered them to a pair of leather chairs behind a glass table. As Scott took his seat, he saw the Ultimate Bet logo embedded in the table, beneath a scrawl of carved writing: WORLD POKER TOUR CHARTER MEMBER.

Pierson noticed him reading the table and pointed with a thumb.

"Cost us a hundred thousand, and worth every penny."

"The table?" Hilt asked, incredulous. Pierson laughed.

"Fuck you. No, sponsoring the tour. Got us unlimited access to advertise on the TV show. Wednesday nights on Travel Channel."

Scott and Hilt nodded, but Pierson just looked at them, then shook his head.

"You guys don't get it, do you? *Wednesday nights on the Travel Channel.* That's national TV."

Scott smiled politely. He knew the show. It was one of a number of poker shows that had launched on television, including *World Series of Poker* on ESPN, which was probably the industry's best-known show. The idea of poker on TV had been a long time in coming, but it hadn't been until very recently that the game had finally made inroads into the medium, specifically because of a pretty interesting invention—the hole cam.

The problem with poker, as a visual sport, was that you couldn't normally see the players' cards—so it was hard to play along with them, because you were only seeing the results of the game after all the cards were laid down, rather than taking part in the action along the way. But the hole cam changed all that, by showing the players' cards as they were dealt, so that the viewer could witness the drama of the game as it unfolded. First instituted on a show in the United Kingdom, it had come to U.S. TV via both the ESPN *World Series of Poker* and Travel Channel's *World Poker Tour*. Scott hadn't realized that Pierson's Ultimate Bet had been a sponsor of the show—but at first, he didn't get the significance. Besides, they'd all sponsored all sorts of shit, from cruises to golf outings to charity tournaments.

"It's a fun show," Scott agreed. "We catch it now and then on the TVs in the sports book upstairs from our office."

Pierson pulled his desk chair around so he was sitting across from them at the table. He leaned toward them, looking like some sort of intense, bespectacled turtle.

"You're not getting what I'm saying. Scott, you know how much revenue we did last week? One hundred thousand a day. Every day."

Scott looked at Hilt. He could see the shock in his friend's eyes. Absolute Poker was doing eight thousand a day—and that was during a good week. A hundred thousand dollars a day? That seemed impossible.

"How?" was all Scott could manage.

Pierson grinned, obviously happy he had gotten through. "The game has changed, man."

"We know," Hilt started. "So many more online sites—"

"No. That's not what I mean. The *game* has changed. Poker. It's gone mainstream, in a major way. Because of shows like ours, and the World Series. It started with Moneymaker winning a bracelet, but it's gone so much farther now, it's straight-up mainstream. And that's what we've done. We've gone mainstream too."

Of course, Scott knew all about Chris Moneymaker, who'd won the *World Series of Poker*'s main event in 2003. Moneymaker had been a regular Joe, an accountant who won his spot in the event by playing a thirty-eight-dollar online tournament at PokerStars. When he won the World Series—going head to head against some of the greatest professional poker players of the era—his $2.5 million prize had inspired a whole new genera-

tion. Moneymaker hadn't trained in dark poker rooms or smoky casinos. He'd learned how to play at home, online. If a guy as average seeming as Chris Moneymaker could win the World Series of Poker, then anyone could.

"One in five Americans played poker last year," Pierson continued. "And those numbers are only growing. More people play poker than play baseball—it's our goddamn national sport. And now it's nationally televised. Travel Channel, ESPN, ABC, NBC."

Scott was starting to catch on. For the first time in history, the two-hundred-year-old game of poker was being beamed into living rooms across America. All over the world too.

Back in 1999, when Scott had discovered the game, poker had been relegated to the back rooms of bars like Stockman's and the frat houses and dorm rooms of college kids. Now it was on TV, right after the Yankees–Red Sox game or the Super Bowl.

"TV changed everything. TV is the key."

Pierson railed on, explaining that Ultimate Bet was advertising on as many shows as it could—and everyone else was doing the same thing. PokerStars had the *World Series of Poker* and the *North American Poker Tour* on ESPN, *National Heads-Up Poker Championship* and *Poker After Dark* on NBC. Party Poker was advertising everywhere, including sports events and shows that had nothing to do with cards.

And through television, these sites were working with the poker shows to publicize a whole roster of poker celebrities who were becoming as well known as professional athletes: Phil Hellmuth, Chris "Jesus" Ferguson, Doyle Brunson, Phil Ivey, Annie Duke. By sponsoring players, sites like Pierson's could further

advertise themselves—through T-shirts, hats, whatever they could get the players to wear. They were after exposure, as much as they could buy—and from what Pierson was saying, because of TV, they could suddenly buy a whole hell of a lot more than Scott had ever thought possible.

As Pierson talked on, Scott was already trying to figure out a way to cut the meeting short and get the hell back on the road. He tried to signal Hilt with his eyes. He didn't want to waste another minute in that office.

Pierson was right. Television was a window into every American home. The faster Absolute Poker could get on TV, the faster it would end up in every American living room.

Go, go, go!" Scott shouted, pushing Garin, Hilt, Shane, and Brent up the cement stairwell in front of him. "It's on in two minutes!"

Scott had just gotten the phone call from their Philadelphia-based advertising company a few minutes earlier: Absolute-Poker.com's first commercial was going to air during the last few seconds of *World Poker Tour*—in the same block as one of Pierson's own ads. Although Scott and his team had gone over the ad a dozen times since the Philly guys handed it in, there was something different about the idea of watching it live. They wanted to see it on the screen just like their customers would.

Scott and Hilt had come up with the concept of the ad during the drive back from Portland to Seattle. Just a thirty-second bump, a simple story that Scott felt captured the essence of what Absolute Poker was supposed to be. A guy at a computer in a

well-appointed apartment, his friends in the next room getting ready to hit ladies' night at a local bar. The friends tell him it's time to go downtown—that the party is about to start. The guy declines; he says no, he's going to pass, he's playing online poker. Then the AbsolutePoker.com logo—and something like "Play it anytime, anywhere."

To Scott, it felt perfect. There was nothing seedy about it, nothing dark. Choosing to play online poker over going to a bar—it was just another form of entertainment, and hell, if you looked at the average credit card deposits of most players, it was an even cheaper, more responsible decision than heading off to ladies' night.

Scott made it to the top of the stairs and burst into the back room of the sports book office, right behind Garin, Shane, and Brent. The room was set up like a lounge, with couches, a refrigerator, and a handful of televisions hanging from three walls. The TVs were usually turned to sporting events, but Scott had called their upstairs neighbor right after he'd gotten off the phone with Philly; all the screens were now showing the *World Poker Tour*, which had just ended. The credits were rolling as Scott took his position a few feet from one of the televisions, his hand resting on Hilt's shoulder. Garin, Shane, and Brent were near a second TV, breathing hard.

And then, suddenly, there it was. The ad went by fast—thirty seconds felt like four heartbeats, maybe five—and then the show was over. Scott blinked, still seeing the Absolute Poker diamond emblazoned on his retinas. Then Hilt turned and raced back toward the stairwell.

"Back down," he said. "Let's see what that did."

The rest followed, nearly knocking him over as he pushed his way back onto the stairs.

A moment later they were in front of Scott's computer, looking at the back-end numbers that told them how many people were registering for the site in real time. Hilt was hitting the Refresh button with his index finger.

At first the numbers were the same as before—a few new registrations, followed by a few more. And then—*Christ.*

Twenty registrations to the website. All new players, all signing up to AbsolutePoker.com for the first time.

Then forty registrations.

Then eighty.

"How is this possible?" Garin whispered.

A hundred registrations. Then a hundred fifty. And it was still increasing, more and more registrations, every time Hilt hit Refresh.

"From one commercial?" Brent said. "Holy shit."

"If this holds up," Hilt commented quietly, "we're going to do twenty thousand in revenue in the next day."

Scott exhaled. From around eight thousand in revenue before the television ad to twenty thousand after. And what would happen when those television ads were everywhere? How many people would be coming to AbsolutePoker.com to play poker? How much money would they be able to generate?

"Is the software going to hold?" Garin asked. There was a tinge of panic in his voice.

Scott ignored him. He caught eyes with Hilt, and could see that Hilt felt it too. Something had changed, something huge.

Scott glanced behind them, and saw that most of their

other employees—maybe forty, fifty people—were now standing around watching the company officers. Scott reached out
and pulled an office chair from in front of the nearest desk, then
climbed up so that he was standing high above the room. He
waited until the place had gone silent.

"Poker is everywhere," he said, hitting each word. "And from
now on, we will be everywhere too. Television ads. And not just
on poker shows. I'm talking sporting events, college basketball,
college football. Wrestling—everywhere. We're not just an online
poker company anymore—we're a marketing company. And the
thing we're selling is the most popular game in the world."

The game of poker had changed, and Absolute Poker was
going to change with it—hurtling into the mainstream.

Maybe Garin had his concerns, but Scott knew it wasn't the
time to slow down.

It was their moment to step on the goddamn gas.

CHAPTER 19

The speedometer had to be wrong.

There was no way the BMW could be going that fast down a road this narrow, or one that was mostly dirt and gravel, with enough blind twists and jagged turns that it was way beyond serpentine. And yet there it was, those bright red digital numbers screaming out of the dashboard, telling Brent that he should be screaming as well. But instead he was laughing, so damn hard that the half bottle of tequila he'd drunk over the past three hours was threatening to tango back up his esophagus and drench the backseat of Scott's car.

That would serve his brother right. It was Scott who was behind the wheel, grinning back at Brent in the rearview mirror every time they took another hairpin turn and somehow stayed on the road, a wild, adrenaline-infused grin that was almost as terrifying as the numbers on the dashboard. When his brother got like this, anything could happen.

"Creo que está loco!" the girl seated on Brent's lap squealed—alerting Brent to the fact that there was a girl seated on his lap. In the same moment, he noticed that she wasn't wearing any pants, just bikini briefs and a T-shirt. Her ample breasts were fighting against the thin material of shirt, dime-size nipples jutting out as she took another swig from the bottle of tequila, which Brent now saw she'd brought with her from the bar. She was either terrified or excited, or both. Brent tried not to stare—because he could see now that his younger brother, Trent, jammed into the cramped backseat of the speeding BMW next to him and the girl, had gone bright red with the effort to do the same. Every now and then, however, the poor kid lost to the urge and snapped a quick glance at that heaving, perfect set.

Brent couldn't blame him. Because Trent really *was* still just a kid, even though he'd turned nineteen a few months earlier. A devout Mormon who'd just gotten back from missionary work in Chile, he wasn't used to Scott and his antics, and he'd certainly never been in a situation like this before.

Trent had arrived in Costa Rica only that afternoon, about six hours earlier. Just a three-day visit, on his way back to Salt Lake City. When he'd gotten to Scott's house, Brent had suggested they take him hiking in the jungle, or maybe to the beach. Scott had vetoed those ideas immediately: *He's just spent the past year preaching about Jesus. We need to take him downtown.*

And so they'd brought him to the worst place on earth, the same spot Scott and Hilt had taken Brent when he'd first arrived in San José. That pink hellhole full of girls.

To Trent's credit, he'd kept himself under control the whole time, refusing alcohol, turning away when the girls tried to throw themselves at him. At one point in the evening a Nicaraguan

beauty had sat right on his lap in the bar, pulling up her tube top to reveal her naked brown chest. Trent had looked away until finally she shrugged and moved on to the next guy at the bar.

Brent wasn't sure, but it appeared the same Nicaraguan girl was actually now up in the front passenger seat, next to Scott, her long arms extended as she gripped the dashboard, brown fingers now turning white. At least it looked like her from the side, the same green tank. She was shouting something in Spanish too, probably about Scott's mental state, but Brent could hardly hear her over the sound of the gravel spitting up behind the tires. Girls like her, and the one on his lap—they'd been cycling through Scott's house at a pretty frantic pace, ever since the company had discovered TV and exploded. There was so much money coming in, it felt like there was a reason to celebrate every single night. Even though most of the twenty thousand dollars in revenue they were bringing in each day was going back into marketing, there was still enough left over to put them all in a different tax bracket—if Costa Rica had tax brackets. Brent wasn't sure what Scott, Hilt, Shane, or Garin were bringing in, but his salary had grown from his original two thousand dollars a month to closer to ten. It was more than enough to have imported his own BMW, which would have saved him from the terrifying roller coaster he now found himself on.

In the distance, out the windshield beyond the Nicaraguan girl's clawed grip on the dash, he saw another turn in the road, marked by a pair of palm trees. At first he felt a surge of relief, because he recognized the trees; they were only about a quarter mile from Scott's house. But then his eyes shifted down, to the road leading up to the trees—and his stomach went tight. There was something weird about the gravel there, the way it was glis-

tening in the moonlight, and he realized that it wasn't just gravel, it was also sand—a lot of sand. Which, if the digital numbers on the dashboard really were real, and not just a figment of his imagination, would make it extremely hard, if not impossible, for Scott to make the turn without hitting—

Suddenly there was a scream and a horrible screech of metal and his whole world lurched up in the air, then flipped over, spinning and spinning, and then . . . nothing.

Y ou okay? You okay?"
Brent opened his eyes. He was looking at the sky. His body was pretty much horizontal, his legs were extended right out in front of him, and yet somehow he was moving, sliding along the gravel on his butt, and then he looked straight up and saw Scott staring down at him, eyes wild, blood caked on his lower lip, hair sticking straight up from his head like a demented halo.

"You okay? You okay?" Scott repeated.

Brent realized that Scott had him by his arms and was dragging him across the road. Brent looked back toward where he'd come from—and saw the BMW on its side, windows shattered, the whole damn front of the thing crushed in like an accordion. One of the palm trees was cracked in the middle, and the other was bent over, like it was bowing to the moon.

"Holy shit," Brent whispered. "Trent."

"He's good," Scott said, relief in his voice. "We're all good. Everybody's good."

They reached the side of the road, and Scott placed Brent

gingerly on the grass. Brent looked over and saw Trent, sitting there next to him. At first glance, Trent didn't look anything like *good*. He was holding a rag to his forehead, and there was blood everywhere, running down both of his cheeks, covering the front of his shirt, trickling all over the grass.

"Oh, man," Brent started, but Trent offered a weak smile.

"Just cut up a little," he managed. "The girls are okay too. But I think Scott's got a broken ankle."

Brent looked over to where Trent was pointing with his free hand. Scott was trying to calm the girls, who were about five yards away, also on the grass, jabbering in Spanish. Neither one of them looked hurt. When Scott left them to cross back to Brent and his brother, Brent saw that he was indeed limping pretty badly.

Scott sat on the grass next to Brent, reaching down to check out his ankle. It looked huge, swollen, and blue, and Scott grimaced as he gingerly removed his shoe.

There were suddenly sirens in the distance—still about ten minutes away, by Brent's guess. Scott heard them too, and seemed to forget about his ankle.

"I gotta get the fuck out of here," he said suddenly.

Brent stared at him. "What? No, man, you gotta get to a hospital. We all have to—"

"No, I gotta get out of here. I'm the CEO of a company. It's gonna look real bad if this gets in the press."

"You got in a car accident—"

"With a couple of hookers in the backseat. No, man, I gotta go."

Suddenly he was up on his good foot, and then he was hobbling away from the road, into the brush. One of the girls, the Nicaraguan, saw him going and for some reason decided to follow,

jogging right past Brent and Trent. She put an arm around Scott and helped him forward, deeper into what appeared to be a field of waist-high bushes and weeds.

Brent watched them go. Then he turned back to Trent, who was also staring after Scott, awe in his eyes. The bleeding didn't look quite as bad as before, but he was definitely going to need stitches. The sirens were getting louder, and the other girl was still babbling in Spanish, but her voice was so high-pitched and she was speaking so fast, Brent had no idea what she was saying. He reached out and put a hand on his younger brother's leg.

"Trent, I'm so sorry, man." The kid had been in Costa Rica less than ten hours, and he'd nearly died.

Then Brent noticed that Trent was smiling.

"Sorry? This has been the best day of my life!"

Brent was on his way to the emergency room to get his brother stitched up when the police finally found Scott crouching in the field of weeds, the prostitute curled up next to him with the bottle of tequila. The officer had his handcuffs out and ready— until Scott opened up his wallet. Two thousand dollars American, and the officer quickly went back the way he had come, leaving Scott and the girl in the field, where Hilt eventually picked them up and drove them home.

CHAPTER 20

There was something uniquely pleasant about the feel of a good hammer against your palm. Maybe it was the weight of the thing, how it pulled at the muscles of your forearm with just the right amount of force. Or maybe it was how it looked, arced back above your shoulder, the steel head of the tool poised in the air with so much pregnant power, so much potential strength.

And then the hammer was flashing downward, tearing through the air in a perfect swing. It hit the cast dead center, spraying plaster all over the newspaper Scott had spread out across the floor of his home office to cover the Oriental rug he'd had imported the week before.

Without pause, Scott brought the hammer back up above his head—and then he heard a cough from the open doorway across the room.

"What the hell are you doing?"

He looked up and saw Garin standing there, mouth agape.

Garin had a laptop open in his right hand, the screen glowing with their revenue numbers for the previous week. Scott wasn't sure how long he'd been there, or even when he'd arrived at the house. Scott had been in the home office for most of the day, his cell phone off. It was a Friday afternoon, and he knew that a lot of their Costa Rican employees would be on their way to the beach, starting the weekend early. Scott had chosen to work from home, to keep from being distracted by the early exodus.

"This thing is driving me nuts," he responded. Then he brought the hammer down again, hitting the cast from the side. This time the cast cracked like the shell of a nut, and he laid the hammer on the newspaper and went to work with his fingers, prying the damn thing open.

"It's only been two weeks," Garin said, stepping into the room. "Your ankle is broken. Didn't the doctor say you're supposed to wear the cast for six?"

"Fuck him. He doesn't have to walk around in it. My ankle feels fine."

Scott got his foot free and tossed the remains of the cast into a trash can by his desk. Then he slowly rose to his feet, carefully putting weight on his injured leg. His ankle felt weak, but it didn't hurt.

"Is this *Apocalypse Now,* descent-into-madness kind of shit?"

At that, Scott had to smile. Before he could respond, Hilt pushed past Garin and into the room. He had an intense look on his face.

"Got another one. This time from an M&A firm in Canada."

Scott stretched his leg. Garin looked down at his laptop.

"How much?" Scott asked.

"Twenty-five million. I told them to go fuck themselves."

Garin looked up, his face blanching. Hilt laughed.

"I'm kidding. I told him we weren't looking for that sort of investment." Then to Scott. "We're not, are we?"

Scott shook his head. Still, it was pretty amazing to hear—yet another firm wanting to make an investment in their company. Even more amazing, he knew that the investment would just be a stepping-stone to an eventual IPO. Because these days that's all anyone was talking about in relation to Absolute Poker—the inevitable IPO.

They were now raking in seventy thousand dollars a day in revenue and signing up players at an amazing rate. And their timing couldn't have been better. The industry had completely exploded in the past month—beginning, of course, with Party Poker's IPO on the London Stock Exchange. That poker company, with the help of Morgan Stanley and DKW, had managed to pull off the largest IPO in the previous decade on the UK exchange. Its valuation had gone as high as thirteen billion dollars on the first day, ending at around nine billion. The founders of the company were now on the *Forbes* list.

Billionaires. Off of online poker.

And almost overnight, the industry had become real. The biggest banks in the world were calling everyone who had a piece of it to see how they could get involved. Major, respectable institutions, with teams of lawyers and auditors and CPAs.

Scott had taken many of the calls himself. He'd given the major firms access to their books, and everyone liked what they saw. One of the biggest banks, with headquarters in London, had gone into specifics; they wanted to take Absolute public—for no less than a billion dollars in an IPO. The only problem was, unlike Party Poker, which had started in such a large way that

they'd been run with an IPO in mind from the very beginning, Absolute Poker had only two years of audited financials; to IPO, they'd need three at the minimum. They'd employed some of the most respectable big banks and auditing firms available, had engaged numerous high-priced legal teams, and had meticulously documented their financials. But they still needed one more year of records.

One more year, and they'd be worth a billion dollars. No problem, Scott had told the London bankers. We'll get one more year on the books. By the end of 2006, they'd be ready to go big—Party Poker big.

So this, now, was their trajectory. If all went well, in one more year they would all be on their way to becoming billionaires.

Between now and then they just had to keep their heads down, keep the revenues flowing, and turn down all the investors who were trying to buy their way into an industry on steroids. But Scott felt they also had to make a few changes—because now that the industry was legitimate and first class, they needed to get respectable—first world.

"It's not money we need," Scott responded. "We're in the due-diligence phase now. We need to look clean and pretty. Look at Ultimate Bet—those offices in Portland were top-notch. We need to look like that."

"You mean we need to get out of Costa Rica," Hilt said. "Open another headquarters somewhere respectable, where we can hire professional talent and make sure the big banks continue to take us seriously."

Scott nodded. He had been going through this with Hilt for a while, and they had already chosen a place they felt was

right for them: Vancouver, Canada. First world, close to the United States, relatively cheap, and with highly educated talent that would look very good to the major European banks and exchanges. They'd even come up with who they thought they might bring in to help open the new office—someone who knew their business intimately and also had a strong background in marketing. The current conversation wasn't spontaneous—it was really for Garin's benefit.

Because Scott and Hilt had also recently come to another conclusion: they needed to make some other changes as well, for similar, somewhat cosmetic reasons.

"Along those lines," Scott said tentatively, "we need to make some slight changes involving the shareholder structures. Specifically, we've decided to tweak the board of directors."

At this, Garin paused, shutting his laptop. He looked from Scott to Hilt.

"What do you mean, 'tweak'?"

"Gray it up," Scott said. "Put a little age into it, because the bankers who look this shit over don't want to see a bunch of twenty-five-year-olds running a billion-dollar company. Some of us can stay on, but we need to switch some out to add some of our older investors."

Garin's face was reddening, and Scott could tell he was getting angry. Scott didn't want this to get personal; it was just business, and good business at that.

"We think that since you're more focused on the day-to-day—the TV spending and marketing, stuff like that—it makes more sense for you to step back."

There, he'd said it. Like pulling off a Band-Aid. Hilt had

remained silent throughout the conversation. Still, Garin kept glancing his way. For a brief moment, Scott thought that something was going to happen—something ugly. But then Garin seemed to slump his shoulders, just the littlest bit.

"I assume you two will stay on the board. And your dad?"

Scott nodded. His dad was good for the image of the company, as a high-powered financial player in Seattle. And he and Hilt—well, they really were running the show. And Shane, now that he was clean, would also remain on the board; his family had put up a significant portion of the money that had kept them afloat, making them and him major shareholders. But the rest of the board would be older, respectable shareholders.

Garin was obviously angered by the change, but in the end he'd have to accept things as they were. A battle right now would be foolish; this was a train that none of them wanted to get off.

Scott turned away, so that he didn't have to look at the cauliflowers of red still spreading across Garin's cheeks. He forced his mind to whirl forward, away from the tension in the room. He had other, more important things to focus on.

Billionaires. Was it really possible? Internet billionaires—the idea seemed hard to fathom. But if things continued the way they were going, it was inevitable—Scott would soon be nearly a billionaire. A nobody kid from a trailer park in Montana, who'd barely survived childhood—on his way to becoming a billionaire.

All they needed to do was get clean and pretty—and somehow stay that way until the banks were ready to take them public.

CHAPTER 21

It was definitely the most difficult pitch Pete Barovich had ever had to make.

He was sitting in the sunlit, tastefully modern kitchen of his brand-new home in Phoenix, Arizona. His hands were cupped around a mug of fresh coffee, and his two Labrador retrievers were curled up at his feet. The dogs were almost as new as the house, both jumbles of puppy energy; even though they'd spent the whole morning running around the construction site that was the backyard—new pool, new Jacuzzi, a deck for barbecue parties, even an outdoor wet bar—they were taking turns pawing at the laces of Pete's shoes. But Pete wasn't focused on the dogs or the coffee; across the table, his wife, Brandi, was sipping from her own mug, watching him intensely. She'd already guessed the theme of what he was going to say, but she was going to make him say it anyway.

"We have to do this," he finally opened.

It wasn't the strongest opening, but this was an unusual situation. Pete had been honing his marketing skills since his fraternity days; he'd become a true expert at selling, not just objects or ideas but the big picture. With Brandi it was different, because with Brandi he had only one option, and that was to be utterly truthful. It was like playing poker if your only move was to immediately lay down all of your cards.

"Fine," Brandi responded, brushing long strands of her brownish-blond hair out of her eyes. At twenty-six, she was a staggeringly pretty woman—a former pageant girl who'd made it all the way to Miss Montana, she should have been way out of Pete's league. More evidence that even back in college, where he'd first met her, he could market snow to Eskimos. "What is it, exactly, that we have to do?"

Yes, she was going to make him spell it out, every word. Because really, it was so damn insane. They'd literally just moved into their new house two days earlier. Adopted the two Labs. Started construction on the pool, as well as the refinishing of the three bathrooms in the gorgeous split-level ranch-style home.

"We have to sell everything. Take a massive pay cut and move out of the country. And we have to do it right away."

Pete laid it out for Brandi, step by step; the bottom line was, he had been dead wrong. He had underestimated Scott and his idea. He had thought poker couldn't work over the Internet—and he had been wrong.

Absolute Poker's biggest competitors were IPO'ing in the billions. Absolute Poker was now generating close to a hundred thousand dollars a day, and had raised more than fifteen million in working capital. The company was being groomed for a

billion-dollar IPO by prestigious banks and hedge funds, who were all hoping to get in on the ground floor of an industry that had taken the financial world by storm.

When Scott had called Pete the night before, offering him a VP job—and explained that they were also in the process of hiring a Canadian CFO and setting up a respectable office in Vancouver—Pete had been forced to admit to himself, and to his friend, how wrong he'd been. To Scott's credit, he hadn't rubbed it in at all; to the contrary, he'd explained that Pete was an important piece in the puzzle, that they needed a guy like him to help get the company to the next step. Then again, Scott had always been very good at telling people what they wanted to hear—and at making people see his way. In Pete's mind, that's really why Scott had succeeded, why he'd been able to build his company from nothing and, in a way, help invent an entire industry out of something that Pete had thought had no potential. Maybe Pete could sell snow to Eskimos—but Scott could sell Scott to anyone.

However it had happened, now Absolute Poker was on an IPO path; all the banks needed were one more year of audited financials and a real, first-world headquarters—with an outstanding accounting department and a first-class CFO. The fact that Scott had turned to Pete to help build the Vancouver office, even after Pete had turned him down numerous times when the company was nothing but a pipe dream—it was humbling.

Pete would have accepted the offer right on the phone, if he hadn't had one last sale to make before he could pack up his suitcase and get on a plane.

"I'm not going to tell you that it's not crazy," he continued to

Brandi, while the dogs chewed at his laces. "Because it's completely insane. But it's also an opportunity we may never have again."

That afternoon Pete and his wife called in an ad to the local paper—moving sale, everything must go. At five thirty in the morning the day after the ad ran, there was a line of fifty people waiting by their garage door. By noon, people were buying the salsa out of the refrigerator, and Pete was trying to figure out how to ship two rambunctious Labradors and an angry wife to Vancouver, Canada.

CHAPTER 22

Three thousand miles, eight days. One hundred twenty cars racing from London to Vienna to Budapest to Belgrade, then everyone loaded onto airplanes and set back down in Phuket, Thailand. Racing again, Phuket to Bangkok, then back on the planes to fly halfway around the world to Salt Lake City. Back on the road from Salt Lake City to Vegas. A concert at the Hard Rock by the rapper Snoop Dogg, then on to Los Angeles, right down the middle of Rodeo Drive—and a wrap party at the Playboy Mansion.

It was the ultimate fantasy, yet it was entirely real; the Gumball 3000 wasn't a race so much as it was a party on wheels, attended by royalty, the ultra-wealthy, movie stars, rock stars—and one group of frat brothers from Montana in AbsolutePoker.com blue racing jumpsuits, flanked by a dozen girls in matching blue tube tops.

Six hours into the wrap party, Scott found himself standing

next to his father on the back lawn of the Playboy Mansion. He was wearing sunglasses, though it was well past midnight, and he was shivering, despite the temperature being in the midsixties. Then again, he was soaking wet; his rented tuxedo clung to his legs and torso, and his cummerbund and bow tie had gone missing. If he had to guess, he'd say the bow tie was floating somewhere in the infamous grotto. When he and Phil had stumbled into the rock-walled cove, he'd recognized the place immediately from the magazine. And just like in the magazine, the grotto had been filled with girls, many of them actual Playmates, all of them topless. Scott had done the only sensible thing—he'd jumped right in, tuxedo and all. Phil had followed. He'd only wished Hilt could have been there too, but Hilt was in the UK, meeting with investment bankers.

So now Scott was soaking wet, but nobody at the party was going to care; it was the Playboy Mansion. And at the moment, Scott had the run of the place. He knew that parked somewhere out front was an F430 Spider, gunmetal gray—the Absolute Poker logo painted across the hood, that AP diamond in the center clinging to the car's perfectly precise curves. He knew that the Ferrari, on its own, would be a spectacular sight; and it was next to a row of some of the most expensive, unusual cars in the world. A Lamborghini Gallardo, a Rolls-Royce Phantom, even a pink Range Rover.

Hef himself, and his bevy of girlfriends, had greeted Scott and his friends at the front door. As premier sponsors of the Gumball, they were at the top of the food chain. Hell, in Vegas, Scott had signed a dozen autographs for being CEO of what was now on its way to being one of the biggest companies on the Internet.

"Soak it in," he said, really to himself as they watched a group of Playmates wander toward them from the direction of the miniature zoo Hef kept on the premises. "A little while longer, and we'll all be living like this—"

He was interrupted by a commotion from behind, and he turned in time to see Garin being half led, half carried from the direction of the grotto. Garin had a foolish grin on his lips and a stream of blood coming from his scalp. One of the security guards who was helping him along was holding what looked to be a bikini top against the wound, trying to stifle the bleeding.

"What the hell?" Scott said as Garin was ushered past.

Garin looked back over his shoulder.

"I guess there's a no-diving policy. There should be a freaking sign."

And then he was gone, on his way to the front exit.

Phil was laughing hysterically, and Scott was just shaking his head. They'd collect Garin on the way out; he'd just have to do his best to keep from bleeding to death, because this party was going to go all night.

CHAPTER 23

Now, that's what I call service," Brent said as he stood next to Hilt in the entrance hall to their lavish two-room suite, staring at the man in the doorway. The man was wearing a gray-on-gray uniform with too many buttons to count and white gloves, and he was holding Brent's perfectly ironed tuxedo shirt out in front of him like it was the flowing cape of a matador. "I called down to ask for an iron, and they send me a guy instead who irons my shirt in five minutes flat."

The man bowed, handing over the shirt, and Brent fished in his pockets for a handful of euros. The man bowed again, taking the tip, and Brent shut the door after him.

"I mean really," Brent continued as he went back to the floor-length mirror on the wall by one of the room's many closets. "You don't get service like that in Costa Rica. Or Montana, for that matter."

"In Costa Rica—" Hilt started.

"The guy would have blown me for that many euros," Brent finished for him. "Fair enough. But he would have done a shit job ironing my shirt."

Hilt laughed, going to work on his bow tie. His tuxedo had come out of his suitcase with the creases perfect and the lapels straight. Brent had no idea how Hilt had managed the feat, especially considering the distance they'd just traveled. Costa Rica to London to Nice, and then, of course, the helicopter. Brent had never been on a helicopter before. The rotors were surprisingly loud, even through the cushioned headphones he'd been given by the pilot. Still, there was something so incredibly upscale about a helicopter trip; he couldn't help thinking the whole time, *This is how rich people live.* It didn't hurt that the view down through the bubble-glass windows was one of the most spectacular on earth: the pristine beaches, twisting roadways, anachronistic castles, and craggy hills of southern France flashing by at 150 miles per hour. Brent would have asked the pilot to slow down if they hadn't already been late for the party.

Nowadays, it seemed like they were always late for a party. Probably because there seemed to always *be* a party. The Gumball 3000 and the Playboy Mansion had been just the beginning; now that they were throwing themselves heavily into high-profile sponsorships and events, they were charting up the frequent-flier miles on a near-daily basis. Celebrity golf tournaments, major rock concerts, television specials, and, of course, huge poker events, all over the world. Brent had seen places he'd only read about before—Paris, London, Tokyo, Hong Kong—and now Monte Carlo, which from the air had looked like something out of a Disneyfied fairy tale, a gilded little enclave of castles and

ornate mansions dug right into the top of a mountain. The cab ride from the helicopter landing pad up to their hotel only amplified the fantasy, the taxi twisting up that serpent's tail of a road. It was not lost on Brent that once a year these same roads hosted the premier Formula 1 race—the Grand Prix—which began and ended right in front of their destination, the famous Hôtel De Paris.

Lavish did not begin to express what the hotel was like. Situated across a manicured plaza from the famed Monte Carlo Casino, the 150-year-old building was a palace of jutting domes and spires, elegant marble columns, arched windows, and ornate stone carvings; a veritable army of bellmen met them at the front steps, ushering them past the statue of a mounted Louis XIV, through the cavernous lobby, and beneath the massive chandelier that hung from the domed skylight, crystal tentacles painting the very air in strokes of reflected light.

Their suite was only slightly less impressive than the lobby: antique furniture, canopied beds, a miniature version of the crystal chandelier hanging from the arched living room ceiling, a balcony with a view of the courtyard and the equally palatial casino. And the party they had come halfway around the world to attend was presumably already in full swing in one of the many private gambling parlors—swank caverns of velvet and marble.

Fitting, that the event was being held in the most famous casino in the world—since it was sponsored by Neteller, the now billion-dollar Internet payment processor that had become the de facto financial pillar of the online gambling community. Nearly three-quarters of AbsolutePoker.com's deposits went through Neteller, and Brent guessed the numbers were similar for all of its

competitors—certainly Party Poker, PokerStars, Full Tilt, and Greg Pierson's Ultimate Bet, which had become the big four in terms of revenue, with AP following in fifth.

"If anybody should be blowing us," Brent continued, taking his shirt into the marble-lined bathroom just beyond the entrance to the suite—one of two similar bathrooms, each nearly as big as Brent's entire old apartment back in Montana, with a soaking tub the size of his first car—"it's the guys from Neteller. They did hundreds of millions of dollars this year, a lot of it facilitating online poker deposits. It's no wonder they sprang for a helicopter. If it wasn't for us, they'd be hustling porn like the rest of the Internet."

Brent exchanged the collared shirt he had worn on the trip from San José for the tux shirt, watching himself in a back-lit mirror as he went to work on the buttons. He noticed that the floor was particularly warm beneath his bare feet. Heated marble tiles, he realized. They really hadn't spared any expense. He shouldn't have been surprised. Neteller was a class act—very different from most of the other payment processors Absolute Poker did business with when Neteller wasn't available to handle a percentage of their accounts.

It was funny—a year before, Brent had never heard of Neteller, or of any payment processors—hell, he hadn't even known that there *were* businesses that processed credit card payments over the Internet. But now he was fast becoming an expert in the financial gymnastics of the online world.

After he'd shifted from customer service to fraud and bank security, he'd assumed that his job title would remain stable for the foreseeable future; when one of the banking guys walked into

his office not three months ago and placed a stack of papers on his desk, he had thought it was just more financials to look over for instances of potential credit card fraud. But then the guy had asked him if he'd be interested in yet another job change; he and Scott wanted to know if Brent would want to be responsible for payment processing—essentially, handling all aspects of the movement of money in and out of the company from players, via the middlemen processors such as Neteller and PayPal.

Brent had jumped at the opportunity. It seemed like a great area for growth, and a chance to learn about the inner workings of a business that was integral to how online commerce functioned. On his very first day, looking through those papers, he realized that Neteller had been overcharging them on transactions; they'd been taking 8 percent off all deposits to the company, when the number should have been closer to 4. One phone call, and Neteller had immediately handed AP a three-hundred-thousand-dollar credit. It had been just that easy—there was so much damn money coming through the business, nobody was going to haggle over a few hundred thousand here or there.

The deeper Brent dug into the processing world, the more he realized that the class acts such as Neteller and PayPal were an exception to the rule. Most of the other processing companies were extremely shady—appearing and disappearing overnight, often incorporated out of island territories that Brent hadn't even heard of and run through banks he wasn't even sure existed; these were companies you gave your credit card numbers to at your own risk. But sometimes they were also necessary; the flow of player money moving in and out of the poker site was constant and hungry, and the middlemen made that flow possible.

Of course, it was only Brent's opinion, but some of what these processors did struck him as taking place in a bit of a gray area—shady, if not outright illegal. As some bigger American banks enacted in-house rules governing the use of their credit cards for online gambling—even though there was no clear U.S. law concerning Internet gaming, other than sports betting—some of these middleman processors set up accounts that effectively hid where the money was actually going. Instead of online poker, the middleman processors would earmark the credit card deposits for items such as T-shirts, golf balls, even online flower delivery. That way, the banks profited from the transactions, Absolute Poker could still earn its rake, and the players could enjoy their poker.

In Brent's mind, even though the means were a little bit shady, when properly implemented, the result didn't seem to hurt anybody. The customers who were giving their credit card numbers to the processors were doing so willingly, because they wanted to play poker. And Brent didn't believe that the banks were actually being fooled; one day their credit cards were being used to deposit a million dollars in money earmarked for an online poker site; the next day, the same million dollars was deposited to purchase T-shirts and golf balls? They knew exactly what was going on, and they didn't care. It was just the way the business worked.

The banks made money. Absolute Poker made money. The players got to play poker. And Brent got an all-expenses-paid trip to Monte Carlo.

Brent came out of the bathroom and retrieved his tux jacket and bow tie from where they were hanging by the bedroom dressing table. Hilt looked ready to go; he was standing by the door to the balcony, bathed in the glow from the plaza lights, the

reflected glory of the ancient casino. Hilt glanced at Brent, who had finally gotten his bow tie to sit straight and was straightening his sleeves over his cuffs, and smiled.

"You look like you're about to get married."

Brent blushed. He knew Hilt wasn't just talking about the tux, or the party they were about to attend. Brent had been opening up to Hilt during the whole trip from Costa Rica; Hilt knew that the new job wasn't the only thing that had changed in Brent's world over the past few months. Right before they'd left for Monte Carlo, his personal life had gone a little bit crazy.

He'd first gotten the news while in Vancouver—he'd gone to Canada as soon as Pete was there, and the team had gotten the new headquarters up and running, on the third floor of a sleek office tower in a prize corner of that city's financial district. Brent had been settling in for an indefinite stay in the Canadian city. The team had really set up a first-class operation, hiring a top-notch CFO with an MBA from one of the elite Canadian schools—a genial six-foot-three, 250-pound Fijian transplant who'd just ended a stint running the accounting department of a Fortune 500 banking giant—and Brent had been looking forward to living in a city where everyone spoke English and the power stayed on twenty-four hours a day. And then, quite accidentally, he'd run into a friend who'd just come from San José; the man had mentioned that he'd recently been at a party back in Costa Rica and had seen one of Brent's ex-girlfriends—a beautiful Colombian national Brent remembered fondly, even though they'd only been together a few months. The friend had casually mentioned that the woman had just had a baby boy—and then, still in passing, he'd said, "And he looks just like you."

It was something Brent couldn't ignore. An hour later he had called her up.

"I heard you had a baby," he'd said.

"I had your baby," she'd responded. "If you want, you can come see him. If you want to never call me again, that's fine too. It's up to you."

Brent had gotten on the next flight to San José. When he met the kid for the first time, he just sat there, staring at him, thinking he looked more like some sort of wrinkled alien than a baby. He'd actually poked the kid a few times, just to see if he was real. And then all he had wanted to do was hug him and hold him. Deep down, he knew. He was a dad, and nothing else in his life would matter as much as that.

Hilt might have been joking, but Brent knew, after the trip to Monte Carlo, that he wasn't going to be returning to Vancouver. He'd be going back to Costa Rica. And it was early to say for sure, but he didn't think marriage was out of the question. That kid had changed everything.

"Let's see how the party goes first," Brent responded, following Hilt toward the door. "If you treat me right, we can skip the wedding and go right to the honeymoon."

Five hours later Brent found himself stumbling down a cement spiral stairwell, out-of-his-mind drunk, searching desperately for a bathroom. In the portion of his brain that was still functioning, he knew he'd taken a wrong turn somewhere back in the casino, but the minute the fifth shot of sambuca had hit the back of his throat, all reason and sense of direction had

gone out the door, and he'd become a man on a mission, navigating entirely on determined, if faulty, autopilot.

The party had been beyond extravagant: a buffet that seemed to go on for miles, offering everything from piles of stone-crab legs the length of baseball bats to vats of beluga caviar that could have filled a sandbox; four working bars staffed by a half dozen staggeringly beautiful bartenders, all amazonian Eastern Europeans who looked like they'd stepped off the set of a James Bond movie. Everyone in tuxes, and everyone on their best behavior. Except maybe Brent himself, who wasn't sure when he'd gone from happily buzzed to frighteningly blitzed.

When that last shot of sambuca hit, he'd known what he needed to do—just not where he could do it. He'd stumbled around looking for a bathroom for a few minutes, before pushing his way through a heavy curtain and into the stairwell—and now he was descending into what appeared to be the subterranean depths of the Monte Carlo Casino, looking for somewhere to throw up.

One more step, foot after foot—and suddenly, his leather loafer slipped on the concrete and he went down, landing on his ass. Then he was sliding forward, step to step, and the motion was simply too much for his stomach to handle. He leaned to the side and the warm vomit spewed out, splashing down the cement stairs right next to him.

Christ. He slid a few more steps down the stairwell, vomiting as he went—and then landed on the floor of a hallway, dazed, head spinning. There was a door right in front of him, another to his right. He knew he had to make a choice. One of them might be a bathroom, he supposed. Then again, it was just as likely that

it was some sort of torture chamber, where they took people who had the gall to vomit all over the most famous casino on earth.

He slowly staggered to his feet. He was about to open the door directly in front of him when he heard the crackle of a radio from behind it; he couldn't understand the French words, but the radio definitely gave him pause. It sounded like the sort of thing a security guard would carry.

He quickly shifted right and headed for door number two.

It wasn't a bathroom—it was even better. A second later he found himself outside in an alley behind the casino. To his left, a narrow road curved up the hill back toward the plaza; elegant lampposts lit the way to his palatial hotel and the comfort of his marble bathroom and canopied bed.

Wiping vomit from his lips, he staggered upward, lamppost to lamppost. It dawned on him as he went that these were the same curves the Formula 1 cars would take, tires screaming against the pavement, as the entire city applauded and cheered.

In Brent's inebriated mind, he was suddenly one of those race cars, tearing through the city—it was a wonderful feeling, a high that felt like it was never going to end.

CHAPTER 24

Pete read through the fax on his desk for the third time, but still the numbers didn't change. His gold-plated Cross pen— etched with the SAE insignia, a gift from the house when he'd handed over presidential duties to the president before Brent— danced in the air, rising and dipping precipitously between his first and second fingers; still, he couldn't bring himself to mark up the document. Because really, what was there to say?

The fax was only the first page of the report that the M&A fund had made of their nearly complete third-year financials, but it told Pete, and everyone else, everything he needed to know. The company's revenues had increased by more than 100 percent, year over year, and they were now funded at a valuation of more than one hundred million dollars. Since Pete was working in accounting and heading up an affiliate team, Scott had asked him to go through the report and add his input, point out things they might need to work on in the last few weeks before they

were set to begin their IPO talks—but there was very little that Pete could think to add. One-hundred-million-dollar valuation, revenues exceeding forty million a year, and all of it increasing at a rapid pace.

Pete spun the pen between his fingers, its gold surface flashing in the sunlight that streamed in off the bay, reflected through the large picture window behind his desk. The view was spectacular, a straight shot through a corner of the financial district to the water, high enough to see over the low pincushion of office buildings, with sight lines to the mountains to the east as well. But in the past few months he'd gotten used to that view; the giant numbers on the fax were much harder to digest.

Still, he had to give Scott something. His salary had already been bumped up twice since they'd launched the Vancouver office and management had hired their new Fijian-Canadian CFO, who went by his first name, Shay. He began to scribble in the margins of the fax about dropping some of Brent's more disreputable payment processors when he heard a tapping on his office door.

He looked up to see Megann Cassidy, one of his marketing department heads—another recent hire, Canadian with an advanced business degree from McGill—standing in the doorway. Her face looked pale, and she was leaning into his office like she was trying to make herself even smaller than her five-foot-five frame.

"Mr. Barovich? I think there's something going on in the lobby."

Pete put his pen down on top of the fax.

"What do you mean?"

"Well, these two ladies came in a few minutes ago," she said, pausing as Pete nodded. Pete had seen them come in; he had been on his way back from lunch and had just gone through the glass doors that led from the lobby into the cubicled Marketing and PR Department when he caught sight of the two women. The truth was, they would have been hard to miss. Both were dressed in dark gray business pants, matching blouses, and heavy gray jackets. One was tall, at least five ten, the other around five seven. Both had dark hair—one in a tight ponytail, the other bunned up on top of her cubic head. Neither had been smiling, which was strange, considering it was Canada. Everyone seemed to smile in Canada.

"Well," Megann continued, "they just showed Lucinda their badges. They're agents with the RCMP."

Pete stared at her. RCMP: the Royal Canadian Mounted Police, Canada's version of the FBI.

"What do they want?"

"I don't know—" Megann started, her voice shaking, and then the phone on Pete's desk buzzed to life, signaling a call from the lobby. He waved Megann away, and she backed out of the office in full reverse, shutting his door behind her. Pete took a breath, then lifted the receiver.

"What's going on, Lucinda?"

The moment Pete heard Lucinda Palmer's voice, he knew that something big was happening. The secretary was as fierce as they came; in her midthirties, she favored leather skirts, high boots, and thick wool jackets, and she had been hired to man the front lobby specifically because she knew how to handle people without ever losing her cool. It was a lesson Pete had learned run-

ning numerous businesses since college: the customer may always be right, but he's often also an asshole.

But this was something different. These women weren't customers, they were federal agents. And Lucinda sounded like she was almost in tears. She told Pete that the women were asking for whoever was in charge. She'd tried to connect them to Shay, but Shay wasn't answering his phone. Shay's secretary had told her that he wasn't there, but Pete knew that wasn't true—Shay had returned from lunch a few minutes before he himself had. So if Shay was avoiding them—well, maybe that wasn't such a bad idea.

"Tell them I'm sorry too, I'm just on my way out."

He quickly hung up and rose from his desk. He crossed to the door of his office, quietly pulled it open, took one step out into the hall—and saw his newly hired CFO about five yards away, down on his hands and knees, literally crawling behind the row of cubicles. The heavyset Fijian cut an absurd figure; all six foot three of him, dressed in a tightly fitting tailored suit and tie, his face inches from the carpet as he tried to stay below the sight line of the women on the other side of the glass wall that separated the cubicles from the lobby.

Pete realized with a start that Shay was heading for the fire exit. Within minutes, the CFO crawled the last few feet to the fire door, then raised himself to a crouch. He looked back at Pete and made a frantic gesture with a tanned hand, telling him to follow. Then the man put his weight into one thick shoulder and leaned into the door. The door came open, and then Shay was gone, sprinting heavily down the fire stairs.

Pete swallowed. He glanced toward the glass lobby wall; he could barely make out the two federal agents, the ponytail

and the bun, as they berated Lucinda. He knew he had to make an immediate decision, because any second now, those women were going to push past the secretary—and God only knew what might happen next.

So he did the only thing he could think of, and dropped to the floor. Hands in front of knees, he crawled toward the fire exit as fast as he could.

Five minutes later he was standing next to Shay at the window of the Starbucks across the street, watching the RCMP agents rifling through his office. He had no idea what they were looking for, or even if they had the legal right to do what they were doing. He and Shay had put three calls through to Scott and the Absolute Poker legal team, but they hadn't heard back yet. He was pretty sure Scott was actually on vacation somewhere in Europe with a girl he'd begun seeing seriously; Pete had heard from Garin that the girl was a real head case, and not a long-term potential—par for the course, since Scott's relationships usually involved so much drama. At the moment, Pete wouldn't have given a damn if she were a spear-toting harpy. He needed to talk to Scott or their lawyers, because he had no idea what they were supposed to do next.

Another twenty minutes went by, he and Shay standing in the Starbucks in near silence, and finally the two RCMP agents left the way they had come, through the building's front doors. Pete and his CFO waited another ten minutes, then decided it was safe to go back inside—via the elevator this time, not the fire escape.

When the elevator deposited them back on the third floor, a loud buzzing sound greeted them. It was coming from the financial wing, where Brent had set up his processing department before he'd gone back to Costa Rica. It took Pete a full minute to realize what the buzzing was—and when he did, his face went a shade paler. *Paper shredders, running nonstop.* He had no idea what, exactly, was being shredded, or by whom. And he decided that he didn't want to know.

Instead, he led Shay into the lobby, where they found Lucinda slumped behind her desk, in tears. After she'd gone through a box of tissues, she told Pete that the RCMP agents had first demanded to know who was in charge—and then they'd demanded to know what, exactly, was going on in the third-floor offices. Lucinda had been both terrified and bewildered; the RCMP couldn't be there to arrest anyone, because they weren't even sure what sort of business the company was in. In fact, as far as Pete could gather from the questions they'd asked Lucinda, the agents were only there because a high-level Canadian official was convinced something illegal had to be transpiring, simply because of the amount of money that was moving through the building in such a short period.

It was ridiculous, sheer harassment—and yet Pete could understand the terror Lucinda was feeling. When she told him that fully three-quarters of the staff had already quit—dropping their ID cards on the lobby desk on their way out—he realized that this wasn't the sort of trouble they could simply get past. He looked at Shay and could see that his CFO was thinking the same thing. If the RCMP had sent agents to harass them in the middle of the day, there was a good chance that it was just the beginning.

Soon there would be more agents, search warrants, maybe even confiscations.

Pete also knew that in the back of those offices there were computer servers engaged in running their hundred-million-dollar business; if the RCMP confiscated those servers, even under illegitimate orders, it could destroy Absolute Poker.

He thanked Lucinda, did his best to comfort her, then accepted her resignation. He told her that they would pay everyone who had quit double their expected severance. Then he pulled Shay aside and lowered his voice. "We need to find a U-Haul truck—fast."

Ten minutes past midnight, and Pete rolled the oversize U-Haul the last few yards into the parking lot behind his office building with the engine off. Shay, in the seat next to him, hunched as low as a 250-pound person could hunch, was sweating beneath his three-piece suit.

"Are we really going to do this?" Shay asked, but Pete didn't answer. He had already spoken to Scott twice, and he knew that they didn't have a choice. As wrongheaded as the RCMP seemed to him, there was no reason to believe that they wouldn't go after their servers next—and that simply couldn't happen. As far as Pete knew, the company hadn't broken any Canadian laws, and the servers were their property. The computers themselves were worth six figures, but the information on them was worth potentially many millions.

Pete got out of the truck, Shay behind him. They made their way through the darkened lobby. When they got to the elevators,

Pete swiped his key card into the after-hours security slot—and instantly discovered that his key card no longer worked. Another really bad sign. He looked at Shay, wondering how they were going to get through, when he heard noise from the far corner of the lobby. He turned to see a cleaning man in a blue janitorial uniform dragging a heavy vacuum cleaner toward the thick shag carpet.

"Wait here," Pete said to Shay. Then he hurried over to the janitor. The man recognized him, of course; Pete and Shay had often worked late since setting up the new offices. It wasn't unusual to see them there well after midnight.

"I think my card got demagnetized," Pete said, offering as easy a smile as he could. "I wonder if you could help me out."

Before the man could answer, Pete pulled out his wallet and took out a fifty-dollar bill. The janitor looked at the money, then shrugged, smiling back.

"Happens all the time," he said. And he handed Pete his own key card. "Just bring it back on your way out. I should be here all night."

Arriving on the third floor, Pete and Shay went to work like men possessed. They found a pair of huge metal roller carts in a supply closet behind Lucinda's desk, then went through the offices, grabbing everything they could get their hands on—not just the huge servers, which were boxy steel cabinets the size of small tables, but also laptop computers, monitors, phones, and any notebooks that looked important. All of it needed to be done in one trip—two people, two roller carts, and enough stuff to fill an entire office floor. Since they could fit only the crucial material, they had to leave behind hundreds of thousands of dol-

lars' worth of equipment. But there was no choice. An hour later, having gotten as much onto the carts as they could manage, they headed for the elevator. Then Pete remembered one more thing. He rushed to his office and retrieved his gold SAE pen. Shoving it into his jacket pocket, he ran back to Shay, and they took the elevator back down to the lobby.

Adrenaline pumping, they began to push the two roller carts across the freshly vacuumed thick shag rug. Just as they reached the doors leading out to the parking lot, the janitor rushed toward them. Pete remembered the key card, yanking it from his pocket and offering it to the man. The man grabbed it, then lowered his voice.

"I just got a call from the owner. He said the cops were on the lookout for anyone who worked in your company. I told him you just left—so you've got about five minutes at the most to get out of here. Good luck."

Pete and Shay sprinted the last few yards to the U-Haul truck, pushing the metal carts in front of them. They threw the computers and equipment into the back, trashing most of it in their haste, then slammed the doors and started the engine.

They could see police lights flashing in the rearview mirror as they pulled away from the office building.

It was 5 A.M. by the time they finally got Scott on the phone. They were in Shay's apartment, in a corner of his brightly lit kitchen, standing a few feet from the refrigerator—because that was where Shay's only landline was connected and neither of them wanted to use their cells.

As Pete had guessed, Scott was somewhere outside of Paris; there was a woman's voice in the background, but it was hard to tell from her accent where she was from. Pete had barely gotten three words across to his friend before Shay had calmly taken the phone out of his hand. Leaning back against a granite kitchen counter, the oversize CFO methodically told Scott exactly what had happened. He explained that after they had left, they had made some inquiries and had found out that the RCMP had indeed opened up an investigation.

Pete couldn't hear exactly how Scott responded, but obviously he wasn't taking the situation quite as seriously as Shay wanted—because one second later Shay's face turned bright red, and everything calm and methodical about him went right out the fucking window. He began screaming into the receiver, *"You better fucking figure this out, and get us legal right now! You better get us some fucking lawyers and get this shit under control—"*

Pete wrestled the phone out of Shay's hand. He gave the man a moment to calm himself down, then put the receiver to his own ear and listened to Scott, who was obviously trying his best to remain rational in the wake of their CFO's meltdown.

"What do you want us to do?" Pete finally asked. Shay had slumped to the floor, shaking his head.

"I want you to get your asses back to Costa Rica," Scott responded quietly. Then he hung up the phone.

Pete replaced the receiver, then dropped to the kitchen floor next to Shay and rested his chin in his hands. Shay glanced at him.

"Are we doing something illegal?" Shay asked.

Pete didn't answer. He didn't know what to say. He had sold his whole life and moved his wife and dogs to Vancouver, he had

been there a few months, and the whole thing felt like it was blow-ing up around him. He was only twenty-nine years old, but even at that young age he knew that this wasn't the way a billion-dollar company was supposed to be run. And up until that moment—that vivid, seemingly frozen moment with his CFO on his hands and knees and federal officers standing in the lobby—Pete had thought that Scott's company was just like any other rapidly ex-panding Internet corporation, providing a service for millions of people, revenues skyrocketing as the world moved online. In just a few weeks they were supposed to start preparing for a billion-dollar IPO. Hell, there was still a fax sitting on his desk in his ravaged office with numbers telling him that the company Scott had founded was worth more than a hundred million dollars at that very moment, with revenues in the tens of millions.

But now he had to wonder.

What, exactly, had he gotten himself into?

And where did they go from here?

CHAPTER 25

Two weeks later, on a Friday night in September, Pete still hadn't quite gotten a handle on what happened in Vancouver. The next few days had been a whirlwind, setting up the rescued servers in an apartment near their raided offices so that the accounts could keep spinning—a hundred-million-dollar company basically run out of a one-bedroom, four-hundred-bucks-a-month walk-up—and then hightailing it out of Canada, wife and dogs in tow. As far as Pete knew, he personally wasn't in any trouble. He hadn't broken any laws that he knew of, and there hadn't been any Canadian federal claims made against Absolute Poker either. But Scott hadn't wanted to take any chances—if the Canadians didn't want them there, they would leave.

That's how it had been with Absolute Poker from day one: if someone wanted to regulate them, they were happy to comply with any and all rules. In the UK, online poker was indeed taxed and regulated, and as Party Poker had proven, you could success-

fully IPO on their exchanges. In many other countries as well, Absolute Poker was licensed and approved, paying whatever fees were necessary—or, in other cases, simply blocking people from playing when a country made it clear that it wasn't legal to play from there. Players from China, for instance, weren't accepted by Absolute Poker; it was as easy as blocking any computer with a Chinese ISP.

But Canada, obviously, was momentarily unclear about how it viewed the business—so for now, Vancouver was done. Pete was in Costa Rica, winding down the Vancouver operations, trying to help the team ready a first-world company for a billion-dollar IPO in a third-world setting. It wasn't easy, but he had no reason to believe they couldn't make it work. Everyone they talked to, from the bankers to the lawyers, believed that the company was weeks away from being valued at over a billion.

He glanced at his watch and realized it was nearly nine thirty; Brandi was going to kill him if he stayed any later. She didn't like living in San José, and she had made it abundantly clear that the stay was going to be temporary. Pete had assured her that as soon as that IPO went through, he would have enough shares in the company for them to live anywhere in the world she wanted.

He flicked off his computer and rose from his chair, his eye-line rising above the edge of his cubicle. Scott had given him one of the larger prefab squares; he didn't have real walls or a window, but at least he had two computer screens and easy access to the kitchen, which was really a pair of refrigerators and a sink out of which spurted water he wouldn't have washed his dogs in.

He reached for his briefcase, tucking a few closing reports on Vancouver into the side pocket, and was about to head toward the

stairwell that led down to the parking lot when he noticed a dull yellow light coming from the far end of the office. Someone was in the very last cubicle, hunched over a computer screen.

Pete knew Scott and Hilt had headed out earlier, Shane was at home, and Garin had taken a three-day weekend to visit relatives back in the States. It could have been one of the Costa Rican employees, but he doubted it; it was extremely unlikely that any of them would have been in the office on a Friday night, especially since it wasn't raining outside—a brief gap in the unrelenting rainy season—and most would be on their way to the beach.

That left Brent. Which was odd as well; since returning to Costa Rica to start his new family, Brent had settled into at least a semblance of a more normal working life—a Friday night was an unusual time to find him at a computer screen.

But as Pete circled around the cubicles and approached the glow, he saw that it was indeed the youngest member of their team. Brent didn't look up as Pete slid into the cubicle behind him, and Pete was about to give him a little shove to wake him up when he saw the way Brent was gripping the edge of the desk beneath his computer's keyboard.

"Hey, man, you okay?" he asked. Brent didn't glance up from the screen. Pete looked toward the glow and saw that the screen was filled with video—an assembly hall of some sort, with wooden chairs and benches, most of them empty, and a scrawl of writing beneath. Pete read some of the words—and saw immediately that Brent was watching a feed, either recorded or live, from C-SPAN. Pete had never watched C-SPAN before, but he could tell that what Brent was looking at was some sort of U.S. congressional session.

"I don't think that I am," Brent finally answered. "I don't think any of us are." His voice sounded strange.

Pete put a hand on his shoulder. "What are you watching? Did something just happen?"

"As far as I can tell, they just voted through something called the Unlawful Internet Gambling and Enforcement Act of 2006. I've gotten like twenty e-mails about it in the past ten minutes. The UIGEA, they call it."

Pete squinted at the screen, reading more of the scrawl beneath the picture.

"It says they just voted on a Safe Port Act. It says it's a bill about protecting our ports from terrorism," he said.

"Yeah, that's the thing. They tacked the antigambling bill onto the Safe Port Act, because they knew nobody would vote against an antiterrorism bill. Most of the people who voted it through didn't even read the antigambling addendum—they just voted to protect our ports. The bill itself, it's basically the same antigambling bullshit a couple of moralizing senators have been failing to get anybody to take seriously for years, but now it's passed through Congress. On the last day of the congressional session, with almost nobody around to even take a look at what they're voting on."

Brent hit keys on his keyboard, pulling up a handful of e-mails he'd gotten from friends across the industry who had been monitoring the legal back-and-forth that had led up to the congressional vote. Pete speed-read through the summaries— and as he got to the gist of each e-mail, he felt the color leaching from his face.

According to Brent's experts, the UIGEA was really the

brainchild of two conservative senators—Bill Frist, a Republican from Tennessee, and Jon Kyl, a Republican from Arizona—who'd come up with the ingenious plan of attaching it as a last-minute amendment to the Safe Port Act—no matter that Internet gambling had nothing to do with protecting U.S. ports from terrorists. The two antigambling senators, who had run for their positions on morality platforms, knew that trying to take down a pastime that millions of Americans were already enjoying was too difficult, so they'd concocted what was essentially a sneak attack.

The bill didn't make *playing* online poker illegal. In fact, the bill didn't even make running or owning an online poker site illegal. What the bill made illegal was dealing in online gambling proceeds. Specifically: *"The Act prohibits gambling businesses from knowingly accepting payments in connection with the participation of another person in a bet or wager that involves the use of the Internet and that is unlawful under any federal or state law."*

It wasn't entirely clear from the bill what constituted a "gambling business," but the addition of the phrase "unlawful under any federal or state law" seemed to give a lot of leeway to prosecutors who wanted to go after an Internet company. All you'd need to do would be to find a state with a particularly harsh definition of *gambling*—and you could use that definition to go after any website that took money from a player living there.

Poker, Pete firmly believed, was for the most part a game of skill. But he also knew that in a few states—New York, for example—there were some pretty wide definitions of what constituted illegal gambling, definitions that could seem to include even games that were mostly skill. So what, exactly, did this

mean? It was a bill; it had now gone through Congress. It still had to be signed by the president, which would take some time. But what did this *mean*?

"This seems crazy," Brent was saying, tapping the screen. "It doesn't target the players. It doesn't even target the game. But it makes the movement of money illegal, if that money is used for illegal gambling. But how do you define illegal gambling? Every lawyer we've talked to says under the Wire Act of 1961 it doesn't mean poker. But for players playing from the U.S.—I guess this is saying it varies state by state?"

Pete rubbed a hand through his hair. "Have you talked to Scott?"

"A few times since these e-mails started coming in. He's pretty pissed about this too. I think some of the shareholders are running around like the building just got set on fire. The lawyers, though—most still believe the legislation isn't clear, especially for a private, international company like ours. And on top of that, the lawyers have brought him and Hilt a fairly radical offer, which they're kicking around."

"What's that?"

"You ever heard of Joseph Norton—the Canadian Indian chief?"

Pete raised his eyebrows. It was a name out of left field, but having just dealt with the Royal Canadian Mounties and taken a look at Canadian gambling law, he had indeed heard of Joseph Tokwiro Norton—the former grand chief of the Mohawk Council of Kahnawake, near Montreal. Norton was a bit of a legend in Canada. Story was, he'd once stopped an RCMP raid by literally blocking federal troops from crossing a bridge into Mohawk

land. An actual armed standoff—First Nations against federal agents with guns and tanks. Norton had negotiated a peaceful resolution and had become a hero in his community. In recent years he had become a successful businessman and had established the Kahnawake Gaming Commission, which licensed and regulated Internet gaming sites. Because he operated out of designated First Nations territory, he wasn't bound by Canadian law; even if there had been any clear rules against poker, they wouldn't affect his business.

"What about him?"

"I think he's about to become the owner of Absolute Poker. He's approached our legal team, made it clear he's interested in buying the company."

Pete looked at Brent. "We're going to sell the company to an Indian chief?"

But when he thought it through, it made sense. Certainly, it added a step between them and this UIGEA bill, and there was no question that under Mohawk law an online poker company would be legal. However, from what Pete was reading, that wasn't exactly what this bill was going after. On a straight reading of the UIGEA, running an online poker company wasn't illegal. Playing online poker wasn't illegal. The only thing that was illegal was accepting money from U.S. players. They were going after the flow of money—and the more Pete thought about it, the more he realized that this was going to change everything.

"It's like Prohibition all over again," he said. "Every company is going to have to go through the same thought process—do we shut down now, just close up shop? Do we cut out of the U.S. market and only go international—even though that would just

about kill us, or any of our competitors, because as an industry, eighty percent of our players are American? Or do we just keep doing what we're doing, take our chances, and hope this is more smoke than fire?"

The way Brent was still gripping the desk beneath his computer, Pete could tell they were sharing the same thought. They were weeks away from starting the process of their IPO, and this was going to ruin everything. This bill, this UIGEA, snuck through on the tail of some antiterrorist Safe Port Act, wasn't just smoke, and it wasn't just fire.

It was Armageddon.

CHAPTER 26

The panic had reached epidemic proportions; Scott could see it in the eyes of every person he passed as he strolled the last few yards through the huge, warehouse-like conference center's main floor, toward the elevators that led into the hotel. They all looked as though they were melting down inside, succumbing to a fever so fierce and virulent, it threatened to consume them.

Only when the elevator doors shut behind him, leaving him alone in the brightly lit, thickly carpeted steel box, buffeted by invisible waves of Spanish Muzac—some version of a Beatles song, Paul McCartney run through a vocal translator and backed up by what sounded like a mariachi band— did he let his body show the toll the last two weeks had taken, allow the true weight he'd been carrying around since the bill had gone through Congress to settle across his taut features.

It had been an emotional roller coaster, from the first minute his phones had lit up with the news about the UIGEA sneak

attack—in Scott's mind, the act had come out of nowhere, tacked onto that Safe Port Act like a legal version of Pearl Harbor, with no warning to anyone in the industry—to the day he and his team had left for Barcelona, for the Internet gaming industry's annual conference. They had planned the trip months earlier, as had everyone else; but nobody could have foreseen that the conference—usually an event marked by partying to excess, good food, and plenty of optimism in an industry that was minting money day by day—would become ground zero for a community facing what appeared to be a mortal blow.

Scott coughed, trying to clear his throat as he watched the digital display on the elevator count upward. He had been talking nonstop since the bill had gone through, and he was in real danger of losing his voice. At first, the calls had all been the same—terror-stricken associates, competitors, and shareholders telling him that it was all over, that the gaming industry, as he knew it, was finished. Even Scott had joined in on the talk of gloom and doom; he'd immediately called Phil, his dad, and told him that it felt like they were done, that they'd have to shut down operations and just move on.

But by the end of the weekend, the calls had started to change in tenor, especially the ones coming from the many lawyers his company employed, who seemed to be split down the middle on what the UIGEA's passage really meant. To roughly 50 percent of the lawyers he spoke to, as a private, international company centered on a game primarily of skill, it wasn't clear that they were within the UIGEA's jurisdiction. Sure, the safe thing to do would be to shut down U.S. operations—which, for Absolute Poker, with most of its players coming from the States, would es-

sentially mean closing up shop—but if they continued to operate, what could really happen? Would Scott, personally, be breaking the law? Not Costa Rican law, for sure. Not international law. Would he be breaking U.S. law?

It wasn't entirely clear. And when, at the urging of shareholders, he and Hilt came up with the plan to sell the company to Norton and the Kahnawake Gaming Commission—for a $250 million promissory note and a portion of future earnings—it seemed a responsible and legitimate way to separate them further from that jurisdiction; certainly they weren't breaking any Canadian First Nations tribal laws by running an online poker company.

It was tough, mentally—the idea of selling the company, parting, even in a small way, with the entity he had built from an idea into a worldwide brand. But there was no denying that the world he lived in was now in a state of flux and chaos. One minute he was weeks away from being a near-billionaire; the next, he was facing a confusing legal battle that nobody he talked to could even give him a straight answer about.

Whatever he felt about the future of Absolute Poker, there was no question that the industry as a whole was reeling. The minute the bill passed, shock waves ripped through the online poker world. Party Poker, which after its multibillion-dollar IPO had become the biggest site, cut and ran from the American market. It paid a $1.05 million fine to the U.S. government and agreed to exit the U.S. market in exchange for amnesty from any future legal actions. And as a result, its value had gone from around $12 billion to around $2 billion—overnight.

The other publicly traded companies followed suit, and really,

they had no choice, because they had to answer to public share-holders who wouldn't face the risk of legal action, no matter how arbitrary it seemed from Scott's point of view. In the blink of an eye, dozens of companies shut down U.S. operations, basically giving up billions of dollars in revenue at the stroke of a conservative Republican senator's pen.

Although Scott and Hilt initially discussed doing the same, they eventually decided not to pull the trigger—at least not yet. For one thing, the venture capitalists and bankers they had been working with to capitalize themselves in preparation for their IPO basically forbade them from exiting the U.S. market. At that point the company had about four hundred employees, and with the vast majority of its revenues coming from the United States, it would be insolvent if it left. Further, UIGEA's jurisdiction arguably wasn't any more clearly damning to Absolute Poker than the original Wire Act had been—even the WTO was in the process of declaring online poker exempt from gaming statutes in a suit brought by Antigua against the United States for hampering its island-based gaming businesses. It didn't seem right that they should commit financial suicide based on what they saw as shaky law.

But even so, Scott knew that post-UIGEA, nothing would ever be the same. The way he understood it, his board of directors had been taking feedback from the lawyers, and had voted that the company was to maintain its U.S. presence. Scott felt left with no choice but to uphold that vote—after which, even though they seemed to have gotten what they wanted, 90 percent of the board had resigned, including Shane, along with a large percentage of the U.S. citizens who worked for the company.

Shane had decided to step down from his position—from the board, and from Absolute Poker as well—not because he believed the UIGEA prohibited Absolute Poker from doing business with U.S. players, but because he simply wasn't willing to risk facing prosecution or never being able to return to the United States.

Nobody wanted to be a cowboy, flaunting the law, even if that law seemed unfair and unclear. Scott felt trapped by the board's decision, but he also knew that if they did somehow go forward, there would have to be rules in place for the U.S. citizens who remained at the company. For the foreseeable future, lawyers told them that they'd probably have to restrict U.S. travel, maybe even ban it altogether. If prosecutors in the United States were going to try to go after them, they'd be looking for Americans on the inside of the poker companies to help build those cases.

Scott clenched his jaw as the elevator slowed near his floor. That he even had to think this way, like he was some sort of criminal for running an Internet poker company—it just seemed so unfair. Why was this happening? Why pass a bill like this, essentially trying to turn a moral issue into a legal one, rather than regulate them, like with cigarettes and alcohol, or give them a chance to regulate themselves? And why didn't anybody see how hypocritical this was? Nearly every state in the United States ran lotteries, which were clearly gambling, and nobody had a problem with that. Many states allowed horse racing, which was clearly gambling, and nobody had a problem with that. Vegas was built on casinos—hell, they'd rallied around the UIGEA, because it protected their established gambling interests and cut down their competition—and nobody had a problem with that. Poker itself was legal in most states, and nobody had a problem with that.

Christ, Scott could go on E*Trade that afternoon, open an account, and roll his entire 401(k) into it, start gambling on the stock market with no advisor and lose everything—and nobody would have a problem with that.

But online poker? Bill Frist was going to rally the American legal system to protect college kids from playing poker over the Internet? To Scott, it was the height of hypocrisy.

The elevator doors whooshed open, and Scott nearly tumbled out into a narrow hallway, with thick carpeting and sconces on the walls. He caught sight of Hilt immediately, at the entrance to the small, windowless conference room, standing with six other people; most looked like lawyers, in suits and ties, carrying briefcases—but right next to Hilt was Greg Pierson, the head and founder of Ultimate Bet.

At the sight of Hilt and Greg, Scott felt his shoulders rise, if only an inch or two—because even in the midst of all the chaos, terror, and misery of the moment, there might just be a silver lining.

Back when Scott was struggling to find a way to get Absolute Poker to the next level, he'd called on Greg for advice; now, with the industry imploding and the ground reeling beneath their feet, Greg had contacted him.

Ultimate Bet, like Party Poker, was a public company. By then, it had grown to be one of the biggest in the business—but like Absolute Poker, most of its customers lived in the States. If it shut down that part of its operation, Ultimate Bet wouldn't survive. Greg was in a real bind; he couldn't ignore the UIGEA, but if he responded the way Party Poker and the rest of the public companies had, it would be corporate suicide.

So he'd turned to Scott, just as Scott had once turned to him.

And over the past few days, Scott had come up with a solution. A crazy, wild, impossible solution. It wasn't going to undo the dramatically destructive results of the UIGEA passage, nor would it erase the threat of what might come because of it—but it was a response that would take advantage of the situation in the best way possible.

Scott painted a calm and cool mask across his features as he hurried down the hallway and followed Hilt, Greg, and the group of suits into the hotel conference room.

Thirty hours later, with $130 million changing hands, a deal was struck. A deal that instantly changed the landscape of an entire industry and put Scott and his friends in the dead center of a brand-new—and exceedingly dangerous—world.

I t was sometime after 2 A.M., but it was impossible to tell for sure, because there weren't any windows. Hell, from where Brent was sitting—sunk waist-deep into a huge beanbag chair in the center of a circular pit of overstuffed pillows, thick velvet drapes, and wicker tables surrounded by ornate, Arabian-looking hookahs bubbling out mysterious blue-smoke concoctions—the place didn't seem to even have walls. The ceiling curved upward, mosque-style, and was dripping with colorful strips of fabric that waved in an artificial desert breeze provided by huge air-conditioning vents. The club was vaguely Middle Eastern, but Brent couldn't be sure, because he wasn't entirely certain where he was. He didn't know Barcelona at all, and the streets of the damn city were as circuitous as those of downtown San José.

He'd been led to the place from the hotel by the three young men who were sharing the hookah pit with him; two were his counterparts from Ultimate Bet, about his age and dressed in similar club garb—black shirt, dark jeans, and a plastic wristband from the mixer back at the conference hotel—and the third was from PokerStars, which, now that Party Poker had dropped out of the American market, was the biggest company on the block. All three did the same job at their respective companies; like Brent, they were in charge of payment processing—which meant that all of them were about to see their worlds turned upside down.

In this new landscape, payment processing was going to change—in a big, big way. Although Neteller claimed it was going to stay in the business—UIGEA seemed unfair and unprosecutable, it said—Brent and his counterparts were very likely going to have to find many new middlemen, and soon, if they were to continue to collect deposits from American players. This meant dealing with the shadier and shadier outfits that would spring up to fill the void left by those who fled fearing criminal prosecution—no doubt charging exorbitant fees and turning what was already a shaky part of the business into something much dirtier. Because anyone willing to handle the flow of money in and out of Internet companies after UIGEA was risking being labeled criminal—and anyone willing to take that risk was probably already a little dirty to begin with.

Brent didn't want to think about what that made him; his name was on most of the financial transactions that had gone through his company since he'd been handed that stack of paper giving him the financial processing job. If anyone at Absolute Poker was flouting the new bill, it was him.

At the moment he wanted to think about anything other than that. He took a deep breath, letting the thick, flowery scent of Moroccan incense blend with whatever the hell was bubbling out of the hookahs, and was reaching for what had to be his fifth shot of rum when a shadow leaped across their pit of beanbags and another guy joined their group. He was lanky, and wearing a poorly fitted suit. *He must be a salesman of some sort,* Brent thought, and as he shook hands around the hookah, Brent heard him introduce himself as another Ultimate Bet employee, in the Marketing Department. His name was Joe or John, but Brent had never been great with names, especially when his throat was full of expensive Spanish rum.

He was barely paying attention as Joe or John—or maybe Joel—starting chatting excitedly about the conference, about some big development that had just been announced on the exhibit floor. He barely noticed as the other Ultimate Bet employees seemed to stiffen, then chatter loudly among themselves, their faces a mix of awe, excitement, and a little fear. He barely noticed anything—until he realized that everyone in the pit was now looking at him, and then he finally caught a few words that were still hanging in the thickly scented air.

"Um, what was that?"

"Did you hear the news?" the new guy said, his voice high-pitched. "Ultimate Bet just got bought out."

"Wow," Brent said, unfazed, reaching for another shot. "By who?"

"By who?" the guy responded. "By you."

Brent stopped, his hand frozen above the shot glass. "No way."

One of the other Ultimate Bet guys nodded. "It's true. I just

checked my phone, got three texts from our CEO. Guess what, Brent—now we all work for you."

Brent's head was still spinning as he sat in the waiting area of the Barcelona airport, just inside Security. He was hung-over as hell, maybe still a little drunk, and he smelled of alcohol, hookah smoke, and decidedly citric perfume. The perfume was French, though he was reasonably certain the girl had been Spanish; he was also pretty sure she was a waitress from the Middle Eastern club, though the night had gotten very hazy after the hookah pit. He'd woken up in a tiny first-floor apartment in the El Raval section of the city—which, he knew from a guidebook, was essentially the red-light district, a bit seedy, but also home to Barcelona's artistic community. So maybe the girl in the leather skirt, leather boots, and nothing else on the futon next to him was an artist? He hadn't woken her up to find out for sure. He'd just checked his phone, seen the twenty or so texts and calls from Hilt telling him he was going to miss his flight if he didn't get to the airport right away, and yanked on his dark jeans and shirt and gone in search of a taxi.

And somehow, he'd actually beaten Hilt to the airport—because he was already sitting there in the waiting area by his gate, his little carry-on bag under his chair, when he saw his brother's main business partner come out through Security and hurry toward him.

"We've still got a few minutes," Brent croaked, his throat still feeling the effects of all that rum. "The flight got delayed. They say ten more minutes."

Hilt nodded, then dropped into the empty seat next to Brent. Hilt looked even worse than Brent felt; it was obvious he hadn't slept at all. From what Brent had heard about the negotiations with Ultimate Bet, it wasn't surprising. Normally, a merger like that would take months of due diligence, haggling, give-and-take. Hilt and Scott had gotten the deal done in thirty hours. A promissory note of around $130 million, $5 million in cash, a profit-sharing agreement—and just like that, Absolute Poker/Ultimate Bet had become the third-largest online poker site in the world. Alongside PokerStars and Full Tilt Poker, the two other major private companies that had decided to stay in the U.S. market post-UIGEA, Absolute Poker was suddenly going to dominate a landscape that had been left open by the desertion of Party Poker and the rest of the publicly traded companies.

Which meant that literally overnight, Absolute Poker's revenues were going to go from around $200 million a year to as much as five times that amount. The amount Brent, personally, would facilitate the processing of would go from $25 million a month to closer to $75 million. It seemed like an insane, impossible number. And not only that: he was going to have to do so in an environment that was going to be more and more like the Wild West, because the rules were now completely uncertain and the middleman processors were going to get even shadier.

"You're going to have to make a decision," Hilt said, continuing a conversation he'd been having with Brent's voice mail. "And if you do decide to stick with us, you'll have to follow some new rules. First, we have to ask that you not go back to the U.S.—it's just too confusing, and we don't know what will happen. So nobody with an American passport is allowed to go through the

U.S. anymore, at least for the foreseeable future. We believe that in the long run, this bill won't hold up—and even if it does, it won't be prosecutable. But for now, if you go overseas, it has to be a direct flight."

Brent nodded. It was a strange thought, not being able to return to see family. It was giving up a lot. Weddings, funerals, birthdays—he'd be cut off from the people he'd grown up with, from parents and uncles and friends. For all of them, it would be an intense sacrifice. He knew that a good portion of the company's American employees had resigned right away, but Brent didn't want to walk, at least not yet. The thing was, his hands were already a little dirty; he'd been running payment processing for some time, and he knew that many of the little things his middlemen had done to get through the banks' sometimes arbitrary rules were probably technically illegal. Forms that earmarked deposits for the purchase of golf balls and T-shirts, instead of gaming, were going to look pretty bad, even if they hadn't hurt anyone, even if the banks had known what was going on.

"If you decide to leave," Hilt continued, "nobody is going to have any problem with that. But if you stay, we're going to bump your salary to twenty-five thousand a month. We're going to jump from four hundred employees to close to a thousand. And now we have offices in Costa Rica, Toronto, Vancouver, Malta, Montreal, Korea, the UK—the list is endless. You're going to be responsible for many of them. As well as almost two million dollars a day in player money."

Brent's hangover seemed to disintegrate as he listened to the numbers. *Twenty-five thousand dollars a month*. It seemed like a fortune. If things stayed like that for a while, he was going to get

rich. *Two million dollars a day*. Hell, all of them were going to get rich. He had no idea how much Scott and Hilt were getting paid. He couldn't begin to imagine. There was no more board, and a Canadian First Nations tribe was officially running the show. He wasn't even sure what roles Scott and Hilt were going to play going forward; for all he knew, they were going to fade into the background and let the company run itself. It was a true empire now, with huge revenues—and a worldwide structure.

"I'm in," Brent said. "One hundred percent."

Before Hilt could shake his hand, a voice broke over the airport intercom in Spanish, then in heavily accented English. Their flight to Malta was about to start boarding. *Malta*. Brent was certain he couldn't find the place on a map—and yet now he was on his way to visit a payment office there—an office that he now ran. A day ago he had been booked on a flight back to Costa Rica, toward his cubicle and his Neteller accounts and his handful of little headaches. Now he was on his way to what Hilt warned him could extend into a three-week around-the-world trip—to offices in a half dozen countries, offices that Brent now ran.

Brent rose to his feet, excited and scared. He reached into the front pocket of his jeans, looking for his passport. Instead, his fingers touched something that felt like crumpled plastic wrap. He pulled it out, looked at the thing—and then his entire body froze.

In his palm was an eight ball of cocaine—three and a half grams of the white powder, rolled into a little plastic-wrapped ball.

"Damn," Hilt whispered, staring at him.

Brent clenched his hand closed, then looked around, at the airport waiting area. Travelers were lining up at the gate not ten

feet away. In the other direction, other travelers were still spilling out of the security area, some repacking their bags and putting their shoes back on.

Brent wasn't sure how the coke had gotten into his pocket, or even whose it was. Maybe the Spanish girl with French perfume, maybe one of the Ultimate Bet guys, God only knew. And he had absolutely no idea how he'd gotten it through security.

He forced his legs to start moving and quickly crossed to a nearby garbage can. Then he tossed the little plastic bag inside and rushed back to where Hilt was standing, still staring at him.

"You've got to be the worst Mormon I've ever met," Hilt said, bewildered.

Brent grinned back at him. Together they joined the row of travelers lining up for the ninety-minute flight to Malta.

CHAPTER 27

"Completely insane, man." Brent's voice croaked out of the speaker on the polished mahogany desk in Scott's home office, mingling with the gurgle from the marble fountains out on the manicured front lawn drifting in through the open French doors that led out onto the two-hundred-square-foot balcony. "Malta to Dubai, then Singapore, Hong Kong, and all the way to Frankfurt. It's like the Gumball rally in reverse."

Scott laughed. He was seated behind the desk, his white collared shirt open to the third button, a Corona in his left hand, his legs up on the desk, flip-flops on his feet next to the telephone speaker. In his lap was a .38 caliber Smith & Wesson revolver. As he listened to his brother his right hand rested lightly against the gun's grip, his finger on the safety. The cool touch of the metal felt strangely comforting against his skin.

"And every meeting has been just like Malta, back in the beginning," Brent continued. "We get in there—this building had

to be like three hundred years old—and everyone just stares at us. 'What do we do?' they ask. 'What do you normally do?' we ask back. 'Just keep doing whatever that is, only now you're doing it for us instead of UB.'"

It was wonderful, the enthusiasm in Brent's voice. Since the meeting in Barcelona and the merger, there had been so many anxiety-filled days and nights, but finally things seemed to be tilting back to a status quo. The new, supersized company was pushing forward on all cylinders.

Even the disaster with Neteller hadn't knocked them down— although it had been scary going for a while. Neteller had been a multibillion-dollar business, publicly traded, handling 80 percent of the processing market. When the two founders, John Lefebvre and Stephen Lawrence, were arrested simultaneously— Lawrence when entering the U.S. Virgin Islands—and charged in a sting operation headed by the U.S. attorney for the Southern District of New York, with help from the FBI, it essentially wiped Neteller from the map. Using UIGEA, the feds alleged that nearly 95 percent of Neteller's $7.5 billion in revenue came from online gambling. The Neteller case struck fear in the companies that had remained engaged in U.S. business—essentially, Scott's company, PokerStars, and Full Tilt, who together now had 90 percent of the market.

For a good week after that, Scott fully expected federal agents to burst through his door at any minute—even though his lawyers had assured him again and again that the fear was unfounded and ridiculous; that he'd done nothing illegal in Costa Rica, where he resided; and that even if someone decided to come after them under UIGEA, they'd have trouble building a

case that implicated him personally, since the company was now owned by the Canadians, and he didn't handle the payment processing, and never had. Then again, the thought that Brent was at risk instead didn't give him any pleasure, but in his heart he truly believed that none of them should be afraid of an unfair law.

Still, the reality of the situation had affected him. Even his closest friends—Hilt and Garin—had commented on his growing paranoia.

Scott glanced at the gun in his lap while Brent went on about his most recent trip to visit processing agents and their financial offices around the globe. Brent's stories were pretty crazy. Since Neteller had gone down, the companies that had filled its place came and went almost daily, and were all shifty, sleazy affairs. They'd open, process deposits for a few days, then disappear, with whatever money they hadn't yet turned over. This happened again and again, yet still there was so much cash coming in that it didn't matter—a few hundred thousand dollars lost was almost immediately washed over by a few million dollars in player deposits coming in. Players never even knew what was happening behind the scenes—they could deposit and withdraw money just as before, without realizing where their money was going and how it was getting there.

But the shady processors and Neteller arrests were just a couple of components that were feeding Scott's paranoia. After UIGEA there had been quite a shake-up at their home office in Costa Rica as they absorbed the much larger Ultimate Bet. As with any merger, there were layoffs, but in a place like San José, layoffs led to death threats. Most had been things Scott could ignore: letters sent to the office, notes scrawled on cars

in the parking lot. But a few of the threats had risen to a real, actionable level.

Getting a gun wasn't hard in a place like Costa Rica, where a hundred-dollar bill was enough to buy you just about anything you wanted and every taxi driver was his own little home shopping business, delivering drugs, girls, and firearms. But personal protection in a place like that didn't stop at a handgun; Scott had made some inquiries and eventually decided to hire a full-service security company. At that very moment, as he sat in his office listening to Brent, there were two bulletproof sedans parked in his driveway, and eight armed bodyguards in his living room. There was another standing outside his bedroom door, where his current girlfriend—Miranda, a fucking gorgeous *tica* with long, braided blond hair and a treacherously curvy body that could have graced the cover of a swimsuit catalog—was still sleeping off the night before.

He knew the number of guards was overkill, but he'd discovered that it was a real thrill going around town with a crew that large and imposing. In fact, after a week surrounded by an armed security contingent, Scott found he felt naked and vulnerable without them. Someone was always there, taking orders, making sure the road was clear; the door was held open; there was never a line for a bathroom. He, Hilt, and Pete would go to a restaurant or a club, and they'd show up in a caravan of armored cars, walk in surrounded by armed men—hell, by that point, they had more bodyguards than the president of Costa Rica.

The head of Scott's security company was ex-military, a guy named Santos, with a scar down the left side of his face and a very dark sense of humor. He talked about killing people as

easily as he talked about the weather. Garin had taken a dislike to Santos from the start, telling Scott these weren't the sorts of people they were supposed to hang out with, that they weren't killers or mobsters, they were Internet entrepreneurs. But Scott reminded him that they were also expats in a country where life was held extremely cheap.

At some moments, though, Scott had to agree—Santos could be a little terrifying. When a laptop had gone missing from the office, Pete had tasked Santos with finding it. Not a day later Santos had brought the missing computer back. When Pete asked him how he'd found it, Santos had shrugged. He'd gone to a known neighborhood thief's house, kicked down the door, waved a gun, and asked where the computer was. Then he'd gone to another suspect's house and done the same thing. By the third door, someone had returned the missing computer.

Garin didn't want a guy like that hanging around, but to Scott, there was something undeniably thrilling about having a private army. And besides, with the amount of money they were generating, they were targets, whether Garin wanted to admit it or not.

"And things got really crazy when we got to Frankfurt," Brent continued, still going through his trip report. "Got a call just as we walked into the office, found out we needed to go to Munich to deal with another shit processor. The guy who runs Frankfurt says, 'Don't fly, take our cars.' He sends us down to the basement—and there were two black Porsches parked next to each other. Holy shit, man, these were nice cars. So we take the cars and we're doing Mach five all the way to fucking Munich."

Scott turned the .38 over in his lap, feeling the weight of the thing, the meaty heft of the grip. Porsches going Mach 5, armed

bodyguards like his own private army to fix any problem, a couple million in revenue a day.

Maybe everyone was right—what did he have to be paranoid about?

Y ou sure this is a good idea?" Shay said from the front seat as Pete stepped out of the back of the taxi, followed by the Costa Rican girl in the tight jeans and white lace top. "We probably should have called first."

Pete shrugged, looking up at Scott's beautiful rented mansion on the hill. Most of the lights were still on, and there were two sedans parked out front, with matching tinted windows and armor-thickened doors and sidewalls.

"He never answers anyway," Pete said. "And besides, she says he's looking forward to seeing her. Who are we to argue with that?"

Shay laughed, getting out of the cab after him. The girl said something in Spanish, but Shay didn't translate, so Pete just smiled at her and nodded. He looked at the girl again as she bent to fix one of the straps of her bright yellow high heels. She was a pretty girl; her nails were a little too red and long, and her lipstick was almost blindingly bright, but she carried herself well for her height, which was all of five foot four. When they'd met her at the bar at Friday's and she'd asked if they could take her to visit Scott, they'd resisted at first. But she'd grown on them; she'd explained that she and Scott had dated a bit a few months earlier, and they still talked on the phone now and again—and she really wanted to see him. It was kind of funny—despite ev-

erything that had happened, some elements of Scott's personality hadn't changed at all from his SAE days. He was still the charming rogue, but now his playland seemed to have shifted from the University of Montana to the entire country of Costa Rica.

Pete headed up the steps to the front door, followed by Shay and the girl. It dawned on him as he reached the entrance that there was a good chance Scott already had a girl in the house; he wasn't in a serious relationship at that point, and there was hardly a week when there wasn't some gorgeous thing in his bed. But still, this one had been very insistent, and she seemed nice; maybe she had long-term potential. Since Pete, Garin, Brent, and Hilt all were in serious relationships now, it would have been nice to see Scott locked down as well. Maybe a good girl would calm some of his growing anxieties. They would all benefit from a less excitable Scott Tom.

Pete knocked on the door, and a meaty bodyguard by the name of Juan opened it. He smiled at Pete and Shay, then smiled wider when he saw the girl, and ushered them inside.

Scott was in the living room, sitting on the couch watching TV. There was a six-hundred-dollar bottle of wine in his left hand. He looked up, waved at Pete and Shay, and then he too saw the girl, and smiled as wide as the bodyguard. The girl ran over to him and gave him a big, wet kiss on the lips. Scott laughed, put an arm around her waist, and without another word led her out the side door to the back lawn, still clutching the wine bottle.

Pete looked at Shay, pleased with himself.

"I think we might have assisted in a love connection—" he started.

But before he'd even finished the sentence, there was a noise

from the spiral stairway to his right, and he looked up to see another girl coming down the steps. She was tall, curvaceous, with long blond hair in tight braids hanging all the way down her back. She was dressed in a pink Juicy Couture sweatsuit, the front zipper down a few inches, revealing the soft curves of her ample chest.

Crap, Pete thought. He glanced at Shay, whose eyes were wide. The girl saw them and smiled amiably.

"Hey, guys," she said, in heavily accented English. "Where's Scott?"

Pete coughed. "I don't know. I think he went to get some beer."

It was a stupid response—there was probably enough alcohol in the place to satisfy an army. Before Pete could come up with another lie, the side door that led to the back lawn opened and the girl with the red nails strolled in, followed by Scott. The girl's shirt was completely unbuttoned, and she was in the process of adjusting her bra. Scott, for his part, was fastening his pants with one hand while taking a swig from the wine bottle with the other.

There was a frozen moment—and then suddenly the room seemed to split down the middle. The girl on the stairs came bounding down at full speed, her braids whipping out behind her. She caught the shorter girl by the throat and threw her to the ground, then leaped on top of her, screaming in Spanish. The shorter girl was screaming as well, trying to use those nails to defend herself.

A split second later, five huge bodyguards raced into the room, two from the kitchen, one from behind Pete and Shay, two

from the backyard. It took all five of them to break the girls up. Finally, one of them got the tall girl over his shoulder and carried her back toward the stairs. Two of the guards grabbed the short girl by the arms and dragged her, still kicking and screaming, out toward one of the sedans.

Scott dropped to the couch, then put his head in his hands.

"And how was your night?" he mustered as the sedan screeched away.

CHAPTER 28

It was a Wednesday afternoon, sometime after two, and Pete was in a rush as he arrived back at the office. He wasn't in the habit of taking two-hour lunches, but there was just so much new marketing to go through he'd started using lunch as a way to meet with his affiliate reps. The way things were going, he would soon be using every hour of the day to cover all the ground he needed to. Too much business was never a bad thing, and in many ways he was in charge now—which was ironic, considering that he was the one who hadn't initially believed in the business, had never intended to join, and was most hesitant to continue after the UIGEA passed.

Yet here he was, rushing up the stairwell to get back to his desk. He had six phone calls to make before five, and two more after that, once the Korean software people came online. All of it had to do with managing marketing projects—a couple of new television shows on cable networks, a few promotions involving

poker tournaments in cities around the world. If UIGEA had scared off the public companies on the London Stock Exchange, it had done nothing to curb the hunger of U.S. television networks. Although officially the online poker sites couldn't advertise money games, they could promote their free games, which easily linked into their real money games. AbsolutePoker.net was all free play, for fun—and that's the site that was promoted in the ads. But AbsolutePoker.com was for money, and that was where a good portion of the players eventually ended up. Because whatever Senator Frist and the good people in New York's U.S. Attorney's Office believed, people still wanted to play online poker—no matter who they had to give their credit card numbers to in order to get there.

Pete reached his floor and headed straight toward his cubicle. It was funny that he still had a cubicle; even though Scott and Hilt weren't coming to the office anymore and were no longer officially acting in any leadership capacity, nobody had yet claimed the one walled office on the floor. Perhaps it would always remain empty; it was kind of a metaphor for the business as a whole. Absolute Poker was a machine without a brain; all the gears still worked, the money still flowed in and out—but it was all automatic now, except for what Pete was doing in marketing and what Brent still did in payment processing. Joe Norton had brought in his own management team, including a CEO and a COO, who called the shots, but in many respects Pete and Brent were the new guard; the old guard had stepped away. Scott and Hilt still cared about the company, still wanted it to succeed. But they weren't living it anymore, day to day.

Pete had reached the entrance to his cubicle when he saw Brent approaching from the back of the office, followed by one

of their in-house programmers, a squat fireplug of a guy named Angelo, a Costa Rican they'd recently hired to take the place of one of the Americans who had resigned shortly after UIGEA had passed. If Pete remembered correctly, Angelo worked part-time in Brent's old fraud-detection department; he checked the software for flaws and made sure the game play seemed kosher—looking for signs of player collusion, things like that. Every now and then the department found something it didn't like, and once in a while a player would get suspended. Nothing serious, but it was important that they monitored themselves as best they could, since there was no overarching regulation and, after UIGEA, it was unlikely there would be anytime soon.

Angelo was a head shorter than Brent, with thick glasses over sunken eyes, and he had one of those faces that always seemed to emit worry. Still, he was a good programmer, and even though he wore the Costa Rican unofficial uniform—shorts, T-shirt, and flip-flops—he was a solid worker.

"Cheer up, Angelo," Pete said by way of a greeting. "The rainy season will be over in four months. And then we only have the mosquitoes to look forward to."

It was a running joke between Pete and many of the Costa Ricans in the office; Brandi's dislike of the third-world country had become grist for a near-constant back-and-forth complaint session. Costa Rica was hot, dirty, lawless, and heavy on insects. The United States was uptight, moralistic, overregulated, and full of religious freaks who pushed Jesus like he was Colombian co-caine. But the look on Angelo's face seemed even more anxious than usual—he wasn't there to sling jokes.

"Pete," Brent said, his voice low. "There's something we need to talk about. It might be nothing—it's probably nothing—"

"What is it?"

Brent led Pete and Angelo into Pete's cubicle and ushered the programmer into Pete's seat. Angelo went to work on the keyboard, pulling up a website. Pete recognized it immediately as one of the more prominent poker blogs—a website called Two Plus Two. As a poker marketer, Pete knew the site well; the online poker community was pretty tight-knit and often rabid, and Pete had spent a lot of time reading through all the blog sites, although recently, he'd been too busy with all of the current promotional work to check in on them.

"What is it now? Someone complaining about our table felts again? Thinks they look too plush? Or is someone whining about not getting a withdrawal on time? If they knew the sleazy fucks we deal with since Neteller went down—"

"No, it's not that," Brent said. "Angelo?"

The Costa Rican began gesturing toward the screen. "This came to my attention a couple months ago, but I've been hoping it would just go away, as these things often do. Just people griping because they lost. But, well, it hasn't gone away; it's actually just getting bigger—"

"Spit it out," Pete said.

"There's been a bunch of players complaining on one of the High Limit tournament forums that three other players on Absolute Poker are winning a ridiculous amount, playing pretty suspiciously."

Pete cocked his head. "What do you mean, suspiciously?"

"Playing almost every hand pre-flop. Then, on the river, when they get bluffed, they seem to always call or raise. If their competition has good hands, they almost always fold. Like I

said, a little suspicious. Anyway, after posting about it, a bunch of players analyzed the play history as much as they could, and now they've e-mailed us, asking us to take a look and see what the hell is going on."

Pete nodded. The truth was, this sort of thing happened all the time—accusations of cheating, either by other players or by the site itself. Usually the accusations were unfounded; everybody who'd ever lost in a casino believed, deep down, that the casino must be cheating. In games that employed some level of chance, strange things happened—and most of the time those strange things looked like cheating. But this sounded like a little more than common paranoia.

"And what did we find?"

Angelo shrugged. "Nothing yet. We're still analyzing all the hand history. It's going to take some time. But the idea that there's a superuser out there—"

He didn't need to finish the thought. Superuser accounts— accounts that could see all the cards as they were dealt, kind of like God mode on a video game—were the ultimate boogeyman of online poker; the idea that there were people on the inside, able to play so unfairly—it wasn't something anyone who worked in the industry ever wanted to even mention. Even the rumor of such an account existing could destroy an online poker company, because the whole industry was built on trust. If the players couldn't trust the online poker companies to keep the game fair, they were throwing their money away. If such a rumor spread on online forums, people would leave in droves. There would be a run on the bank.

There was a reason Absolute Poker had always been at the

top of the industry's rating lists: it took the security of its game very seriously.

"Send out a press release," Pete said, both to Brent and the engineer. "Explain that we've looked into this, that our investigation is ongoing—but that there is zero evidence that there's any cheating going on, or that anything like a superuser exists in our software. Nip this in the bud. A rumor like this could kill us."

"But what if—" Brent started. Pete shook his head.

"No what-ifs. Even a whiff of something like this can cost us millions. This has to end here. These guys are just jerking each other off, trying to find a reason why they lost money. Everyone gets paranoid when they lose. It's human nature."

Pete waited for them to file out of his cubicle, then headed toward his phone. He couldn't spend any more time on bullshit accusations from a poker forum. He had TV accounts to deal with.

Like he said, this had to end here.

A few days later Angelo and Brent were back in Pete's cubicle—and this time, both their expressions were equally grim. Not only had the situation not ended with the press release, it had gotten a whole lot worse. In fact, it had turned into something that might bring the entire company down.

"This can't be right," Pete was saying as he dropped into his office chair. He was only a few pages into the report Angelo had pulled together about what was going on, but already he could see—it was worse than anything he could have imagined.

"I'm afraid it is," Brent said. He looked at Angelo, who nodded.

"Does anybody else know about this yet?" Pete said.

"You mean apart from everybody on the poker blogs?"

Pete swallowed. His face was heating up, and he could feel the sweat beading on the back of his neck. "I mean Scott."

Brent shook his head. "I don't think so."

They'd have to bring it to him right away. Because if what he was looking at was true, even just the broad strokes, it was a disaster.

According to Angelo's report, the Absolute Poker press release had landed in the online forums like a lead balloon, but at first the complaints that continued to crop up all over the blogs were just that—complaints, without evidence, just more griping by losing players.

But then things took an unusual turn. A new player, who'd been hitting the AbsolutePoker.com tournaments under the handle CrazyMarco, had previously lost another tournament under what he considered to be suspicious terms. A player named Potripper had played almost all his hands pre-flop, then had played almost perfectly from there on—folding whenever he was up against a better hand, betting when he had the higher cards. It was almost as though he could see what everyone was getting dealt.

At the time, CrazyMarco had e-mailed customer service at Absolute Poker, asking for a play history for Potripper and the tournament. It turned out that, for whatever reason—either by mistake or on purpose—someone at Absolute Poker had e-mailed back an Excel file including the entire play history—everyone's cards, the history and information on everyone in the tournament's e-mail accounts. This was a staggering breach of protocol;

even worse, when CrazyMarco eventually looked through the file—spurred on by the Absolute Poker press release, which he felt had brushed aside a legitimate suspicion of cheating—he discovered that Potripper had indeed been cheating somehow. Playing the way he was playing simply by chance or skill would have been like winning the lottery ten times in a row. The only thing that explained his play was that somehow he could see everyone's cards, as they were dealt.

That was bad enough, but then things got really ugly.

Because upon analyzing the IP addresses and user details that had been provided by the anonymous Absolute Poker employee along with the hand history, it appeared that there was an observer account—number 363, to be exact—associated with Potripper's winning play—and that both 363 and Potripper's IPs could be traced back to Costa Rica. Once the blogger sleuths got hold of that information, it was just a few more steps, a little more research—and they'd uncovered the e-mail associated with account 363.

That e-mail was scott@rivieraltd.com. And according to the bloggers, that e-mail linked directly to the founder of Absolute Poker.

Scott Tom.

CHAPTER 29

Eight hundred thousand dollars. He really screwed us. He really screwed *me*."

Pete felt like he was in the presence of a volcano that was seconds from erupting. A moment of tense silence swept through the room as everyone at the dining room table watched Scott struggling to regain control of his features. Pete had seen Scott mad before—even in college the guy could be volatile—but this was different. This was terrifying.

The moment had been building all through dinner. Even though the conversation had remained light, avoiding the obvious topic—the reason for the get-together in Scott's house—Pete could see the emotion roiling behind Scott's green eyes. By the time dessert was served, it was obvious he was using every ounce of willpower to keep that emotion from bursting forth until the dishes had been cleared and the wives and girlfriends had retired to the living room, the better to avoid getting hit in the crossfire.

Scott had been upset when Pete and Brent first told him about the discovery of the cheating scandal and where the players' intricate sleuthing had led them. Now that he'd had a chance to piece together what had happened himself—and had discovered how his name and reputation had been dragged into the depths of the scandal, without his knowledge—he was absolutely livid.

The e-mail had indeed been linked to his profile, though it was an e-mail he hadn't used for a long time. And the 363 account, it turned out, was in fact an old account also linked to him that had been deactivated years ago; it had been one of the employee accounts the Koreans had initially given them to keep tabs on the beta test, way back when they had first launched AbsolutePoker.com. Furthermore, when they traced the IPs of where number 363 and Potripper were being employed, it appeared that both accounts were being run through ports in computer networks linked through Absolute Poker's home servers: the cheating was coming from inside the house, so to speak.

Eventually Scott had been able to piece together what had happened. Sometime, perhaps as early as summer of 2007, a database programmer in Korea attempting to speed up back-end communication routines had inadvertently disabled the time delay in the software used to monitor game play. At some point after that an employee in Costa Rica had discovered this mistake—and had realized that with no time delay built in, it would be possible to see the cards as they were dealt, in real time. This employee had further realized that by using one of the old employee player accounts—number 363, to be specific—he could escape notice, because the old accounts often had large money balances. And since the account was linked to management, it

wouldn't catch the attention of anyone in the Fraud Department, no matter how often it was being played.

From there, it hadn't taken long for Scott to discover the cheater himself. Scott hadn't been to the Absolute Poker offices for some time, and neither Pete nor Brent had made use of his computers since he'd stepped back from his official leadership role—but that didn't mean the computers had lain dormant. It turned out that one of the operation managers who'd worked part-time under Angelo had engaged account number 363. When he'd realized how easily he could beat the game, seeing all the cards as they were dealt, he'd gone to work with an unknown number of accomplices and had managed to swindle almost eight hundred thousand dollars from tournament players, observing the cards with account 363, then parroting that information to other handles—Potripper among them.

Worst of all, he'd done all this while inadvertently implicating Scott and the Absolute Poker headquarters.

It was appalling, and personally devastating to Scott, whose reputation was now being trashed on the poker blogs. The perception that he would somehow knowingly be involved in betraying the company he'd built—a company that was now bringing in two million dollars a day—by cheating his players was difficult to bear.

They'd immediately fired the person responsible, who besides being an operation manager was a close friend of Scott's—and had finally admitted to the public that they'd discovered the source of the scandal and had done their best to fix the software security issues. They had also responded by paying back anyone who had played against the cheating player accounts. But it wasn't enough,

and they all knew it. Online poker was an unregulated industry; trust was something companies earned, and once players stopped trusting a company, they found somewhere else to play.

It was Pete who finally broke the silence at the table—surprising himself, because he couldn't even match Scott's angry glare.

"Let's look at this rationally. This is out now. It's been picked up by news organizations. The blogs, newspapers, it's gonna be on goddamn *60 Minutes*. We've already had a run on the bank. A week ago we were averaging two million dollars in revenue a day. Now that's been cut by more than fifteen percent. We're seeing withdrawals of around eight hundred thousand—a day."

The numbers were sobering. Pete had been monitoring the press and the blogs, and the issue felt like it was only growing, not going away. Absolute Poker was being linked in everybody's mind with cheating. This scandal was ruining the brand they had worked so hard to build.

"People are scared," Pete continued. He wasn't sugarcoating it, that was for sure. "The press is getting worse. At the end of the day, this is the largest online scandal in the history of gaming. It's a big deal."

"I know it's a big deal," Scott shot back. "And we're paying everyone back who lost. Hell, we're paying people back who would have lost anyway, even if this shithead hadn't cheated."

"That's not the point. It isn't really about how much was stolen. These guys sitting around playing poker twenty hours a day have nothing better to do than write and talk about this shit. This has become a soap opera. Ninety-nine percent of what everyone is saying is false—but we can't ignore the one percent that was true."

"We're getting goddamn death threats, Scott," Brent said, his voice so low it was almost a whisper.

Everyone looked at Scott, who finally laced his fingers together against the table, getting his anger in check. He spoke carefully, picking his words as if with tongs.

"I'm not even running things anymore. I've been gone awhile."

He seemed to resolve something internally; it was as if a shade was drawing shut behind his bright green eyes.

"Maybe it's time I made it official."

Scott understood that if they didn't get this scandal under control and behind them, it would cost the company much more than the money the cheater had stolen. But more important to Scott than the money was the company he had built, with his sweat and his blood and his passion—and he didn't want to watch it disintegrate.

He cared too much to ever let that happen.

The North American Sabreliner twin turbojet sputtered to life, then began rolling slowly toward the private strip of runway on the back lot of Santamaría International Airport. Up in the cockpit, the two pilots were finishing up their flight check, speaking in Spanish with each other and the tower, their voices carrying back through the open cabin of the midsize private business jet to where Scott, Hilt, Hilt's gorgeous blond wife, and Scott's girlfriend were opening a three-hundred-dollar bottle of champagne.

It was taking all four of them to attend to the bottle, because they were already a little buzzed, even though it was half past

noon on a Monday. It had been a long weekend already, but they were now officially on vacation, taxiing toward the first hop on a weeklong Caribbean tour. The trip would begin with a refueling stop in Colombia, then extend through a handful of islands that promised white-sand beaches, palm trees, infinity pools, five-star hotels—and limited access to wireless networks.

It was a bittersweet moment for Scott, seated by the window in the back of the small plane, one hand on his girlfriend's arm, the other gripping a crystal champagne flute. Officially stepping down from his role at Absolute Poker had been more difficult than he'd ever let on to any of his friends; only his father knew the torment he had gone through as he'd made his leaving known to the shareholders and packed away whatever remained of his life at the company into cardboard boxes to be stored in the basement of his rented home. He'd never dreamed of his company growing so big—but he'd also never imagined that one day he would have to step aside, especially under such dark circumstances. Not just the cheating scandal caused by one of his employees, but what the UIGEA had wrought. Only his dad fully knew how painful it had been for Scott to watch himself go from being an Internet wunderkind, days away from being a billionaire, to having to separate himself from the company, forced to explain away his association with an entire industry that had overnight been tarnished by what he saw as an unfair and hypocritical act of Congress.

But here he was, in the back of a private jet with his closest confidant, who was struggling with the champagne cork as the plane bumped and jerked over the poorly paved runway.

The private plane had been Hilt's idea; none of them had

ever been in a private plane before, and it just seemed fitting. They were going out in style. At the moment, Scott didn't want to think about anything other than the trip to those white-sand beaches, those five-star hotels.

"Here we go!" Hilt shouted over the rumble of the twin turbojets churning to full power. They'd turned down the runway and were now gaining speed. There was a loud *pop*, startling Scott, but then he saw the cork pinging off the cabin ceiling and laughed. He tried to hold his glass steady as Hilt poured the champagne.

Then he turned forward, toasting himself as he watched the front of the plane lift upward, inch by inch, the front wheels coming off the runway, the nose tilting toward the sky.

And suddenly, a violent shudder reverberated down the right side of the cabin. Before any of them could react, the nose of the plane plunged back down to the runway—and there was an incredible noise, like a gun going off, as the tires blew. The pilots were screaming in Spanish, and Scott dropped his champagne glass, gripping the seat in front of him. He could see the pavement still flashing by through the front windshield. They had to be going 150 miles per hour, skidding on those trashed tires, the entire plane shaking and jagging like it was about to tear itself apart—and even worse, Scott could now see the end of that runway, a grassy field extending toward a fence and a grouping of what appeared to be steel pylons . . .

And then the plane hurtled off the pavement and into the field. A second later, they slammed into the first pylon; the windshield shattered inward, an entire section of the plane's nose shearing off. The cabin dipped down, and then they were

spinning. One of the wings was caught in the grass, and jet fuel sprayed in through the cockpit, drenching the interior of the cabin. Part of the wing snapped off—and then everything went still. The plane was tilted halfway over, and there was a gaping hole where the cabin door used to be.

Scott's mind went blank as his reflexes took over. He grabbed his girlfriend in one hand, yanking her out of her seat belt. Then he was diving forward over the seats. Hilt and his wife were right behind him as he leaped through the opening and landed feet-first in a ditch, two feet deep in noxious jet fuel.

All four of them lost their footing as they struggled to crawl out of the ditch, but they didn't stop moving until they were a good three hundred yards from the wrecked plane. When Scott looked back, he saw the first fire truck pulling up. He dropped to his knees on the grass, watching with Hilt and the girls as the fire truck sprayed the crash site with foam from a giant, high-powered hose. They were all bleeding from scratches on their hands and faces, and they reeked of jet fuel—but somehow, they were alive.

By the time they were released from the hospital—more a precautionary stay than due to the severity of their cuts and bruises—word of the accident had already made it onto a variety of online local and international news sites and was rapidly spreading through the blogs. Scott's phone was gone, lost somewhere in the wreckage, which was now entirely presided over by agents from the FAA, since it had been an American-built airplane. They had to use Hilt's phone to check in with everyone to

tell them that they were okay. By the second person they'd called, they'd realized that the story, spreading electronically at first, but eventually into newspapers as well, was turning into something out of a Hollywood thriller.

"This is ridiculous," Hilt said as he hung up the phone. "Now they're reporting that there was three million dollars and a bunch of coke in a suitcase in the back of the plane, and that you're on the run to Colombia. I've never gone near cocaine—and where the hell did they get the three million dollars?"

Scott shook his head, bewildered. He was watching an urban legend generating right in front of him, and there was nothing he could do about it. What the hell—it was just too perfect to fight. A high-flying American cowboy from Montana, founder of an online poker empire, fleeing Costa Rica to Colombia with a suitcase filled with millions of dollars and mountains of coke.

"If you've got to go out," he said finally, laughing, pulling at one of the bandages on his hands, "may as well go out with a bang."

CHAPTER 30

If Pete had thought things would return to normal after Scott exited in his faux blaze of glory, he couldn't have been more wrong. The Absolute Poker cheating scandal that the bloggers had uncovered, as bad as it was, was only the tip of a much, much larger iceberg. This time, however, they were facing a problem they hadn't created, but had inherited—or, more accurately, had bought.

The whispers had started right after Barcelona, but everyone had been too busy dealing with the massive jump in their business and the payment-processing fallout of UIGEA to take any real notice. Just as with the Absolute Poker scandal, the whispers were coming from players, via poker blogs; but this time, as soon as the rumors reached Pete in his cubicle in San José, he took them extremely seriously and reacted as quickly as he could. He'd learned his lesson—covering up suspicions of scandal only made the scandal worse—and this time the scandal appeared to be so

much bigger from the outset that no number of press releases would make it go away. It would take months to get to the core of what had happened, but once Pete had his proof, he intended to act, and to put everything out in the open, as clearly as he could.

When the time finally came, he turned the office that Scott no longer used in their San José headquarters into a sort of war room. The walls were covered in charts and graphs, most culled from the blog sites, a few developed by his own in-house software guys. He'd set up a small round table in the center of the room, which he, Brent, and Angelo were now seated around. Computer printouts, faxes, and studies sent from Korea were piled high around them; many of the detailed reports that went along with the studies were actually in Korean, but Pete had gone through enough of it over the phone with C.J. that he knew the gist of what they had found.

It had taken thirty people, and more than a million dollars in investigative fees, to build the evidence on the table in front of them. And Pete was now certain; just as many bloggers and players had been posting over the previous six months, there was a continuing and severe cheating scandal taking place at the tables of UltimateBet.com. The Absolute Poker cheating scandal had been relatively short-lived and had cost players between six and eight hundred thousand dollars. The Ultimate Bet scandal, according to Pete's research, had possibly gone on for years, dating all the way back to at least 2005, and had probably resulted in many millions of dollars stolen from players—perhaps between ten and twenty million, if not more.

Even worse, Pete and his investigators believed that the cheating went all the way up to the top levels of the Ultimate Bet

corporate brass. Pulling IP addresses had given them names and profiles way up in the hierarchy of their former competitor. Once he'd compiled the evidence, Pete had confronted UB's leadership directly; he'd shown them his evidence of back-door programs, irregular play, chip dumping—all of it. And they'd just dug in their heels. But there was no way Pete could let this go.

It was too staggering a find. It was only a matter of time before it became public, because the players analyzing the suspicious play of many Ultimate Bet accounts were uncovering more evidence of cheating every day. Pete also intended to put out a press release about what he'd found, and to get the Kahnawake Gaming Commission involved. The news was going to seriously impact the business—and the value of the entire company.

From what Pete could see, all of this had been going on before they bought Ultimate Bet during the Barcelona conference—and had continued since.

"They fucked us," Pete said, as Brent and Angelo leafed through the pages for the hundredth time. "Whether they did it knowingly or not, they fucked us big-time. And they're still holding that promissory note for around a hundred and thirty million dollars. We're supposed to pay them a hundred and thirty million bucks for a company with this shit at its core."

Brent's shoulders sagged. "This is going to cost us. But I'm not sure what we can do. We can't go after them in court. I mean, what court? What jurisdiction? Certainly not the U.S. How do we deal with this, legally?"

Pete shook his head. He had given this a lot of thought. "I don't think we deal with this in court, at least not initially. I think we handle this old-school."

Brent looked at him. Angelo started to fidget in his chair.

"What do you mean, old-school?"

Pete grinned. "You remember Hell Week, back at SAE?"

"Of course."

"I think it's time we bring Hell Week to Central America."

And then Brent was grinning too. Angelo looked at both of them, then forced a grin as well, although he had no idea what the hell they were talking about. Angelo couldn't possibly understand—but those cheating fuckers at Ultimate Bet were about to get a taste of all-American fraternity life, SAE-style.

CHAPTER 31

The limousine was pitch-black, its bulletproof windows tinted so dark they were like glassy bat eyes, flashing intermittently as the bright slice of moon blinked down through gaps in the thick jungle overhang. The road was so narrow, the curves so steep, that at times the long, sleek car seemed to be tilting almost ninety degrees from horizontal; the four overweight men jammed together in the leather-lined, sectioned-off backseat were sweating through their tailored suits, emitting gasps of fear whenever the car tilted a little too precariously toward a steep ravine or came a little too close to a jagged rock face.

The men weren't sweating just because of the treacherous road. The air-conditioning in the car had been turned off, which was particularly torturous because they were presently deep in the hills outside of San José, and it was weeks into the region's humid season. Not that Costa Rica had a season that wasn't humid, but these men were not used to the tropics, or the

third world. They had flown in from London, Vancouver, and Portland. They were businessmen, middle-aged, two with law degrees. And they had fully expected a modern hotel, a glass-walled conference room, maybe a tray filled with Starbucks in Styrofoam cups.

Instead, they had been met at the airport by three burly security men, wearing obviously visible sidearms right out in the open. They had been ushered into the back of the limo and driven directly into the jungle.

Two hours had gone by like that, the limo twisting up and down the narrow road, and the men were about ready to break down. Thankfully, it was only another ten minutes before the car finally slowed to a stop, angling into a dirt clearing in front of what appeared to be a single-story wooden shed. Through the heavily tinted windows, it was hard to make out much about the decrepit building, but there were obvious holes in the thatched roof, and there was a pair of mangy-looking dogs tied up near what appeared to be an outhouse next door.

"Christ," one of the men uttered. The three armed security guards didn't respond. One remained behind the wheel, the engine running, while the other two came around the car and opened the passenger doors.

The suited men stumbled out into the thick jungle air, stretching their legs. One of them looked like he was going to throw up, but he managed to contain himself. Then a security guard pulled a long metal wand out of his jacket pocket.

"Strip down to your underwear," he said gruffly.

One of the men laughed. The guard stared at him with narrow eyes. He didn't put his hand on his holster, but his fingers

twitched in that direction. The businessman stopped laughing, then glanced at one of his colleagues.

"Are you serious?" the businessman asked. "Absolutely not. We will do no such thing."

"You strip, or there's no meeting. And you can find your own way back to the airport."

The second security guard began to head back toward the car. The businessmen looked at one another. One of them cursed.

Then, slowly, they started to undress.

It took a full five minutes for the heavyset men to get down to their underwear, each suit piled up on the dirt in front of them. They stood there with pasty flesh, boxer shorts and white Hanes briefs, beads of sweat rolling like marbles down trembling legs.

The guard stepped forward and began waving the wand over each man, then over the piles of clothes. None of the men noticed that the wand was actually a television remote control affixed to a car antenna, or that there were no buttons, lights, or batteries involved. They just waited, terrified and sweating, for him to finish.

When he was done, he gestured for them to head into the shed. The men looked from him to their clothes.

"Like this?" one of them asked. "Can't we get dressed?"

The guard shook his head. "The boss says you guys go in like this."

Cursing even louder, the four businessmen, still in their underwear, hurried toward the shed door.

It wasn't until the men were back in the car, still buttoning and zipping up their clothes as they headed back down the jungle

road, that Pete and his negotiating team, still in the dank, stark confines of the shed, which reeked of goat dung and rotting produce, let themselves burst into hysterical laughter. Pete actually fell to the dirt floor, he was laughing so hard, and it was a good few minutes before he finally caught his breath.

The plan had worked perfectly. Those businessmen were worth tens of millions of dollars, were at the top echelons of what was formerly a publicly traded company—and there they were, in their freaking underwear, agreeing to anything and everything Pete and his team put forward. Pete had accused them of stealing $25 million, then demanded that they cancel the $130 million debt, in exchange for a simple $1.5 million payment. Furthermore, he told them he fully expected a renegotiation of their profit-sharing ratio, and that he intended to pay back whatever he could that had been stolen from players over the past half decade.

The businessmen had agreed to every last demand. Pete couldn't help but feel proud of himself. He wasn't just a master at marketing; if his time as SAE president had taught him anything, it was how to pull off a damn good fraternity hazing.

CHAPTER 32

It was a few minutes after 9 A.M. on a Friday, one of those perfect April mornings that makes living in Costa Rica worth it, despite all the negatives. Any argument Brandi could make about third-world conditions, the traffic or the smog or the power outages—none of it had any resonance on a morning like this, against that sun, that breeze, the smiles on every face in the office. Pete was the only one who seemed to be working at his desk in his cubicle, while everyone else was already making plans for the beach; but really, he was thinking more about playing golf that afternoon with Brent than he was about poker revenues and television buys. His mind was already on a golf course, his eyes following an imaginary white ball as it arced across the aquamarine tropical sky. He didn't even hear the phone ringing on his desk until an accountant who happened to be walking by, tapped his shoulder and pointed at the receiver.

The voice on the other end of the line barely cut into his day-

dream. It was one of his advertising contacts, a guy who was part owner of a poker magazine.

"Pete, I think you're getting hacked."

The man's voice sounded pretty anxious, but Pete knew it wouldn't be more than a minor irritation. Over the previous few months, as the art of hacking had become more in vogue, they'd dealt with a handful of hack attempts, and usually it was just some kid in Russia or China taking a shot at their software for no reason other than boredom.

"Thanks for the heads-up," Pete responded, watching that spinning golf ball in his head. "I'll get someone to take a look at it—"

"I think you better check it out for yourself," the magazine owner said, and then he abruptly hung up.

Pete sat up in his chair. He was still sure it was nothing—the business had been going so well since they'd dealt with the Ultimate Bet scandal and resumed building their player base until it was almost as high as it had ever been—but the tone of his contact's voice had gone from anxious to something far less identifiable. He put the receiver back on its base, then powered up his computer. A second later he typed in the address for Absolute-Poker.com.

And his heart nearly stopped in his chest. His entire screen was taken up by the official seal of the United States Department of Justice. Pete stared at the big eagle holding the branch, at the official-looking titles, at the red border, and then he started to comprehend the words.

This site has been seized . . .

Pete's first thought was, *Shit, this is a serious hack.* And then

a much darker thought crossed his mind. He quickly typed in the domain name for PokerStars, their main competitor who had stayed in the U.S. market. A second later he was staring at the same DOJ seal, the same horrific words:

This site has been seized . . .

He quickly typed in the address for Full Tilt Poker, the other major poker site that had U.S. customers.

This site has been seized . . .

His next thought was, *What are the chances that the three biggest poker websites in the U.S. are getting hacked at the same time?* And then he closed his eyes. He knew it was impossible. It hit him right then.

This was real.

This was *it*.

"Everyone!" he shouted, his voice reverberating off the cubicle walls. "Get on your computers. Go to the site."

There was a pause, and then a handful of gasps. The sound ran like an infection from cubicle to cubicle, as everyone else in the office went to the site as well. Then he heard someone cursing—followed by the sound of a phone crashing into a wall. Without thinking, Pete brought his hand up in the air, turned it into a fist. And before he could even comprehend what he was doing, he crashed it down against his keyboard, again and again. The plastic shattered, keys raining across his desk.

Through all of the scandals, the cheating, the RCMP raiding Vancouver, everything, it had never really been *it*. Even before he had been with the company—the Caribbean bank failures, Shane's addiction, Scott's car crash, the UIGEA—it had never been *it*.

But in that split second, Pete knew that it was over.

After Vancouver, his wife had asked him, *When do you quit?* And he'd answered, *When it's no longer a gray area. That's when we get out.*

In that moment, Pete knew—it was no longer gray. It was black-and-white, and it was time to get out.

B rent had one hand on the steering wheel, the other tapping at the controls of the MP3 player built into his dash. He was trying to find just the right music for the short drive to the office. He was a little late, but he didn't think anyone would care. Then again, he was pretty much the boss now—well, him, Pete, and a few others. They'd been sharing responsibilities since Scott and Hilt had left, and everything was going so well, nobody would have even cared if he'd taken the entire day off—turn the afternoon of golf he'd planned with his friends into a three-day weekend. Golf, beach, hanging out with his wife and two kids— Christ, now it was *two* kids, two amazing little balls of energy, one five, the other a little over one—crazy to even think about.

And then his cell phone was ringing. He abandoned the MP3 controls and put the speaker to his ear.

To his surprise, it was his lawyer.

"Brent, you need to get to the office right away, and call me as soon as you get there."

Brent raised his eyebrows, because he'd never heard his lawyer sound like that.

"Why? What is it? Did someone die?"

"We just got a fax from New York. It's an indictment. And your name is on it."

It felt like the universe was crashing down around him. He needed to get off the road, immediately. He was still a good ten minutes from the office, but the beach traffic was snarling in front of him. He yanked the wheel to the right, driving into the parking lot of a gas station, then slammed on the brake.

"What do you mean, indictment? Who's indicting who?"

"The U.S. Attorney's Office for the Southern District of New York, with the help of the whole DOJ. They've shut down all the sites, and they're bringing up ten of the principals on charges."

"Wait, what? What charges?" Brent's voice was little more than a croak, echoing around the car, blending with the noise from the traffic crawling past the gas station. "Which principals?"

"The charges range from operating an illegal gambling business to bank fraud to money laundering."

Money laundering. Bank fraud. The words reverberated in Brent's head. This wasn't about whether poker was a game of skill or risk. These were real, criminal charges. These were the kind of charges they threw at actual criminals.

"Who does the indictment name?"

"It looks like they picked two people from each of the big three poker companies that continued to operate in the U.S. after UIGEA, and a payment processor. Two from PokerStars, two from Full Tilt, and two from Absolute Poker. From Absolute Poker, they picked you—and your brother."

Brent lowered his head to the steering wheel.

"It gets worse," the lawyer continued, his voice seeming so damn far away. "They've seized all the company funds they could get their hands on. Seized all the domain names. The payment processors—it looks like they're just disappearing, a lot of them taking players' money with them . . ."

Brent was barely listening. His eyes were welling up with tears.

Money laundering.

Bank fraud.

"This is what it looks like," he whispered to himself, "when everything comes crashing down . . ."

Some people just knew how to live.

Scott put his feet up on the wooden banister, staring out over the white-sand beach, watching the soft waves lapping at the seashells. The carved-driftwood balcony of the small, elegant restaurant at the five-star hotel where he was staying was crowded—mostly well-dressed tourists finishing up breakfast, planning their day on an island that could only be properly described as a true paradise—but Scott had found a nice, quiet corner in which to relax by himself. His girlfriend was still up in the room, sleeping off a night of dancing in the hotel bar. Soon Scott would rejoin her, and they would hit the beach—or not; there was a nice big Jacuzzi in their suite, overlooking those same soft waves. Hell, he thought to himself, he could stay in that suite all day. He could stay on this beautiful island forever.

And then he felt a trembling against his thigh—his cell phone, jammed into the side pocket of his bathing suit, on vibrate mode. He thought about ignoring it, but decided it could only be good news. It was that kind of a morning.

He got the phone free and placed it against his ear. To his surprise, it was Hilt on the other end of the line. As far as he knew, Hilt was in Panama, setting up his new home. Now that

they were no longer involved in the company, they had gone off in different directions. Hilt had landed in Panama City and was working on new business ventures, using that fierce brain of his to begin his empire-building anew. Scott was still searching, but the wonderful island of Antigua had seemed as good a place as any to start.

"Hey, buddy," Scott said, watching a seagull hop just out of reach of the waterline, bouncing on legs the thickness of twigs. "You should get your ass over here, this place is awesome—"

"Scott, stop and listen. The site was just shut down by the Department of Justice. The U.S. Attorney in Manhattan filed an indictment against you and Brent."

Scott laughed. "April Fools', right? You're a bit late, fucker. It's the fifteenth—"

"This isn't a joke. I'm e-mailing you the indictment right now. It's gonna take you an hour to read through the whole thing, but they're trying to get you on running an illegal gambling venture, bank fraud, money laundering, and a bunch of other shit. It's coming from New York, because of their broad gambling laws—but Scott, this is a real indictment, with real jail time at the end. The lawyers I've talked to said you could be facing a lot of years—"

"Wait, what?"

"Scott, listen to me! You and Brent were just indicted."

Scott blinked. This couldn't be happening now. So many years had passed, so many hurdles had been overcome—why was this happening now?

"Why *me*? I'm not even there anymore. Brent's been dealing with those fucking processors—but why is my name there?"

Hilt didn't answer. The blood was rushing through Scott's head. He couldn't believe what Hilt was saying. He'd never been charged with anything more than a traffic ticket in his life. He hadn't done anything wrong. He'd lived pretty hard, he'd gone through some crazy shit—but in his mind, he hadn't done anything *wrong*.

"This is insane. Hilt, what should I do?"

Hilt still didn't say anything. Scott knew what his friend was thinking. It could have been any one of them named in there. It felt so arbitrary and unfair. The U.S. government could have addressed the business in so many other ways. It could have come up with regulation, it could have demanded taxes, it could have even filed a cease and desist. But it had gone right for the jugular.

Still holding the phone, Scott stood up from his chair. He found himself stumbling back from the banister, toward the small tiki bar in the corner of the restaurant's balcony. When he got there, he ignored the smiling bartender and pointed toward a bottle of tequila on a low counter behind the man.

As the man poured him a shot, he spoke low, into the phone.

"I'm gonna fight this," he said, trying to sound hard. But inside he was falling, spiraling down toward a deep hole that had been with him his whole life. He'd climbed so far out of that pit—but now he was plunging right back down.

"Scott," Hilt was saying, "you need to talk to the lawyers. This is going to be big news. The newspapers are already calling it Black Friday. Maybe you can go to New York and make some sort of deal."

Scott hung up the phone. He knew Hilt had his best interests in mind, but Scott wasn't going to New York. He was going

to stay right where he was, in Antigua, as long as he could. He truly believed, in his heart, that he was innocent, and he wasn't going to throw himself into hell because of an indictment that had come out of an unfair, poorly written law.

He had built a company out of an American pastime. He'd created a way for the Internet to provide a game of skill to people who wanted to play it, and now he was being persecuted for it. He'd come from nowhere, and had built a billion-dollar company—and now it was all gone, a multibillion-dollar industry destroyed in the stroke of a pen, and he was facing jail time.

No, he was going to stay right where he was.

CHAPTER 33

Lawyers, lawyers, and more lawyers. Phone calls, e-mails, faxes. Long hours sitting in glass-walled offices, staring at documents that barely made sense, poring over numbers that never added up. Day after day, week after week, and yet still it just kept spinning on and on, a never-ending marathon, so mind-numbing and heavy that by the end, when Brent finally made his decision to turn himself in, he was actually relieved.

Of course, the decision hadn't been easy. And at first the thought of what he, personally, was going to do had taken a backseat to how he and the company would deal with the fallout of what everyone now called Black Friday.

An entire multibillion-dollar industry, gone in a single day—the fallout was astronomical, and almost instantaneous. The minute those three websites were seized, their assets frozen, hundreds of millions of dollars in players' accounts were suddenly put into jeopardy, and much of those millions disappeared in the

blink of an eye. Likewise, an entire marketing and advertising field vanished—perhaps a hundred million dollars in television sponsorships alone. Overall, throughout all the industries affected, perhaps as much as ten billion dollars evaporated. But to Brent, and to many millions of people around the globe, the biggest disaster fell on the players themselves, many of whom were facing personally devastating losses.

Though PokerStars had enough capital on hand to pay back many of its accounts, Full Tilt and especially Absolute Poker were facing true catastrophe.

Brent saw it happening right in front of his eyes. Almost immediately a large number of his payment processors—shady middlemen in the best of times—simply disappeared, along with whatever money they owed players and the company. At that same moment, Brent and Pete were also facing the forced firing of more than four hundred employees, most of them in Costa Rica, all of them demanding severance, whatever salaries they were still owed, whatever benefits the laws of their country mandated. And on top of all that, of course, there were the lawyers—not just his, but the company's, the shareholders', the employees'. Everyone now needed a lawyer.

From the very first moment that the site was frozen, the money began to evaporate—faster and faster, and it looked like it was only going to get worse.

The first thing Brent tried to do was to submit a proposal to the U.S. government to help the players reclaim at least a portion of the money they'd deposited into the site to play poker. By his calculations, the company had about fifteen million dollars in cash, another forty-five million in receivables. His plan gave the

players precedence over other debts—and, by his numbers, would have gotten them about seventy-five cents on every dollar they'd deposited.

Unfortunately, the government turned his plan down, for a variety of reasons. They were in the process of building their case, and the most important thing to them was their investigation, and taking down what they considered an illegal industry. The lengths they'd already gone to were impressive. Brent learned from his lawyers that beginning back in 2009, the Department of Homeland Security had created a fake payment processor, called Linwood Payment Solutions, which was really staffed by U.S. federal agents. Linwood had actually processed close to fifty million dollars in poker money, while the feds gathered evidence against Brent and the others named in the indictment. Brent himself had dealt with Linwood—signed his name on forms that were now entered into evidence against him.

Clearly, the government was not interested in Brent being involved in cleaning up the fallout that Black Friday had caused; the only thing they wanted from him was cooperation—in the case against his company and the industry as a whole.

And with two young kids at home and a Colombian wife, whom he desperately wanted to bring back to the States to try to restart a normal life, Brent had taken the government's request for cooperation extremely seriously—until his lawyers explained what "cooperation" really meant.

It wasn't a matter of telling them a few stories and giving them details about how the business worked. If he cooperated, he would have to speak out against anyone the government

wanted to target. His friends, his fraternity brothers—and, of course, Scott. There was even talk of Brent having to wear a wire.

In exchange, Brent would get a guarantee of no jail time and no forfeiture of assets. But even so, he simply couldn't do it. His brother was his hero, and despite everything that had happened, his brother would always be his hero.

The brief conversation he'd had with Scott right after the indictment hadn't changed anything—although it had been incredibly tense and had started on a very harsh note. The minute Scott had gotten on the phone he was shouting in Brent's ear:

"Why is my name on this fucking thing?"

But Brent's response had brought him back into the reality of the moment. "Why are you asking me? My name is there too."

And after that, it had just been two brothers talking about a future they'd almost had, a past they'd shared, and what all of them would do next. Scott was going to stay in Antigua. He'd probably end up trapped there, a fugitive; Antigua wouldn't extradite him, because there, running an online poker site wasn't illegal, it was a respected line of work. Pete had gotten on the first plane to the United States, taking his family with him. Garin was remaining in Costa Rica—even though at the moment it seemed a little terrifying. Right after the indictment, Scott's house was raided by Costa Rican agents, who'd literally carried out everything of value they could find. Hilt was in Panama; technically, he was free to go where he wanted, but he was going to avoid setting foot in the United States, because the last thing he wanted to face was a subpoena. None of them wanted to be forced to speak out against one another.

And that left Brent. He had a wife, two young children, and no job, and he was facing a near future of lawyers, lawyers, and lawyers. All he wanted was for all of it to be over.

So he'd made a decision—not to cooperate fully, but to turn himself in.

Over the next few weeks his lawyers had begun to negotiate his surrender with the U.S. government and the U.S. Attorney's Office. The government had quickly agreed to drop most of the gambling and money-laundering charges, but Brent would have to plead guilty to some form of bank fraud. Even so, the prosecutors were willing to admit that it was fraud without any loss to anyone—without any real victims. In fact, the people being defrauded were making money, not losing it, and most were willing participants.

Although the sentencing guidelines for what he would plead guilty to were between twelve and eighteen months in federal prison, his lawyers, and the prosecutors, were confident that his past, and his willingness to surrender, would translate to a sentence of probation. Maybe he'd have to pay a fine, but he'd be home, he'd be free, he'd be with his family.

In the end, the plea had seemed the right thing to do.

On July 21, 2012, even though the Department of Justice's own attorneys argued for leniency, Brent Beckley was sentenced to fourteen months in prison for his role in running an online poker website. The very prosecutors arguing the case had agreed that there was no evidence that Brent had caused losses to any banks or any individuals. Despite this, the judge enacted a

sentence that, in his words, "makes clear that the government of the United States means business in these types of cases."

After the sentence was handed down, Brent found himself standing in the back of the courtroom, surrounded by eight members of his extended family. Everyone around him was crying, and Brent himself was in a state of near shock. Even so, he did his best to stay upbeat.

"It's not cancer," he said as he gave them each a hug, one by one. "We'll get through this."

Even through his shock and sadness, there was a sense of relief. Because for him, at least, it really was over.

EPILOGUE: THE AFTERMATH

Brent Beckley is currently serving fourteen months in a minimum-security federal prison situated on the grounds of a supermax outside of Denver, Colorado. He is taking culinary classes while in prison and hopes to work in the restaurant industry upon his release.

Garin Gustafson and Shane Blackford are both happily married, working together as business partners and entrepreneurs, and are still living in Costa Rica. Garin visits Montana frequently, and Shane has a new baby daughter and is still actively involved in his NA and AA fellowships.

Pete Barovich finally listened to his wife and got his family on the first plane out of San José after the federal indictment. He has since relocated to Phoenix, Arizona, where he runs his own business.

Hilt Tatum remains in Panama City. Since leaving Absolute Poker he has started various businesses and currently works in private equity while commuting back and forth to the UK to finish up business school at Oxford University.

Scott Tom remains trapped on the island of Antigua; although he is not technically a fugitive—since he was on Antigua when the federal indictment came down, and thus isn't *fleeing*, but remaining still—the feds currently consider him "at large." Despite the fact that he presumably earned millions of dollars as the creative force behind Absolute Poker, and was once days away from becoming an Internet billionaire, he now lives in what could be accurately described as a gilded cage.

The industry of online poker took a huge hit on Black Friday; billions of dollars vanished with the stroke of a pen, and millions of players saw their poker accounts disappear. Even so, most legal experts believe the U.S. online poker business will one day make a regulated, taxed, and extremely profitable recovery. In July 2012, PokerStars agreed to pay a $731 million fine to the U.S. government; part of that settlement included a deal in which PokerStars purchased what remained of Full Tilt Poker. The newly merged company has since resumed operations; in January 2013 it announced that it had purchased a brick-and-mortar casino in Atlantic City, gaining a foothold back in the American market. Even more significant, one month earlier, in December 2012, the Department of Justice's Office of Legal Counsel finally and officially clarified its position on the 1961 Wire Act as it applies to the online gaming business. According to U.S. deputy attorney general James Cole, the OLC analyzed the scope of the Wire Act and concluded that it is indeed limited to sports betting. In other words, the DOJ now officially believes that online poker should not face criminal prosecution under the Wire Act.

Whether these developments open the door to the resurrection of the U.S. online poker industry remains to be seen.

PHOTO APPENDIX

March 2002: Group shot on the scouting trip to Costa Rica. Garin Gustafson, Gary Thompson, Phil Tom, Shane Blackford, and Scott Tom. *(Courtesy of Garin Gustafson)*

September 2002: First trip to meet with Korean software programmers—a partnership begins. C. J. Lee, Garin, and Victor Kim. *(Courtesy of Garin Gustafson)*

June 2006: Garin at the Gumball 3000 finale party in the Playboy Mansion.
(Courtesy of Garin Gustafson)

Absolute Poker
software in the
beta testing period,
depicting the initial
design of a virtual
poker table.

The foam-covered aftermath
of the crash of the private
plane, from which Scott and
Hilt somehow emerged alive.
(Courtesy of Oscar Hilt Tatum IV)

ACKNOWLEDGMENTS

First and foremost, I am grateful to the many individuals within this story, named and unnamed, who opened up their lives to me over the many months it took to research this amazing tale. I am also indebted to my wonderful editor, Peter Hubbard, and the team at William Morrow. I am also, as usual, grateful to Eric Simonoff and Matt Snyder, the best agents in the business. Many thanks to my Hollywood brother Dana Brunetti and the incomparable Kevin Spacey, as well as Mike De Luca. I would also like to thank my secret weapon, Jeff Glassman, and his associate Michael D'Isola. Many thanks to Barry Rosenberg, Megann Cassidy, my incredibly supportive parents, and my brothers and their families.

And most important of all, thank you Tonya, Asher, Bugsy, and our newest addition, Arya—you make it all worthwhile.